'Move over Sanderson, there's
Mike Sl

'If *Master of Sorrows* established a fresh new mark on modern epic fantasy, then *Master Artificer* carves a brightly burning glyph [...] Call has created a rare blend of story innovation, authentic characters, and a finely crafted, diverse world'   *Fantasy Book Review*

'This riveting second instalment in *The Silent Gods* series reveals a complex magic system that rivals Brandon Sanderson's. As Ainnevog's journey explodes across the pages, taking dark turns towards a darker destiny, it will keep you reading into the early hours of the morning'   *Sean Reads Books*

'A wonderful mix of the old and the new, and the ending had me begging for just one ... more ... chapter. I'm very impressed with Justin Call's debut, and I'm looking forward to seeing where this series goes. If you're a fan of coming-of-age stories, magic schools, and the idea of what's right and what's wrong, then *Master of Sorrows* is the book for you'   *The Fantasy Inn*

'*Master Artificer* takes everything you thought you knew in *Master of Sorrows* and burns it to the ground in order to bring forth something new and glittering from its ashes'
A Cat, A Book, and A Cup of Tea

'This is an adventure well-worth embarking on, one filled with monsters, gods, deception and betrayal'   *booktopia.com*

MASTER ARTIFICER

THE SILENT GODS: BOOK TWO

JUSTIN CALL

This paperback first published in Great Britain in 2021 by Gollancz

First published in Great Britain in 2021 by Gollancz
an imprint of the Orion Publishing Group Ltd
Carmelite House, 50 Victoria Embankment
London EC4Y 0DZ

An Hachette UK Company

1 3 5 7 9 10 8 6 4 2

A CIP catalogue record for this book
is available from the British Library.

ISBN (Mass Market Paperback) 978 1 473 22292 2
ISBN (eBook) 978 1 473 22293 9
ISBN (Audio) 978 1 409 17607 7

Typeset by Deltatype Ltd, Birkenhead, Merseyside

Printed in Great Britain by Clays Ltd, Elcograf S.p.A.

www.gollancz.co.uk

For Coco, whose sacrifices enable my successes

* chaenbalu-unconfirmed

LUQURA

profile of Locks of Luqura
by Rosel Dogass
medium mid-summer's height

Copper Lock   Gold Lock
Lower River Gate   Upper River Gate

45 15 18   35   14 15 12

Typical Times to Traverse

Arthon Quarter

High Quarter

Merchant Quarter

Dens &w Quarter

River District

Upper River District

Old Low Quarter

←N

BRIDGE
PRIVATE GATE
MINOR GATE
CITY GATE
RIVER GATE
WALL
ROAD
CLIFF

SCALE 1:12,000

ENTRANCES TO UNDER-CITY PASSAGE

Beware the Deceiver who bears the remnant of Keos.

Having wrestled with His spirit, he will seek the throne of Earthblood.

Having deceived His worshippers, he will seek to turn them against Him.

Be vigilant, therefore, and watch for the dawning of the Age of Rebirth.

Then Keos the Third shall rise in His glory and sweep the pretenders from Luquatra.

And these are the signs by which ye shall know Him:

His arm shall raise the Hand of Keos, and His breast shall bear the mark of His enemies.

Dressed in the blood of His servants, He will adorn Himself with the bones of His people.

Though Heir to the sons of Odar and the daughters of Lumea, His magic will be pure and His spirit will remain whole.

Look for these signs, therefore, children. For when He rises again, He will reward those who are faithful and punish those who doubted, and the magic that resists Him will be turned against those who wield it.

Our Saviour and Destroyer.
The Master Artificer.
The Darklord.
Keos Reborn.

'The Faithless and the Fallen', excerpt from the Book of Terra

The story so far...

Annev de Breth has fought for years to become an avatar of the Academy of Chaenbalu, battling the other boys at the academy to prove himself and balancing the demands of his training along with his role aiding his mentor, Brother Sodar, a priest who runs the village chapel.

In his final avatar tests, Annev finds himself at a series of crossroads: first, whether he will accept the academy's teachings or embrace Sodar's; and second, during the test itself, whether he should work as a team with his friends or focus on achieving his own goals. Whatever he chooses now will determine his future ...

But no path is ever smooth, or without its surprises. After completing a special mission in the Brakewood for Elder Tosan, head of the Academy of Chaenbalu, Annev finds himself unexpectedly promoted to the status of Master Avatar and sent on a magical artifact retrieval mission to the township of Banok. With him are his two rivals: Fyn, the school bully and Annev's nemesis; and Kenton, a boy who has betrayed Annev and his friends before ... and who secretly loves Annev's sweetheart, Myjun.

United in their goal, the three boys enter Banok and confront Janak Harth, the crippled merchant who holds the Rod of Compulsion they have been sent to retrieve. Using all of their hard-won skills and working together for the first time, they battle both the merchant and his thralls for control of the artifact, only to have it stolen from them in their moment of triumph by a young thief named Sodja Rocas, a noblewoman from the capital city of Luqura. In the subsequent chaos, Fyn chases but fails to catch her, while Kenton sees his moment. He traps Annev in Janak's burning study, hoping to kill his rival.

Trapped with no prospect of escape, Annev does the only thing he can: he removes the magical prosthetic arm he has worn since childhood, and kept hidden from all at the Academy, who would condemn and murder him if they learned the truth: that Annev, like the keokum they despise, can use magic.

Annev is forced to leave his prosthetic to burn, along with the rest of the merchant's possessions, and he finds himself confronted with another choice: he can flee with Sodar and escape Chaenbalu once and for all, abandoning his dream of being an avatar and marrying Myjun; or, he can try to stay, understanding that the Academy will never accept him as he is, and that to preserve his secret he would have to search for a new prosthetic by breaking into the Vault of Damnation where the stolen magical artifacts are kept. Making his decision – that he must at least try to preserve his new status as Master Avatar and win the woman he loves – Annev uses a magic elixir to outrun Oyru, a shadow assassin, and races back to Chaenbalu before his companions can report their failure and his death. He creates a faux limb (filling his long-sleeved glove with straw) and then breaks into the Academy's lower levels, heading for the Vault of Damnation with Myjun's help. But just as they reach the Vault, Myjun discovers Annev's missing arm and, horrified and betrayed, knocks him unconscious.

When Annev wakes, he's a prisoner in the Academy's dungeons. Elder Tosan, Myjun's father, demands that he confess to being a Son of Keos, cursed with the talent of magic; but the interrogation is interrupted by true monsters – the humanoid *feurog*, with skin made of metal and stone – who have invaded Chaenbalu, broken through its circle of protection, and murdered many of the villagers and students. In the resulting chaos, Annev escapes his cell – blinding Kenton with a magical liquid and imprisoning his traitorous companion. As he makes his escape, Annev arms himself with an assortment of magical artifacts from the Vault of Damnation to aid him in saving the village.

Free of the dungeon, Annev reunites with his friends and his former adversary Fyn, and together they help fight the feurog intent on slaughtering the remainder of Chaenbalu's inhabitants. With the monsters finally defeated, Annev finds his mentor Sodar ... only to be confronted by the shadow mage behind the attack: Oyru, an elite assassin of the fallen god Keos.

Together, Annev and his friends injure Oyru and trap the assassin in the town's collapsed well ... only to be condemned by Elder Tosan, Myjun, and the Academy's surviving masters and ancients. The headmaster attacks Annev using a dark rod, but Sodar steps in, protecting Annev with a shield of air ... until it fails, and Sodar is murdered by the magic of Tosan's hellfire wand. Annev uses his magic artifacts ... but he cannot hold out for ever. When all hope seems lost, he reaches for anything that might aid him and is surprised to find the Hand of Keos: the cursed prosthetic forged by the Fallen God of Earthblood thousands of years ago. Using it to repel Tosan's attack, in grief and desperation, Annev immolates the headmaster and nearly kills Myjun, who falls deep into a rift in the earth.

Stunned by the destruction of their home, Annev, his friends Titus, Therin and Fyn, and the few survivors prepare to leave the destroyed village and make a new life in Luqura. Sraon, the village blacksmith and secret ally of Sodar, offers to lead the party along with Brayan, the Academy's former quartermaster. Annev has his own goals, having found he's unable to remove the Hand of Keos now attached to his missing arm, and hoping someone in Luqura can help. Meanwhile, Brayan explores the Academy's rubble and finds a cryptic note suggesting that the *feurog* attacked Chaenbalu in concert with the Academy's witwomen because 'the Vessel' – Annev – had been discovered.

As the group departs, Oyru remains trapped, roaming the tunnels beneath the Academy. There, he finds Myjun being tortured by *feurog*, who are attempting to pour a magic liquid (*aqlumera*) on her scarred face. He watches her kill her attackers and then approaches the bitter young woman, inviting her to become his apprentice. In exchange, he offers her a mask that will heal her ... and promises to help her achieve her own goals: finding and killing the boy who betrayed her and left her for dead.

Prologue

Kenton crashed against the door just as the drop-bar fell into place. A heartbeat later, the peephole slammed shut and the key turned in the lock.

'Ainnevog!' Kenton shouted, pounding on the metal. 'Keos burn your bones! I'm going to kill you. If I ever see you again, I will *kill you*!'

His vision blurred and he stepped back from the door, his retinas burning with an increasingly intense pain. He screamed as he rubbed his eyes and wondered what damnable liquid Annev had splashed in his face.

'*Ainnevog!*' he howled, cursing. The pain spiked, as if twin daggers had suddenly plunged into Kenton's skull, and he collapsed backward to the ground. He wrestled with the pain for several long minutes, trying to wipe away the burning liquid that was consuming his vision, but every second brought a new level of agony, a new torment that sought to rule him.

Kenton wept, his salty tears searing like acid. He sobbed and clawed at his eyelids as he begged for the pain to end.

But it did not – it *would* not. Instead, Kenton felt the pain seep deeper into his skull. He shrieked, imagining the acid boring through his brain, and he abandoned his remaining sanity. His bloody nails tore again at the flesh covering his eyes, now peeling back the lids as though they were molten wax. This brought a new sensation of pain, but it was quickly swallowed in the ocean of agony consuming his lidless eyes. Kenton's fingers groped for the epicentre of his torture, straining to pluck the first orb from his skull even as his mind reeled at the horror of the idea. It was a desperate act, but blindness would be a mercy – even death was preferable to this. His bloody fingers were pressed around his eye, his body tensing in anticipation of what was coming ... and then he stopped. In one lucid moment, Kenton realised he was no longer touching the soft membrane of an eyeball, but the smooth, unyielding surface of a glass sphere.

My eyes ... ? Kenton flinched, his face twitching as if to blink, yet unable to do so for lack of eyelids. He probed again, disbelieving, and felt the truth of it. He would have cried out – would have sobbed again, this time in the knowledge he would spend the rest of his life as a lidless freak, a monster whose eyes could never close – but a second revelation stopped him: the pain had finally ceased.

Kenton sucked in a chestful of air, gasping in relief, and softly touched his eyes again. It was a wonder they had not dried out, but the glass spheres seemed to require no lubrication, no tears or moisture. Kenton consciously tried to blink again and found the action both unnatural and unnecessary.

Damn you, Annev, he thought. *What have you done to me ... and what have I done to myself?* His fingertips drifted to the remnants of his eyelids and he found the tissue foreign; instead of ragged chunks of bleeding flesh, they felt wreathed in hard leather, his own skin now stiff and inflexible. The sensation faded as he moved his fingers over his eyebrows and cheekbones, and dis-appeared completely when he touched his cheeks, nose, lips and forehead. The old scar on his cheek remained – the liquid Annev had thrown into his eyes had not reached the mottled flesh – but the horror of Kenton's lidless gaze would trump any scars the masters had left him.

Kenton looked around the empty cell, surprised that he could still see. He cautiously dabbed the blood from his eyes, expecting his prodding to provoke another bout of pain, but it had dis-appeared entirely. Even his missing eyelids didn't seem to bother him. His vision had grown clearer. With each passing minute, his eyesight seemed to grow stronger.

Keos take you, Annev. What did you do to me? Kenton allowed himself another moment to wallow in his sorrows then forced himself to his feet.

A rusty trapdoor had been set into the ceiling of his prison cell. Could it be that easy? Kenton doubted it, but he had to try all the same. He mounted the carved steps leading to the hatch in the ceiling and tried to push the portal open. Nothing. He pushed harder, bracing his feet against the stone and heaving upward with his shoulders and back. Still nothing. Maybe it was rusted shut, or maybe it was barred from the other side. Probably both, though Kenton supposed it didn't matter. That trapdoor wasn't budging. He turned his gaze on the rusted metal and peered at the luminous liquid trickling from its edges. As he stared, he saw a vortex of colours, images, and impressions: bright flashes of emerald and violet, the cold breath of hoarfrost and the hot steam of molten metal. Out of nowhere, a swarm of spectral faces filled his vision and Kenton stumbled backward, missed his footing, and toppled down the short flight of stairs to the ground. His elbow cracked against the floor and his head snapped against the stone, sending him into a daze.

'Cracking hells!' he swore, awkwardly rubbing his head and elbow. *What* was *that? Ghosts? Ghosts with children's faces?* He shook himself, trying to regain his bearings. *Burn me, but that was strange.* Kenton rubbed his glassy eyes once more, vowing to stay away from the rainbow-hued liquid, then stared numbly at the door instead, trapped, dizzy and sore. When his vision began to blur, he cursed Annev once more and concentrated, bringing it back into focus only for it to blur again and then clarify, revealing a translucent wooden door and the empty hallway just beyond it.

'Silver staves,' he breathed, almost reverent.

Kenton reached out and touched the door, his fingers brushing the solid frame despite its intangible appearance. As Kenton focused on his hand instead, the door seemed to solidify once more and the internal workings of his own hand were revealed: flesh and bones, blood vessels and sinew. He continued to stare, aghast, as his vision slowly penetrated the flesh of his arm before once more revealing his cell door and then the hallway beyond. The sensation was startling. Kenton lowered his arm and the walls

3

came back into sharp focus before fading into translucency again. He would have blinked if he'd had the ability to do so. Instead, he continued to stare, shocked by what his new glass eyes couldn't help but see. With literally no effort, his vision bored deeper into the walls, penetrating further as he stared at nothing.

I can see through things, he thought, attempting to reconcile this new world view. *I can see through the walls . . . through the earth itself.*

Curious about the extent of his new vision, Kenton turned his gaze to the ground and strained to see how far into the depths his sight could reach. Within seconds, his vision had penetrated the floor and discovered another cell beneath his own, the latter appearing disused and sealed off. It was in such disrepair that Kenton doubted anyone at the Academy knew of this second subterranean level beneath the Academy's dungeons. Kenton let his gaze sink further into the ground, leaving the forgotten cell behind as he gazed through moist earth and solid rock. He needed no light to see, though his magic sight perceived little besides more clay and stone.

Kenton returned his vision to the hallway outside his cell and clearly saw the path leading to the stairs, which then climbed towards the surface. He traced the path upward, and only then found he was unable to peer through the ceiling into the confines of the room above. He opened his eyes wide, trying to take in everything around him, twisting and gazing around his cell. It took only a few moments to see there was an aberration in his vision: a spherical space above his head which was impervious to his new-found powers.

I wonder. Kenton calculated his location and confirmed his suspicions. *I can't see into the Vault of Damnation*, he realised. *Curious.* He dismissed the riddle and went back to searching out any potential means of escape. Unfortunately, his magic vision couldn't help him: the stone walls and metal door of his cell were solidly constructed, and the trap door above his head and cell door were immovable – as he discovered by bruising himself again trying to open them in turn.

Kenton growled. He hated waiting, but it seemed that was all there was to do. He slumped back down. He was exhausted from the previous night's activities, and as he sorted through the events of the past few days, the final tests and his doomed struggle to become an avatar, he found himself reflecting on the Test of Judgement, recalling his bitterness at nearly winning the contest . . . then being thwarted by Annev, Titus, and Therin.

He lay back on the cold stones, trying to put it all out of his mind, wondering if it was possible to sleep with his eyes permanently open. His eyes rolled backward a few times, the promise of sleep tantalizingly close, but then the cold ache of lying on the floor seeped in and his consciousness reeled itself back from whatever oblivion he'd been about to find. In the end, he huddled into a tight ball and his exhaustion finally claimed him.

Kenton woke when the stones beneath him started shuddering violently. He was disorientated, confused by what he was seeing – or not seeing – as his brain shifted from the dreams of his mind's eye to the physical world he perceived with his lidless glass eyes.

The curse of his supernatural sight had grown while he had slept. Now his vision revealed new spectrums of light: lazy reds and frenetic violets, their invisible waves keenly visible to his magic eyes. Kenton looked down and saw the floor where he had slept was a mix of reds and oranges, fading to yellows and greens. He touched it tentatively and felt a trace of his body heat where the reds were brightest. *I can see* warmth? *How is that possible?*

The earth shook again, rocking the walls of his prison cell, and Kenton huddled down, lowering his centre of gravity to steady himself, but it was the very stones that ached and heaved beneath him. He heard a loud *crack* and looked up in time to see a fissure open in the prison wall, just a finger's breadth wide but enough to trigger a surge of panic in his chest. A second heave of the earth and the fissure widened to a hand's breadth, its fingers spiderwebbing across the walls, floors, and ceiling. The crack touched the corner of his cell door and there was a terrific squeal of metal and rock as the door abruptly buckled under the weight of falling rock. Kenton threw himself into the farthest corner of his cell, buried his head in his arms, and prayed to a god he didn't believe in, asking the heavens to spare him from an ignominious death in the bowels of the Academy. Stone tumbled down around him, glancing off his shoulders, arms and back. Another clamour of tumbling rock and stone followed ... and then an echoing silence.

Kenton cautiously lifted his head, trying to squint through the dust in the air – which did him no good without eyelids. He gingerly checked his arms and extremities and, though bruised and bleeding, it seemed he had escaped any serious injury. It was then that he exhaled into the billowing cloud of stone dust and saw his prayers had been answered: his cell door had bent and buckled.

Kenton approached the door with all the caution of a man dying of thirst being offered a glass of water. This was his miracle, his only chance to escape a death he did not deserve and a fate that was not rightfully his. With trembling hands, he grasped the twisted metal frame that had once imprisoned him and measured the crack between the crumpled metal and broken rock. Was it large enough to squeeze through? He doubted it, though he would try anyway. First, he grasped the metal door with both hands and pulled, commanding it to yield to his meagre strength. The metal protested, squeaking but not bending or budging. Kenton spat a mouthful of curses in response, all sense of reverence or gratitude disappearing, and then he yanked again in a fury, pulling with all his might at this crumpled barrier between himself and freedom. Twisting in his bloodied hands, the portal finally relented, its broken hinges swinging free before toppling to the earth with a clang.

Kenton paused, looking around for anyone racing down the corridor to shove him back into Annev's cell. Stillness met his gaze: nothing but silence in the hallway and from the floors above, which was even more unnerving than the possible sound of approaching footsteps or even the clatter of crumbling earth and rock.

The Academy was quiet. Far too quiet.

What had Carbad said to Tosan just before leaving Kenton to guard Annev? It felt like another lifetime ago: *Chaenbalu is under attack! ... Monsters. Demons made of metal ... They're inside the Academy!* The remembered words rang in Kenton's skull, but the physical world remained silent.

Whatever had happened, he couldn't stay here. Kenton took a deep breath, immediately coughed on the rock dust that still hung in the air, then took a cautious step out of the cell.

The hallway was warped and strewn with rubble. The ceiling likewise hung at a nasty angle, sloping down and narrowing as it approached the stairwell that was his escape route. Kenton began to jog down the hallway, not caring if the masters or ancients saw him, practically willing them to appear. In fact, it would have been a relief to see them.

But they didn't appear. No one raced down the stairs to investigate the noise he'd made. No one turned the corner to be surprised by Kenton's new scars and lidless eyes. No one came to call him a failure, a keokum, or a Son of Keos.

No one came at all.

Kenton reached the foot of the stairs and used his magic eyes to see what lay above him. He saw the winding stairs, saw where they branched off to the archives and the Vault of Damnation ... and he saw a body, its features so mutilated he couldn't guess its identity. Its robes were so dirty, so mangled and so bloody, he couldn't tell whether they'd belonged to a student or a master avatar.

Kenton's magic sight retreated, instinctively pulling back from the spectacle. He quietly breathed in the smells and the silence as his hand crept up to touch the old scar on the side of his face then traced the hard skin that had formed around his lidless eyes. As he did so, he caught a faint glimmer of light shining on his hand, as if his skin were glowing. Kenton pulled his hand away, surprised, and the glow disappeared. When he brought his hand up a second time, he realised the light was not coming from his hand ... but from his glowing eyes, their ghostly light illuminating his fingers.

Before Kenton might have laughed or wept, but now he took this new change in his stride, accepting that he was becoming something else – that he *was* something else.

He took the first step, prepared to see what changes had been wrought above while he had been changed below.

Part One

Now the Third Age of the world was marked by the birth of the Younger Gods. Yet when they awakened to their divinity, their father was absent from them. Yea, Keos had removed himself from the face of Luquatra, and he forsook his children that he might nurse his wounds and gather his strength for the day that he would rise again in glory and power.

And the number of the Younger Gods was five, for they had sprung from the Breaking of the Hand of Keos, and they retained a portion of his strength. And they awoke to a world of chaos and blood, for Keos had forsaken his worshippers and they did war one with another. And the Younger Gods took pity on the people of Keos, and as they succoured the Terrans they gained worshippers of their own. In this way, the Younger Gods began to usurp Keos's stewardship over *t'rasang*.

Now Sealgair the Hunter claimed dominion over the Animals of Luquatra, and those that followed him could commune with creatures great and small. Yea, and there were some among them who could even take the shapes of animals.

And Garadair the Gardener claimed dominion over the Plants of Luquatra, and those that followed her were friends of the forest. Yea, and there were those among her worshippers who could manipulate plants, directing and accelerating their growth. And there were still others who could speak to the plants, seeing and hearing the world through them.

And Cruithear the Creator claimed dominion over the Minerals of Luquatra, and those that followed him were hearty folk who loved the earth's secrets. Yea, there were those among them who could shape earth and ore with their bare hands. And there were still others whose bodies bore the strength and weight of the earth.

Now Sealgair, Garadair, and Cruithear had claimed

stewardship over all that was Earth and Blood. And they counted themselves wise for this purpose, for their people did flourish, and so it seemed no stewardship had been left to either Dorchnok or Tacharan.

Yet Tacharan the Changeling was a cunning one. And he said, 'Our siblings claim dominion over All That Was and All That Is. Therefore, I will claim rulership over All That Might Be.' And Tacharan became the God of Chance, and his worshippers called him the God of Doom and the God of Fate, and his people loved all that was arcane, whether prophecies of the future or the mysteries of the afterlife. And they loved their secrets even more than the people of Cruithear.

But Dorchnok the Trickster was no less cunning. And he said, 'My siblings are the Gods of All That Was, All That Is and All That Might Be, and they have left naught for me to rule. Therefore, I claim dominion over All That Is Naught, and I shall be the God of What Is Not.' And Dorchnok made a home in the World of Dreams and became the God of Shadows. And those that followed him were exiles, dreamers, and death-dealers, the displaced and the disfellowshipped. Yet Dorchnok ruled none of these, for he dictated that his worshippers should govern themselves. Nevertheless, he blessed those whom he favoured, and he was fickle in his favourites.

So it was that the five Younger Gods divided the people of Keos, flattering his worshippers and claiming many for themselves. Yet the majority of the Terrans remained true to Keos and continued to worship him in his absence, for when Keos rose from his isolation they believed he would seek communion with the faithful and that many would be raised to become Bloodlords – and so it came to be, and their faith was rewarded.

But the unfaithful were not rewarded. Yea, Keos did visit the Younger Gods in his wrath, and he ordered them to submit to his will and bring their worshippers back into his fold. But the Younger Gods spurned Keos, for they were proud like their father and they asserted their own divinity.

Yea, and they claimed that Keos was a maimed God and that his power was diminished. And as their evidence, they pointed to the forge at Thoir Cuma, which had ever been a sign of Keos's strength, and they showed that it had been cast down and a temple of Tacharan had been raised in its place. And thus did Keos fail to establish his supremacy over them.

A fragment recovered from the Ruins of Speur Dún:
'The Council of Keokumot' from the Book of Terra,
translation by Sodar Weir

Chapter One

Annev jolted awake and looked about, trying to gain his bearings. A mix of bracken, pine, maple and spruce surrounded him. He was in the Brakewood, but not at its heart. He lay almost at the edge of the wood itself, if not close enough to see the treeline that marked the end of the forest and the beginning of the plains that led to Banok and Luqura – and that revelation provoked Annev into remembering the previous night: the shadows of the Brake had crept up on them as dusk fell, and despite consistently heading in a northwesterly direction and being near the end of the forest, they'd never managed to penetrate the Brake's western treeline. As the shadows overtook them and night fell, they'd agreed to set up camp and continue the next leg of their journey in the morning.

It was morning now – late morning, actually – and Annev's friends were bustling about the camp, stowing their things back in the apple cart. Annev looked up from his blankets and saw Brayan's towering figure hitching the black mare to its harness. The round-faced Titus was assisting him and gave Annev a wave as he saw that he had awoken. Annev nodded back and stood up, stumbling into Therin as he did so. The thin boy splashed half a bucket of water across Annev before tripping over his own feet and spilling the second pail. He surveyed the two half-full buckets and his own wet clothes.

'Morning, Master Glove.' Therin scowled, pouring the contents of one bucket into the other, then handing the now-empty bucket to Annev. 'Master Blacksmith wants us to fetch him some water. Since you've gone and spilled half of mine, why don't you be a brother and fill this one back up?' He smiled, but his eyes were flat.

'Master Glove?'

Therin groaned, pulling the bucket back. 'You know, you're a bit dense when you wake up.' He indicated the thick, soot-stained smithing glove on Annev's left hand. Annev had fallen asleep wearing it, though he recalled that had been a conscious decision.

'Glove,' Therin said, waving his fingers in front of Annev's face. '*Master* Glove. Because you're a master avatar now, you know?' He paused. 'It's a joke.' Annev only looked more confused. 'Forget it. I'll refill the bucket.' He pressed the full one into Annev's hands. 'Take that to Sraon – then do yourself a favour and douse your head in it.' He waited till Annev accepted the bucket then hurried back in the direction he had come.

Annev watched him go. As he did, Titus walked over and threw his arm across Annev's shoulders, though he did so with an effort.

'Ignore him,' the blond boy said. 'Therin's grumpy because he was woken up for chores and you got to sleep in.'

Annev looked about the camp and saw everyone's bedrolls were packed. 'Why didn't he wake me up?'

'Because I said I'd brain him with my axe if he disturbed you.' Sraon stepped from behind a tree with a cord of wood in one arm and a woodcutter's axe in his free hand. He carefully set the latter in the back of the cart along with the wood then picked up his halberd, which had been leaning against a tree trunk. 'The last few days have been traumatic and you're still recovering. I thought it best if you slept.'

The words stirred up fragments from a recent dream, but Annev was unable to hold onto them. Had he been talking with someone? Yes. A strange man dressed all in black. And he had said ... no. The memory was gone. Annev shook his head.

'Thank you for the consideration, Sraon, but from now on I'd prefer to rise with the rest of the party.'

The blacksmith bowed deferentially. 'Very well, Master Annev.' He took the pail of water then gestured for Annev and Titus to open their empty waterskins. As Annev opened his, his belly rumbled.

'Any breakfast?'

'We saved you some grouse,' Sraon said, topping off both bags. 'It's on a skewer on the other side of the cart.'

'Everyone else has eaten?'

Sraon nodded. 'To be honest, I thought you'd be up earlier. Titus did try to wake you for breakfast, but when we saw how deeply you slept, I decided to let you rise on your own.' He placed the emptied bucket back in the cart and waved for the boys to tie off their skins. 'That's it then. We can push on now.' He looked around. 'Where did Therin get to?'

'He spilled the other bucket,' Titus said. 'He went to refill it.'

The blacksmith grunted. 'I only asked him to fetch two pails because I guessed he'd spill half the water bringing it back.' Annev smiled and Sraon shook his head. 'Go fetch the lad, Titus.' The boy ran off. 'Pack up, Annev. You can eat while we walk.' Annev complied, noting how easily Sraon fell into a leadership role despite his claim of being a simple blacksmith. Sraon seemed not to notice the dissonance between his words and his actions, though, and Annev wasn't about to point them out.

The swarthy blacksmith gazed about the wood, his eye alert. 'I'm eager to leave this forest behind,' he said to no one in particular. 'Never much liked the way the shadows play tricks on you.'

Annev stopped in the midst of rolling up his blankets, but the blacksmith had already gone to help Brayan break the rest of their camp.

Shadows ... tricks. Why does that sound so familiar? Once again, he tried to recall the details from his dream, but he was too awake now and the impressions were fleeting. He packed his bedroll into the cart and strapped his sword to his waist. As he grasped the sword's hilt, Annev felt an unnoticed tension ease from his body.

The wavy kris blade – or flame-blade – was properly called a flamberge, a name that was doubly appropriate for this weapon, which possessed the ability to summon fire along its undulating edge. Annev had plundered it from the Vault of Damnation in Chaenbalu, along with the handful of other magical artifacts in his possession, such as his Boots of Speed and his dragonscale cloak. He wasn't entirely certain how he felt about stealing cursed magical items – he had been trained to place them inside the Vault, not steal them from it – but the flamberge had helped him defeat both the metal-maligned *feurog* and the seemingly invulnerable Oyru, a Kroseran warrior who was also a member of the Siänar and one of the six elite assassins of Keos. That memory gave Annev pause, both because he had never confirmed the death of the shadow assassin, and because it sparked another memory from his half-forgotten dreams.

Shadowcaster.

Clesaiche.

Dorcha Sionnach.

Three different names for the God of Shadows.

I dreamed that Dorchnok visited me. The details suddenly crystallised in Annev's mind: a man with pale skin, bright purple eyes, curly black hair, and a black moustache and goatee; he had been dressed all in black, his clothes shifting between darkness and smoke.

Could he really have been visited by the Younger God of Shadows – the God of Dreams? It hardly seemed plausible, even with everything that had happened in the past few days ... but if so, what had he wanted?

He tried to warn me about something. About someone. Annev tried to recall more, but that was all he could remember.

It was just a dream, he decided. It wasn't real – it *couldn't* be real. It was only nerves. Anxiety about leaving Chaenbalu, coupled with the uncertainty of what he would find in Luqura.

Only something *was* pursuing Annev – he couldn't deny that. Kelga and Janak had been after him, as had Oyru. The *feurog* and the shadow demons – the eidolons – were connected too, though Annev didn't know exactly how. And while Kelga and Janak had been destroyed, Oyru might still be alive. In fact, the more Annev considered it, the more he was certain Oyru *had* survived and that the Shadow Reborn would eventually track him down, intent on bringing him back to the Fallen God of Earthblood.

But Annev wouldn't voice those concerns to the others. They had plenty to worry about without his suspicions, and he planned to leave them at the first opportunity. No one knew that – not even Sraon – and Annev meant to keep it that way. Staying with the group was selfish when his presence endangered their lives, and as he became attuned to the others, Annev saw they sensed this, too. He observed it in their posture, the way they leaned back when he passed or settled a hand on their weapons belts; he saw it in their eyes, the way they stared at his gloved hand yet wouldn't meet his gaze. He'd even caught a glimmer of it from Therin when the boy had lashed out at Annev for spilling his bucket of water.

They were all afraid of him – and they had good reason to be. Even if Annev currently controlled the glowing hand hidden beneath his smithing glove, he was being pursued and their proximity to him put their lives at risk.

Annev kicked dirt onto the embers of the campfire and stowed his pack, earning a nod from Brayan on the other side of the wagon as he rechecked the straps harnessing the black mare to their repurposed apple cart.

Titus returned with Therin, who tossed his empty bucket into the back of the wagon. Before Annev could say a word, the taller boy pointed at him. 'I wouldn't have spilled the water if that bastard blacksmith had only asked me to fill *one* bucket. All right? I'm not stupid.'

Annev held up his hands, hoping to soften his friend's ire. 'I never said you were, Therin.'

'Annev doesn't need to when it's so obvious to the rest of us.'

The trio turned as Fyn appeared from behind a silver maple, a broad falchion resting on his shoulder. Twin maces were also strapped to his back and he had a brace of throwing knives wrapped around each of his forearms.

'Where have *you* been?' Therin asked, ignoring Fyn's insult and asking Annev's question for him. 'And why do you look like a walking armoury? I thought we were supposed to leave our weapons in the cart.'

'I was scouting the trail. Figured I might run into some *feurog* and wanted to be prepared.'

Therin and Annev nodded at this, their memories of the metal monsters still fresh in their minds.

'Also,' Fyn continued, 'Sraon says we might see bandits on the road today. Figured a show of force might deter aggression.' The larger boy sheathed his sword then gestured back the way he had come. 'Found us a way out of the forest where the brush isn't too thick. We should be able to pull the cart out of the Brake within the hour.'

'Excellent,' Sraon said, appearing behind Annev and the other two boys. 'We'll leave immediately.'

'There's something else,' Fyn continued, looking more thoughtful. 'I found a young woman – a witgirl from the Academy. She's alone, and she won't say a word. She's also carrying something. A small bundle.'

'A witgirl?' Annev repeated. 'Who?'

'I don't remember her name. She's blonde. Friend of Myjun.'

Annev's breath hitched at the mention of his former crush, yet as he struggled for words, Therin immediately perked up. 'You found *Faith*? She's *alive*?'

'Yeah, Faith. She's not talking, though. Walked the other way when I approached. She's ... well, I don't think she's all there. She kept singing some tune I've never heard before and pretended she couldn't see me. I didn't get a good look at what she was holding but I think it was a child. A baby.'

An infant from the Academy, Annev realised, *probably taken from the witwomen's nursery. But how? And why is she alone?* He looked to Sraon and the blacksmith nodded.

'Brayan and Titus, go with Master Fyn and see if you can bring Faith here. We can see to her needs, and I'd like to ask her some questions.'

'At once,' Brayan said, nodding fiercely. He gestured for Titus to follow between him and Fyn, then picked up his heavy war maul.

'I'll come, too!' Therin declared, dashing to join the trio, and soon all four had disappeared into the forest.

Sraon watched them go, then eyed the skewered bird swinging from the side of the cart. He looked at Annev. 'That's yours, but it'd be kind if you saved it for the lass. If I don't miss my guess, she'll be hungry.'

'Of course. She's welcome to it.'

The smith winked at Annev with his one eye. 'Good lad. We can get you something when we stop in Banok.' He shook his head. 'It's a wonder how she got out here. And if she survived the Academy's fall, maybe others did, too.' Sraon scratched his chin as his eyes dipped to look at Annev's gloved hand. Annev impulsively flexed his fingers and the smith turned away, pretending not to notice.

Self-conscious, Annev found an excuse to stalk into the woods, rubbing the back of his soot-stained glove. Through the tough leather he could feel the outline of the thick gold caps reinforcing his metal knuckles. Just below, on the back of his hand, was the symbol of the God of Earthblood: a war hammer floating above a smoking anvil. Annev's fingers drifted down to the back of his hand and he shuddered.

I'm using the Hand of Keos. The same hand that imprisoned and slaughtered hundreds of thousands at the Council of Keokumot. The same hand that fought my ancestor Breathanas during the Battle of Vosgar. I am wearing the hand of an evil god ... and I can't remove it.

Brayan and the three boys returned a few minutes later, but Annev kept his distance. He stood at the edge of the clearing as Faith approached, her slender figure encircled by the others. As Fyn had said, she was holding a small bundle in her arms, cradling it the same way a mother would hold a small child.

And she was still humming the strange tune: from the hoarseness of her voice and the haggard look in her eyes, Annev guessed she had been singing all night, yet she still sang it – a lilting song that was both sad and sweet.

Sraon approached the haunted witgirl, openly sympathetic. 'Morning, lass. You're a good distance from Chaenbalu. Are you all right?'

Faith continued to hum her song, oblivious to Sraon's questions. She seemed aware of her surroundings, though, for she stopped walking when the others halted near the ashes of their campfire.

'You're safe here,' Sraon said. 'I was just wondering how you got out this way.'

Faith stroked the bundle in her arms, her eyes distant, and continued to hum, not meeting anyone's gaze.

'Faith,' Therin said, his voice uncharacteristically tender. 'You're with friends.'

The woman half-turned, her gaze looking past Therin's shoulder. Such a small thing, yet they all seemed to sense its import.

Therin swallowed, glanced once at Annev, and looked back at the filthy witgirl. You can talk to us, Faith.' He paused. 'We're all leaving Chaenbalu. Headed to Banok. You can come with us if you like.'

Faith's tune faltered and her humming grew quieter. Slowly, she turned her eyes towards Therin, staring through him until she blinked and her gaze focused on his face. Therin smiled, looking for all the world like she'd kissed him on the nose.

'What's that you got there, girl?' Sraon said, stepping closer. 'A child?'

Faith looked up, saw Sraon's one eye staring at her, and drew back, her face suddenly wild. A stream of words burst from her lips, their cadence matching the tune she had been singing. Annev caught the first few – something rapid about darkness and light – and then his vision blurred, his mind growing hazy. He tried to focus on the girl again, blinked, and realised she was gone.

'Keos!' Brayan swore, jumping back. 'Where'd she go?'

They all looked around and were each as confused as the next. 'It's as if she was never here at all,' Sraon said, voicing what they all had been thinking.

'You mean ... she was a ghost?'

'She might have been, Titus. How else to explain it?' The blacksmith swallowed, his grip tightening on his halberd. 'Never liked these woods,' he muttered. 'Let's move out. The Brake Road isn't far, and we have supplies to fetch before we roll on to the capital.'

Chapter Two

The black mare and supply-laden apple cart trudged through the forest, their progress slowed by frequent stops to clear brush from the path or lift the wagon when it reached terrain it could not surmount. The group had become effective at overcoming such obstacles, though, and soon they broke through the Brakewood's treeline and rolled along more quickly. They reformed with Annev and Therin flanking the cart, Sraon and Fyn leading the party, and Brayan and Titus following behind. Within a half-hour they reached a hard-packed road just north of the Brake, and from thence their progress towards Banok and Luqura was brisk.

The party had been travelling west on the East Road for less than an hour when they met their first group of travellers. Five men on horses wearing black armour led a second group of about twenty-five men on foot, the latter dressed in simple farmers' clothing with red bands tied about their arms and pikes on their shoulders. Sraon eyed the group warily before directing the rest of the party to move off the road and let the soldiers pass.

'Conscripts,' he whispered. 'Don't make eye contact, keep your weapons hidden and keep walking.'

Fyn swore as he hastily shed his assortment of weapons, dumping them unceremoniously into the wagon. Annev likewise unbuckled his flamberge and removed the spiked vambrace that doubled as a shield and buckler, and the rest wordlessly followed suit, doing as Sraon directed. The soldiers seemed about to pass them by, until one of the black armoured men pulled his roan horse about and trotted in front of their apple cart. Sraon cursed, just loud enough for Annev to hear, and halted their black mare. Everything came to a standstill, with the mounted man blocking their path and then pointing at Therin.

'You, boy! Where are you headed?'

Therin bit his lip then glanced over at Sraon. 'Uh ... Luqura?'

The man on horseback grunted then spurred his horse to flank Therin. 'You don't seem so sure. Perhaps what you meant was Borderlund.'

'Borderlund?' Therin echoed, his head shaking as his gaze rose to meet the soldier's. 'That's east. We're headed west.'

'You *were* headed west. You're travelling with us now – to Paldron.'

'Hold up,' Sraon said, frowning. 'What's this about?'

The soldier trotted his horse back over to Sraon, and Annev finally risked a glance up at the man on horseback. Although the black metal plate obscured the man's bulk, he seemed of a size with Annev and Fyn. He wore no helmet, his head was bald, and a nasty scar ran the length of his skull, its line tracing down his cheek and disappearing into a fiery red beard.

'You the leader of this party?'

'Of sorts.' Sraon looked up, his dark eyes meeting the soldier. 'I suppose I could ask you the same question ... but I don't see any epaulettes. No ribbons. You wear no sign of rank at all, actually.' He saw the soldier's cheeks and ears redden until they almost matched his beard. Sraon smiled. 'Unless the Paldron Army has changed its marks of office some time in the last two years, I'd say you're a sergeant, maybe even a lieutenant, who's been sent to conscript men.'

'Who are *you*?' The scarred soldier demanded, his hand grasping the hilt of his sheathed sword. 'How dare you challenge—'

'Or perhaps you're just a bandit,' Sraon continued. 'You're in a foreign kingdom, after all, and you've presented no documentation or writ of conscription. You haven't even told us your name or that of your superior officer. If you *are* of the Paldron Army, I believe we are entitled to continue our journey to Luqura unmolested.' He paused. 'Unless you're bandits, of course, in which case we are entitled to defend ourselves and our possessions, and

King Lenka will hunt you down once he hears you are preying on weary travellers.'

The red-bearded officer blustered then snapped his fingers at another of the mounted soldiers. The second man rode over, leaving the rest of the soldiers and conscripts to wait on Sraon and Annev's party. 'Show him the writ, sergeant.' The veteran pulled a folded piece of parchment out of his saddlebag and handed it to Sraon.

'I am *Captain* Alcoran,' the first soldier said, scowling. 'And your king has given me permission to conscript men for the war in Borderlund.' Alcoran waited a few seconds for Sraon to study the document then snatched it back from him. 'This writ grants me the power to conscript any men of fighting age.' He surveyed Annev's party. 'Which would include all of you. So, as I said, perhaps you *were* going to Luqura. *Now* you're marching to save the Darite Empire from the monsters beyond the River Kuar.' Alcoran reached into his own saddlebag, pulled out a handful of red armbands and threw them at Sraon's feet. 'Put those on. And bring your cart and horse with us.'

Annev held his breath, wondering what the blacksmith would do. Brayan and the rest seemed frozen in place too, while one of Fyn's hands slowly dipped into the sash at his waist. Apparently he'd kept at least one weapon on his person. Annev caught the boy's eye and Fyn stopped moving but didn't let go of the hidden dagger.

Sraon looked down at the red strips of cloth lying in front of him and shook his head. Instead of picking them up, he turned and reached inside the apple cart. Alcoran whipped his sword from his sheath and levelled it at Sraon's chest.

'One more move, peasant, and I will skewer you.' The captain's eyes glittered, daring Sraon to challenge him. 'Now pick up those armbands.'

Sraon laughed and used two fingers to casually direct the blade above his shoulder. Alcoran's frown deepened, but then Sraon's other hand slowly withdrew a small package from the cart. Keeping his eyes on Alcoran, Sraon unwrapped the twine and oilcloth securing the parcel, then slid a yellowed piece of parchment from a tarnished metal cylinder. Sraon carefully opened the document and passed it to the bald captain, who read it, his lips moving as he did so.

'You're a slaver from Innistiul?'

'That is what the document says.'

Alcoran looked back at it, parsing the words again, then rolled the parchment up and tapped his chin with it. 'This is an old writ. Show me your mark, slaver.'

Sraon's scowl deepened but he pulled down his shirt to show a dark red scar in the shape of a single-masted sailing vessel branded on the back of his shoulder. Beside it was a second brand in the shape of an open hand. Before Annev could study the marks closely, Sraon pulled his shirt back into place.

'King Lenka might have given you permission to press-gang his people into your border war,' Sraon said, straightening his shirt, 'but King *Cheng* has done no such thing.'

Alcoran studied Sraon for a moment, then looked back at Brayan, Annev, and the other avatars, evaluating each in turn. 'These aren't Innistiulmen. They're still subject to Lenka's decree.'

'These men are my slaves,' Sraon said, surprising Annev and the rest of the party. 'Are you threatening to deny me of my property?'

Alcoran snorted. 'Since when does an Innistiul slaver travel alone with five unchained slaves? These men are your *companions*, and they are citizens of Greater Luqura – or possibly Borderlund. Either way, I'm conscripting them.'

'We *are* his slaves,' Brayan said, stepping up from behind the cart. He had slid his war maul from wherever it had been hidden and now it rested casually on his shoulder. 'Are you calling our master a liar?'

Alcoran eyed the war hammer. He nudged his horse back a few paces then turned to look at Annev. 'Is that true, boy? Are you a slave to this man? Think hard before you answer. You could find your freedom serving in the Paldron Army.'

Annev took his cue from Brayan. 'I've served Master Sraon my whole life. He treats us well, and I fancy I have more freedom following him than your conscripts have following you.'

The captain smiled, his eyes cold. 'Your whole life, you say? Yet you are Darite by the look of things, and all Darites are born freemen. How is it, then, you have served this man your whole life?'

The rest of the group froze, all eyes turning to Annev, who did not dare to look back at Sraon for help.

'I'm only half Darite. My mother was an Ilumite.'

'An Ildar!' Alcoran sneered, hawked, and spat into Annev's face. He turned back to Sraon. 'You'd execute that one if you knew what was good for you. Ildari always bring trouble. Sometimes they even carry magic.'

Annev felt the weight of more eyes turn to him as he ducked his head. Sraon saved him this time, though.

'The boy has been a good slave, just as his father was a good servant. And I assure you, he hasn't shown an inkling of affinity for magic.'

No, Annev thought, *I've shown rather more than an inkling.* Instead of responding, he kept his head down in subservience, not even wiping the spittle from his cheek. It was no different than when Fyn used to pick on him, actually.

Alcoran looked at the rest of the party, eyeing Brayan in particular. 'And the rest of these slaves,' he said, addressing Sraon. 'Are they Ildari as well, or something even more abominable?'

'Simple Darite slaves,' Sraon said. 'Brutes and sneak thieves, for the most part. Imprisoned until I purchased them – legally. If you take them, you will have to reimburse me for the loss of property.'

Alcoran scowled, eyeing them all darkly. 'I don't see any brands on these men, Master Slaver. They aren't your property if they haven't been marked. You know the law.'

'Aye, better than you it seems. Codex eleven-dash-two of the Innistiul Code of Human Procurement states a slave need not be marked as such if they consent to their master's ownership, either verbally or in writing. They fetch a better price at market when they aren't branded, and these here are perfectly loyal. Never had cause to brand them, nor will I so long as they remain dutiful.'

'So loyal ... yet you choose not to brand them so you might one day sell them. This seems inconsistent – and I am familiar with the Innistiul Codex, Master Slaver. Borderlund has its own flesh trade and I recall Codex eleven–dash–two differently. Does it not say that an unbranded slave must consent by word *and* by writ? If you are travelling with unmarked property, you must carry your receipts.'

Sraon glowered at the man, his swarthy face turning a dark red. 'You have heard them state of their own free will that they are my property, Captain. The writ is a formality for situations in which the slave might recant.'

Once again, the captain looked over the party, his eyes sparkling. 'Do you hear, men? Your master has given you leave to depart his company. He has no writ and you carry no brand. If you desire to leave his employment, you can become a freeman now and join my soldiers in Borderlund. There is food aplenty, clean uniforms, dry beds. You'll earn three pips a day to start – a whole copper wheel – more, if you stay with the company for at least a year. What say you?'

The others glanced between Annev and Sraon and slowly shook their heads. Alcoran watched it all then snorted. 'Too stupid to seize your own freedom when it's offered.' He spat at the ground and Sraon frowned at him.

'I'd like my writ back now, Captain.'

Alcoran didn't move to return it. Instead, he glanced back at his soldiers, who were getting restless, then turned to scrutinise each member of the party in turn.

'They'll run away the moment you enter the city. That one especially.' He pointed at Fyn. 'I can see it in their eyes. The ones that won't bear the yoke of another man.' He pointed at Annev. 'Him, too – and he's Ildari besides. You should brand him now and save yourself the trouble when he runs out on you. If he causes any trouble, they'll pin it on you.'

'Thank you for the warning, Captain. Now, my writ?'

Alcoran half-crumpled the yellowed parchment in his hand and trotted his horse close to Sraon, eyes cold. 'I could rip this up,' he said, his voice just above a whisper. 'Take all of you by force. We have the men.'

'You could, but you won't,' Sraon answered, eyes glittering.

'King Cheng sells almost as many slaves to King Alpenrose as he does to King Lenka. If he learned that his emissaries were being accosted on the roads, he might cease trade with Paldron.'

'He wouldn't, though. Cheng is too greedy.'

'Then he would buy your Terran stock at half price and sell them back to you for double.'

Alcoran weighed Sraon's words then tossed the document at Sraon, who caught it deftly. The captain sneered then spat at Sraon's boots.

'Safe travels, Master Slaver.'

The soldier turned his horse about and rejoined his company. Shortly thereafter, the Borderlunders resumed their march and the red-banded Luquran conscripts fell in line behind them. Annev and the rest watched them go, and then all eyes slowly turned towards Sraon. The blacksmith looked from Annev to the rest of the party, shrugged, smoothed out the crinkled parchment in his hand, then tucked it back in the tarnished cylinder. After rewrapping it in oilcloth, he returned the package to the apple cart.

Annev and the other avatars looked at one another, no one needing to articulate what they were all thinking.

No one except Therin.

'You were a *slaver*?'

Sraon sighed, turning to face the youth. 'I was a lot of things before I came to your village. You may not realise it, but some of us had lives before coming to Chaenbalu. I had several. In one of those, yes, I was a slaver.'

'Huh.' Therin continued to stare open-mouthed, as if he had just seen a pixie or sprite. 'Huh,' he repeated.

Annev couldn't deny his own surprise at Sraon's revelation. *A slaver*. The knowledge pricked his conscience, reminding him of something Myjun had once said to him: 'Sraon never tells people what he did before he came to Chaenbalu. Don't you find that a little odd?' At the time, Annev *hadn't* thought it odd. He knew the man had learned smithing in Odarnea, the northernmost tip of the Empire, and he knew Sraon had fought ogres on the Cunnart Isle – where he had lost the eye he kept covered beneath a black patch – but this new piece of Sraon's past was unanticipated.

Innistiul – the slaver isle – lay very close to Cunnart, and both were just a day's travel from Quiri, the capital of Odarnea. All the details made sense, but they painted a new portrait of the blacksmith that did not match the image Annev had built in his mind. 'He's a good man,' he'd told Myjun. 'I see him every Seventhday.'

Annev bit his lip, wincing at the memory of Myjun's retort. 'He's a *smith*, Ani. Like the *Terrans*? They worship Keos and they're *all* smiths.'

Annev shook his head, attempting to dismiss the memory and repress the pain that came whenever he thought of the dead woman. He was rarely successful.

I killed her, he thought, reliving the terrible instant when the earth had opened beneath Myjun's feet. *I would have burned her alive, just like Tosan, had she not fallen into that pit first. Screaming. Calling my name.* Annev closed his eyes, forcing himself to acknowledge what he had been too blind to see before.

Myjun had not been a kind person. Like her father, she had been prejudiced, manipulative, full of pride and spite. She had wanted Annev dead – had wanted Sodar dead, too, which Annev could neither forget nor forgive. In some ways, she even shared blame for the priest's death, though the bulk of it lay with Annev for his own foolishness, and with Tosan for committing the deed.

Annev forced himself back to the present.

Sraon was a slaver – or he had been. That didn't make the man evil, but it didn't make him good, either. It also raised a lot of questions Annev had thought he had answered.

Who exactly was Sraon? What other secrets filled his past, and why had Sodar trusted him? Had he known? Like the old priest, the blacksmith was more than he pretended to be. Unlike him, he seemed more prepared to discuss his past.

'Come on,' Sraon said again, shaking Annev from his dark thoughts and spurring the other party members into action. 'We can sell the grain and seed we took from the Academy at the trading post outside of Banok. If memory serves, we'll need plenty of coin to pay the gate fees in Luqura.' He passed the mare's reins to Fyn and started walking. Once they were moving, things felt a little less awkward.

Annev watched as Therin slowed his pace to join Titus and Brayan at the back of the cart. He whispered something to Titus and the two talked in hushed voices, which made Brayan visibly uncomfortable, his meaty fist continually reaching up to scratch his thick neckbeard. But the quartermaster held his tongue, pretending to ignore the conversation between his plump apprentice and the lanky brown-haired youth.

Near the head of the group, Fyn seemed unaffected by Sraon's revelation. He had paused long enough to retrieve his twin maces from the cart and secure the weapons on his back where he was accustomed to carrying them. This morning he had also tied his dirty brown dreadlocks into a thick ponytail, which stiffly swayed as he marched in silence beside Sraon. As Annev watched, he caught Fyn sneaking furtive glances at the blacksmith's back. What was that expression? Awe? Respect? Whatever it was, Fyn seemed more impressed than anxious about Sraon's past.

Annev frowned and trotted up to the taller boy, who glanced to the side and slowed his pace a bit so they walked a distance behind Sraon.

'What?' Fyn asked, not bothering with pleasantries.

Annev's eyes darted between Sraon's back and Fyn's face. 'Yesterday, you said you were only coming to Luqura with us because Sraon knew someone who would pay for your avatar skills.'

'That's right.'

'*All* of your avatar skills ... or just the ones that involve those maces?'

'Whichever pays best, I suppose.'

Annev considered his next words carefully. 'You could have conscripted with those Borderlunders – if you just wanted to fight, that is.' Fyn nodded and Annev continued. 'I expect an army provides lots of opportunity to fight. Just seemed like something you might enjoy.'

Fyn smiled. 'You trying to get rid of me, keokum?'

Annev smiled in turn, knowing the jibe was meant to be friendly – sort of.

'The opposite, actually,' Annev said. 'I'm not sure what I'll find in Luqura. Sodar never said much about his plans once we left Chaenbalu, and I won't know this Reeve fellow from my own arse. I'd feel safer if I had friends about, just in case.'

'We're friends now, are we?'

Annev hesitated. 'Sure. Closest thing to it, anyway.'

Fyn snorted. 'Look, Annev. I might no longer want to kill you, but that's a far cry from calling you a friend – and I don't want to chain my fate to you any more than I wanted to tie myself to that army jackass. I'm my own man, and now that the Academy is gone I can go where I want and do as I please. I intend to do exactly that.'

Fyn's words echoed Annev's unspoken feelings. 'Luqura is a big city, though. It'd be nice to know someone's watching your back – like at Janak's palace. We worked well together then.'

'We got the job done – mostly – but I wouldn't say we worked well together.'

Annev chuckled. 'I suppose you did leave for me dead – well, Kenton did anyway.'

Fyn answered with a smile and a shrug, then chewed his lip. 'The problem is we both like to lead, and I'm not comfortable following you around like ol' Titus back there. That boy's got his nose shoved so far up your arse, he could tell you what you ate for breakfast.'

'Very eloquent,' Annev said, grimacing. 'I suppose you're right, though. I'm no more likely to be your lackey than you are to ...'

'Shove my nose up your arse?' Fyn provided.

Annev again laughed in spite of himself. 'Yeah.' They walked in silence and Annev could hear that Therin and Titus had stopped talking too. He looked ahead and saw why: Banok's city walls had come into view, along with the people and tents outside its southern gate. They were approaching the trading post. Annev turned to take his former place flanking the apple cart as Fyn spoke up again.

'I'm not saying we can't work together in the future, you know. Just saying ... well, I don't know what I'm saying. I want to keep my options open.'

'I can accept that. I suppose that's what I'm doing, too. I don't

31

know what I'll find in Luqura, or what kind of person Reeve will be. Just want to get this damned glowing hand off my arm.'

'You could always cut it off.'

Annev scoffed, finding little amusement in Fyn's joke, but when he saw Fyn's thoughtful face, he was less certain. 'Wait. You're serious?'

Fyn nodded. 'You've already lost one arm, right? What's it matter if you lose a bit more flesh? That hand could fall off right now and you wouldn't be any more or less crippled than if you had cut it off yourself.'

They were almost to the trading post now, and the gates of Banok lay beyond the clustered tents. Annev slowed his pace, letting Fyn go on ahead, and looked down at his elbow, considering it.

As if reading Annev's thoughts, Sraon dropped back to join him and tapped the glowing hand covered by the old smithing glove.

'You and I will be splitting from the group when we get into the city. There's someone I want you to meet – someone who might be able to help with that arm.'

'Who?' Annev asked, feeling a little of his growing tension ease.

'A smith,' Sraon said. 'Goes by the name Dolyn.'

The group strode into the trading post and Annev took note of Banok's now-familiar walls, providing a backdrop to the outdoor market, which was new to him. The latter was packed with merchants hawking their wares, with accents ranging from rustic Odarnean to primitive Markluan and exotic Alltaran.

'Fresh fruit from Fertil Hedge! So sweet, you'd swear it's magic!'

'Soft silks from da fa' east! Warm furs from Tir—'

'Paldron steel! Axes 'n' swords! Pots 'n'—'

'Horses! The best stock of the Green Froch, at better prices than you'll find in Desbyr!'

The trading post itself was little more than a collection of tents, carts, and mercantile booths designed to be packed up or carted back to the safety of Banok's walls before dusk. Annev hadn't seen any signs of the mobile marketplace less than three days ago, but then he, Fyn and Kenton had all arrived in the night.

Only three days ago, Annev thought. *So much has happened since*

then. Tosan sent us to Banok to retrieve Janak's Rod of Compulsion.
Sodja Rocas stole the rod from under our noses. Kenton left me to die
in Janak's burning palace. Oyru chased me from Banok to Chaenbalu.
I escaped a cell, plundered the Vault, and fought off the feurog. *I saved*
Sodar ... and then I had to watch him die. Annev grew sombre at
that thought, and a masochistic part of him refused to stop there.

And then I killed Tosan and Myjun. I killed the masters and ancients.
I killed everyone who was still in the Academy when it collapsed, because
I couldn't control myself. Because I couldn't control this.

Annev glowered down at the large smithing glove and found
himself making a fist with the cursed golden prosthetic.

Annev and Sraon left the rest of their group at the market and
passed through Banok's city gates without so much as a sign or a
watchword. A black-clad guard with a short, blue-trimmed cape
glanced at them as they passed by but gave no signs of recognition.
That shouldn't have surprised Annev – not all of Banok's watch-
men had been ensnared by Janak's Rod of Compulsion – yet he
feared being recognised all the same. His gut had told him that at
least one of those men would be guarding Banok's gate and would
recognise Annev.

But the guard didn't spare them a second glance. Even the
blacksmith's missing eye didn't seem to faze the man – further
evidence that prejudices from Chaenbalu were not quite the same
as those in the outside world.

'Quit gawking and keep moving,' Sraon said, pulling Annev
along. 'If Dolyn still lives here, she'll have her smithy in the craftsmen's district.'

'She? I thought you said Dolyn was a blacksmith.'

'I did. Women can be smiths, too.'

'Yeah, but ... it's not common.'

Sraon snorted. 'Maybe not in Chaenbalu. Takes a special sort of
person to shape metal, and Dolyn is just such a one.'

'What makes you think she can help me remove this hand?'

'She's special, like I said. I met her through smithing.' He
grinned, remembering. 'She came to Banok to practise her craft
and give me a friendly bit of competition. Well, she managed that,

and then some. Dolyn can turn a bit of iron as good as anyone, but she's also got quite a skill with smaller work. Goldsmith. Silversmithing. Very versatile lass. My clumsy hands couldn't compete with her graceful ones, so I soon found folks only came to me when they wanted sturdy work. Horseshoes. Hoops for the cooper. Nails. Maybe the odd farm tool or a pot that needed mending. I could understand it, but though I may not be an artisan like Gwen, I've got more skill than that. I was wasted here, and when Sodar invited me to come to Chaenbalu, I went gladly.'

'To replace my father.'

Sraon slowed and turned his one eye on Annev. 'You know about that, do you?'

Annev nodded. 'Yes, I know. Sodar explained that much, at least.' Sraon grunted. 'You knew Sodar before Chaenbalu, though, didn't you? I mean, he was more than two thousand years old. You must have met him before Banok.'

'Aye, I did.' They picked up their pace along the street again. 'I first met Sodar as a child. In Innistiul.'

'Before you became a slaver?'

Sraon wobbled his head back and forth. 'Yes and no. You've heard how some folks are born into slavery? Well, that's the way in Innistiul. Except I wasn't born a slave. I was born a slaver. Family business. Didn't have much choice, least not as a child on the Isle. You learn the craft, and you think it's the same way the world over. Wasn't till I met Sodar that I learned how backwards we had it.'

'How old were you?' Annev asked, getting wrapped up in the tale. Sodar had never shared many details of his life, nor had Sraon – not in all the years they had known each other in Chaenbalu.

'Not more than five, I think? I don't recall why Sodar had visited the Isle, but he brought Thane and Tuor with him. A woman, too, though I don't recall her name.'

'You knew my father?'

'Not really, no. Tuor was a few years older than me, and we weren't exactly playmates. Sodar knew my father, though, and that's how I came to be introduced to him. He told stories in court. Used a bit o' magic to enhance the telling.'

'Sodar was a storyteller? He performed for folks? Like Yohan the Chandler?'

Sraon snorted. 'Yohan couldn't tell a tale from his tallow. He only told stories at night, and only then to sell more candles – and he didn't enjoy it the way Sodar did. You could see it in the way he gave his sermons. They all verged on being more story than moral. No magic, though. Not with those ancients and masters watching.'

'Not with *anyone* watching,' Annev said, his tone sour. 'Not even to save my parents when I was born.'

Sraon squinted at Annev. 'Might not have been anything he could have done, lad. The whole village stoned them to death while he saved you. Wish I coulda been there. Maybe two of us could have stopped it but ... well, that's the past. All those folks have gone now. Dead or pulled into those damnable shadows ...'

Sraon fell silent, and Annev suddenly remembered how Alanna, the widowed seamstress, had been pulled from his fingers. Deep into the shadepools cast by Oyru and his eidolons.

'Right,' Annev said, trying to change the subject, 'so tell me more about Dolyn – or is it Gwen?'

Sraon smirked and turned down one of Banok's many side streets. The walls pressed in around them, narrow and half-covered by Banok's overhanging rooftops.

'Not Gwen. She signs her work "Dolyn", but I reckon that's on account of her wanting folks to buy her wares without knowing a woman forged them.'

'And why do you think she can help remove this hand?' Annev asked, returning to his earlier question.

'Ah,' Sraon said, his one eye glinting. 'I'll leave Gwen to explain.'

'Wait ... you just said—'

'This is her,' Sraon said, teeth flashing. He halted in front of a squat stone building with a soot-stained door. 'Mind your manners. You're a guest. I'm an old colleague and a competitor – and the only one she tolerates calling her Gwen. She's Dolyn to you. And we have history. That gives me licence to wag my tongue a bit. Don't think that gives you the same privilege.' He raised his hand to knock. 'And don't believe everything she says, neither. Specially not about me.'

Annev nodded, though he could hardly think what else Dolyn could reveal about the old blacksmith. Sraon had been a slaver – a practising one, if that writ and slaver's brand were authentic – and he was an old friend of Sodar's, a master at keeping secrets who had a hundred or more lives and kept them all secret from Annev. Sraon might be no different, so Annev would be paying very close attention to anything Dolyn the Smith said about the reformed slave-trader.

Chapter Three

Sraon knocked his meaty fist against the soot-stained portal and let the echo die inside the unmarked smithy. They waited ten heartbeats and then Sraon knocked again. No answer. The smith adjusted his eyepatch, his brow furrowed.

'Her sign's gone. Might be she's moved.'

'How long since you've seen her?'

'Years and years,' he admitted, still frowning. 'I didn't make it a point to visit her, mind – we weren't close – but my contact said she was still here.'

'Your contact?'

'Aye. A farmer called Gribble. Sometimes, when Sodar needed something, he'd send me to Banok. If he wanted something special, or I didn't want to show my face much, I'd ask Gribble to help. When you left for Luqura on that retrieval mission, Sodar asked me to get him to send a message to Reeve in Quiri. Told him it was urgent, and Gribble promised to speak with Tukas – our contact in Luqura. I figure Reeve's got that message by now. Counting on it, in fact.'

'But what does Gribble have to do with Gwen?'

'*Dolyn*,' Sraon said. 'Only *I* get to call her Gwen, and only then if I'm tweaking her nose.' He knocked once more, louder. 'Gribble gets me information about a few folks in the town,' Sraon continued. 'People of interest, you might say. Janak Harth was one of those. Gwen's another.'

'Why?'

'She'll tell you herself. If we can find her, that is.' He mumbled this last part.

Annev looked up and down the narrow alley. 'This seems an odd place for a smithy. Your forge is open to the air, but I don't even see any windows here. Wouldn't that get incredibly hot? And then the smoke and the steam. Seems like a terrible place for forging metal and stoking fires.'

Sraon was looking around. 'Smaller work is done on a smaller scale. You don't need raging fires and billowing smoke if you're forging jewellery and the like. Still, you're not wrong. That's part of Dolyn's mystery. It's also what led me to suspect there was more to her forging than simple handicraft.' Sraon's tone had dropped to a whisper now and his eyes were shifting about, taking in the street, the rooftops, and nearby buildings, particularly those with windows.

'Wait,' Annev said. 'What're you saying? Is she a keokum?'

Sraon sucked air between his teeth. 'Gods, but that's offensive, Annev. I know it's what you were taught, being raised in the village, but folk that use magic are not keokum. They're blessed. Talented folk. That's why they call it the "blood-talent" – why they used to, anyway – and why we call them artisans. Though it's unlikely you heard them called that in Chaenbalu.'

'No,' Annev agreed, trying to adjust to this new perspective. 'But Dolyn can use magic? Like Sodar.'

'Not quite like Sodar. But I'll let her explain, assuming we find her.'

'Find who?'

As one, Sraon and Annev turned to see a middle-aged woman standing at the other end of the alley. The newcomer had broad shoulders, a narrow waist and muscular arms that seemed fit enough to wield a smithing hammer – or crack a man's skull if the occasion demanded.

'Gwen!' Sraon said, grinning broadly. 'It's been an age! You still look strong enough to wrestle a bear.'

'Aye,' the woman said, taking two long strides to stand beside the door. 'And you're still ugly enough to mistake for one.' She set down a heavy sack beside her door and nodded at Annev, eyeing his glove. 'What's this? New apprentice?'

'Mm. Might say that.'

'Or I might not?' Dolyn said, eyes knowing.

'Could we talk inside? I've a favour to ask.'

'Sraon Cheng wants to ask *me* a favour?' She laughed. 'I wouldn't mind having that to hang over your head. Well, come on in then.' She hooked a finger into her belt, pulled out a large key, and unlocked the door. She swung it wide open and Annev muttered his thanks, stepping in after Sraon.

The smithy was clean, if a bit dark, which Dolyn fixed by throwing back the sash and opening the shutters on the opposite wall, revealing that the indoor smithy was deceptively spacious. It took up the entire floor of the building they had entered, as well as the adjoining two-storey building. Several tables had been set up as individual workstations, and at a glance he saw the traditional hearth, a smelter, a forge, and an oven.

Annev took a hesitant step towards the tables, remembering Sraon's admonition to mind his manners, and spied a variety of tools and implements he could never have imagined: crimpers and crackers, complicated vices and delicate chisels. There was a tiny anvil and a matching smithing hammer, a variety of pliers and pincers, and half a dozen barrels of water. He took it all in and shook his head.

'So many tools!'

Gwendolyn set down her bag with a clink of metal. 'Do you know any poets? Do you even know what a poet is?'

Annev's cheeks burned red. 'Of course.'

Dolyn raised an eyebrow at Sraon and they shared a smile, implying they were enjoying some joke at Annev's expense. She grunted.

'How many tools does a poet have?'

Annev stared, caught off-guard by the question. 'Um ... none? I mean, well, his voice I suppose.'

Sraon chuckled but Dolyn looked unamused. 'A poet uses words. How many words are there in the world?'

'Well,' Annev said, determined not to make a fool of himself again, 'for a skilled poet there's the Darite language, plus Ilumite and Terran. Then there's the old Darite tongue, and the glyphs of power ... given all the words in the world – written and spoken – I'd imagine there's several hundred thousand. Maybe several million.' He paused. 'I take your point to be that, at least compared to a poet, what you have here is a beggar's hoard. Is that right?'

A glint had returned to Dolyn's eye. 'Maybe you're brighter than you look.' She smiled. 'This boy isn't your apprentice, Sraon. Who is he? What is he to you?'

The one-eyed blacksmith chuckled. 'You've got me. I've shown Annev a bit of forge work – just the basics, mind – but he's actually Sodar's apprentice.'

Dolyn seemed to perk up at this, eyeing Annev more closely. 'So you're lettered then? That smithing glove threw me, but I can see it now. Too much muscle in those arms to be some scribe or deacon, though.' She looked at Sraon. 'How much does he know?'

An awkward silence filled the room. As it grew, Annev could feel his stomach twisting into a knot. Why had Sraon been so cagey about his relationship with Dolyn? And why did he think another blacksmith would be better able to remove the Hand of Keos? Annev could only come up with one answer to that question, and it drove a spike of fear into his heart.

'He suspects only,' Sraon said, breaking the silence. 'I haven't told him anything, but he's guessed a bit from your smithy.' Annev swallowed, the pit in his stomach growing wider.

'Has he now?' Dolyn eyed Annev more closely, stepping closer as she sized him up. 'He's got the gift. Yes?'

Sraon's face was suddenly serious. 'The gift ... and something else.' He glanced at Annev. 'Show her.'

Annev hesitated, then slowly slid the smithing glove from his hand, his eyes fixed on Dolyn's face. He'd barely drawn the cuff down before the light started to spill out, illuminating the room. Dolyn gasped, her hand flying to her mouth.

'Keos,' she breathed, eyes widening. 'This isn't ... no. Is it?' She looked astonished.

'Show her, Annev. All of it.'

Annev tugged the glove off his hand, exposing the artistry of the brilliant gold fist beneath. This time when Dolyn saw the hand, she didn't curse. She beckoned Annev closer with trembling fingers, her gaze suddenly reverent.

'May I?' she asked. Annev nodded and Dolyn carefully touched the gold prosthetic, her fingertips tracing the smoking anvil, the floating hammer, and the words inscribed on the palm and back of the hand. Annev flinched as she caressed the limb. Though made of metal, his golden skin was somehow more sensitive than the flesh of his right arm.

Dolyn's lips moved silently as she read the Terran inscriptions on his palm: *Memento Semper. Numquam oblivisci.* She turned his hand over, mouthing the words written there: *Aut inveniam viam aut faciam.* When she looked up, her stare pierced Annev.

'You know what this is?'

Annev nodded, suddenly finding his voice. 'Can you ... help me take it off? It's cursed. It frightens me. I need help.' His voice cracked at the end, but he kept the tears from forming. Barely.

'I ... don't know. I can try.' Dolyn glanced back at the prosthetic, her head shaking. 'This is powerful magic, Sraon.'

'We're aware,' the smith said, his expression dour. 'Saw its power first-hand.'

'Did you now?' Dolyn's gaze shifted between them, then her eyebrows suddenly shot up. 'That beam of light shooting out of the west, about a day past. Was that you? Was that *this?*'

'You saw that?' Annev asked, eyes widening. 'All the way from Banok?'

Dolyn nodded. 'Not often you see a pillar of light shooting into the sky, much less one as bright as the sun. Brighter probably, seeing as it was midday when we saw it.'

'We?'

'Of course. Whole damned town saw it. Practically all anyone spoke about, till dusk fell anyway. By then folks had ascribed it to some sort of Regaleus celebration put on by the Druids or a group of Ilumites.' Dolyn sniffed. 'Nonsense, of course. Druids don't practise that kind of magic, and the Ilumites are too smart to call attention to themselves. Not here in Daroea, anyway.'

'That's good to know, Gwen, but can you help the boy?'

41

Dolyn glared at Sraon, but there was no fire in it. 'I can try, but what you really need is an Artificer.'

'Artificer?' Annev repeated, pulling his hand back. 'But ... aren't they Terran?'

Dolyn laughed. 'And what do you think I am?'

The bottom fell out of Annev's stomach. He stepped backward, mind reeling. 'No, you wouldn't ... You can't be.' He looked at Sraon, eyes widening in panic. 'Why am I here, Sraon? Why did you bring me here?'

The one-eyed smith raised his hands and patted the air as if to calm Annev's wild suspicions. 'Dolyn's not Terran, lad – not the kind you're thinking of anyway. She's an Orvane – *New* Terran. She belongs to the tribe that shapes metal and minerals.'

'You mean ... she worships Cruithear?'

Dolyn nodded, and Annev felt the bile rising in his throat. Janak Harth had made a deal with Cruithear. The God of Minerals had promised the crippled merchant new legs – a new body – in exchange for capturing Annev.

Annev looked to the door. Dolyn's muscles tensed in response, and Annev dropped into a battle stance, prepared to fight or run if she tried anything. It was an effort of will not to attack when Sraon's hand fell on his shoulder.

'Easy, lad. This is why I wanted Dolyn to tell you herself, to avoid any misunderstandings.'

'She worships *Cruithear*, Sraon. Her God is hunting me!' Annev folded his arms in front of his chest and suddenly realised the Hand of Keos had begun to warm, its golden metal – once cool – now felt hot against his chest. He hastened to pull the thick smithing glove back on.

Sraon suddenly looked uncertain. He glanced at Dolyn, an eyebrow raised, and his hand fell to resting on his holstered halberd. 'That true, Gwen?'

The woman's eyes fell on Sraon's hands and she took a small step back, her hands held where they could be seen. 'Did you come here to threaten me, Sraon?' Dolyn sniffed. 'Don't accuse me of ill motives. I doubt there's a God or Goddess who wouldn't like to see the bearer of the gilded Hand of Keos.'

'That's not an answer, Gwen.'

'Technically, it is. And I'll remind you that you're in my house. In my smithy. *You* came to *me*. I did not seek you out.' She waved at the door. 'You're welcome to leave whenever you like.' She glanced at Annev just as a tendril of smoke escaped from beneath his smithing glove. The boy tried to wave it away, chagrined, but it was too late. Dolyn shook her head and took a step back. 'Forget the hand. You should both go.'

'Hold on, Gwen,' Sraon said, stepping aside before the woman could push him back through the door. 'Don't be like that. Please. The boy needs your help.'

'And I don't need trouble,' Dolyn said, her arms folded. 'I don't care what he's got fused to him. I don't let folk insult me in my own home – and stop calling me Gwen! I'm not some barmaid or farmer's daughter. It's Dolyn. Not Lynn. Not Gwennie. Not Doll. Dolyn. You know that.'

'Dolyn, *please*. For the boy's sake, look at his arm. You've got the talent. I'm helpless here.'

'Everyone's got the talent,' Dolyn muttered under her breath. 'Just some of us know how to make use of it.' She frowned, pulled a lock of brown hair behind her ear, and looked between Annev and the glowing hand, shaking her head. She froze when she met Annev's frightened eyes, though. Annev nodded – a silent plea – and she gave a great sigh of defeat. 'I'll try, Sraon, if the boy will trust me. But only because we've got history – and I won't make any promises. What you really need is an Artificer.'

'An Artificer,' Annev repeated, remembering. 'You mean ... like Urran?'

Dolyn raised an eyebrow. 'You know about Urran?' She grunted. 'Well, he'll be of no help to you, so you can forget about him.'

'Wait,' Annev said, incredulous, 'Urran is still *alive*?'

Dolyn grunted. 'He was an ageless one, so he could be lurking about somewhere. Maybe. Been missing for almost two millennia though, ever since he stewarded that damn mission to reclaim the diamagi. My guess is he's dead.'

'The diamagi ... you mean the Lost Artifacts?'

'Yes. Probably not the sort of thing Sodar would know about – or any other Darites for that matter – but it's no secret neither.' Annev absorbed this.

'I say you need an Artificer,' Dolyn continued, 'because their specialty is artifacts – how to make them, how to use them – and not just the lesser artifacts that the rest of us can make. I mean *real* artifacts. The great ones that don't lose their power.' She tapped the glove covering Annev's glowing hand. 'Like this. Like the Hand of Keos.' Dolyn stared at the glove as though she could see right through it. 'Gods, boy. There are people who would kill to get that artifact, and they'd cut off their own hand to use it.' She paused. 'How *did* you get it? That hand has been missing since Keos fell at the Battle of Vosgar, almost a thousand years before Urran went missing.'

Annev looked at Sraon, who shrugged. 'Whatever you feel comfortable sharing, Annev. It's your tale, not mine.'

Annev looked Dolyn over carefully, still suspicious. Could he really trust this woman? *Should* he trust her?

'You're worried I'll send Cruithear after you,' Dolyn said, as if reading his mind. She nodded slowly. 'You're right to be cautious. I'm a priestess of Cruithear, Annev – one of his most devout.'

Annev was caught off-guard by Dolyn's candid admission, and it took all his composure not to bolt for the door. Worse, the smithing glove now itched his skin, and he had to force himself not to check if the leather garment was burning.

'That's why Sraon brought you to me,' Dolyn pressed, still studying Annev. 'Orvanes have a special talent with minerals and metals, and you won't find another priest or priestess of Cruithear who knows half as much as me. There is a chance I can help you.' She paused. 'Would you like me to explain further or have you heard enough?'

'You'd let me leave? If I wanted to go, I mean. You'd let me?'

Dolyn snorted. 'What? You thought I'd chain you to my forge? Force you to recite prayers to Cruithear?' She sniffed. 'If Cruithear wants you, I wager it's because of that cursed artifact you're wearing. And you came here asking me to remove it. That serves both

44

our interests.' She extended her hand, palm open. 'So will you let me try? Or will you race out of here like a startled sheep?'

Annev relaxed a bit, though his cheeks flushed hot with embarrassment. Sheepish was precisely how he felt. He cleared his throat, looking anew at the tools filling the workroom, wondering if any had the magic necessary to remove his cursed golden hand. 'Sodar didn't teach me much about Terran or Orvane magic. How would you do it? What tools would you use?'

Dolyn raised both of her calloused hands, turning them towards Annev. 'These.'

Annev frowned, not understanding, and Dolyn reached into the sack of metal she had lugged into the shop and plucked out a gold shard nearly as large as her fist, easily worth five solari. She began turning the yellow metal over in her hands, her strong fingers working and stretching the ingot as if it were clay. Annev watched in fascination as she first moulded the raw metal into a band, then shaped it into a bracelet. As she traced her finger around the edge, delicate lines began to spread from her touch, turning into a subtle filigree. She turned the metal over for Annev to examine, and he slowly took the proffered band and scrutinised it more closely.

'It's beautiful,' he said, suddenly realising how great the gap was between Sraon's smithing work and Dolyn's artistry. She made the master blacksmith look like a journeyman apprentice. Annev passed the delicate bracelet back, his awe plain on his face.

'Thank you,' she said, taking the gold band. 'I'll finish it off later, use some of these tools to add more detail, maybe knock out some of the lines.' She set the bracelet down next to the cold forge fire. 'That hand, though. It's not simple gold. It looks like gold because that's how Keos fashioned it, but he forged it from something else. From the stuff the Gods and the world itself were made from.' She paused when she saw Annev's eyes had begun to widen.

Annev hesitated. 'It's made of *aqlumera*,' he said at last, watching Dolyn's reaction.

A small smile tugged at the corner of her mouth. 'Not so ignorant after all, then.' Dolyn beckoned for them to follow to the far end of her workshop, where she unlocked a strong-box and pulled out a vial of brilliant, glowing liquid; its colour was something akin to molten gold, yet the light it emitted shifted between all the colours of the rainbow.

'*Aqlumera*,' Gwendolyn said, carefully setting the tiny vial into a wrought-iron display stand. 'Just a few drops – I doubt it would fill my palm – but just this much is worth a king's ransom.'

Annev scoffed. 'You're joking.'

'Not in the slightest. I saved a king's life once, and he gave me the choice between this tiny vial or twelve chests of gold.' She chuckled. 'King Cheng likes to gamble, even when he's paying his debts. Lucky for me, I knew which was more valuable.' She tapped her nose, grinning. 'I've never seen someone so mad to be free of a life debt.' She looked at Sraon. 'You ever hear about that?'

The blacksmith frowned. 'You know very well I wouldn't have. Washed my hands of that lot decades ago.'

'Of course,' Dolyn said, admiring the light cast by the tube of liquid-metal magic.

Annev stared at the vial and swallowed. A king's ransom? He'd splashed twice that amount in Kenton's face when he'd made his escape from the Academy's dungeons – and that was just what he'd caught trickling into his cell from the Vault of Damnation. How much of it must have trickled away to form the waste pit at the back of his cell? Annev was dumbfounded by the notion that something so valuable was locked away beneath the Academy, utterly wasted.

Then he remembered the seemingly bottomless pool of *aqlumera* that had dominated the heart of the Academy's Vault. The magic liquid had leaked from there into Annev's prison cell. If Dolyn was right about the value of the stuff, then the ruined Academy sat atop an unfathomable amount of wealth.

The Orvane was still staring at the vial. 'The only problem with owning such a treasure, as Cheng may have understood, is not knowing what to do with it. It has infinite uses, but I can only choose once – and I only have one chance to get the forging right.' She tsked, then returned the glowing vial to her strong-box.

'So now you know what made that arm of yours. And you know the Artificer who forged it – the God of Earthblood himself.' Dolyn eased herself down onto a nearby stool. 'I'm your best chance to remove it, though honestly I'm not sure I can help you.'

Annev exchanged a meaningful look with Sraon. The blacksmith raised both hands unhelpfully and Annev returned his gaze to Dolyn, his expression earnest. 'I don't trust your God,' he said, 'but I might be persuaded to trust *you*. The truth is I need your help, and I think it's in your interest to help me.'

'I don't disagree.' Dolyn nodded at his arm. 'Take off that glove again. Let me see it.'

Annev did, forcing his emotions to remain calm as the golden hand once again filled the immediate space with its soft, yellow light. Dolyn stared at it, not daring to touch it a second time. As they all watched, the light in the room seemed to pulse in time with Annev's breathing.

Dolyn studied the artwork inscribed on the palm, then shook her head. 'Here's the heart of it: I can try to remove the prosthetic with Orvane magic, but this was forged with a unique blood-talent – using the blood of a God, no less – so I'd be tampering with things I don't understand. It's a different kind of magic – not even Terran, if I'm being honest – and attempting to separate the gold hand from the flesh of your arm is as dangerous as trying to smelt something with that vial of liquid magic.' She gestured at the strong-box behind her. 'I could try, though. Cruithear knows I'm not above taking a gamble, and he'd bless me above all other smiths if I succeeded ... but you should know the risks. Could be I free you from that golden arm, but if things go awry, we could have a repeat of yesterday's light show.'

Sraon cleared his throat. 'Maybe it's better if we push on, lad. If Dolyn can't help you safely, we'll have to trust to Reeve to get the job done.'

Annev wasn't sure he agreed. Reeve was from the same brotherhood as Sodar – neither an Artificer nor a Terran. His talent was with skywater, not earthblood. What chance did he have of removing the cursed prosthetic? Annev didn't know, but he had a good guess that Dolyn would be his best chance of removing the arm. Even if Annev could find an Artificer like Urran – if one still lived – the chances of their helping him seemed no better than Dolyn's, and it was likely that any Terran Artificer would try to capture Annev and bring him back to Keos. Dolyn had been clear her only interest was in the prosthetic – a fair trade in Annev's opinion, considering all the grief it had caused him – so while he wasn't at all sure he could trust her, he felt he had to make the attempt.

I just pray to Odar that I don't get us all blown up.

'Sraon, wait.'

The blacksmith had already been saying his goodbyes to Dolyn. 'What is it?'

'I want her to try.'

Sraon frowned, his emotions plain on his swarthy face. 'You're sure? You heard what Gwen— er ... what Dolyn said. If this goes wrong, you might end up in a worse state.'

Annev nodded, his mind made up. When Dolyn saw his expression, she took them to her walk-in kiln at the back of the room. The large furnace was sealed by a heavy iron door, which, when Dolyn opened it, revealed a second iron door at the back of the kiln. Dolyn led the way inside, lit a candle, and beckoned for Sraon and Annev to follow.

Chapter Four

Dolyn sat down opposite Annev, her single candle lighting the table and the secret underground room.

'My heritage isn't common knowledge,' she said, 'nor is my affinity for magic. I may be Orvane, but that's still Terran as far as most Darites are concerned. Most folks wouldn't hire me or purchase my wares if they knew. Others would vandalise my smithy or try to drive me out of town.'

Annev understood that reaction well from his childhood in Chaenbalu. As far as the villagers were concerned, possessing a strain of Terran blood was enough to get you ostracised or exiled. Being a full-blooded Terran would likely have meant death – like possessing magic – though Annev couldn't recall anyone being executed for the former crime. It seemed that Banok was more cosmopolitan than Chaenbalu, but its prejudices were similar.

'Is this an escape tunnel then?' Sraon asked. There were only two chairs and no other furniture, so the one-eyed blacksmith remained standing.

Dolyn nodded, gesturing at the door she had just closed, and at yet another door at the opposite end of the room, which was locked and barred. 'That leads outside the city walls, though I've never had cause to use it, praise Cruithear.'

Annev shifted in his chair, made uncomfortable by both the epithet and the setting. 'Why are we down here?'

'You're wearing one of the most powerful artifacts ever created, boy – probably *the* most powerful artifact ever created, if you exclude the diamagi. And since the staff, the hammer and the flute are as lost to this world as the Gods who made them, that makes your golden hand the most dangerous thing this side of the veil. If something goes wrong when I try to remove it, I want to minimise the damage. Being ten feet underground should help somewhat.'

Annev wanted to laugh. Just ten feet? At Chaenbalu he had carved chasms in the earth almost a mile deep. How tall had the Academy been? How many rooms had it held? It was a mountain of rubble now. No, ten feet of earth over their heads would do nothing except ensure they got buried alive.

Still, Annev had made his decision, so he didn't object. He laid his arm on the table and stretched the glowing hand towards Dolyn. This time it was the smith's turn to look uncomfortable.

'Before I start,' she warned, 'I will explain what I intend to do. Given the hand's volatility, it would go well if you do not resist my probing.' Annev nodded his understanding and she seemed to relax a little. 'How much do you know about Terran magic? Or Orvanish magic?'

'Nothing,' he said, 'or next to nothing. I know it uses earth-blood, not skywater or lightfire. And I know its art is physical, not mental or spiritual.'

Gwendolyn raised a hand. 'You were right the first time. You know nothing – less than nothing, maybe, which is more danger-ous.' She rubbed her temples, causing the candlelight to flicker. 'Everything is connected. Everything is the same. Earthblood. Skywater. Lightfire. It's all *aqlumera*.'

'Do you mean that abstractly?' Annev asked, his expression doubting. 'You don't mean they're really the same – just that they're similar.'

'I mean they're *connected*, just like I said. When you look up at the stars, are you seeing starlight or the sky? When you sit beside the embers of a hearthfire, can you tell me where the wood ends and the ash begins? Are the cinders more lightfire or earthblood? You cannot *say* these things, you can only *sense* them. There are no clear divisions. Do you see now why it is foolish to say only Terrans use earthblood? Or only Darites use skywater?'

Annev glanced at Sraon and the blacksmith shrugged, unable to offer any insight. Annev felt the same – what did he really know of magic? How much had Sodar kept from him? How much had Sodar actually known?

'Why do I need to know this?'

'Because I need you to trust I know what I'm doing – and because if you trust me, I'll be more successful at helping you remove the artifact.' She gestured. 'Please put your arm on the table.'

Annev slowly did so, mulling over her words. 'I'm not as ignorant as you think.' He tried to keep his tone even, not wanting to seem petulant. 'I know how Darite magic works, and I understand how the three depend on one another—'

'Eight,' Dolyn corrected, taking his hand in her own.

'What?'

'There are eight magics.'

Annev was suddenly less certain of himself. He squirmed in his seat, both uncomfortable with Dolyn's revelations and her prodding his prosthetic. 'You're talking about the magic of the Younger Gods?' he asked, trying to make it sound like a statement rather than a question. His voice peaked at the end, betraying him.

Dolyn nodded, her fingers tracing the arabasques and filigree of the artifact. 'Can you feel this?'

'You're just touching it right? Not using magic yet?'

'Correct.'

'Then yes, I can feel it.'

Dolyn lightly brushed her fingertips over his reinforced knuckles. 'This, too?' When Annev flinched at the tickling sensation, Dolyn shook her head in wonder. 'No hairs on your metal skin, but you can sense the slightest pressure. Incredible.'

Annev cleared his throat, increasingly uncomfortable with Dolyn's light caresses.

'Eight magics,' he prompted, 'but the Younger Gods are just extensions of Keos. It's just more Terran magic – not actually a different *kind* of magic ... right? Eight or three, it's all the same. It's all *connected*, like you said.'

'It's also a great deal more complicated than that.' Dolyn tapped her chest with her thumb, her other hand still gripping the wrist of his glowing prosthetic. 'I'm an Orvane. Among us, there are two castes of magic: the Ironborn and the Stonesmiths. Which do you think I am?'

'I don't know. You moulded that metal earlier, so that should make you a smith. But it was metal, not stone ... so maybe you're Ironborn?'

'You should have stopped at "I don't know",' she chided, though her smile was encouraging. 'I am a dualist – both Ironborn and Stonesmith – though smithing is my primary talent.'

'And that makes you?'

'A Forgemaster,' Dolyn answered, reasserting her grip. 'Calm yourself now. I'm going to prod you with just a bit of my magic. Nothing transformative. Nothing destructive. Just need to get a sense of the resistances at work here.'

Resistances. Annev didn't like the sound of that, though he tried to keep his composure. 'Sure. Fine.' Not the most confident answer, but at least his voice didn't crack. 'What, um ... I mean, how many castes of magic are there?'

'Twenty-two, for now.'

'For now?'

'Over the ages, the three prime magics evolved into twelve distinct castes. After the Breaking of the Hand of Keos, the five New Terran magics were born. They've since formed ten castes of their own, though I expect there will one day be twenty. When that happens, there will be thirty-two artisan types, not including dualists.'

Annev's eyes widened as he digested what Dolyn was saying. 'So there are eight kinds of magic – three for the Elder Gods and five for the Younger Gods – and that makes twenty-two magic castes ... and each of those can be combined to create a different type of artisan?'

'Exactly. And every artisan will have their own strengths and weaknesses. Just because you were born a Stonesmith doesn't mean you can shape stone. Maybe you can only shape metal. Maybe you can only shape certain *kinds* of stone. I've known Stonesmiths who can only shape quartz, but are masters with it. And I've known smiths that can't shape the earth at all – neither metal nor mineral – but they can transverse *any* inorganic substance. Trap them in a metal cage beneath a mountain of stone, and they will climb right out, laughing the whole while. But trap them in a cage of fresh-cut green wood – or a living cage, which the Druids grow – and they're powerless. How do you classify that? How many types of artisans can there be? It's impossible to separate the magics, or define where one begins and another ends, but we still try. That's what I mean when I say everything is connected.'

Annev flinched as a cold chill ran up his wrist and forearm. His fist involuntarily flexed and Dolyn hissed through her teeth. Annev forced his grip to relax and the priestess shook the fingers that Annev had nearly crushed.

'Are you all right?' Annev asked, chagrined.

'It's fine. Just startled me. You've got quite a grip.'

'What did you do?'

'Prodded a nerve, I think. Our bodies have them ... and, it seems, so does this artifact.'

Annev felt his anxiety spike and instinctively tried to shift their conversation back to Dolyn and her blood-talent. 'So how does your magic work? What does a Forgemaster do?'

'Stonesmiths have an outward focus,' Dolyn said, her eyes and fingers still searching the prosthetic. 'They can manipulate the earthblood around them, usually by touching it with their hands. Ironborn have an inward focus. Instead of transmuting ore or earth, they can change the composition of their bodies. Make their skin hard as rock. Bones as strong as steel.'

Like the feurog, Annev thought, though he kept that to himself.

'There are costs to using magic, though,' Dolyn continued. 'My people consume precious minerals – mostly iron and calcium – and then there are side effects like this.' She pulled back the hair coiled behind her head and Annev glimpsed a metallic patina dusting the back of the woman's neck. He schooled himself, stifling a reaction, but was unable to prevent the Hand of Keos from pulsing with a bright yellow light. Dolyn glanced at the prosthetic then back at his face, her expression blank.

'Your hand grew very warm just then.'

'Did it?' Annev said, his voice cracking once more. He cleared

53

his throat then took his arm off the table. 'Just give me a second to work the feeling back.' He flexed his fist as Gwendolyn studied him, her eyebrow raised.

'So there are side effects to dwimmer-crafting,' he said, his tone casual. 'Like with glyph-speaking or spellsinging, but instead of depleting your *quaire* or augmenting your *lumen*, you're transmuting your *t'rasang*.'

Dolyn was silent, then nodded. 'The effects can be minimised – even reversed – but only by someone who truly understands the craft. A meddler with no mentor could easily turn themselves into more of a monster than a man.'

Again, the connection between the *feurog* and the Orvanes seemed impossible to ignore. They each bore the same deformities, though Annev couldn't fathom what to make of that. It made his skin crawl, and he began to reconsider his decision to accept Dolyn's help.

Janak Harth, Annev thought, suddenly remembering the mad merchant who had enslaved half of Banok. *He had made a pact with Cruithear. Would Dolyn know about him? She's a priestess of Cruithear, from the same town as Janak, so she must know something.* Annev opened his mouth to ask, but Dolyn continued.

'You should understand that magic is never free – there is always a price. Even for this. Whatever magic I employ on your hand today will have a rippling effect on me, probably a strong one.'

That sobered him. Annev had been thinking so hard about saving himself that he hadn't stopped to consider what he might be asking of a stranger. Knowing that Dolyn was willing to sacrifice her own safety to help him made Annev ashamed of his suspicions. He tamped them down and instead bowed in thanks. 'I understand,' he said, head still lowered in appreciation. 'Whatever sacrifice is required, you should know that you're saving many people's lives – not just my own.'

Dolyn snorted. 'You need to stop claiming you understand anything. Your mentor didn't educate you properly, and I've barely scratched the surface. I might paralyse myself. My bones could turn to mud, my blood to sand. So, I'm going to be very careful, and if I stop midway through, now you know why.'

'Do you think that's likely?' Annev asked, his anxiety returning in crashing waves. 'Could you get hurt that badly?'

'Probably not. I know what my body can sustain, and I have enough of the Ironborn talent to strengthen me, to let me withstand things that would stop a less skilled artisan.'

Annev looked again at the brass patina speckling the back of Gwendolyn's neck. *She's halfway to becoming a* feurog *... can I really trust her to do this? Can I even ask that of her?*

'Do you want to continue?' Dolyn asked, as though reading his thoughts. 'I'm confident none of those things will happen, but if you want to stop, I understand.'

'I trust you,' Annev said, though he wasn't sure his words were true. 'Just ... tell me what we need to do.'

Dolyn gestured to his prosthetic. 'Back on the table.'

Annev did so with only the slightest hesitation. Dolyn gripped his wrist in both hands once more, her face a mask. 'I've tried looking for magical triggers to release your hand. Now I'm going to try working on the bond itself. Open your mind. Let your spirit soak into your body and pull its essence towards the surface of your skin.'

'What do you mean?' Annev asked, trying to calm his nerves.

'Most people keep their thoughts, fears and passions close. They guard them, physically and mentally, careful not to let their body language give away their feelings. I need you to open your mind to your body. Immerse yourself in your thoughts and then push that energy – your soul – outward. If you do it right, you'll feel a pleasant glow in your skin. A sense of balance, of connection. When you have it, I should be able to sense how the prosthetic is connected to you. If I can see those threads, then I can disentangle it from you and physically removing the artifact should be quick and painless.' She eyed him intently. 'Try it.'

Annev slowly exhaled, then turned his mind inward, trying to feel through Dolyn's instructions. First he focused on his physical aches and pains, those that lingered from his injuries in Chaenbalu, but he quickly sensed this was not what the smith needed and shifted to the thoughts and fears he was loath to remember, let alone examine. He sorted through these emotions, shying away from those that were too sharp, too painful to handle. Eventually he found something he was comfortable handling: a smothered resentment towards his friends, and a prickling anger about this fool's errand to Luqura. Annev didn't like being shunned by his companions, but he didn't want to be responsible for anything bad that might befall them either. He was sceptical about finding Reeve waiting for them in Luqura, and even if they did, Dolyn had been clear it was unlikely the Arch-Dionach could help Annev. So why was he going? Why had he agreed to any of this?

For Sodar, Annev realised. *I'm doing it because it's what he would have wanted. And to protect my friends, because this is the only way I can keep them safe from me and my curse.*

'Let your spirit free, Annev. Let your emotions flow.'

Annev closed his eyes and thought of Sodar once more. His heart began to race. He did not want to dwell on his memories of the old priest, did not want to recall either his well-meaning lies or his fatherly love.

But the memories came anyway, like water bubbling up from a hot spring. He relived his last days with the priest in bright flashes, culminating in Sodar's death at Elder Tosan's hand. Alone, grief-stricken, Annev had unwittingly bonded the golden Hand of Keos to his stunted arm. He'd killed Tosan and half the Academy's masters, then lanced the towering edifice in half and collapsed it on itself. Last of all, he remembered Myjun, her betrayal and subsequent death. It had been an accident, but she'd still died by his hand – by the Hand of Keos, which he had been wielding.

Was it really an accident? Annev wondered, his thoughts flowing freely now. *I wanted them all dead. I wanted to crush the Academy and destroy the village in rubble and ash. I turned the fire towards her ... towards that screaming ...*

Sraon gasped behind him and Annev was startled back to the present. Gwendolyn's eyes were wide and her hands raised as she stared down at Annev's glowing prosthetic, which had now taken on a more lively light: instead of its dim yellow glow, barely noticeable in the daylight, the hand shone with a brilliant orange fire. Annev's breath caught in his throat and he instinctively clenched the hand into a fist. The orange glow flared, turning red.

'Annev ...' Sraon said, his tone measured, cautious. 'Please don't blow us all to bloody pieces.'

In other circumstances Annev might have laughed, but there was nothing funny about the pulsing red flame shrouding his fist. Instead he took a deep breath and slowly let it out, calming his mind. As he did, the fire shrank, its light paling to yellow and then sinking back into a soft, white glow. Annev gently opened his hand and a tiny slip of smoke wafted up from his fingers. On his palm, the second half of the Terran inscription still glowed with a dull orange fire: NUMQUAM OBLIVISCI.

Never forget.

Annev blinked. Where had he learned that?

He hadn't. He shouldn't have known the meaning of the inscription ... yet there it was. Annev's stomach twisted into a sour knot. He slowly turned the hand over and read the words on the other side: *Aut inveniam viam aut faciam.* This inscription was not glowing, and Annev hadn't a clue what the words meant. The pit in his stomach slowly shrank and he began to breathe easier.

'Interesting,' Dolyn said. 'Maybe we should try a different tactic.' She eyed Annev, sizing him up. 'What kind of art do you perform?'

'Mm?'

Dolyn waved a hand at the still-glowing prosthetic. 'Ignore that – and whatever you were thinking of when it started to glow like a forge fire.' She shivered. 'Tell me about *you*. Your magic. How did you access it before?'

Annev thought about it. 'Sodar trained me in Darite magic.'

'Right, so what was he? There are four fields: Breathbreaker, Stormcaller, Shieldbearer, Mindwalker.'

'I'm not sure,' Annev said. 'Sodar didn't really talk about magic like that. I overheard him talking to another artisan once. The other man called him ... a Breathbreaker, I think.'

'So he never tried to find your focus? Never tested your magic?'

Annev laughed in spite of himself. 'He tested it almost every day! But I was never good at accessing my powers. I didn't manifest any kind of ability until a few days ago, and even then, it

57

didn't match the way Sodar said magic worked. It was ...' Annev fell silent, remembering Sodar's words.

Like a keokum.

'It wasn't what he'd expected.'

Dolyn studied him. 'I guess that makes sense. You'd have to be special to get that thing to weld to you.' She frowned. 'You're a puzzle, Annev.'

A long moment passed and then she smiled. 'I like puzzles, though. Tell me. What were you doing when you first accessed your magic? What happened?'

'I was using an artifact – a Sword of Sharpness. I couldn't get the glyph to work for me, though, so I ...' He remembered how he had extended his awareness into the blade. He had sensed the weapon's purpose, its essence. Then he had shaped his own essence and pushed his will into the sword, magnifying its power.

Was Dolyn asking Annev to do something similar now – to extend himself into ... himself? If he could get a firm grasp on that, if he could extend his mind and his will to the edge of his being, perhaps ...

Annev emptied his mind of thought and emotion and settled his focus on his core, where his spirit dwelt. These were abstract concepts for him, but he recalled using Sodar's sword, Mercy, to chop through Janak's soldiers. He also remembered finding his fiery flamberge in the Vault of Damnation and using it to scythe through the metal limbs and stone skin of the monstrous *feurog*. He had sensed the source of that weapon's power and magnified its intensity until the heat was powerful enough to shear through iron and stone as easily as flesh and bone.

Annev's arm began to tingle at the joint where the prosthetic joined his stunted forearm. He took note of it, recalling the sensation as familiar but not paying it attention before. This was important. He wasn't sure why or how, but there was something at work here, and while Annev couldn't say what it was, it tickled at his memories.

Annev relaxed, letting the memory go. He opened his eyes – surprised to find he had closed them – and looked up at Dolyn.

'I think I can feel it ... that connection you spoke of. There's a twinge in my arm – a tingling. I'm not sure how to describe it.' He extended the gold arm towards Gwendolyn, open palm facing her. 'What comes next?'

Dolyn slowly reached out with both hands, taking his arm by the wrist and forearm for the third time. This time, though, she laid her left thumb on his palm and her right thumb at the seam of the prosthetic. 'Keep your focus on that connection but relax your mind. I'm going to see if I can sense where you end and the arm begins.' She paused. 'This may be uncomfortable, so try not to fight it. Empty your mind – and please don't ball your hand into a fist. The prosthetic seems to respond to gestures used for dwimmer-crafting. I think there is some residual muscle-memory stored there from its last owner.' She trailed off, not daring to speak the name they were all thinking.

Keos. What muscle memories had the god left behind in the golden artifact? What atrocities had he committed while wearing it? Worse yet, what acts could Annev inadvertently commit with the cursed prosthetic?

If Dolyn's warning had been intended to inspire calm, it had the opposite effect. More than ever, Annev wanted to be rid of the damned thing. He couldn't bear the thought of more destruction, like that in Chaenbalu. Another place burned, another friend dead or lost because of him and his glowing hand.

'Do it,' Annev breathed, his teeth clenched.

Dolyn closed her eyes. 'Your spirit ... it's holding tight to the arm. Ease up, boy. Relax. You're not fighting anyone, least of all me.'

Annev nodded, forcing his muscles to unclench and redirecting his thoughts to more pleasant things.

But it was like fighting a river current. The negative thoughts and emotions were always there, ebbing and flowing around him. He tried to summon a positive memory, but he kept failing. Thinking of winning the stealth contest in the Academy's nave made him think of kissing Myjun, and that made him think of her betrayal and death. Thinking of winning the Test of Judgement just reminded him how Tosan had unjustly stolen his victory and given it to Therin. Thinking of Sodar ... he couldn't. Some wounds were still too fresh.

Annev startled as he felt a hand drop onto his shoulder – Sraon's hand.

'I'm here for you, Annev. Whatever happens. We all are.'

That's true, Annev thought, his anxiety easing slightly as Dolyn pressed at his flesh. *I have Sraon. And Titus and Therin. Not to mention Fyn and Brayan.* Annev smiled, remembering how the Academy's former quartermaster had spoken for him in the village square when no one else had. How Brayan had stood up to Tosan and taken Annev's side when all others were too afraid to do so.

Fyn was another matter entirely. He'd been a bully, a constant pain and a galling irritation. He had also been a dangerous adversary during the Academy's tests. But something had changed. Somehow, they had become reluctant allies. It was a strange and thrilling shift in their relationship, and Annev still wasn't sure how he felt about it.

'There it is,' Gwendolyn hissed through clenched teeth. 'I can feel the connection, where the *aqlumera* has merged with your flesh and spirit.' She slowly exhaled, her eyes half-lidded, then began to trace the surface of his skin with delicate invisible patterns.

'Dwimmer-crafting,' she said between laboured breaths, 'requires motion of the body. Certain gestures, certain movements, call on the magic inside us and the world around us.' The smith rose from her seat, her arms entwining Annev's in a martial dance of flowing movement that almost mirrored the patterns of the arabesques inscribed on the surface of the golden arm.

'If I can persuade the metallic elements that they aren't part of you ... if I can draw the *aqlumera* back into the arm itself ...' Beads of perspiration had begun to dot the smith's face. She clenched her jaw, head tilted to one side, and her elbows began to quiver. She drew her hands along the surface of the oversized arm, her fingers caressing the golden skin, drawing down to clutch the glowing hand in her rough palms.

Annev jerked as he felt something yank at the marrow of his forearm. The sensation came from somewhere deep inside – deeper than flesh or bone could possibly reach – and the pain that followed was like fiery claws tearing at his soul. It transported Annev to another time and place. Instead of sitting in Dolyn's underground kiln, he stood before a hellish army of monsters, roaring with bloodlust.

At the opposite end of the clearing, a young man with a glowing silver staff faced him. Lightning arced from the weapon, lancing Annev, followed by a rolling wave of immolating fire. Annev growled in frustration and pain, absorbing the magic and then attempting to hurl it back at his adversaries.

The room shifted again and Annev gasped as arcs of blood-red lightning burst from his hand, throwing Dolyn against the wall. All around them the air crackled with heat and the stench of burned flesh.

'Gods!' Sraon swore, dashing from Annev's side to aid the fallen smith. 'Gwen, are you all right?'

The Orvane shuddered, her breath coming in deep, ragged gasps. She rose to her feet, though, which Annev took to be a good sign, and to his relief he didn't see any visible injuries.

And then Dolyn raised her hands, turning them, revealing the arabesques and inscriptions carved on Annev's golden hand, which had somehow transferred themselves to hers, burning their likeness into the surface of her palms. He stared blankly at them, wisps of smoke still rising from the charred outline of the war hammer floating above the smoking anvil. On the opposite hand, Annev could plainly read the mirrored letters of the inscription on his palm: *MEMENTO SEMPER. NUMQUAM OBLIVISCI.*

'I'm sorry,' Annev stammered. 'I didn't mean to—'

Dolyn raised her burned palms between herself and Annev. 'It's my fault,' she said, wincing. 'I found a thread and pulled at it. The connection ... it's like nothing I've experienced – slippery as a fish but harder to grasp. The *aqlumera* has been forged into the shape of a golden arm but its spirit ... it's something else. Something wild and untamed.' She stared at her burned hands, fingers trembling. 'It was beautiful,' she said, almost whispering, 'like nothing I've ever held or forged. As ephemeral as fire. Soft as silk, yet stronger than steel.' She shuddered, closing her eyes, and tears streaked down her face.

'I'm sorry,' Dolyn said at last, her glistening eyes meeting Annev's. 'I cannot remove the hand.'

Chapter Five

The Shadow's apprentice stalked among the sun-dappled shrubs of the Brakewood, her muscles tense, her green eyes sharp and shining beneath her golden mask.

'When do we leave?' Myjun growled, her teeth gritted in pain.

Oyru raised a single eyebrow. 'Why would we leave?'

Myjun's breath quickened, her fists flexing at her side, the cords of her neck tense with emotion. 'To kill that bastard, Ainnevog! To avenge my father! You promised me blood, you kraik, and I want it.'

'You have barely killed before,' Oyru said, matter-of-fact. 'The stench of death has not yet stained your soul. You have no experience.'

'But I *have* killed. You saw it yourself in the tunnels.'

Oyru stepped deeper into the glade, the shadows of the trees soothing him. 'I saw you murder two mindless creatures – and you let the third *escape*. My other apprentices began as trained killers.' Oyru shrugged. 'You are not ready to pursue your vengeance, let alone obtain it.'

Myjun's eyes remained fierce beneath the blood-streaked golden mask. 'You wish to test my commitment?'

How quickly I forget, Oyru thought, *that the Mask of Gevul's Mistress makes its wearer an insufferable bitch.* He would have laughed – or cursed, or sighed – if he cared enough. Instead, his thoughts were cold. Pragmatic.

She must be humbled. Steel must be burned and beaten before it can be tempered and taught its shape.

'I do wish to test your commitment … among other things.' Oyru raised his hand and drew on the void, channeling the energy of the Shadowrealm to forge a thin double-blade of nether in the palm of his hand.

'This is a shadow construct,' Oyru said, flipping the knife in his hand. 'It is a physical manifestation of another plane of existence. One whose essence overlaps with this world but whose substance is anchored in another dimension of reality. I have drawn it into this world – summoned it from the nether – but its form is unstable.' Oyru flipped the knife high above him. It reached its arc and began to fall, the twin blades spinning lazily in the air. Oyru reached out as if to catch it, but before he could grasp the black shard, it evaporated into smoke and nothingness.

Myjun stared at the assassin, her pale eyes still fierce and challenging. 'What is the point of this except to prove you're a rotting conjuror?' She spat at Oyru's boots, though the gesture was diminished by her saliva slapping against the inside of the golden mask.

'I will teach you how to find your prey,' he said, unfazed. 'I will show you how to track him. How to capture and kill him. To do that, though, you must give heed to my instruction. You must learn to be as deadly as I am in the dark, if you wish to be equally powerful in the light.'

Myjun laughed, though there was no amusement in her voice. Instead, each spike of sound was like a needle driving into Oyru's skull.

'Teach *me*?' she scoffed. 'I need learn nothing from you, demon. I have been trained by the greatest fighters in the Darite Empire. I am a *warrior*.'

'Truly?' Oyru said, his face blank.

'Truly.'

Oyru flicked his hand towards Myjun. A dark star of metal flew from his palm, its four points trailing wisps of ethereal smoke. The spinning construct thudded into Myjun's shoulder, slicing deep into her ragged red dress and the flesh beneath.

Myjun's hand flew up to clutch her injured shoulder. 'You rotting *kraik*! Why'd you do that?'

'You are a warrior, are you not?' Oyru gestured at Myjun's injury and the black star of metal dissolved into smoke and nothingness, exposing the red wound further.

'You *attacked* me!'

Oyru forged three new shards of nether and casually hurled a second volley at Myjun.

She dodged to one side, throwing herself to the ground and evading the first throw. A second trio of spikes followed them a heartbeat later, and Myjun flinched as two plunged into the ground beside her. The last thudded into her calf and she screamed in pain.

'Gods!' she cried out. 'What in the hells are you doing! Do you want to *kill* me?'

'If I wanted you dead, you would be. The fact you are still alive proves you had *some* martial training, but I wouldn't call you a warrior.'

'Then you underestimate me,' Myjun said, her voice cracking beneath the pain. 'I am a skilled assassin, trained by the masters and witwomen of Chaenbalu.'

'That means little to me, especially when your masters were so easily overrun by the *feurog*.' Oyru dismissed the five throwing spikes in the dirt. The last spike, the one buried in Myjun's calf, he left as a reminder of her weakness.

'Why would you do this?' Myjun sobbed, prodding her injury. 'What does this teach me? I can't walk, and now Annev is going to get away!' She sniffed. Beneath the mask, her green eyes sparkled with tears.

Could it be, Oyru marvelled, stepping towards the injured woman, *that I have misjudged this one so poorly? Could she truly be so weak?* He began to kneel beside his apprentice, intending to remove the throwing spike. Before he could reach it, though, Myjun jerked the void-shard from her leg, spun around Oyru's kneeling form, and jammed the shard into his left hamstring. She twisted hard, then pulled savagely at his shade-bound flesh.

Oyru grunted, half in shock, half in pain. Before he could recover, Myjun plunged the spike into his back once. Twice. Thrice.

64

Then she swung her fist sideways and slammed the nether-spike into his neck, just beneath his jaw.

The assassin gurgled then coughed, blood dribbling from his lips. Myjun leaned over his shoulder and hissed in his ear, all trace of her former anguish gone.

'I told you. I *know* how to kill.'

Oyru reached up, his black-gloved hand patting the young woman's, reaching for the spike. Myjun's hand fell away and she hobbled backwards, still on her knees. She stared, incredulous, as Oyru grasped the twin-pointed shard ... and ripped it free. A spray of blood pulsed from the wound, spattering his black rags, Myjun's mask, and the shrubs on the forest floor.

Oyru held up the spike, and the young woman gawked as Oyru casually dismissed the construct back to the Shadowrealm. He forced a smile, teeth stained red, and saw Myjun's eyes widen further. He knew what she was seeing; he could feel the nether streaming into him, the shadows swarming to fill the gaps in his flesh, healing what should have been several mortal wounds. He coughed again, but instead of spitting blood and bile, he felt the blood in his lungs shift into shadow-vapour and he exhaled a cloud of inky darkness, its essence spilling from his lips like an airy waterfall, its mass somehow heavier than the surrounding air.

'What are you?' Myjun asked, both disgusted and horrified.

'I am your master.'

'Then what have I apprenticed myself to? The Lord of Shadows? To Keos himself?' Myjun shuddered, her disgust magnifying. 'You are as foul as the one I hunt,' she breathed, full of contempt.

'I have no doubt that I am worse.'

'Then why should I serve you? What makes you think I would be your apprentice?'

'Because you already *are*. Because you are just as corrupted by magic. And ...' he paused, 'because *I* am not the one who killed your father. I am not the one who *betrayed* you.'

At these last words, a fire seemed to kindle in Myjun's emerald eyes. 'He lied to me. Made me fall in love with him – a bloody *keokum*! I hate him. I hate everything he is – every lie he told me, every word he whispered to me. Death is too good for him ...

but his life is all I can take from him. He took my father from me. My beauty, my face, my life. He took *everything*. Annev,' she said, trembling with rage, 'must die.'

Oyru studied the young woman. The sharp edge to her voice was a contrast to the soft curves and alluring gaze of the cursed artifact. Its twin streaks of bloody tears were no less out of place, more sad than gruesome as they trailed down the mask's perfectly crafted cheekbones.

Oyru chided himself for letting the magic of the artifact lull him into seeing anything other than the dangerous girl beneath. Her anger made her feral. Bloodthirsty. There was a cunningness to her eyes and a quickness to her movements – Myjun had not lied when she called herself a warrior. She had indeed been trained to kill, though it was clear she had not much practised the art, let alone perfected it. Still, she had potential, more so than any of his previous apprentices. It had been over two decades since the last one had stabbed him ...

Larissa dan Karli, Oyru thought, remembering, *and only when she had nearly finished her apprenticeship*. He hadn't even begun training Myjun, unless he counted stabbing her. She had good instincts.

She reminded him of Oraqui.

'You will notice you moved faster the second time, and faster still when you attacked me. This is the magic of the artifact – the Mask of Gevul's Mistress. Your pain fuels it, gives it power. And it, in turn, feeds you. When you are injured, you will move faster. When you feel pain, you will strike harder. When you suffer the most, you become the greatest threat. The mask will also speed your healing and recovery, though that is not its primary function. It cannot make you invincible, though it might convince you that you are. But while it cannot save you from a mortal wound, whatever does not cripple you will make you stronger.' Oyru rose to his feet, standing above Myjun. 'This is your first lesson. Embrace your pain. Agony is your ally and suffering is your sword.'

Oyru slapped Myjun's gilded face, making the metal ring out. Myjun reeled, tumbling backward, rolling awkwardly with the injuries to her shoulder and calf.

'And this is your second lesson,' Oyru continued, his voice cold as Reotan ice. 'I am not your friend. I am not your ally. I am your master and you are my apprentice – my *servant*. You will obey me in all things and without question. If I tell you to plunge a dagger into your breast, you will do so. If I tell you to sear your skin, you will reach into the flames and press the coals to your flesh. Do you understand?'

Myjun hissed, climbing to unsteady feet. 'You would make me a slave then. A whipping-maid for your cruel fancies.'

'Yes. If I wish.'

She growled, her injured leg unable to bear her full weight, and rocked back, lowering herself to the earth once more. She paused. 'But you will help me kill my father's murderer – my betrayer? You promise you will help me find and kill the demon that calls itself Ainnevog?'

'I will.'

Myjun nodded, her ragged breath beginning to slow. 'Then it is worth it. Show me where he is that I may kill him.'

Oyru sniffed. 'You are not ready.' Myjun opened her mouth to protest but the assassin held up a single finger, forestalling her objections. 'I will tell you when that time has come, and I say it is not that time. Your martial skills are considerable, particularly when paired with the magic of your mask, but you are not perfect. You could not pluck my weapons from the air and hurl them back at me, much less evade my attacks.'

Myjun scoffed. 'You caught me by surprise and hit me twice – in the shoulder and the leg. I stabbed you *five* times, and three of those blows would have killed you if you weren't some Keos-be-damned shadow-spawn.'

She was right, of course. Not just about who had bested whom, but about his damnation and his otherworldly powers. True, he hadn't been trying to kill her in earnest, and she had surprised him, but he had been incautious *because* of his certainty that she couldn't harm him – not permanently. He never would have been so careless, so reckless, if he had felt he was in any real danger.

It was refreshing, after decades of training obedient apprentices. Oyru had given her the mask and then provoked her into fuelling it with her pain. He had injured her, and then left her

67

the nether-spike instead of dismissing it. He had given her the opening, the training, and the means ... and she had taken it. She had baited him then gutted him like a fish. He should have expected her attack, should have been waiting for it.

He would have to be more careful. Especially as she *had* bested him.

'You are right,' Oyru said at last. 'You are not without skill, and the mask enhances it. You surprised me, and that is no small thing.'

How many times had he done this? With how many apprentices? He had lost track of the faces and the names. The gilded mask had replaced them all, erased as surely as if they had never existed before putting on the mask. And when he looked at them, he thought of only one face. One name.

Oraqui.

It was strange to feel nothing when thinking of her – no pain or anger, no regret or sorrow, no longing or love. Time could do that. It could not 'heal all injuries' as the poet Nilanteska had oft asserted, yet it was still the only balm to give him a clip of relief. Not wine or women. Not murder or self-flagellation – not even his own death had eased it. Time was the only remedy, it seemed, and even that could not have quenched his anguish without the second ingredient in his secret salve.

Obsession. Oyru could never bring Oraqui back, just as he could never follow her. But he could craft a *new* Oraqui. He moulded each new apprentice into Oraqui's replacement, shaped her into something better than the original. And if he failed – if the duplicate proved inferior to the original or no longer pleased him – he could break her and start anew. He had done it hundreds of times, and each time he felt a little more relief, a little more distance. It was as if each of their deaths deadened him further. He felt so little now it was sometimes difficult to rise above his own apathy and follow his master's instructions.

Capture the Vessel. Bring him to me. Alive.

It seemed such a simple task, and yet Oyru had lost the boy. He had never failed before. He had never needed to report to the First Vampyr with the *reasons* for his failure. Oyru wasn't even sure what he would say to Dortafola. Much better to treat his mission as incomplete than failed. An ongoing task with an indefinite timetable. Dortafola could always correct him of that assumption. Till then, Oyru's mission to capture Ainnevog had not changed. He would bring him to Fala Tuir, as instructed, and to hell with his promise to help Myjun.

But she needn't know that, and he would not tell her. He needed allies. Something more formidable than a corrupted wood-witch or the perverse creatures that served her. He had his eidolons, of course – the shadow demons that begged to be released into this world – but that wasn't enough, he realised, not if he was going to remain in the Physical Realm for this long. To capture this particular quarry, he needed an ally who could fight in the sunlight as easily as he could fight in the shadows. He needed someone like Oraqui to keep his own demons at bay.

For the first time in decades, Oyru *needed* an apprentice. He needed an ally who was dangerous enough to aid him but not enough to be a threat to him.

'You are not ready,' Oyru repeated, studying Myjun, 'but I will teach you. I will finish the education begun by your witwomen and witmistress, and you will begin your second school of study.' He waited, knowing she would ask.

'Studies? The only thing I want from you is Annev.'

'I do not know where to find him.'

'But you said—'

'That I would teach you *how* to find him.'

'And kill him,' Myjun added, her eyes flinty behind the static mask.

Oyru allowed his silence to speak the lie for him. 'You have much to learn, apprentice. I can teach you so much about pain, and survival ... and betrayal.' He watched her, but the maiden behind the mask didn't flinch.

Good.

'But you have already learned some of these things. Today I want to discover the extent of your affinity for magic.'

Myjun scoffed. 'I don't have magic. I'm not cursed like you.'

'Aren't you? You are scarred. You were betrayed and abandoned. You wear a cursed mask.'

The apprentice shook her head. 'But I am not a flaming *keokum*.'

Oyru stepped towards the young woman, his eyes gleaming. 'You don't understand. That mask only bonded to you *because* you possess magic. The only question that remains is what kind.' He tilted his head, a thought occuring to him. 'Your father wielded that obsidian wand. He used artifact magic to melt that well and seal me inside.'

'Do not speak of my father.'

'Why? Because it pains you? Do you hold affection for the dead man who lied to you?' His lean figure towered over her prone body. 'Your father used a Luminerran hellfire wand. Where did he get it?'

'From the Vault of Damnation, I guess. It holds artifacts from every corner of the world. Finding and using it would have been a simple task.'

'Finding it, perhaps – but not using it. Hellfire wands can only be wielded by those with both Terran *and* Ilumite blood.' He waited, letting his implication sink in.

'How *dare* you accuse my dead father of magical degeneracy.' Her words were saturated with menace and disgust.

'It is not such an uncommon thing,' Oyru said. 'Even in a backwater like this. The Terrans have been trying to dilute your bloodlines for centuries, seducing your mages with their talentless loyalists; weakening or perverting the Darite potential for magic. It seems to have backfired in your case, though, likely due to the injection of Ilumite blood. You don't often see that in Daroea – not unless someone has coupled with a slave ... or a whore.' He watched closely as he stoked her anger, her muscles tensing as he spoke. 'Most likely the interloper was a man and the woman was too ashamed to admit her child was the issue of an Ilumite. Perhaps a wandering Dragonrider raped your grandmother, or an Auramancer twisted her emotions till she couldn't help but—'

Myjun lunged at him with a primal scream, bounding off her good leg as she swung a fist at Oyru's jaw. The assassin sidestepped, anticipating the attack, but didn't notice her other hand darting for his leg. The woman's fingers struck hard, thumping into his hamstrings. He felt the limb go numb as Myjun landed on her good leg then awkwardly rolled to her injured one.

Oyru took a stumbling step backward, surprised by his now petrified limb and barely avoiding a fall. He phased the immobilised leg into the shadows then brought it back to the corporeal realm to restore its full function, though he felt increasingly drained by the effort.

'I see that you find the truth distasteful.'

'You talk too much, sorcerer,' she said, her teeth gritted. 'You insult my dead father when you should be teaching me how to find his killer.'

'And to do that effectively, I must probe your magical capabilities.'

'So *test* me,' Myjun said, her words both an invitation and a threat.

The Shadow Reborn studied the girl's wounds, which were bleeding less fiercely than they had just moments ago. The mask was working. He looked back at the forest.

'Follow me, little degenerate, and we'll uncover the curses your mixed blood has brought you.'

Chapter Six

They walked more than a mile, with Oyru leading them towards the heart of the Brake, sometimes following animal trails but just as often forging a path through the brush. Myjun followed close behind, limping and cursing the whole way, but the assassin paid her no mind. He scaled a boulder-strewn hill with the grace of a mountain cat, then slid down a treacherous slope on the opposite side.

Demon, she thought. *I've apprenticed myself to an actual demon. If his training doesn't kill me, I may kill myself.*

Myjun tried to follow, but she couldn't keep pace with her new master. She stumbled over the boulders, her blood dappling their stone faces, then – tired and full of self-hatred – she pitched herself over the side of the hill. When she finally rolled to a stop, the assassin stood above her, head shaking.

'You are weak.'

'And you are a sadist. I don't have demonic magic to heal me.'

'Don't you?'

'No!'

'You have your mask. It will heal you – eventually.'

Eventually. The lie seemed so obvious now. Myjun sneered beneath her mask, furious that she had allowed herself to be tricked by a shadow-spawned keokum.

'Everything you say is a lie,' she hissed. 'I see that now. The mask has only imprisoned me, so you can give up the charade.'

'I have not lied. The mask *will* heal you.'

'Then why am I still in *pain!* If it's healing me, why don't I feel any better?'

Oyru cocked his head to one side. 'I thought you understood. The mask can heal your body, but that is secondary. Its true magic comes from focusing your pain into energy, which you can channel to be faster, stronger, more alert. If your pain subsides, that focus is diminished and the magic fades. Do you understand what that means? Do you see why the mask can never *fully* heal you?'

Myjun gave a mewling growl that transformed into a frustrated roar. 'What good is your magic, then?' She flung a fistful of wet pine needles at the assassin. 'What advantage does it bring me? Too little pain, and I gain no benefit. Too much, and I am crippled by it!' He was trying to break her. That was the only explanation she could fathom for this prolonged torture. But Myjun would *not* break.

'If your pain has crippled you,' Oyru said, 'it is because you have allowed it to.'

'*You* crippled me!' Myjun screamed. 'You're the reason I'm lying here in the muck instead of hunting down my father's killer.'

'Am I?'

'Yes! What are you trying to prove? That I'm weak? That I'm not worthy to learn your secrets?'

Oyru looked down at her glaring golden face, his expression serene. 'You are not helpless. You are not crippled. You are lying on the ground because you are afraid.'

'I'm lying on the ground because you stabbed me – twice.' She paused, suddenly hearing his words. 'What do you mean, I'm afraid?'

'You're afraid of pain,' he said. 'You have not embraced it – you have not *owned* it. If you had, you'd still be walking and we would not be having this conversation.'

Myjun fell silent, thinking. Her emotions told her she was being attacked – that Oyru was trying to hurt her, trying to humiliate and punish her – but something in his tone made her reconsider. Had she truly fallen because of her own weakness? Or had she instead done it to inconvenience the Shadowcaster?

'You're insane.'

'That's irrelevant. Now ... stand up. I need to see your aura.'

She lay on the ground for just long enough to irritate him, then growled beneath her mask and forced herself onto her knees and then her feet, her right leg bearing most of her weight. The moment she was standing, Oyru grasped her shoulder, causing her to flinch – yet she did not pull away; instead, Myjun watched him intently as the assassin prodded her wounded shoulder with his thumb. She hissed, tensing, but Oyru paid her no mind. His other hand reached down to probe the injured thigh, as intimate as a lover, as casual as if it were Myjun's own hand exploring the wounded flesh. Myjun swallowed, uncomfortable yet unwilling to retreat. She had allowed herself to fall once already; she would not give him an excuse to call her weak again.

'Tell me what you feel,' Oyru said, his attention divided between the girl in front of him and the invisible aura that seemed to surround her.

'What do you care?' Myjun growled, still tense. Instead of answering, Oyru jammed his thumbnail into her injured shoulder. Myjun shrieked, trying to pull away, but the Shadow Reborn held his grip, forcing his thumb deep into the bloody gash. She batted at him, clawing his face with her other hand, tearing flesh – yet he paid her no mind. Myjun's skin tore further, her wound opening wider.

'What do you *feel*?' Oyru demanded, his tone as merciless as death.

'Pain!' she shouted, struggling to break free, still clawing at his eyes and mouth. 'I feel pain!'

'Not good enough.' Oyru snatched her attacking hand, pulled it from his face, and twisted her wrist behind her back. He held it there, pinned, as the shadows repaired his injured face. 'Describe the *way* it hurts. Is it superficial pain or does it hurt down to your bones?' He dug his thumb deeper, widening the gash further. She screamed, barely able to form a coherent sentence. 'Take your time,' Oyru said, his speech steady, his breathing even. 'I can wait as long as it takes.'

Myjun clamped her mouth shut. Sharp blasts of air spurted from her nose, hard and fast.

I am stronger than this! she told herself. *I survived the Academy and its training. When the monsters came for me, I broke them. I will not let this break me.*

Slowly, her breathing steadied until she exhaled a shuddering breath. 'It hurts to the bone,' she said through gritted teeth, still tense as a coiled spring. 'It feels like a knife ... or a worm burrowing into my flesh.'

'Good. What else do you feel?' He pulled her wrist tighter, raising it behind her back.

Myjun took a sharp breath then slowly let it out again, ragged. 'My arm,' she said, her voice turning into a squeak. 'You're going to break it!'

'You know this? Your pain has somehow turned you into a Seer?' Oyru bent her arm further, bones creaking beneath the pressure. Myjun gasped and fell to the ground, but Oyru held his grip. He forced her further, bending her forward till the mask was inches from the Brakewood's soil.

Don't break, she told herself. *Don't break ... don't break.*

'You are no Seer,' he continued, 'but your blood-magic is something else – something special. I will discover what it is.' He waggled his thumb in her bloody shoulder, probing flesh, nerve, and sinew. This time she did scream. The pain was unbearable, greater than anything she had ever experienced, and she kept waiting for him to finish, for the torture to end, but the assassin didn't stop. He continued, probing deeper, as if unaware of his actions or their effect.

'Please!' she wept, surprising herself. 'You'll cripple me. Stop – *please!*'

Oyru held her firm, lowering his face. 'Focus on the pain,' he whispered, almost tender. 'Let it fuel you, but don't let it rule you.'

Myjun shuddered again, her sobs softly muted by the golden mask – yet she did not cry out again. *I am already broken,* she told herself, and found it was true. *I am shattered ... there is nothing he can do to break me further. Right?*

Without letting go of her wrist, Oyru slid his bloody hand from Myjun's shoulder to her elbow, holding her in an arm lock. She grunted, a new wave of pain and fear flooding her, but she didn't scream.

'Which hurts more,' Oyru asked, 'your shoulder or your arm?'

'My arm.' The words were forced, but she spoke clearly.

'But I have not broken your arm,' Oyru said. 'So why should it hurt more? Why should your injury hurt less than the *threat* of injury?'

'Because ... I'm afraid.'

'So, your fear is greater than your pain?' Myjun hesitated again and Oyru tightened his grip on her elbow, forcing her face into the soil. 'Answer me,' he said, his voice calm yet unrelenting.

'Yes,' she growled.

'What are you afraid of?'

'That you'll hurt me *more*! That you'll scar me ... *cripple* me.' She whimpered at the end, twisting slightly as she fought against Oyru's grip, but she couldn't escape without breaking something.

'I am not the one holding you captive,' Oyru whispered. 'You are.'

Myjun wanted to cry, to submit or relent – yet something stayed her. She *could* be strong ... but she also had to admit she was broken. She needed to embrace both her strength and her shattered edges. Accepting that was the only way she could escape.

She paused, her breath so still, they both knew what would come next.

With a sudden jerk, Myjun spun away, her wrist breaking free even as her elbow gave way, the tendons rupturing, the joint dislocating as muscle tore from bone. She roared in pain, which became anger. And then defiance, as she stood.

Chapter Seven

'Good,' Oyru breathed, his eyes drinking in the sight. 'Never again be a slave to fear. Never be afraid of pain. It is your ally, and you are its master.'

The girl was panting like a dog beneath her golden mask. 'You *broke* my arm.' She spoke in anger, but this time her words possessed a controlled fury – a focus – that had been lacking in her previous threats. That was good. The steel was being tempered, though her full conversion would take much longer. Oyru wasn't sure he'd have enough time to properly forge and hone her – not before Dortafola called on him again. Still, he didn't want to rush the process. It was the one thing that gave him joy. Perhaps if they travelled to Riocht na Skah ...

'I didn't break anything,' Oyru said, matter-of-fact. '*You* did. You possessed the strength to free yourself from my grasp, no matter the cost. By accepting that, you have become invulnerable to further breaking.'

'Invulnerable?' She almost laughed. 'You call *this* invulnerable?' Myjun lifted her flopping forearm, the limb hanging askew.

'I call it ... progress.'

This time Myjun did laugh, a crazed keening that was sharp as a knife and hot as a forge.

'You're still a monster,' she growled, once she had composed herself.

'Yes,' Oyru admitted. 'And now so are you.' He gestured at her arm.

The girl turned away, her expression hidden behind the golden mask. 'Perhaps. But now my weakness has become my strength.'

Oyru grunted, surprised by how quickly this one learned her lessons. 'Does your arm still hurt?'

'Of course it hurts, you kraik! My bloody arm is broken.'

'Yet you aren't weeping. You aren't pressed with your face to the ground, pleading for your life. How are your other injuries? Where I struck you with the nether-spikes.' He pointed to the girl's bloody shoulder and thigh.

'You are one flaming—' Myjun cut off as though suddenly realising something. Her eyes narrowed and she inspected her wounds, first probing the soft flesh of her leg then prodding the bloody holes of her dress. As her fingers moved more vigorously, her eyes began to widen. 'They're *gone*?' She spat the word out as if it had an unpleasant taste. 'How is this possible?'

'The Mask of Gevul's Mistress,' Oyru said. 'I promised its magic would heal you, and I explained how your pain would fuel it. Physical pain, emotional pain – it is all the same. As long as you hurt, you cannot *be* hurt.'

'Then why is my arm—'

'Still broken?' Oyru said. He turned his back on her, surveying the Brakewood. 'It will heal too, eventually, but there is a limit to the mask's magic. It can't regrow a severed limb or bring you back from the dead. Greater injuries require greater sacrifice, and there is only so much you can give before there's nothing left.'

Oyru paused, staring into the darkness beyond the trees: there was a shadepool out there, nearly two miles east. He hungered to find it, to plunge back into the Shadowrealm – the doorway to the World of Dreams – and lose himself in its nethereal void. Staying in the Physical Realm for too long always had that effect on him, as if being carnate somehow reminded his body of its actual age, yet the truth was both more exotic and mundane.

The Shadow Reborn needed to sleep.

It seemed ironic that, as a half-man accustomed to living in the Plane of Shadows, Oyru could ignore nearly all physical appetites, yet he couldn't deny his body's need for sleep. Like all humans, daily existence in the Physical Realm cost the assassin a portion of his cognitive vitality – an arcane essence called 'somnumbra', which could be replenished by mentally touching the World of Dreams – but shadow mages also used somnumbra to access the Shadowrealm and manipulate the nether.

Yet Oyru was no ordinary shadow mage; he could store and utilise more somnumbra than any other being in the Physical Realm, but he also expended it more rapidly. Maintaining a physical presence in the real world was taxing – something a true shade could only do for minutes at a time – so Oyru became subject to the strengths and weaknesses of both species. He could survive in the Physical Realm for days at a time, but the sleep deprivation left him weak in body, mind, and magic. Conversely, when Oyru slept he could not simply send his mind to the World of Dreams like a human shadow mage; he had to *physically* move to the Plane of Shadows and saturate himself with its pure somnumbra. Once he had absorbed enough essence, he could return to the Physical Realm and dive into the waters of reality. He would then navigate its currents like some nethereal leviathan, submerged and slowly expending his breath before resurfacing in the Shadowrealm to capture another chestful of somnumbra.

But I have been under the waves for too long, Oyru mused, rubbing his bleary eyes. He deduced that his growing irritation at Myjun, and his poor reaction-time when the girl attacked him, was related to his deficiency of somnumbra – not that it excused his failures.

I'll give her a training exercise, Oyru decided, *something that will occupy her attention for a few hours while I regain my strength.* It would take at least that long for her arm to heal, and once she was whole it would be easier to test her magical abilities. He turned from the Brake and settled his gaze on his apprentice.

'Without more pain, your arm will be slow in healing ... so I must subject you to further suffering.' He paused, waiting for the woman to object – to curse him or otherwise refuse his tutelage. She did not disappoint.

'My arm is already healed, you—' The girl stopped, her lips quivering, her mouth contorting into a bestial growl before roaring, '—*orspkocugu!*'

Oyru froze, more surprised by the girl's curse than her claim.

'You ... speak Southern Kroseran? *Bunun benim dil oldunu biliyor mosun?*'

Myjun sniffed. 'My father taught me many languages, but your demon tongue was not among them.'

'If that were true, you would not have understood my question.'

'*Git kendini beyzhar!*' she snapped in defiance.

The assassin's mouth fell open. He stared, on the point of laughing ... and then he *did* laugh. He hadn't done it in centuries, and it came out as a dry cackling cough, almost painful in the way it rattled his chest and contorted his face; it felt unnatural, but it also felt *good*. All the same, he forced the emotion down deep into his belly, let it simmer, then waited till it died.

She doesn't realise she's speaking my tongue, he thought, his emotions back under control. *She must be using her* lumen *to communicate – it's unconscious ... instinctive.* Yes, that was it. She was using her Ilumite magic to swear at him, which would make her an Auramancer or a Soulrider, possibly a combination of the two. That would make things interesting, particularly as she was wearing the Mask of Gevul's Mistress. He could do great things with that combination.

'You say your arm is no longer broken,' Oyru said at last. 'Show me.'

Myjun rolled across the ground, snatched a large stone from the forest floor, and hurled it at the assassin's head. He sidestepped easily, yet his eyes fixed on her elbow – the same one she had used to throw the rock.

'It *is* healed.'

'That's what I said.'

'Don't be petulant.' Oyru tried to focus on the puzzle of the girl's miraculous healing – but it was no use. With every passing second his mind was becoming more clouded, his body more fatigued. It was as if the somnumbra was draining from him much faster than it should have.

Her magic, Oyru realised. *She's siphoning the somnumbra from me ... sucking the cognitive life-force right out of me.* That could only mean one thing. *She's a Soulrider, for sure. Possibly something else, too, but her primary talent ... is soulriding.* Oh yes. He was going to have a lot of fun with her – but first he needed to rest; if he stayed around the girl any longer, her presence would forcibly thrust him into the Shadowrealm.

'Your healing is exceptional,' Oyru said, clarity breaking through his increasingly hazy mind, 'but it needs to be tested.' He summoned a void blade, bent to the floor, and scooped up the oblong rock Myjun thrown at him. With a several quick strikes of his shadow construct, he chipped the large stone into a cruel-looking knife: one side was jagged with saw-tooth spikes, the other thin, straight and sharp as a razor. There was no handle, though the dagger was nearly as long as his forearm.

'This is your blade,' the assassin said. 'Until I say otherwise, it will never leave your hands. You may not carry or use any other weapon.' He held the knife up for Myjun to see. 'You claim you are a warrior but you have only shed the blood of two monsters. Tonight you will change that.' Oyru tossed the long knife and she caught it deftly, wrapping her hand tight around the blade despite the blood oozing between her fingers.

'Does it matter what I kill?'

'Impress me,' Oyru said, his form fading into shadows and mist. '*Try* to impress me – without hunting Annev. That prey is for another day.'

The sharp lines and colours of the Physical Realm faded from Oyru's vision, and the sounds of the forest became muted and indistinct, portending his arrival in the next world. Yet before he disappeared entirely, the Shadow Reborn heard the muttered reply of his apprentice.

'One day I will hunt *you*, conjuror.'

Oyru permitted himself a small smile as his shadow-bound body fell into the next plane of existence. He had chosen his apprentice well. She had strength, vitality, and magic.

He hoped he wouldn't have to kill her, like he had all the others.

Chapter Eight

The corpses lay everywhere. In the stairwells, the hallways, the storerooms. Everywhere Kenton looked, he saw death.

Most of the bodies belonged to men – acolytes, avatars and ancients that Kenton had known personally, if not very well – but there were children among them, too, and a few women. In fact, Kenton was surprised to see so few women, given how many of the masters and ancients had been killed, but so far he had only encountered two fallen witwomen. The first, Witwoman Nasha, lay in the nursery surrounded by the corpses of dozens of dead infants. The second woman Kenton hadn't known well – just another one of the many teachers that had instructed the witgirls – but her death had been so grisly Kenton had difficulty banishing the bloody images from his mind. Her jaw ripped from her skull ... her chest cavity emptied of its organs ...

And then there were the corpses of the monsters themselves. Disfigured humanoids made of sharp metal, rough stone and mutated flesh. Nightmarish creatures. In some places their mangled bodies littered the ground like dry leaves scattered by the wind. In others they were piled atop one another. A fleshy mound of twisted metal, rock and refuse. They lay crushed beneath fallen archways, suffocated by collapsed tunnels, and chopped into bloody pieces that lay across the shattered stairs and broken corridors.

Gruesome as it was, Kenton couldn't even close his eyes to it. He'd lost that ability when the *aqlumera* had scarred him – when Annev had injured him — and had no respite from the horrors.

That bastard, Kenton thought, remembering his pledge to kill his former reap mate. *If I see Annev again, I'll gut him like a fish and feed his entrails to the crows.*

His magic vision captured the interior of the Academy in perfect clarity, letting him peer through the stone and mortar, past the crumbled walls and fractured pillars, into every dark corner of the ruined Academy.

Not every corner, Kenton thought, looking down the dark steps leading back towards the Vault of Damnation. The magic fires in his eyes smouldered as he studied the void marking the Vault, their fiery light flickering as he concentrated. Whatever magic protected the room prevented his supernatural vision from piercing its walls, leaving only inky blackness that dissipated once he looked away. Kenton could see the body lying outside the Vault's great ironwood portal, though, and while he couldn't see the dead man's features, his cursed eyes revealed the man's identity.

Narach, he thought, feeling little sympathy for the dead man who might otherwise have been his mentor. Kenton was grateful to have escaped that fate and found himself curious how the sour old man had met his demise. Had the demonic creatures killed him? That seemed likely, and those same monsters were almost certainly dead. It seemed they had also failed to break into the Vault of Damnation.

Just as well, he thought, stepping carefully through the remains of a ransacked storeroom. *Nothing down there but cursed magic, and I need to find a way to the surface.*

He was still searching for a hallway or corridor that led above ground and was beginning to despair. Every path he had found had been closed off, and it seemed impossible that so many of the Academy's secret entrances and exits had been demolished by accident. Even the paths shown to him by Duvarek, the dead Master of Shadows, were sealed. More and more, Kenton suspected the demolition had been an act of sabotage, that the intruders had sealed the exits to ensure no one escaped. Whoever had done it had been thorough.

The metal monsters had received help, Kenton decided. How else could they have penetrated the Academy so thoroughly? How else would they have destroyed *every* staircase and tunnel that led to the surface? Kenton had found exactly one intact corridor that still led to the first floor, but once there, every hallway had been sealed off. It was too neat. Too much of a coincidence. Certainly, some of the destruction had been an accident – a side effect of the upper floors collapsing upon the lower ones – but the storage chamber Kenton was currently studying seemed to have been demolished intentionally.

Once again, Kenton was trapped. He had only escaped his cell by good fortune, and now fate was toying with him. He retraced his steps, searching for another tunnel, another path to salvation.

But there were none. Kenton was alone with the dead, and not even his magic eyesight showed him an answer to his puzzle.

I can't go up, he thought, *and I can't circumvent the cave-ins. If I go down to the lower levels, could I find another tunnel?* It seemed logical. The Academy's collapse had sealed off many corridors, but it might also have opened new ones.

I wish I still had Annev's sword, Kenton thought, remembering how easily it had carved the stone at Janak's keep. *If I had just kept it from Narach, it would still be in my room. At least then I could cut my way out.*

A new thought stopped him dead. Had Narach actually taken the sword into the Vault of Damnation? Kenton had assumed so, but the decrepit Master of Secrets was very particular about how he catalogued his artifacts. Might he have left the sword in the archives, to be properly catalogued at a later date? Could he have left it in his bedchamber? The latter seemed unlikely, but the former ...

Kenton shuffled along the dark hallways, using his magic sight to guide him. He had no need for a torch and stepped over the cold bodies as easily as the loose stones and broken tiles. His mind was focused on his goal.

When he reached the stairwell leading down to the archives room, he stopped and allowed his vision to penetrate the floor below. He saw his own bedchamber, which he had only slept in for half a night before chaos had erupted and Annev had locked him up. Then he glanced into Narach's bedchamber and examined the man's austere furniture: a bed, a clothes chest, a small table. No sword.

84

Kenton's gaze shifted into the archives. As his vision penetrated the walls, Kenton felt the stark power of the Vault of Damnation attempt to negate his supernatural vision, its magic growing stronger as he looked at things closer to the wall. He glanced away, still frustrated by his inability to squint or blink to clear his vision.

And then he saw it: a long table displaying the Sword of Sharpness. An open book, stylus and inkpot lay beside the silvery artifact.

Kenton raced down the steps two at a time, skipped over the bodies littering the corridor, and leapt across the threshold into the archives room. The black haze of the Vault felt almost palpable here, but Kenton ignored it, dancing around the fallen bookshelves and snatching the sheathed shortsword from the table.

As soon as his hand touched the cloth-wrapped hilt, Kenton felt the magic rush into him.

I am air that cuts like a knife, it seemed to say. *I am the wind and the rain that shapes the mountains and the hills. This sword is my sheath and I am its blade. Call on me and I am yours. Wield me and I will bring Mercy to your enemies.*

Mercy, Kenton thought. That was its name. That was how the sword viewed itself. The blade itself was not sentient, but the magic that forged it – the *blood* inside it – was still alive. Somehow.

Kenton tightened his grip on the weapon. *I shall wield you,* he thought. *You are mine and I am yours. While you are in my hand, our will shall be one.*

He felt a thrill as the sword seemed to respond to his thoughts, extending its magic towards him, grasping his mind as firmly as he held its hilt. They *were* one. The sword – Mercy – was his.

We must go to the surface, Kenton thought, not knowing why he addressed the sword this way, yet feeling it was the right thing to do. *We must go where the air is fresh, where the rain falls and the sky can kiss your blade.*

The sword thrummed in his hand, as if in response. *Air*, it seemed to say. *Follow the path of the air.*

And then Kenton felt it – he *saw* it as the sword perceived it: a draft of air flowing down from the stairwell, its cool breeze coming from some unexplored chamber.

Follow the air, it seemed to whisper. *Follow the voice of the Skyfather – the way of the wind.*

Kenton turned from the table, holding the sheathed sword in front of him like a silver divining rod. The blade quivered ever so slightly, its metallic soul yearning to feel the breeze from the surface, and Kenton followed it, seeing that Mercy was leading him back towards the staircase. His pulse quickened and he started up the steps before he felt the cool displeasure of the sword's magic.

Follow the wind, it whispered, urging him back down the steps, back towards the Vault of Damnation and the Academy's dungeons.

But we must go up.

No, Mercy whispered back. *We must go* out. *The wind knows the way.*

Kenton hesitated, then trusted Mercy, his boots soft on the broken steps. When he reached the landing leading to the Vault of Damnation, he felt Mercy urge him deeper into the Academy's bowels.

Kenton took a deep breath and descended the next flight of stairs, his feet slowly drawing him closer to the origin of the draft at the bottom of the stairwell, past the cells lining the corridor, all the way to a locked door adjacent to his former cell. Kenton stuck out his hand and felt the soft whisper of air coming from beneath the cell door. He almost laughed.

Calling on the sword's magic, Kenton slid it into the door jamb and sliced through the deadbolt barring his entry into the room. He kicked the door open and was rewarded with the source of the draft: a crude tunnel at the back of the prison cell, its rough-hewn walls leading up towards the surface. He had missed it from the upper floors, his vision blocked by the Vault of Damnation.

Kenton knelt down in front of the tunnel, his right hand on Mercy's hilt, his left probing the black earth and sharp stone. Clearly someone or something had dug this tunnel deliberately.

Kenton ducked his head into the hole then eased his shoulders inside. The thick smell of rock dust filled his nostrils along with the sweet tang of clay. He clawed at the ground, felt the rough soil beneath his fingernails, and angled his body upward so his magic eyes could peer straight ahead: the tunnel climbed upward for perhaps two dozen feet, but some loose earth and rock had been piled there, partially blocking the passage. Kenton crawled farther into the tunnel, the stones grinding against his knees as he slid Mercy ahead of him, pointing the way.

When he reached the blockage, Kenton called upon the sword's magic once more, extending and shaping the air that sheathed the weapon. Using the thin draft of air to guide him, Kenton slid Mercy between the fallen stones and began cutting away the rubble. It was slow work, for while the artifact held a keen edge, he still had to apply force to push the blade through the rock. Even then, the shortsword was better adapted for piercing and slicing, less so for carving or digging. After a few minutes, he had to pause to clear away the mound of dirt and debris piled in front of him, shovelling the loose dirt and rock aside with his bare hands and dumping handfuls of rock and earth back into the prison cell.

If I have to dig the whole way, I'll kill myself, Kenton thought grimly, though that wasn't strictly true. He had found food and water in the storerooms above – not enough to feed an academy filled with teachers and students, but enough to keep a man alive for a year or two. He wasn't going to starve to death or die from thirst. Nor did he lack for oxygen, so it seemed the air underground was still circulating despite all the cave-ins and collapsed tunnels.

Hold on, he thought, as he trudged back to collect more rubble. *I can see how much farther it is to the surface. All I need do is look.* He chided himself for his foolishness and turned towards the tunnel. The Vault of Damnation still blocked part of his view, but as he took a few steps closer, Kenton's magic vision reasserted itself and he had a clear view of the shaft he had been widening: the blockage was shorter than he had thought. With a little work, he could clear the remainder of the cave-in and the rest of the shaft would be easy to scale. He smiled and hastened to the tunnel, not relishing the bruises he was developing on his knees, then carried two more armloads of dirt back to the empty prison cell. With most of the debris cleared he used Mercy again, cutting away more rock and shaping the tunnel into a squarish crawlspace.

Skrrit. He thrust Mercy into the stone.

Snikkt. Snikk-snikk. He sliced through three more pieces of rock.

Kenton set down the sword and began working on the rubble again. As he did, he saw the faintest glow of light – actual *daylight* – reflect from somewhere farther up the sloping passage. Kenton slid another armload of the soil and rock away from the opening, then pushed his head and shoulders inside the area he had cleared. As he craned his neck, he caught the faintest sliver of light shining from the tunnel's distant exit.

'Thank the Gods,' Kenton breathed, instinctively shifting his vision so that his magic sight revealed what had been difficult to see before.

The tunnel ramped upward at a steep but easily climbable angle. After bypassing the cell where Annev had imprisoned him, it skirted the Vault of Damnation and ascended past the archives floor and the level above. It reached fresh air a hundred feet beyond the watchtower at the northern perimeter of Chaenbalu.

He'd found a clear path to the surface, more than half a mile in length and almost perfectly straight.

Kenton pressed further into the tunnel, trying to force his way past the narrow neck of the underground passage. Solid rock pressed into his shoulders, clawing at his red master's tunic and the flesh beneath. His heartbeat quickened as he felt the stone threaten to pin his arms against his body.

'Nope, nope, nope,' Kenton growled as he extricated himself from the tight passage. Once he'd backed up several feet, he lifted Mercy again and began cutting away another foot of stubborn earth.

Kthhhunk. The sword slid into the dirt. *Ssssssnikt. K-snikt.* He pulled the blade sideways into the stone, widening the passage.

Snikkt. K-k-k-crack.

The earth groaned.

Then the ground above him shuddered.

'Bloody b—'

A thunderous ton of dirt and rock collapsed atop Kenton, breaking his ribs, crushing the air from his lungs, and pinning his head, arms and legs.

The dim light from above immediately winked out, and Kenton's vacant eyes stared at nothing but the cold gloom of his subterranean tomb.

Chapter Nine

Annev and Sraon trudged through Banok's narrow streets with their heads bowed and a pall of silence hanging about them.

'I don't want Titus and Therin to come with us to Luqura,' Annev said slowly, after working through his thoughts.

Sraon nodded as though following all Annev had left unsaid. 'That's probably for the best. What of the others?'

'Fyn will be fine. Titus will probably stay with Master Brayan, and I doubt I can do anything to get rid of you. If you're still willing, you're the only one who can help me find Reeve.'

'Aye,' Sraon said, finding no complaint with Annev's deductions. 'The boys won't like it much, but I agree it's the safest thing. If Brayan keeps them company, they should be fine here. I'll point him to Dolyn's smithy and the two of them should be able to keep the boys busy while we're gone.'

'Whatever is hunting me won't stop when I find Reeve, not even if he can help me remove the hand.' He turned, squinting at the blacksmith. 'I mean to leave them behind for good, Sraon. I can't be responsible for their safety.'

'Fair enough, but you can't tell them that – especially not Titus. If you try to say goodbye, they'll fight you and they'll chase you. Tell them you'll come back, though, and you might persuade them to stay.'

'You want me to lie to my friends?'

'Who's to say you're lying? Might be fate and fortune carry you back here faster than you think.'

'In which case they would be in danger – again – and I would need to leave again.'

'So wait, and explain it to them then. Might be you never need have the conversation.'

Annev muddled it over. He could leave them and lie to them, as easy as promising to be back before the week's end and then never seeing them again, but he felt they deserved better than that. At the same time, he felt leaving Chaenbalu was a chance to write his own narrative and he didn't much like the taste of starting that with lies and deceit. Sodar would have done it that way, no doubt, but Annev had no interest in a life built on lies and deception.

Thinking of the dead priest, Annev glanced down at the glowing hand hidden beneath Sraon's smithing glove and remembered Sodar's words: 'Some lies can protect us, and truths can kill us. Given the choice between the two, which would you prefer?'

Annev knew his answer now – he wanted *the truth*. Any other choice meant someone was influencing his actions, and that he was acting on incomplete information. It meant someone was manipulating him. He wanted to know the truth, to know all the forces that challenged him, and then take his chance. But could he choose the same for his friends?

Damn it. It was the same choice Sodar had been forced to make: to protect his friends by lying to them – and protect himself by continuing to hide his hand – or to put Titus and Therin in danger by telling them the truth. A truth that would likely come back to endanger him.

They walked back to the market square in silence, and Annev couldn't come to an answer that sat well with him. He wanted to be honest with his friends, but he suspected Sraon was right. No amount of earnestness or reason would deter Titus from hitching his wagon to Annev's.

As if thinking the boy's name had summoned the chubby steward, Titus suddenly separated himself from a growing crowd and ran up.

'Annev! Did you see? Banok has jugglers – *Ilumites*! And some other exotic folks I've never seen or heard of before! There's a ranger – a beast lord from Alltara – and a soothsayer! Annev, his skin and hair are as white as milk – and his eyes! Annev, they're *pink*. Can you believe that? Come and see!'

What's this? Annev wondered, though he didn't wonder long. Titus pointed into the crowd and he saw the knives flipping over the heads of the gathering townsfolk. The group had gathered near the southern entrance of the marketplace, and as Annev neared he saw a lean man in bright red leathers juggling four throwing knives high overhead. As Annev pushed through the edge of the crowd, he saw the man had three dozen more knives strapped to his calves, arms, chest, back, and thighs.

Therin suddenly appeared at Annev's side, barely noticed amidst the spectacle before them.

'I can do four knives,' he bragged. 'Hell, I can do *five*.' As Therin spoke, though, the man in red spun and reached into his bracers – and suddenly there were six knives cycling through the air above the juggler's head.

'Huh,' Therin said, now looking impressed. 'Well, that's … wow. I wonder how many he plans to put in the air.'

Annev was equally impressed by the spectacle, though Titus's words echoed in his mind. *An Alltaran ranger … and a soothsayer with pink eyes and white skin.* Annev's gaze drifted away from the juggler and searched for the other two party members. When he didn't see them he looked back at the juggler: the fellow was handsome – tall and blond, lightly tanned, with an angular face and a muscular build – but his face was also criss-crossed with delicate white scars, and his thin moustache vaguely reminded Annev of Master Ather, the Academy's Master of Lies. There were other oddities about the man's appearance, not just his face or his features but also the way he moved and spoke. It was like watching a dancer or listening to someone speak the lyrics to a familiar song. The effect was mesmerising.

'He's an Ilumite merrymaker,' Sraon whispered, walking up beside Annev.

Annev glanced at the blacksmith. 'The crowd doesn't seem to mind his being a foreigner.'

'No, merrymakers are often well received – and Banok is more cosmopolitan than Chaenbalu. Even in the village, Ilumites were tolerated as a novelty – a spectacle – not something to be feared.'

'You're talking about my mother.'

The blacksmith slowly nodded. 'I never met her, though I knew her reputation from folks in the village. She made quite a stir when she married your father.'

'Aegen,' Annev said, still watching the juggler. 'Sodar told me her name was Aegen.'

'She was a talented singer, as I heard it. It's a mark of an Ilumite – the spellsinging, or spirit-singing as some call it. They've got the grace of the Gods in them. You can see a touch of it in this fellow, the way he moves and flows.' He pointed to the juggler. 'Bright clothing is another indicator, as is the blond hair, though there are enough blond Darites that you can't tell by that alone. There's another sign, too, apart from the spellsinging and dweomer-dancing, that is. Can you see it?'

Annev studied the lithe performer, observing his movements as he began spinning knives under his legs and catching them behind his back.

'His necklace,' Sraon said, leaning closer. 'You see what's on it?'

Annev squinted until he spotted the bronze medallion swinging on a chain about the man's neck. He took a step closer, almost pushing into the clearing around the man, and saw it was engraved.

'What's on it?'

'A dragon and a phoenix,' Sraon said. 'Tesked – Lumea's first flame. And Rogen – Lumea's last hope. Both are symbols of the Ilumite faith.'

'Tesked the dragon and Rogen the phoenix,' Annev repeated, their names sparking some old memory from one of his conversations with Sodar. 'What else did you call him? A merrymaker?'

Sraon nodded. 'Merrymakers are entertainers of sorts. Not Ilumite specifically, but a lot of them fall into the trade on account of the singin' and storytellin'.'

'Are they different from a bard then?'

'As different as a king is from a commoner, I'd say! Bards sing and tell tales, for sure, but you're unlikely to encounter a true bard outside a king's court. Merrymakers come in all sorts – jongleurs, knife-throwers, musicians, actors, poets. This one juggles, and I expect he's got other talents up his sleeves. Since he's an Ilumite, too, I'd bet my good eye he has a strong singing voice, or a musical instrument stashed somewhere. Probably both.'

Annev kept watching the spectacle, and the smith slapped a hand on his shoulder. 'You and the lads enjoy the show. I'll let Brayan know our plan, see if he's had any luck selling our grain. Help Fyn keep an eye on the wagon, too.' He gestured to the apple cart and the tall youth standing outside the perimeter of the show. 'If this were Luqura or Quiri, there'd be a thief working the crowd about now.'

Annev blinked, dropping a hand to his belt pouch, and felt his cheeks flush with panic – the pouch was empty! The mantis-green sack and all of its contents . . . it was gone! Annev's stomach twisted as he catalogued the items he had lost through his inattention: the magic phoenix lantern, Breathanas's banners – Sodar's translation of the Speur Dún manuscript!

Just as Annev's bowels began to turn to water, he felt a wave of embarrassment. He'd stowed the bottomless bag inside the tunic pocket where he normally kept his lockpicking tools. He touched his chest pocket, felt the sack inside his tunic, and knew his possessions were safely hidden. He smiled, feeling a bit foolish, and turned to see if anyone had noticed.

Sraon had found Brayan, who was now unloading the dozen or so sacks of grain, seed, and flour the group had pilfered from the Academy's unmolested storerooms. Just beside him, Sraon chatted with a fat man in broad silk pantaloons, the latter gesturing towards another vendor who sold fruit, cheese, and bread. On the other side of the cart, Fyn was watching the merrymaker's show, paying neither Annev nor the cart any mind. Meanwhile, Titus and Therin had fully joined the crowd forming the half-circle around the Ilumite entertainer. Fyn raised a hand to his mouth, yawning, and began to turn away just as the juggler spun in a circle and snatched two shortswords from his back. There was cheering as the larger weapons joined the six spinning daggers circling over his head.

Fyn turned back to watch the show.

'Hello!' the merrymaker shouted, flashing his brilliant white teeth at the crowd. 'My name is Kryss Jakasen, but most folks call me Red-thumb. If curious why, keep watching my act— ouch!' The juggler pulled his right hand to his mouth, briefly sucking his thumb, then snatched a falling dagger and continued the performance.

Therin laughed, whispering to Titus. 'He didn't actually cut himself. Those knives probably aren't even sharp.'

The merrymaker danced over to Therin, light on his feet. 'Not sharp, you say? Didn't cut myself, you say? The world's best performer, you say? Ah, but if only that were true.' Without missing a step, the man wiped his bloodied thumb on Therin's cheek, streaking it red. Therin quickly wiped away the stain, drawing laughter from the crowd.

'No, I may not be the world's best juggler, sir, but I am an *honest* one. Ouch!' This time the crowd laughed at the merrymaker's perceived injury, then the laughter changed to a roar when he marked Therin's other cheek with his left thumb, drawing a second red stain across his skin.

Therin jumped back. 'Blood and bones,' the boy swore, rubbing vigorously at his face.

'Indeed!' Red-thumb said, continuing his patter. 'I've bloodied many bones in this profession. Catching the knives isn't the most difficult part, though.' Matching actions to words, the juggler leaned forward, caught his shortswords behind his back and sheathed them, all while juggling the six smaller knives. The crowd clapped in amazement, and Annev remembered Sraon's warning to stay alert for thieves preying on the spectators.

He had expected to see a young boy, dressed in rags or nondescript clothing, so it took him a moment to spot the merrymaker's true accomplice standing between the apple cart and the back of the crowd. She wore a fiery orange dress with a yellow shawl draped across her shoulders. The woman's bright auburn hair had been plaited into two loose fishtail braids that hung down to her chest and swayed merrily as she wove her way through the crowd. Having spotted her, Annev let his gaze flick between her and the merrymaker's act.

No sign of the ranger or the soothsayer, though, Annev thought, his curiosity still piqued by Titus's earlier description.

'No,' Red-thumb drawled on, still smiling, 'the hardest part is maintaining a rhythm you're comfortable with. When someone else dictates how fast or slow you must juggle, that's when things get dangerous.'

The woman in the orange dress suddenly leapt forward, dashing to the front of the crowd as she pulled a simple wooden flute from beneath her shawl. As she spun to face the crowd, Annev could see she was almost twice his age and quite beautiful. Glancing at Red-thumb, she held the flute to her lips and began to play a soft, haunting melody.

Suiting his actions to her music, Red-thumb threw his knives high into the air while sheathing a single pair of knives, deliberately slowing his juggling to match her pace. 'Ladies and gentlemen, may I present my sister – Luathas!' The woman gave a slight bow to the crowd, eliciting a dull murmur and some light clapping, then she picked up the pace of her tune. Red-thumb adjusted his own rhythm, pumping his knives into shorter, tighter arcs.

Hmm. I guess she's not the thief after all.

Annev continued to keep an eye on the crowd but didn't see anyone else moving among the spectators. There were two men that caught his attention, though. The first wore a cowled, hooded robe – dark grey, almost black – with his hands and arms tucked deep inside his sleeves. As Annev watched he caught a glimpse of pale white skin beneath the man's hood.

That's the soothsayer, Annev thought, marking the man for further scrutiny, *which means the other man is the ranger.*

The second fellow sat apart from the crowd, his studded leather armour and fur-trimmed boots setting him apart from the merchants and townsfolk gathered to watch the show. He also had two shortswords strapped to his back, though these were accompanied by a pair of wooden tonfas on his belt. The ranger knelt to rub the head of what looked to be a small weasel nuzzling his boot, and then the creature scampered off to frolic amidst the crowd. No one else seemed to notice it. Annev found his own attention drawn back to watch the merrymaker and his sister.

She's an Ilumite, he mused, *just like my mother.* Annev felt a dull pang of loss at that thought, despite never having known his parents. Aegen would have been just a few years younger than Luathas. Would she have worn the same clothes? Shared the same features? Annev watched the woman's slender fingers as they slid along the length of the flute then hastily banished such morose thoughts from his mind.

'Fortunately for me,' Red-thumb said, still spinning his blades, 'my sister has never been good at playing the flute. Can't carry a tune in a bucket, and she stutters and stops almost as much as she blows and whistles.'

Luathas punctuated her song with a shrill piercing note, then kicked her elder brother in the shin. The crowd laughed and Red-thumb cursed as he cut another finger. Therin stepped back before the merrymaker could mark his face again, and the crowd roared with laughter. Red-thumb smiled, this time wiping his bloody thumb on his sister's cheek. Luathas's eyes flared and she picked up her pace yet again, her fingers dancing across her instrument.

The crowd began to 'ooh' and 'ahh' as Red-thumb bit his lip and drew another pair of knives from his bracers. Luathas played faster and Red-thumb drew a second pair from the bladed bandolier over his chest, adding them to the mix. Faster and faster. Another pair of knives. Then another.

The crowd murmured in amazement, starting to count the number of knives flying through the air over Red-thumb as he added them. Annev joined in. *Ten. Eleven. Twelve knives? Can't be right. That's impossible.* But Red-thumb was achieving the impossible. The juggler's hands moved so fast they were a blur, with each silver throwing knife arcing high overhead before spinning gracefully downward, flipping into Red-thumb's fingers and then rocketing back up.

Luathas played faster and faster, the notes blending into one beautiful voice. Red-thumb tried to match her, but it was clear this last feat was too much even for the master juggler. Finally, Luathas finished with one last flourish of speed, her final note ringing out across the market. At the same time, Red-thumb kicked a plank of wood that had been lying at his feet and snatched up the board. With stunning precision, the merrymaker caught each of the knives as they plunged rapid-fire, point-first into the wood. When the last dagger had fallen, Red-thumb turned the plank towards the audience, holding it aloft to prove that he had indeed juggled twelve glittering pieces of razor-sharp metal. The crowd roared. Red-thumb bowed, flipping the board as he did so, and Annev read the words the merrymaker had inscribed on the other side: DONATIONS WELCOME!

Chapter Ten

The crowd continued to applaud as Luathas pulled out a worn leather sack and made her way through the audience, collecting coins. When she passed Fyn and then Titus and Therin, the three boys shook their heads apologetically. The woman gave them each a smile. When she came to Annev, he was about to give the same silent excuse as the others, but remembered the bottomless bag in his chest pocket. Annev spoke as the woman started to turn away.

'One moment. I may have something for you after all.'

Luathas stopped, turning to face Annev as he withdrew his magic pouch and fished around for some coin. He found something metallic and extended it to the woman – and was as surprised as she was by what he held.

The misshapen copper was heavier than it looked, its edges rough and uneven. The faces were also a bit worn, but on the front one could just barely see a casting of the Staff of Odar dividing a wind-tossed sea from a lightning-streaked sky.

Annev swallowed as she silently took the copper penny from his hand. He had seen that coin once before. Sodar had showed it to him, and he knew what the flautist would see as she turned it over in her hand: a picture of a war falcon – part smith's hammer, part billhook – with the long-handled weapon floating ominously above a smoking anvil. The coin was almost five-thousand years old and had come from a brief time when the people of Daroea and Terra shared currency.

Annev doubted anyone present would have understood the coin's origin, let alone its relative worth, yet the auburn-haired woman seemed moved as she rubbed the coin between her fore-finger and thumb. She looked up at Annev, her hazel eyes bright with tears, and studied the features and contours of his face. Suddenly her eyes widened, first in realisation, then as if in fear. With a gasp, Luathas took a quick step back towards her brother. Red-thumb had sheathed his throwing daggers by then and stepped lightly to his sister's side.

'Luathas?' Red-thumb looked between Annev and his mute sister, then noticed the coin she clutched in her palm. With a frown, Red-thumb reached out and plucked the metal disc from her fingers. He examined both sides of the penny, amusement spreading across his face, then held it up to Annev.

'Did you give this to her?' Annev nodded. A smile spread across the merrymaker's face. He licked his lips, about to say something, then stopped, taking in the cart beside Annev and the three boys who were edging closer to their conversation.

'Thank you for the donation,' Red-thumb said, palming the ancient coin. 'Your generosity is humbling.'

'It's just a copper wheel,' Annev said, finding his words. 'I doubt it has much value.'

Red-thumb studied Annev with his cloudy blue eyes, then took the coin pouch from Luathas and showed Annev the contents: the purse was empty. Annev frowned.

'I'm not sure if you've noticed, son, but we're Ilumites.' Red-thumb dropped the misshapen copper into the pouch. 'People rarely give us coin, no matter how good the show.'

'Oh.'

Just then, Sraon and Brayan returned from selling their goods. The blacksmith jingled a small handful of coins in front of him, smiling. 'It's not much, but it should help us pay those gate fees.' He turned to Luathas and Red-thumb, eyes tightening. 'Hello. Quite the show you put on. You are very talented, Master Merrymaker.' He flicked a copper in the man's direction and Red-thumb caught it with a bow and a sweeping flourish.

'You don't know the half of it,' Titus said, joining the conversation. 'He juggled almost a dozen knives – at the same time!' Therin and Fyn stepped up beside Titus and Fyn nodded his agreement.

'It was pretty good,' Therin said, wetting his fingertips with saliva and wiping them on his cheeks. 'Could have done without the blood, though.'

'Blood?' Sraon asked.

Red-thumb raised both shoulders and plastered on a mischievous grin. 'Part of the cost of the show.' He gave the bag and coin to Luathas who continued working the crowd, and then he held up both hands, showcasing the hundreds of tiny white lines that scarred his thumbs and fingers. The merrymaker squeezed the fleshy pad of one thumb and a fresh drop of blood oozed from the cut. 'The name's Kryss, but folks call me Red-thumb – for obvious reasons.'

Sraon turned his good eye on the merrymaker, studying him, then finally extended his hand to the Ilumite entertainer. 'Sraon Smith.' Red-thumb took the blacksmith's hand and shook it obligingly, leaving a faint spot of blood on the man's wrist. Sraon looked down at the red smear and smiled. 'Red-thumb, indeed.' He looked between the juggler and the retreating flautist then turned to Brayan.

'Master Brayan, would you take Titus, Therin and Fyn and get the provisions for the rest of our trip? A little fresh fruit ... maybe some dried meat and cheese. It'd go a long way to complementing those parsnips.' He gave his handful of coins over to the hulking quartermaster.

'Happily, Master Sraon. I am at my best when tallying and distributing supplies.' He looked to the boys. Come along. I'll teach you how to stretch our coin.'

Titus cheered, hurrying to follow Brayan, and the other boys followed less enthusiastically. Fyn tossed a glance over his shoulder at Annev, raising an eyebrow, though he said nothing.

Sraon turned back to the merrymaker. 'Is Kryss the name your clan gave you?'

Red-thumb's smile faded somewhat. 'Tesked is my birth name, though only my sister calls me that. Truthfully, I prefer Red-thumb. It's a friendly name, and that's a boon in my trade.'

'Tesked,' Sraon repeated. 'Named after the first dracolum?'

A broad smile broke across Red-thumb's face. 'Why, Master

Smith, you are a man of rare breed!' He shook his head. 'A Darite acquainted with Ilumite culture. Tell me, how do you know so much of my people?'

Sraon's face grew sombre. 'I was once a slave-trader.'

Red-thumb's mirth vanished and his body tensed, his eyes flitting between Sraon and Annev. 'Once?' he asked, his face growing hard as his right hand drifted towards a knife.

'In my youth. I was born in Innistiul – though I no longer call it home, nor do I call its citizens my brothers.' Red-thumb's face seemed to soften at hearing this and he stopped reaching for his blade. Meanwhile, Sraon pressed on, his gaze falling to the ground. 'I spoke with some of our captives and learned what I could of their culture – *your* culture – which eventually persuaded me to leave Innistiul and my family for good. Some years later I met a priest named Sodar, who taught me a great deal more about Ilumites. With time, he persuaded me to join the Guardians of the Well.'

Red-thumb's eyes lit up, its hardness evaporating. 'You're a Dionach Tobar?'

'I'm not an artisan, no – I don't possess the gift – but I do hold to the faith.' Red-thumb nodded, understanding. 'What of yourselves?' Sraon said, glancing between Red-thumb and Luathas, who had returned from collecting donations. 'Do either of you possess Lumea's grace?'

The merrymaker smiled. 'I suppose I do, though not of the magical variety. Like yourself, I am simply an adherent of the faith. A Keeper of the Flame, but not Dionach Lasair. My sister ...' Red-thumb looked to Luathas who gave an almost imperceptible nod of the head. 'My sister once possessed the gift, but she lost her voice when a Bloodlord attacked our family. She no longer sings Lumea's song. She no longer speaks at all.'

'I'm sorry to hear that,' the blacksmith said, looking truly grieved. 'I heard the song of the Dionachs Lasair once. It was an experience I shall never forget.'

Red-thumb bowed his head. 'One day, Lumea's voice will be heard again. Perhaps on that day my sister will also sing.' He laid a hand on her shoulder and she smiled up at him. 'Until that time,

Luathas contents herself with the flute. I also play, though I prefer the harp.'

'So you do more than juggle knives.' Sraon caught Annev's eye. 'I told you as much, didn't I, lad?'

Red-thumb grinned. 'I juggle, I dance. I sing and play. I can tell stories and recite poems with the best of the merrymakers – but that is not my *true* calling.'

'Oh?' Sraon asked, surprised. 'Which art do you call your own?'

Red-thumb snatched up a satchel lying on the ground near his plank of wood, pulled the straps over his shoulders, and gave Sraon and Annev a conspiratorial grin. 'You call my profession an art – and that is correct, though most would not deem it as such. Yet I know the truth of things, and I share that truth with you.' The entertainer stretched his arms to the sky as if embracing the world and everything in it.

'I, Red-thumb, Ilumite bard and betimes merrymaker, am a treasure-hunter of the highest calibre. I hunt for mythologies, legends and tall tales, and I share them with others when I entertain. But my true passion comes in tales of treasures. For,' the Ilumite boomed in his powerful baritone, 'what is more poetic than a treasured tale containing the tale of treasure? And if that tale of treasure is true, whence the treasure's trove? And if one finds the treasured trove and, within, the treasure true, do we not become part of that tale, and thus a treasure ourselves?'

Sraon and Annev glanced at one another and Luathas took the opportunity to elbow her brother in the ribs. The bard winced, though his grin did not diminish.

Annev scratched his ear. 'I'm afraid you've lost us, Master Merrymaker.'

Red-thumb gave a deep bow. 'My apologies, Master ...?'

'Annev.'

Red-thumb bowed deeper. 'Master Annev. Excellent. Our benefactor has a name.'

Sraon glanced questioningly at Annev but the boy shook his head, not wanting to explain. Fortunately, Red-thumb continued.

'What I meant to say was, while I enjoy hunting for stories, I also like getting paid for my labours – and merrymaking is a poor profession. Treasure-hunting, though ... that can pay extremely well.'

Annev raised an eyebrow at this. 'Only if you know of buried treasures?'

Red-thumb laughed. 'I know of *scores* of them! But less than half the stories I know are true, and the rest are rarely worth hunting. I seek the few that are worth my time.' He stepped forward, eyeing first Annev then Sraon. 'May I ask who it is that leads your party?'

The sudden change in topic gave Annev pause. To his mind, the blacksmith was clearly leading the group, but why should Red-thumb care? Why take an interest in Annev's group at all? If the question took Annev by surprise, though, he was even more surprised by Sraon's response.

'I am young Annev's steward, though he, in truth, leads our party.'

Red-thumb nodded as if this were exactly what he'd expected. He looked back at Annev. 'I know this is impertinent as we've only just met, but my sister and our companions are travelling to—'

'Look out!'

Annev spun towards the speaker and was surprised to see the albino soothsayer standing beside their half-empty apple cart. Closer still was the Alltaran ranger. Annev blinked and suddenly the ranger's tonfa was swinging past his nose, appearing as if from nowhere.

CRACK! Something small and dark flew over Annev's head.

'Gods!' Sraon swore, pushing Annev to the ground. 'Stay down, boy!' The smith fell atop him in a heap, but Annev was quick to regain his feet. The albino stood beside him along with Red-thumb and his mute sister.

'There!' The merrymaker shouted, pointing. 'Down that alley!'

The group turned and Annev spotted a silhouetted figure fleeing down an alley mouth. The ranger holstered his tonfa and dashed after the assailant, both disappearing into the shadows.

Beside Annev, the albino swept back his grey cowl, revealing hair as bone-white as his skin, though his smooth skin and sharp eyes suggested he was nearly the same age as Sraon. He stooped to the earth, picked something up, and held it for all to see: a crossbow quarrel. The albino studied first the quarrel and then Annev with intense pink eyes.

'You are hurt, Master Ainnevog?'

Instead of responding, Annev dashed off after the ranger and the would-be assassin, hurtling past tents and stalls crowded with hawkers and customers.

'Annev!' Sraon shouted. 'Wait!'

But Annev was already gone, having called on the magic of his Boots of Speed. Within seconds, he reached the alley where the ranger had disappeared, barely catching a glimpse of him as the fleeing assassin dashed behind a row of vendor stalls with the Alltaran in close pursuit. Annev took another step and nearly tripped over a heavy crossbow. He left it where it lay and hurried after the ranger, catching him as he reached Banok's city wall.

'There!' The Alltaran pointed to a cluster of booths selling woven rugs and artful tapestries. 'Behind that red wall hanging!'

Annev reached the stall three steps ahead of the ranger and tore the hanging aside, chagrined to find only a blank stone wall behind the drape. 'Where did he go?'

The ranger inhaled deeply. 'I swear he was here.' The man tilted his head to the side, inhaling. 'The attacker's scent lingers. He was here. He should still *be* here.' The foreigner pressed his nose to the city wall, smelling its bricks. 'I don't understand it. It's as if he vanished into the rock.'

Annev looked up at the looming city wall, his hand pressed to the stone, and tried to imagine his attacker scaling it unnoticed. He swore.

Just like Faith, Annev thought. *Vanished into thin air ... unless the assassin went through the wall?*

'Are you all right?'

Annev turned to see the ranger studying him. 'I'm fine. Just upset we didn't catch him.'

'You're not even winded,' the ranger said, obviously impressed. 'Few, even among my countrymen, can match my speed.'

'Ah,' Annev said, understanding. 'I did not truly best you.' He hesitated, wondering if he should say more, then decided he could probably trust the ranger with one of his secrets. He lowered his voice: 'My boots are enchanted.'

'Excuse me!'

The pair turned to find a sweaty merchant glowering at them. 'You gonna buy that?' he asked, pointing at the tapestry still gripped in the ranger's hand. The Alltaran stared blankly at him. 'Then get the hell out of my stall! You're scaring away my customers.'

Annev doubted that, but he and the ranger complied all the same, returning the way they had come.

'Thank you for saving my life,' Annev said, extending a hand. 'My name is Annev.'

'Well met.' They shook hands. 'I am Corentin, a Shalgarn from Alltara, though my companions call me Mad Cat.'

'Mad Cat?' Annev repeated. 'That's a strange—' He saw the man's eyes for the first time: yellow with black, oval pupils, the same shape as a cat's.

'Not so strange,' Mad Cat said with a grin.

'Oh!' Annev said, surprised. 'Yes ... I see why.'

The Shalgarn walked to the fallen crossbow, picked it up, and offered it to Annev. 'Are these common in your country?'

Annev took the heavy weapon. The stock was made from metal and the string of braided wire. 'I've never seen its like,' he marvelled. 'I can't imagine being strong enough to load it without assistance.'

'Expensive, too,' Mad Cat agreed. 'That's the tool of a master assassin. At a distance, it could probably punch through plate mail.'

'How did you knock that quarrel out of the air?'

'I almost missed it. My eyes and reflexes gave me an advantage – similar to your boots, I think.'

'You mean ... an enchantment?'

'A blessing,' Mad Cat corrected, 'though the effect is the same.'

'Annev!' Sraon called, running across the market square to join them as they emerged from the crowded row of booths. 'What were you thinking, running off like that?'

'I was thinking someone had tried to kill me and I didn't want them to get away.' Annev handed Sraon the crossbow to examine. 'I'm not sure how he eluded us. We chased him straight to the city wall and then he just ... disappeared.'

'Are you injured?' Sraon asked, drawing them back towards the group still surrounding the apple cart.

'No,' Annev said, speaking to the entire group. 'The bolt didn't even graze me.'

'That's a relief,' Red-thumb said, and Luathas was quick to nod her assent. 'It's a fine thing Corentin and Jian were here, else your journey might have ended here.'

'Jian?' Annev said, looking towards the hooded albino. 'You shouted the warning, yes?'

The pale-skinned man bowed his head. 'As you say, Master Ainnevog. It was foreseen.'

'And you knew my name,' Annev continued. 'My *full* name ... though we've never met.'

The pale man inclined his head again. He glanced to Red-thumb for assistance but Sraon interjected before the merrymaker could speak.

'We had just finished our introductions. The pale fellow is Jian Nikloss, a Yomad from Terra Majora.'

Jian bowed a third time, his hands clasped in front of him. 'A pleasure.'

'Master Nikloss possesses a talent for sensing what cannot be seen by the common man,' Red-thumb explained, twisting his moustache. 'It grants him limited precognition of people and future events. It's also been a popular trick among the small villages ... but I sense Jian has not showed us the full extent of his talents.'

Annev stared openly at the white-skinned man, half in disbelief and half in suspicion. 'You mean ... you can see the future?'

The Yomad made a strange gesture with his hands and shook his head. When he spoke again, Annev noticed he spoke with a slight accent. 'Like seeing,' Jian said, 'but not seeing. Small window to see the world. Short time to see and hear.'

Annev tried to process this. 'Did your magic tell you my name then – and save me from that crossbow bolt?'

Jian bowed again. 'As you say, Master Ainnevog.'

Annev touched the hem of his smithing glove, a fire churning in his gut. *First Dolyn ... and then the Ilumites, the Shalgarn, and the Yomad. In one day I've met the worshippers of Cruithear, Lumea,*

Sealgair, and Tacharan. That can't be a coincidence – and the wood-witch said I would be hunted by the Younger Gods, which means someone here probably has ulterior motives. Annev frowned at the soothsayer, unnerved by his appearance.

'You wonder about my other talents,' Jian said, teeth flashing. 'I have many,' he continued before Annev could answer. 'Seeing. Speaking. Summoning. Not common to have these all.'

'What do speaking and summoning entail?' Annev asked.

'I talk to . . .' Jian searched for the word. 'People who go to holy lands,' he said at last. 'I call them and hear them. Sometimes they speak. Sometimes I speak.'

'You speak with the dead?' Annev ventured.

Jian made the strange gesture again, once more shaking his head. 'Not dead. *Lumen* and *quaire* move to holy lands. They live. *T'rasang* remains in this world. *T'rasang* is dead.' He hesitated. 'But I can speak to *t'rasang,* too. Sometimes it answers. Sometimes it no answers.'

Mad Cat cleared his throat and all eyes turned to him. 'Your pardon, but your leader has admitted to owing me a life debt.' The ranger indicated Annev. 'I would claim it, but I have already promised my aid to these two Ilumani.' Mad Cat pointed to Red-thumb and Luathas. 'Because I have pledged myself to them, his life debt is transferred to them as well.' The ranger nodded as if he had completed some formal contract. 'That is all.'

'Life debt?' Annev asked, turning first to Sraon and then to Red-thumb. The former swore under his breath while the latter merely stroked the patch of hair beneath his bottom lip.

'Mad Cat is Shalgarn,' Jian said, nodding sagely. 'Life debts are common in Alltara.' He held up a finger. 'But I also have claim to your life. I shouted the warning to you, and I had told Mad Cat to protect you from flying harm.'

'You foresaw the crossbow bolt,' Annev said, filling in the gaps in the soothsayer's broken Darite. 'You had a vision that I would be attacked, and you told Mad Cat to save me.'

'You are wise,' Jian said, bowing his head once more.

'Our party is bound for Luqura on a mission of grave import-ance,' Sraon said testily. 'We cannot be waylaid by life debts and strange customs.' He inclined his head slightly towards Luathas. 'No offence intended, mistress.'

Mad Cat frowned. 'I am confused. You cannot mean you will shirk your debts.'

'No,' Sraon said again, 'but we have commitments we must keep, just as you have yours.'

'Ah yes. This I understand.' Mad Cat looked between Red-thumb and Jian Nikloss. 'A favour, then. It is customary to exchange a favour in such cases as these.' He turned back to Annev. 'You will grant us a boon, yes?'

Annev then saw the game for what it was. This was probably what the foreigners had been after all along. *Just another way to trap me,* he guessed, suspicious.

'Am I permitted to ask the nature of the boon before it is requested?'

Red-thumb gave a smile that was all teeth. 'I think we can allow it.' The merrymaker gestured to his group. 'I am seeking additional members of our troupe.'

'Stop right there,' Sraon interrupted. 'Not a one of us will be joining your clan. We have our own mission to fulfil.'

Red-thumb laughed, his hands waving in front of him. 'No, no. We are seeking *specific* members. My Yomad friend here has even divined some of their names.' The merrymaker raised two fingers. 'We are seeking a Druid from Fertil Hedge and an Orvane named Dolyn. We came here looking for Dolyn, but Jian's magics have failed to unearth him.'

'If we can direct you to Dolyn, will that fulfil my debt to Mad Cat?' Annev asked.

Red-thumb looked at him gravely. 'Might do.'

'Dolyn is a woman,' Sraon interjected, 'who has been absent from the village these past few days ... but I doubt she'll join your troupe. She runs a very successful smithing operation in the Gold District. Deals in fine metals mostly, but she can work damn near anything.' He shrugged. 'Find her if you like, but don't discuss her heritage in mixed company. You seem cosmopolitan enough, Master Red-thumb, but not all folks are so accepting of foreigners.'

Mad Cat whispered something to his white-skinned companion, and Jian tugged his grey cowl back to cover his hair and face.

'Indeed,' Red-thumb said, nodding in agreement. 'And that is why I seek your help. You see, the fifth member of our party lies in the capital city, and Luqura has become altogether unwelcome towards the people of my culture.'

'That's an understatement,' Sraon said, shifting his eyepatch. 'When was the last time you visited Luqura, Master Red-thumb?'

The merrymaker smiled. 'Ah, Master Sraon. This will be my first visit to your capital city.'

'Then, for your own good, I suggest you postpone your visit . . . indefinitely.'

'You are referring to the Ilumite slave trade, which has been imported from the north – from Innistiul.'

'Yes,' Sraon huffed. 'I haven't seen the capital in some time, but I've heard that King Cheng's influence has almost eclipsed King Lenka's, even there, and I fear what will happen when the old man passes, particularly with Innistiul's hooks so firmly embedded in the city's commerce. If you are intent on travelling to Luqura, you are likely to find yourselves captured, branded, and enslaved.' He paused, glancing at the cat-eyed Shalgarn ranger and the pink-eyed albino soothsayer. 'I expect the rest of your troupe will meet a similar fate – worse, perhaps. If you openly walk the streets, they'll scoop you up and sell you off quicker than you can blink.'

'Which is precisely why we need a chaperone in the city. Someone to vouchsafe for us while we track down the last member of our troupe.'

Sraon shook his head. 'I've already granted your boon, Master Red-thumb. I've told you where to find Mistress Dolyn, and I've given you fair warning that you aren't likely to persuade her. Best to give up this quest of yours before you endanger your life and that of your friends.'

Red-thumb raised his open hands and arms. 'That I cannot do.'

Sraon sniffed. 'Then I wish you good health and good luck in your travels.'

Chapter Eleven

'Master Ainnevog still owes a debt to *me*, yes?' The group turned to look at Jian, who had raised his hand in mild objection.

Sraon frowned, scratching at his eyepatch. 'Could be. What do you want?'

'To travel to Luqura … with you.'

Sraon spat. 'Come on, Jian. I just explained why I can't do that.' He turned to Red-thumb and Luathas. 'I even said I was a former slaver. Doesn't that bother any of you?'

'You do not understand,' Jian pressed. '*They* are not going. *I* am going.'

'Well … damn.' The blacksmith looked at Annev, his expression helpless. 'This will probably bring us more trouble,' he said, lowering his voice to a whisper.

'It's not my first choice,' Annev admitted, glancing sideways at their would-be Yomad companion. 'Would denying the life debt bring us *more* trouble, though?'

'Hard to say. Are you superstitious?'

'Not especially, though I might make an exception in Jian's case.'

Sraon sighed. 'Probably wise, given that he serves the God of Fate.' He leaned closer, his voice dropping to a whisper. 'It just seems a little *convenient*, you know?' Annev held up a finger then turned his attention back to Red-thumb and the rest.

'Excuse me. I'd like to discuss this proposal in private.'

'Of course.' The knife-wielding juggler bowed and the two groups separated a few dozen paces.

'What's convenient?' Annev asked once they were out of earshot.

'Everything,' Sraon said, his face hard, his eyes grim. 'I've seen set-ups like this before – even participated in a few. It's common enough in the Empire.'

'What is?'

'The game – the *long con*. It's like they had us marked the moment we joined their audience. Probably as soon as they saw the provisions in our cart.'

'You think they plan to *rob* us?'

'At the very least. Just think back. Red-thumb marked Therin during the show, probably to signal who to target. Then you gave him that coin and he turned his attention to you. He asked who our leader was, and a few minutes later ...' Sraon clapped his hands in front of Annev's face. *CRACK*.

Annev glanced sideways at Jian, Red-thumb and the rest. 'You think they arranged the attack.'

'I'm not even sure there was one. That Mad Cat fellow would've had to move impossibly fast to stop that bolt – maybe he was holding the bolt the whole time. Jian shouts to get our attention and then *BAM* – a quarrel sails over your head. Convenient, yes?'

Annev nodded. 'I never did see my attacker's face – and Mad Cat could have pointed me in the wrong direction at the end.' He scoffed, feeling a fool. 'They really have been playing us. I bet Luathas isn't even mute.'

'I'm sure she reads lips,' Sraon countered, his back turning to face the woman. 'Seems likely this group is exactly what they seem to be – a novelty act by performers and charlatans, the kind of rogues who prey on the charitable and the gullible.'

'And I nearly fell for it.'

'We're still not out of the woods with them. That life debt nonsense puts us in a bind.'

'Why not just say no?'

Sraon hesitated. 'Because it's possible they're telling the truth.'

'But you just said—'

'I know what I said, and I still think I'm right. But I could be wrong – been wrong plenty o' times before – and I'd hate to be wrong about this.'

'Why? Wouldn't it be safer just to assume?'

'Aye, it would be, but you'll recall I have a history of treating Ilumites poorly, and I'm not proud of it. If they're telling the truth – if they're not just a bunch of rogues parroting the stereotypes – then I want to help. It'd go a small way towards cancelling my debt against their people.'

'Then let's be smart about it. Jian can come with us – just Jian – and we keep a close eye on him. Maybe he slips up and tells us what Red-thumb is really after. Or maybe he's telling the truth and we help Jian locate their last contact.'

Sraon considered it then nodded. 'Agreed.'

'Do we tell the others your suspicions?'

'No, I don't think so. One of them might try to take matters into their own hands.'

'You mean Fyn.'

'Well, yes. I was trying to be tactful.'

'Tact is wasted on Fyn.' Annev glanced towards the merry-makers. 'Best to let them know our decision.'

'Aye, better make it quick, too. The others are returning.'

Annev glanced up just as Brayan and the rest reached the apple cart. Each boy deposited an armload of supplies, and then the quartermaster handed out dried meat and apples. Fyn stared suspiciously at Annev.

'Master Red-thumb,' Annev said, once he and Sraon rejoined the Ilumites' group. 'Who is your contact in Luqura?'

The leather-clad rogue smiled. 'Another treasure-hunter of sorts – a noblewoman.'

'Do you have her name?'

'Of sorts. My hooded friend here calls her "the Raven" or "the Sooted Rook". Makes me think ol' Lady Fate can't keep her corvids straight – that or Jian keeps mixing up the translation.'

'There is no mixing up, Tesked.' Jian spoke without raising his pink eyes from the ground. 'All names are masks. They are true and not true. Sometimes she is the Raven. Sometimes she is the Rook. She wears her names like different faces. Also, Fate is not a lady. He is Tacharan, the God of Doom.'

'And now you see why I had wanted to bring everyone,'

Red-thumb said to Annev. 'Finding the missing members of my troupe is its own treasure hunt, especially with this soothsayer leading us.'

Annev nodded, remembering the cryptic way Kelga had spoken to him in the Brakewood, and the way Janak had spoken of the Oracle's answers. 'Prophecies aren't always clear. I don't trust them myself.' He glanced at the albino. 'No offence intended, Master Nikloss.'

The soothsayer lifted his hooded face, a small smile touching his lips. 'I take no offence. Fate is my master ... but he is a cruel lord. Even to me, his face is masked.'

'Hold on now,' Sraon said, lifting a hand. 'Annev and I had agreed to let Master Nikloss join our caravan as payment for Annev's life debt – and we'll do our best to keep him safe while we're in Luqura – but I won't agree to any faerie chasing.' He looked at the merrymaker. 'Master Red-thumb, if you don't know the name of your contact, then we can't help you find her. You can understand that, yes? Luqura is the second largest city in the Empire, and riddles about birds and noblewomen won't get us any closer to—'

'I know who she is,' Annev said, saying the words as he realised, with a shock, that he did know.

'What's this now?' Sraon said, all eyes turning to Annev. 'How could you possibly know?'

Annev peered at Jian Nikloss who still wore his small, knowing smile. 'If I gave you her name, would you know if I was right?'

'Names are masks. If the mask fits, it is right.'

The soothsayer's cryptic answer did not surprise Annev. In the Brakewood, Crag had tried to make the wood-witch speak plainly using both threats and talismans, and that had only been half successful.

Fate, it seemed, would not be denied his riddles.

'You seek Sodja Rocas, the daughter of the House of Rocas in Luqura.' He looked to the soothsayer and Jian nodded in confirmation. 'Sodja is also a thief and a heartless killer.' He glanced between Jian, Luathas, Mad Cat, and Red-thumb. 'Why would you want her to join your troupe?'

There was an awkward silence.

'Wanting and needing are almost never the same,' Red-thumb said, once more speaking for the others. 'A good king does not want to burden his people with taxes, but he will do so out of need. Our own need is no less great and requires us to seek out this Sodja woman – the Sooted Rook – so she can help us solve our puzzle.'

'All for a piece of a treasure?' Annev said, his tone mocking.

Red-thumb didn't take offence. Instead his eyes gleamed with a fierce passion. 'The *best* kind of treasure, Master Ainnevog. The kind they sing about in stories and will remember for ages and ages to come.'

Annev sniffed. 'What treasure is that?'

Red-thumb smiled, his roguish demeanour suddenly overcome by a beatific zeal.

'We're going to end the Silence of the Gods.'

'I take it back,' Sraon boomed, his thick hands helping Brayan secure the supplies in the cart. 'He's not a charlatan or a con artist. He's a madman – a religious zealot.'

'That doesn't explain the performance with the crossbow bolt.'

'No,' Sraon admitted. 'I won't take it all back, then. They're still performers – talented ones, too – but they're also zealots, and that makes them more dangerous than thieves. They have an agenda – and I don't doubt they'd justify any act that furthers their goal.'

'Who's this now?' Therin asked, piping up from the other side of the cart.

'Never you mind, lad. Just get the last o' the foodstuffs into the wagon.' Sraon surveyed the tidy cart and nodded. 'This should last us a week. More than enough for the short trip to the capital.'

'Brayan says we might get there before nightfall tomorrow,' Titus added for Annev's benefit. 'It'd be faster if we all had horses, but two days is a modest pace with all of us walking. Do you know he's been there twice on retrieval missions?'

'Many years ago, Titus.' Brayan hand-fed the black mare from a bag of wild oats, his emptied hand stroking her neck after each mouthful. 'Regardless, I think we should camp outside the city's walls when we arrive tomorrow. The capital is a big place, and evening is a poor time to get acquainted with it.'

'I agree,' Sraon said. 'Matter o' fact, I was just talking with Annev about how it might be best for some of our group to stay here in Banok.'

'What?' Titus's face scrunched up with emotion. 'You want to separate us? Won't that make us *more* vulnerable?'

'Not for those staying behind – you'd be safe, probably even get lodging with my smithing friend, Dolyn.'

'You want *me* to stay behind?' Titus looked to Annev, his expression hurt. 'Annev, you want me to come with you, right? Me and Therin?'

Annev glanced at Therin whose attention was split between following their discussion and eating a giant sugar apple. 'Titus,' Annev said, 'I don't want to leave anyone behind—'

'Good,' Titus said, as if that settled it.

'—but I will,' Annev continued. 'It's not safe on the road or in the capital, and being around me is more than half the danger.' He lifted the gloved Hand of Keos, its size slightly out of proportion with the rest of his body. 'Sraon's friend Dolyn tried to help remove this. She tried – she tried very hard – but she failed, and she was hurt.'

'*She* hurt herself?' Fyn asked, finally breaking his silence.

Annev fixed the boy with a glare then stopped himself. 'She was hurt because of me. The prosthetic hurt her because I couldn't control it.'

'Is she *dead*?' Therin asked, spitting out a piece of apple.

'No! She just ... her hands are burned, and she's a smith so that's a big deal. In fact, that's another good reason for some of us to stay behind. Gwendolyn would probably appreciate the help while her hands heal.'

'Did you say Gwendolyn?' Brayan rose to his full height. 'Gwendolyn Goldsmith?'

Sraon nodded. 'You know her, then?'

The quartermaster shrugged, his cheeks reddening above his neckbeard. 'Barely more than an acquaintance ... but yes. Lost a few arm wrestling matches to her.' Sraon grunted, evidently unsurprised.

'I'm still coming with you, Annev,' Titus declared, his chubby face resolute. 'I won't abandon you. I promise.' His eyes travelled to the quartermaster. 'You'll come, too, won't you, Brayan?'

'I'm not sure,' Brayan said, eyeing first Sraon and then Titus. 'Annev and Sraon should be fine in the city – the blacksmith has been there more than I, it seems – but it sounds as if Gwendolyn could use our help.'

'*Annev* needs our help.' Titus looked at Therin. 'You're still coming to Luqura, right, Therin?'

The scrawny boy pitched his apple core away. 'I'm with you two – till Annev melts us all, anyway.' He laughed at his own joke, though no one else shared his mirth.

'Okay,' Sraon said, resigned. 'Brayan, will you stay and help Dolyn?'

'Certainly. Might be I can help with her forge work, and that's not something the boys are apt to do.'

'Good enough. There's one last issue to discuss, then. We'll be travelling with someone else – the soothsayer, Jian Nikloss, from the troupe of entertainers we saw earlier. Red-thumb has some business in Luqura. He can't travel there himself, so we're taking Jian in his stead.'

'Why are we doing this?' Fyn asked, his hands resting on his sword belt. 'Weren't you just saying it's dangerous to be around you?'

'Yes,' Annev said, answering slowly, 'but I don't have much choice in the matter.'

'Like hell you don't.'

'No, really,' Annev said, his tone becoming more heated. 'While you were with Brayan, someone tried to shoot me.'

'What?' Titus dropped the reins he'd been hitching to the wagon. 'Are you okay? What happened?'

'So *that's* what you two were talking about.' Fyn smirked as if he'd discovered some saucy secret. 'So who was it? Did you kill them?'

'Fyn,' Brayan rumbled. 'This isn't the Academy. There are

different rules out here, and you need to learn them.' He looked at Annev. 'So what did you do?'

'Truthfully, not much,' Annev said, 'The shot came from over there.' He pointed to the alley mouth just beyond the market square. 'We chased them but could only find their crossbow.' He still wasn't convinced the attack had been real, but he chose to follow Sraon's advice and keep his suspicions to himself.

'But why—'

'Did you see—'

'How did you—'

Annev threw up his hands, halting their questions. 'I'm fine – everything is *fine*. I knew someone would come after me. I just hoped it wouldn't be till we reached the capital.' He looked at his companions' puzzled faces, and swore. 'You all remember the monsters that destroyed Chaenbalu? They were *sent* to the village by someone – by humans or maybe demi-gods, I don't know – but they were meant to kill or capture *me*.' He waited another moment for that to sink in. 'The destruction of Chaenbalu hasn't stopped the people who are after me. Today they sent a stranger with a crossbow. Tomorrow it could be poisoned potatoes, or an old woman with a knife, or some new devilry we've never seen before.' He paused, letting them see his sincerity. 'When I find out who's hunting me, I'm going to end them. Till then, I've got assassins behind me, the godsdamned Hand of Keos hanging from my arm and a constant preoccupation with trying not to pick my nose or scratch my arse with it.'

As a group, Annev's companions stared at him in horror.

Good, Annev thought. *Give them something to think about.*

Therin opened his mouth to say something then, and Fyn was just a heartbeat behind him, but Titus interjected before either boy could speak.

'That's settled then. We're definitely not leaving you.'

Fyn groaned and Therin's mouth snapped shut. Annev hoped to argue the point further, but he was then interrupted by a tug at his elbow. He turned and saw the grey-robed man standing just outside the circle of their discussion.

It seemed he was stuck with the lot of them.

'This is Jian Nikloss,' Annev said, abandoning the argument. 'Are you ready, Jian?'

'Yes, Master Ainnevog.' He patted a black bag hanging from his waist and gestured to the larger drawstring knapsack slung over his shoulder. 'I do not have a horse, but I will not slow you down.'

'He's the Pale Man!' Therin said, eyes widening. 'The Ghost Man with the dead eyes!'

'Therin!' Sraon snapped. 'Don't be rude.'

'It is not rude, Master Cheng.' Jian's pink eyes slid to the blacksmith and then back to the wiry wide-eyed boy. 'Avatar Therin names me true. I am the Pale Man. The Ghost Man. I have other names and other masks, too – Dead Eyes, Seer, Necromancer, Marrow-Lich – none of these names offend me, even when they are spoken in fear, hatred or ignorance. They are simply my names.' He looked at the rest of the group. 'If I gave you names, would you fear or hate me? If I spoke the truths written on your faces, would you spit in mine?' He smiled, his teeth white as chalk. 'Some would, I think – but I will not say your names. Not unless you ask me to share them, or Master Ainnevog demands them.'

Titus and Therin exchanged looks with one another, neither one sure what to make of the soothsayer's words. Sraon tugged on his eyepatch and Fyn stayed silent, his hands firmly on his weapons belt.

'Well,' Brayan said at last, breaking the silence, 'I guess you're the fellow taking my place in the caravan.' The quartermaster extended his hand and Jian took it without hesitation, his blue-veined palm looking small in the giant's gentle grip.

'That is a new name,' Jian said, smiling broadly. 'Thank you for bringing it to me.'

'Er ... you're welcome.' Brayan glanced sideways at Sraon, one eyebrow raised, and finally released the soothsayer's hand and scratched his head. 'Right then. I'll grab my war maul and, uh, maybe some supplies. That all right, Sraon?'

The blacksmith nodded. 'Will you go straight to Dolyn's?'

'I think I might, yes. Feels strange walking the streets here – I'm used to skulking around at night, you know.' He shifted, his massive shoulders heaving in a bear-sized shrug. 'I'm sure I'll get used to it.' He turned to Titus. 'Take good care of the mare. You're still the Steward of Husbandry, after all.'

Titus's eyes were suddenly bright with tears. 'We'll be back in a week, Brayan. We'll be quick.'

'Sure,' Brayan said, sounding a little choked. 'Just a week. Don't worry if things stretch a bit, though. I'll be here waiting for you.' He forced a smile.

'You'll find Dolyn in the craftsmen's district, Brayan. If you hurry, you might also run into those merrymakers Jian parted with. Seems they have business with her, too.'

'Do they now?' Brayan swiped his hammer and a sack from the wagon. 'That juggler puts on a good show. Wouldn't mind seeing him perform some more – his sister, too. Fastest fingers I've ever seen on a flute.'

'Aye, better than Nikum, even!' Sraon winced as he spoke the dead carpenter's name.

In the silence that followed, Annev had the awkward sense that everyone was fighting not to stare at him. *Because I'm to blame for everyone who died in Chaenbalu,* he thought. *It doesn't matter that Nikum was murdered by the* feurog *or that I fought to protect him from the monsters. Somehow, they're all my fault. The babes in the Academy's nursery. The students and the witwomen. The farmers, masters and ancients. They're all my fault . . .*

Instead of meeting their non-gazes, Annev looked beyond Jian, past the market and towards the city's southern gates. The milling crowd filled his vision, and he tried to banish his memories of the destruction he had caused. He blinked.

That girl in the crowd . . . she looks familiar. Then it dawned on him. *She's back. The ghost is back.*

'Odar's balls!' Therin shouted, loud enough to spook the horse. 'It's Faith! Titus, are you seeing this?' The boy gestured at the girl Annev had seen: a young blonde woman with a freckled nose and a ragged shift, a bundle clutched tightly in her arms. The light seemed to pass right through her, as her body did not obstruct Annev's view of the market or of Banok's town walls.

Titus shrieked. 'She's a ghost, Therin! She followed us here from the woods.'

'She's still carrying that dead baby,' Fyn said, his right hand shifting to his sword hilt.

'Is she still singing?' Therin asked, his eyes locked on the shade now marching towards them.

'She's a ghost-*witch*!' Fyn snapped, his sword clearing his scabbard. 'I bet she's casting a hex now, to punish us for her death.'

'Sraon,' Annev said, drawing the name out as he fought to keep the panic away. 'Are you seeing this? She's ... glowing, right? And you can see right through her?' Faith's spectre stood just a score of paces away now, her eyes vacant, distant.

The blacksmith nodded, his mouth agape. 'Aye, lad. That's what I'm seeing.'

'How is this possible?'

Sraon shook his head, eyes fixed. 'Dunno.'

The girl's clothes were torn and ragged. Her lips moved as she walked – as she stumbled – and Annev heard the first echoes of a familiar tune.

She's definitely holding a dead baby, Annev thought, unable to look away as she approached. *And she's singing the same song as before. Sad and sweet ... about darkness and light.*

Somewhere on the opposite side of the square, a woman screamed and a clay jar shattered to the earth. In that same instant, the group's trance seemed to break and the ghost gliding towards them winked out.

Vanished.

'Keos,' Fyn spat. 'Is that ghost going to follow us all the way to the capital? I figured we'd left her in the Brake with all the other shadow magic.'

Brayan was staring open-mouthed at the place the young woman had been standing, his grip white against the black wrapping of his maul. He licked his lips. 'Right then. I'm off.' He shook as if trying to banish Faith's ghost from his mind. 'I'll, um ... see you soon, Sraon.'

The blacksmith's eyes were tight. 'Good luck, Master Brayan. Tell Gwennie I said hello.'

'Gwennie?'

'Yeah. She loves that.'

Brayan nodded absently, too distracted to catch the nature of Sraon's joke. 'I'll do that, Sraon. Safe travels.' He strode off, his sack of provisions forgotten on the ground where he'd dropped it. Therin danced over, picked it up, and slung it back onto the cart.

'All right, boys! We'll need a brisk pace to get there. Master Nikloss, try to keep up, but do tell me if you need to ride. These boys are all in their prime, so there's no shame if you can't match them.'

'Thank you,' Jian said in his strange accent, his round eyes unblinking. 'Are you also in your prime?'

'Me? Oh I do all my exercise with these.' Sraon flexed his massive forearms and biceps. 'I may not get winded easy, but my legs are my slowest part.'

Jian's pale lips pursed into a button of a smile. 'No part of me is fast, but Fate propels my feet. I shall not slow your pace.'

Sraon fell in front of the cart and took the horse's reins. He clicked his tongue as he did so and the mare immediately fell into step with him, pulling the wagon and its contents. Fyn strolled beside the cart, and Titus and Therin quickly fell in behind the wagon. Annev followed and Jian Nikloss soon trotted along beside him, his feet stepping quiet on the earth and cobblestones.

'A strange vision,' Jian said once they had passed the gates and the trading post. 'Who was the young woman?'

'You saw her, too? The blonde girl with the torn dress?'

'And the child,' Jian said, nodding. 'The poor babe sleeps deep. If it is not fed, I fear it will die soon.'

Annev's steps faltered. 'The baby? You think it's *alive*?'

'Without question.' Jian shifted his knapsack. 'I have a talent of speaking with spirits, you will remember, and the child will become one soon. The girl, too, if she does not let herself sleep.'

'Can we help her? There must be some way to reach her.'

Jian shook his head. 'Her path lies in another direction.'

'But you say she's on the brink of death?'

'She has moved beyond Death, Master Ainnevog. She has transcended, and your paths will not cross again in this life.'

Annev exchanged a look with Therin, resigned. Faith was a ghost – they had all seen it – and Jian's words did not help.

'It would be lovely if she were still alive,' Therin said, his expression full of mourning.

'I know,' Annev said, placing a hand on the boy's shoulder. 'If I could, I'd bring them all back – all the innocents that died when the *feurog* attacked and the Academy fell; all the infants from the nursery, and the acolyte children.'

Annev glanced back at the city gates, half-believing their conversation would conjure the young woman's ghost for a third time, forcing her spirit back into the ether. He peered through the thin cloud of dust rising behind them, but still saw no one. As he returned his gaze to the road, though, he couldn't shake the feeling that the witgirl's dead eyes were lingering on his back, trailing them as their party followed the westbound road.

Chapter Twelve

The sun had just passed its zenith when the group lost sight of Banok's trading post, the rays warming their faces as they moved west along the East Road. Along the way, Annev took in the wide farmland and distant villages dotting the landscape, constantly searching for his first glimpse of Luqura's city walls. He had seen the city from afar only once before, its parapets lit by lantern light and only barely visible from the top of the Brakewood's tallest hill, and he was eager to repeat the experience.

How long ago had that been? The last day of Regaleus had been Seventhday – the same night that he, Fyn, and Kenton had embarked on their mission to Banok – and though that seemed a lifetime ago, it had been less than two days.

He had buried Sodar yesterday. Just a day ago the man had still been alive. Sodar had died on the Firstday of Fourthmonth, and this week would have been the old man's half-birthday.

Annev let out a deep breath, allowing some of the pain of that loss to sink in. He had never stopped feeling it – not for a single minute since the priest had passed away – but he'd been ignoring it like a rotten tooth, too afraid to probe and see how deep the damage was. Maybe in a month or a year that pain would fade, but a day was nothing. Less than a blink in time, and every moment filled with grief that he could not share or express. It choked him. He was surrounded by friends and companions, but he was also alone. Without Sodar, he would always feel alone.

Annev slowed until he walked behind the dust cloud kicked up by the apple cart, then matched the cart's brisk pace. Jian walked somewhere just ahead and to the side of him, as if uncertain whether to walk with Annev or join Titus and Therin. As a result, he hung between the two, his pace faltering then picking up once more.

Annev ignored him. He ignored the world rolling by. The sounds of the road became muted and the conversations of his friends distant, as he remembered walking the Brakewood's paths with Sodar, collecting herbs, gathering firewood and springing animal traps. He tried to think of the old man not as he wanted to remember him, but as he truly was. Surly. Always ready with his dry wit and his deep wisdom. Always trying to teach him something – especially when he didn't want to be taught. Annev knew he'd find most of Sodar's papers in the bottomless sack – not just his Speur Dún translation, but also the endless notes Sodar kept on every topic that interested him. Annev suspected not one of the priest's lessons had disappeared when he died. In time, Annev would find those notes and learn everything Sodar still had to teach – he'd read every note, study every scribbled piece of chickenscratch – but not today. Today, Sodar's lesson was one of mourning, and Annev feared it would be the hardest lesson the priest had taught him.

'Sodar,' Annev breathed, saying the name just loud enough that only he could hear it. 'I'm so angry at you. How can you be dead? You should be here, telling me how stupid I am without ever quite coming out and saying it. You should be here chiding me and pushing me ... telling me how proud of me you are.' Annev pulled his dragonscale cloak tight, the air around him feeling suddenly chill, and wiped a tear away. When he dropped his hand, he saw Jian was strolling next to him once more. The Yomad was unsettling quiet.

'It is difficult saying goodbye.'

Annev didn't care to explain. If the soothsayer truly spoke with spirits, he knew enough already.

'You will see him again.'

'Excuse me?'

'Your friend, with the strong heart and the wrinkled hands. You will see him again.'

Annev pressed his lips into a thin line, uncomfortable at Jian intruding on his grief.

'I don't think so, Master Nikloss. Sodar is with the All-father now. I'll only see him again in dream, or in death.'

Jian swept back his hood, nodding thoughtfully. 'I heard spirits sometimes visit the dreams of the Kroserans. I did not know this was also true for your people. Have you seen him then? In dreams?'

Annev shook his head.

Jian nodded as if that were answer enough. 'In my country, the dead do not visit us in dreams. We call them to us in this physical life.' He gestured at the dirt road, the trees, the brown fields. 'Our dead are all around us. We surround ourselves with death and gain strength from it.'

'But you do not truly see your dead. They are still in the after-life.'

Jian shook his head. 'Tacharan is not like the other Gods. He is not jealous of his treasures. He sends them to his children. We speak with our dead, we eat with them. They are never far from us.'

'That's ... nice.' Annev fought to keep his tone neutral. 'Your families must be quite large then. Lots of ghosts standing around, telling stories?'

'In my household, yes, but this is rare. Most Yomads no longer share the blood-talent, and those that still carry it prefer to culti-vate its primal half.'

'Primal half?'

'Necromancy. Instead of valuing what the dead can teach us, they manipulate what the dead leave behind. They are deaf to our ancestors – they cannot hear or see their spirits – so they force their bodies into servitude. The dead that should be revered and worshipped have instead become servants, labourers, and slaves.' Jian bowed his head and tsked. 'The balance is not right. The spirits complain against the living, and the living fear the dead.' He inhaled deeply. 'That is why I travel away from my homeland. The spirits tell me to travel far to the south, to the old shrines of Thoir Cuma and beyond. There, in Shalgar, I met Corentin – who'd had a vision of a Lightdragon urging him to find two

Ilumani in Western Daroea. The spirits agreed with the words of the dragon, and so we found Tesked and Luathas.'

'Oh. That's ... great.' Annev smiled weakly, having little to say to that. 'You're helping Red-thumb end the Silence of the Gods then?'

Jian nodded. 'It has already begun. Yesterday a fire woke in the sky. Keos spoke to us. Wrath and sorrow filled his heart, and he smote those who awakened him – all as prophecy foretold.'

'You think that yesterday's noon-fire came from Keos?'

'*Noonfire*. Yes, that is a good name for it. The noonfire spoke for Keos.'

Annev shifted his gloved hand behind his back, feeling anxious. 'That's ... quite a story – and you say the spirits have confirmed it?'

Jian's soft lips puckered into a tiny smile. 'That is not the way of the spirits. They are lost sometimes, too, you see. They make mistakes, but they can also see things we do not.' He looked at Annev, his pink eyes bright with clarity. 'Just like Kelga could see things! Do you recall? She had a touch of the necromancy, too, but she was more of a Seer.'

'Kelga?'

'The Wood-Witch, the Crone of the Brake. She should have seen this herself, but she was as blind to her passions as the necromancers in my homeland.' Annev was almost cringing at his words. 'When you hold yourself open to the spirits, their messages are open to you. But when you hoard your knowledge, Fate gives you more riddles to solve.'

'Did you know Kelga?'

'No, not in life.'

'In death?'

Jian wobbled his head. 'I am not dead, so I do not know her in death, either.'

'Right, but—'

'I know Kelga because her spirit cries out to me. She pleads for your death and whispers dark words in my ear.' Jian smiled. 'She is full of much humour, you know? I try not to laugh out of respect for the dead, but she is a real bitch.'

126

Annev suddenly snorted, taken off-guard by the soothsayer's abrupt change in language. Titus and Therin glanced back at him and he had to wave them off.

Jian's smile broadened. 'I have said something amusing?'

'Yes,' Annev said, drying his eyes. 'The others wouldn't understand it ... but yes. Kelga was a real bitch.'

'A Wood-Bitch.'

This time Annev laughed out loud, his chortles catching the attention of even Fyn and Sraon. He put his head in his hands and shook himself, forcing the laughter down. 'You're a funny man, Jian. Has anyone ever told you that?'

'I have been told I am funny-looking, yes.'

'No, no. I mean ... wait,' he said, suspicious. 'Are you teasing me?'

Jian steepled his fingers in front of his chest and gave a deep bow, his bleached-white, bowl-cut hair blowing lazily in the wind. 'You are wise, Master Ainnevog.'

Annev smiled in spite of himself. 'I doubt that very much.' He cleared his throat. 'So, Jian. You said you are a Seer, but you also know some necromancy.'

'Yes. Among my people, this makes me a Marrow-Lich. It is a rare thing, and it was of great interest to Master Red-thumb.'

Annev was still keen to pursue his line of thought. 'Does that mean ... I mean, your necromancy – it makes dead things move, right? That's the idea?'

'Yes and no.'

'Okay,' Annev said, trying a different tactic. 'Could it ... could you use your necromancy to take off someone's prosthetic? Like if they were wearing a fake arm or a leg. Could you use your magic to make the limb obey you instead?'

Jian seemed to think about this. 'A strange question.' He scratched a tuft of blond stubble on his chin. 'Necromancy is related to the magic of the Stoneshapers – the Old Terrans that made golems from clay and stone, iron and earth. The Yomads have lost this talent – but for one skill, that is.'

'What is that?'

'The Flesh Golem. Necromancers use the memories stored in

the body to remind it how it once moved. When they tell the body to remember its patterns, it reanimates. Bones knit to bones. Flesh holds to flesh. The dead walk – or to speak truly, the *t'rasang* walks.'

'But what if the necromancer needed to make someone's *prosthetic* move? Could he do that using the blood inside the person's body?'

'Now you speak of a Bloodlord's powers. Only they can manipulate the blood inside a man's body, and only if there is an open channel to it.'

Annev sighed. 'Never mind.'

'I believe what you mean to ask,' Jian continued, 'is whether I can use my necromancy to remove the Hand of Keos from your body. Is that right?'

Annev walked in stunned silence, then—

'Yes.'

'Hmm. May I see it?'

Annev looked around to be sure there was no one else in sight, then reluctantly extended his left fist. He opened his palm and slid the smithing glove from his hand.

And there it was – the Hand of Keos.

A band of white-gold surrounded the wrist and sparkled in the daylight, reflecting the sun's brilliance. The reinforced golden knuckles spoke of power, strength, authority. It was a gauntlet, as much as a hand. Annev ignored the smoking anvil on the back of his palm, his attention drawn this time to the tiny inscription surrounding it, so delicate he hadn't given it much thought until today: *Aut inveniam viam aut faciam*. On the other side, in much larger block lettering, it read: 'MEMENTO SEMPER. NUMQUAM OBLIVSCI.'

Jian stared open-mouthed, his pink eyes flitting between the beautiful scrollwork and artistic etchings. He swallowed. 'This artifact ... it carries the blood of a God.'

'The blood of Keos.'

Jian shivered. 'It is ... not dead. The blood is still alive inside. You feel it, no? The heartbeat of the Gods. *Tum-tum, tum-tum*. It is strong. I feel it there.' His hands reached out, just an inch from touching the golden prosthetic, but then he reeled back, his head shaking. 'No, Master Ainnevog. Death magic will not remove this hand from your body.' He slowly exhaled. 'Death himself will not remove it. This magic is beyond both me and my Lord. It may be that only Keos himself can remove it, or perhaps an Artificer of supreme skill and power.'

'An Artificer ...' Annev said, crestfallen, '... like Urran.'

'Precisely. A man of such skill might be able to help you, but my talents would be useless. I am sorry, Phoenix Child.'

Annev slipped the glove back on, still disappointed. 'Do you realise you keep changing people's names?'

'Pardon?'

'You keep giving people new names. You just called me Phoenix Child – and earlier you called Sraon "Master Cheng". Do you know that you do that?'

'I do not do it on purpose. Please forgive me if my naming has offended you.'

'No,' Annev said, lowering his hand to his side. 'It's as you said before. A name is just another mask we wear.' He glanced sidelong at the soothsayer. 'Do you know any of my other names?'

Jian studied him. 'Are you asking for the Ritual of Naming, Master Ainnevog? It is not something you should do lightly. Naming another can have dramatic consequences. You must be certain it is something you want.'

Annev frowned, uncertain he understood the question. 'I have been named before – by Kelga. I just wondered whether the Fates would tell you something different.'

'Fate usually speaks with one voice.'

'No prophecies then,' Annev said, suppressing his disappointment as he wrapped himself in his cloak once more.

Jian smiled. 'I thought you did not like prophecy.'

'It's not the prophecies themselves I hate. It's the not knowing – the lack of understanding – and the feeling that someone else is tugging your strings. It makes me angry. Makes me want to do something drastic just to prove them wrong.'

'Ha. I am familiar with those emotions. Among us Seers, we would say you are gambling the present against the future.'

'I ... don't follow.'

'It means that by doing so, you are sacrificing your choices in the present to change the future. Even if you win, you have still lost in the present. And if you lose, then your gamble has cost you both.' He tsked. 'You cannot fight prophecy. You can reinterpret it, reimagine it, reshape it maybe – but you cannot fight it. The future will not be denied its present, and the present is built upon what is already past.'

'That's what I don't like! It sounds like you can't change your destiny – that your path is set for you.'

'You do not think this is true?'

Annev shook his head. 'I find my own path.'

'Like your hand.'

'Hmm?'

'It translates as "Find a way, or make one". You choose your own path. You find it or make it, but it is yours alone. No one chooses for you. Yes?'

'Ah ... yes. I guess that's true.'

'Do you know the story of Chade Thornbriar, the Kroseran Voidweaver?' Annev was unsure. 'A long tale. Tragic. Perhaps I will tell it another time. The lesson is that when we run from Fate, we are only running from our future selves. After wearing many masks and taking many names, we become the thing we are running from.'

'And if fate gives you a terrible name – an *evil* name?'

'Then I would accept it and seek to understand its nature.'

'And what if fate named you the Son of Seven Fathers?'

'Son of Seven ...' Jian slowed and then came to a halt. Annev stopped with him and saw the man's knees wobbling beneath his robes. 'Who spoke this name to you, Master Ainnevog? Another Seer?'

'It is what Kelga named me.'

The albino licked his lips. 'Damn.' He started walking again, a little unsteadily. 'You have been named once, then. I shall not tempt Fate by naming you again.'

'Fair enough.'

They walked in silence for a long time after that. Eventually,

Annev grew bored of the silence and felt drawn to his friends' laughter. He jogged to catch up to the apple cart, and this time Jian did not try to match his pace.

The sun was just setting on their first night on the East Road when the group crested the hill hiding Luqura's distant stone walls from view. They paused as a group and took in the sight.

Luqura was big – much bigger than Annev had initially guessed.

Until his failed mission in Banok, the small village of Chaenbalu had been the only town Annev had known. Seeing Banok's size and scope had opened Annev's eyes to the wider world, and he had guessed that Greater Luqura's capital would be at least five or six times larger yet.

In reality, it was far beyond anything he had imagined. Towering rock walls stretched around the capital, its foundations laid at the foothills of the northernmost tip of the Vosgar. A full dozen of Banok's townships could have fit within those walls, which were themselves bisected by two gleaming threads of silver that fell from the Vosgar's snow-capped mountains and then wound their way through the city's southern gates. One river flowed west and to the south while a second emerged at the north side of the city and flowed northwest where, Annev knew, it would eventually reach the distant Kingdom of Odarnea and its own religious capital, Quiri.

'Jings! It's huge.'

'Aye, Therin. Jings is right. She's a beauty, with the sun setting behind her like that. No dawdling, though. Darkness falls fast, and we'll want to set up camp off the road somewhere safe while there's still light. Don't forget, we've another full day of walking before we reach those walls tomorrow.'

'We should press on towards the city,' Fyn said, his eyes hungry for what lay beyond. 'If we camp a bit closer, we could get there before dark tomorrow.'

'We've been over this, Fyn,' Sraon said, tugging his halberd out of the cart. 'Evening is not the time to be rushing headlong into Luqura. Thieves and bandits will be thick on the roads then, searching for folk in a hurry – folk not watching their sides or their backs. Some might be waiting for the gate guards to turn us away – which happens often at night – and then we'd be desperate for shelter. They'd wave us over to their fire, and if we were stupid enough to join them, the patrols wouldn't even find our bodies in the morning.'

'Is that true?' Titus asked, suddenly frightened. 'Are people that terrible out here?'

'Not usually, no. Some folks really do want to help – but I've travelled with men who were that terrible, so I'm wary of things like that.' He peered at Fyn. 'You want to run ahead and strike camp on your own, lad, you're welcome. Maybe you'll even make the gates afore they close tomorrow. But you'd still be camping on the street, and you'd still have to watch for bandits tryin' to cut your throat and steal your coins. Myself, I think you'd be better served staying with us – and I'm sure we'd be better served, too.'

Fyn tugged his dreadlocks. 'Fine. We'll do it your way. Day after tomorrow I'll be free of you lot anyway. I'll either find someone to pay me for my avatar skills ... or I'll use them myself and turn the city into my personal playground.' He smiled at that thought, dark eyes gleaming. 'Luqura doesn't know what it's in for.' He elbowed Therin. 'What do you think? How much gold could you steal in a night? If you could break into any shop or mansion in the city, what would you carry away?'

Therin's eyes widened as he considered Fyn's not-so-rhetorical question. 'Not so much that they'd miss it ... but enough that I could play cards and dice for a weekend.'

'None o' that,' Sraon said, his eyes searching the road. 'I promised I'd find you some honest work – and I just told you lot we need to hurry. Come on. We can set up camp down by that gully. Should be easy to keep watch o' the road without havin' others watch us. No fires. Just blades and bedrolls.' He tugged the mare's reins. 'Hurry now, lads.'

Chapter Thirteen

Myjun stalked the Brakewood like a predator searching for prey. Everything had felt more visceral – more *real* – since she donned the Mask of Gevul's Mistress. She could smell the richness of the damp earth, the pungent odours of animal urine and dying flora. She could feel the soft caress of the air around her and knew instinctively she was downwind of her target. She heard a swift trickle of water coming from the south, and she knew she was close to the stream that fed Chaenbalu's mill pond. She saw the crisp details of the trees, the shadows, and the wary things that lurked behind both.

Most of all, though, Myjun felt pain. Her elbow had mended and her flesh had healed, but her body still ached from the injuries she'd sustained. Stranger still was the realisation that she *liked* it. That she *needed* it. She ached with the fear she might one day lose that pain, for if it left her, she might have to endure those other emotions ... and face the knowledge that her father was dead. Worse, she would have to face up to the fact that though he had taught her magic was evil – that they should destroy anything carrying its taint – *he* had shown himself tainted with its foulness ... and she had become tainted in the process.

So she didn't grieve for him. She only hated him.

Annev had betrayed her, too. He had hidden his darkness from her – his deformity *and* his magic – and he had tried to ensnare her in it. He had led her on. He had wanted to *marry* her, for Odar's sake! Why had he done that? She could have chosen anyone, and Annev had ruined her with his charm and determination.

Why had he deceived her? Why her, of all people? She felt like such a fool. He had lied to everyone in their godsforsaken village. Everyone except that Keos-loving priest. How *dare* he hurt her like that? Think he could court her, that he could *bed* her, that he could *infect* her with his magic?

But I was already infected, Myjun thought, tightening her grip on the stone knife. *My father's foulness is a part of me. His tainted blood – his* magic *– is in my veins . . .*

The thought of it made her sick. When she felt that same tainted blood coating her sticky palm and fingers, she wanted to retch. The only thing that distracted her was the pain of the knife biting into her flesh. *And I've made it worse,* she thought, *by putting on this mask and apprenticing myself to a demon. Does that make me worse* than him?

No, she could not – would not – accept that.

She was sprinting through the trees now, running hard on an animal's trail. She had its scent, strong and musky, and she knew she was closing in for the kill. As she ran, she cut away the remains of her tattered red dress, exposing the reaping clothes beneath, freeing her further.

I'll kill him . . . just like he killed my father.

A large bristled boar darted from the brush ahead. Myjun angled towards it, thinking nothing for her safety or the immense size of the beast. She had no idea how she would kill it – her stone knife was small compared to its thick hide – but she trusted that she *would* kill it. Nothing could stand before her fury. She would fight on, even if it tore her guts out and spread them across the forest. Fight on until she had slaughtered it.

The boar trampled through the brush with wild abandon, aware it was being hunted. Its enormous tusks ripped through the shrubs and overgrown grass like a scythe through the wheat field. The beast veered left, crashing into the sluggish water of a trickling stream then scrabbling up the embankment on the opposite side. Myjun reached the ravine and jumped, easily clearing the muddy stream and closing the gap between them.

I will kill you, she swore, breathing hard beneath the flawless golden mask. *I will cut your throat and drink your blood. How* dare *you run from me!*

The boar galloped faster yet, regaining its lead and heading directly for a dense grove of ochroma trees. Myjun followed, knowing she could corner the animal amidst the tangled brush and thickly settled trees. Yet as she approached, she caught the faint smell of death wafting from the grasses ahead. She saw bones piled there and careened to a halt, stopping just outside the ring of trees.

What am I doing? She screamed at herself. *Ochroma trees ... I'm going to get myself killed!*

Inside the grove, the boar spun in a circle so that its curved tusks faced Myjun. It shrieked and squealed, pawing at the dirt as it dared her to come closer, unaware of its own danger.

But Myjun held her ground. She had seen the bones now – the bodies of other creatures that had wandered into this shaded copse – and she remembered the warnings her father had once given. Fortunately, the chase had not overcome her caution.

Barely.

Ahead of Myjun, the boar moved backwards, keeping its eyes locked on her, not seeing the looping vines untangle themselves from the branches overhead. Not seeing as the codavora twisted its long body, dangling lower until it hung just above its squealing prey.

Myjun hissed at the reptile, stomping as she did so, and the boar stepped backward, falling directly into the other predator's trap. The ring-snake's body suddenly dropped from the overhanging branches then coiled tightly around the boar's chest and neck. The swine squealed one more time – high and frightened – before the snake's brown body strangled the breath from its lungs.

Myjun raised her eyes to the trees, searching for more of the codavora. She couldn't see any, but she did not doubt they were there, camouflaged among the misshapen branches, waiting for her to enter their circle of death.

Codavora. Ouroboros. Ring-snakes. The Brakewood's silent assassins. Her father had warned her of their nests south of Chaenbalu, and described them in detail, but this was the first time she had seen one of the serpents in the flesh.

Myjun turned from the ochroma grove and the snake's feast, still clutching the sharp stone knife in her raw and bloodied fingers. She had missed her kill – her chance to prove herself to Oyru – and with the snake distracted by its meal, killing the codavora would be an insufficient challenge. The failure made her angry, full of hate and spite and a dark craving to rip out the throat of the next creature to cross her path.

But it also made her pause. Myjun was the hunter, not the prey, yet she had almost run headlong into another predator's trap. That had been foolish. She would have to be more cunning from now on, more cautious. To take down something big enough to impress Oyru she needed to plan instead of chasing the first monster she encountered. What *had* she been thinking? Chasing a wild boar with a stone knife. It was incredible – complete and utter idiocy.

Yet a part of her refused to see it as foolishness. Some dark voice inside her – her own voice – disagreed: *You are the* huntress! *You do not* wait *for your prey to come to you – you chase it down. You do not* hide *– you stalk and hunt and* kill. *You are the golden blade. The mask of fury.*

The mask.

It was the mask, Myjun realised. It was feeding on her emotions, pushing her to act rashly when she wanted to keep a clear head. And when she tried to think, it overwhelmed her with emotions: the pain of her father's hypocrisy and death, Annev's deceit and betrayal, her own self-loathing. It filled her with anger, spite, and malice. It blinded her to the world around her, made her act irrationally.

But then … it had strengthened her, too. Hadn't she felt its power while chasing the boar? The way her stride lengthened as she jumped the brook and ran through the trees? It kept urging her to focus on her pain, physical or emotional – and when she did, she felt stronger for it. She was sharper, more alert to the world around her and more prepared to confront it.

But it had still almost killed her.

Myjun took a long hissing breath then turned south, her feet carrying her in the direction of the Brakeroad. On the other side lay the Vosgar, a dark forest that was much older and deadlier than the Brake. She had never crossed its border, firmly delineated by the old trade road connecting the capital city of Luqura to the eastern kingdom of Lochland. Rumour said monsters lived in the woods. Keos spawn. None ventured in, not even the masters or the ancients, and very little ventured out.

Behind her mask, Myjun bit her lip and tasted blood. She could go there now, freely – no one alive had any reason to stop her – but she hesitated.

Did she really want to enter the dark forest? Or was the mask pushing her to do so? It was difficult to be sure which thoughts were hers and which came from the cursed artifact, but she supposed it mattered little in this case: Oyru had told her to kill something impressive while he was gone – as if impressing him mattered to either of them.

Still, Myjun felt a keen desire to test her own limits, to break the boundaries that had so long confined her. She wasn't the Academy's witgirl any longer. She wasn't the blushing head-master's daughter or the doe-eyed teenager that had fluttered her eyelashes at the acolytes and avatars. She was the woman in the golden mask. The daughter of a dead man. Cursed apprentice to an assassin who was more demon than human. She had pledged her soul in exchange for the opportunity to kill Annev, and in so doing she had sworn herself to Keos.

She was a monster, exactly like those she despised.

The Vosgar beckoned. A place for magic, monsters, and demons. She was one of them now, wasn't she? Didn't she belong there? Didn't she *deserve* to be there?

She was running through the woods again, breaking through the treeline and crossing the rut-covered road, dashing headlong towards the Vosgar's dark eaves and towering pines. As she ran, her vision turned red and hazy. She reached the end of the road and felt her breath burn in her chest, as though her lungs were bursting, as though she were drowning in a river of blood.

She sped into the trees, snatching spiderwebs from her face and hair, her lungs screaming for air. She took that pain, and she ran and ran and ran. Time and distance blurred into dark evergreens, black soil, and sloping hills. In the distance, Myjun heard wild animals baying and ran towards them, her blood pushing her onward. Daring herself, or the mask, or both to break.

I am a monster, she repeated, forcing herself to run harder, faster. *I am gilded death. The shadow's knife. Demon apprentice. Servant of Keos.*

The cry of wild animals grew louder, and Myjun instinctively knew they were hunting her. She had entered their domain after all, making either a threat or an offering. They had to bring her down, and within a minute they had surrounded her, running with her as if they'd been hunting her since she had entered the Vosgar.

The predators and their prey.

Myjun caught the scent of the wolves a moment later – dark, feral, musky – the smell of sweat and earth and something not quite human. There was also a tang of blood in the air. A taste of their recent kill. There was a flash in the darkness behind her and she glimpsed bright eyes and white teeth in the shadow.

Myjun ran faster and the wolves fell back slightly. They had her scent now. They would hunt her down.

But Myjun was not prey. She held her knife ready, her hand both sticky and slick with blood, and the double-bladed stone dagger firmly embedded in her flesh. She howled, eager for the hunt. They should be running from her, but they didn't understand the nature of the thing they hunted. She roared in ecstasy and agony then shouted her challenge again. This time the beasts snarled their own reply.

The predator and her prey.

They weren't far behind now. They had a plan and were closing in on her and she on them. Her heart beat faster, ready for the coming confrontation, eager to test her ferocity against theirs.

As she kept running, her lungs reached a new level of pain ... yet her breathing was somehow getting *easier*. Somehow, despite all her experience to the contrary, her pain was literally strengthening her; in spite of her exhaustion, in spite of not having eaten or drunk anything in two days, she felt *stronger*.

Yes! She exulted. The pain washed over her, filling her with power.

The harder she ran, the more she hurt. Yet the more she hurt, the more alive she felt.

A large wolf flew past Myjun's elbow, nipping at her flesh. She had sensed it coming, though, and brought her arm up, narrowly evading the attack. The beast's impossibly large head raced beside her and she flipped herself into the air without breaking stride, hooking one arm around its neck as she rolled over its tall back, slicing her knife across its throat as she did. The wolf gurgled and growled, surprised by her speed and alarmed by its injury. It ploughed onward for another dozen paces, too stupid to know it was dead, then crashed to the earth.

Myjun was running again, still clutching her knife, still wary of the rest of the pack. The beasts were all around her now, those which had overtaken her turning to meet her head-on. With a sudden leap, Myjun danced up the trunk of a nearby tree. Two large wolves flew past her, slowed, and attempted to turn. Another wolf came from the side, jaws snapping as she reached a tree branch.

But Myjun didn't slow or stop. She was still intent on her next kill. As the first two wolves slowed down, she jumped, using the branch as a springboard, and slammed into the nearest creature. The size of all three wolves surprised her, and she adjusted her plans as she saw these were no simple wolves, no ordinary wolf pack – these were dire wolves. Huge, monstrous beasts that stood shoulder to haunch with horses. They had sprung from night-mares, fabulous tales meant to frighten children away from the Vosgar.

But this was no fable, and Myjun was no child. Her stone knife sliced into the wolf's face with all the force of her fall behind it, so deep through one eye that she almost lost her weapon in the beast's skull, but terror and adrenaline kept the stone knife firm in her hand. The rest of her body crashed down on the dire wolf's back and she wrapped her legs around it, literally riding it through the brush. It bucked and fought her, wheeling and screaming with pain. Other jaws snapped at her as Myjun rode the half-blind beast through the dark woods. The other wolves ran beside her, nipping at the black flanks of the wolf she rode as the dire wolf shook itself, trying to dismount her. Myjun gripped the wolf's fur tighter still, prying her knife free of its eye socket and then slamming the blade into the wolf's other eye. This blow was lethal. The creature collapsed beneath her, toppling onto its side, and she skidded across the forest floor with barely enough warning to roll away, her fingers slick with her own blood and that of the wolf. Myjun pushed all thought of it away as its companions slammed to a halt beside her and began to circle.

The first was a silvery-white monster, its fangs as long as her hand and sharp as any dagger. A smaller grey wolf heeled beside it and howled, mourning the loss of its pack mates.

Myjun had only one eye for them, though, for she heard the third and final wolf racing to join the pack, running with all the rage that Myjun felt boiling in her own chest. This was the pack leader – she could sense it, could *smell* it – and the yellow-eyed monster wanted blood.

Myjun's blood.

Myjun turned fast enough to see the brown-black body leap over a fallen pine, its bone-white teeth glistening with drool and crimson saliva. It dived for her throat and she instinctively brought the long knife forward, driving it hard into the wolf's lower jaw until it pierced the beast's throat and up towards the dire wolf's brain. Its paws scrabbled, the great jaws clamped shut, and too late Myjun realised she'd raised her other arm to block the attack, shoving it deep into the dire wolf's maw.

Distantly, through the sound of her own scream, Myjun realised her arm was injured, that it was attached to her elbow by mere threads and filaments, broken bones and bloody gobs of flesh. That didn't matter yet. What mattered now was the kill. The hunt. So instead of worrying, she forced her arm deeper into the wolf's throat, found the place where her knife had pierced the flesh, and pulled it upward, sawing at the muscle and bone.

The beast's jaws broke, the lower half unhinged from its skull.

Myjun carved upward with her knife and cut the tendons still holding the jaw to its skin. The wolf keened, blood gurgling in its throat, and Myjun sawed in the opposite direction, tearing the wolf's lower jaw from its head entirely, gouting blood. The wolf trembled before falling against Myjun, convulsing in its final death throes.

Her half-severed arm free of those jaws, Myjun swung to face the remaining two dire wolves. Neither had moved, though the smaller grey wolf had ceased its howling. Something terrible gleamed in the eyes of the silver wolf, and Myjun wondered fleetingly if this was a female, perhaps the mate of the black male she had killed earlier, and their cub.

The silver bitch howled, though not in challenge. Her shoulders weren't tensed for attack, but for flight. Myjun had won, the two wolves were going to run.

But something hungry had awoken inside Myjun – something painful and lusty, full of hate and malice. She needed death – needed to *kill* – and these two animals had challenged her, had threatened her, had hunted her.

They deserved to die.

Myjun took a step towards the silvery she-wolf and the grey cub, her green eyes full of enough hate and murder to rival any creature the Vosgar saw fit to send against her.

The dire wolves ran. First the cub and then the she-wolf.

Myjun took a step forward then stopped, feeling dizzy with the loss of blood. The intensity of her pain was making her lightheaded.

No, that wasn't right. It was the *absence* of pain. When Myjun had been in the thrall of her bloodlust, the pain had made her feel invincible. She had shrugged off her devastating injuries and swelled with the strength of a dozen warriors. But now the challenge was gone. Her foes were vanquished, and her pain was creeping to a dull whine instead of a furious roar. And with the lessening of the pain came a moment of clarity: her arm was destroyed, savaged and broken; it was likely she would lose the limb.

Myjun glanced down and saw the horror that waited there: shards of white bone and gleaming red flesh. The hand was recognisable, untouched even, but the limb was raw and ravaged. She stared at it, the horror slowly sinking in.

I'll be like him ... *like Annev.*

It was justice, of a kind – a cruel and twisted justice. She had pledged her soul to Keos, had sworn to serve his servants, and in less than a day he had marked her as his. Just as the assassin had promised.

But if Keos was her Dark Lord now, where was his help? What aid did he offer that was worth her soul?

The thoughts were half curse, half prayer – and to her astonishment Keos answered her: as she stared at the mangled limb, the red and purple veins began to creep towards one another, the seep of her blood slowing as they knitted themselves back together. Bone splinters fell away and the fractured pieces shifted to realign themselves. Bloody flesh crawled across white bone, the bloody threads shifting between vermilion, claret and amaranth. The sheath of skin slid forward, white with blood loss yet painted in crimson. Flesh paired with flesh and her savaged limb pulsed pink and alive. Whole.

Keos had healed her.

The cursed mask had healed her.

Her own pain had healed her.

Myjun realised she had fallen to her knees, in awe at her miraculous self-healing flesh. She flexed the fingers of her left hand, working the new muscles in her arm, and stood, still marvelling at the blessing she had been given, at the curse she had accepted.

And then her stomach rumbled and Myjun remembered with sharp clarity that she had not eaten in days. She thirsted for water. She hungered. She listened to the sounds of the forest, its wildness surrounding her, embracing her. Like the cold waters of the mill pond or the near palpable darkness of the Academy's lower halls.

The forest seemed to be holding its breath, as if waiting to see what Myjun would do next. She raised her left hand to her face and traced the golden lips of her mask. It was flawless. Impervious. Immutable. She traced the edge of her jaw and felt where the metal ended and her flesh began. She tried to pull the mask off, to uncover her mouth and teeth, to free herself of the cursed artifact so she might eat and drink.

But the mask did not move. Its golden curves clung tight to her flesh, undaunted and immovable.

With a trembling sense of anticipation, Myjun brought the point of the stone knife up to the edge of the mask and slid the blade along the metal, easing it between the mask's golden chin and her neck.

Pain – she felt the knife slice through her skin, its edge unable to separate the mask from her flesh, only capable of shearing the skin from her face.

She pushed on, cutting deeper, heedless of the injury she was doing herself: if she did not remove the mask, she could not eat; if she did not eat, she would die.

A howl of pain broke from her dry lips, echoing beneath the golden mouth of Gevul's Mistress. Myjun pressed on, pushing the knife beneath the mask with one hand, trying to lift it away with her other, the pain fuelling her bloody attempt to free herself from the mask's golden prison.

Blood poured down her neck, dripping onto her shoulders, breasts, and belly. She felt her tattered black reaping clothes soak in her blood, felt the warmth and stickiness of it as it coated her body and painted her flesh.

She had carved the knife up to her forehead now, and a terrible giddiness flooded her followed by a sudden horror. The stone knife seemed to grow heavy in her hands and dropped away from her face. Her empty left hand came up to join her right on the mask, heavy as a brick, slow as winter's death. She imagined pulling up the mask to reveal her flayed flesh, raw and gory. She imagined removing it, then imagined finding her former companions Coshry and Faith in the woods, stumbling into them as they screamed at the monster she was. Myjun imagined them cursing her, spitting at her, stoning her – but then she imagined being free again, imagined water coating her parched throat. The thought weakened Myjun's knees and her fingers pulled of their own accord.

The mask did not move.

Myjun clawed at where the knife had sliced, sought out the cut she had made and tried to tear the bloody thing from her face.

But the cut was already healed by the mask's magic. A new terror bloomed in Myjun's gut then as she realised the depth of the curse: the Mask of Gevul's Mistress would not let her die, would not let hunger or thirst destroy her. She would grow hungry, thirsty, dizzy – the pain and fear of starvation and dehydration would constantly plague her – but Myjun would not die. Instead the artifact would feed on her anguish, magically fuelling her body in a perverse kind of symbiosis.

Dread filled her gut, and that too fuelled the mask. She swore in anger, cursed at the pain of her deception – and the mask drank it in. Its magic melded with her rage and she felt the strength flow back into her, filling her with the need to hunt and fight and kill once again.

So she ran – and she hunted. She preyed on the arrogant and the unwary, felling devious predators and magical monsters alike. She killed and thrilled and filled her belly with the scent of blood and the taste of devastation. Dusk came and still she ran and hunted and killed. A skittering spider dropped on her, its fangs sinking into her bicep. She stabbed the keokum through the head, severed its legs, cephalothorax and abdomen. A giant bear with the head of a lion and the eyes of an owl fell upon her when she marched into its cave. In half a minute she had gutted the beast, wrenching its bowels from its belly, then left, heedless of the carnage she had left in her wake.

She encountered dozens of keokum – mythic monsters spawned from the broken hand of Keos – and she killed just as many, sating her bloodlust with the fallen creatures. As she butchered the beasts, Myjun could almost feel her physical hunger being sated by the violence – could almost feel her thirst for water being quenched by the arterial mists of blood.

Almost.

The pain still gnawed at her, the needs of the flesh – to eat and drink – were still deeply ingrained in her, but she now realised the strength she had gained by forfeiting her reliance on such things. She didn't need to sleep, eat or drink; she needed only to hurt, to hunt and to kill.

The woods were darker now, transformed into looming shadows and ghostly figures that grasped with black limbs and bony fingers. Myjun stooped beside a stream of water and plunged her red hands into the wash, the stink of death and blood floating away as her fingers grew cold and numb. She splashed her gold face next, washing the blood from her metal mask, and was surprised by the taste of water and blood trickling down through the eyes of the mask to moisten her dry lips. She peeled the stone knife from her bloody hand and set it on the ground beside her then splashed her face again, delighting in the unexpected taste and touch of the cold water. Again she splashed her face, her tongue savouring the salt and blood from her injured hand as it mixed with the ice water.

Downstream, something roared in the darkness, a feral screech that seemed both hungry and alien. Myjun reached for her long knife, her magically healed hand fumbling for the stone razor ready to be cut anew, biting deep. The screech came again, closer this time, and Myjun's hands came up empty. Her heart rose in her throat: the pain that had fuelled her – the thirst for violence that had enhanced her senses and honed her reflexes – seemed dull now, muted somehow. The loss of her magical strength had come with the comfort of water, leaving her feeling sluggish … cold … tired.

Something large and vaguely reptilian stalked towards her in the deepening gloom, the moonlight reflecting off soft, slippery scales punctuated by knobby bones, spikes, and horns; a wide head with a pointed snout sniffed at the air, its flexible neck stretching like an uncoiling serpent, rising almost a dozen feet in the air. When the beast stood less than fifty paces away, it reared back on powerful legs, raised its clawed arms, and shifted its sinuous body, its corded muscles pulsing with veins that glowed in the night.

Myjun forced herself to glance away, to search the earth for her fallen weapon. She spotted it at the edge of the stream and snatched it up, its sharp edge biting deep in a familiar and comforting way. As the blood ran and the pain blossomed, she felt her senses grow clear once more. She smelled the foul lizard's pungent odour – rotting flesh and bitter iron – and saw its muzzle twitch at the scent of her own fresh blood.

A serpentine tongue snaked out of the draken's maw as it tasted the air and found her taste to its liking. The monster opened its jaws to shriek a challenge, and sprang into the air.

Chapter Fourteen

The draken leapt over two dozen paces, halving the distance between itself and Myjun. As the beast landed, it belched a vile spray of blood and acid, filling the air with acrid smoke and showering Myjun. She instinctively raised an arm to protect her eyes from the burning liquid then stepped back as a gobbet of the foul-smelling mucus splashed across her forearm. The slime burned her skin, foaming and bubbling as it stretched to drip down her hand and elbow.

Good. Fill me with pain so I can kill you that much quicker.

She whipped her injured arm at the creature, flinging her blood and the draken's own acidic mucus back into the monster's face, but it paid her no mind; instead, the beast's tongue flickered in and out, tasting Myjun's scent again before lunging a second time, its maw wide for the kill.

This time Myjun was ready. She dodged the diving draken, rolled away from its jaws and slipped behind a withered spruce as the creature tried to spray her with its acid breath again. A mouthful of blood and mucus splashed and sizzled against the tree's bark – and then Myjun was on the move, sprinting to flank and disembowel the great beast.

But the draken was too quick. As Myjun reached its side, the flicking tongue and serpentine neck had stretched to intercept her, blocking her path to the creature's soft belly. The monster's long snout crashed into Myjun's side, tossing her into the air. She twisted, rolled, and regained her footing just as the draken's jaws opened wide to clamp down on her. Myjun slashed out with her stone knife and the blade cut through the monster's leathery flesh as easily as it had gutted the owl-bear and the giant spider. The draken roared, reared back on its haunches, and swiped at its injured snout.

Myjun saw her opening and lunged, plunging the knife into the draken's belly and slashing downward. She expected to see entrails plop from the creature's guts, but something resisted the pull of her blade. She spun away as the beast dropped down, meaning to crush her, and suddenly their eyes were only inches apart.

The serpent blinked, its slitted eyes narrowing as it growled its displeasure. Myjun stared as the draken's flapping skin began to repair itself, the raw red flesh of its snout stitching together, erasing the injury Myjun had delivered moments before.

Damn.

Myjun's own acid-burned flesh had begun to tingle with re-newed health, but she wasn't healing as fast the blood drake.

Double damn.

Myjun spun, sprinting through the trees, trying to get as far from the beast as possible. Behind her the draken roared in challenge, giving her a few precious seconds head-start. The boom and crash of dead trees being knocked aside announced its pursuit – and the huntress became the hunted.

Myjun tightened her grip on the knife, its double-bladed edge biting deep, igniting her pain and fuelling her speed and stamina. She flew through the woods as fast as any beast or human, her heart racing in time with the beat of her feet against the ground. She crested a hill and jumped, hurtling through the trees and rolling back to her feet, her pace never slowing.

Behind her, the draken snarled, crashing through the under-growth, broadcasting its closeness. Its heavy paws thudded into the soil and Myjun danced off a fallen log, spinning away into a dense copse of trees. Two heartbeats later, the draken collided with one of those trees, the trunk snapping as the giant crashed into it before bracing its long tail against the splintered remains and rocketing itself forward, closing the distance between itself and its prey.

Myjun ran, unable to think, her emotions dulled as the magic of her mask siphoned her pain to fuel her body. She ran for a cluster of boulders, instinctively aware this would be her last stand. This was where she would die.

She spotted a narrow crack between the rocks, the opening just large enough to admit Myjun's slender form. She dived sideways into the crevice, the rough boulders scouring flesh from her arms and legs as she fell hard to the earth. A second later, the blood drake crashed into the heavy stones, its serpentine neck crunching into a coil as its snout punched into the narrow crevice. The beast roared and tried to force itself further into the hole, its head wriggling, its jaws snapping.

Myjun scurried back from the monster's sharp teeth and rolled into something round, yielding and sticky. There was a buzz in her ear and she drew away, allowing a swarm of insects to rise up from the nest she had just crushed. Thick black bodies pelted her skin, their hard shells clacking against each other as scrabbling legs and pinching mandibles sought a hold on her flesh. Myjun screamed as they bit down, a thousand strong pincers tearing at her flesh, crawling under her clothes, fighting to dig under her mask.

Outside, the blood drake screeched and reared its head back, its sharp claws swiping at its snout as the black beetles tore into its soft flesh. With a roar, the draken coughed acid and blood, the ichor spuming from its lips as it tried to burn the insects from its mouth and body.

Inside the crevice Myjun continued to scream, her body raw and bleeding as the swarm fought to consume her faster than the mask could heal her. She rose to her knees then fell back to her side, the stone knife slipping from her grasp as the beetles stripped the flesh from her palm and fingers. Myjun tried to crush the ravenous insects, but their tiny bodies resisted all but the fiercest pressure, yielding only when she smashed them against the boulders. For every beetle she killed, a dozen more took its place. If not for her mask, the swarm would have choked her to death. She had to choose: leave the beetle nest and confront the draken ... or stay and be consumed one bite at a time.

Myjun started to move, but before she could flee, the blood drake roared, lowered its muzzle, and sprayed a cloud of acid into the churning black crevice to rid itself of the pests. The effect was instantaneous: insects clacked and chittered, popped and crackled, their bodies sizzling as heads and abdomens burst. Red ichor rained down on Myjun, her already tattered flesh bubbling and broiling beneath the cloud of dead insects and acidic mucus. Beneath the gold mask, she opened her mouth and screamed, a wail of pain that was both ecstasy and agony. She trembled, unable to move, unable to breathe, as the cloud of acid filled her lungs and threatened to choke her, to consume her.

The spray of acid stopped as the blood drake pulled back its maw. Sizzling saliva rolled down the rock walls, the sliding mucus dragging the dead beetles' bodies with it. Myjun stared through half-burned eyelids as the rapidly healing draken started to swipe at the boulders, its long claws digging beneath the stones, pulling back the earth until one of the boulders shifted. With terrible strength and cunning, the blood drake's long-fingered paws pressed into the crevice and pulled back the stones, leveraging one boulder until it rolled away, exposing Myjun's limp, burned body to the monstrous keokum.

Its mouth opened to claim its prize.

Myjun's hand flew up, her long stone knife stabbing hard into the draken's lower jaw and sticking fast, impossible to free. The blood drake screeched, enraged by her final deception – and then it clamped down on her, its teeth crunching into her body, a dozen ivory daggers stabbing into flesh, piercing Myjun's chest and lungs, stomach and organs. She coughed blood as the draken dragged her from her hole and flung her about like a rag doll, her head whipping back and forth, her spine threatening to snap.

Beneath the gold mask, Myjun's pain was matched only by her frustration and fear. Her arms were pinned by the monster's crushing jaws. With no weapon and no means of freeing herself, a pressure built up in her head and chest, an intense claustrophobia accompanied by the rage of denial. She screamed – a raw, primal thing – and felt a heat fill her chest, lungs, and throat. Knives blossomed in her hands – not the cold stone of the handle-less blade she had left in the draken's mouth, but the sharp fire of her rage that felt tangible in her burned and bloodied fingers.

With a ferocity matching that of the draken, Myjun stabbed her knives into the roof of the monster's mouth and carved outward, slicing deeper until the beast wailed, dropping her to the forest floor. She turned and saw the blood drake's reptilian eyes glaring down at her. This time Myjun did not hesitate. With all her remaining strength, she drove the soulfire blades deep into the blood drake's eyes, its pupils burning out in a flash of fire and light.

Without so much as a whimper, the twenty-foot creature slumped to the earth, its serpentine neck flopping onto Myjun's prone body just as the blades in her hands winked out, their fire extinguished.

Myjun choked and fell beneath the collapsed draken, her head rolling back, staring up at the dark forest canopy and the bright stars overhead. She felt her body grow lighter as her consciousness drifted up towards the twinkling stars and the shadowed tree limbs, and she lay there watching the sky gently lighten with the dawn. Something shifted in her vision, and the shadows around her seemed to morph into something more tangible. A booted foot tipped her chin sideways, and she thought she glimpsed Oyru's shadowed form above her, his hands on his hips. Before he could say anything, the world around her turned dark and deathly quiet. The chirrups and burps of beast and insect fell away, and the first glimmers of light became cold and black and endless.

Chapter Fifteen

It hurt to move. To groan. To breathe. Everything hurt. He was broken. The *world* was broken.

Kenton stared at the soil covering his lidless eyes. He couldn't blink the dirt away and found it didn't bother him enough to care. His glass eyes were not the problem.

It was his body. The falling stone had broken something – several somethings, based on how he ached – but he couldn't move any of his limbs to test how badly he had been injured.

He was trapped. Pinned beneath a mountain of loose rock, dirt, and soil.

Not like this, Kenton thought. *I won't die like this.*

His breathing was shallow – a thin stream of air that he struggled to pull through his nostrils, with the rocks that had piled around his head creating a small chamber of air.

But for how long? How much air had he used up while he was unconscious? How much air still remained? He was already getting light-headed. A bad sign.

Kenton calmed his racing heart and unfocused his vision, allowing his cursed sight to push through the veil of dirt and grit now covering his fiery glass eyes. After a moment, he found he could see the stone pinning his head. A few seconds after that, he perceived what lay beyond it.

More dirt and rock. The tunnel – the entire passage – had collapsed on itself. Kenton further extended his sight, allowing his focus to penetrate hundreds of feet of earth and gravel, emerging at last on the surface. He glimpsed sunlight, the shadow of the

North Tower, and the dark trees of the Brakewood. He tried to sweep his magic vision to the side, but that only brought the surrounding earth and rock back into focus.

Odar's bearded balls, he thought, cursing. *How do I get out of this?*

He couldn't claw his way to the surface. He didn't even have Mercy any more – the sword had fallen from his grasp when the stones crashed down on his hands and fingers. Kenton tried to shift his bruised legs and found them pinned by the rubble. He opened his mouth but earth slid between his lips, threatening to choke him.

He was suffocating.

Panic swelled in Kenton's chest. His heart beat against his rib cage like a wild animal trying to break free.

He was going to die down here. He couldn't breathe. The tunnel was blocked. There was no air. Keos incarnate, he was going to *die*. As his panic rose, a sensation of heat started to overcome his vision. The claustrophobia was palpable.

NO!

Kenton felt the word rise inside him, an embodiment of his will and his rage, his strength and his fury. It silenced his thoughts and fears, shouting back at the darkness.

No! He shouted again, defiant. *I will not die here. I will not die buried and forgotten. Not here, not now, not ever.*

NO!

His thoughts roared into the silence and were answered with the same. The soil above him pressed against his eyes and skin, no longer cool to the touch. He wanted to scream but clenched his jaw instead, to keep the earth from flooding his mouth a second time.

Annev, you bastard, he thought. *When I get out of here, I will hunt you down, stake you to a pit, and pile rocks atop you till every bone in your body breaks.*

But Kenton knew the lie for what it was: he was a dead man. Even if his spine wasn't broken, he was as good as paralysed. The rock held him so fast he could barely twitch his fingers.

But he *could* twitch them. That was something. He *wasn't* paralysed, as he had originally feared. He moved his fingers again, shifting the earth that buried them, and felt something cool and metallic brush his skin. A voice spoke to him – the voice of semi-sentient blood-magic.

I am air, it whispered. *I am the knife that sheathes the sword.*

The corner of Kenton's mouth twitched. He had found the sword – he *hadn't* lost it. His fingers wormed through the soil, clawing up the artifact's cloth-wrapped grip.

A rock shifted and Kenton's hand seized the blade.

Hello, Mercy.

He tried to pull the sword free, but it was stuck fast. He concentrated on its magic and focused the sword's edge, shaping it into a blade that could cut the stones.

Careful now, he thought. *Don't want to cause another cave-in.* He almost laughed at that. What else could happen? What worse thing could the Gods do to him?

As if in reply, the sword's magic edge slipped free of its prison, pivoting to chop through the stone that had pinned it. The rocks around Kenton shifted as well, and the stone that had pinned his forehead slipped down to press against his nose and mouth. His eyes bulged. The thin stream of air he had been breathing was suddenly cut off.

Terror struck. Kenton flailed and thrashed, gripping Mercy with all his strength and forcing his wrist to shift the sword back and forth, chopping further through the surrounding stone and earth. He kicked out, screaming at the pain of his injured legs even as he dislodged some of the stones around his calves and ankles. A hole opened somewhere behind and beneath him, giving him further room to move, and he squirmed backwards, dragging his face along the stone that suffocated him. It cut into him, tearing his nose and lips.

Kenton didn't care. His upper lip split apart and then his mouth came free of the stone and he spat out the dirt that had threatened to choke him – and then he could *breathe!* Never before had air tasted so sweet, not even while sucking it a mile beneath the earth with his tongue caked in blood and dust.

It was glorious – yet his ordeal was far from over. The slanting stone still crushed Kenton's nose and his head remained stuck. He screamed, feeling impotent. Claustrophobic.

Trapped.

'Noooo!' Kenton shouted into the darkness, fighting to free his arms and face. The stone slid another inch, cutting deeper into his flesh, squeezing him. He felt the *krick-crack* of his nose breaking and howled again. Wordless. Primal.

Kenton thrashed with all his strength against the earth holding him. He gripped Mercy tight in his hands, demanding that it aid him, that its magic might break the chains of his prison. A ferocious howl tore from his throat as Kenton yanked his sword arm free, pulling the magic blade through the stone. With little room to manoeuvre he spun the hilt in his fingers, scything Mercy through the rock. The blade *snikkt* through the stone pinning Kenton's face and he jerked his head downward, tearing his nose free — what was left of it. Before Kenton could celebrate, the heavy stone shifted again, its jagged edge dashing against his skull, stabbing into his glass eyes.

'Aaaagh!'

Kenton expected them to shatter — had *known* they would — yet the magic spheres that had replaced his organic eyes held firm.

Praise Odar, Kenton thought, taking another breath.

But it seemed the God of Skywater did not hear him, for seconds later the stone had slid even further, its impossibly heavy weight pressing the hard orbs deep into his skull.

It was agony — the sliding crush of death, like the weight of a mountain slowly descending onto his skull. A pressure filled Kenton's head as he raged beneath the relentless onslaught of rock and gravity. He screamed, dirt and blood spitting from his ragged mouth — and while his roar was wordless, three familiar words still rang inside his head:

NOT . . . LIKE . . . THIS!

Wrapped in his rage, Kenton focused his magic sight and began to channel the mounting pressure behind his eyes. He glimpsed a penetrating view of the crushing rock — a flash of stone behind stone — and then a bright yellow beam erupted from his eyes, obliterating the heavy rock that had pinned his skull. Fragments of molten rock showered his face and neck, and Kenton's head slid free of his tomb. He dragged his arms free a moment later and pulled Mercy with him, sliding the blade down and to the side. The enchanted weapon pushed through the stone then jerked downward as it slid into empty air. Rocks and gravel tumbled into the void and Kenton followed, rolling into the vacuum. For a full second he was floating in the air, and then the ground rushed up to slam into him. More rocks followed, and Kenton raised his arms to shield himself from the falling earth and stone.

When the rock fall finally eased, Kenton took his trembling hands from his face. He lay on his back, his head turned sideways as a cloud of dust filled the tiny room – a room with a familiar rainbow-hued light.

No . . . Gods no. I can't be back here again.

But he was. In his mad attempt to escape the cave-in, Kenton had inadvertently carved his way back into Annev's prison cell.

He was right back where he had started.

Kenton started to laugh. It was a joke – a tremendous, gods-awful joke. All that searching, all that nearly *dying,* just so he could end up here. Again. Tears threatened his eyes, but he found himself laughing all the harder. It hurt – he'd broken his cracked ribs in the fall – but he kept laughing in stuttering stops, and the dusty prison walls echoed the sound back to him.

I'm going mad, he thought. *Something has come loose in my head, and I've gone mad.*

As the cloud of dust started to settle so did his laughter, and Kenton marvelled at how much improved his vision had become since he'd first left the cell. He glanced at the walls, peering through them again, into the adjoining prison cells. It was easier now, almost instinctual. He glared at the rusty trapdoor mounted at the top of the stairs.

My vision . . . that magic fire I just summoned. Could I use it to break into the Vault? It was a fair question, though Kenton instinctively shied away from experimenting with anything so volatile, particularly beneath the weight of the crumbling Academy.

I'm not even sure how I summoned it, he told himself. *Or that I would want to again.* He stared at the ceiling above him and growled when a black barrier thwarted his magic eyesight.

I still can't see into the Vault of Damnation. Probably has a hundred useful things that would help me break out of here. Some weapon like Mercy or . . .

The sword. Kenton had briefly forgotten the weapon.

Ignoring his aching ribs and injured legs and face, he rolled himself out of the rubble and crawled through the fallen dirt and debris, searching. Then he stopped and chided himself: he didn't need to search; he need only *look*.

And there it was, buried beneath a pile of dirt and rock near the base of the carved stone steps. Kenton clawed away the loose rubble and reclaimed the weapon, feeling the familiar tingle of its magic as he did so.

I am Mercy. I am the air. I am—

'Yes, we've been over this.'

Kenton snorted, suddenly realising he was talking to a sword.

I need to find a way out of here before I really do go mad.

He forced himself to climb the stone stairs, each step bound in pain and exhaustion. When Kenton reached the top of the carved steps, he paused to take a breath and then called on the sword's magic, sharpening its edge into something supernatural. He felt the artifact respond, the magic pulsing in his hand, and then he raised the weapon to the edge of the locked door. A tiny stream of liquid light trickled out from the corner of the trapdoor. Kenton briefly glanced at the magic liquid then turned away, not wanting any more of the ghostly visions he'd seen when he last peered into its depths.

With his attention focused on the stone surrounding the ancient trapdoor, Kenton guided Mercy's blade until its invisible sharpened edge found the crack dividing stone from metal. He felt the compressed blade of air slide into the rusted metal, as smooth as steel parting silk. The iron flayed then flaked away as he forced Mercy farther into the Vault, pushing it upward till the cross guard met stone. He gripped the hilt with both hands, preparing to saw through the sealed door, then thought better of it and shifted his left hand to grasp one of the sword's quillons. Still grasping Mercy's magic in his mind, Kenton jiggered the blade around the perimeter of the trapdoor. The metal shrieked, bands and bolts buckling, the old boards breaking, shuddering and shattering. At almost the same time, a tremor seemed to shake the earth as the entire cell – the entire *Academy* – groaned with the weight of shifting rock and earth pressing down on it. There was a sharp *CRACK* as the wall to Kenton's right splintered, spidering outward to engulf and then shatter the lower half of the carved stone steps.

Kenton jerked the sword free from the fractured trapdoor and threw up a hand, shielding his eyes from rock dust and splinters, though he could still see through the muscle and bone of his fore-arm: the trapdoor above him had been twisted from its hinges, broken by the very stones that had once supported it. The ground shook again, spreading the crack in the wall until its opening was as wide as his waist. Loose dirt and earth tumbled into the cell and Kenton tumbled backward, crashing to the floor. The rumbling roar of the earth continued as more jagged rocks and pounds of dirt poured into the cell, threatening to smother him. Kenton scrambled to his knees, Mercy still in hand, as the fissure shook the room and the floor began to shift beneath his feet. He saw the crack spread – saw the pit opening up, threatening to drop him into the forgotten lower dungeons. A chunk of ceiling crashed down from above, glancing off his shoulder, and Kenton realised he was going to be buried alive a second time unless he took action. He jumped to his feet, instinctively leaping onto the remaining rough-hewn stairs, then scrabbled up them to reach the former prison hatch.

With the walls still shaking, their stones shifting and crumbling around him, Kenton thrust Mercy into the fractured trapdoor and cut away the last hinge of metal and wood, dropping the rusty portal into the crumbling void below. Kenton flung his chest into the opening in the ceiling and dragged his legs up after him, pulling his feet into the luminescent chamber above. He panted heavily, gazing about for further destruction, but the cacophony below felt distant now, its rumbles barely noticeable in the larger chamber he now occupied.

Rolling onto his back, he sucked air through gritted teeth in short breaths of pain, grunting against the fierce reminder of his still-broken ribs. As he did so, his vision shifted, taking in the details of his surroundings. He recognised the rainbow-hued light from his prison cell and saw it magnified a thousand times over, filling the room with an eerie incandescence. He then glimpsed the spokes of liquid magic radiating out from the room's centre – bright as a beacon on a moonless night – and he watched as the light illuminating the room shifted in colour: first red then purple then blue ... Every colour of the rainbow shone on his face as he stared in awe at the rows of shelves lining the dome-shaped chamber.

He had finally entered the Vault of Damnation.

As if the revelation somehow weren't enough, the grinding and groaning beneath Kenton suddenly ceased. The earth stilled, and he sensed he was no longer in danger of being buried alive.

It wasn't simply because the ground had stopped shaking, though. It was something he *sensed*, something he knew instinctively, like being able to use Annev's magic sword, or understanding the purpose and intent of every artifact he had ever touched.

The room – the Vault itself – *was* an artifact, an enchanted chamber designed to conceal and protect items cursed with the taint of sorcery, blood, and magic. The earth itself might crumble around Kenton, but within these walls he was safe. Outside he was a scarred freak, but in here, the eyes of Gods and men were blind to him and he was blind to them. A profound sense of solitude struck him, a solace he had never known or wanted but which nevertheless brought him peace. As he basked in the shifting glow of the room's magic light, Kenton accepted the truth of its perverse embrace: he had never really belonged at the Academy. He had not belonged because he had unknowingly been the very thing they hunted – a vessel of magic. How ironic to discover that the Vault he had long sought to avoid now seemed a place of refuge.

Surrounded by other artifacts of damnation, Kenton no longer felt out of place. He had pretended to be like the other acolytes and avatars, but he held more in common with these tools – these crafted artifacts of semi-sentient magic – than he did with any of his peers. The relics would never judge him, Kenton realised – never spurn him. They would never love him, either, but that was no loss. Kenton was a monster, and now he no doubt looked like one. Torn lips and broken nose. Lidless eyes and scarred flesh.

There would be potions in this room that might heal the former, but the latter would always be with him. He slowly raised a hand to the scars covering his cheekbones, tough like hard leather around his flaming glass eyes.

Kenton was a keokum now. A freak. Something to be hated and feared for the magic he carried and the mark of Keos he now bore. The sooner he accepted that – the sooner he stopped thinking of himself as one of *them* – the better off he'd be. This new change – his scarred face and cursed magic – had crystallised something within him.

To hell with Tosan and the Academy, he thought. *It seems they're all dead now, anyway ... I'm alive and they're dead – and none of their rules could save them.*

It seemed so silly now, all of those rules. Fighting to pass the Test of Judgement, to become an avatar, to earn his place as a master. Even then in his moment of greatest triumph, Tosan had tried to sweep him under the rug, condemning him to serve in the Vault with that decrepit Master Narach. And now those bastards were all gone – either dead or fled – and Kenton owed them nothing.

And Myjun? Kenton had seen few signs of the witwomen or their apprentices. Was it possible they had escaped the Academy's destruction?

Kenton didn't know. If they had, though, Myjun might have escaped with them. And if she was alive, she was no longer under Annev's spell – she had *spurned* him. Maybe Kenton could ...

But no. Annev had spoiled that, too. Even if she lived, she wouldn't be interested in Kenton. Not with his scarred face. Not now. No, Annev had damned him as surely as he'd damned himself; if Myjun had known he was trapped underground, she would have taken her fickle heart and left him to rot in that cell.

Damn them all.

Kenton gritted his teeth. He hated Annev for revealing the truth of his living lie, for stealing every hope and dream he had ever aspired to have or hold. Keos burn him, but he would visit wrath and blood on that one-armed kraik if they ever crossed paths again. To do that, though, Kenton had to escape, which meant embracing the magic he had denied for so long.

Kenton sat up and stiffly inhaled the stale air of the Vault, his tongue writhing beneath the bittersweet tang of magic. It reminded him of blood, of copper and fermented sugar beets. He felt its echo penetrate his bones, a power both vast and ancient. He sensed its source at the centre of the room: a brimming pool of golden liquid that radiated the rainbow-hued light. Kenton suspected that even his normal eyes would have seen the magic in the air. Now he could see the magic itself, like a vapour of steam rising from a pot of boiling water, and he followed it to see the glowing fountain. He saw the notches cut into the rim of the pool and saw how they fed a series of spokes radiating from the fountain's edge. Runnels had been cut into the floor, their perfect paths guiding the magic liquid towards the perimeter of the dome-shaped room.

Kenton didn't understand glyphs or wards the same way Tosan and Narach did, nor could he recite texts of scripture as easily as Annev or Sodar, but he had a talent for sensing the subtleties of the magic around him. He'd always been able to, though he'd kept his talent hidden from the ancients at the Academy. He had even tried to convince himself that the whispers weren't real, that he was imagining a pseudo-sentience in the artifacts he held.

But Kenton had never quite convinced himself of that lie. For him, the buzz and hum of magic could be loud or soft, high or low, yet each one communicated a unique purpose or intent. The artifacts themselves weren't really talking to him – not with words – but he still interpreted it as such. He could feel their voices thrumming around him. Focused and precise. Constant and inflexible. He'd grown accustomed to ignoring it. But standing here, in the heart of the Vault, Kenton felt the drumbeat of magic pounding his skull like never before. The voice of the chamber echoed inside him, telling its purpose.

Hide. Protect.

Kenton's eyes followed the spokes of white-gold liquid trickling away from the pool of magic, their streams disappearing to feed an underground matrix with rainbow-hued light. He still couldn't see through the chamber walls, but he knew enough to guess where those spokes led: out to the standing stones surrounding

Chaenbalu's perimeter. The twelve streams were equidistant from each other, their lines pointing in the cardinal, intercardinal, and ordinal directions. If he could somehow escape the Vault and trace their paths, Kenton guessed each one would terminate at a standing stone, their liquid magic humming beneath the earth's surface, its tune matching what he felt in this room.

Hide. Protect.

Kenton had felt that power just two days ago at the western perimeter of the village, the strange tug of magic coming from the worn and weather-beaten rock. He had paid it no mind then, being distracted by his mission to Banok with Annev and Fyn, but he'd wondered if his companions felt it too. He hadn't asked them. To do so would have risked revealing his magical affinity. Now, instead of ignoring it, he embraced that resonance and felt the room's magic envelop him.

Kenton turned his eyes from the pool and stared at the Vault's contents, barely able to fathom the vastness of the treasures hoarded there. He limped towards the nearest shelf and saw it contained a collection of amber bottles filled with their own glowing liquid – a substance entirely different from the magic pooling at the centre of the room. Kenton looked more closely at the bottles, his *aqlumera*-blessed vision revealing what human eyes could never see: an alchemical mixture that would heal the body and invigorate the mind. He wasn't exactly sure how he knew that until he spotted the glimmer of magic floating at the centre of each bottle.

Blood, Kenton thought. There was no crimson blob or streak of red, nothing to smell or taste, no way to confirm what his eyes and instincts told him – yet Kenton knew he was right. What's more, he knew the blood was special; it had come from a Terran who possessed the power to heal himself at an extraordinary rate. Kenton reached out, touched one of the bottles and felt the magic respond to him.

You are hurt – but I can heal you. Drink me. Become one with me. Remind me who and what I once was.

Before he'd even processed what he was doing, Kenton found he'd lifted the bottle from the shelf, uncorked its top, and raised its murky orange-gold contents to his lips.

What am I doing? he wondered. *This could* kill *me. Why in the five hells would I drink it?*

But he knew what was in it: blood – an *Inquisitor's* blood. This last thought came half from him, half from the amber bottle.

I will heal you, the magic whispered. *Let me show you what I can do.*

Kenton slowly upended the glass bottle, the liquid sliding past his teeth and tongue. He swallowed, felt the oily amber bile roll down his throat, and though he coughed, choked and sputtered, he drank it all.

It tasted like ash and orange peel, like cinders and saffron, and it burned going down – but not *too* painfully. As it coated his throat, he felt its warmth spread throughout his body, filling him with heat and headiness. His nose tingled and he felt the magic essence shift something in the broken cartilage. The fire reached his broken ribs next and burned his pain away in a tide of fiery citrus and smoky honeywine. He inhaled – the pain in his side gone, the aches of his bruised legs and other injuries having vanished – and he smiled.

'Damn, but that's good.' He smacked his lips, trying to taste the magic he had felt while holding the bottle, but it was gone.

Curious, he thought, reaching for a second bottle.

I can heal you, the blood-magic whispered, potent once again. *I will cleanse your poisons, mend your injuries. Only taste me . . . taste me . . .*

Kenton put the bottle back on the rack, his suspicions still aroused. Something was wrong here. He let go of the bottle and his eyes drifted to the next shelf. A mixed assortment of glass vials and bottles sat benignly on the shelf, some filled with powders, others with watery liquids or viscous oils. He touched a smoky vial filled with swirling green vapour, peering into its depths.

Die.

The voice-that-was-not-a-voice seemed to pulse in the back of Kenton's head.

Expire, it whispered. *Cease.*

And then a second voice sprang up, its throbbing rhythm altogether different from the first: *Grow,* it seemed to whisper. *Spread . . . expand.*

It was a conversation, he realised. Two blood magics were speaking to each other, drawing on each other's power. As he listened, Kenton had a vision of green spores spreading to fill his lungs, their essence choking him. Killing him.

He set the vial back on the shelf and shuddered, suddenly wondering if the cave-in really had driven him mad. The voices . . . they weren't real – there was no audible sound coming from the artifacts – yet he could still feel their intent, as if they were communicating with him on a more primal level. Kenton touched another bottle, this one filled with grey powder, and focused on the sensation he knew would come.

Nothing.

No sensation. No magic pulse.

Kenton lowered his eyes, his magic vision peering into the depths of the bottle, and it was as if a door in his mind had been flung open.

Touch me, the powder whispered into the recesses of his skull. *Touch me . . . and touch nothing. Rub me into your skin – let me become your skin – and I will protect you. You will feel nothing. I will shield you. Touch me, and let me be the last thing you ever feel.*

Ironborn, Kenton thought, as if tasting the magic on his tongue. *You were once called Ironborn.*

Yes, the powder echoed, its magic pulsing in his hand. *I am Ironborn, and you will be too if you touch me . . . touch me . . .*

Kenton put the bottle of grey powder back on the shelf. He understood now. He knew what to look for. A sly grin broke out across his face as he reached for one of the bottles of amber liquid.

Drink me, the blood-magic whispered. *Let me heal you. I can—*

Inquisitor, Kenton thought, practically tasting the words on his tongue. *You were a Terran Inquisitor. Your magic heals.*

YES! It practically shouted at him, its magic pulses quivering in a euphoric kind of anticipation. *Drink me!* it pleaded. *Remind me who I once was.*

It was the blood, Kenton realised. There was a drop of human blood in every one of these artifacts. He ignored the voice in his head and replaced the bottle. The voice grew quieter once he let go of the artifact, but he could still hear it ... so long as his vision stayed on the bottle.

So why hadn't he noticed it before? Had he just been ... blind to it? Had his magic sight somehow unlocked something more than supernatural vision? He turned his eyes to the ceiling again then reached down to where he had lain Mercy. He touched the corded hilt, now leaning point–down against the shelf in front of him, and he listened.

I am air, the sword seemed to whisper, its voice quiet in his head. *I am the magic that sheathes the sword ...*

Kenton grunted. *So, I can sense the sword's magic without using my eyesight ... but not the Elixir's magic. Why?* He had no answers for that, so he turned his magic vision back on the sword, studying its edge. The pulse of magic throbbed loud in his head, almost shouting.

Ah, he thought. *The eyes amplify my existing ability. Touching it helps me focus on the magic, and looking at the artifact while I touch it makes the magic scream back at me.* He concentrated, peering at the sword's silvery sheen, and he could practically see the shimmering air pressed thin around the blade: pink and blue, and sharp as any razor. Sharper. He tried to divine what kind of blood had been used to forge the artifact and lost his sense of it. He tried again, peering at the steel then letting his eyes unfocus. His vision seemed to shift, sliding into a new spectrum of light and colour.

What were you? Kenton thought. *Who were you?*

Shieldbearer, the sword seemed to pulse. *I compress the air. I protected Sodar. Now I will protect you. Sodar?* Kenton's mind reeled.

You were Sodar's *sword ... and the old man gave you to Annev.*

The weapon seemed to pulse in affirmation.

This is unreal, he thought, not for the first time. Was the sword sentient? Did it have a spirit?

I am Mercy, the blade pulsed, as if trying to answer him. *I am the air and the ice. I am the razor's edge. I am the blood of the Shieldbearer.*

All right, Kenton thought. *Semi-sentient then.* Like the blood used to forge the artifact somehow remembered what it once was – or *who* it once was. Yes, that seemed right.

Kenton leaned the sword against the shelf once more, his eyes sliding away from the blade while his vision remained in that eerie, unfocused place where magic shone like fire. He stared at the myriad artifacts sitting placidly on the Vault's thousands of shelves – and nearly lost his breath.

Amulet of Incorporeal Form.

Gauntlets of Indomitability.

Boots of Stillness.

Belt of Strength.

Circlet of Malice.

The room throbbed with the pulse of whispered magic. A silent susurration of whispered wants and promised power.

Wear me. Hold me. Drink me. Wield me. Break me.

I will warm you. I will silence you. I will strengthen you.

I will show you the path. I will stop their arrows.

I will hide you from their eyes. I will guard you from their lies.

Use me. Take me. Taste me.

Remind me who I am ... what I once was.

Become one with me.

Kenton twitched, overwhelmed by the silent voices in his head. He turned his eyes to the floor and his perspective shifted back to the mundane world. He clutched his hands to his temples then slowly looked up again, observing the room's contents.

This was how he would escape. How he would take his revenge, just a step away, one shelf up or down. All about him lay the artifacts of damnation, and Kenton understood every one of their secrets.

Barely two days ago, Tosan had brought Kenton to his study and named him Master of Curses – an insult and a condemnation. Now, as Kenton examined the magical hoard surrounding him, he found himself warming to the title.

Kenton would make the masters and ancients pay for abusing and abandoning him.

First, though, he would hunt down Annev, and teach the Master of Sorrows the true meaning of his name.

Chapter Sixteen

Kenton hadn't been hasty in his assessment of the Vault's treasures. Instead of grabbing the first magic glove or dark rod he encountered, Kenton took the time to work through the full extent of the Vault's store. He didn't just want the best or most useful items. He wanted the ones that would pack easily, the ones that wouldn't weigh him down or take up too much space. Even after he'd found the Belt of Strength, he was selective about how much gear he could reasonably carry with him out of the Vault.

Until he found the Cloak of Secrets.

The cloak was a marvel. The moment he saw it, he knew he had to have it – had to touch it and unwrap the secrets it contained. The fabric was black, smooth as melting ice and near as slick. Even his magic eyes tended to slide away from the material, as if some filament of shadow had been woven into its fibres. *I will hide you. I will keep your secrets safe. Wrap your burdens in my folds. Let my pockets hide your blades. Your toys. Your poisons. Your lies and deceptions. Give them all to me and I will keep them safe. I will hide them from the light – hide them from the world – and you shall walk unfettered by their presence.*

It wasn't till he draped the cloak round his shoulders, though, that the cloak shared other secrets: *I have seen the world and know its secrets. If you wish, I can show them to you, take you to their lands . . . to their hidden places.*

That was a trap. That was how the cloak had ensnared its previous wearers and abandoned them in a void beyond this world. He could sense the cloak's anticipation as it tried to lure him towards the darkest secrets hidden in the folds of its fabric. He could even catch a glimpse of them – worlds of shadow and shade, dream realms and nightmare lands. If Kenton wrapped himself in the Cloak of Secrets and expressed a will to travel to one of those places, the cloak would take him there – and leave him there. One more secret hidden in its depths, one more owner left in the void.

Kenton wasn't falling for it.

'Your magic,' he said, speaking aloud. 'It is Kroseran ... Void-weaver magic?'

The hum of the cloak's magic hesitated. Could it hear him? Could it understand him? Kenton doubted it, but he kept talking all the same.

'The man who crafted you – whose blood you bear – he could manipulate the fabric of this world. Could use it to move between those places ... yes?'

The magic throbbed around Kenton's shoulders, filling his senses with an impression of the artifact's blood-magic and the person it once belonged to: soft and sensual, sharp and clever.

A woman, Kenton realised, *with hair black as night and skin pale as the moon*. She reminded Kenton of another woman – younger, almost as pretty, and no less dangerous.

Sodja Rocas, Kenton thought. Who had stolen the Rod of Compulsion which he, Fyn and Annev had gone to great lengths to steal from Janak Harth. They were connected somehow ... similar blood. Kroseran? Yes, that was it. Both women were Kroseran. Worshippers of Dorchnok, the God of Shadows. It surprised him how much he could learn about the world and its magic simply by listening to the whispers of its artifacts.

So interesting. Kenton stared at the strand of blood-magic woven into the cloak's fabric and saw its magic reflected back at him, written as plainly as the inked words in an open book.

Oh yes, this cloak held *many* secrets. Kenton reached into the pocket at his elbow and drew out the slender black wand concealed there.

Ebony wood. Surprisingly flexible. As long as his forearm and inscribed with iron-grey runes that shone in the room's magic light. Kenton peered at the runes and smiled again.

Wand of the Void. Kenton felt the rod's magic echo in his head. If the Cloak of Secrets were a door to another world – a trap for the unwary – then this rod was the key to that door. So long as he held the wand, he could safely enter the worlds concealed within the cloak and return as he chose.

Kenton chuckled. Then he laughed, loud and long, a booming cackle that echoed within the confines of the Vault. He really did feel lighter, really did feel as though the cloak had lifted his burdens. He didn't need to be so choosey when the cloak could carry any items he wished. He didn't need to fret about how to escape the Academy. Not when he wore the door on his shoulders and carried the key in his hand. He began to sweep artifacts into the pockets of his cloak almost at random, pausing just long enough to memorise each one's purpose: a glove that could sense the emotions of whomever he touched; a tome that held a hundred forgotten libraries and ten thousand forgotten books; a slender key that would open any lock; a pair of rings that would bond the wearer of the first to the will of the second. Kenton slipped the latter onto his finger and put the former in his pocket – just so he'd be prepared.

And then he spotted the Ring of Remembrance. Kenton picked up the bauble, confirmed its significance, and slipped it onto the middle finger of his left hand. His thoughts immediately began to crystallise, the impressions and thoughts of the world around him recorded with perfect clarity and stored within the ring. He smiled. No more hard choices lay before him, only the easy work of studying each artifact, recording its magic, and then storing the item in the infinite folds of his cloak. He hesitated when he came to an earthenware jug that would not fit in any of his pockets, but it turned out all he need do was shroud the vessel in his cloak and will it away. He swished the fabric, flipped the cape back – and the jug was swallowed by the Cloak of Secrets.

But how to retrieve it? He had not placed the jug in one of the cloak's pockets, so how could he summon it again? He meditated on this, then discovered he need only flap the cape of his cloak while thinking of the item he wished to recall – and there it was, sitting at his feet. Easy as breathing. Another flip of his cloak and the jug vanished once more.

Damn, but I could get used to this.

Few artifacts were safe from Kenton's hands after that. He swept whole shelves into the void hanging loose about his shoulders. Bags and bottles. Garments and gold. Jewels and weapons. He stopped when he came to a glaive that stood taller than his head and shrugged. He didn't have to take everything, after all – just *almost* everything. He chose to keep smaller, useful items close about his person: a powerful Amulet of Regeneration, its enormous garnet filled with the blood of a dozen Inquisitors; Boots of Silence, capable of hiding Kenton's entire body in a soundless void whenever he activated its magic. He found a pair of trousers made from the skin of a black panther and slipped them on, invigorated by the grace and speed of the animal it had belonged to and the Shalgarn ranger who had been bonded to it. He felt keen and cunning, strong and quick. His thoughts were clear and his body felt hale and hearty.

Kenton looked around at the rest of the Vault's contents. He hadn't even taken a fifth of the artifacts, and yet he had stolen enough to fill a dozen wagons.

'It is enough,' he said, speaking to the remaining artifacts as if they were people: silent watchers, quiet listeners, prisoners waiting to be released from their cells.

Yes, it was enough. He could always come back for more if need required it.

Kenton pulled up the hood of his black cloak. He arched his shoulders, stretched, and pulled the night-black garment close about his body. The world had scorned him. The Academy's masters and ancients had persecuted him. Elder Tosan had mocked him. Annev had cursed him.

They would all pay.

The secrets he had plundered from the Vault of Damnation – the artifacts the masters and ancients had spent generations coveting, stealing, and storing – they would all come back to haunt them now. That's what he was, after all. No longer the Master of Curses, but the Lord of Damnation.

Now to leave this prison, do I simply use the Cloak's portal magic . . . or do I make a final attempt to claw my way out? If Kenton attempted the latter, he now had a wealth of artifacts to aid him, so it seemed his success would be assured. By contrast, using the Cloak would be simpler, but that same simplicity made Kenton suspicious: the artifact seemed to *want* to trap people with its void magic, and that impression made him reluctant to use it.

Kenton laid his hand on Mercy's hilt, its magic voice somewhat muted by the glove he now wore on his right hand, and circled back towards the Vault's entrance where he stared in silence at its massive ironwood portal. He rubbed his stubbly jaw and summoned the slim skeleton key he had found earlier. He approached the door and examined its cylindrical lock, instinctively knowing that it wouldn't fit but thinking he had to try anyway. As he suspected, the artifact was designed to open mundane locks – but not magical ones. He replaced the key in the pocket of his cloak and glanced to another corner of the room, his magic eyes peering through the shelves to study the hole where the rusted trapdoor had once barred his entry. He could leave through there . . . but he didn't like the notion of returning to that damn prison cell. If an aftershock brought the Vault down on his head, his artifacts might prevent him from getting crushed to death, but he could still suffocate. He could still be pinned beneath a hundred tonnes of rock and earth, kept alive by his magic but trapped by the stones.

Looking for alternatives, Kenton found his attention drawn back to the stream of glowing liquid trickling down into the compromised prison cell below. His eyes followed where the stream escaped the chipped runnel carved into the Vault's floor, and he followed that back to the pool of rainbow-hued light shining from the centre of the room. As Kenton drew nearer to the pool of liquid magic he noticed the radiating rows of shelves and bookcases all terminated a few dozen feet away from the raised wall circumscribing the fountain and the liquid magic it contained.

Thus far Kenton had deliberately stayed away from the pool, his gut filling with a sense of dread any time he looked towards it. That dread seemed a pale thing now that he had equipped himself with the Vault's magic, though, and he forced himself to take a cautious step towards the wide stone wall. He glimpsed the magic pooling inside, and when he leaned over to study the depth of the luminous liquid, Kenton realised precisely what he was looking at.

It was a well – a deep well brimming with the rainbow-coloured light of liquid magic. The stone wall encircling the magic barely reached his hip, and there was no bucket or rope to draw out the luminous substance, but its surface was tantalizingly close. Just a few inches below the lip of the containing wall. Close enough that he could reach down and scoop up the liquid with his palm.

Kenton took another step and leaned over that wall, dazzled by the shifting light and colours reflected back at him: the magic was translucent; he could peer down into the depths of the well, seeing a natural shaft that plumbed deep into the earth before stretching out to fill an underground grotto. Kenton peered into those depths, transfixed by the light and colour he saw there, captivated by the aura of magic that seemed to waft up from its depths.

Aqlumera.

The mythical combination of *quaire*, *lumen*, and *t'rasang* wasn't supposed to be real. It was a symbol of unlimited potential. A legend and a lie. The impossible stuff from which the Gods and the world had been made. Kenton had never believed it – not once in all the stories he'd heard had he given credence to the myth, nor had he guessed its nature when Annev had splashed him with the stuff – but now, standing at the well's precipice, Kenton found he could not deny it.

The grotto far beneath his feet was alive with fire and ice, crackling and freezing. A prism, reflecting the infinite paths of the future. An instant later, it seemed to boil with the froth of life and death, growth and decay, stagnation and regeneration. It was earth and metal. Air and water. Light and fire. It flowed with purpose, as if the liquid itself were alive.

It *was* alive, Kenton realised. Amidst the currents of magic he could see the spirits of the dead and the unborn. The faces of children and infants who had left this life too early, the pinched and grimacing faces of old men and women who had long since perished. They churned among the magic, swimming in it, trapped by it. The more Kenton stared, the more he felt they *were* the magic ... as if their very souls formed the white-gold liquid and rainbow-hued light that shone from it. The spirits seemed to float before him, caught between this world and the next. He stared, transfixed ...

... and one face rose from the morass, gaining form and figure: the spirit of a man, tall and lean, with a short cropped goatee and a stern face.

Elder Tosan.

With a wail and a roar, the spectre lunged for Kenton, forcing itself from the *aqlumera* and rushing for him. Before he could pull away, the spirit plunged into Kenton's eyes, filling him with a cold wash of dread, despair, and anger.

You! the spirit hissed inside Kenton's skull.

Tosan? Kenton reeled back from the edge of the well. *What in the bloody—*

You, Tosan continued, *have magic, Master Kenton. Like that cursed keokum, Ainnevog. You were hiding amongst us this whole time ... right under my nose.*

How are you doing this? Kenton stumbled into the shelf behind him. *How are you in my head?*

How indeed? Tosan snapped. *This was supposed to be like Bron Gloir – supposed to send me to the nearest living person so I could exorcise their soul and take possession of their body, not trap me inside here with you.*

Did Annev bring those metal monsters to the Academy? Kenton wondered. *Did they* kill *you? I searched but never found you among the dead ...*

Kenton could feel the spirit searching his memories, sifting through them the way the Master of Coin sifted through his clips and coppers. He flinched, pulling himself out of Tosan's spectral grasp.

The headmaster's dry laugh seemed to echo inside his skull, its tone filled with contempt. *You loved my daughter, Master Kenton? Just like that damned spawn of Keos. You wanted to infect her with your taint too ... Fortunately the Gods have seen fit to carry her out of this world. You will never have the chance to taint her, and she will never see the monster I have become.*

Myjun, Kenton thought, barely able to string his thoughts to-gether. *I was hoping she had escaped. How … how did she die?*

A vision appeared in his mind; he saw through Tosan's eyes as Annev raised a golden hand filled with fire, its palm bright as the sun. Myjun stood next to him, her hands clutching his chevron-patterned robes, terrified for herself and her father. Annev screamed and a cylinder of fire lanced out from his palm. It raced towards Tosan, slowing as he consciously forced the memories to play at half-speed then quarter-speed. Slower still. Slow enough that Kenton could feel the heat wash over Tosan's outstretched arm, melting his fingers and gold ring, his hand and his arm. Myjun was trying to run when she was blasted by flame. She twisted away, thrown backward, and then Tosan's eyes filled with the orange fire of his own immolation. His body burned and his spirit tumbled like a leaf in the wind, leaving Tosan disorientated … until he felt himself drawn steadily downward, pulled down towards the Vault of Damnation.

It wasn't supposed to be like this. Tosan practically snarled in Kenton's mind. *My soul was supposed to transfer to another body. I was supposed to cheat death, not get sucked down into this pit. Damnation took me – the Vault took me. The ritual must have failed, somehow. I don't know. It worked for Bron Gloir, but he was a Soulwalker …*

The headmaster grew quiet and Kenton felt his stomach churn.

Annev killed Myjun, he thought. *He killed her and I wasn't there to stop it.*

You couldn't have saved her, Tosan replied. *Neither of us could. His magic – that Keos-be-damned hand – nothing could stop it. It ripped me from my body and tore her from this world. He killed her like an angry devil – like Keos incarnate.*

A fire bloomed in Kenton's belly, full of fury.

Annev had killed Myjun. He had tricked her, stolen her heart away from Kenton, then murdered her when she rejected him.

I will destroy him, Kenton thought. *I will turn everything he holds dear against him. I will destroy everything that brings him joy. I will fill his life with such misery and despair he will pray for death to deliver him from his private hell. And then I will show him who the real architect of his sorrows was … before I kill him, slowly and painfully. He will plead for an end, but it won't come quickly. It will—*

Not come from you.

Kenton's plans for vengeance foundered on Tosan's cool voice. *You will not harm Ainnevog because I will administer the boy's punishment. I will bring the boy to judgement, and I will do so using your body. Your presence will not be required.*

Once more, Kenton felt the grasping talons of Tosan's spirit sink into him, forcing him backward, pushing his own spirit from its corporeal home. Kenton tried to fight back, but it was like grasping at water. He could not get hold of himself. He could not stop the implacable force that bore down on him, nor could he gain enough traction to push back. He felt something tearing inside him, felt the force of Tosan's angry will ripping him out of his mind. His identity, his psyche … it flowed past him like sand through his fingers.

At almost the same time, Kenton felt a second pressure pulling on him, tugging his soul towards a distant and merciful oblivion.

It was the *aqlumera*, Kenton realised, as his spirit fought the seductive force. In contrast to the precise blows and direct attack of the headmaster's spirit, the magic coming from the pool washed over Kenton in pulsating waves, eroding his sense of self and slowly drawing him towards the pool of liquid light. He heard the disembodied voices of the dead, pleading for another chance at life, calling to him from the *aqlumera* – and he realised he was screaming with them. He battled to stay in place, to fight Tosan's ferocious push and the *aqlumera*'s relentless pull.

But it was no use. Kenton was dying, and the headmaster's disembodied spirit was taking possession of him.

Part Two

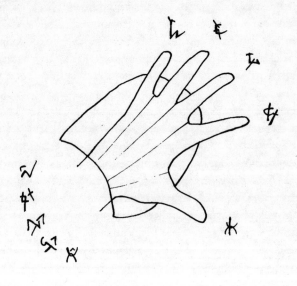

I do not see Odar's will in this. I'm not certain I have ever truly heard his voice ... yet I feel certain that he would approve of my decision. I take delight in the irony of using the very tools of Keos against him and his servants. And so I have begun my studies in earnest [...]

I confess that I feel a thrill when I confront the magic that taints me. I do not believe Keos calls to me, nor Lumea, nor Odar himself. The magic seems to have a life of its own, independent of Gods and men. Beneath the taint of Keos, I perceive a promise of life and a certainty of death. It is bigger than all of us. Sometimes I feel swallowed up in it, barely able to resist it. I feel it calling to me now, though I compose these thoughts from several floors above the damnable magic [...]

The text calls them Earthshapers, and while I care little for the name or the corruption it represents, it is connected to another piece of lore that has captured my attention: an Ilumite-Terran hybrid known as a 'Soulshaper', which has much in common with the Ildari hybrids known as 'Soulwalkers'.

According to the text, it is possible for Soulshapers and Soulwalkers to cheat death itself. The book is vague about the specifics and it is too early to draw my own conclusions, but my hypothesis is that these Soulshapers could move their souls to another vessel upon their death. Such a feat would match the mythic tales of Bron Gloir ... yet I cannot ignore the evidence, nor can I write this off as fancy. I intend to tease out the clues about how it may be done. The narratives of Bron Gloir himself might provide some. If I can find the secret, it would be a great boon for the Academy. [...]

The narrative of Bron Gloir shows promise. I've sent Duvarek north to see if he can recover anything of value, but I don't hold out much hope. Too much time has passed since the rite of Bron Gloir and the dissolution of his damnable order. Yet if there are records to be found, they must either be here in this Vault or else in the ruins of Speur Dún [...]

I am tantalizingly close. I have translated every word of that moth-eaten tome of black magic, and I can only conclude that the Elixir recipe is incomplete. Thankfully, Duvarek's crude copies of the Speur Dún mural have helped illuminate the rite itself – there is little guesswork there, and they match the Bron Gloir mythology – but I am missing something. Some element of transmutation that is required for a Soulshaper, but different for a Soulwalker. I have experimented with several elements, but none have yielded a sensible concoction. Until I discover what that is, I am at an impasse. I hate to pause these feverish studies – I am so CLOSE! – yet I fear I must. Perhaps a renewed dedication to my calling will convince Odar of the righteousness of my endeavour, and then he will reveal the answer to me [...]

Ring-snake venom! Its properties are mutative. Arcane. Possibly keokum? Might be the catalyst to solving Bron Gloir's immortality spell. Needs testing [...]

I think I have it. The Elixir ... it resonates with the tone and timbre of deep magic. The venom was the key, as I suspected, yet it is still missing the final ingredient: the blood of a living human sacrifice.

I confess that I am vexed. I cannot proceed without imperilling my life. Even for the purpose of my studies – even to unlock the secrets of immortality – I cannot bring myself to complete the ritual until crisis and circumstance demand it. Instead, I must content myself with carrying an anelace prepared with the Elixir. In this way, I cannot be caught unawares when the need and opportunity arises. I have no doubt that both will, for why else would Odar curse me with the tainted blood of Terran and Ilumite lineage? It must be for the purpose of solving the riddle of the Elixir, in accordance with the will of the All-father [...]

Baron Harth has captured Duvarek, and Keyish confirms the Master of Shadows is enthralled to the baron's Rod of Compulsion. It seems I have underestimated the cripple ... but no matter.

I am sending Ainnevog to deal with the merchant. He has demonstrated his loyalty to the Academy by executing that fat pedlar, and he found and killed Kelga, whom I have searched for these many years. Avatars Fyunai and Kenton will accompany him, and the irony is not lost to me. Between the three of them, there is not a soul in Chaenbalu who is more wilful, nor one who is more capable of resisting the dark rod's influence. Myjun is the one exception to this, but she has not undergone the reaping. I will spare her from it for as long as I am able to deny the longings of her heart.

I only pray that her heart longs for the things that will keep her safe, for I cannot imagine losing Myjun as I lost Lana. I would damn the world itself and sell my own soul to Keos to protect my daughter [...]

— *Excerpts from Elder Tosan's journal*

Chapter Seventeen

After another easy day of walking and a few breaks for meals, Annev's company drew close to Luqura's city walls around the same time they'd established camp the previous night. This time Titus and Sraon took the first watch and Therin and Fyn were assigned second. In spite of Sraon's warnings about bandits roaming the hills, and perhaps because of his precautions, both watches passed without incident. Therin shook Annev awake for the third watch, and by the time Annev had extricated himself from his blanket and bedroll, the scrawny avatar had already dropped onto his bed and drifted off to sleep.

Annev shook his head in mild amusement then noticed Fyn standing awkwardly over the sleeping soothsayer. Annev hurried over, pulling on his cloak, and stopped next to the adolescent weaponsmaster.

'Trouble?'

Fyn inclined his chin towards Jian. 'He's an ugly one, ain't he?'

Annev frowned. 'It's not his fault, Fyn. People are born like that sometimes.'

'Yeah, and if he'd been born in our village, he wouldn't have lasted the week.' He sniffed. 'Strange to see folk like this – older folk who haven't been culled. Makes you wonder.'

'Wonder what?'

He lifted one hand. 'How much of what they taught us was true ...' He lifted the other. 'And how much was a lie? If people like *him* are wandering around – and he looks about as dangerous as Titus – then maybe there was never any cause to kill those people.' Fyn lowered his hands. 'You're some kind of exception, too, right? I mean, you're missing a hand. They should have killed you a long time ago ... but they didn't, and nothing bad really happened. You grew up with the rest of us, did the training and lived in the village. It's only these last few days that have been crazy. So, it makes me wonder.' He paused. 'Is that weird?'

'No, I don't think that's weird.'

Fyn nodded, satisfied. 'I never really liked the masters and ancients. I mean, I liked the structure – I liked knowing where I fit into things, and I liked being at the top of those things – but you were right to question what they taught us. I don't think any of us really felt good about it ... but what could you do?' He scratched his head. 'I guess, maybe I shouldn't have picked on you so much back then.'

'Fyn ... are you trying to apologise?'

The large boy sputtered, squared his shoulders, and snorted. '*Hell* no. You were a cocky prick and deserved every beating I gave you.' He snickered then turned thoughtful again. 'Nah, I was just thinking it will be different in the city. All the rules we had to follow at the Academy ... they don't apply here. People are different here – they *think* differently. It may take a while to find out where we fit in.'

Annev shrugged. 'I don't *care* if I fit in. I'll find my own way. Always do.'

'Yeah, you do.' Fyn looked over at Annev, squinting in the dark. 'Just don't go blowing things up the first week, all right? Give me time to get my feet wet.'

Annev smiled. 'No promises.'

'Damn.' He punched Annev in the shoulder. 'All right, I'm headed to bed.' He strode over to his bedroll and began tugging off his boots. 'You can wake whitey on your own, okay? His pink eyes give me the creeps.' He pulled the blankets up to his chin, then turned over.

Annev paced the camp for a minute, his gaze drifting between each of his slumbering companions before returning to rest on Fyn. The boy's chest rose and fell in imitation of sleep, and Annev found himself smiling, still finding it hard to believe he'd found an uneasy friendship with the former bully. His eyes slid away towards the walls and dim lights of the sleeping city. Flickering torches marked out the guards who patrolled the length of the wall, and a few small campfires burned just beyond the city's gates. Annev hoped Sraon had been wrong about bandits molesting the people at those fires, but it was impossible to tell in the dark. He didn't hear any screams, though, nor had Fyn mentioned any disturbances during his own watch, so he liked to think those people were sleeping safely, too.

Something shifted near his feet and Annev looked down to see Jian Nikloss rising from his bedroll. The Yomad blinked, his pink eyes reflecting the starlight. Annev nodded at him and he shuffled off his furs to stand with Annev in the pre-dawn light.

'We should move higher up this hill,' Annev said. 'Easier to survey the camp while keeping an eye on the road.' Jian remained silent, and they moved far enough away that they wouldn't disturb their sleeping party but close enough they could still keep a watchful eye on them. Annev's gaze shifted between the road they'd come in on, the parapets surrounding the city, and the darkness surrounding their camp.

'You should know that what you told your friend was wrong,' Jian said.

'Hm? You were awake?' Jian nodded and Annev gave a soft laugh at the revelation. 'What did I tell him? What did I get wrong?'

'You said that this' – Jian pointed to his white skin and pink eyes – 'was not my choice. That is not true.' The soothsayer ran a pale hand through his white hair and pulled out a clump, its fibres as brittle as straw. He turned the patch over in his hand then scattered it to the earth. 'I was not always death-touched. When I was closer to your age I had brown eyes, black hair, and dark brown skin. Things changed when I began using magic – my skin grew lighter, my eyes turned red and then pink.' He shrugged. 'This is what happens to Terrans who use magic, even New Terrans who worship the Younger Gods. We change in our skin. In our eyes. Sometimes in our blood and bones.'

'I ... hadn't known that – not before I met Dolyn. She has

a bit of brass on the back of her neck, but I didn't realise the connection.' *Marked by Keos*, Annev thought involuntarily, then banished the thought. 'Is it the same for everyone?'

'Among my people? No. I do not know precisely how it is for the other tribes, but in Terra Majora Seers with the blood-talent change quickly. White skin and changes in eye colour are normal – the most common red, white, and black – but the transformation can be more extreme.'

'Extreme how?'

Jian gave a sickly smile devoid of mirth. 'Necromancers manipulate the elemental, so their changes are more primal. They reflect their chosen forms. Bone-walkers look more skeletal. Flesh-walkers come to look like the dead they raise – scabrous and unclean.' He shuddered, eyes half-closed. 'When I must make the dead walk, I use only the recent dead who have transitioned peacefully. Nothing rotten. Nothing with decay. I do not deal with angry flesh or awaken spirits best left undisturbed.'

Annev frowned. 'Why are you telling me this, Jian?'

'Because I have travelled far to speak with you.'

'I thought you travelled south to find Red-thumb and Luathas?'

'I said I felt compelled to leave my homeland and seek answers. When I travelled south, I found the ranger and the Ilumani, and their goals aligned closely with mine, but the prophecies did not push me to find *them*. I sought the Vessel, the one bearing the Hand of Keos, because the spirits said he would bring change to my lands.'

Annev didn't like that at all. 'Well, I'm not sure what the spirits told you, but I'm not going to Terra Majora – wherever that is. There are lots of strange people looking for me – looking to *use* me – and I don't want any part of it.'

'Mm. Perhaps I am mistaken then.'

'But you don't think you are. You wouldn't travel across half a continent, or insist on travelling with us, if you weren't sure you were right.'

'Four continents, actually – Western Daroea, Eastern Daroea, Terra Minora, and Terra Majora. The world is a vast place, to be sure.'

'Wow. That is a ... long journey.'

'And you at the end of it. The Master of Sorrows, Vessel of Keos. Saviour and Destroyer. I would not have believed it if I had not seen you with my own eyes. Even yesterday at the market, I wasn't sure. Not until you showed me your golden hand.' He sighed, content. 'I hope to be there beside you when you scour the rot from my homeland. It will be a great day, truly.'

Annev grimaced, more uncomfortable now. 'I'm not scouring anything. In fact, I'm getting rid of this.' Annev raised his gloved hand. 'As soon as I find my contact in Luqura, I'm removing the cursed thing and then getting the hell away from all this prophecy crap.'

Jian's smile faltered. 'You will not help my people?'

Annev raised both his hands, helpless. 'Jian, I don't *know* your people.'

'This is why I tell you about them.'

Annev shook his head, more emphatic. 'They're strangers who live half a world away. I have no argument with them and no love for them, either. No reason to cross four continents to aid or destroy them. Even if I did, I don't *want* to.'

Jian seemed to think about this. Behind him, Annev could see the glow of the pre-dawn sun rising in the east.

'You are very much like Chade Thornbriar, I think. You will take your own path, but you will still arrive where Fate places you.'

Annev had a tight smile on his lips. 'No one is placing me anywhere. I'm my own person. Fate will figure that out eventually.'

'And if he does not? If he keeps meddling in your affairs?'

'Then I'll find out where Fate sleeps, break down his gates, and shove his shattered prophecies up his pretentious—'

Jian erupted with laughter. 'Yes, yes!' he said, still laughing. 'That is good, yes! Do that – haha – do that and we will see. We will see how Fate likes to have his arse paddled for a change. Haha, yes!'

Annev stared at the strange pale-skinned man, unsure where his laughter was directed. In the end, he supposed it didn't matter. He rubbed his jaw, felt the roughness growing there, and reminded

184

himself he'd have to look for a razor in Luqura. He glanced back over Jian's shoulder to see the first rays of dawn alight and prodded his companion.

'Come on. Time to wake the others. We'll see if Fate has any surprises for us in the capital.'

'Haha – and if it does, you will paddle it, yes? Heehee.'

'I guess we'll see, won't we.'

Chapter Eighteen

'That'll be one lunari—'

'What?!'

'—and six copper wheels.'

'That's preposterous. If I want to get robbed, I'll stay outside the walls.'

'Then stay outside the walls. Next!'

'Hold on now! It's a copper per family. I'm no foreigner. I know the laws.'

The guard at the gatehouse peered at Jian, who kept his face hidden in the shadows of his hood. He studied Titus's blond head and Fyn's dirty brown dreadlocks, then he glared at Sraon's swarthy skin. He shook his head. 'If you're a family, then I'm your uncle. Next!'

'*Hold* now!' Sraon shouted, less at the guard and more at the line of angry citizens edging to get by him. The blacksmith ignored the throng, though, pushing back on a lad of sixteen who tried to elbow past him. He reached the cart, tossed aside a bag of apples and stale bread, and pulled out his writ of slavery. 'I meant to say this here is my *property*,' Sraon said, waving the writ at the guard. 'That's what I meant to say – and if you go collecting slave taxes I'll fetch the Guild after you.'

The guard glanced at the writ then sniffed. 'Still a lunari for the wagon.'

'It's a half-empty apple cart! I'm here to *buy*, not sell, dammit.'

'Then pay your lunari and move on. Next!'

'Hold!' The blacksmith grumbled a bit then proceeded to count out the coin into his palm. 'Two silver staves ... and two shields.'

'Four shields.'

'Three.'

'Fine. Next!'

The guard snatched the coin from Sraon and their group squeezed through one of the smaller gates cut into the sally port of the eastern Merchant's Gate. A second guard brought the apple cart around to the main entrance, and the blacksmith was obliged to part with his fourth copper before the wagon and its contents were released to him.

'Bloody thieves, the lot of them.' He spat. 'How a farmer can afford to bring a wagon to market every morning, I'll never know.'

'I thought you said you'd been here before,' Fyn said, eyeing the mob with half suspicion, half awe.

'Aye, and every time it's a fight just to keep yer teeth.' He knuckled his eyepatch. 'Least they didn't tax us for the weapons. I've seen them pull that stunt before. Thieves and cut-throats, the lot of them. Come on. You don't wait around the gates unless you're lookin' to get pickpocketed.'

The group pushed their way along the main thoroughfare, occasionally stopping when the press threatened to separate them.

'Wow,' Therin said. 'I've never seen so many people in my life – and look what they're wearing!'

Annev was no less intrigued by the variety of clothing and the strange ornaments everyone seemed to be wearing on the hems and cuffs of their dresses, jackets and trousers. One woman wore plinking metal bells, while her companion sported clacking wooden balls. A man in a fitted beige suit wore what appeared to be tiny chimes, the slender metal tubes tinkling with music as he waved to a passing carriage. It was deafening, and Sraon tried to shoulder past the lot of them, his eyes fixed on the road ahead while his hands clutched tight to his coin purse and the mare's reins.

'Annev and Fyn, watch the wagon. Clobber anyone foolish enough to stick their hand inside. Master Nikloss, you might want to stow your travel pack and knapsack. They're likely to be cut from you otherwise.' As he said this, a small boy of about seven strolled boldly up to the opposite side of their cart, reached over the wall, and plucked a bag of food right out from under Therin's nose. Annev shouted a reproach and jumped over his side of the cart, but by the time he'd reached Therin, the urchin had disappeared into the crowd with their entire supply of bread and cheese.

'Sorry,' Therin said, looking sheepish. 'There was a woman with a snake – a big one, all brown and black and red. I swear you could see the shape of a *rat* inside it – big as my head! Never seen anything like it.'

'Stay focused!' Sraon boomed, eyes roaming the crowd. 'There'll be plenty o' ringers in the crowd – weird things, strange sights, folks with no clothes on. They're all distractions to help the street hustlers get their hands on your purse.'

'No clothes?' Therin said, eyes scanning the crowd once more. 'I missed that!'

'Focus!'

'Where are we headed?' Annev asked as they finally broke free of the main road.

'Reeve should be meeting us in the Old Low Quarter, near the southern riverside docks at a place called The Bottomless Cup. We'll bed down there. Not likely to draw a crowd till later this evenin', though, so I figure we can take care of Jian's errand first. We'll head south towards the High Quarter. Most of the nobility live there, so you've a better than even chance of finding your Sooted Rook gal over there.'

'Sodja Rocas,' Annev said, nodding. 'Makes sense. And if she agrees to go with Jian ...'

'Then they can make their way back to Banok without us. Debt paid, problem solved.'

'Fantastic.'

They turned down another cobblestone-studded street and moved in a southerly direction towards the Vosgar's piney foothills. A moment later, Fyn stepped up close to Annev, his tone low.

'Who is Sodja Rocas?'

Annev's eyebrows shot upward in surprise. 'You don't

remember? We met her at Janak's palace.' Fyn looked perplexed, and then Annev remembered. 'That's right! Your hearing was shot after you blasted Janak's wheelchair to pieces.' Fyn nodded, looking irritated. 'Do you remember the thief who stole the Rod of Compulsion?'

Fyn sniffed. ''Course. First time a girl has ever got the best of me.'

Annev tried not to roll his eyes at that – the witgirls had bested them all during the competition in the nave, after all – but he let the comment slide. 'That was Sodja, of the House of Rocas here in Luqura. She's *nobility*, Fyn. Her family is a few steps away from the throne.'

Fyn processed this. 'So why are we going to see her? To get that rod back?'

'Not exactly. Jian is trying to recruit her for some treasure-hunting quest Red-thumb is engineering.'

'Treasure, eh?' Fyn raised an eyebrow, intrigued. 'Why hasn't anyone talked to me about this?'

'Because it's not the gold and silver type of treasure – at least, I don't think it is. Red-thumb said something about ending the Silence of the Gods.' He shook his head. 'I've got enough problems with the Gods as it is. I'm not keen on waking any of them at the moment.'

'All right, so we're visiting Sodja.' He paused. 'And you think she'll be happy to see us? Annev, she practically knifed you the last time we saw her, and then she left you chained to a corpse – in a burning building, no less!' He chuckled at the memory then sobered. 'What happened there, anyway? Kenton was supposed to free you, but he tried to sell me some tripe about the roof collapsing and you being buried alive – or burned alive, I don't remember which. Seemed strange. I figured he just decided to off you.'

'Glad you were so concerned for me.' Annev looked around, ignoring Fyn's questions. 'So, what's your plan? How long are you sticking with us?'

Fyn sucked his teeth. 'This Sodja Rocas business sounds interesting. I wouldn't mind seeing her again, so long as it doesn't end with a knife in the ribs. I'll stay to see how it plays out.'

'So I can count on you if things get rough? To keep the knives out of my ribs?'

'Yeah, why not.'

The group walked the road dividing the Artisan and Merchant Quarters until it branched right. Instead of following the main road into the heart of the mercantile district, Sraon followed the wandering thoroughfare and then made a beeline for the wide river bisecting the city.

'Why are we going north?' Annev asked, still trying to orient himself to the city.

'We've got to cross the eastern river first.' Sraon gestured with his hands. 'This one is the North Tocra, which flows towards Quiri. If we had used the bridge on the main road, the fees would have been tremendous. A slight detour into the River Quarter makes the bridge taxes far more palatable, though. This is also where they store the boats for long-term docking.'

Annev nodded in understanding as the stench of fish guts grew thick in the air and the heavily ornamented outfits suddenly vanished, replaced by rough homespun and stained smocks. At the river bend, groups of workers laboured to load and unload cargo from skiffs, boats, and rafts. Sraon brought them to an area where still more workers were loading goods into carts and wagons, then he called a halt and began unloading the apple cart.

'Strap on your weapons and load your packs. We'll put the rest on the horse.'

'You're gonna leave the cart?'

'Yep. It's slowing us down, and we don't have licence to sell it. If we were caught trying to, the city guard would clap me in chains till I paid the fine – which, I'm sure, would be more than the value of the cart.'

'Then why bring it inside the city at all?' Annev asked, perplexed. 'You paid that guard a full moon just to take the wagon inside. We could have dumped it earlier and saved some coin.'

'Trust me, this was cheaper.'

'How?'

'Guards are under strict orders to keep the poor out. Come in with nought but the clothes in your pack and you'll be payin'' more than the rest. Tourism tax. City tax. Capital tax. Gate tax. Road tax.' He spat. 'Have a cart and they let most o' those slide.'

Annev scratched his jaw, the ways of the city still a mystery to him. 'But don't we want the cart?'

'Not once we get to the High Quarter. Only carriages allowed there – unless you've got a licence to vend.'

'Licence to vend?' Fyn swore. 'What's wrong with this place? Do I need a licence to spit?'

'No, but they'll fine you for doing it in the High Quarter – so mind your manners, each of you. If you behave like commoners, you'll end up with the riff-raff.'

'Riff-raff?' Therin asked, scratching his nose.

Sraon gestured at the many fragments of wood floating down-river. 'River rafts – riff-raff. Some folks use barges to transport goods short distances. If you wanted to skimp on hiring a boat, you could risk floating your goods on one o' those.' Annev stopped to watch as a group of labourers hauled some long splinters from the water's edge. 'I wouldn't gamble my life on it, though. Things of low quality have a tendency to get broken in this city.' As he said it, Annev noticed the river flotsam – torn burlap sacks, smaller fragments of lighter-coloured wood, and the horrible bloated bodies of the raft's former crew.

Sraon led them to one of the many footbridges spanning the river and began to haggle over the cost of the toll. Annev marvelled as, yet again, Sraon dipped into his purse. The toll man nodded when he'd received the proper number of clips, and then two rivermen blocking the entrance stepped aside, allowing Sraon to lead the mare and the boys across. They hurried after him, up the suspended walkway and over the rope bridge, its boards swaying beneath their feet. The mare seemed reluctant to cross, but Sraon was quick to place himself and Fyn on either side, shielding the animal's eyes from anything but the planks below. When they were halfway across, Titus pointed to the city's north-western horizon and they all stopped and stared at the scores of other bridges connecting over the flowing water. As he turned, Annev saw a second river that flowed away from the city, its current carrying goods west towards the ocean and south towards the lower half of the Empire. According to Sraon, a large canal had been dug between the two rivers, with a river lock and sluice set into it, allowing goods from one western-flowing river to be moved to the northern-flowing river and vice-versa – but Annev did not see it.

'Where's the lock?' Annev asked, squinting at the horizon. 'Aren't the rivers connected?'

Sraon chuckled. 'One detail I forgot to mention. The lock is *underground*. A few hundred years ago, they dug the canal between the Old Quarter and the Lower River District, but that pinched commerce on the streets, so eventually they sealed up the lock and laid roads over the top of it.'

'You mean,' Therin said, eyes widening, 'there's a whole underground canal *right under* those streets?'

'Aye.'

'Big enough for boats to sail through? Even galleons?'

Sraon quirked an eyebrow. 'I doubt you could tell a galleon from a galley – but if the latter were short-masted … aye. There's a whole network of tunnels beneath the capital that's built for commerce. Regular folk don't use it – just the wealthy who can afford the service routes, plus a few bandits who abuse the system – but the canal is part of that. Everyone else travels above ground, and that includes us.'

'And *this* is the North Tocra,' Annev said, pointing at the river flowing beneath their bridge, 'and the far river is the South Tocra?'

Sraon nodded. 'Those are Luqura's greatest assets. Everyone pays to ferry goods upriver to the city, and the two rivers carry everything away. That's why they say, "Gold flows into Luqura and water flows out."'

Annev took it all in, whistling at the complexity of the operation, and then the toll man behind them shouted to move along lest they overburden his bridge. The group did so, and the scene on the west bank was similar to what they'd seen on the other side, with the hustle and bustle of rivermen going about their labours. They veered south and Annev watched as signs of economic disparity once again distinguished the boundaries of the neighbourhoods, with the labourers from the River District on their right and the wealthier citizens from Merchant Quarter on their left. When they reached a grand plaza at the very heart of the city, Sraon led them into the winding streets of the Merchant Quarter and the group began its slow climb towards the noble houses at the southern edge of the city. As they walked, the quality of the men's smocks became sturdier. The women's dresses became finer. The paint on the buildings seemed fresher. Even the streets looked cleaner.

'We're approaching the High Quarter,' Sraon said, nodding to the manicured trees that began to dot the sides of the streets. 'There'll be fewer workmen and more guards here, so pay less attention to your purse, and mind your feet and your tongue. Step outta the way o' the carriages, but try to stay off the footpaths. Those are for nobility to stroll on.' He gestured to the road. 'Stick to the gutter, keep your heads down and your eyes forward. No one should bother us till we get farther along. Although ...' He paused. 'Master Nikloss, would you mind riding the mare for a bit? Means fewer boots clogging the road. Therin, you can take the reins.'

They all did as Sraon instructed, with the blacksmith leading the group and Fyn and Annev trailing at the back. Titus followed close behind Sraon, his hands clutching the edge of his light-ning-embossed battle buckler, his knuckles white. Therin and Jian walked in the middle of the procession, the former with his eyes swivelling all around him, the latter riding with his head and face hidden by his grey hooded robes.

'Where'd all the common people go?' Therin asked quietly, after they'd walked for perhaps a mile. 'All the vendors and the beggars. They disappeared back at that last street. Like a wall kept them moving any farther west.'

'Those funny ornaments are back, too,' Fyn noted.

'We just entered the High Quarter,' Sraon explained, head swivelling to watch the sides of the road. 'Any beggars caught here are imprisoned as thieves – unless the guard's of a mind to let them go, in which case he'll beat them and drop them in the river.'

Therin's face was solemn. 'Is it dangerous for us to be here?'

'Yes.'

'Then why *are* we here?'

'Because with his fair skin and hood up, riding the mare, Master Nikloss passes for a low-born noblewoman – which, I suppose, means I should be callin' her *Mistress* Nikloss. You and Titus are her pages, and Masters Fyn and Annev look like sellswords I've hired with the bit o' coin she's paid me to keep her safe. Someone stops us, we stick to that story. Jian needn't speak – that's what she's hired me for – and the upshot is we needn't walk in the gutter. If we're stopped we can ask directions to the Rocas Estate. Tell 'em we're acquaintances of Lady Sodja. That should be enough for any reasonable guard.' He eyed Titus. 'That buckler's outta place, though, lad. Pass it here. I'll keep it safe till we get to the Low Quarter.'

They marched along for perhaps another mile, stepping aside only once as a carriage bumped along the road and threatened to spook the mare. Therin kept a tight grip on the reins, though, and they trotted farther into the heart of the High Quarter. They entered a spacious plaza with an ornately sculpted water fountain at its centre, and Sraon paused to get his bearings. A few dozen paces away, a dandy in a puffed collar strummed a lute for a lady with pearls dangling at the hem of her colourful silk dress. On the opposite side of the fountain, a man with a bald head and oiled moustache wore a fantastically embroidered vest and extolled the superior quality of his three Ilumite slaves – all of whom he described as adept performers, contortionists, dancers, and singers.

'The passion of Lumea flows through them like sunlight brought to life by the master jeweller's ruby. No common slave is their equal. No simple courtesan can match their grace or beauty. Hear them – *see* them. Let their song kindle a flame in your heart and their touch fill your loins with fire!' He smiled at a nobleman who stopped to examine the youngest of the three performers. 'A good eye, sir. Very good eye. Do you own a concubine, milord? No? Ah, you cannot know true passion until you've felt the joy of bedding an Ilumite savage.'

'Right then,' Sraon whispered, ignoring the slaver's banter. 'The road opposite the water lilies leads to King Lenka's palace. A few of the grander noble houses lie down that way, too – big, fat estates with acres o' land – but the rest have smaller mansions down these side roads.' Sraon looked between Annev and Jian. 'Any notion as to the wealth or influence of this Lady Sodja?'

'That is not known to me, Master Cheng,' Jian said, raising his hooded face to peer at the one-eyed blacksmith. 'But I suspect your friend will know. He approaches now.' Jian lowered his face again and they all turned to see the slaver circling the fountain, whose eyes lit up when he recognised Sraon.

'Lord *Cheng*? But this is unprecedented! What are you doing here in Luqura?'

Sraon started, then laughed aloud. 'Farthinand Caldaren, you old rascal! How is it *you* are here? Last I heard, you were trying to woo one of my cousins. A fat one. Emeralda, yes?'

The moustachioed slaver laughed, one finger twisting his curled moustache while the other patted his forehead with a scented handkerchief. 'That was an age ago, Sraon! Where have you been? I settled for some low-hanging fruit – a Luquran woman wanting to expand her family's interest on the Isle. Much prettier, too – and a wild cat in the sack. Hoo-hoo!' He raised his voice. 'But none so passionate as the Ilumites you see before you! Now, madame. Do not be shy! Take a good hold of that glute. You see? Firm, strong. He will entertain you and your daughters, I guarantee! Stamina for days. Strong fingers from harping. He comes with sterilisation papers. Well-healed, mind, so you can start the moment you get— No? Very well. Perhaps another time, milady.' He waited for the older woman and her manservant to pass out of earshot then turned back to Sraon.

'So, what brings you to Luqura? Where have you been all this time? Not still playing pack-mule to that heretic, are you?'

'No, no. I opened a smithy in Banok some time back, then moved south when business got too competitive. You know me. Never one for conflict.'

Farthinand laughed at this, a deep, throaty bellow that shook his embroidered vest, exposing his brown nipples. 'Sraon, you bring conflict with you like it's in demand at the market.' He shook his head, moustache flailing. 'You should come back north. I know some folk who'd be happy to see you.'

'And a lot more who'd be happier not to, I'd wager.'

'Eh, true enough. The Illustrious King Cheng, Fourth of His Name was a solid prick, though. King Cheng the Fifth is proving a sight more magnanimous. He's opened more trade with the southern lands and expanded our interests in the north. The people love it. Gold runs through Innistiul like spoutwater after a thunderstorm. You'd do well there, Sraon. And you're not far from the throne yourself.'

'Enough,' Sraon said, abruptly raising his hand. 'You know why I left.' He glanced sideways in Annev's direction. 'In any case, I'm not looking to re-establish old friendships – present company excluded. I'm looking for the Rocas Household.' Sraon jerked a thumb at Jian who sat primly atop the black mare, his posture perfectly suited to the role of a low-born noblewoman. 'Mistress Nikloss has some business with one of its members – a young lady named Sodja.'

'Ah, you'll want to see Matron Tiana then. Down the King's Road half a hike. You'll know it by the cherry trees – it's the only estate that has them. Be careful, though.' He lowered his voice so Annev had to lean close to hear. 'Tiana has her hand wrapped good and tight 'round King Lenka's balls, so don't piss her off. You remember Phoeba Anabo? The dark-haired lass who made eyes at you whenever you came to court?'

'Aye,' Sraon said, looking uncomfortable. 'I remember her.'

'Well, King Cheng made Miss Anabo the consul to King Lenka five years back, and now she runs most of the legitimate slave trade here in Luqura – along with the Rocas family – so don't step on any toes.'

'I'll keep that in mind.' Sraon winked with his one eye. 'Thank you, Frani. You've always had my back.'

'Of course! No matter how the winds are blowing, you can always count on Frani as a friend. When your business is finished, you should come visit my home in the Merchant's Quarter. Meet my wife, Magatha.' He patted Sraon on the back, leaned in close, and whispered a joke that got a chuckle from the olive-skinned blacksmith. They shook hands then, grasping wrists, and parted ways.

'Old friend?' Annev asked once they had passed the sculpture of the merfolk dancing in the water fountain.

'Aye. I knew Frani in the old days, before I was old enough to shave. Time was we were closer than family. Blood brothers and the like. Different paths, though.'

'Did he say you're a relation of the king ...?'

The blacksmith sniffed. 'Distant relation, and no love lost there.' He chewed his lip. 'Whatever politics has the Chengs invested in Luqura doesn't concern me, nor are they likely to welcome my sudden appearance, so keep your knowledge to yourself. Call me Sraon Smith. Safer that way.'

They proceeded down the King's Road, making sure to stay out of the path of a group of high-born noblewomen and their entourage. A half mile farther on and they passed a pair of guards who nodded curtly at Sraon but did not stop them. Tall houses gave way to lush gardens and fragrant orchards. Painted gates tipped with sharp metal stakes formed along the walkways, and the cobblestone road transitioned to patterned brickwork. Far ahead, a few miles closer to the Vosgar's hills, a shining castle rose atop a cliff facing the final bend in the river.

'King Lenka's palace,' Sraon said, knuckling his forehead. 'Jewel of Greater Luqura. Crossroads of the Empire.' He chuckled. 'Technically, the Crossroads are that underground canal you couldn't see – or maybe that dirty plaza at the edge of the Merchant Quarter ... but noble folk don't like to be reminded of that. This' – he swept his hand at the cliffside castle – 'is a much grander image.'

'Cherry blossoms,' Annev said, pointing at a gated orchard between the South Tocra and the King's Road. Tiny flowers floated in the wind, carried by the breeze and the promise of spring. The blossoms cycled down to the road and spiralled pink and proud around the legs of the mare.

Annev spotted the silhouette of a crow every hundred paces, its image cut into the iron posts marking the estate. Another half mile and the brickwork lining the road swept to the side to open a passage through the gated orchard and towards the mansion. Sraon cleared his throat.

'All right, Master Nikloss. You think you can manage your own affairs from here?'

'Once I have met Lady Rocas, yes. Till then, your assistance is still appreciated.'

'Right then.' Sraon touched his collar, rubbing his neck. 'Titus, lad. Why don't you take back your buckler, just till we finish our business. Stay alert, eyes forward.'

They approached the mansion, the cherry blossoms swirling around them like a fragrant whirlwind. The mare's hooves clattered on the stones as they passed between the blooming trees. Acres of them – acres and acres, stretching around the mansion and filling the wide orchard with their swirling petals.

Somewhere nearby, a gong tolled, its tone long, low and flat. The blossoms seemed to part just then, and the mansion's front gate came into view.

And then they were there, standing at the entrance to the fortified mansion, its front door just a stone's throw beyond an iron gate. They all stared dumbly at the crow's profile in the metal, and then Sraon raised a hand to knock. It rang out, soft and hollow – impotent. He knocked again, more loudly. Again, the sound died in the wind. He cleared his throat.

'Hullo!' He rapped a third time. 'Hullo, is—'

The gong rang out a second time, its sonorous *bong* seeming much closer. This time when it died, though, a voice rose up to replace it.

'What is it? Who is this? Pyodr, are you expecting guests?' The voice was nasal, low-pitched, and had a whine to it that set Annev's teeth on edge. 'Pyodr!' the woman shouted. 'Are you expecting guests!'

'No!' This from the house – a voice that, though male, had a higher pitch than his female counterpart.

'What?'

'NO!'

'Well, send the bloody manservant to answer the—'

The door swung open, revealing a stout nobleman in a stained waistcoat and black trousers. He squinted at the sight of them then shouted at the air: 'Daunia! What is this?' He turned back to them.

'Who are you? Are you with the Slaver's Guild?' The man cupped a hand to his mouth and shouted into the orchard. 'Daunia! We have guests!'

'Well, who is it?' A pinch-faced woman in a black dress appeared in a swirl of cherry blossoms. She clutched the side of the house as though out of breath. 'What's this all about?' she screeched, as if offended by their mere presence. 'You're not here to make a withdrawal, are you? I've told them a hundred times, if you need to make a withdrawal, you have to schedule it with Tiana – or Ketrit, if you can't get a hold of her. It's not like we keep the keys hanging on a hook, or the ledger on a pedestal in the lobby.' She eyed the group, her nose scrunched as if she couldn't bear the smell of them.

'We are not with the Guild,' Sraon said, speaking loud enough for both man and woman to hear him, 'nor are we here to make a ... withdrawal.' His head swivelled between the fat man and the fatter woman. 'Whom do I have the pleasure of addressing?'

The obese woman – Daunia – scowled, her creased face looking even more sour. Meanwhile, Pyodr flashed a white smile, though its warmth never reached his eyes. He snapped his fingers and a young woman appeared from behind him, a set of keys jangling in her hands. As the maidservant went to unlock the gate, Pyodr stepped forward, hand extended, then he folded the same arm in front of his chest and gave a slight bow.

'Pyodr Saevor.' He spoke with a slight accent, his lips puckered slightly as he spoke. 'And you are?'

'Sraon Smith.' The blacksmith bowed as the gate swung inward. 'My patron,' he gestured to Jian, who still rode the mare, 'wishes an audience with the Lady Rocas. Is she at home?'

The fat woman fluttered forward. 'You cannot simply come here and expect to be received! Who is your patron? Where are the guards? Get out of here!'

'Oh hush, Daunia. They're here, aren't they? They've announced themselves, haven't they? Stop acting like you're some godsdamned lady of the house.' Pyodr waved to them. 'Come in, please. Ignore my wife – she's supposed to be *on her walk*!' He shouted this last bit with his hand cupped to his mouth, his words entirely for the sour woman's benefit.

'Like hell I am!' Daunia trotted forward, her arms paddling in front of her, as if she were swimming through the blossoms. 'These rotting cherry trees,' she said, spitting at the petals. 'I'd rip them out if they hadn't been so bloody expensive to transport here.'

'You touch a branch of those trees and Tiana will flay the skin from your arse.' He nodded curtly at Sraon, his tight smile never leaving his mouth. 'You have business with Matron Tiana? She is expecting you?'

'Not exactly, no.' Sraon stared at the open gate, as though unsure he wanted to enter. 'Truth be told, we're here to see the *young* Lady Rocas – Lady Sodja.'

'Sodja?' Pyodr repeated the name as though he'd never heard it before. He turned to his wife, his beady eyes turning shrewd. 'Daunia,' he said, sickeningly sweet, 'when was the last time you saw the Lady Sodja?'

Daunia sputtered, something that was half laughter, half offended choking. '*Sodja?*' She spoke as if the name held some hidden meaning. 'Why, I'm not sure, Pyodr.' She stopped beside the servant at the gate, her wide body now blocking the path between the open gate and the mansion. She eyed the group, her piggy eyes scrutinising Jian. 'I haven't seen Sodja in *ages*, Pyodr. In fact, we've been looking for her, haven't we?'

'I should say so,' Pyodr said, trotting over to stand behind his wife. 'Been looking for months.' He tucked his thumbs into his waistcoat. 'Been worried something awful for her. Have you seen her in any of that time?'

Annev sensed a hint of a threat in that question. Sraon seemed to sense it, too, for he glanced briefly at Annev and Jian before shaking his head. 'No, I'm afraid we haven't. My patron had hoped to find her here. Some business we were hoping to discuss.'

'Ha.' Daunia turned on her heel and tromped into the house. 'If you've got a grievance with that bitch, you can get in line!' She slammed the door, leaving Pyodr and the serving woman outside. Mr Saevor snorted as the young woman went to unlock the front door.

'Do forgive my wife,' Pyodr said through clenched teeth. 'She comes from the old blood,' he said, raising his voice again to be sure she heard it, 'and it tends to sour with age.' He glanced over his shoulder, peering first at the door then up at the mansion's second-floor window. Annev followed his gaze and spotted a dark figure standing there, shrouded behind a gauzy grey curtain.

Pyodr turned back, pretending not to have noticed it. 'If you do happen to cross paths with Lady Sodja, we would be extremely grateful to know her whereabouts. Her mother has been desperate to speak with her about a matter of some urgency.' He licked his lips, eyes shifting between the members of the party. 'There's, uh ...' He coughed, clearing his throat. 'If you could see your way clear to bringing the young woman home, Matron Tiana has promised a substantial reward.' He spoke this last bit as if from a script, not a trace of emotion or tenderness. Then he smiled again. 'Good day.'

And before Sraon could respond, the man slammed the gate shut, flitted up the steps to the front door and disappeared inside along with the servant. A heartbeat later, the door closed behind him, the bolt turning in the lock with an audible *click*.

Chapter Nineteen

'I'm sorry, Master Nikloss,' Sraon said as they returned to the King's Road. 'It is an unsatisfying way to repay a life debt, but I see no other way we can help you.'

'You do not see another way,' Jian said, 'because the future is not a stone – fixed, immovable. Instead, it is a river. Its direction is known, its course is set, but the path it takes changes as we step into its waters.'

'That's not what you told me on the road yesterday,' Annev said, walking alongside Jian and the mare. 'You said a man can't outrun his destiny.'

'Indeed,' Jian said, pulling back his hood to let his bowl-cut hair blow in the wind while there were no guards in sight. 'Fate often finds us on the road we take to avoid it.'

'So which is it? Was today's fate unavoidable? Should we have stayed away from the Rocas Estate?'

'No. Fate led us here, and he will lead Sodja Rocas to us – to you.' He gestured to Annev and the others. 'I will ride with you until she reveals her face to me. Then I will invite her to join Red-thumb's quest and she will agree.'

'Why?'

'Because she must. Because her fate is tied to the Ilumani and their purposes align. Because her fate is tied to you and your companions.'

Annev looked at Sraon, suspicious. 'Which means our fates are also tied to Red-thumb's quest?'

Both of Jian's pale eyebrows lifted. 'Of course. It has always been so, or have you not noticed? The coin you gave Red-thumb. The life debt owed to me and Master Corentin. This journey to Luqura.' He gestured to the estates lining the King's Road. 'All of this is fated.'

'All right,' Fyn said, stepping forward to join the conversation. 'All I'm hearing is a lot of chatter when we've wasted half the day and the blacksmith has been spending our coin like water on wash day. I said I'd play along till we met up with this Sodja, but that doesn't appear to be happening, so ...' He pointed at Sraon. 'You said you knew people who would pay for our avatar skills. Well, from the looks of things Luqura is full of money, and I haven't seen a copper clip of it, excepting what you've been spending.' He hiked up his weapons belt. 'Now, are you going to deliver on your promise, or do we need to part ways so I can find work myself?'

Sraon swivelled his head, his one eye glinting. 'I'll hold to my end of the bargain, Master Fyn, but if you'd like to leave now and take your chances against the city, you're welcome to do so. You may have noticed it's got some strange customs? Easy to run afoul of the law, for misunderstandings to turn into crimes – with quite dire consequences.'

'I don't plan to run afoul of the law *accidentally*—'

Sraon bared his teeth in a wolf's grin. 'Then there's an entire underbelly to Luqura with its own codices you may need to study. The Beggars' Guild, Thieves' Guild, Assassins' Guild. Even the whores have a union, though I doubt you'd be looking for that kind of work.'

'And what would you know about any of that?'

Sraon scratched the socket beneath his eyepatch, still grinning. 'Times were that slavery in Luqura was a mean affair. The men of Innistiul sold their goods on the Black Market, in the slums beneath the city. So we *knew* the dark side of Luqura. Since then, some of it has moved above ground ... but not all of it.'

Fyn seemed mollified by the explanation. 'Well, I'll stay close to you then – but I want to meet some of these people soon. Today.'

Sraon was already watching the road again. 'Won't take us long to get back to the River District. From there, it's a straight shot to the Low Quarter and the Ash Quarter.'

'Ash Quarter?' Therin spoke up. 'What's that?'

The blacksmith paused in the road and slashed his finger in the air, drawing lines out of nothing. 'This is the High Quarter, right? Ain't nothin' out here but the nobility and the king's castle. Above that you've got the Merchant's Quarter and the Open Market. Circumscribing most o' that is the River Quarter, but that's divided up into the Upper River District and the Lower River District. Most of it is reputable – riverboat captains, labourers and the like usually have their homes in the Lower River District. You get too far from these foothills, though, and you end up in the Low Quarter.'

'Is that the northern or western edge of the city?'

'Both, I suppose. New Low Quarter is in the north, but it's mostly full of low nobles and the likes. The Old Low Quarter covers the western side o' the city. Runs right up to the canal, so lots of sailors like to dock there. Cheap lodging. Guards aren't too keen on breaking up the fights either, so they mostly let the locals sort it out.'

'Sounds like my kind of place,' Fyn said, eyes full of mischief.

'Aye, I thought so too. Easy enough to find work in the Low Quarter, especially if you've got special talents and you're not picky about the type o' work.'

'So what's the Ash Quarter?' Therin said, piping up again. 'Is that the worst of the lot?'

Sraon nodded then beckoned them onward, setting the pace for the rest of the group. 'A terrible fire rolled through the Old Low Quarter a century ago. Lots of warehouses were burned, several thousand died. The city washed their hands of it. Said it was too expensive to rebuild. Too dangerous – meaning it was too dangerous for merchants and nobles. For the common folk, it was open land – the whole lot rent- and tax-free, which is saying a lot in Luqura. The poor fled there in droves. Packed the place in tight. But it's filthy, dangerous, lawless. You go there, you're taking your life in your hands.'

'So that *is* the worst of the lot.'

Sraon held up a finger. 'Deep inside the Ash Quarter, at its heart, you'll find the place where they dumped all those burned bodies – the Boneyard. *That's* the worst o' the lot. There were too many folk to bury and not enough incentive to do so, so they heaped 'em up. Turned one whole city block into a charnel house. No sane person would live there, so the insane chose to make it their home. You know the type – the *real* criminals. Not the rogues who form guilds and make laws about whose purse you can cut. I mean the real sadists. The cut-throats, the necrophiles, the witches, and the mad men.' He shook his head. 'You go to the Boneyard, it's because you have no choice. You go because someone or something is *making* you go there.' He shuddered. 'If you know what's good for you, you'll stay well away, lads. Stay away from the Ash Quarter, and don't go anywhere near the Boneyard.'

Titus looked to Annev, his face pale. 'I wish Master Brayan were here with us.'

'Aye, lads. He was good to have watching your back – but so is Master Fyn here, and Master Annev, and I'm no slouch myself.' He sighed. 'Anyhow, we're headed just west o' the Upper River District. A fine establishment called The Bottomless Cup.'

'You've been there before?' Fyn asked, eyes flinty.

'Well, no, but old Farmer Gribble spoke of it often. Said we should ask for a man named Tukas. And if everything went according to our plan, Tukas will have sent on ahead to Quiri to fetch Reeve.'

'Right,' Fyn said. 'That friend of the priest Annev is supposed to meet.'

'A friend of *Sodar's*,' Sraon corrected, holding up a hand to forestall Annev's own interruption. 'Aye, and Reeve is another priest – of sorts. He knows some Darite magic.'

'You mean his magic doesn't come from artifacts?' Titus said, eyes wide. 'He's a real wizard? Like the ones you hear about in the stories?'

Sraon chuckled. 'Sodar was a real wizard, too, Titus – just like the stories.'

'I guess he was but I ... I never thought of him like that.'

'Exactly as Brother Sodar liked it. This other fellow, though – Reeve – he's somethin' else. To hear Sodar tell it, he's a celebrity amidst the Order. Said he's got more magic than any three brothers combined – though I suppose that's to be expected of a high priest.'

'So Reeve is the head of Sodar's brotherhood?' Titus asked. 'No one is higher than him?'

'No one save Odar himself, an' good luck talkin' to him.' The smith smiled. 'I've met Reeve once or twice. Nice enough fellow. Not as good as Sodar, mind, but he's a clever sort. Knows his way about the world, as they say. Not the most sociable though – at least not when I lived in Quiri.'

'I know of this Reeve,' Jian said, nodding. 'He is known to Master Red-thumb as well. I am certain he will want to speak with him.'

'Beggin' your pardon, Master Nikloss, but wanting ain't the same as doin'. Dionach Reeve is a busy man. He won't have time for your eccentric treasure hunts.'

'As you say, Master Cheng, but Fate has a way of changing our priorities. To end the Silence of the Gods will require a servant of each God, one blessed with their full favour.' He pointed to himself. 'Like me. I am a Marrow-Lich – a Seer *and* a Necromancer. Not common among my people, but necessary to achieve Fate's designs. Master Corentin is a Shaman – a Beastmaster *and* a Skinchanger – also rare among his people. And the Lady Sodja, she too is special. Kroseran by birth. A servant of Dorchnok. She possesses the skills of a Shadowcaster and the very rare talent of the Voidweavers. The latter has been extinct in Krosera for centuries. Only by visiting this distant branch could Red-thumb find his Dark Lady – the Sooted Rook.'

Annev and Fyn glanced at each other uneasily. They had seen Sodja in Janak's palace – a lithe woman dressed in grey and black, her clothing cut to look ragged despite the expensive fabric. She had reminded Annev of Oyru in the way she moved and dressed – but the similarities had ended there. Had she possessed shadow magic like the assassin? Annev didn't think so, or at least, he didn't recall seeing her use any in Janak's study. Her skills in combat and skullduggery had been such that she'd stolen the Rod of Compulsion from Fyn and neutralised Annev without resorting to any kind of arcane magic.

But she did lock that manacle around my arm, Annev thought, remembering how he had lost his first prosthetic. *And it wouldn't have locked unless she used magic.*

'Jian,' Annev looked at Fyn, 'you're saying Sodja Rocas has shadow magic, yes?'

'Certainly, Master Ainnevog.'

'Does that mean her family possesses magic? Those people at the mansion. They didn't seem ...'

Jian's lips pursed into the bud of a smile. 'Sodja's mother has a dormant strain of Voidweaver magic – laid silent by the incestuous inbreeding of the Saevor family. Sodja's father, though. He carries the Shadowcaster blood, strong and vibrant. When the two mixed, it reawakened the old magic. I suspect Sodja's siblings will have the same blood-talent, but I would have to taste them to know for certain.'

'Taste them?' Titus asked, looking sick.

'Their blood, yes.' Jian said, as if this did not require any explanation, and pulled up his hood.

Fyn stepped up to Annev's shoulder and whispered, 'Don't look now, but we're being followed. Something – someone – has been trailing us through the orchards.'

Annev fought the urge to turn his head. 'How long?'

'Since we left the estate.' Fyn gestured at the row of cherry trees marking the end of the Rocas Estate. 'A puff of blossoms goes up, like something is throwing them in the air. Maybe running between the trees. Maybe jumping.'

Annev felt sheepish not to have noticed it himself. 'Where are they right now?'

'About parallel with us. I think he or she aims to pass us, without being noticed. Keep an eye on that west orchard.'

Annev did so, his eyes straining to peer sideways at the long rows of blooming peach trees that filled the next noble family's orchard. At first he didn't see anything, but as they moved past some flowering fruit trees, Annev spotted a glimmer of green and brown rushing between the trunks of the orchard, its movement marked by the delicate puff of falling peach blossoms. He turned his head towards the movement, but as soon as he did, it stopped.

'There,' Annev said, his voice low. 'I can't see it, though.'

They kept walking, Therin trying to scare Titus with the imagined horrors they might encounter in the Low Quarter. Sraon punctuated the increasingly wild speculations with the reminder that the Ash Quarter and the Boneyard were in the northwestern corner of the city, whereas The Bottomless Cup lay to the south – but Therin paid him no mind, describing charred ghouls, soot-blackened cannibals, and blood-spattered necromancers. Sraon cleared his throat at this last part, and it took Therin a moment to realise Jian was smiling down at them from his horse, his pink eyes shining with silent amusement.

'I ... uh.' Therin looked around for help but didn't find any. Finally, Jian saved him.

'You are right to fear the Necromancer, Avatar Therin, for those that deal in death rarely value life.'

'But, um, aren't you ...'

'A necromancer, yes.'

'But you don't, uh ... you're not that scary. I mean, you do *look* scary. Pale skin. Pink eyes. It's creepy enough, right? But you don't, uh ... You just seem ... I don't know.'

Jian nodded. 'And if my mouth were covered in blood? Or a host of the undead followed, slaves eager to serve me, would you fear me then?'

'Uh ...'

'Yes, I think you would – I *know* you would. Now understand, Avatar Therin, that I value life and death equally. I do not spend life easily, nor do I lightly call upon those who have passed over to the Realm of Spirits. Life and death should both be respected.'

Annev had one ear on the conversation while he watched for puffs of peach blossoms in the orchard to his left. He was fairly certain their tail was now ahead of them, for he no longer saw the fluttering petals. The estates they were passing had begun to diminish in size and scope, and the brickwork road had transitioned back to cobblestones. Carriages had started to pass on either side of the road, and the city guard patrols had begun to give the group more careful inspections. Jian pulled his hood close, once again taking on the role of a noblewoman with her retinue. They had almost reached the plaza with the merfolk fountain when they were finally challenged, not by the city guard, but by a fat man wearing an open leather vest, its pockets festooned with heavy gold chains and oversized jewels. More than one chain snaked up from the man's pierced nipples, their opposite ends tethered to his studded nose and bottom lip.

'What is this rabble with an Ilumani slave on horseback?' The man shouted, waving his naked arms to gather the attention of both the nobility and the guard. 'Rebels – no doubt! See how they hide their faces. How they carry their weapons in defiance of custom and conduct!'

Annev frowned, noting that the speaker was himself wearing a sheathed scimitar and a pair of ornamental daggers. The man opened his vest wide, fingering the hilt of one dagger while his thumb stroked the chain piercing his flesh. Annev wondered how he could hope to defend himself with such piercings, but then he noticed the caravan of warriors forming up behind the speaker and knew they would answer any calls for violence. Like the chain-pierced warrior, these men were large, heavily muscled and carried scimitars of their own, but they were unencumbered by decorative piercings and chains of office. Instead, their swarthy skin was tattooed and their right shoulders were branded with the marks of their house and trade: a feral cat and a double-masted sailing vessel.

Sraon stepped forward, his face dark as a storm cloud. 'You *dare* to call the Royal House of Cheng a rabble?' he barked. 'On your knees, slaver!'

The chain-festooned man hesitated. 'I beg your pardon?'

'You may not have it – on your *knees!*' Sraon spun, grabbed the hilt of the man's scimitar and unsheathed the weapon in one fluid motion. The guards that had been racing to answer their master's summons came to an uncertain halt.

'This man has insulted the Royal House of Cheng. I demand an apology or I shall take his tongue.'

The city guards looked at one another, as if convinced they

were standing in front of a madman. The Innistiul soldiers, however, seemed unsurprised by Sraon's demand. Not one moved to unsheathe their swords.

'Your lordship,' said one of the guards, 'not all of Innistiul's customs are honoured here. If you have a grievance with this man, you must take it up with the high judge or one of the local magistrates.'

'Or the consulate,' Sraon said, straightening. 'As this is a matter between slaving houses, Consul Anabo may resolve our dispute.'

'That would be ... acceptable.'

'Unless this man would like to apologise for his insult and withdraw his accusation. Then he can keep his tongue and we can be on our way.'

The slave captain sputtered. 'Do you even know who I am? Why—'

'Elar Kranak, Second Dan, Noble Lord of Innistiul.'

The slaver's mouth dropped open. 'I ... How do you know that?'

'I am Sraon Cheng, First Dan, Archon of Innistiul.' He tapped the scimitar to the man's jaw. 'Now, on your knees and apologise, or I'll send these guards for the Lady Consul – and you know how that will go.' Sraon stuck out his tongue and bit it. Elar paled and fell to his knees.

'I am sorry, ah ... Archon Cheng. Forgive me. I was told you were another.' He glanced at Jian who still sat ahorse, eyes trained on the ground. 'This ... foreigner you escort. May I ask—'

'You may not.' Sraon threw the scimitar to the cobblestones in front of Elar. 'I accept your apology and expect your tribute to make its way to our coffers. I will let Magistrate Bliven know to expect it. Ten solari should be sufficient.'

Elar paused, halfway to his feet. 'Ah ... yes. Of course, Archon Cheng. Very gracious.'

Sraon moved past the man, flicking the gold chain attached to his left nipple and nostril. The slaver hissed in pain but said nothing, and the rest of the party followed Sraon through the plaza and then the Upper River District in silence.

Chapter Twenty

Myjun woke to find Oyru kneeling at her side, a mass of bloody black bandages heaped beside her. 'Where am I?' she hissed, the mask seizing her emotions before she was fully conscious.

'South of the Brakewood. About a mile outside a town named Hentingsfort.'

'The Brakewood,' Myjun growled. 'I was in the Vosgar ... west.'

'You were. And now you are here.'

'But ... the draken?'

'A good question. I found your knife – what was left of it – but I do not think you killed the monster with it. Something else.'

'It's dead then.' She tried to relax and found the pain was too great. She forced herself to stand instead, and though it pained her more, she felt stronger for it.

She thought of the blood drake, its snapping jaws clamping down and savaging her. She touched her belly and was momentarily surprised to find no scars, no sign of the damage the beast had done to her. 'I killed it,' she whispered.

'Yes.'

'And it ... killed me.'

'Almost.' Oyru stood. 'The mask attempted to heal you, but the injuries were too great and its magic too slow. Your spirit entered the Shadowrealm and was prepared to move on to the World of Spirits. Instead, I brought your physical body to the Shadowrealm to reunite the two, and then I brought you back to the Physical Realm. Whole. Complete.'

'How is that possible?'

Oyru's finger caressed her golden brow and temple. 'The mask's power was not sufficient to heal you, yet your body survived after your spirit had gone.' He tapped the gold mask. 'Something else – some other power – was at work to heal you. While you were unconscious, I used the shadows to examine you and found a second piece of gold, embedded in your flesh next to your eye.'

Myjun raised a hand to the bridge of her nose, traced her left eye and touched her temple. 'Metal,' she said, '*in* my head?'

Oyru nodded. 'It contained the blood of a Terran Inquisitor.' He stared at her. 'Do you know how this shard found find its way into you?'

Myjun remembered her father standing between her and Annev, his arm held protectively in front of her as he blasted the one-armed keokum with his hellfire wand. She recalled her horror when Annev unleashed his fury on Tosan, his body suddenly consumed by liquid flame and demonic rage. Charred bits of her father's hand and arm had blasted into her. She remembered the searing pain as her face ran hot with bloody fire and the liquid metal of her father's molten ring. Annev had scarred her – had *ruined* her – and then he had dropped her in that hole, sealing her away to be tortured by the monsters who had destroyed the village.

'I was injured when the monsters captured me,' Myjun said, the hatred choking her throat. 'They did something to my face – poured something on it.'

'*Aqlumera,*' Oyru said, his voice neutral. 'Liquid magic. It healed you and cursed you – but the Inquisitor blood came from somewhere else.'

'My father,' she said, remembering the curse that he bore and the shame that she felt from it. 'He had magic.'

Oyru shook his head. 'This is different. You have an *artifact* buried in your skull, and it is augmenting the healing powers of your mask.' He stared at her, his eyes dark as waters beneath the new moon. 'Where did the artifact come from?'

'My father's gold ring,' she said, the truth of it suddenly coming to her. 'He claimed Odar had blessed him with the ability to sense when others were lying ... but I suspected the ring might be an artifact. He was wearing it when Annev killed him.'

'Could he also use the ring to heal himself?'

'I don't know,' Myjun said, swallowing the bile that rose in her throat. Speaking of Tosan brought back her father's hypocrisy and his cursed blood. 'My father believed artifacts could only be used by those with strong wills and pure hearts. He said that he alone, the headmaster of the Academy, could be trusted to use them with prudence and piety.' She wanted to laugh, but instead she sneered. 'He was a self-righteous, hypocritical bastard.' She spat, though without any saliva behind it – she had learned that lesson since donning her mask and she didn't care to repeat it.

'That ring contained a blood-talent.' Oyru was unfazed by her anger. 'And the *aqlumera* may have augmented that power.'

'And the mask ... ?'

'Has augmented it further. Whatever your powers were before you became scarred, the combination of Inquisitor ring, *aqlumera* and mask has made you something ... exotic. Something un-expected.'

'A monster – like you.'

'You could say that.'

Myjun scoffed. 'It didn't stop me from dying, though.'

'You were only half dead – and that is an experience I can relate to.' He looked towards the fields at his left and then towards the Brakewood on his right. 'It should not have been possible for you to slay the blood drake, not with its superior ability to heal. I am impressed.' He returned his gaze to Myjun. 'Now for another test – *three* tests, actually.' He twisted his fingers, flicked his wrist and a bloody rag appeared in the palm of his hand.

'I abducted a local farmer and hid him nearby. This belongs to him.' He tossed the rag to Myjun. 'Hunt him down.'

'Then what?' Myjun raised the cloth to her mask and inhaled. Even behind the gold metal, she could smell – could practically taste – the blood. The coppery taste of rust. The bitter iron tang of life ... and death.

'Finding the farmer is the first test. The second is to get answers from him.'

'What questions would I ask a stupid farmer?'

'You'll know when you find him.'

'And the third test?'

'Something special – something that might explain how you killed that draken.'

Myjun's eyes narrowed. Her reaping clothes were blood-soaked, ragged and torn. Her body had healed, but the hunger and thirst she had felt while running through the Vosgar had been awakened once more. She ached for sustenance, for fuel ... for pain.

'I will find the farmer.'

Chapter Twenty-One

Myjun studied the man tied to the chair, his face bruised, blood oozing from his scalp, shoulder, ribs and arms. The hot, sticky scent of trickling blood left her feeling sick and horribly hungry. The desire for hot, dripping flesh between her teeth made her tremble. She craved meat now more than she ever had. Something about its smell – the rawness of it – made her thrum with primal need.

She had begun to suspect there was another way to feed herself, after she'd killed the dire wolves. She'd felt the rush of satisfaction, the barest alleviation of her hunger, and she'd become more certain while hunting the Vosgar's other monsters.

Myjun had to kill.

Denying the urge was like refusing to eat. The mask's magic could channel her hunger pains into its own sustenance, but that was weak broth when what she craved was red meat. The need to kill called to her, tempting her with the promise of stolen strength. Myjun knew she wasn't a vampyr ... but she couldn't deny that she was becoming a monster.

The farmer's legs and arms were bound by thick cords of shadow, their nethereal fibres as strong as steel. He was gagged with the other half of the bloody cloth Oyru had given her to track him, and when Myjun tossed her scrap on the floor, the man's attention flicked to where she lurked in the shadows. His eyes searched the darkness for her, stopping when he saw the glint of the golden mask stained with bloody tears. He shed his own tears then. They streaked down his cheeks, wetting his fuzzy white stubble. He sobbed, shoulders hunched, and a feeling of disgust bloomed in Myjun's belly.

This man – this *creature* – was less than human. She saw that with clarity now; this farmer was as inferior as the prey that cowered before the hunter.

'What ...' he sobbed, unable to form the words. 'Wha ... what do you want?'

Myjun watched him, the shadows lengthening inside the old barn. Chickens clucked outside and a horse snorted from a nearby stall. She caught the scent of a milk cow further down, its udders full to bursting, and the man sobbed again. She remained silent. Truthfully, she had no answer for him, and even if she had, she doubted that she would have given it.

She hated him for his weakness – hated him for reminding her of her own weaknesses.

'Find out where his family is hiding.'

Myjun had known he would come, had sensed his nearness – not quite a physical presence, but close enough that it did not matter.

'You ask him.' The words cankered her mouth, her lips dry from lack of water.

'No,' Oyru said, appearing beside her, 'this is your second test.'

Myjun stepped from the darkness into the square beam of light that shone through the barn's open loft. 'Tell me where your family is,' she hissed.

'I don't have any family. Just me.' His face was streaked with dirt, his cheekbones purple-black in the darkness.

'I don't believe you. Where is your family?' she repeated.

'Gone.'

'Gone *where*?' She felt the heat rising behind her mask, her temper flaring.

'They are gone,' his voice quavered. 'Please. Don't hurt them.'

Myjun studied him, seeing if the magic inside her would respond to his words. She felt nothing, though, and she turned the frustration of that failure upon the farmer.

'You're lying to me,' she said, stepping closer. 'You try to save them – to *protect* them – but your lies only endanger them.'

'Please, let me go. I've done nothing wrong!'

'I don't care,' Myjun said, surprised that she spoke the truth. 'I

216

don't care if your hands are stained with the blood of a thousand women and children.'

'I would never—'

I don't *care*,' she repeated, 'if you are the world's holiest saint. I don't care if you're a dutiful father and a loving husband.' She leaned forward, whispering into his ear. 'I don't *care*.'

'Then why do this to me?' the man blubbered. 'Why ask for them?'

Myjun sniffed. She had asked because Oyru had told her to ... which made her uncomfortable. Why *did* the assassin want to know about the farmer's family?

'Tell me where they are,' she repeated, 'or I will gut you like a fish and hang your bloody bits for them to find when they return.'

'No! Please, you can't. My wife ... my children.' He sobbed.

She looked back at Oyru, then gestured in disgust at the wailing creature tied to the chair. 'What is the point of this?'

'Did he tell you the truth?'

'He hasn't told me anything.'

'Then you are failing the test. You hunted him. Now catch the scent of the truth and track it down.'

'It is not the same thing,' she growled.

'Try harder. Find the truth.'

Myjun studied the shadow mage's dark silhouette. *Find the truth*, she thought, her anger with Oyru and the farmer growing hotter by the moment. *Damn them both. I'll tear the truth from his bloody corpse.* She turned back to the farmer, her green eyes smouldering.

'Tell me where they are,' she urged, her voice near as cold as the assassin's, 'and I will let you go.'

'Wh-why are you doing this?'

'Ah-ah.' She reached for the farmer's throat, her fingernails tracing his jaw and jugular. 'I ask the questions. Now tell me.' She paused. 'Tell me ... the name of your cow.'

'The what?'

She raked her fingernails across his face. 'No questions,' she hissed. 'Just tell me ... the name of your cow.'

'G-G-Gertie,' he stuttered. 'Her name. G-Gertie.'

'Gertie,' Myjun repeated, her senses open to the truth he spoke.

217

'That's a good name. I believe you ...?'

'Da–David. The name's David. Folks call me Old Davey.'

'Old Davey,' Myjun repeated. It seemed true enough, though she couldn't say what made her sure of it – her gut, maybe. Or perhaps it was magic. 'Old Davey,' she said again. 'And you're married?'

'Y–yes.' True again. She was getting the sense of it now.

'And you have children.'

'Yes.'

'Thank you for being honest, Davey. I hate it when people lie to me. Bad things happen. You understand?'

'Yes.' He seemed to be calmer now, the answers coming easier.

'Excellent. And their names, Davey.'

'Sam, Palmer, Little Deidre ... and Dawn.'

True again, she thought, though it rankled not to know how or why she knew. *Time for the tougher questions ...*

Davey's voice cracked and the pleading leaked back into his voice. 'By the Gods, they're just children. They've done nothing – *I've* done nothing.'

'Shhh.' She slid a finger down his lips, pressing them closed and following her intuition. 'Now tell me, Davey, this family you love so much. Did you *save* them, or did they abandon you? Did they run when my shadowy companion captured you?'

The farmer sagged. 'How do you know these things? Who are you?'

Myjun slapped him. Hard. Davey's head reeled, his eyes spinning. 'I ask the questions,' she growled. 'Forget again and I will start spilling guts over this barn. Understood?'

'Yes, yes! Dear Gods, merciful Odar. Please, yes!'

'Good,' she purred. 'You see how easy it is to tell the truth?'

'Yes,' he said, head lolling as if drunk on his terror. 'Yes. Yes, God – I see.'

'Oh, I'm not your god, Davey. Your god, the All-father, has abandoned you right now – but *I* am here, and I am very real.' She leaned close, her mask just inches from his face. 'So, tell me now – tell the *truth*. Where is your family?'

The farmer hesitated – just for an instant – then shook his head. Myjun's intuition screamed at her. *He knows exactly where they are*. The truth of it was clear to her, just as it had been clear when he was lying.

'Tell me where you sent them! Which farmhouse are they hiding in? Which aunt did you send them to?'

Davey's eyes widened, but he said nothing.

Myjun's temper flared at his silence. She snatched up a pair of sheep shears, stepped back and snipped off the man's left finger. At his scream, she snipped more. *Snip. Snip. Snip.* Four fingers gone, and now he was choking on the tears and the pain. Myjun only stared at him, her anger still hot, her rage still rising.

'Tell me now – and if you lie, I will start on your other hand.' Despite all the blood, Myjun's voice was level. 'Where have they gone?'

'My sister's home,' he wept, 'in Hentingsfort. Dear Gods, have mercy, please.'

Myjun stared at him, her brow furrowed in concentration. The man had spoken the truth ... but not the *whole* truth. Something was wrong. Something was *missing*. What was it? A truth and a lie perhaps? She drove back her anger at being lied to before she jammed the shears into his neck. Instead she steadied herself, forced him to look her in the eyes.

'You lied to me.'

'It's the truth, I swear it!'

False. Something about the man – a dim glow that seemed to pulse as he spoke – suggested he was lying to her still. She gritted her teeth and shook her head. 'They are with ... the sister of your dead wife Charlyn – but they are *not* in Hentingsfort? They are further east of us ... along the Brakeroad.'

'Witch,' the man breathed, his voice strangled, choked. 'You're a damn *witch*! Why do you care? What do you want from us!'

She swung her arm back and drove the shears point-first into Davey's neck – or would have, had Oyru not caught her by the wrist and saved the farmer's life.

'He lied,' she hissed, pulling her hand free, '*and* he disobeyed me.'

'The mask is making you act rashly. You must control your emotions.'

She wanted to punch the shears into the assassin's face. Instead, she stilled her shaking hand and glanced at the farmer. 'What do you care for him? He's nothing – *less* than nothing.'

'How did you know about Charlyn and Hentingsfort?'

Myjun hesitated. 'I don't know,' she said, answering truthfully. Oyru studied her more closely then nodded.

'How did you know he lied?'

'The light,' she said, unthinking. 'It pulsed around him.'

'Was the light there before he lied?'

'I don't know. Maybe.' She considered it. 'Yes, but I had not noticed it.'

'Look at him now. What do you see?'

Myjun stared at the farmer, his mutilated hand bleeding onto the floor, his face pale, almost white. If his fingers weren't tended to he could bleed to death. Myjun huffed – he had lied to her – and she was about to look away when she noticed a flicker of colour around him. A silhouette of light she had thought was simply the glare from the sunbeam overhead. She squinted at it now, fixed on it, trying to *see* it ... but there was nothing to see. It was only an impression, an *aura* that she observed less with her eyes and more with ... something else. She wasn't sure what.

'He's glowing. There's some kind of aura surrounding him.'

'Describe it.'

'Yellow? Maybe white. It has ... streaks of blood in it. Red and pink.'

'And when he lied?'

She thought about it. She hadn't really *seen* colours – it was something she had felt more than saw. So what colour did it feel like? What did it remind her of?

'Not black ... not purple,' she said at last. 'Something between the two.'

'You have a talent for auramancy,' Oyru said, nodding. 'I cannot see it, but I feel the inverse of it. It is the opposite of shadow magic – the dark and the light.'

'And?'

'And,' Oyru continued, smoothly materialising so that his face became corporeal, a floating head amidst the darkness, 'that means you have a talent for auramancy *and* soulriding – and, if the blood wyrm's death is any indication, bladesinging. That is a rare combination. Very rare, when your father was only half Ilumite. You most likely possess the fourth Ilumite blood-talent as well: lightslinging.' He pointed at the farmer. 'It should be easy to execute him with your magic.'

Myjun scoffed. 'What magic?'

'You summoned soulfire blades to kill the draken. It burned out its eyes.' He pointed at her. 'With the full Ilumite talent, you can conjure fire and blades of light, you can throw lightning. You can bend the light around yourself – turn invisible – or you can reflect it and create illusions. Some of those skills will be hard to master and some will come naturally, but as my apprentice you will master them all.'

She stared at the assassin. 'I can't do any of that. Not a damn piece of it. Besides,' she added, not caring in the slightest, 'your farmer is dead. You let him bleed out.'

Oyru shook his head. 'Half dead is not truly dead.' And with that, he stuck his hand through the farmer's chest and gave Old Davey's heart a squeeze. The man's eyes shot open and he screamed as if woken from a nightmare – except *this* was the nightmare, and Oyru would not let him leave it so easily.

The Shadow Reborn slid his hand free then pointed at the terrified farmer, the blood from Davey's severed fingers slowly pooling at his feet. 'Kill him,' he said, 'using your magic. Use your soulfire blades, or fire, or lightning. I don't care how, only that you do it.'

'This is the third test?'

'Yes.'

Myjun sniffed. 'Fine.' She stomped over to the dazed farmer whose eyes were already drifting closed, and slapped him across his weather-beaten face. His eyes popped open once more, and he spat at her. In an instant rage, her hands reached for his throat.

'NO!'

Myjun stopped, frozen by the intensity of Oyru's voice. The cold apathy that always marked the man's speech had vanished, replaced by a piercing anger. And then, quick as a summer storm, it disappeared. The iciness returned, harder than before. Colder.

'Do *not* touch him. Feed your anger and frustration into him, all your pain and fire. Lash him with it. *Burn* him with it.'

Myjun stared at the dying farmer, his face bloodless, his body slack and unmoving. She felt little anger for the man – disgust and hatred, yes, but her rage had subsided as the man's life-force ebbed away.

She did feel frustration, though – a tiny flower of hatred that burned with the fire of being unable to kill the man, of not being allowed to strangle him. She was angry at Oyru, angry that he believed she could do this, angry that he could *compel* her to do it.

And yet ... she had done it before. She tried to remember how, to draw out the memory. Blood and claws. Teeth and scales. Beetles gnawing at her flesh, the acid-blood spewing from the draken's mouth. Burning and pain, the frustration and anger as its jaws clamped down on her, piercing her flesh. Myjun dug deeper, immersing herself in the pain of the moment – that moment when she longed to die but continued to live.

She screamed, the sound ripping from her throat. She screamed and screamed ...

Light sparked in her hands – tiny flames, white-hot and incandescent – and then they winked out. Myjun panted with exertion, her voice raw with emotion.

'Beautiful,' Oyru whispered, standing in the dark once again. 'Absolutely beautiful.'

'Pointless,' Myjun snapped. 'A useless spark.'

'Not so.' Oyru gestured at Old Davey who had fallen silent once again, the blood still dripping from his severed fingers, but slower ... slower ...

'Try taking his pain and fear – and using them to fuel your magic.'

'I don't ...' Myjun stared at the farmer, watched the aura around him begin to dim.

Could she do it? She knew pain fuelled her mask and made her stronger, faster – but could she steal that same pain, those same emotions, from other people? Could she turn *their* pain into *her* strengths? A spark lit inside her, its intensity fuelled by the possibility, by the *need* to try ...

To burn. To break.

Myjun reached out to the dying farmer, allowing her emotions to feed off his. It was easy – easier than she expected. She felt the man's aura peel away from him and Davey's eyes flew open, more horror in his face than she had ever seen during her interrogation.

He screamed at her, terrified. 'What are you doing!'

Rage. Pain. Frustration. Disgust. Hatred. All of his emotions were hers, channelled through her, strengthening her – and as her power grew, his fear grew, too. Terror. Pain. Fear. Agony. Despair. An endless feedback loop that fed the spark inside her until it blossomed into a flame. That flame found its home in her arms, condensing, sharpening as twin points of light sprang from her palms – sharp white blades of pure spirit, an aura of emotion and fire, light and energy. The blades grew into daggers … into swords. She realised she was screaming, was venting her pain with her ragged and intense voice, as sharp and piercing as any blade. Old Davey screamed, too, his pale face filled with a terror as pure as her hatred.

Then she struck, her soulfire blades scissoring together to snip the farmer's head from his shoulders. His skin burned as they slid into his flesh, his eyes bursting into flame, an otherworldly light pouring from his mouth.

The pain that filled Myjun's body, the hunger that penetrated her soul, suddenly evaporated in place of a sense of fullness. The sensation startled her, awakening her senses to a world that had grown dull beneath the endless aches and pains.

She was not hungry. She was not thirsty. She was … alive with the rush of life and a feeling of fulfilment, the thrill of having taken a life and being given one. Beneath it all, she still felt the influence of the mask – the sharp need for pain and the malice that accompanied it – but these were distant now, their sharpness abated by the euphoria of the moment.

And suddenly they were gone – the rush, the joy, the thrill – all vanished. Her hunger and thirst were still diminished, but along-side a void, a wide chasm of need … and a new kind of hunger that would not be satisfied by food or water.

'You would be a Soulblade, I think – a Soulrider and a

Bladesinger – but the *aqlumera* and the Inquisitor ring have tainted your magic. Forged it into something new. Something *wonderful*. You aren't spellsinging. You are ... soul-shrieking.' A queer smile touched the corner of Oyru's mouth then – an emotion so foreign, so out of place, that it sickened Myjun to see it.

'A Soulscreamer. Light-bending and soulriding may be challenging for you – certainly more difficult than for a full-blooded Ilumite – but that jagged edge ... that raw *power*.' His expression morphed into a sadistic grin. 'Oh, yes. You are my sharp little knife. My bloody Oraqui.'

Behind them, the husk of the dead man slumped forward, his skin and bones as dry and brittle as burned charcoal. When his soulless body hit the ground, there was a faint crackle of light, a soft sigh and then silence.

'Come,' Oyru continued, not missing a beat. 'The people of Hentingsfort await us.'

'What's in Hentingsfort?' Myjun might have been angered to ask before, but her feelings still floated beneath the memory of her soulfeasting. She hungered for more – more blood, more death, more soul-sucking. She craved it, needed it like a lusty lover or starving mendicant.

'Another test,' Oyru said, beckoning towards the door. 'The last before I take you beyond Reocht na Skah and the heart of the Shadowrealm.'

'You will take me ... into the shadows?'

The assassin led her outside, into the sunlight and then the deep shade of the Brakewood. 'Yes, but Hentingsfort first. You've only just discovered your power, and the shadows are far more dangerous than an old farmer tied to a chair. Hentingsfort is a village, with its own town council and militia. A few hundred people.'

'And what will we do when we get there?'

'What else? We will fight and kill. We will sup on the souls of the weak. Drink the darkness and the light.'

Myjun shivered in anticipation, eager for the taste of blood and the thrill of the hunt. She would dine on death – she would slake her unquenchable thirst and satisfy her insatiable hunger. She shuddered at the thought of it and followed the assassin into the woods.

Chapter Twenty-Two

Tosan's spirit fought Kenton, as precise and relentless as a mason chipping at a block of stone. At the same time, Kenton felt fragments of himself being washed away, drawn inexorably downward into the *aqlumera*. He felt disorientated, as though he were spinning into an abyss.

Kenton reached out, grasping for any anchor, and seized on his love for Myjun and his hatred for Annev. An instant later, Tosan loomed over him, and it was as though they wrestled at the edge of some spiritual void.

'My daughter is dead!' the former headmaster shouted, his attacks pushing Kenton towards oblivion. 'If you had kept Annev in his cell' – *push* – 'she would still be alive!' *Push. Shove.*

Kenton's spirit stood at the brink of the *aqlumera*. His grasp on himself slipped and he felt his feelings for and memories of Myjun grow faint ... distant.

Tosan shoved again, threatening to tumble him into the yawning abyss. 'I had wondered whether you had helped him – whether you had *freed* that monster from his cell – but then I saw you were just inept. Unable to save yourself, unable to save my daughter.' *Push. Shove.* 'Her death is as much *your* fault as his!' Tosan struck, his blows hard enough to shake Kenton to his core ... yet Kenton's grip on his twin loves and hatreds remained, and he clung ferociously to his life and control of his body ... and, by so doing, he realised how to fight back. Entangled with the man's psyche, Kenton sensed Tosan's own doubts and fears – his weaknesses, the things he loved and most wanted to protect. The former headmaster truly cared about very little, but two things stood out: his dead daughter and the ruined Academy.

'*You* couldn't protect the Academy! You blame Annev and me for its destruction, but you were the one who struck the first blow. It was *your* magic – your hellfire wand – that sparked the tinder. Everybody in Chaenbalu died because of *you*!'

'No!' Tosan roared, his grip slipping. 'It was that boy – that one-armed keokum took everything I loved – everything *you* loved!'

Kenton wavered, struggling to regain control. Annev *had* destroyed Kenton's life ... but it was Tosan's fault, too. Kenton had been trapped in the prison cell, unable to fight. Tosan had been above ground, fighting the monsters. He'd been trying to protect his daughter – and he'd succeeded ... right up until he'd attacked Annev.

And then Kenton saw the headmaster's weakness ... his most terrible secret. The truth of it hit Kenton like a bolt of thunder.

'You *let* him kill her.'

Tosan stumbled, shaken to his core, and they stood on equal ground once again.

'No, I tried to *save* her! You weren't even there!' The headmaster clawed at Kenton's psyche, trying to regain control. 'I *died* trying to protect her.'

'I can see into your memories, Tosan. You thought Annev wouldn't hurt you so long as Myjun stayed by your side. You used her as a shield to protect yourself – and she *died*!'

Tosan faltered, his doubts creeping in, pulling his certainties apart, and when he stumbled again Kenton shoved – hard. The vengeful spirit reeled back, his psyche tipping backwards into the void of *aqlumera*.

'*No!*'

But it was too late. Kenton flung the old man away, forcing him out of his body, and Tosan's spirit tumbled back into the magical abyss, his essence swallowed by the liquid magic.

Kenton took a shuddering breath, in possession of himself once again. He was alive, but pieces of his psyche had been splintered, their pieces swept away by the battle with Tosan. Kenton had clung tightly to major things – aspects of himself that he most identified with, the things that anchored him – but smaller details had been torn away, pulled down into the consuming void of *aqlumera*. He tried to recall the names of his favourite poisons, his preferred weapons, or his companions at the Academy ... but they were hazy. He was surprised to remember that he favoured fighting with the tachi – a piece of himself that had nearly been lost – but he could not recall if he had a favourite colour or food.

As Kenton quietly gathered himself, he found other splinters that were decidedly *not* his memories. His thoughts of Annev and Myjun remained, but they were tainted by a feeling that was almost patriarchal. His thoughts and impressions of the Academy were similarly possessive, and rooms he had never entered now felt familiar.

Kenton lay on his back, his fiery glass orbs staring sightlessly at the curved ceiling of the Vault chamber. Cautiously, he eased himself into a sitting position, then rose to stand in front of the pool of *aqlumera* once more. This time he did not peer into its depths; he would not tempt fate, or give Tosan a second chance to possess him. Instead, Kenton reached into his Cloak of Secrets and withdrew a long black scarf – an artifact that made its wearer more commanding, more likely to be followed. He wrapped it around his head and tied it tight over his lidless eyes, hoping it might lend some protection against further attacks to his soul. It didn't impede his supernatural vision, and Kenton turned his back on the glowing font, returning to the trapdoor.

I have to try one more time, he thought. *The Cloak is too risky, and with these new artifacts I should be able to forge a way out of here.*

Kenton cautiously navigated the fallen stone and broken rock and returned to the broken cell door, ignoring the collapsed tunnel he had dug with Mercy. Once safely free of the cell, he renewed his exploration of the Academy's subterranean passages, hoping he might find a new, unexplored path to the surface. He had little hope, yet after wandering the gloom for just a few minutes his sharpened vision led him to a new section of tunnels. He started to follow the twists and turns as if on instinct, first warily and then with increasing confidence, as if he knew these tunnels. A moment's reflection revealed the truth: he did remember them, but they were Tosan's memories. One of the fragments the Eldest of Ancients had inadvertently left within him.

Selfish prick, Kenton swore, not for the first time. *Trying to cheat death by stealing* my *body . . . my life*. He sniffed, the irony not lost on him. *And now I'm using his memories to escape*. The notion brought a smile to his face, though it was quickly tempered by the thought that Myjun was still dead, and that Annev had been the one to kill her. It reignited his sorrow and rage, though his feelings were dulled too. Kenton no longer felt like himself, and he worried about the long-term consequences of his struggle with Tosan.

It was dusk when Kenton finally emerged, led by his vision and Tosan's memories, and saw a flickering campfire between the town well and the Academy's stables. A group of men whispered there, and it wasn't long before Kenton recognised the varied voices of Master Carbad, Ancient Denithal and the other surviving teachers from the Academy.

Kenton watched in silence, trying to decide whether to approach and announce himself or sneak away and leave Chaenbalu for ever. As he listened, though, a plan slowly began to form, one that might utilise Tosan's stolen memories and increase Kenton's chances of taking his revenge.

Edra surveyed the haggard men surrounding the campfire. They were a pitiful lot, made worse by squabbling between themselves. *Like a pack of dogs fighting over a soup bone. But this soup has lost its savour.*

The former Ancient in the Art of Warcraft looked at the ruins of the Academy. It had been his home. With its towering grey walls and stout wooden doors, the Academy was more than a building: for the infants that were brought through those wooden doors it was a nursery; for the boys tutored there it was both a school and a sanctuary; for the men that survived their training and lived to go on retrieval missions, the Academy was a comfortable home and a familiar friend. The one constant in an otherwise bleak life.

And it had been sheared in half in a matter of seconds, tumbled to the ground and melted to so much slag and cinders. It was a crushed husk of its former glory. The stained-glass windows that once rivalled the greatest cathedrals of Luqura were all shattered when the edifice collapsed. The Academy's familiar dark rooms and narrow halls had caved in, forming an impossible, impenetrable warren of tunnels – Edra knew, because he had tried to get through. It was a tomb now, a crypt for both his fallen brethren and the monsters that had invaded their small village.

Edra shuddered, recalling their grotesque corpses: feral men with twisted metal woven through their bodies, stone clubs for limbs and teeth filed to razor-sharp spikes. Edra felt the bile rise in his throat as he remembered the mangled bodies of both friend and foe. Broken limbs, sheared torsos, shattered faces. More than once, he'd tried to move a stone blocking his path, only to discover it was not a stone at all, but a monster's severed limb.

It had been dangerous work, trying to explore. Bringing a torch into the confined spaces often led to the smoke forcing Edra back out after a few minutes of searching, yet without light it was near impossible to navigate the maze of fallen stone. Some paths suddenly dead-ended. Others spiralled upward. Sometimes the ground itself would tremble – an aftershock from the earth-rending battle between Ancient Tosan and Annev – and the paths would either shift or collapse in on themselves.

Edra's home – the only place he ever felt safe and at peace – had become a deathtrap.

'We should leave. This place is dead and so are the villagers. You are talking nonsense, Carbad.'

Edra glanced up at Ather, the slender Master of Lies, and nodded in agreement. The man's words echoed his own thoughts, and it was the first thing remotely resembling wisdom he had heard from the lot of former masters.

Unfortunately, Master Carbad was deaf to it.

'We *must* rebuild, Master Ather. For the good of the Order, the Vault of Damnation must be exhumed, its foundations rebuilt and its walls reclaimed.' The spindly Master of Operations twisted his ash-stained robes. 'The Academy *must* rise again.'

'It can't be done,' said Murlach, the Master of Engineering. 'The foundation is unstable. The Academy was built atop that grotto centuries ago, and that fool boy must have blasted a hole down to its core.' He ran a hand through his greasy black hair, drawing attention to the shock of white that now graced his forehead. 'If the Academy must be rebuilt, it would be better to start work on a solid foundation – preferably one far away from here – instead of atop some shifting hole that is bound to give way and swallow up our efforts.'

Ancient Denithal shook his head in disagreement.

'We cannot build the Academy somewhere else. The Vault of Damnation is *unique*. It protects the artifacts from detection – it is the only reason the Academy was built here in the first place! The *aqlumera* is also irreplaceable – if unstable – so we cannot simply build another Academy, let alone another Vault.'

'Which is why we must stay,' Carbad declared, seizing hold of the conversation once again. 'I'm certain that with Master Murlach's ingenuity we can safely excavate the building.'

'Even if it were possible, I would need a hundred labourers just to dig out the foundations,' Murlach snapped. 'We don't have the resources to—'

'We can *find* the resources,' Carbad said, his cheeks flushing. 'We can bring scores of villagers from Banok and Luqura and *force* them to rebuild. We will take farmers from their fields and bring them and their families to till the ground and re-establish—'

'You're insane.'

All eyes turned to Aog, the brooding Master of Punishment. Despite his towering stature, the stony-faced man had always been soft-spoken and solitary. As the Academy's de facto executioner, he was also adept at silencing other men with an almost casual indifference. Since the Academy's destruction, he had not spoken a word. It seemed fitting to Edra that he chose to speak now, to say what the others had been thinking but were afraid to articulate.

Carbad sputtered, wanting to object but unable to find the words. Edra smiled at that; it was uncharacteristic for Tosan's former lapdog to be speechless, and it was even rarer for Aog to find words where Carbad could not.

'Cut off a man's head. He dies.' Aog jerked his head at the Academy. 'Tosan is dead. So is the Academy.'

'I can *replace* Tosan. I managed the Academy and the village while Tosan was in charge, and I assisted Ancient Windsor for almost a decade!'

Denithal sputtered, rising from his seat next to the low-burning fire. 'You aren't even an Ancient, Carbad, let alone *Eldest* of Ancients. If anyone were to replace Tosan, it should be *me*.'

Edra spat into the fire in disgust, and all turned and looked up at him. His hands had drifted down to the sword sheathed at his hip.

'No more of this garbage,' Edra said, forcing his hand away from the comforting hilt. He felt the veins bulging on his neck, the tightness of his clenched jaw, and tried to relax. His body was aching for a fight – but this was not the fight he wanted. 'We've been retreading this argument for two days, and you seem intent to drown us all in it.' He punctuated his accusation by pointing a finger at the grandfatherly Denithal. 'You're *twice* as old as any of us here, Den. You were two decades older than Tosan. You were passed over for the title of Ancient for years because you're an *alchemist*. You're not a leader. No one has ever asked you to be one and no one wants to follow you. So stick to your potions and stop pretending we care what you think.'

Denithal blustered, patting his robes as if searching for some defence against Edra's words – but they were true, and the other masters knew it.

Edra wasn't finished. He turned to Carbad, saw the smug smile on the man's face, and slapped him. The Master of Operations' hand flew to his mouth and he drew it away bloodied, eyes wide with shock.

'How *dare* you—'

Edra slapped him again. This time Carbad kept his mouth shut, though his eyes gleamed with hatred. Edra nodded.

'Aog is right. The Academy is dead – and you're an *idiot*, Carbad. We can't rebuild this. We can't even salvage the artifacts trapped in the Vault. Even if we could get down there, what would we do? Trade artifacts for food or gold in Luqura, after spending our lifetimes collecting and safeguarding them?' Edra heaved a great breath. 'Chaenbalu is dead,' he repeated. 'Brayan was right to leave for Luqura, and I wish I'd had the sense to go with him.' The

Master of Arms looked around at the six other men surrounding the fire and saw Der, Ather and Murlach nodding in agreement. Aog ran a hand over his shaved head, letting his silence speak for him. 'It's settled, then.'

'Not quite.'

Edra raised an eyebrow, surprised to hear a voice of dissent coming from the direction of the Academy. He turned, prepared to clout whomever it was until he saw the man climbing out of the Academy's ruins. The newcomer wore long robes the colour of ash and thunder clouds, with a black cloak over his shoulders and thick cloth wrapped around his eyes. A dazzling array of jewellery adorned his neck, forearms, and gloved hands. Edra's eyes locked on a particularly entrancing gold and ruby amulet. As the figure walked towards them, Edra couldn't help but feel there was something familiar about the stranger ... about the way he walked ...

'Tosan?' Edra asked, taking a step forward to see the man emerging from the rubble more clearly. With the setting sun shining behind his head, it took Edra a second to realise the truth.

'Kenton?'

The newly raised Master of Curses continued to pick his way between the stones, and when his blind gaze fell upon Edra, he felt his blood run cold. Something was different. Edra blinked, trying to shake the chill he felt when he looked at the shrouded young man. 'We thought you were killed in the attack,' he said. 'We tried to search the Academy for survivors, but ...'

'But you failed to find me.' Kenton stopped in front of Edra and looked the Master of Arms up and down, as if he could see through the thick blindfold that covered half his face.

Edra shivered in spite of himself. Had the boy grown taller? When had he become so intimidating? And what had happened to his eyes? 'Yes ...' he said slowly. 'It's been two days since the Academy fell ... and we've searched but we seem to be the only survivors. We were just discussing what to do.'

'You've been debating for days,' Kenton said, managing to glower through his blindfold at each man around the fire, 'and you haven't done a damn thing but sit here.'

Master Carbad stumbled forward, apparently willing to stand

up to Kenton despite having crumpled before Edra. 'Who the *hell* do you think you are, whelp? You're barely raised from an acolyte – and then only because the *real* masters were too drunk to raid Janak's keep, which you *failed* to do anyway. Tosan made you Master of Curses because he was so embarrassed of you.' He paused, suddenly horrified. 'Is that where you got that clothing? That jewellery? Did you *plunder* the Vault?'

Edra had wondered the same thing. Kenton seemed to be dressed head to toe in cursed artifacts. He licked his lips, appreciating how dangerous Kenton might be if those items really had come from the Vault.

As if Kenton could hear Edra's thoughts, the former Master of Curses raised his hands and gently removed his blindfold. Edra gasped and Carbad stumbled backward, tripping on his robes: instead of eyes, tongues of rainbow fire burned inside the boy's skull, giving him the appearance of both demon and angel; it was as if his eyes had been burned away, replaced by orbs of fire, and their gaze pierced Edra to his very soul.

Keos, he thought, biting his cheek to keep from uttering the curse aloud. *The boy is a ghost ... or a demon? He's like those wraiths that attacked the village.* As Edra watched, the flames dancing inside the boy's eye sockets seemed to shift from orange-red to purple-black. He swallowed hard.

The young man let his eyes meet that of every man at the fire-pit, matching them glare for glare, daring anyone else to challenge him. 'Yes, I plundered the Vault – and you should, too. Every one of you.' Kenton paused, turning to Carbad. 'Except for you, Master Carbad. As you possess no magical affinity, you are of no use to me.'

'What? Of *course* I can't use magic. None of us can! We aren't bloody keokum.'

Kenton gestured at Edra, Denithal, and the rest of the masters, excluding Carbad. 'Each of these men possesses magic, though they may not know it. I can see it burning inside them. It has shaped their natural abilities. Pushed them into the roles they now possess. Stealth, deception, engineering, alchemy, arms ...' He studied Aog. 'And the administration of death.'

Edra squinted at the former Master of Curses, trying to reconcile the quiet, dark-haired boy he remembered with this powerful, confident man. The side of his face was still scarred from when Master Ather had beaten the boy bloody, but instead of hiding the disfigurement behind his long dark hair as he used to do, Kenton seemed to be displaying the scar. Displaying it . . . and his eyes.

This was not the same boy that Tosan sent to apprentice with Master Narach. He was stronger . . . and Kenton knew it. *Those eyes*, Edra thought, shying away from Kenton's uncovered gaze. *It's like staring into a firepit and realising the flames are staring back at you.*

'I can use all of you,' Kenton said, taking in all of the weary masters and ancients. 'I can make each of you stronger than you've ever dreamed. I've been given a gift.' He indicated his eyes. 'I can see magic in all its forms. I understand artifacts in a way Master Narach could only wonder at, and I can use that ability to give you the tools to fulfil your new mission.'

'And what mission is that, Master Kenton?' The question came from gnarled old Denithal, whose sour expression suggested he was honestly weighing Kenton's words. 'Our mission was to find cursed artifacts and bury them in that godsforsaken Vault. How does using those artifacts help us fulfil the Academy's mission?'

'As you said, the Academy is dead.' Kenton turned his burning eyes on the alchemist. 'Its mission, though admirable, is also dead. We can no longer hunt down magic artifacts and hope to secure them in the Vault. Besides, there is no way to sustain life here.'

'Then what do you suggest?'

Kenton ran a finger down the side of his scarred face. 'The Academy was a defensive operation. Our forebears hoped to defeat the evils of magic by hiding their tools in the bowels of the earth. But that was folly. You can see what it earned us.' He gestured at the ruins of Chaenbalu – from the rents in the earth to the burned-out shell and fractured corpses littering the ground. 'A Son of Keos brought monsters to our home. Shattered it. Burned it to the ground. One boy brought all this upon us, and we were powerless to stop him.'

Edra glanced at the other masters and saw Der and Murlach

nodding. Denithal and Ather seemed to be weighing Kenton's words, and Aog watched in mute silence. Edra, however, was growing more concerned. *How does he know about Annev and Tosan? Kenton was inside the Academy when the fighting started. He couldn't have seen Tosan's death ... but he* knows. *Somehow, he knows.* Edra swallowed. If he had entertained any thoughts of ignoring the young Master of Curses, he discarded them. The avatar they had sent to the archives room, to be forgotten in the dust and catalogues, was not the man that had risen from the Academy's ruins. Kenton had changed, and it ran deeper than the clothes he wore or the fire in his eyes.

'Annev scarred me with his magic when he escaped his prison cell,' Kenton continued, his eyes smouldering. 'He took my eyesight and cursed me with *this*.' He gestured again at the flames that filled his eyes. 'But I will turn this curse back upon him. I will hunt him down and punish him for what he has done to us ... to Myjun ...' This last bit was mumbled so softly that Edra wondered if he had heard correctly. The boy cast his eyes down at the earth, as if peering at some distant scene below the surface, but after a moment he looked up again, into the faces of his captive audience.

'The Vault of Damnation has failed, so as the surviving masters it falls to us to contain the curses once stored there. We must atone for those failures by embracing our own damnation.' Kenton reached into his robes and pulled out five ruby amulets – smaller replicas of the one he wore – and passed one to each man around the firepit. He ignored Carbad, a slight that was not missed by the former Master of Operations. 'Each of you will come with me into the Vault where I will arm you.' He gave an amulet to Edra. 'Once you are each properly outfitted, we will seal this tomb and hunt for the Son of Keos who brought this destruction on Chaenbalu.'

Murlach weighed the amulet in his hands. 'You're saying *we* have magic?'

'An affinity for it. Yes.'

'Then are we not also damned?'

'This is *insanity*!' Carbad shouted in a fury. 'You have no authority over us! How dare you say we must ... what? Serve you? *Follow* you?' he scoffed. 'Stupid boy – and look at his eyes!' Carbad turned, appealing to the others. 'He's a Son of Keos *himself*, tempting you into a pact with the God of Blood and Bone so he can seal your will to his!'

Edra cocked his head, listening to Carbad more closely. He didn't like the bookish Master of Operations – he was always too dry, too uptight – but his words actually made sense. Perhaps Kenton *had* made a pact with Keos. It would explain his eyes.

Kenton seemed unperturbed by Carbad's arguments, though. He walked calmly over to the man and lightly placed two fingers on the side of his neck. The master's eyes bulged, his mouth dropped open and he fell backwards, dead as a stone.

'Keos,' Edra whispered.

Kenton looked directly at Edra. 'Yes. I'm indeed touched by Keos, and it is his touch that allows me to use the artifacts. His touch has made me stronger.' He gestured dismissively at Carbad's body. 'He was weak. He failed to protect this village, and he earned his own damnation.' Kenton swept his burning eyes over the rest of the men. 'Every one of you is also touched by Keos. You're as damned as I am. But with that curse comes the power to wield these accursed artifacts. With that curse comes strength.' He opened his grey robes, pulled a bone-white dagger from a sash and dragged the knife's edge across his open palm, drawing blood as he did so. He held out the wound to the five remaining men and, within seconds, the cut began to heal itself. Within a few breaths the wound had completely sealed. With the men still watching, Kenton laid the flat of the knife atop the blood that had pooled in his now-healed palm. A heartbeat later, thin red veins began to pulse beneath the surface of the blade, and the artifact siphoned the pooled blood away.

'Bloody bones,' Der swore. The swarthy Master of Stealth scratched his stubbly face, mesmerised by the magic. He glanced down at the amulet in his hands, then up at the destroyed Academy. He shrugged and pulled the trinket over his neck. 'I'll take some of that.'

Kenton gave a slight bow, then looked at the other masters. Ather slowly pulled his amulet over his neck and no one objected.

On the other side of the firepit, Aog studied the tear-shaped ruby attached to his own golden chain then dropped the latter over his head. Murlach did the same and then Denithal, grumbling, followed suit. All eyes turned to Edra, who sighed.

'Damned if you do ...' Edra glanced down at Carbad, then draped the amulet around his neck. 'Damned if you don't.'

A faint smile touched Kenton's lips. 'Just so.' He replaced the black blindfold over his eyes then unsettled them all by seeming to stare through the cloth. 'We are the Sons of Damnation, and none who harbour magic will stand before us. Our goal is not to reclaim or confiscate magic – it is to *obliterate* it. To destroy every artifact and every wielder of them. To convert or kill any who are similarly damned. That is how we will redeem ourselves, and that is how we will find and destroy Annev.' He turned towards the Academy's ruins. 'Follow me.'

Edra fell in line behind the Master of Curses. It felt odd to follow someone half his age, someone he had tutored, but this boy – this man – frightened him. Edra wasn't sure the sum total of his life's actions warranted damnation, but following Kenton seemed to tip the scales in that direction.

'Keos take us all,' Edra whispered under his breath, and they made their way into the bowels of the fallen building.

Chapter Twenty-Three

Despite Sraon's guesswork, The Bottomless Cup was more or less as he had projected. Labourers from the Old Low Quarter and River District sat at tables eating and drinking their lunches with an enthusiasm that almost matched that of a master avatar on feast day. Sraon had then surprised everyone with a handful of clips to buy food and drink.

'I've got to see about stabling the horse and finding our contact,' he said, by way of explanation. 'You're all adults. Find a table and order something. Master Nikloss, I expect you to keep an eye on the boys. Just keep them out of trouble for five minutes.'

'I thought you said we were all adults!' Therin protested, though he took the offered clips.

'Aye, and that's why I expect you to keep an eye on Master Nikloss in turn. Don't let anyone bother him or each other. Shouldn't take me but five minutes to handle the horse but finding Tukas may take longer. Can you all handle that?'

They all nodded, Titus with the gravity of a boy intent on the task assigned to him, and Fyn and Therin in a way that suggested they already had other plans for their coin. Annev glanced around the room, saw some rivermen playing cards and guessed that's where his friends would be once the blacksmith went about his errands.

'We'll keep an eye on them,' Annev said, watching as the pair snuck off to gamble away their coppers. 'How much coin do we have left?'

Sraon hissed, holding a finger to his lips. 'Not something to discuss in a public place.'

'Didn't you say this was a safehouse for the Dionachs?' Annev asked, lowering his voice.

'No, this is a *vetting* house. You want to meet with the Dionachs Tobar, you come here and say the right things to the right people – probably to Tukas, but it could be one of his agents. If we satisfy him, he'll take us on to the safehouse. Then we won't be paying room and board while we wait for Reeve to show up.'

'How long do you think that'll take?'

'My guess is two weeks. Could be more, could be less. It all depends on how quickly Tukas passes our message to the Enclave – and how long it takes Reeve to extricate himself from their politics. My understanding is that's the slow and complicated bit.'

'So we won't be staying the night here.'

'No, not unless something bad has happened to Tukas – and if something has, we'll be moving on anyway.'

'Okay.' Annev held up his coins. 'Do you want me to grab you anything?'

The blacksmith shook his head. 'Worry about yourself, Master Annev. I'll give you some road advice, though. Never miss a chance to rest your eyes, fill your belly or empty your bladder, because you can't know when your next chance will come.'

Annev smiled. 'Fine, but hurry back. I don't trust Therin or Fyn to stay out of trouble for too long.'

'And I'm starting to have second thoughts about Master Nikloss.'

'Huh?'

Annev turned to see the albino soothsayer had joined Fyn and Therin at the gambling tables. The rivermen were amused by the trio, laughing and whispering to one another, though they were quick enough to take the newcomers' coins and deal hands of cards. Annev shook his head and waved Sraon off.

Meanwhile, Titus had found a seat at an empty table, its surface sticky with beer. He waved Annev over and the two of them sat down before hailing a motherly serving woman who took their coin and fetched them each a plate of roast chicken and fried turnips. Therin joined them just as their food arrived and confessed to having lost his coins already. Not to the rivermen, but to Jian Nikloss.

'It's like he knows what I'm holding before I do,' Therin said, seizing a piece of Titus's turnip and shoving it into his mouth. '

'How do you two even know how to play cards?'

Therin looked at Titus, who began to laugh. 'We played cards almost every night in the bunk rooms – well, every night we could sneak a deck away from the masters.'

'What did you wager?'

'Favours mostly. Sometimes chores or dares. We didn't usually have coin, but it was great when we did.' He snuck a piece of Titus's chicken. 'Easy come, easy go, though. Right?'

Annev didn't want to engage. He had one copper clip left, and he didn't care to spend it heedlessly. He found himself wishing for his stipend on becoming a master avatar, but the coins had been lost – or stolen from him – when he was thrown in the Academy's dungeons. He huffed, guessing Fyn still had *his* stipend. The thought left Annev feeling a bit sour, particularly as Fyn seemed to be doing well at the gambling table that afternoon.

Annev pulled out Sodar's bottomless sack to distract himself and began to rummage inside, looking for anything of interest. Amazingly, he found nine copper spears, a pair of copper stars, three silver staves, and a single silver moon. That brightened his mood considerably, but it also left him wondering what other treasures remained hidden in the bottomless sack, if he thought to search for them.

Annev dropped the coins back into the sack and plunged his hand in once again, feeling for Sodar's Speur Dún papers. He found them quickly enough but found himself returning them again, uninterested in Sodar's dry translation of the ancient scriptures, regardless of their Terran origin or their damning perspective on theological matters, and a little heartsick to see his mentor's handwriting.

Annev fished in the sack again and drew out a different stack of papers. He glanced through them and was surprised to see this packet was in a stranger's handwriting. Even so, Annev spied some places where Sodar had added his own notes, either as revisions or as an addendum to the original.

What's this? Annev thought, curious what had summoned this particular document into his hands. He had been idly thinking about the mysterious crossbowman in Banok and speculating that the attacker had been one of the Siänar, the six elite assassins of Keos. Oyru had been one of them, after all, and Sodar had said there were others.

Sure enough, as Annev read through the documents, he saw they dealt almost exclusively with the Siänar. And while Annev couldn't guess at the author's identity, it was easy to identify Sodar's tightly packed scrawl correcting the manuscript.

Annev glanced over at Jian and Fyn and saw they were still busy at the gambling table. Therin and Titus were likewise occupied, engrossed as they were in the food and their conversation. Satisfied, Annev turned his attention to the mysterious papers.

> *My reading suggests The Six rarely associate with one another and, at best, tolerate one another. Sometimes, they will work together to hunt a common enemy, but this is rare.*
>
> *It is my belief that Dortafola communicates the will of Keos to The Six, and I suspect the vampyr's servants operate beyond the purview of the established Terran theocracy, which reports directly to the Terran God-king, Neruacanta . . .*

Annev skimmed the next page, skipping ahead.

> *Shachran has been confirmed as one of the living members of The Six. This is remarkable as he is a Darite who has somehow managed to pervert his racial connection to quaire to enable him to summon the undead. I cannot fathom how such a thing is possible as that taint is only found among Yomadic sorcerers, yet it seems Shachran has found a way to subvert the very laws of blood-magic.*

Sodar had added:

> *Blood-talents not limited to genetic ancestry! Must share with Reeve the next time he complains about my studies.*

Annev smiled at this, catching a glimpse of his mentor's often subversive nature. *Even amidst the Dionachs Tobar,* Annev thought, *he challenged what others assumed was truth. He was never content to accept what others told him.* Annev's smile deepened, recognising that much of his own stubbornness came from a life lived with the priest.

He skipped ahead again, skimming notes on Oyru, the Shadow Reborn, which only guessed at details Annev could already confirm from his confrontation with the assassin – though it did speculate about an apprentice, which he found interesting. He read about Mollah, the Whispering Witch, with more interest and saw Sodar had noted she was probably an Ilumite Lightslinger and Auramancer. Next came the Faceless Beggar, whose peculiar abilities allowed him to move unnoticed through the general populace.

> *Dortafola's remaining tomes say only this of him: 'Travelling light through Narj [sic] and found a man hanging from a tree. Unconscious but not dead. I cut him down and revived him. Refused to give his name and does not talk much. Soft spoken . . . The Narjman has accepted my offer to join the Siänar. He may prove useful after all.'*

The Faceless Beggar, Annev thought, *Mollah the Whispering Witch, and Shachran the Necromancer. With Oyru, that's four of the Siänar.* He flipped another page. *Bratóg Blacktongue could be a fifth . . . and there's one more.* Annev skimmed the rest of the manuscript but found no further notes on the Siänar, and only one further addition from Sodar:

> *Saltair the lizardman. One of the lesser keokum. Works as a mercenary in Odarnea, Innistiul, and Western Ilumea. Reeve has encountered him a few times. Described him as an adept tracker and fighter. Black scales can change to match surroundings. Bite is venomous. Carnivore. Keeps himself robed when travelling in cities and has a swaying gait when he walks. Most dangerous in the forest and the water. May not be wholly loyal to Dortafola?*

And there the manuscript ended.

Annev stared into space, his stomach twisting into knots at the thought that any one of these monsters might be searching for him: a seductive fire-breathing witch, an ancient necromancer, a venomous lizardman, a faceless stranger. Then there was the Yomad, Bratóg Blacktongue, about whom the manuscript said very little, or Oyru might be trying to finish what he started in Chaenbalu.

Damn, Annev thought, suddenly feeling paranoid. Six assassins – six servants of the vampyr Dortafola, who served Keos. But what was the likelihood that one of the six had been responsible for the crossbow attack in Banok? Having learned a little more about them, Annev felt the chances were small. Maybe the Beggar – the 'Narjman' – but it seemed amateurish, even for that cypher.

So, who had ordered the attack? What had precipitated it? Could Sraon be right, and the Ilumites had been behind it to gain Annev's trust and help? Annev didn't know, but the whole thing felt wrong somehow, and Sodar's notes on the Siänar had done little to address his concerns. He shoved the papers back into Sodar's sack and started to draw the string tight, then stopped.

The artifacts, Annev thought. *The ones I stole from the Vault. I never took the time to study them.* He shoved his hand back into the sack, suddenly giddy at the prospect of examining his half-forgotten treasures. Moments later he withdrew the four items: a simple copper ring, a second ring sculpted to look like a pair of entwined silver–gold snakes, a lacy handkerchief, and a nondescript wooden rod. Annev placed all four artifacts on the table and picked up the handkerchief first, resting it lightly on the palm of his hand as he attempted to identify its magic.

Annev breathed slowly, concentrating. As he inhaled, he caught the distinct smell of something floral – roses? Cherry blossoms? – and then the scent was gone. Curious, he held the scrap of cloth up to his nose and sniffed. *A bouquet of flowers,* Annev thought. *Lots of different flowers.* He sniffed again, let his lungs fill with the perfumed air, and exhaled. He felt invigorated – the more pungent smells of the pub now overwhelmed by the fresh scent – yet he perceived no additional magic within the artifact. He turned the handkerchief over and studied the fabric, noting that tiny runes for air, water and *quaire* had been stitched into the border of the napkin.

Vanity, Annev thought. Some noble had commissioned an Artificer to create a scented handkerchief. He scoffed. *Pure, stupid vanity*.

Annev scooped the handkerchief back into the bag and moved onto the copper ring. It was a heavy thing, unadorned and just large enough to fit on his forefinger, and it gave him no clues as to its nature while it rested in the palm of his hand. He couldn't know without slipping it on, so he braced himself, glanced at Therin and Titus, then pinched the ring between the fingers of his gloved prosthetic and slipped the copper band onto his right hand.

Annev's vision blurred and suddenly turned a misty-red. He blinked as motes of crimson floated in front of his eyes, and the world pulsated around him in sync with the throb and thrum of the heartbeats in the room. Annev stared at his friends, leaving the ring on in his surprise, and then he began to notice the heartbeats of his two friends pulsing at different speeds. Titus's pulse was high and fast as he listened to Therin's story, while Therin's beat low and steady ... until he surreptitiously reached over and plucked a morsel of chicken from Annev's plate. Therin's eyes were fixed on Titus, yet Annev saw the boy's heartbeat quicken as he noticed Annev had spotted his theft. At the same time, Annev noted that his own senses were heightened – he could smell the rosemary on the turnips, the roasted chicken, Therin's bad breath and Titus's sweat. He focused on these last two scents, doing more than smelling them – he was *tasting* the air. His tongue and nose tingled with Fyn's musk, and he knew without looking that the other boy was leaving the gambling table.

Annev swallowed, unnerved by the throbbing mist of blood that seem to fill the room. With growing unease, he slipped the copper ring from his finger and dropped it back into the sack, and the world shifted back into normalcy. He breathed an audible sigh of relief, his stomach starting to settle again, and thought that perhaps this wasn't the best time to examine the artifacts. The task needed more privacy, and for him to be less anxious.

Before Annev could bag the remaining items, though, Fyn and Jian plunked themselves down on either side of him.

'He cheats,' Fyn said, pointing at the Yomad. 'I should have won that last trick – I had a winning hand – but he called me anyway.'

Jian raised a finger. 'I, too, had a winning hand. My choices were then to call or raise.'

'He raised me right to the top of my winnings!' Fyn said, slapping the table. 'Then he took the whole godsdamned pot and left those rivermen reeling.' He shook his head. 'You'll need to watch yourself, Jian. If I felt like you were cheating, those dock workers sure as hell will be thinking the same thing.'

The pale-skinned Yomad pulled his hood up, suddenly self-conscious, though Annev caught a small smile puckering the man's pink lips. 'I apologise, Master Fyunai. I have never played games of chance before as they are unpopular in Terra Majora. Was I *not* supposed to win?'

Fyn sputtered. 'You can win if you like, but not by too much – or too easily. You do that, people won't like playing with you. Or, worse, they'll come back to reclaim their winnings.'

'Then I should return the coins to our friends. That would unburden their souls, yes?'

Fyn slapped a hand to his forehead and dragged it down his mouth, shaking his head. 'You try to explain it,' he said, waving at Titus, Therin, and Annev. 'I'm going to grab a drink.'

'I thought you lost all your coin,' Therin said, looking sullen.

Fyn snorted. 'I'm not an idiot – I *always* keep something back.'

Therin grunted in response, his hand slowly reaching up to swipe another roasted turnip. This time Annev slapped his hand away and the boy pulled back, full of mock offence.

'Master Ainnevog,' Jian said, his white fingers prodding the two items still lying on the table. 'What are these treasures you have before you? I sense Yomad magic.'

'Hmm?' Annev looked down at the wooden rod and the snake ring. He picked up the latter, examining the silver snake and its gold twin: they were twined together, each biting its own tail.

'Codavora,' he said, remembering Tosan's description of the ring-snakes.

Jian nodded. 'Ouroboros.' He extended his hand. 'May I see?'

Annev dropped the artifact into the Marrow-Lich's palm. Jian turned it over, his fingers rubbing the metal. 'Yes,' he said, returning it to Annev. 'There is a connection in the silver serpent, but it is not strong. Like a prophecy ring, but less potent.'

'Precognition?'

'Yes, that is the word. The magic ... it will push you towards the fate that Fate has ordained.'

'The what?'

'Excuse me. That translation is not well.' Jian paused. 'It will direct you to the *destiny* that the *God of Fate* has set before you.'

Annev frowned. 'Not sure I like that – I don't want fate trying to control me, or Tacharan, or anyone else for that matter.'

'Of course not, Master Ainnevog, but this merely whispers what is soon to come. It is less a question of Fate and more one of ...' He twisted his fingers in the air, as if trying to summon the right word. 'Threads? Promptings? I do not know the word in your language – but put it on, please. Experience is better than description.'

Annev did so, if reluctantly, carefully working the smaller ring onto his right pinky finger. Despite the bulkiness of the golden prosthetic, it was surprisingly dexterous, and he was able to slide the ring into place on his flesh hand as if it belonged there. Annev waited but felt nothing. 'What, uh ... what should I feel?'

'The future,' Jian said, as if that should be obvious. 'Come. Try.' Jian held up his open palm then stuck his hand behind his back. 'How many fingers?'

Therin leaned over, studying whatever Jian held behind his back, then he looked back at Annev and nodded encouragement.

Annev hesitated. 'Uh, I don't know. Should I?'

'Guess.'

'I suppose ... maybe three?'

Therin's eyes widened, his head nodding in sync with Jian's. 'Very good, Master Ainnevog. You see how the ring prompted you?'

'But it didn't tell me anything,' Annev protested. 'I guessed – I got *lucky*.'

'Yes!' Jian said, slapping Annev on the shoulder. 'That is the word I searched for. *Luck*. This is a Ring of Luck.'

Annev frowned. 'You've seen these before?'

'They are not common, but yes. The silver snake contains the magic of seeing without seeing. It prompts you with feelings of the future – a Yomad blood-talent.' He pointed at the gold snake. 'The other serpent usually contains the blood of an Ilumite, to help inspire positive feelings, or to sense the feelings of others.'

Titus and Therin both looked at Annev, the former with awe and the latter with covetousness.

'Can I borrow it, Annev?' Therin asked, his voice filled with longing.

'Not right now, Therin.' Annev slipped the codavora ring from his finger and dropped it into the bottomless sack. 'These came from the Vault of Damnation – I picked them up when I was trying to escape my prison cell – and I'm still not sure what they do.'

'Jian just said what it did!' Therin protested, his voice rising. 'You've got a *good luck* ring. You should share it! I mean, you've already got tonnes of great stuff from the Vault. And I only want it so I can play another hand of cards. That's all, I swear.'

'No,' Annev repeated, dropping the unidentified wooden rod into the sack too. He cinched it tight and replaced it in the interior pocket of his tunic. 'Magic can be ... unpredictable. We shouldn't experiment with it here.'

'Fine,' Therin grumbled, huffing, 'but next time I could use a spot of luck ...' Therin's eyes suddenly widened. 'Wait a second. Jian, did you use your magic when we were playing? Did you *know* what cards we were dealt?'

Jian surveyed the table innocently. 'Is that improper, Avatar Therin? I am new to your games of chance, but I was told that was the goal – to guess your opponents' cards and to bid when you have the winning hand.' He looked between Titus and Annev, his cheeks flushing. 'Have I done something wrong, Master Ainnevog? Steward Titus?'

The boys looked at each other, Therin scowling and Titus and Annev trying to suppress their laughter. Fyn returned just then and sat down at the table, a mug of ale clutched in his fist. He took in everyone's expressions.

'What did I miss?' he asked, slowly raising the mug to his lips.

Therin pointed at Jian. 'He cheated. At cards.'

Fyn raised an eyebrow. 'Did he admit it?'

'Yes!'

'Jian,' Fyn said, his face solemn, 'did you admit cheating?'

'Yes, Master Fyunai. I apologise. It seems I did not understand the rules of the game.'

'The first rule of cards, Jian, is that you never, *ever* admit you were cheating.'

'But ... was I not cheating?'

Fyn shrugged. 'That depends. The way I see it, cheating is part of the game.'

'Wait,' Therin said, his face darkening further, 'were *you* cheating?'

Fyn looked affronted. 'I never cheat.'

'Only ... you just said—'

'That I never cheat.' He raised his mug. 'Neither does Master Nikloss, isn't that right, Jian?'

The soothsayer lowered his face into his hands. 'I do not know, but I fear Avatar Therin is correct.'

'No,' Fyn said, placing one hand on Jian's shoulder and another on the coins the man had stacked atop the table. 'We *never* cheat – and if we do, we don't admit it.' Fyn winked at the Yomad and Jian cocked his head at him, confused by the gesture. Then he looked down at the table and saw part of his winnings had disappeared. He smiled then.

'Ah ha! I see, *yes*. Very clever. The game continues after the cards have been played. Very good! An excellent lesson, Master Fyunai.'

Annev could only shake his head and laugh. He pushed his half-eaten meal towards Therin. 'You can have the rest. Eat fast. Sraon just walked in.'

He went to meet the blacksmith.

'Everything go all right?' Annev asked when he got close, made anxious by the look on Sraon's face.

248

'Took care of the horse,' the smith sniffed, 'but I had the damnedest time finding Tukas.'

'So you couldn't contact the Dionachs?'

'Well, that's the real question, isn't it? I spoke to a few promising folks, dropped the passwords I knew. No one responded, though. Didn't get a single solid reply. Made me feel half mad – and I don't doubt the folks I spoke to felt the same way.' He chewed his lip. 'The whole thing makes me uncomfortable.'

'You think something happened to Tukas – or to the Order?'

'Aye, maybe.' He stroked his chin. 'Then again, it could be nothing. Either way, we'll need to wait a spell and see if the Order sends anyone to check on us. Might be they want to confirm our identities.'

'But that's what the password is for, isn't it?'

'Aye,' Sraon said again, looking worried. 'I see you've all stayed out of trouble.'

'More or less,' Annev said, lowering his voice. 'Master Nikloss may have accidentally cheated a table of rivermen at cards. So far as I can tell, though, no harm was done.'

'Is that right?' Sraon gave a crooked grin. 'That fellow is certainly full of surprises.' He passed Annev two coppers. 'Get me something to eat? My feet are sore, and I'd love a minute to rest my heels.'

'Sure,' Annev said, taking the coin. 'Be right back.' He jogged over to the bar and tried to wave down the serving woman who'd brought them the chicken and turnips. She was busy with another patron, though, so Annev was waiting at the bar when a dark-haired man sidled up beside him.

'Hard to get people's attention around here,' he said by way of conversation.

Annev grunted in response, distracted and disinterested. Instinctively, he lowered a hand to his purse – empty as it was – then turned his shoulder to the man.

'Sometimes, even when looking for someone, they can be right in front of you, calling your name even, and you still don't see them.'

Annev turned to look at the stranger more closely. The fellow was of middling years, had dark brown hair, brown eyes, and an unassuming posture.

'Tukas?' Annev said, studying the man's reaction.

The stranger's relief was evident. 'I understand you'd like to see one of our ... family?'

Annev guessed at the man's meaning. 'Yes. Is he close?'

'He's already in the capital – lucky for you.' Tukas nodded at the door. 'Let me speak with our mutual friend and then I'll bring you to the safehouse.' He gestured at Sraon's table. 'Have your friends ready to move.' Then he slipped off his stool and headed out the front door. Annev watched the man go, beginning to feel there was something odd going on, but before he could articulate it Sraon joined him, his calloused hand landing on his shoulder.

'All right, Annev?'

'I ... think so, yes.' He tried to smile. 'I think I just spoke to Tukas.'

'Did you now?' Sraon looked around, his eyes searching the crowd. 'So where is the bastard? And why didn't he speak to *me*?'

Annev gestured to the door. 'He just left to get Reeve.'

'Reeve is *here*? In Luqura?'

'That's what he said. I asked if he was in the capital and he said yes.'

'That's ... strange.'

'Right?' Annev said, his anxiety growing. 'You didn't think he'd be here for a week yet, and then Tukas said—'

'What did this man Tukas look like?'

Annev shrugged. 'Hard to place. Medium build. Tanned skin. Sort of ... average looking. Nothing really stood out about him.'

'His hair? His beard? Did he ... Well, hold on now.' Sraon's eyes suddenly brightened, his attention locked on the entrance to the pub. 'Tukas said he was sending for Reeve?'

'Yeah,' Annev said, his own attention turning towards the door. 'At least, I think so.'

'Well, I may have just spotted him.'

Annev squinted at the two men who had just come in, expecting one of them to bear some resemblance to Sodar, but neither man matched Annev's expectations. Instead of a priestly fellow in blue robes, a dirty, bald-headed beggar had entered, followed by an Innistiul slaver.

'Who?' Annev asked, still uncertain.

'He's coming right towards us.'

Annev watched the two men approach, uncertain which he'd rather was Reeve. The slaver glowered at Annev and Sraon for an uncomfortable moment, then turned and walked away.

The ragged beggar approached them. He stank of urine and faeces. A thick beard obscured most of his face, and he carried a crude walking staff for support. When Annev saw the man's dirt-encrusted fingernails, he cringed and drew back.

But the beggar kept coming closer. He glared at Annev and Sraon with one crooked eye, then ignored them for the bar keep.

'Whisky,' the fellow said, his voice cracking. 'I'll take a dram of fire water.'

'Oy!' The barman scowled. 'What have I told you about comin' in here? Take your godsdamned filth and get out.'

The beggar didn't move. Instead his body went slack and his face turned blank and unresponsive. The barman swore and dropped a hand beneath the bar, clearly searching for something – a weapon, if Annev guessed correctly.

To Annev's surprise, Sraon saddled up to the foul-smelling man and asked, 'Have you come for the fire or the water?'

The beggar's blue eyes squinted through muck and unwashed hair. 'Water,' he said, eyes shining. 'Clean air and fresh water.'

The barman raised a cudgel from behind the bar, his eyes dark. 'Now don't go botherin' my customers or I'll—'

'It's fine, neighbour. I think our friend will be leavin' after we have a chat.' Sraon dropped a coin atop the bar, his eyes never leaving the beggar. 'Why don't you fetch our friend something cheap to drink.' The barman muttered something rude under his breath and took the coin.

'Are you acquainted with skywater?' The beggar nodded once, watching Sraon. 'And might we accompany you and share our water with one another?'

A faint smile appeared amidst the stranger's overgrown beard.

'It is fine to share the blessings of Odar,' the ragged man whispered – and then he winked. 'Come. I'll take you some place safe.'

Sraon's face fell. 'Are you expecting trouble?'

'You tell me,' the beggar said, indicating the door.

Annev turned and saw the first Innistiulman was now accompanied by Elar Kranak, the slave master from the plaza who had confronted Sraon. Other Innistiul slavers filed in behind him and started spreading out amongst the bar's patrons, their number including the armed guards who'd been with Elar at the merfolk fountain. Sraon swore aloud and turned away from the slaver's searching gaze.

'I'd bet my good eye he's not here by accident,' Sraon whispered in hushed tones, his face turned towards Annev. 'Get the others, quick, and don't be obvious about it. Take them out the back door.' Annev nodded. 'Take our new friend with you and I'll meet you by the stables if you can manage it. Don't get separated.' Sraon rose and ambled towards the back of the pub, his gait unhurried. Annev waited half a minute, his attention divided between Sraon's retreating figure, the dirty beggar at his side and his friends still sitting at the table.

'You must be Sodar's boy,' the stranger said, examining Annev with a strange twinkle in his eye. 'I've heard a lot about you. All good things.'

'And you are ...?'

'You haven't guessed?'

Annev had, and he'd hoped he was wrong. Such a ragged, stinking man ... he was nothing like Annev had expected. But then the beggar smiled, his mossy teeth gleaming with amusement, and Annev knew his fears were correct.

'You're Reeve,' Annev said, stomach churning, 'the High Priest of the Dionachs Tobar.'

The filthy man's smile widened further, revealing a missing molar. 'That I am.'

Chapter Twenty-Four

Just then, Elar pointed one thick arm at the table where Jian, Fyn, Titus and Therin were sitting. The slavers moved, signing to one another in an unfamiliar handspeak.

'We've got to run,' Annev whispered as he took a step towards the table. He looked at Reeve, who hadn't moved from his seat at the bar. 'I don't suppose you have any tricks for getting us out of this?' As Annev spoke, the barman returned and slid a cup of water roughly across the bar, its contents sloshing in front of Reeve. The man dipped a finger into the spilled water, his blue eyes sparkling. 'My boy,' the high priest said, tracing a glyph in the surface of the liquid, 'I've got much more than tricks. Gather your friends. I'll take care of anyone who tries to stop you.'

Annev did, as much trusting the dung-stained priest to know his business as he was eager to leave. He reached his friends' table seconds before the Innistiul slavers.

'We need to go.' Annev didn't bother to lower his voice. 'Out the back door – right now.' Titus and Fyn were on their feet. Jian stood a half-second later, followed by Therin.

'What's going on?' Therin whined, his quick hands scooping the remaining food from the others' plates. 'We're not really leaving, are we?' He noticed the slavers hurrying to encircle their table, a chicken bone half-raised to his mouth. 'Oh,' he said.

'Run!' Annev shouted, grabbing a chair and hurling it at the nearest slaver. Fyn had the same idea, for he followed up a half-second later, hurling both his and Therin's chairs at the warriors closing on him. Titus scurried towards the back door and Jian followed him, his robe and hood pulled tight to his body.

'Blood and filth!' Therin swore as another slaver tried to grab him. He mashed chicken bone and turnip into the man's face, then grabbed Fyn's flagon and smashed it against his skull. As he fell, another Innistiulman took his place, but Therin was already running to join Titus and Jian at the back door of the pub.

'These men are convicts!' Elar bellowed, his bulky form blocking the front door. 'By the accord of King Cheng and King Lenka, I claim them as my property, slaves to House Kranak.'

Many of the bar's patrons had been edging out of the way of the fight, but this gave them pause.

'A gold solari to anyone who brings me one of those boys!'

Suddenly half the patrons were on their feet, tipping chairs and tables in their haste to get at Fyn and Annev. The group of rivermen who had lost their coins to Fyn and Jian were quickest, rushing to grapple Fyn from behind. The hulking boy shoved off the first two attackers, but most of the rivermen matched his height and build, denying Fyn his usual advantages. Annev spun one man, punching him in the side of the face, but then a slaver grabbed Annev from behind, twisting his arms and shoulders and forcing him to the ground.

With a roar, Annev tore his gloved golden hand away from his attacker and used the superior strength of his prosthetic to grab the man's calf and crunch his shin bone, shattering it with such force that white fragments pierced the skin. The slaver shrieked, falling to his knees, and Annev punched him in the skull with his metal fist. Blood and matter flew from the man's mouth and nose, half his face caved in from the force of the blow.

Annev swore beneath his breath, shocked to see the strength of the magic artifact. He had no time to regret his brutality, though, and turned to punch the nearest of the rivermen holding Fyn. The man tried to dodge, which only gave Fyn the momentum he needed to free his arm. He unslung one of his maces and slammed it into the man still holding him. The riverman fell, blood gurgling from his mouth, and the other backed off, leaving Fyn beside Annev, his second mace freed from its sheath.

'It's like we're back at Janak's palace,' Fyn said, breathing hard and grinning like a fool.

'Yeah,' Annev said, hesitating to draw his magic flamberge. 'But these aren't thralls. They're just servants and labourers. I don't want to kill them!'

'Kill or be killed,' Fyn said, spinning his bloody mace. 'Those have always been the rules.' They backed towards the other end of the pub together, Annev's hand resting on his sword hilt.

The slavers advanced, their scimitars flying from their scabbards, but the remaining rivermen hesitated, uncertain their prize was worth the cost.

Reeve suddenly appeared between Fyn and Annev holding a bottle of liquor. He upended it, and rapidly traced a rune in the air with the falling alcohol.

'*Reo-amais-amaisect-amas!*' The liquid glyph held its shape, frozen in mid-air, held by the magic of Reeve's words.

Then it tinkled like broken glass and fell to the earth.

A cloud of dense fog suddenly filled the air, hung for a moment, then crackled into frost. A heartbeat later a gust of wind blew the frozen air across the bar, scouring slavers and patrons alike with a cold wind and tiny needles of ice.

'Come on!' Reeve snapped, tugging the two boys out through the back door, racing together out of The Bottomless Cup and into the alley behind the bar. A dozen feet away, Sraon stood with Therin and Jian beside the saddled black mare. Titus sat astride the beast, his hands clutching tight to the saddle pommel.

Reeve dashed ahead, his strides sure. 'Follow me,' he said as he passed the blacksmith and the soothsayer. 'And hurry!'

They ran north, boots thumping the cobblestones as they navigated the streets of the Old Low Quarter, Reeve at the head of the group, his quick pace taking them down one side alley and then another. Annev wondered if they were in the clear just as a monstrous shape in shining black plate jumped down from one of the rooftops, blocking their path.

Reeve shouted in surprise, but didn't hesitate to fling a blast of magic at the attacker, this time hurling him back over the rooftops in a whirlwind of air and a crackle of lightning.

'Wow!' Therin shouted, still sprinting. 'Did you guys see that?'

They ran on, expecting another ambush. Time seemed to crawl as they hurried through the increasingly derelict streets behind Reeve. Five minutes became ten, then twenty, and the group became increasingly sure they were not being pursued. When they passed a section of burned-out buildings, Titus spoke up from atop the mare, his voice just above a whisper.

'Is this the *Ash Quarter*?'

'Yes,' said Reeve. 'We're nearing the safehouse now. Quiet.'

They slowed as Reeve led them into a crumbling tenement, the building mostly destroyed and its beams burned to cinders. On the other side Titus dismounted and they led the beast through the rubble of more fallen buildings, past the firepits of homeless Luqurans and into the shadow of a burned-out cobbler's shop.

'Leave the horse here,' Reeve said, helping unload the mare. 'It's too recognisable.' Sraon nodded, unloading the last of their supplies, and they said their goodbyes to the one horse they had taken from Chaenbalu.

'Goodbye, horse,' Titus said, rubbing the mare's muzzle, his eyes misty. 'Maybe you'll find us again before we leave.'

'Maybe she will,' Annev said, but he doubted it. They were in a rough part of the city, and the hard faces staring from the windows seemed as likely to eat the horse as ride her.

The foul-smelling priest led them down another alley, away from the mare and into a dark, unlit tunnel. Minutes passed as they walked in darkness, their footsteps echoing back from the narrow walls. Eventually, they turned a corner and Reeve pushed a rusty iron door open, taking them back out into the waning afternoon light.

'Almost there,' Reeve said, darting through the crumbling wall of a burned-out hovel that connected to another, larger building, its locked oak door barring admittance.

'Is this ... a rectory?'

'It was,' Reeve said, indicating a rotting bed and broken furniture. 'And this used to be a church.' He poured out the remains of the bottle of ale he still carried, wetting his fingers in the alcohol.

With the brown liquid running down his fingers, he sketched a sloppy glyph on the surface of the old church door, then whispered something to the soot-stained wood. There was dull *whump* and a puff of ash blew out around the door. The filthy man rubbed his bald pate and turned the handle, opening the once-locked portal.

'This is it. Go on now.'

Sraon entered first, followed by Titus, Therin, Fyn and Jian. Annev was last, and Reeve closed the warded door behind them, sealing them all inside in the dry, ash-blown edifice.

'So Sodar is truly dead,' Reeve said, eyes damp.

'Yes,' Annev said, struggling to keep his own emotions under control. A single candle flickered on a charred altar in the corner of the room, its tallow burned down to half its original length. Outside, the shadows had lengthened as afternoon became evening and evening became night.

'And you didn't come because of Sodar's letter,' Annev said, his voice returning, 'You're here because you lost contact with Arnor.'

Reeve nodded. Since arriving at the safehouse the high priest had been transformed. He'd washed, dressed in a dark blue robe, and had even taken a razor to his beard and unkempt hair, trimming the former into a neat goatee and the latter into a short shock of spiky hair crowning the halo of an otherwise bald head. The change was a relief to Annev, the wizard-priest more resembling the image he'd formed in his head. Though he still looked a good deal younger than Sodar.

'I knew Anor wouldn't have much luck convincing the old man,' Reeve said, his angular face looking stony and severe now that it was uncovered, 'but I thought his visit would soften Sodar up for my own entreaties. I left just a few days after Arnor left Quiri, stopped in Ankyr to meet with another of our civilian contacts, and then came here to meet with Tukas and Keezel. Neither had heard back from Arnor ... and then Keezel disappeared. She had been my contact in the eastern part of the city, in the merchant district, so Tukas and I spent a few days seeing if we could discover what happened to her.' The priest scowled, his blue eyes turning as dark as a stormy sky. 'Tukas disappeared during our search. That's why Sodar's letter never reached me. Tukas wasn't there to get it from our contact in Banok.'

'Farmer Gribble,' Sraon said, nodding. 'There's a good chance the letter is still with him then.'

'Most likely.'

'Hold on,' Annev said. 'If Tukas is missing, who did I speak to in the pub? Wasn't he your messenger?'

'No messenger,' Reeve said, exchanging a worried look with Sraon. 'It was luck that brought me to the tavern, though I've been checking it often of late. Tell me, what did this messenger look like?'

'He was ... well, just average. Medium height. His hair was sandy ... maybe brown?' Annev tried to think but couldn't recall the face of the man who'd approached him. 'It's fuzzy. I don't even remember what he asked me. Only that he said he was going to fetch Reeve.'

'Or maybe,' Sraon said, his eyes narrowing, 'he went to fetch Elar Kranak.'

'That ... actually makes sense.' Annev frowned as something niggled at the back of his mind. He had just read about a Siänar who could go unnoticed in a crowd. Could that have been the person he'd had spoken to?

'Well,' Fyn said, interrupting his thoughts, 'I'm glad some of this makes sense to you, because it makes absolutely *no* sense to me. Like, why did this priest come to us looking and smelling like a rotting garderobe? And what in the five hells happened at that pub?' He stood and pointed at Reeve. 'Did you freeze those people? Are they dead?'

'It was more of a heavy frost,' Reeve said, also standing, 'and I doubt it killed anyone. As for my appearance ...' Reeve glanced at the stinking rags and curls of brown hair he'd left in the corner of the chapel. 'It's been a rough journey, with many searching for me. Folk are less likely to stare at the man behind the beard when he smells like horseshit.' He smiled then sniffed his wrist. 'Perhaps I got carried away.'

'No,' Sraon said. 'It was perfect. That pub was crawling with spies – folks lookin' for you, and for us, too. I wish I'd known it was compromised.'

'You couldn't have known,' Reeve said, dropping a hand on Sraon's shoulder. 'We didn't know it ourselves until two days ago.' He sighed. 'I'm glad you made it, though – even if it was just to share the sad news about Sodar. That's one priest I never thought I'd outlive.'

The nave fell silent, each tending to their own thoughts. Night had fallen and the sounds of evening activity outside marked a change in the mood of the Ash Quarter's inhabitants; instead of the silent scuffle of street urchins prowling the alleys, they could hear the distant shouts of a brawl breaking out. There was a scream – and then the streets were quiet once more.

'So,' Annev said, breaking the silence, 'do you think you can help me remove the Hand of Keos?'

Reeve rubbed his close-cropped goatee as if expecting to still find his beard there, then his hand fell away. 'I can certainly try. Let me take a look at it.'

Annev began tugging the smithing glove from his left hand. As the tough leather peeled back from his forearm, a faint glow began to fill the room, its brilliance nearly equal to the guttering candle. Reeve sucked in a deep breath, squinting against the dim light.

'Remarkable,' he said, studying the artistry covering the golden prosthetic. 'It's just as I remember it.'

'Remember?' Titus asked, perched on a pew. 'You've *seen* it before?'

'That I have. Probably the same place Sodar saw it.'

Annev bit his lip. 'Sodar? I never got to show it to him.'

'He would have recognised it. We were both there when Keos fell. We saw him die – saw his hammer and his golden hand fall to the earth. The hammer was given to the Halcyon Knights along with the other diamagi – the Staff of Odar and the Flute of Lumea – but our order kept the Hand of Keos. Kept it safe until the Steward of the Hand disappeared anyway. It seems we've been backsliding ever since. Losing artifacts ... losing people.' He shook his head. 'But that is my concern – and yours is removing that hand.' Reeve turned his palms upward. 'Bring it here, Annev.'

He did so, holding his breath as he rested his golden arm in the hands of the Arch-Dionach Tobar. The blue-robed priest traced the filigree and arabesques carved into the metal. He turned the prosthetic over, reading the inscriptions carved on both sides of the hand. He prodded the palm, flexed one of the fingers. He scraped his fingernail along the reinforced knuckles and white-gold bracelet.

'Do you feel any of that?'

'I feel all of it,' Annev said. 'It's not the same as my real hand, though. It's almost like I'm wearing a glove or a gauntlet ... but it doesn't feel restrictive. The gold metal is sensitive, like skin – *more* sensitive in some ways – just thick and hard, almost like a callus. I can feel the texture of the metal, but I can also feel my blood pumping beneath the surface. It's also very dextrous. Not clumsy at all.'

'And your old prosthetic – the one that Sodar obtained for you? What happened to it?'

'It was lost. Burned in a fire.'

'I see.' Reeve prodded the seam between the pink flesh and the golden arm. 'It really is remarkable. An artifact forged by the God of Craft.'

'You mean Keos,' Fyn said, interjecting once again. 'Keos made that.'

'Correct.'

'I've never heard him called the God of Craft.'

'He's been called many things – the God of Art, the God of Creation, the God of Men – but those names have all fallen into disuse, particularly among our people. Now you only hear of the Fallen God – the God of War, the God of Earthblood. Keos is all of those things, or he was when he was alive.'

'But you think Keos is dead?' Annev asked, keeping his voice neutral.

Reeve nodded, slow and steady. 'Yes, I think so. Sodar believed differently, I know. But there was much we didn't agree on. Still, Sodar was a good man. The Order will miss him, as shall I.' Reeve let go of the prosthetic, his hand stroking his beard. 'As for your arm ... I'm going to need some of your fluids.'

'My what?'

'Fluids,' Reeve repeated. 'Your blood, saliva, tears. Even your urine would be helpful.'

Annev's mouth fell open just as Therin began to laugh.

'You want his *piss*? Annev, are you going to give him your piss? That's disgusting!'

Reeve cleared his throat. 'Unlike Sodar,' he said, the hint of a growl to his voice, 'my studies have concentrated on glyph-speaking using *quaire* – skywater. I'll need to draw glyphs on your arm, and I could use water, but since the hand is attached to you, the spell will be exponentially more effective if I use your fluids. Of course, this is all theoretical. If I could, I would ask a Terran Artificer to help you ... but I wouldn't know where to find one. Even if I did, they'd be as likely to kill you and steal that golden hand. It's an important part of their religion, you know. Almost as important as the hammer – *more* important, in some ways.' He licked his cracked lips. 'I could attempt to separate you from the artifact by removing the vacuum that holds it to your flesh. That should be easy enough, but this is also an abnormal artifact. It's bonded to you in a way that goes beyond mere flesh and blood.'

'That's what Dolyn said.'

'Dolyn?'

Sraon raised his hand. 'Smithing friend o' mine. Lives in Banok. She's an Orvane – New Terran lass, nice girl – and a Forgemaster.'

'Truly?' Reeve said, his expression revealing nothing. 'That's fortuitous. A Forgemaster would be an excellent second choice, in lieu of a true Artificer. What happened?'

'Well, ah ...'

'She burned her hands,' Annev said, interrupting Sraon. 'Or maybe *I* burned them. She got burned and I nearly blew up her smithy.'

'I ... see.'

'Odar's *balls*, Annev!' Fyn swore, backing away from the glowing prosthetic. 'When were you gonna tell us *that* part? "Nearly blew up her smithy!" Just like you blew up the Academy? And half of Chaenbalu?'

'Hmm. This may be more complicated than I originally thought

261

– a *lot* more complicated.' Reeve tutted his tongue against his teeth, clearly thinking. 'Perhaps we should wait. The hand doesn't seem to be doing you any actual harm, and I'd like to have the resources of the Enclave before I attempt anything.'

'You mean you want to take me to Quiri?'

'Yes.'

'I'd ... rather not.'

'I think it's necessary, Annev. Even with my skill, it's a remote chance that I'd be able to remove the prosthetic without another artisan's assistance. I was willing to try anyway, but if the Forgemaster failed ...' Reeve shook his head. 'Better to take you to the Enclave. The other Dionachs could help, and that would significantly improve our chance of success.'

'That's all then? We just wait till we get to Quiri, then try again?'

'Well ... there is one more thing that might improve our chances.'

Annev grimaced, knowing the Dionach had likely saved the worst for last. 'What is it?'

Reeve's eyes ran over the rest of the party. 'Do you know the story of Bron Gloir?'

'Bron Gloir?' Titus said, perking up. 'Of course! That was the best of Ancient Benifew's stories. The Man with a Thousand Faces. The Last of the Halcyon Knights!' He grinned. 'Everybody knows his story.'

Annev looked from Titus to Reeve. 'Sodar told me Bron is real,' Annev said, speaking slowly. 'That he's ... still alive. He said Bron has been protecting the Oracle – it was a special mission given to him by the Order.'

'What Oracle?' Fyn asked, eyebrows furrowing. 'What mission? What's this about?'

Annev waved him off. 'I'll explain later.'

'Does it have to do with Jan—'

'*Later*, Fyn,' Annev said, now glaring. The other boy glowered back, his fists clenched, but controlled his flash of anger and sat again. Annev turned back to Reeve. 'Why did you mention Bron?'

'Because it's as you said. Bron has the Oracle but it hasn't been working properly, not for a few centuries now. It used to respond to anyone's questions, but then it started becoming more selective about who it would answer. About a century ago it declared it would only respond to five people.' He held up his hand, counting off on his fingers. 'The Man with a Thousand Faces, the Crippled Warrior, the Gilded One, the Cursed Leader, and the Vessel of Keos.' He cleared his throat. 'Obviously Bron is the Man with a Thousand Faces. The others were a mystery, though, and we didn't want a vessel of Keos controlling the Oracle, so Bron went into hiding. I think, though, that this golden hand' – he gestured at Annev's prosthetic – 'makes *you* the Vessel of Keos. You aren't serving him – you aren't a true Son of Keos – but you are wearing his hand and that means his power rests on you.'

'So you think the Oracle will talk to me?'

'Yes. Which means you can ask it how to remove the hand.'

Annev looked at Fyn. 'This Oracle ... what does it look like?'

'The Oracle itself? Like a djinn or a sylph – all air and water but with the shape of a human and a mind to match the gods.'

'Yes, I've heard the stories. I meant what does it *inhabit*. Where does the Oracle live? I assume that, if Bron Gloir is protecting it, it must be held within some vessel or talisman.'

Reeve stared at Annev for a long moment, his face a mask. 'Of course. The Oracle has had many different homes over the millennia, but most recently it was contained within a brass lamp.'

Janak's lamp. Annev wondered if Fyn had also put the puzzle together, but the boy seemed more intent on studying the exits to the room. Annev licked his lips, thinking to press his luck. If his guess was right, then the Oracle was currently in the ruins of Chaenbalu ... but that would also mean Janak Harth had stolen the lamp from Bron Gloir sometime in the recent past. Was that possible?

'Do you know where the Oracle is located right now?' he asked.'

'With Bron, I would assume.'

'Right. And you know where Bron is right now? You know how to find him?'

Reeve raised both hands and wobbled his head. 'It's complicated.

263

Bron is a hard man to keep track of. A Man with a Thousand Faces – he can become any person he wishes.' Reeve chuckled, though the sound was dry, bitter. 'Bron only checks in once a year, just before Regaleus. That was last weekend – another reason I've stayed here in Luqura – but I haven't heard from or seen him.'

'So Bron has gone missing, too. Just like Tukas and Keezel – and Arnor. Just like all the other members of your order.'

Reeve stared hard at Annev, his expression cold. 'You heard Arnor talking to Sodar?'

'Yes, and I heard all about your intrigues. The rebellion that had to be quelled. That the Order is imploding.'

'It has stabilised.'

'Has it? You said that you lost both Tukas and Keezel while you were here in the city. Now it seems Bron Gloir is in the wind. That doesn't sound stable to me.'

'Annev,' Sraon said, a hint of reproach in his voice. 'The Arch-Dionach is here to help. Don't badger him.'

'I want the truth,' Annev said, his tone not quite apologetic. 'Sodar kept a lot of secrets, and he told just as many lies. I know they were all meant to keep me safe – and I loved him for that – but it was hard to trust him.' Annev pointed at Reeve. 'How do I know you're different? How do I know I can trust you, let alone the Order?'

'You want the truth, Annev? You can't.'

'Excuse me?'

Reeve cleared his throat. 'You can't trust the Order. We have done our best to eradicate its divisive elements, but people are still disappearing. One of us, at least, cannot be trusted ... that's why I wanted Sodar to come back. I knew he could be trusted, that in spite of our philosophical disagreements, he would always do what was in the best interest of the Order. I hoped that others would see him as a rallying point. That with his presence – and yours – we might turn the tide. We might begin to recruit again, and find those members who have gone into hiding. You could train with us – become *one* of us.' He stopped, apparently uncertain what more to say.

'The truth, Annev, is that I need your help as much as you need mine. More, perhaps. I know I can trust you and Sraon, and if you have vouched for Therin, Titus and Fyn, they would also be welcome at the Enclave.'

This seemed to set everyone else back, Annev in particular. He looked at his friends, uncertain what to say.

'Annev,' Titus said quietly, 'if going to Quiri would help you remove that arm – and help Reeve – I would do it.'

Annev studied his friend for a moment and then glanced at Reeve. 'What do you want with them? They don't have any magic. They can't become Dionachs.'

'That remains to be seen,' Reeve said, his expression more thoughtful. 'Sodar told me that your acolyte and avatar companions from Chaenbalu have exhibited extraordinary abilities – talents that could only be explained by an untapped potential for magic. He believes it was so common among the students and masters that none thought to question it – that the impossible became commonplace.' Here Reeve looked at Annev's three companions, his eyes searching. 'I expect all of you have a touch of the blood-talent, though what form it might take I can't say. The Enclave could help identify your talents and develop them.'

'Hold on,' Therin said, intrigued. 'You mean ... we could learn magic – *real* magic?'

'We're not going there to learn magic, Therin. We're going to help Annev.'

Reeve smiled then, and Annev knew the high priest had won Titus over – probably Therin, too. He was less sure about Fyn and himself.

'I ... don't know, Reeve. I need to think about it.' Annev paused, suddenly aware that the soothsayer was missing. 'Where's Jian?' he asked, surprised he had not noticed the man's absence.

'Upstairs,' Sraon said, pointing to a soot-blackened set of stairs at the back of the room. 'Said he needed to meditate or somethin'. I told him it wasn't safe, that the floor would probably collapse at any moment, but he just smiled in that queer way of his. Said he'd know if it was dangerous. He's still up there, so far as I know.' He squinted at Annev. 'I guess you're wantin' to talk to him – talk privately?'

'If he can see the future,' Annev said, leaning closer, 'it'd be helpful to get his opinion. See if he thinks going to Quiri is a good idea.'

'And you'd trust him?'

'No ... but I'd like another perspective. I want to consider my options before I make my decision.'

'You should really be gettin' some sleep,' Sraon said, brows furrowed. 'In fact, we should *all* be gettin' some sleep.' He said this last to everyone. 'I don't care to light another candle, and we all need the rest. Been a long few days.'

Titus yawned as if to emphasise his point, and Therin matched it with a yawn of his own. This produced a chuckle from the grizzled blacksmith and he waved the boys away, his argument already won. 'Go find yourselves some benches, lads. Rest your eyes. I'll take the first watch.'

Therin grumbled at this, but still followed Titus to the opposite end of the room to collect his bedroll. Sraon gave a small smile then peered over at Fyn, expectant. The boy stared back, unmoving, then finally rolled his eyes and joined the others.

Sraon was about to say something more to Annev, then stopped. 'I know that look, boy,' he said, then waved at the charred steps. 'Go on. If it's safe enough for him, I suppose you'll be fine. Just watch yourself – and test the floor before you step.'

Annev climbed the burned staircase leading to the second floor.

Chapter Twenty-Five

'Master Nikloss?' Annev said, emerging at the top of the stairs. He squinted into the darkness, his feet sliding cautiously along the blackened floorboards, alert for any snapping wood.

'I am here, Master Ainnevog.' The man's voice came from the heart of the darkness, muted despite its proximity. Annev reached out, felt a wall in front of him and turned the corner to see Jian sitting cross-legged in front of a strange symbol drawn in ash. Annev came closer, careful not to disturb the symbol. It wasn't until he stood just behind the soothsayer, though, that he really saw the image inscribed in the soot.

'Is that the Hand of Keos?'

Jian nodded, his pale skin still visible in the dark. 'It is, but not the hand you wear now – the hand that was lost.'

Annev looked more closely, sitting down next to the Yomad. Using the glow of his golden hand for more light, Annev studied the five pairs of glyphs drawn near each of its fingers.

'These look like Old Darite,' Annev said, pointing at the symbols, 'but they're modified somehow. I can't read them.'

'They are the symbols of the Younger Gods and their servants. Each finger represents one God.' Jian pointed at the thumb. 'Tacharan stands apart from the other four. He is the God of What May Be, and it is through him that I see what cannot be seen.'

Annev stared at the carefully drawn hand, puzzling over the ten symbols drawn there. 'You mention the servants. The Younger Gods are represented by the fingers themselves. The glyphs … represent their mages – the artisans who serve them?'

'Just so.' Jian pointed to the two symbols inscribed at the tip and base of the thumb. 'Necromancer and Seer. Each serves Tacharan.'

'But as a Marrow-Lich you're both.' Annev opened his mouth to ask a question then guessed the answer. Studying the symbols, he drew a new glyph in the ashes between them, a combination of the symbols for Seer and Necromancer. When he finished, the soothsayer pursed his lips.

'You are wise.'

Annev shrugged. 'I've studied glyphs and runes. I can't use them, but I understand their meanings. These aren't so different from Old Darite.'

They sat in silence, the only light in the room now coming from Annev's glowing hand.

'Jian, can you tell me my future?'

The albino hmmed to himself. 'Yesterday you scorned prophecy, today you seek it?'

Annev frowned in the near darkness. 'Unlike yesterday, today I am at a crossroads. I need some advice. I need to know what will happen if I go with Reeve, or if I decide to stay here.'

'And you think I can tell you.'

'Can't you?'

'I can foretell your future, Ainnevog de Breth, but you may not understand it. Prophecy is a double-edged sword, filled with things that *may* be. Many paths but no certainty. There is an inherent duality – an *ambiguity* – in foretelling.' Jian's delicate mouth formed his peculiar smile. 'You should know from the beginning that when speaking of the future I cannot speak plainly, even if it is my desire.'

Annev remembered the wood-witch's riddles. Even when threatened, Kelga had spoken ambiguously. 'I understand, Jian. I still need answers, and I think you can give them to me.'

The soothsayer studied Annev, eyes fixed on his. 'And are you prepared to sacrifice your blood for this knowledge? I will need to taste it if I am to give you a proper foretelling.'

'Oh.' Annev hesitated, suddenly uncertain. 'That seems … wrong.'

'Blood is *t'rasang* – the meta-metaphysical.' Jian drew another symbol in the ash between them, beneath Annev's symbol for a Marrow-Lich, and Annev recognised it.

'That's the symbol for *aqlumera*.'

'Correct, and this ...' Jian drew the marking for *t'rasang* just above *aqlumera*. '*This* is the symbol for blood. It combines the heat of lightfire, which fills our bodies with warmth; the liquid of skywater, which flows through our veins; and the essence of our being – our metaphysical flesh. When a Seer consumes the blood of another, they glimpse that essence. They fore*see* and fore*tell*.'

'And fore*taste*?' Annev said, with black humour.

Jian blinked at him, his face blank, then he smiled – a real grin that showed his teeth. 'Yes, Master Ainnevog. Foretasting! An excellent observation.'

Annev's smile dimmed. 'So ... you need my blood – for the foretasting, er, foretelling then? That ... makes sense.' He glanced from the symbol down to his sword and started to unsheathe the blade.

'Allow me, Master Annev.' The Yomad drew a sleek dagger from his robes, its edge razor-sharp, its point as fine as any needle. 'I will be careful with your *t'rasang*.'

Annev gritted his teeth and extended his right hand, palm upward. The Marrow-Lich turned it over and the blade sliced precisely into Annev's flesh – a tiny nick at the back of his hand, just below his thumb. Annev hissed, instinctively drawing his hand backward, but Jian's mouth was already pressed to the incision, sucking at the wound. Annev grimaced, disgusted – and then his mouth fell open.

By the dim light of his glowing prosthetic, Annev saw red veins rise to the surface of the albino's snow-white skin. Crimson branches spread out from the corners of Jian's mouth and crawled like spiderwebs across his cheeks, neck, and throat. When they reached his eyes, a translucent cloud spiralled outward from Jian's pupils, his pink irises turning a milky white. The image was un-settling, reminding Annev too much of the wood-witch's cloudy white irises.

Meanwhile, Jian continued to suck the blood from Annev's wound, the sensation both sensual and grotesque. He was about to pull away, uncomfortable, when the soothsayer stopped, his eyes staring blankly as the blood dripped from his dark red lips.

'What do you seek, Son of Seven Fathers?'

Annev fought his déjà vu as he recalled Kelga giving him the same name. He swallowed back bile and forced himself to speak.

'Tell me,' he said, the questions he'd been holding so tight rushing up to spill out at once. 'Should I go with Reeve to Quiri? Should I join the Order of the Dionachs Tobar and continue my training? Can Reeve actually remove the Hand of Keos?' He realised he had asked too much, that he might have violated some arcane rule that one was to follow when questioning a Seer.

If he had offended the Marrow-Lich, though, he gave no sign of it. Jian's lips parted, as if on the point of answering. Then his blank gaze turned to Annev, his lips wet with fresh blood. 'You will learn the truth of things if you go to Quiri – but it will not make you happy, and you will not join the Dionachs Tobar.' Annev was about to ask another question, but the Marrow-Lich was not finished: 'The High Priest of Odar *can* remove the Hand of Keos, but he will only do so if the Vessel aids him first.'

'If I *aid* him ... and how will I do that?'

'Find the First Dracolum, join with the fragments of the Broken Hand, and forge the Sword of Seeking. You must tell Reeve how to recover the Staff of Odar to earn his help.'

Annev stifled a laugh, barely able to believe what he was hearing. 'Is that all? Find the Lost Artifacts of the Gods!' He laughed again.

'No,' Jian's voice was neutral, emotionless. 'You must set his house in order, find the Man with a Thousand Faces and recover the Oracle of Odar.'

Annev didn't know what to say to that. He would have laughed again, but Jian's words seemed deadly serious, and the tasks he laid out impossible. Instead, he held his injury and steadied himself, preparing to speak the question whose answer he most feared.

'Who hunts me ... and why?'

Jian stared into space again, licking his lips, savouring the blood. The answers came hesitantly now, as if the soothsayer was having difficulty articulating his visions. 'The Siänar hunt the Vessel for their master. The Terran God-king, the God of Minerals, and the God of Doom hope to usurp the Fallen God's power by controlling the Vessel, or destroying him.'

'And I am the Vessel?' Annev asked, his voice quavering.

'The Shadow God and the First Vampyr seek to turn the Vessel against itself. If they succeed, you will become a slave to the Terrans, your friends will denounce you, your name will be cursed above all others, and you will only find joy after embracing Death.'

Jian's breath was laboured now, the white clouds covering his eyes beginning to dissipate, the bright red lines receding from his pale skin.

'Wait!' Annev said, sensing the foretelling was at an end. 'I need to know! Why were Janak Harth and the *feurog* after me? Who was the crossbowman in Banok?'

'Tools,' Jian said, shaking his head. 'Tools and former tools of Cruithear.'

'But what does that mean?'

Jian blinked, his face ghostly pale as the final milky wisps disappeared from his eyes, then he slumped backwards nearly falling to the floor.

Annev was quick to steady him. 'Jian, are you all right?'

The soothsayer nodded, his voice weak. He looked up at Annev with his pink irises. 'The *t'rasang* is depleted,' he said, voice cracking. 'I pushed too hard, I think.'

'I'm sorry, Jian. I won't ask anything else.'

The frail man shook – part nod, part convulsion, and then coughed, his body shaking violently. 'I was afraid of naming you, and I was right to be. I have joined my fate with that of the Herald.'

'The what?'

'It is as the prophecy says: "For the honour of His naming, the Herald shall plead mercy and receive it." My fate is now tied to hers ... Death comes to claim me ... I should prepare myself to ensure Death cannot claim more than is his due.' He smiled faintly. 'Do not trouble yourself, Master of Sorrows. I will protect you from that at least.'

Annev was unwilling to accept the soothsayer's dark words – but then a scream rose from the level below and Annev's blood ran chill.

'Sraon, Annev! There's a dead man down here!'

Chapter Twenty-Six

'Who is he?' Annev asked as they gathered around the dead man. Therin had found the body while searching for something to use as a privy – and the corpse had toppled out when he opened a small closet. It was difficult to tell how long the man had been dead; there was no stench or overt signs of decay. The kill didn't look fresh, though – ragged bite marks on the shoulder, neck and thigh had clotted with purple-black blood, and the dead man's eyes were jaundiced.

'That's Tukas,' Reeve said, scowling. He brushed the man's thick blond hair back and tried to smooth close his eyes, but the muscles were too rigid. The corpse stared at them, a rictus of pain on his frozen, snarling face.

'What do you suppose happened?' Sraon asked, though it seemed to cost him something to ask the question. 'These marks. It looks like an animal bit him.'

Reeve nodded. 'It's a message that we're not safe here. Not the Dionachs, not our civilian members; not in our safehouses or out there on the street.'

'We should go, right?' Titus said, torn between cowering and packing. 'We should run!'

'They want us to run. They want us afraid – that's why they left Tukas here instead of laying an ambush for us,' Reeve said, his face hardening. 'No signs of struggle, no footprints in the ash. But they tucked him here, neat as a peg, to prove our own house isn't safe.' He paused. 'Your friend is right, Annev. We need to go.'

'To the Enclave?' After speaking with Jian, the thought of the place filled Annev with foreboding.

'Yes. Our allies can help you, and your friends can be tested for the talent. Maybe even start their training.'

'To use magic?' Therin was sceptical. 'Three days ago we were in Chaenbalu – being trained in the dangers and evils of magic – and now you want us to bloody well learn to use it?'

'Well ... okay then.'

'More or less, yes.'

'Has anyone seen Jian?' Annev asked. The soothsayer had come downstairs with him, but now the man was nowhere to be seen in the chapel.

'Aye,' said Sraon. 'He's right over ... well, he *was* standin' right there.' He walked to the nave's entrance and tested the door, then he tried the door to the rectory and it opened.

Reeve looked up from the glyph he had been drawing on Tukas's forehead. 'That door shouldn't open. I set a ward on it.' He turned to Titus and the others. 'Go and pack your gear. You may also want to look away for this.' Titus did so, but Therin and Annev looked on, curious.

The high priest mumbled a quick prayer then whispered a word to the corpse. In an instant, all the moisture in Tukas's body fled from him, drying the man into a withered husk – and then less than a husk: skin flaked away and was followed by muscle and bone. In seconds the petrified corpse had been reduced to earth and dust.

'Holy hells,' Therin breathed.

'What?' Titus said, turning around.

Reeve waved them both off. 'Tukas's body had already begun decomposing, but it was stunted by something – a toxin or poison – so I restarted and accelerated the process. We couldn't leave him here like that, and we don't have time to bury him. Now, what's this about the Yomad? He can't have left.'

'Well he's not down here nor upstairs, but the door to the rectory is open.'

'But the ward ...' Reeve strode to the door and cursed. 'The glyph has been broken. He's escaped.'

'Escaped?' Titus said, looking more frightened by the minute. 'Was he a prisoner?'

'Not a prisoner, boy,' Sraon said, eyeing Reeve. 'But he's a stranger and a Terran – New Terran, I'll grant you, but Terran all the same. I wasn't sure we could trust the man, so Reeve set some wards to be safe.'

'If he's an enemy, we're in grave danger,' the Dionach said. 'Gather your things. We're leaving the city now and heading straight for Quiri.'

'Not me,' Fyn said firmly. He had his pack and bedroll stowed and his weapons sheathed. 'I'm staying in Luqura.'

Sraon and Therin eyed him, somewhat surprised, but Reeve and Annev simply nodded.

'Your choice, boy. But I would encourage you to leave the safehouse.'

'I'm not an idiot.'

'That's good to hear. You might even survive the week.'

Fyn ignored him and looked to Annev. 'You're really going with him? Seems like a real tugger.'

'I think so. I mean, I'm not sure but ... yeah. I'm going.'

'Then I guess this is goodbye.'

'I guess so.'

Fyn had a strange look on his face. Before Annev could determine what it meant, though, it was gone. 'Try not to burn down any more villages?'

'No promises,' Annev said, only half successful at keeping a smile from forming. 'What do you plan to do?'

'Not sure,' Fyn said, unconcerned. 'Whatever it is, it'll be a sight better than following you around – or being stuck inside the Academy.'

'I always thought you liked the Academy.'

'Are you kidding? Annev, *nobody* liked the Academy. That's why we hated you so much, you know? You left every day, you had *privacy*.' He sniffed then added, 'We made the best of it, though. You know? Kept waiting for our chance to leave – to go on retrieval missions and stuff – but your burning down that building was the best thing that ever happened to me.'

Annev wasn't sure how to respond to that. He knew people had been inside the Academy when it collapsed – their lives were on his conscience – but Annev had never thought it might equally have made someone's life better.

'Well,' he said, still uncertain what to say, 'good luck and all that.'

'You too.'

Annev stuck out his hand, knowing immediately that it was the wrong thing to do, which was confirmed when Fyn stared at the gesture, one eyebrow raised. After several long heartbeats, he took it and shook. 'See you around, Annev.'

Annev released Fyn's hand and, in that moment, saw something moving at the corner of his vision. He turned ... but there was nothing there. Titus and Therin were packing their things – Annev had never unpacked his – with Sraon just behind them, his hands resting on his halberd while he chatted quietly with Reeve.

There was a sense of urgency, but nothing was out of place.

Fyn scooped up his pack and headed for the doorway, glancing back one last time before he—

'What in the five hells—?'

There was a thunderous growl from above Annev's head, drowning out all thought and sound, and then something heavy crashed to the floor, a scaly body gleaming in the near-darkness, its form almost invisible until a cloud of ash puffed up from the floor and its camouflage adapted to match the dark grey swirls. Annev watched, stunned, as a whip-thin tail lashed out and knocked Reeve backwards. An instant later, the creature lunged, its teeth clamping Sraon's shoulder as he tried to raise his halberd.

In a flash, Annev understood what was hunting him – what had killed Tukas and had been stalking them since leaving the Rocas Household.

It was Saltair, the venomous Siänar lizardman.

Titus was screaming, Fyn was scrambling to draw his weapons, but Therin had been faster. He snatched a dagger from his belt and tried to stab the monstrous creature, but the blade only skittered off the reptile's back, drawing its attention from Sraon and towards Therin. The boy swore, stumbled backwards and hopped over the nearest church pew. A heartbeat later, the monster crashed through the charred wood, breaking the bench to splinters and beginning to dispel the magic that had camouflaged its black scales.

Annev drew his sword free, and when the fiery flamberge cleared its sheath, the flames revealed the monster they faced: it was taller than Brayan – over seven feet – with enormous bulky shoulders, a muscular chest, and a tapered waist; its arms and legs were thick with corded muscle and the black scales shone in the firelight; a set of hooked claws tipped each four-fingered hand, and an elongated neck supported a head that seemed almost draconic – not a frog, nor a serpent or crocodile, but something between the three, with a final dash of humanity that made the creature seem more alien than if it had been entirely monstrous.

A long tongue snaked out of Saltair's mouth, tasting the air, and then its head swivelled to face Annev. 'Veschel,' the creature hissed, its pointed teeth gnashing together as it struggled to pronounce the words. 'Do not rezhisht.'

Annev lashed out with Retribution, the fiery blade crackling as it swung towards the lizardman's head. The monster hissed, lurching backwards to dodge the blade as its tail wrapped around Annev's ankle and yanked him to the ground. Fyn leapt forward, his fluted maces held aloft, but before he could engage the reptilian mercenary there was a deafening *boom* and the back wall of the chapel exploded outward. The boys were thrown from their feet and Annev glimpsed the dishevelled high priest and the injured blacksmith tumble through the hole in the back wall to the alley beyond. Annev stared in disbelief as Reeve lifted Sraon onto his back, as if the smith were light as a feather – and they disappeared into the darkness, not even sparing a glance for the boys he left behind.

He left us, Annev thought, rising to his feet. *That bastard left us.*

Saltair was up a moment later. Its head swivelled about, taking in the hole in the wall. 'No tricksh,' the lizardman hissed, biting off the ends of each word. 'The falsch priest has gone. You will come with me.'

Now Therin was pulling Titus towards the hole in the broken wall, silently urging the smaller boy to follow. Titus resisted, his eyes full of horror as he looked between Annev and the monstrous keokum. Annev met his eyes, discreetly gesturing for his friends to run, then stepped forward to distract their attacker.

'Your name is Saltair,' Annev said. 'And *you* should run.' He tugged the smithing glove from his left hand and the prosthetic's light shone like a dim beacon in the darkness. He held the golden fist in front of him like a buckler and raised the flamberge in his right hand, its flames casting dancing shadows across the room.

The humanoid tilted back its head and laughed, a harsh scraping sound like dry nails dragging across a slate chalkboard, ending with a hacking cough. Then the monster's eyes were on him again. 'Saltair doesh not run. Othersssh run from him.' The beast's mouth opened wide at this, a terrifying smile that exposed long rows of needle-sharp teeth.

'You'll have to run ... if you mean to hunt us.' Annev and Fyn started to back towards the rectory door, Saltair taking a step towards them. Behind him, Titus and Therin began to ease themselves out of the hole in the back wall.

Annev took another slow step, and Saltair did the same. The Hand of Keos began to grow brighter, and the lizardman raised a hand to shield his eyes from its glare. At the back of the room, Therin was helping Titus out, the round-faced boy almost clear of the crumbling wall when he slipped against a broken stone, tumbling out of sight. Saltair spun, his head angling so the sunken ear holes in his skull could pinpoint the noise. At the same instant, Annev and Fyn turned and dashed through the dilapidated rectory into the street and broke into a flat sprint. A roar went up behind them and they heard the lizardman crashing through the church pews, knocking them aside as he ploughed towards the rectory door.

'This way!' Annev yelled, hoping to rejoin Titus and Therin.

'Rot that!' Fyn swore, running in the opposite direction. 'You're on your own, remember?'

Annev watched the boy go, an ache in his gut, before taking to his heels again and circling around the chapel to find his friends. A heartbeat later, he heard the lizardman crash onto the street, his monstrous form leaping from the ruined rectory and smashing the old paving stones beneath his heavy, long-toed feet. Annev glanced backward, saw Saltair was fixed on him, and bolted down a side street. He had no time to regroup with his companions. Indeed, the only way to keep them safe was to lead the monstrous reptile away from them.

Far behind Annev, the lizardman took a flying leap and landed atop the wall of another charred edifice. The building's stones sagged beneath the creature's weight, crumbling under him, but Saltair was already leaping into the air, his powerful legs throwing him onto a roof just ahead of Annev.

'Blood and ashes!' Annev swore, skidding on the street to plunge down a dirty alley he'd just been passing. He had no plan, and he was still holding the flamberge aloft, using it and the prosthetic to light his path. He ducked down another alley then dashed across a wide street, his Boots of Swiftness letting him outpace the lizardman. He flew down another side street then dodged into a narrow space between two squat warehouses and froze there, his blood thumping in his ears, daring to hope he might have lost the keokum in the twisting confines of the Ash Quarter.

A heavy crunch echoed from the building to Annev's right, and he looked up to see Saltair's serpentine head peering down at him from above.

The flames, Annev realised. They lit the obstructions in his path, but also made him easy for Saltair to track in the darkness of the Ash Quarter. Annev extinguished the sword's magical fire and sheathed the blade. With an effort, he forced down the glowing light emanating from the Hand of Keos, almost – but not quite – extinguishing it. Annev's eyes fought to adjust to the darkness around him. The alley was too narrow for the broad-shouldered monster to enter, for which Annev gave a silent prayer of thanks. He listened to Saltair stomp over the roof of the warehouse then spotted a battered door farther down the narrow alley. He sprinted for it, found it locked, and threw his shoulder against the singed wood. It crunched under his weight, but the portal held firm. Then Annev threw his golden fist at the wooden barrier, the boards splintered and the door collapsed inward. He entered the cavernous building then stopped, waiting to hear if Saltair would follow from above.

A second passed.

Five seconds.

Ten.

Whump. Something heavy landed on the raised roof far overhead.

Annev suppressed a grim smile and dodged back into the narrow alley, his boots swiftly carrying him through the space between the warehouses and out the other side. Once there, he ran in the opposite direction from Saltair, doing his best to keep his footfalls as silent as they were swift.

He must have run half a mile, weaving intermittently through the side streets, before he slowed and ducked under the awning of an abandoned shop. He was breathing hard, more from adrenaline than actual exertion, and his hands were shaking. He took a deep breath and tried to calm himself.

Jian's gone, Annev thought, *ran off before this even started – and Reeve has Sraon, so they're probably safe. Fyn is on the run and tough besides. He'll stay hidden. Maybe make his way back to the Low Quarter. Titus and Therin . . .*

Annev swore. Once his friends thought they were safe, the two boys would come looking for him – he was sure of it. Therin would hesitate and Titus would be frightened, but their loyalty would win out.

They'll get themselves killed. I should have forced them to stay in Banok with Brayan. It would have been kinder than this.

But what if his friends had found Reeve and Sraon? The Dionach had his magics, and Sraon could fight if he wasn't too injured. They'd be fine.

Then again, they might stumble into Saltair . . . or the Boneyard.

Keos, but Annev hated not knowing. He had no way to track his friends without circling back and risking another encounter with Saltair, and he had no idea where they might be.

But that wasn't true. He *did* have something that might help him find Titus and Therin through the grubby darkness of the Ash Quarter – he even had something that might help him guess which direction they had gone.

With a stifled curse, Annev reached into the bottomless sack and pulled out the magic copper ring and the Ring of Good Luck. He slipped the bands onto his forefinger and little finger just as he had done in the pub, and his senses reeled from the combined magic of the two artifacts.

As before, Annev's vision was clouded with a blood-red mist, but the effect was far less, perhaps because there was no one nearby. As he peered through the darkness, though, he could see the pulsing heartbeats that marked the hidden inhabitants of the Ash Quarter – a derelict lying in an alley, a family of three adults and two children huddled in the darkness in a nearby building. Using the ring he could smell their nearness, and taste their blood, their anxieties, their fear. Annev's stomach churned at the impressions given by the copper ring, but when he took a deep breath he also caught the scents he had hoped to find – the faint hints of musky sweat, unwashed bodies and the iron taste of blood that was strangely familiar to him.

Annev could sense where Titus and Therin had gone – could practically taste them on his tongue; they were headed north, their pace slow as they edged closer to the rotting stench of the Boneyard. Worse, Annev caught the spicy scent of the Innistiul slavers, no doubt led by their master, Elar. Before Annev could think to curse his friends' bad luck, he also caught the whiff of Fyn's unwashed dreadlocks and the metallic tang of Sraon's swarthy skin; Fyn seemed to be moving northeast towards Annev's position, while Sraon stumbled south. He smelled the smith's blood then, too – his open wound soured by the taint of Saltair's venom.

Poison, Annev thought, its wrongness combining with Sraon's blood. He could practically taste the acidic venom, its potency ... its proximity ...

But where was Jian? Annev tried to sniff out the Terran necromancer, but his scent was too hard to track. Too faint, too unfamiliar.

Did he foresee the attack and not bother to give us warning ... or did he betray us?

Annev froze, his attention suddenly fixed on the mists surrounding him, on the slow pulse of the cold-blooded creature stalking towards him, trying to outflank him from a nearby side street. His first instinct was to run – to flee back into the darkness and rely on his boots to save him – but Saltair would keep tracking him, using his reptilian senses to sniff Annev out exactly as Annev had sensed the location of his friends.

Annev's right hand slid to the flamberge at his hip, and he itched to unstrap Toothbreaker from his back. Instead, he waited. He focused on the magic of the copper band, allowing it to amplify his senses, then tapped into the power of the silver-gold codavora ring. He wasn't sure how to access its magic, but he tried to let his mind relax while thinking of Saltair flanking him … approaching from the side. The lizardman preparing to spring, leaping into the air, his powerful legs extending to stun Annev with a kick to the head.

An instant later, imagination became reality. The keokum leapt from his place in the shadows, legs extended, and Annev turned to meet him, sword unsheathed. Just before the two collided, Annev closed his eyes and forced Retribution to burst into white-yellow flames. Saltair hissed, open-mouthed, as his hands rose to cover slitted eyes. At the same instant, Annev dodged, evading the kick and slashing the lizardman's thigh. Hot metal met black scales, the wavy blade searing and sparking as it cut into the creature's flesh. Saltair howled and crashed into the wall. Annev pivoted, his sword still extended.

Summoning the full heat of the flamberge, Annev shifted its colours from yellow to blue and thrust his blade at the fallen Siänar, attempting to skewer him. Instead, Saltair's claws swung outward, throwing the blade wide of the mark. A second clawed hand swung at Annev's chest and he blocked it with the Hand of Keos, its gold metal glowing fierce in the darkness. He tried to grip the monster's forearm – tried to break it as he had the Innistiul slaver's shin in The Bottomless Cup – but Saltair was too fast, his tail whipping around Annev's ankle and dragging him to the ground. The monster struck, twisting so his jaws snapped down on Annev' shoulder.

Annev screamed as the glistening fangs clamped down, trying to pierce the dragonscale cloak. The artifact held, though the mounting pressure was agony. Trusting the artifact to protect him, Annev smashed his golden fist into the lizardman's skull. Saltair flew backward, the force of the blow ripping out several of the teeth trapped in the dragonscale cloak. Annev sprang up, watchful for Saltair's tail.

The lizardman rolled to his feet, his monstrous form stretching to its full height before hissing in challenge. Annev had his sword at the ready, his gold prosthetic poised like a vambrace or a buckler. Saltair eyed the two artifacts, his slitted eyes shifting between Retribution's flames and the eerie glow of the Hand of Keos. His posture shifted, relaxing.

'We do not need to fight,' the monster growled, chewing his words. 'Come with me now. Leave your friendsssh, your false prieshht.'

'I think we've had this conversation before,' Annev said, his attention focused on Saltair's bobbing tail. 'I'm not going with you, and I'm not leaving my friends.'

'But you have already left them, Chozhen One. They are dead – or *will* be dead. Let them go . . . and come with me.'

'Come where?' Annev said, stalling as he tried to predict Saltair's next attack. He remembered the shop's tattered awning then and a plan formed in his mind.

The keokum gave a wide grin full of poisoned needles. 'It dependsh.'

'On what?'

'On whether Dortafola will match the price of the Rocash family.'

The beast sprang forward, his tail snapping for Annev's sword arm as his clawed hands swiped at the boy. Annev parried one blow with his golden hand and spun Retribution to slash at the mercenary's tail. The blue-white blade sizzled through the black scales, scything three feet of flesh from the monster's body. At the same instant, Saltair's other hand raked across Annev's throat, his hooked fingers ripping chunks of flesh from Annev's neck before the keokum stumbled backwards, surprised and unbalanced by the bloody loss of his tail. His throat burning, Annev hacked at the awning overhead. The soot-stained canvas fell atop the lizardman, entangling him, and Annev hacked again, his flamberge slicing clean through one of the monster's arms.

With a tremendous roar of frustration and pain, Saltair sprang up from the street and landed on the roof of the shop, evading Annev's killing blow. Another roar followed, and then the charred and bloody canvas fell to the street. Annev listened, waiting for another attack, but instead he heard the keokum retreat across the rooftops, his reptilian screeches fading with the scent of his cold blood and sour venom.

Chapter Twenty-Seven

Annev was hazy from the pulsing mists of scarlet. He sheathed his sword and slapped his hand to his neck, the blood running freely through his fingers. *I'm bleeding out. Fast.*

Keos, he was going to die out here.

No, Annev thought, fumbling for the bottomless bag. *The bandage . . . I can stop this.* Using the golden prosthetic, Annev tore the bag free from his tunic then awkwardly stuffed his massive fingers inside the sack, searching, searching. He pinched a thin shred of fabric between his thumb and forefinger and pulled, carefully extracting the tattered remains of his old Shirt of Regeneration.

Thank the Gods.

Annev leaned heavily against the shop, feeling distant from his body. His thoughts were clear, but he felt tired, weak. With agonising slowness, he looped the strips of white cloth around his neck, pulled his other hand away and tied the makeshift bandages tight around his throat.

The effect was instantaneous. Annev felt the flesh beneath the bloodstained wrapping begin to knit back together. He felt more alert, more warmth, and the opaque crimson mists began to dissipate, dwindling until they were once again a transparent fog painting the Ash Quarter in shifting hues of scarlet and vermilion.

Annev counted ten slow breaths. He was alive. Saltair had escaped, but Annev was *alive*. His breathing steadied and his pulse quickened.

Titus and Therin, he remembered, *they were headed into a slaver trap!* In his need to save his own life, he'd forgotten about his friends. Annev focused on the magic of the copper ring and sought them out once more, questing to feel where the two boys had gone.

There. They were a few blocks northwest of him and Annev began to run in that direction, unsteady at first but then his Boots of Swiftness sped him through the streets like an arrow shot from a bow. As he ran, he noticed that his breathing remained slow and even, as though his stamina were somehow able to match the speed of the boots.

It's the shirt, Annev thought, remembering wearing it while fighting the *feurog* in Chaenbalu. *It grants rapid healing . . . and increased stamina. I'd forgotten that.* It suddenly seemed unwise to remove the bandage, even if he was healed, so Annev raced on, neither slowing nor tiring. He entered the Boneyard within seconds, the stench of death and decay almost overwhelming. The pulses of life that indicated the Ash Quarter's inhabitants had also diminished, leaving only the faintest traces around the darkest people hidden in the Boneyard's shadows. Annev avoided those shadows as he raced towards his friends at the heart of the Boneyard.

Barely a minute later, Annev reached a massive warehouse covered in dark script and arcane symbols he did not recognise. There was a pile of mismatched bones heaped outside the main entrance to the warehouse, and while most looked old – picked clean by the passage of time or some gruesome scavenger – some were so fresh they had probably been hacked from their previous owners that very night. Annev tried not to dwell on that grisly prospect and focused on what was inside the warehouse.

Titus and Therin were there, their hearts thudding in their chests. The pair stood inside a massive ring of . . . something. Something old that stank of death. Annev followed his nose to a draft of air and a small hole punctured through a wall. He peered into the darkened gloom, his vision further aided by the magic of the ring, and quickly saw what his nose had not so easily identified.

Bones . . . corpses. A massive heap of the dead, piled shoulder-high, both those that had perished in the fire decades ago and those that had been heaped atop them since. As Annev used the magic of the copper ring, though, he caught another familiar scent

– one he had expected yet feared to find: Elar Kranak and his score of Innistiul slavers. Annev stepped back from the hole then and stared through the walls of the warehouse until he spied the dim outline of their living bodies pulsing with heat and blood.

But there was something else, too – a scent that was vague but familiar. Clean but cold. Annev tried to get a fix on the smell's origin, tried to see the owner's blood pattern, but it was too faint in the mists.

Jian? Was he in there, aiding Elar and the Innistiulmen? It was difficult to say with certainty since he was less familiar with the soothsayer's scent, but he suspected he was right.

Annev huffed then tried to reach out with his other senses: he couldn't hear anything from inside the massive warehouse – its occupants were too distant, and while the magic ring enhanced many of his senses, it did not affect that ability. He could *taste* them, though. The sharp tang of Innistiul spices mixed with the salty sweat of the anxious slavers. Given their proximity to Titus and Therin, Annev had no doubt his friends had been captured, yet the bulk of the slavers seemed anxious. Why? Because they stood in a warehouse stinking with corpses ... or because of some-thing else?

Annev steeled himself and pulled the smithing glove back over the Hand of Keos, extinguishing its eerie light. Then he drew Retribution, mindful not to let the flames ignite until he was ready.

On a whim, Annev recalled how he had used the blade, and tried to imagine the flames alight but near invisible – ghostly ... sub-red. He cautiously fed that thought into the artifact, and it started to thrum with magic and heat. With the aid of the copper ring, Annev could see the intense flames surrounding the magic sword in the way the red mists swirled about its blade, yet those flames were invisible to his naked eye. Relieved, he unslung Toothbreaker from his back and buckled it to his left hand and forearm.

I'm as ready as I can be, Annev thought, feeling small and scared in spite of his magics. Could he free Therin and Titus? Could he attack the slavers without endangering his friends? Annev didn't know – he had no plan at all – but he had an idea about what might happen inside and, as he considered it, the idea developed in his mind. It became a premonition.

The codavora ring, Annev thought, relief washing over him. *Jian said it could give me glimpses of the future.* He leaned into his hopes to save his friends, letting that inform the ring, and opened his mind to what he might encounter inside the warehouse.

Guards patrolling the perimeter of the room, their torches lit in anticipation of someone's arrival. Elar standing in the centre of the room, his soldiers grouped around him as he questioned Titus and Therin regarding the whereabouts and intentions of Annev, Sraon and the rest of their company. Annev had glimpsed that inside. The boys would have few answers, he knew, so Elar would try torture: first pain and humiliation, then disfigurement ... and finally death.

But Annev would stop it. He would carve a new entrance into the wall at the opposite side of the warehouse and stalk inside like a thief, invisible in the darkness. The dead were heaped in every corner. Annev would bypass them, racing for the circle of the dead at the centre of the large room, with the living congregated inside. Annev would leap into the group of soldiers and unleash his fury on the slavers, a living whirlwind of death—

And Elar would behead his friends.

Annev tried again, this time leaping straight for Elar. He would decapitate the slave master in one stroke and then turn to free his friends—

And the Innistiul soldiers would cut him to pieces.

Annev imagined using stealth to free his friends. He would stalk the perimeter of the room, creating distractions to draw out each of the torch-bearing soldiers and killing them in turn. One torch would get snuffed out and Elar would send another man to investigate. A second torch would go out and Elar would sense a threat. He'd have some men watch the prisoners while he ordered more torches lit, more light brought forth. Annev saw Elar split his men into three companies: one to watch Titus and Therin and the other two to sweep the warehouse. Annev would hide amidst the dead, would dart between the larger patrols and then come at Elar from behind; he'd turn and see the killing blow just as it landed. Their master dead, the smaller company of soldiers would strike against Annev – and they would die. He'd free his friends, and Titus and Therin would hold their ground while he fought the remaining soldiers. He'd take a wound to the arm but he would fight on. Ten soldiers would be reduced to eight, then seven. Another wound, this time to the leg. A sword would slip through his defences, stabbing him in the chest. He'd hear a cry, and realise too late it was his friends.

The two guards with the torches had slit Titus's throat. Therin screamed and stabbed the man in the chest, and the second guard split his face in two.

In every attempt, his friends died. Annev was left dying.

It was hopeless.

Annev slumped against the warehouse wall, the premonition fading, his eyes vacant as despair filled his soul. He couldn't save them. Through the haze of red mist, Annev saw Elar had drawn his scimitar and was using it to menace his friends, prodding Therin until bright crimson lines blossomed across the taller boy's chest.

Therin was bleeding. Titus would be crying. They'd both be terrified, wondering why Annev and Sraon and the rest had abandoned them – and Annev just sat there, paralysed.

A heavy hand fell on his shoulder. Annev choked on a curse and spun, prepared to kill whoever stood behind him, but was instead greeted by a familiar face.

'Fyn!' he whispered in shock. 'What are you doing here?'

'I followed you, idiot.'

'How? Why?'

The taller boy shrugged, blood rushing to his cheeks. 'I ... I didn't want to leave without knowing everyone else got away. That's all.'

'Odar bless you, Fyn. Titus and Therin need our help.'

'They're in there?'

'Yeah. You remember that slaver, Elar? He's got them. Him and his rotting soldiers.'

Fyn gave a slow sigh. 'Did you kill that lizard thing?'

'Maimed it – lopped off an arm and a tail. It could come back, but it's not likely.'

The boy grunted. 'You think it's working with the slavers?'

'Honestly, I don't know. We can ask Elar – once his men are dead.'

'Right. How many men?'

'Almost two dozen – but Fyn, we have to move fast. They're torturing them.'

'You got a plan?'

Annev thought for a moment, reimagining the scenario he had last played out. 'I think this will work – and I don't have any other options.'

Fyn unsheathed his falchion. 'Fill me in as we go then.'

Chapter Twenty-Eight

Annev stalked through the shadowy warehouse, his quick steps evading the patrolling guardsmen and their torches. Behind him, Fyn skulked in the opposite direction, his falchion held in his right hand and a parrying dagger in his off-hand. Annev could only see him with the copper ring's aid, which he used to match his pace to Fyn's. Together they edged around the perimeter of the warehouse, intent on the nearest pair of torch-bearing soldiers.

At the centre of the room, a fifth guard held a torch over Annev's friends, the other soldiers and Elar Kranak. Titus was pleading for the slave captain to let them go.

'—told you everything. Please! We were helping Jian enter the city. He needed Sodja Rocas's help – him and those Ilumites in Banok – but they didn't say why. You've got to believe us – please! No one told us anything!'

'Oh, I believe you,' Elar said, toying with the chain which ran from his nose. 'I'm sure you wouldn't lie to me.'

'We wouldn't!' Therin shouted, tears streaming down his face. Titus echoed his words and the slave captain smiled, his scimitar dancing along Therin's flesh. He flicked the sword and scythed off the boy's left nipple. Therin screamed.

'Why?' Titus sobbed. 'Why would you do that!'

'Because pain is an excellent motivator,' Elar said, wiping his sword on Titus's tunic. 'Because your friend Sraon Cheng humiliated me in front of Luqura's nobility. And ...' He sheathed his scimitar and took a hot iron from his torchbearer. 'Because I can.' Elar pressed the slave brand against Therin's bare chest. The wiry boy screamed and his knees buckled, though the Innistiul slavers kept him standing, his bound hands and elbows held high overhead.

Annev's fury raged within him, propelling him across the open room until he stood just behind the first torchbearer. Across the warehouse he saw Fyn do the same, embracing his target as he killed him. The firelight flickered as the soldier died, but Fyn caught the torch before it could hit the ground, and he took his place in the circle of patrolling guardsmen.

Annev moved next, his hand reaching for the nearest man's torch as his sword hacked into the guard's neck. He could have been quieter – might have punched his belt knife through the man's ribs as he'd been taught by Masters Edra and Duvarek – but he was too angry for caution, his indignation too hot. Thankfully, the thud of the man's rolling head and the sputtering cough of his severed neck went unnoticed amidst his friends' screams.

Annev walked his torch to the nearest corner of the room and braced it carefully inside the socket of a grinning skull. He danced away from the torchlight then, a shadow amidst shadows again, and wove through the blind spots between the remaining guards. When he stood a few paces from the light cast by the centre torchbearer, he checked to make sure Fyn mirrored him on the opposite side of the warehouse. And then he waited.

'Keos burn me,' one of the guards swore. 'Hey, Mik! You put your torch down? Riles?'

'Not me,' Riles said, waving his crackling torch from the other side of the room. 'Hollett left his, too.'

'The hell are you doing?' Elar shouted, stepping away from Therin. 'This is no time for a piss!' When no one replied, Elar handed back the slave brand and waved for a handful of his men to investigate, though not as many as Annev had originally hoped.

That's still a dozen inside the ring, Annev thought. His heart beat fast in his chest. *Even with Fyn, I'm not sure we can take a dozen.* Annev tried to use the ring, envisioning Elar approaching Therin and Titus, his scimitar poised to strike. Annev didn't need to see more – he knew how this played out. He had to act now and hope Fyn would back him up.

Annev ran, vaulting into the air and landing inside the ring of corpses just as the Innistiulmen found the dead guards. They shouted in alarm, Elar moved to strike, and Annev evaded a blow from one soldier's scimitar. He swung his flamberge, intercepting Elar's sword before the blade could decapitate Titus. The slave captain hissed in frustration.

'He's here! Capture him if you can! Kill him if you must.'

The dozen men inside the ring had been focused on Annev but turned in confusion as Fyn bowled into the backs of their ranks, his falchion and main-gauche stabbing two different slavers in the neck. The soldiers keeping Therin on his feet released their captive to join the fight, but Annev slammed Toothbreaker into one man's face, then swung Retribution in a flaming circle. The metal slashed at the second guard's eyes and Annev shifted the flamberge's ghostly fire into bright white flames. The guard fell back, burned and blinded, and Annev spun to catch the falling sword of a third slaver attacking from the rear, this one still holding the hot slave brand. Toothbreaker caught the swinging scimitar in its teeth and Annev twisted, snapping the blade in half. The slaver growled and seared Annev's ribs with the slave brand, making him howl in pain. Meanwhile, Titus and Therin had scavenged weapons of their own, and Therin chopped a scimitar into the man's neck. The Innistiulman stumbled forward, Therin's blade buried in his spine, and he collapsed into the ring of corpses.

Behind Annev, the guard who'd been struck by the vambrace climbed to his knees, his sword sweeping for Annev's legs. Annev sensed the attack and spun away, using Toothbreaker's prongs to punch a second slaver in the chest. Titus slashed his reclaimed dagger across the first man's throat and the four boys regrouped at one end of the ring.

In the confusion, Elar had climbed over the mound of decaying corpses and escaped the ring. Fyn had killed two more guards, and seven Innistiulmen lay scattered within the corpse ring. Five still faced them, their scimitars drawn, and more than twice that number stood beyond the ring of dead bodies, Elar with them.

'Fools!' Elar shouted. 'You may as well cut your own throats because I'm going to skin the lot of you! And to hell with Tiana

293

and her lizard freak. Hammer and anvil – now!' the slave captain ordered, and his men began climbing over the mound of corpses as the five remaining soldiers began to edge towards them.

Damn, Annev thought, gritting his teeth. His seared ribs burned. Therin had fared little better with two injuries inflicted by Elar. Annev tried to imagine a way out, but every premonition ended in their deaths.

No, Annev thought. *There* is *a way out of this.* The vision came to him in a rush. He saw his hand clenching, the smithing glove smoking as fire blossomed around his fist. He saw the Innistiulmen hesitate as they saw their death before them. Titus looked to Annev with hope as Therin and Fyn backed away. The ball of fire grew, enveloping Annev and then his friends – Titus melted into blood and ashes as it touched him. Therin screamed. Elar shouted for his men to attack, and the world erupted in fire ...

... and when it was done, the Ash Quarter was truly nothing but ash with Annev alone at its epicentre, untouched yet utterly broken. He would live and they would die. That was their remaining way out.

Annev's fist began to clench even as the tears began streaming down his cheeks. He didn't want this, but he would try. Maybe he could control it. He felt the emotion building inside him and forced it into the Hand of Keos. Smoke began to rise.

Burn them all.

Annev raised his fist just as the soldiers began to scream. He closed his eyes, not wanting to see the realisation of betrayal on Titus's face – then stopped. That screaming *hadn't* been part of his premonition. Annev opened his eyes and was horrified to see the men standing atop the corpses were being pulled down into the heap. Bloody nails and bony fingers tore into their flesh, flaying it from shin and thigh bones as the slavers sank deep into the undead. At the opposite side of the ring, the Innistiulmen nearest the corpses were dragged down in a whirl of chomping teeth and tearing fingers.

Titus screamed. *Fyn* screamed. The four boys pressed together, and Annev felt the heat in his palm shrink beneath the terror that gripped him.

'Run!'

Annev turned towards the voice – towards *Jian's* voice – and saw the faint outline of the necromancer standing in the far corner of the room. Darkness surrounded him, though the magic of the copper ring illuminated a faint outline of pink-grey flesh, almost invisible, as if he were already dead.

'Run!' the Yomad shouted again, his mild voice barely audible above the shouts of the dying slavers. 'Take your friends and flee, Ainnevog de Breth! It is not your fate to die here tonight.' As Jian spoke, the corpse ring nearest Annev shifted. Skeletal hands and feet pulled the wall of undead back, and a path to safety opened before them.

'Go!' Annev shouted, guarding his friends' escape. Fyn went first, dashing through the narrow opening, and Titus and Therin followed. Annev came last and the remaining Innistiulmen pursued him. Just as he cleared the corpse ring, the tide of undead flowed back over the two slavers, their faces disappearing amidst a sea of death.

'This way!' Fyn shouted, leading Titus and Therin to the exit.

Annev glanced back at Jian. Elar and his two remaining torchbearers stood between Annev and the necromancer, the latter now illuminated by torchlight.

'Jian!' Annev shouted, his feet carrying him towards the albino soothsayer. 'Come with us!'

'No, Master Ainnevog! My journey ends here and I will not cheat it.'

'You don't need to *die,* Jian!' As Annev spoke, skeletons began to rise from the corners of the room, their fleshless arms outstretched. Annev paused, seeing them, and took a step back towards the hole he had carved in the warehouse wall. Elar and two remaining slavers seemed to have similar thoughts and turned to flee towards the exit. A wall of *nechraict* rose up around them, cutting them off. Still, Jian held his ground at the opposite side of the warehouse.

'Master Nikloss!' Annev shouted, still not understanding.

Then he saw it – through the red haze of the copper ring, he glimpsed the monstrous figure that leapt down from the rafters, his razor claws and heavy feet slamming into the Marrow-Lich's back. Jian crumpled beneath the weight of the one-armed keokum and Saltair's gaping mouth clamped onto the man's head, ripping it from his body. The undead monsters chasing Elar and his soldiers dropped to the earth, as if their magic strings had been cut.

Saltair turned and spat the albino's head towards Annev. In the guttering torchlight, Annev glimpsed the pulsating stumps of the lizardman's arm and severed tail and saw they were growing back, the new skin shining with wet-black scales. The tail was almost restored, and the arm was regrowing the severed hand, its clawed fingers small and delicate.

'Keos,' Annev breathed.

At the opposite side of the warehouse, the lizardman roared in defiance.

Annev stepped back, his vambrace and flamberge held in front of him as he anticipated the monster's attack. Elar and his soldiers spun to face Annev as Saltair leapt for him, his long legs launching him through the air.

A glittering spear of ice whipped over Annev's head and slammed into the lizardman, its point breaking on the monster's black scales as it sent the keokum flying in the opposite direction.

Annev stared, and a strong hand fell onto his shoulder, turning him around.

'Reeve!'

The Arch-Dionach grimaced. 'Come on, boy! I don't have enough *quaire* to smash through that monster's armour, and Sraon is badly hurt.'

Sraon! Annev thought, remembering his injured friend. *He was bitten by Saltair.* Reeve dashed for the exit and Annev followed, running through while the high priest turned, spat on the wall and drew a glyph in his saliva. He muttered something under his breath and the hole in the wall shimmered, reflecting the moon-light.

'Shield of air,' Reeve said, pulling Annev along once again. 'It won't last long.'

'Wait,' Annev said, shaking off Reeve's hand. 'Titus and Therin – and Fyn! Did you see them?'

'They're with Sraon. Had to circle back for the mare, tie Sraon to the saddle, and then hunt you four down.'

Anger blossomed in the pit of Annev's stomach, replacing the relief he had felt at hearing his friends were safe. 'You left us – you *left* us!'

Reeve huffed. 'You may be Sodar's boy, but I don't *know* you – and you don't know me. I had to choose between saving a man's life or *maybe* finding his lost friends. Do you think I chose wrong? Would you have abandoned Sraon?' Reeve's expression was fierce.

'I ... don't know.'

'And that hesitation would have got everyone killed.' Reeve pushed Annev ahead of him. 'Sometimes you have to make hard choices. You have to accept that, no matter what you do, some people may die – and sometimes those people are your friends – and the best thing you can do is help the person in front of you.'

Annev baulked at the truth in the Reeve's words. 'You *left* us to die,' he repeated.

'Aye,' the high priest said, his expression grim, 'but then I came back for you, didn't I?'

Annev had no answer for that, so he kept his mouth shut and allowed Reeve to lead him through the twisting confines of the Ash Quarter. His conscience prickled, and he remembered those moments before Jian saved them. Was he angry with Reeve, or with himself?

I would have killed them all – I would have burned the Ash Quarter and everyone in it. I was going to do it ... before Jian saved us. He sacrificed *himself for us.*

Annev didn't understand it. The man could see the future, yet he had chosen to place himself in harm's way to save Annev and his friends – four strangers he barely knew.

He knew I was going to destroy the city, Annev thought, remembering the soothsayer's final words: 'I should prepare myself to ensure Death cannot claim more than is his due.'

He wasn't saving us, Annev realised. *He saw that I was going to kill everyone, so he sacrificed himself to save them all – and to save me.* It was a sobering thought, and one which made Annev twice indebted to the man.

'Down there,' Reeve said, pointing to a side street. 'They should be just ahead of us.' They jogged down the road towards the city's northwestern gate, Annev being careful of his pace so as not to reveal the secret of his boots or of the bloody scarf tied about his neck. He remembered his other artifacts then, having grown accustomed to the crimson mists colouring his vision. Annev tugged the copper ring off his thumb and the world suddenly inverted itself, the darkness around him growing thick as his senses grew dull. With reluctance, Annev tucked the heavy copper band into his pocket, though he left the silver–gold codavora ring in place. Its magic had been invaluable, after all, and it seemed less ominous than the eerie red mists that accompanied the copper band.

An Inquisitor ring, Annev thought, the name springing up from somewhere deep in his subconscious. Had he heard the name before? Its magic was undeniably Terran, and its properties seemed to resonate with the little he knew of Bloodlords ... but Annev couldn't remember hearing the phrase before, and the thought troubled him more than he cared to admit.

They were approaching the city's western wall, where the North Tocra river ran adjacent to the city's gatehouse.

'They won't open the gate to foot traffic till morning, but they'll allow boats to sail downriver. We'll get passage on the first raft out of here. If we have to, we can disembark at Ankyr and switch to a faster ship.'

'Does the Tocra run all the way to Quiri?'

'Close enough. It can take us to the ocean and then to Helmstook Inlet, which is Quiri's ocean port.'

'Will we get there in time to save Sraon?'

A trace of fear broke through Reeve's gruff demeanour. 'I don't know. That damn keokum left some kind of poison in Sraon's wounds. I tried to force it out but his best chance of survival lies with the Enclave.'

'Thank you,' Annev said, a little reluctantly. 'If you hadn't acted so fast, Sraon would probably be dead.'

Reeve nodded, then slowed his pace. 'There they are,' he said, pointing to the small group clustered around the torches by the river docks.

Annev dashed ahead to join his friends, embracing Titus then starting to hug Therin before the boy stopped him.

'I'm not up for hugging any time soon,' the boy said, gesturing to his bloody pectorals. 'And I've been branded besides – that smarts worst of all.' He pointed at the ribs on Annev's right side. 'You get branded, too?'

'Yeah. Bastard got me right before you cut him down. We need to get them bandaged and out of sight before anyone decides we're runaway slaves.' Annev remembered the bloody artifact wrapped around his neck and quickly untied the scarf. Without explaining, he pressed the magic cloth against Therin's skin. The boy cried out, cursing, then swore again when Annev pulled the cloth away to reveal a shiny scar where his left nipple had once been.

'You healed it!' Therin said, carefully prodding the puckered flesh. Instead of answering, Annev pressed the rag to Therin's second injury, a second scar quickly forming where there had only been burned flesh. Therin hissed through his teeth then rubbed the blood from his chest and shook his head in disbelief.

'That's an improvement,' he laughed, fingering the red sailboat-shaped scar. 'Be nice if it also took away the slave brand, but I won't complain since the pain is gone.'

Annev realised the rag still hadn't healed his own injury and lifted his shirt, holding the rag to his burned flesh. He gritted his teeth as the cloth made contact and he felt the injury begin to heal. Annev wiped the blood away when he was done, and though the slave mark remained – a red and lurid scar – the injury no longer pained him. Annev moved quickly to the black mare and the limp body lying atop her.

'Sraon?' Annev laid a hand on the blacksmith's neck and was chilled by what he felt. No pulse. Was the man already dead? Annev held his breath and focused, praying to feel some sign of life beneath his fingertips.

There was something – Sraon was alive – but his pulse was faint … very weak. Annev examined the bite marks on the man's neck and shoulder, the skin mottled purple and turning black. He lifted the man's eyelid, saw it dilate and a hint of jaundice beginning to form at the edge of his eye.

'Don't put that cloth on him!' Reeve shouted, seeing what Annev was thinking. 'It could seal the poison beneath his skin! The venom has already clotted the wound.'

'Right,' Annev said, winding the bloody cloth back around his neck. 'I'll leave him alone.'

'Good.' Reeve turned to Fyn. 'Any news of any boats or rafts preparing to launch?'

'Not sure it's the craft you're looking for, but the dockmaster said a slaving ship is sailing for Innistiul within the hour. That's to the north, right?'

'Yes,' Reeve said, his expression dark. 'They are usually well supplied, too. And fast.' Reeve looked over Annev and his friends. 'I understand if you're reluctant, but I think this boat is our best chance to save Sraon.'

Both Titus and Therin looked to Annev, who looked at the dying blacksmith. 'We'll take it.'

'Good lad. I'll make the arrangements then.' The high priest went to speak with the dockmaster, leaving Annev with his friends.

'You okay with this?' Annev asked, his question directed at the group.

'No,' Therin said. 'But I'll stay below deck. Not that keen on spending more quality time with any Innistiulmen.'

'It's fine, Annev,' Titus said, though he looked grey. 'Anything to save Sraon.'

'Fyn?'

The boy shook his head. 'You know I'm staying, and we've said our goodbyes already.'

Annev sighed. 'I was hoping you'd changed your mind.'

'Nah.' He glanced at the mare and the unconscious blacksmith. 'I hope he gets better,' Fyn said, then nodded to the rest of the group. 'Good luck with that arsehole.'

Therin snorted at that and even Titus grinned.

'We'll look after each other,' Annev said, eyeing his other companions. 'I'm grateful that Reeve escaped with Sraon, but I think we've all learned not to trust him. He'll do whatever is best for himself and his order, and I don't think we figure high on his list of priorities.'

Fyn grunted in agreement. 'Well, good luck. If you come back to Luqura, come and find me.'

'Where will you be?' Titus asked. 'What do you plan to do?'

Fyn smiled. 'The Academy taught us to be thieves and cut-throats, and this place is filled with silver and gold.' Fyn gestured at the city, which was beginning to brighten with pre-dawn light. 'I aim to take my share of those coins.'

Therin grinned. 'That almost sounds like fun.'

'Well, don't think of joining me – except you, Annev. You want to join my gang, I can always use a second-in-command.'

'I don't want to hitch my wagon to your cart any more than you want yours tied to mine.' He smiled in spite of himself. 'Therin's right, though. From what I've seen of Luqura, it'll suit you. Good luck.' He stepped in closer, whispering: 'Watch your back. The lizardman, Saltair, is still alive. He killed the necromancer right before we escaped.'

'Keos,' Fyn swore.

'And Fyn ... his limbs grew back. He'd already sprouted a new tail and he's nearly regrown his hand. If you cross paths with him – run.'

'All right.' Fyn slapped Annev on the shoulder. 'Take care of things up north and watch after these idiots.' He left, and Annev felt a slight pang at seeing him go. Before he could dwell on it, though, Reeve was back.

'He decided to stay in the city?' Reeve asked. Annev nodded and the priest shrugged. 'I suppose it'll save on passage. Bring the horse around. The dockmaster will show us to the boat.'

'Did you get the name of the captain?' Annev asked, feeling a slight premonition from his magic ring.

'Why? You know many Innistiul slavers, aside from the ones trying to kill you?'

Annev shook his head. 'Just one – an old friend of Sraon's.'

Reeve quirked an eyebrow. 'What was his name?'

'Farthinand Caldaren. Sraon called him Frani.'

The high priest blinked then smiled. Then he laughed. 'Well, if that's not the damnedest coincidence. The dockmaster said it was a fellow named Caldaren. That's a bright piece of luck there – fated, one might say.'

Annev glanced at the codavora ring on his finger then thought of the soothsayer's prophecy, how Jian had advised him not to run from his fate. He frowned, remembering the Yomad's final sacrifice. He was grateful that Frani was sailing them north, but all the same Annev couldn't help feeling that sometimes fate was a real pain in the arse.

Chapter Twenty-Nine

Myjun glowed with an indescribable feeling of strength and vitality, power and purpose. She was a bright light in the darkness, a candle in the night. She burned with the brightness of every soul in Hentingsfort – every man, woman and child – and held their auras tight around her, a cloak against the wind, a blanket to shelter her from the night. She raised a hand to her mask, its gold metal slick with the blood of a hundred or more souls. She had fought and killed and won. She fed herself with life, fuelled herself with its power, bright as a beacon in the midst of a storm.

Except she *was* the storm. She was the death that all men feared – the spectre that promised no quarter, no remorse, and no mercy.

'You look ... radiant.'

Oyru's words were lost within the fire that still filled her. 'I am the bright death,' she said, feeling as though she stood at the centre of a whirlwind.

'The bright death,' he repeated. 'The golden glamour – the Gilded One.' He stared at her until she turned to face him, their eyes meeting across the void. 'You are my beautiful Oraqui – and you are ready to join me in the darkness.'

The assassin's words slowly penetrated her fog of euphoria and she blinked, the intoxicating rush of emotion slowly fading as the world solidified around her.

Blood and ashes. Death and decay. Fire and smoke. Hentingsfort was rendered as much a husk as Old Davey had been after his soul was consumed by her blades. She stared at it, unseeing, unfeeling.

She tried to focus, to remember what had brought her there – to remember why she had to kill, why she *wanted* to kill.

Ainnevog. I must find and kill Annev.

Myjun blinked again, as if that might clear the fog from her mind. 'I will not,' she croaked, her voice strained from screaming. 'I will not,' she tried again, 'go with you to the shadows. You promised to help me find and kill Annev. I will not find him there.'

'I promised to aid you – and I have done so. I have shown you your strength, helped you hone your weapons. I showed you your potential.' He held up a finger. 'But not all of it – not your *full* potential. These people, this village. It is nothing. Easily lost and easily forgotten. Its people were weak. The Shadowrealm is another matter. It is a harder place; its denizens are sharp. You must hone your skills there – *strengthen* yourself there.'

Myjun focused on the carnage surrounding her – at the broken bodies and the burning homes, at the smoke and the slaughter. She had done this – she and Oyru. They had broken the village together, had hunted its people and scoured it clean of all life. They had killed them together, a bloody, fearsome frenzy.

And she had loved it – had relished it, *craved* it.

'Annev is not *there*,' she repeated, her anger slowly returning, the malice seeping back into her voice. 'I will not delay my vengeance for ever.'

'And I promise you shall have it – and more – but first you must complete your training.'

'And what is this if not training? What other purpose is there for these tests?' She would have been shouting now, if not for the screaming she had done while wielding her soulfire blades. Her voice came out no louder than a hoarse whisper. 'My training is complete.'

'Your training,' the assassin said, his intensity surpassing her own, 'has just *begun*. You think you are hard now? Clever? Strong?' He shook his head. 'You are a child, and I will make you a warrior.'

Myjun eyes narrowed. 'What is in the Shadowrealm? What is so important that you take me there?'

'It is a means to an end. I need time to train you properly and time flows differently there. The closer we get to Reocht na Skah, the slower time passes in the real world. It also overlaps the World of Dreams, and a place of dreams and nightmares is a fitting place to train your skills and hone your magic. Armour and steel are useless there, against the shadow and light we both possess. There is a more practical reason, though. Moving through the World of Shadows allows us to travel faster, which is necessary if we are to reach the ironwood forests of Alltara.'

'Alltara?' Myjun's lip curled. 'That's on the opposite side of the world. You'd have to cross the old Darite Empire and the cursed lands of New Terra. It would take *weeks* to sail there – months, more likely.'

'We need only walk – and it will seem as though many days pass, perhaps a year or more – yet we will arrive as fast any boat could sail.

'You want me to wait a *year* to kill Annev? No.'

'The one you call Ainnevog – Annev – is no minor threat. He bested me, and I am far more dangerous than you. Perhaps together we could defeat him, but I will take no risks in facing him again. You will accompany me to Alltara, and on the way I will teach you the secrets of making armour that is as hard as steel but as light as your own skin. You will do this, or I will end your training now.'

'Why do I need armour when I can heal?'

'Because healing is no replacement for protection, and avoiding an injury is always preferable to healing it – a lesson you should have learned from your fight with the draken. A blade through your heart would kill you, and there is no healing decapitation or dismemberment.'

Myjun thought of Annev's stunted limb, and her horror and disgust on discovering it. She could not – *would* not – suffer that damnable fate. Monster though she may be, she had taken the Mask of Gevul's Mistress to *hide* her scars. If she lost an arm, it would all be for naught. She would be ugly. Crippled. *Lessened*.

'I will do what it takes to have my revenge, even if I must follow you into the shadows before I can exact it.'

'There was never any doubt.'

The shadepool at the edge of the clearing was black as night and mirror-still. Myjun gazed down at its inky darkness and a tumultuous sense of nausea bloomed in her gut.

'Enter,' Oyru whispered, his tone almost reverent. 'Survive this barrier, and we can begin the next stage of your training.'

Myjun stepped closer, her eyes searching the liquid blackness. 'What does it—'

He pushed her, just a nudge from his fingertips, but it was enough to knock her into the pool of shadows. The darkness swam around her calves and ankles, cold and merciless, and then the ground beneath her softened, growing insubstantial. She tried to move, tried to leave the pool, but something was drawing her down into the darkness. She looked down, saw the tentacles wrap around her thighs – pulling, twisting – and she began to scream, calling out for her blades. The sparks ignited in her hands ... but the magic would not come and the soulfire sputtered and extinguished. Now hands reached from the shadows, grasping at her, so many that she couldn't fight them all, or stop them dragging her deeper into the shadepool. Her gaze locked on Oyru, feeling both betrayed and frightened, but his pitiless eyes simply stared back at her, watching as the eidolons seized her shoulders, as they pulled her down and drowned her in shadows so thick she could not draw breath.

Myjun clamped down on her instinct to scream, to cough, to struggle. She stared into the darkness, unable to say if her eyes were still open. She waited for her lungs to burn, for the mounting need to breathe to eventually overwhelm her.

Nothing.

Myjun stood in a void, wrestling with tangible shadows that longed to consume her, surrounded by shadow demons that clawed at her heart, body and spirit, trying to claim that spark that lived inside her.

And she denied them. She held tight to the fire within her and used it as a weapon, wielding it against the monsters that tried to possess her and making them shrink back, blinded by the brilliance of that flame. Myjun grew bolder. She felt the heat rise in her chest and felt her anger grow with it. She *denied* them – and felt the strength of her own spirit, the same spirit that had fought the blood drake ... and *won*.

Myjun was not dying, was not drowning. She lived amidst a sea of darkness. She stood tall amidst a storm of shadows. The monsters clawed at her, pulled at her, screamed at her ... and she screamed back. A volley of light lanced from her mouth, blasting the shadows into tattered dreams and faded memories.

When her voice broke, the light shone bright in the palms of her hands. Her soulfire blades, bright with heat and crackling with life, illuminated the darkness.

Oyru watched her battle from the shadows beyond the light, his profile flickering as the shadows wove around him, forming into thin plates of armour. His grey lips twisted into a smile, and then the darkness coalesced around his hands, stretching as he formed the nether into long, black flyssas. He pinched the cloth hanging around his neck and drew it up to cover the bottom half of his face as Myjun fought the shadows around her to a fragile peace.

'Welcome to the Shadowrealm, Gilded One. You are now *tabibito* – Planeswalker. You are not my equal ... but you are no longer my apprentice. Walk beside me now, and we will brave the darkness together.'

Chapter Thirty

Kenton studied the men standing to attention amidst the rainbow-hued light filling the Vault of Damnation. No longer dressed in robes of simple crimson or austere black, the Academy's former masters and ancients now stood armed with myriad powerful magics uniquely suited to their experience, skills, and blood-talents. Among them, the most contrasting were Master Der and Ancient Denithal: the former Master of Stealth was invisible amidst the shrouds of black mist wafting about him, whereas the Academy's wizened alchemist had opted for a sober white tunic and mask that protected him from the bevvy of magical liquids, powders, and poisons he now carried about his person. Some of those elixirs would grant Denithal almost inhuman speed and strength – a clever surprise, given his otherwise feeble form – and other concoctions would allow him to trap, sedate or kill those unfortunate enough to oppose him.

And Denithal was the least of the five men Kenton had fashioned into the Sons of Damnation. Aog's giant, armour-clad body now seemed so imposing that Kenton wasn't sure he could still navigate the Academy's collapsed tunnels – and Master Murlach, Master of Engineering, seemed positively alien in his collection of whirring gears, clicking cables, and clanking pincers. Kenton had outfitted him first, and by the time he had equipped the other four men, Murlach had made dozens of modifications to adjust and improve his artifacts. Kenton had lost track of the impact of those changes, and he didn't care. These men were pawns – expendable soldiers in his war against Annev. Kenton needed them to stand against his enemy – he had seen, through Tosan's memories, the destructive power of Annev's cursed golden hand; he only needed their skills and their blood-talents, their experience and their numbers.

Yet the honest truth was Kenton hated them. He detested the crotchety Ancient Denithal and his cowardly potions. He despised Master Murlach for his clever fingers and his punishing traps. He envied Master Der and Ancient Edra for their closeness with Kenton's former mentor, Master Duvarek. Most of all, Kenton hated Ather, who had given Kenton his fateful scar and, by his reckoning, merited a painful death for the senseless disfigurement. No, Kenton didn't give a copper clip what happened to them, so long as they helped him find and kill Annev. Perhaps then – when Kenton had had his revenge for losing Myjun's love to Annev's charms, and then her life to Annev's hand – he might extend his revenge to include the deaths of Ather and any other masters who survived the slaughter.

But Kenton could be patient, and it was easy to feign allegiance to the five men helping him. He had done the same thing with Annev, Titus and Therin, and then again with Fyn and his cronies. Few sought Kenton's friendship, and fewer still obtained it. Master Duvarek had been perhaps the only person to manage it ... and then Elder Tosan had ordered Kenton to kill him.

I owe these men nothing, Kenton reminded himself, *and they are indebted to me. They will be my tools to wreak bloody vengeance.* And he had taken care to ensure his control over them. The five magical amulets would indeed heal the men who carried them. They would also enable Kenton to read their thoughts and detect their location. Other artifacts allowed Kenton to ensure his Sons of Damnation would remain obedient to his will. Chief among these were the slave and master rings he had first taken from the Vault and which he had subsequently shared with Master Aog. The slave ring glinted dully on the Master of Punishment's left hand, and Kenton smiled, knowing he could use the master ring to take full control of the hulking killer any time it suited him – like now.

'What are your orders, my lord?'

Kenton's smile deepened, knowing Aog's choice of words would only inspire the others to be similarly submissive.

It was almost too easy.

'We'll go to Banok first. That's the only town Annev has ever visited and it's the closest township to Chaenbalu, so it's the first place he's likely to go.'

'Makes sense,' Ather drawled, stroking his razor-thin moustache with his Gloves of Persuasion. The powder-blue silk garments were nowhere near as powerful as the Rod of Compulsion Kenton had attempted to steal from Janak, but they would give the former Master of Lies a powerful influence over any he touched – any except Kenton, of course.

'Good,' Kenton said, his desire to throttle the man growing with every moment he stared at him. 'Let's get moving, then.'

'There's just one little thing that's bothering me,' Ather continued, as if Kenton hadn't spoken.

'Which is?'

Ather gestured at the pool of *aqlumera* glowing in the centre of the room. 'Why are we leaving that here? Outside the village, an ounce of that stuff could make us rich as kings. Why leave it here for someone else to find?'

'We're *not* merely leaving it here,' Kenton explained. 'We are going to *seal* the Vault by collapsing the tunnels. No one will be able to find the village except those that once lived here, and they will be unable to excavate the tunnels.'

'Right,' Ather said, his voice as smooth as oil on water. 'That's the part that vexes me, see. Seems poorly thought out to leave that much treasure buried under ten tonnes of rock and dirt. Be better for us to carry a bit out and put it to some use, you know?'

Kenton's patience had worn thin. 'I've told you that liquid is dangerous. If you go near it – if you even look too closely at it – you'll imperil your soul.'

The other masters seemed mollified by this explanation – even Denithal, their master alchemist, nodded his head in mute agreement – yet Ather remained unconvinced.

'That's all well and good, I suppose.' Ather stepped forward and rested his gloved hand on Kenton's shoulder then turned his gaze on the boy's face, his eyes looking into Kenton's as though his face weren't covered by a thick blindfold. 'We should really gather a few vials of the liquid, though ... don't you think?'

'No,' Kenton said, sliding the scarf from his eyes so that Ather could see the flames that burned there. 'I really don't think that's a good idea.'

Ather flinched, his heart thudding loudly in Kenton's ears as he withdrew his hand and let it fall to his side. 'Right then,' Ather said, his eyes sliding away, unable to meet Kenton's. 'We'll just head back upstairs then.'

'Good,' Kenton said, watching the man retreat to the back of the group. 'Anyone else?'

Edra slowly raised his hand.

'Tell me.'

'Well,' the former Master of Arms began. 'Do you plan to leave tonight – seeing as how it's dark and all? Might be a good idea to sleep here and leave in the morning. If that's all right with you, I mean.'

Kenton nodded. 'An excellent suggestion, Edra. We can camp here tonight and leave in the morning.' He left the chamber then, not bothering to ask the others. He knew where they were and what they were thinking, after all. He had no need to police them. It was more important that they remained fearful of him – that they learned to obey him – and that wouldn't happen if Kenton seemed to be waiting on their pleasure or advice.

When he reached the surface, Kenton turned his gaze westward, towards Banok and the intervening woods. His magic vision let him pierce the veil of night and the gloom of the forest, but the distance between Banok and Chaenbalu was too great for even his supernatural vision. He contented himself with the thought that he would soon be on Annev's trail.

'Hello, Master Kenton.'

Kenton turned, his fiery eyes focusing on the last person he expected to see.

'Witmistress Kiara,' he said, as much to himself as to the woman standing before him. 'I thought ... are the other witwomen with you? Did they survive?'

311

'Sadly, no.' The grey-haired witmistress turned her own eyes to the west, as if she too sought to pierce the distance between Chaenbalu and the next township. 'I am all that remains of the Witcircle. I am also the last living Bride of Fate, and the only one who knows what happened the night you were imprisoned beneath the Academy.'

Kenton felt his blood growing cold. 'What do you know?'

'I know a great many things, Master Kenton. Secrets that even your deceased headmaster could not have told you ... not even after he tried to possess your body.'

Kenton stared at the woman, his fiery eyes flaring. She did not even deign to look back. 'I see you know some of *my* secrets, as well,' Kenton said, his voice low and intense. He studied her again, his eyes passing over her ageless face. 'What is it you want from me?' he said, cutting to the chase. 'If you know so much, why have you stayed hidden – and why have you sought me out?'

This time the witmistress did look at him, her grey eyes as cold and hard as winter steel. 'You are planning to find and kill the boy known as Ainnevog, yes?'

'Yes.'

'Why?'

'Because he ...' He stared at her. 'You already know the answer, don't you?'

'Yes, but I wish you to speak it aloud – to make certain you also know the answer.'

Kenton watched the witmistress with smouldering eyes, then retied his black scarf over them. 'I need to kill him,' Kenton said, his voice barely above a whisper, 'because he stole Myjun from me, and then he killed her.'

'So, you believe she is dead.'

Kenton snorted. 'Annev couldn't have her – she didn't want him when she knew about his hand – so he killed her.'

'Who told you that?'

'I saw it through Tosan's eyes – and the masters confirmed it. They saw her blasted by fire before the earth swallowed her up. Saw Annev bury her alive.' His voice choked and he struggled to keep it from cracking altogether. 'Annev *has* to die,' he continued, slightly calmer. 'He deserves it. He lied to the Academy, he—'

'Be honest, Kenton. You don't give a damn about the Academy … and truth be told, neither do I. That's why we brought the *feurog* in. Scour it clean. Leave no witnesses. You understand, I'm sure.'

'You … the *feurog*?'

'Yes, my boy. Please keep up. Those gruesome monsters all twisted with stone and metal? Those are the *feurog* – failed experiments of the demi-god Cruithear. He abandoned them and we made use of them – our little secret army. When we discovered Annev was … who he is … we opened the tunnels and brought the *feurog* in to cleanse the village.'

'You …' Kenton breathed, his voice barely above a whisper. 'You … and the witwomen. *You* killed everyone? You murdered the villagers and destroyed the Academy?'

'Through the *feurog*, yes. We euthanised the new reaps – sad thing, that, but it would have been worse to abandon them in the Academy. Wailing until they died from the cold, from thirst and starvation.' She tsked, head shaking. 'No, much better our way – and not all of the witwomen were part of our little cabal, so we had to kill the others.' She shrugged, as if discussing the casual murder of her colleagues were as inconsequential as spilling the milk at teatime.

'You killed the infants … and then you murdered the other witwomen. Why?'

'Because they would have murdered us – they *tried to* – once they discovered our plans. That damn witgirl – my assistant, Faith – caused a lot of unnecessary trouble. Many deaths that could have been avoided.'

'Why … why are you telling me this?'

'Because you are the Cursed Leader. Because you plan to hunt the Vessel – and I can't allow that.'

'The Vessel,' Kenton repeated, eyes narrowing. 'You mean Annev.'

'Precisely.'

'You want me to *spare* Annev?' The witmistress nodded and

Kenton shook with dry laughter. 'You really are insane then. Destroying half the village and all your companions, then coming to me ... to spare Annev's life?' His laughter died like a withered reed. 'I have pledged to kill him – and the Academy's former masters will help me do it.'

Kiara glanced back at Kenton's tunnel. 'They seem more trouble than they're worth, but I suppose it's novel for you to lead anyone – and you *are* the Cursed Leader.' She shrugged again.

'You're not going to stop me?'

'Oh, I am. Just not by fighting you. I've come to persuade.'

'Then you're wasting your time, not to mention revealing your hand. You should have stayed in hiding, should have fled from all of this.' He gestured at the ruined village. 'When the Sons of Damnation and I leave here tomorrow morning, I will sink the Academy to its foundation and finish what Annev started. Then we will hunt him down and kill him.'

'And you're certain there is nothing I can say to change your mind?'

'Nothing,' Kenton repeated, his voice cold as ice.

'Then you will not be moved to hear Myjun is still alive? That I could show her to you?'

Kenton stared at the old witmistress, the fire in his eyes growing dim and then hot once again. He tilted his head sideways, watching, studying her.

'You ... are telling the truth. You *think* it is true, anyway.'

'You can judge for yourself.'

Kenton glanced between the grey woman and the tunnel. He could hear the echoes of the masters and ancients discussing whether they had missed any artifacts of note.

'Send them on ahead to make your camp. Put Aog in charge, then use your little ring to command them from afar.'

'You know about the ring.' He shook his head, a queer smile twisting his lips. 'Of course you do. You seem to know all my secrets.'

'Not all, but most. Tacharan, the God of Doom, grants the Brides of Fate certain advantages, lends us certain insights.'

'You can see the future, that's what you're saying?'

'Just fragments. Visions. Old riddles given new meaning. Sometimes I get premonitions or promptings. Rarest of all are the revelations that come with perfect clarity.'

'Such as?'

'Such as coming to persuade you to leave off your vengeance ... for now, anyway.'

'And Myjun?'

'Come with me, Master Kenton. Follow me to the shadepools in the Brakewood and I will show you that Myjun is very much alive – though she will not remain that way unless you are prepared to aid her when she needs you most.'

Kenton tried to imagine it, the impossible reunion he longed for but knew could never be. 'She ... would not like what I have become.' He raised his hand to the hard leather of his cheeks, the flaming spheres of his eyes. 'She would call me a demon – she would run from me.'

'Perhaps the girl you once knew would run, but now ...' Kiara splayed her hands. 'Who can say what monsters will do?'

Kenton's magic eyes studied the soul of the Academy's former witmistress. He did not sense any deception there, but he was wary nonetheless.

'Very well then, Mistress Kiara. Share your secrets.'

Chapter Thirty-One

Kenton stared deep into the shadepool, his attention fixed on the images within. Amidst the darkness, he saw two people walking together, each one dressed in black rags. The man wore plates of black armour and had his face half-covered by a scrap of black fabric. By contrast, the woman wore no armour and her face was covered by a delicate golden mask. Kenton watched her move – the way she walked or stopped to examine the world around her – and he immediately knew who she was.

'Where is she?' Kenton demanded, his eyes burning with intensity.

'Near ... and also far. She has entered the Shadowrealm, a plane of existence that overlaps our own but which remains distant and alien.'

'Like the Spirit World?'

'They are similar. The World of Spirits is farther still, though it overlaps in much the same way.'

'She is dead then.'

'No.' Kiara waved her hand at the shadepool and the darkness shifted, forming images of overlapping grey discs, some dark and some light. 'We inhabit the Physical Realm, ruled by the Elder Gods and the Younger Gods of Plants, Minerals, and Animals.' Kiara gestured at the pool again and a spinning white disc separated itself from the others.

'Overlapping our world are the other three planes of existence: the Plane of Shadows, the World of Dreams, and the Spirit World. Our actions here cast shadows, silhouettes of reality, in the Shadowrealm. When we sleep, our consciousness touches the World of Dreams – and when we die, our spirits travel to the Spirit World.' Three grey discs rose from the shadepool, their edges overlapping with each other and the white disc.

'All three parts of our soul – mind, body and spirit – converge here and anchor us in the Physical Realm, yet it is possible to travel to the other planes if you possess a special connection to skywater, earthblood, or lightfire.'

'And Myjun is in the Shadowrealm. She's there physically?'

'Correct.' Kiara waved her hand once more and the shadows reformed into the hazy image of the woman in the golden mask and the man in black armour.

'Why?'

Kiara grunted. 'Some secrets remain secrets. But' – she held up a finger – 'I can give you three vital pieces of information. First, Myjun will return *here* – to this very shadepool – in less than a year's time. Second, she will be coming to hunt Annev as well. Third, if you are not here to stop her – if you are not here to *save* her – then she will be killed.'

Kenton stared at Kiara, unable to deduce the woman's motives. If she was lying, it was an elaborate lie – and one that placed the blame for Chaenbalu's destruction squarely on her own shoulders. If she was telling the truth, though ...

'Why are you telling me this?'

'Because your current mission runs counter to my own. You seek to find Annev and kill him. I seek to use the Vessel for another purpose – a purpose I cannot achieve if he is already dead. But now perhaps our desires run parallel to one another. You sought vengeance because you believed Annev had killed the headmaster's daughter – your would-be lover – but those motives were misplaced.'

Kenton was grateful that the darkness hid his reddening cheeks from the witmistress. He wondered how many of the Academy's witgirls and witwomen had known about Kenton and Myjun's short courtship.

It doesn't matter a whit now, though. According to Kiara, they're all dead ... and Myjun is alive.

'Maybe,' he said. 'But if Myjun will be here in a year that still gives me plenty of time to find Annev.'

'Less than a year – and you don't *need* to find him. He will be here too.'

'Why wait when I can find him sooner?'

Kiara shook her head. 'If Annev is not here then Myjun will not be here either. She will be lost to you for ever.'

Kenton's hand drifted to the bone dagger at his hip. He felt a powerful urge to kill this woman, not just because she was manipulating him, but for destroying the village, the Academy and everything they represented – everything Kenton had been working towards. In some twisted way, Annev's escape from prison, the loss of his eyes, and Myjun's death were her fault. She had brought the monsters here; their attack had drawn Tosan away and led to Kenton being alone with Annev.

But no. Kenton had chosen to stay in that cell. He had allowed Annev to goad him, and then blind him. Kenton's hand stopped.

'So, I wait for Annev – a few weeks or months, maybe a year. Then what? What am I saving Myjun from?'

'From death. From the shadows. From herself.'

Kenton frowned. 'From the man she is with?'

'*Half*-man – he is a shadow reborn – and he is her master.'

'Master?' Kenton's lip curled. 'Myjun has no master.'

'She is as much a captive to herself as to him. That is why she needs you to save her – *not* to interfere with Ainnevog. Do you understand? If she kills him, she will be killed. If you kill him, you will never see her again.'

'That's no guarantee she will want to see me – or that she wants to be saved.'

'Some mysteries we must solve for ourselves.'

'I suppose.' He paused. 'Why do you want Annev so much? You and your Brides of Fate destroyed the village ... for what?'

Kiara gave a sly grin. 'You do not seem too upset by my part in Chaenbalu's destruction.'

Kenton sniffed. 'I didn't much like the people who lived here ... and they didn't care for me. Why should I care now that they're dead? The only person I cared about is in the Shadowrealm.'

Kenton looked back to the shadepool and the images that floated there. 'Very well. If it will save Myjun then I will play my part.'

Kiara nodded. 'Then our paths have momentarily aligned.' She gestured at the shadepool. 'So long as you remain here with me, I can show you Myjun's location. You will know when she is about to return.'

'And what is *your* path, Witmistress?'

Kiara waved at the shadepool and the image of Myjun and her master faded into darkness. 'For many decades now, the purpose of the reap has been to find babies with the potential for magic and bring them back to the Academy.' She cocked her head at Kenton, sensing his surprise. 'What? You thought you and Annev were the only ones?'

'Why?'

She sighed, head shaking. 'It all comes from fear, I suppose. The Academy was founded many centuries ago, when a sect of preachers claimed the priesthood had been corrupted and that all magic, including artifacts, was evil. They persecuted any who believed otherwise, and soon left the Church to form their own sect in the heart of the Brakewood. When they left, they stole many of the Church's treasures, including artifacts of legend such as the Hand of Keos. The heretics believed it was their sacred duty to either guard or destroy such magic. Ironic then that they chose to hide in Chaenbalu, home to a radiant fountain of pure *aqlumera*.'

'The Vault,' Kenton interrupted. 'You're talking about that liquid in the Vault.'

'Just so. The Vault was built atop the fountain, the Academy was built to protect the Vault, and it trained young zealots to fill it with other stolen artifacts – but not all of the founders were true believers. One among them, Pomela Witsom, was a Bride of Fate, following a prophecy that the Vessel of Keos would be raised among these heretics. So she joined the group before they splintered, married Elder Cornett – who would become Chaenbalu's first headmaster – and she in turn became the first witwoman. On the surface, Pomela took charge of delivering infants for the Academy and the village. Then she began training other witwomen to assist her in "saving" other untainted children from the world. They were midwives initially, but gradually Pomela found women gifted with the blood-talent. A handful were like her – Yomad priestesses with Darite complexions, already Brides of Fate. The rest were brought in one at a time and indoctrinated.'

'Indoctrinated,' Kenton repeated, turning the word over in his mouth. 'They all joined your cult then?'

Kiara stared at him – not quite a glare, but close. 'Those with too little magic or too little sense remained regular witwomen. Through our work, those without magic have been winnowed out of the Academy, and the ones confiscating magic – the ones that are taught to hate it more fervently – are also the ones carrying the blood-talent.'

'That's perverse.' Kenton paused, considering. 'So are you a Darite orphan or a New Terran infiltrator?'

This time Kiara did glare. 'I am a Yomad from New Terra.'

'But aren't you all stolen from Darite villages, like the avatars?'

'In every reap we bring in a few infants from Alltara or Old Terra, to keep the old blood alive and to be sure we are thorough in our search for the Vessel. None of us had imagined he would be *born* in Chaenbalu, let alone to an Ilumite mother … but such is the challenge of prophecy. We see the future, but only darkly.'

'And that's why it took so long to realise Annev was your Vessel.'

'That, and that meddling priest, Sodar.'

Kenton studied the old witmistress, her iron-grey hair and piercing eyes. She still hadn't revealed why she wanted Annev, and he was of a mind to discover her secrets. But if she was right – if Myjun really was alive and would need his help – then he had no reason to leave. He could even still send the Sons of Damnation on ahead to search Annev out. His connection to their amulets would keep him appraised of their actions, and he could remain here and keep an eye on Myjun through Kiara's magic scrying.

Until she was of no further use to him.

'Very well, Witmistress. I'll spare Annev … for now. In exchange, you will tell me more about your order – these Brides of Fate. Tell me who they are – or were – and why they exist.'

'Mm ... and you will not harm Annev? Neither directly nor indirectly?'

'So long as Myjun remains alive and you can show her to me ... yes.'

'Bargain struck, then.' The grey woman offered her palm. Kenton hesitated, then he shook it. As he did so, the air in the room seemed to shudder, the magic in his eyes flared, and for an instant it seemed as though he were holding the bony hand of a flaming skeleton.

Part Three

LUQURA

The origins of the Six are shrouded in myth and mystery. Such tales – involving monsters, traitors, and keokum being directed by the merciless vampyr Dortafola – are often greatly exaggerated, though on occasion the truth seems more fantastic than fiction.

One case that is frequently misrepresented is that of Valdemar Kranak, the first Darite to abandon his calling as a priest and scholar so that he might instead support Dortafola and his Siänar's malign designs. According to the surviving records, Kranak was born towards the end of the Age of Kings and was raised as one of the Dionachs Tobar. He made the ageless covenant with an unknown Terran priest at the turn of the century and leveraged his longevity at the University of Neven nan Su'ul to become a Magister of the First Order. It has been rumoured that Kranak lobbied for the position of Arch Lector and was denied the coveted role, possibly due to his sympathies with Terran scholarship. If true, this might have been the impetus for Kranak's later betrayal of both the University and the city ... but we shall leave such unfounded speculation to lesser scholars.

What *has* been confirmed beyond doubt is Valdemar Kranak's role in the destruction of the University, and the razing of Neven nan Su'ul and the province of Gorm Corsa. Terran propagandists have attempted to paint Kranak as a benevolent intellectual who was later demonised by the Halcyon Knights, but public record and eyewitness testimonies show he was instrumental in bringing the Terran Bloodlords to the city, precipitating the retreat of the Darite Empire from Gorm Corsa and the rest of Eastern Daroea (now New Terra). The evidence suggests Kranak began by fomenting unrest among the student populace around the beginning of the Third Age.[†] Having gained support among the University's more radical students, Kranak began hosting nightly lectures questioning the accuracy of certain Darite history books, which were already disputed by Terran scholars. The content of these lectures became more and more occult, with at least one claiming that Neven nan Su'ul had been founded by the Terrans rather than the Darites. As the Terrans pressed further and further west, expanding beyond Terra Majora and into Eastern Daroea, Kranak's lectures led to heated disagreements with other magisters which (in a few cases) escalated to physical blows.

It is unclear when Valdemar Kranak's lectures descended from genuine scholarship into Terran propaganda, but the surviving records of censure state the magister was brought before Arch Lector Gale-Dana'y and ordered to stop questioning the Empire's doctrine. As ordered, Kranak disbanded his evening classes, only to be suspended when he was discovered meeting privately with students to further his pro-Terran agenda.

On his return to the University following his suspension, reports indicate Kranak was a changed man: his lectures had been sanitised of all their former inflammatory content and he publicly disavowed the arguments he had made in support of the Terran government. The change would be utterly remarkable, were it not for our own knowledge of Kranak's later betrayal. Many scholars, including my colleague Alice Quenby, have argued that Valdemar Kranak was approached by Dortafola during his suspension, and invited to join what later became the Siänar. This is a persuasive argument, particularly as the dates of Kranak's suspension align with what little we know of the Siänar's first creation.

– 'The Siänar', The Complete Histories of Luquatra by Kyartus
Gairm

† Kash Mikla, a survivor from the razing of Neven nan Su'ul, claims to have seen Kranak leading a calvary of Bloodlords against the University's own students (a testimony that has

since been widely debunked as no mounts were used during either the city's siege or the final rout of its citizens); on the other hand, the folk poem 'Vaul of the Fall' describes Kranak as a scholar whose 'love of the masses brought death to his classes when nechraict rose up from their graves,' suggesting that necromancy played an integral part in the city's final destruction. Finally, Crystal Gooden – one of my esteemed colleagues from Southmarch – has suggested Kranak used Terran shadow magic to infiltrate and attack the University, giving rise to his later moniker 'The Shadow'. It seems more likely, though, that Kranak's nickname arose from his ability to silently pass through the University's halls (a common effect produced by most Breathbreakers).

Chapter Thirty-Two

Fyn plucked the apple from the vendor's cart without breaking stride and continued his stroll along the River District's promenade, a wide road that hid the underground canal connecting Luqura's two rivers. Commerce was brisk here, and the guards were plentiful, but the opportunities for filling his pockets vastly outnumbered his chances of getting caught. By contrast, the merchant and noble districts had too many eyes watching their vendor stalls and too many swords guarding the nobles' purses. He'd noticed the mansions were less well guarded, though – and contained greater riches besides – so Fyn entertained himself with the idea he might rob the homes of Luqura's upper class at night, while picking pockets and lifting goods from its lower class during the day. People in the Ash Quarter tended to carry their most valuable possessions on themselves, anyway – their burned hovels being too insecure to leave valuables unprotected and unmolested.

All Fyn needed was a base of operations, and a gang to speed his acquisition of wealth and power. Territory was easiest to take in the Ash Quarter – it was free, if he could keep and defend it – so he'd spent most of his first two days scouting the Lower District for a good headquarters. He had found a promising corner that was well away from the Boneyard and just a few blocks south of the unburned portions of the Lower District, and he was trying to settle on a tenement when he sensed someone – several someones from the sound of it – approaching from behind.

Instead of turning or fleeing, Fyn took his time eating his apple and continued his stroll down the trash-littered street. At the first blind alley, he turned and ducked inside, knowing his pursuers would be close behind. As he melted into the shadows, he checked his weapons and waited for the expected ambush. He didn't have to wait long.

Six thugs appeared at the mouth of the alley, their leader at the front, sniffing for blood.

'Is it that same one you saw yesterday?' the largest one asked. He carried a heavy, rounded stick that resembled a battered rolling pin, and his face looked almost cherubic in spite of his imposing figure.

'Shh,' the leader hissed, his eyes darting around the alley, searching for Fyn. 'Don't spook him, Siege.'

'What's to spook?' a third one said, a buxom woman as large as the man with the rolling pin – probably bigger – carrying what looked to be a fisherman's gaff.

Of the three that hadn't spoken, one hung back, presumably to guard the mouth of the alley, and the other two shot forward, exploring the shadows and hoping to flank their prey.

Fortunately for Fyn, he'd chosen this exact alley yesterday with the purpose of flanking *them*. He smiled from his hidden vantage point, circling behind the group and approaching the man they'd left as their lookout.

Halfway into the darkened alley, Siege gave a whoop as a snare tangled his foot and pulled his legs out from under him. On cue, Fyn yanked a hidden rope and a sack full of bricks dropped onto the woman with the gaff, knocking her weapon from her hands and quite possibly knocking her out entirely.

'It's a trap!' the leader bellowed, doubling back to the alley mouth. 'Quinn! Way! Grab Siege and Poli and get the hell out of—'

Fyn swatted the back of the man's skull with an improvised slapjack and sent him sprawling atop the body of his unconscious lookout.

'So you're the infamous Fisher King,' Fyn said, leaning over the fallen figure, 'the Serpent of South Ashes … the Terror of Tumbledown Street.' He gave a dry laugh then kicked the man between the legs – hard.

'Oof!' Fisher doubled over on himself.

Fyn glanced back down the alley, his cold eyes meeting Quinn's as she helped the larger woman, Poli, clamber out from beneath the bricks. Siege had nearly freed himself from his snare and was searching for his cudgel, which seemed to have rolled away when he'd fallen. Meanwhile, the sneaky one – Way – had slipped a knife from his pocket and was slowly advancing in Fyn's direction.

'Should have thrown that at my back while I was kicking Fisher. Since you didn't, either you don't know how to throw, you have no intention of actually killing me ... or you're scared shitless.'

'I ain't scared of a little chickenshit like you,' Way swore, still advancing. 'What are you? Twelve? Probably don't even have hair on your fruits.'

'Given the choice between my fruits and his ...' Fyn kicked the Fisher King in the head, knocking him out cold. 'I think I'll stick with mine – hairy or not.'

'You got a mouth on you, don'tcha?'

'Very observant – now let's move this along.' Fyn nodded at Way's weapon. 'You gonna throw that or am I gonna take it from you?'

The lithe man snickered, though he checked to make sure Siege and the others were backing him up. 'I think I'll wait till you start running, then I'll throw it at you.'

'You'd miss – and I'm not running.'

'We outnumber you, boy. Poli's got reach with her gaff there, and you don't want to mess with Sigs. Jolly sort, but he's a killer an' no mistake. Arms like a bull. Crush your skull like an egg.'

Fyn noticed the man didn't mention their other associate, Quinn, who was scaling the rightmost building in an attempt to get behind him.

Amateurs.

'Bulls don't have arms, arsehole – and I'm getting bored.' He hurled his apple core at the man's face, distracting him just as Quinn leapt from the shadows. He had expected a knife thrust, a hammer blow or a hatchet swing – he'd seen the crew use all three in the day and the night he'd been stalking them – but Quinn surprised him with heavy gloves ending in curved iron nails shaped to look like bear claws. *Tekko-Kagi*, Fyn realised, dodging the attack. *Very interesting*. Quinn swung again and Fyn stepped aside, placing the young woman between him and Way. When she swung a third time, he stepped into the attack, grabbed Quinn's wrist and thrust his hips. The small woman's feet came off the ground and Fyn spun, slashing her other clawed hand at Way. The sneak cursed, stepped back and tried another angle. This time, Fyn tossed Quinn over his shoulder and into Way, sending both attackers sprawling.

'You lot work for me now,' Fyn said, not even winded. 'Your contract with the Fisher King has ended.'

'Rot that,' Poli said, her gaff hook extended. 'I'm going to gut you like a fish, boy. No one drops bricks on me and walks away.'

Instead of answering, Fyn reached down and plucked a small purse from Fisher's tunic. He jingled it in one hand then tossed it to Siege. 'What's your cut of the loot?'

'Rule of quarters,' Siege answered, eyeing the sack in his hand with equal parts greed and suspicion. His rolling pin disappeared into his tunic. 'One-quarter for us. Three-quarters for Fisher. He says it's for the Guild – to pay them for the right to work the street.'

'That's a new one,' Fyn said, snorting. 'So, who's in on it? The city watch? The Thieves Guild?'

'Only one Guild matters,' Poli said, lowering her gaff. 'The Slavers Guild.'

'You're not from around here, are you?' Quinn said.

'Like you can talk. Where'd you get those?' He gestured at the Tekko-Kagi. 'You make them? Steal them?' The woman hissed at him in response, her black hair falling to cover half her face.

'He's *definitely* not from around here,' Way said, slapping Quinn on the shoulder. 'Ain't you never seen the Pits?' he said, studying Fyn. 'They put 'em on fighters all the time. Makes 'em look fierce.'

'Only they don't know how to use them,' Quinn whispered.

'And you do?'

The woman nodded, her clawed hands crossed in front of her chest. Fyn studied the group, watching their body language for another attack.

'You're Quynh-Chi, though they keep calling you Quinn. My guess is you're Kroseran, with the Tekko-Kagi. You brought here as a slave?' The woman didn't respond, though she did lower her hands to her sides.

'Ford Siegeman,' Fyn continued. 'Siege – or Sigs. What'd you do before Fisher brought you into his gang? Work in a bakery or something?'

Siege grinned. 'Me and Poli worked the docks – I *do* like to bake, though. You ever eaten pizza pie?' Siege's smile grew. 'It's Darter food – delicious.'

'Maybe you can bake me one sometime.'

'Heh. You find me an oven and the right ingredients, I'll bake a score of 'em.'

'What's Darter food?'

'Darite-Terran,' Way said, thumbing his chest. '*I'm* a Darter. David Sanhueza. People call me Way.'

'I had figured that's 'cause you help Fisher find the way into places.'

Way shrugged. 'I do that, too. How long you been following us? What do you want?'

'Long enough – and I want to be your new crew leader.'

The others shared a look, a few of them glancing at Fisher, who was starting to stir. Siege hefted the bag of coins, considering. 'Why would we follow you?' He studied the maces, falchion and other weapons strapped to Fyn's body. 'You cut a mean figure with all those blades, but you're half Fisher's age.'

'I'm twenty,' Fyn lied. 'And if he's over forty, it's time he started looking for softer work.'

'Kill him,' Fisher coughed, rising to his knees and elbows. 'Stop chatting the bastard up and kill him!'

'They could try,' Fyn said, not bothering to look at the fallen crew chief. 'Or I could tell them where you're hiding that extra coin you claim is for the Slavers Guild.'

Poli frowned, her grip tightening on the gaff. 'That true, Fisher?'

'He's lying!' Fisher rose to his feet, slid a butcher knife from his coat and waved it at the rest of the group. 'You know Neldon checks the books. He'd tell you if I wasn't square.'

332

'Would he?' Way asked, taking a step towards Fisher. 'Neldon's from your old crew. Maybe he's in on the take. It'd be nice to ask him, only he seems to be sleeping on the job.' He nodded at the unconscious lookout then glanced at Fyn. 'You kill him?'

'I don't kill people for doing their jobs – not even if they're bad at it.'

'What's that supposed to mean?' Fisher said sharply, taking a step in Fyn's direction.

'People talk, Fisher.' Fyn had no idea what he was talking about – he'd only been in Luqura for a few days, and that wasn't enough time to gather much more than gossip. He had a hunch, though, and he was following it. 'Wait for Neldon to wake up,' Fyn said, planting his feet. 'He'll tell you what really happened to the old gang. After that, I bet you won't want to follow him.'

Fisher charged, butcher-knife-first. Fyn stepped wide of the blade, catching the crew leader's wrist. He pulled Fisher forward, carrying his momentum in an arc as he dipped his knee and guided the man's knife up under his ribs and into his own chest cavity. The bald man coughed, eyes wide, as hot blood started to pump from his chest, his raggedy shirt soaked in sticky redness. Fyn let go and Fisher dropped to his knees, blood spurting from between his lips. He collapsed and the rest of the gang stared open-mouthed at their dead chief.

'The way I see it,' Fyn said, stepping smoothly away from the convulsing body, 'you have three choices. One: you can attack me now – and when I've finished killing all of you, I'll look for another crew to become my gang. Two: you follow me, and I'll earn you more money than the Fisher King ever could.'

'And the third option?' Way said, still clutching his dagger.

'Three: you walk away – for now. I'll find another gang and start claiming territory. Eventually, though, we'll be back to one and two. You can join me now and get the early rewards ... or I can bury you and build my empire on your ashes.'

Siege and Poli exchanged a look and Fyn knew he had them. Way would follow the majority – he seemed to be the cautious type – and Neldon didn't get a vote since he was unconscious. That left Quinn. Fyn watched her, and she was studying him in

333

turn, chewing her lip, her almond eyes flicking to the flanged maces on Fyn's back.

'Even shares for everyone in the crew?'

'No. I get three shares, and my second gets a share and a half. Everyone else gets one.'

'Who's your second?'

'One of you, I suppose. I'll let the five of you decide who you trust the most.'

'Neldon,' Siege said, and Poli nodded her agreement.

'The lookout?' Fyn was sceptical.

'He's our medic,' Way said, sheathing his knife. 'Used to be a scholar, a doctor. Something like that. Fell on hard times and ended up in the Ashes with the rest of us.'

'Does he fight?'

'If he needs to, he can throw a decent punch. Got a terrifying manuballista he uses for bigger jobs. Usually he keeps the books, though. Patches us up when we get hurt. Talks to the Guild if Fisher's busy.'

'All right,' Fyn said, wiping his hands on his trousers. 'Neldon it is. Of my three shares, one goes into a strong-box for funding bigger jobs.'

Quinn frowned. 'What about the Guild?'

'What about them? They can go hang themselves.' The five gang members looked at one another and sheathed their weapons. Quinn scoffed, spat and went to check on Neldon. Fyn eyed them, feeling he'd missed something.

'You don't get it,' Way said, stepping close enough that Fyn kept an eye on the man's hands. 'The Guild controls most of what happens in the Ash Quarter, the Undercity, the Boneyard – even the Low Quarter and the River District. Everything except the Merchant and Noble Quarters – and they're close to controlling them, too. If you ignore the Guild, they'll send the Watchers after you.' He shook his head. 'You can keep your shares and your delusions. *No one* crosses the Guild.' The rest of the group shouldered past, and Fyn realised he was losing them. He had to think quick.

'You know the lizardman who works for the Guild – some keokum freak? Me and my last crew nearly killed him.'

The gang froze. Neldon was starting to wake and Siege helped him to his feet.

'You're blowing smoke and ashes,' Quinn said, her voice husky. 'No one crosses the Guild – and no one fights Saltair and lives.'

'Ask around. We cut off his tail and his hand. Might be you can even find the pieces somewhere. I hear he can grow them back – but we still got him.' He sucked at his teeth. 'Think about it. If you want to join my crew, be back here in three days and I'll tell you what I have in mind.'

The gang bled away into the street with Neldon tottering between Siege and Poli. Way hung back, taking in Fyn's weapons, his clothing and his face. Finally, he inclined his head.

'Three days?'

'Yeah.'

'And you've got a plan.'

'I do.'

Way grunted. 'You got a name?'

'Fyunai. People call me Fyn.'

'Fyn,' he said, trying the name on his lips. 'Fyn the Feared ... Fatal Fyn.' A queer smile quirked his lips. 'I'll ask around about Saltair. If what you say is true ... well, then count me in.'

Fyn inclined his head and the man slunk away, rejoining his gang. Once they were all gone, Fyn gave a deep sigh, looked down at Fisher's body ... and threw up.

It wasn't the sight of the corpse, nor did he feel guilty about murdering the crew chief – the way Fyn saw it, he'd had it coming. No, what made Fyn spray his lunch across the alley was having no idea what to do about the Slavers Guild or their stranglehold on Luqura's underworld ... and he had exactly three days to create a workable plan. It almost made him wish Annev were still in the city.

Almost.

Fyn wiped the vomit from his lips and steadied himself against the wall. A flutter of movement caught his eye and he looked up to see a lithe figure in a raven mask staring down at him – watching.

From the Slavers Guild? Fyn wondered, remembering Way mentioning their Watchers. But if the Raven worked for the Guild, she gave no indication of it. Instead, she tilted her head, saluted him with two fingers, and slid the mask from her face.

'The hell?' Fyn swore. The black-clad woman danced away across the roof of the building and disappeared from sight.

Fyn watched her go in disbelief. He couldn't imagine why she would be following him – or why she'd have any interest in him after fleeing Janak's palace with the Rod of Compulsion. Yet he suspected he'd see Sodja Rocas again in the not-too-distant future – a thought that was not altogether unpleasant.

Chapter Thirty-Three

The stars were bright overhead as Sodja walked among the cherry trees surrounding her family's estate. She reached the edge of the orchard and drifted over to the pool of super red arowana, the gleam of gold and copper scales beneath the water reminding her of the flames that had consumed Janak's study during her escape with the Rod of Compulsion. Sodja touched that rod now – cool, slender and heavy in her pocket – and she thought of her encounter with the three thieves who had started the fire. That had been six days ago – and only four days since the thieves from the Brakewood had come back to Luqura to look for her.

Sodja knew very little about the thieves' mysterious organisation. Their members were supposedly worshippers of Odar, though Sodja couldn't say how confiscating magic artifacts benefitted the God of Skywater. Sodja's older brothers, Ketrit and Rista, had even encountered a few cultists while going about family business in Luqura, but Rista had been the only one to capture and interrogate one of the thieves, and the man had not long survived Rista's ministrations.

By contrast, the three cultists Sodja had encountered had been little more than boys – although the muscular one with the dreadlocks seemed a little older. Maybe even her age. Sodja smiled, remembering his poor attempt to track her back to Luqura. He'd been adorably angry when she'd used her shadow magic to disappear in front of him – and the string of curse words had been so malevolently creative, Sodja had been tempted to reappear just to let the fellow give chase a bit longer.

It didn't hurt that he was easy on the eyes.

At the time, Sodja guessed she would never see the young man again – he would hoof it back to the Brakewood, and that would be the end of it, despite her taunting the boys with her name, even encouraging them to retaliate against her family. Their arrival on her family's doorstep had been a welcome complication ...

... and their leaving her family home without a lick of protest was an unwelcome surprise. No trouble at all for the Rocas family, despite her efforts. It was so frustrating – all that effort to turn new enemies and former allies against her family ... for nothing. Sodja had been wondering if it was even worth following them out of the High Quarter when Saltair had emerged from the mansion in pursuit and made the decision for her. Sodja watched him track the group into the Ash Quarter and attack them, watched him chase the boy with the glowing golden hand – the same one she'd left to die in Janak's study – and then she'd watched that boy defeat first Saltair and then Slavemaster Kranak.

That reversal had been wonderful – exactly what Sodja had hoped for – but it had also left her with a hundred unanswered questions. Were the boys still working for their Brakewood cult? Had the boy with the golden hand lost his arm in Janak's burning study, and where did he get that obscenely powerful prosthetic? From Janak's collection? Sodja would have sought answers, but the one-armed boy and his companions vanished from the Boneyard, leaving only bodies in their wake ... and abandoning the handsome boy with the dreadlocks. His actions suggested he had no intention of rejoining his companions. If anything, he seemed to be hoping to settle into Luqura.

Another puzzle.

Sodja kicked a loose pebble into the dragonfish pond. Red-gold scales flashed in the water. She sighed. It was late and she needed to finish her errand before the servants woke and guards changed their shift. Sodja walked on, passing the last of the five pools and coming to a long row of hedges dividing the ornamental ponds and orchards from the grounds beyond the Rocas family's keep.

It was still dark – closer to twilight than dawn – yet as Sodja approached the back of the mansion her eyes easily pierced the gloom, catching glimpses of the paths that ran right up to her family's doorstep. Shaped like a giant wedge of cheese with a bite taken out of it, the Rocas Estate was narrow at the front, penetrating deep into the heart of Luqura's High Quarter. As one moved away from the mansion's entrance, though, the grounds flared out and opened into the gated hedges and orchards that her family privately cultivated.

Sodja studied the street, seeing no carriages had been parked overnight at the front of her family's home. That was good. No midnight visitors or urgent demands from the slavers. All would be quiet inside with little chance of surprise, though Sodja always anticipated complications as a matter of personal and professional pride.

Sodja ignored the front door and instead traced the path she would have to climb to reach her mother's private balcony at the corner of the mansion. A collection of chiselled grey fieldstone formed the base of the keep, making it an easy ascent, but Sodja paused after taking a single step towards the wall.

At the opposite corner of the mansion, Sodja spied a tallow candle burning in the bedroom window just above a tall iron trellis. Her heart burning, Sodja steered away from the balcony and towards the window. A rose bush climbed the iron trellis, though the shrub had not been tended in years and its thorns were dry, impotent things. As she climbed, the familiar rusty metal dully squeaked beneath her weight and the desiccated plant crumbled beneath her touch. When Sodja reached the window, she slipped a hand inside her shirt, grasped her lockpicking tools, then stopped to listen. From inside, Sodja could hear a woman's strong voice.

'Absence. Periphery. Shadow and shade. Smoke and vapour. What is made, is unmade.'

Sodja knew the litany. On a hunch, she moved her hand from her shirt and pushed on the glass. A sad smile touched her lips as the window swung inward, and she crept into the chambers as quiet as a breeze.

Inside the room, a single candle made the shadows flicker and lit the fluid motions of an old woman sitting in front of it. Though her eyes were crinkled with crows' feet and her chin was no longer as firm as it once was, Sodja could see glimpses of the woman's youth and beauty: high cheekbones, a pert nose in a heart-shaped face and raven-black hair that, though streaked with grey, still retained most of its colour. Her eyes were closed, though if she had opened them, Sodja knew those, too, would be beautiful – keen grey eyes with a hint of an almond shape to them. Sodja took a step forward and bowed her head in respect.

'Hello, grandmother.'

The woman at the candle tilted her head in Sodja's direction, as if acknowledging her presence. She did not open her eyes, though, nor did she address her grandchild. Instead, the Rocas family's oldest matriarch bowed her head and continued her chanting.

'Bone of my bone. Shadow of me. Blood of my blood. Shadow of thee. Absence. Periphery. Walk and be free.' As Bella spoke, her careful fingers guided a bone needle and black thread through the strips of tattered black and grey cloth sitting atop her lap.

Sodja watched in fascination, though she had seen this many times in the past four months. Day and night, the woman sewed together rags while chanting gibberish to herself. She had to be coaxed to eat or drink, and Sodja regularly found the servants couldn't be bothered. Cups of tepid water and bowls of uneaten food sat uncollected beside the woman's bed, inviting flies and other vermin. If not for Sodja's nightly visits, she thought the woman would have died some months ago.

'If the senile old biddy wants to starve herself while stitching rags together,' Tiana had said, 'who am I to stop her?'

Rista had laughed at that – he laughed at anything cruel – while Ketrit was silent. That hadn't surprised her either. Sodja's eldest brother rarely said anything, and while his visits to their grand-mother hadn't been as frequent as Sodja's, the man still saw her on occasion.

And now Sodja had to visit Bella in secret. Ever since running away from the mansion – ever since finding the ledger and dis-covering her mother's secret – Sodja had been unable to visit her grandmother openly. It had been two months, and Sodja remained surprised that no one thought to wonder how Bella still survived when the servants and Sodja's family rarely tended to her – a fact evinced by the acrid smell of an overflowing chamber pot. Yet each group seemed to think the other must be privately tending to the old lady, for no one questioned how the dishes disappeared every night or why the chamber pot was magically empty every morning. She couldn't manage every day, true, but Sodja tried to keep her vigil, and so far she had evaded discovery. The young woman sighed and followed her nose to the vessel brimming with night soil.

It hurt Sodja to think how sharp her grandmother had been – so vibrant and strong, reining in Rista's cruel tendencies, keeping Tiana in her place – but then grandfather Gadish had died and Bella had never been the same. Vintan died a year later, and though her father's death had deeply wounded Sodja, it had broken her grandmother entirely.

Sewing rags and chanting was something new, though. No one knew where her grandmother had found the fabric, but it materialised one day in Bella's room and thereafter never seemed to leave her hands. Always stitching, sewing, weaving. Binding greys to blacks, and blacks to deeper blacks. It would have been distressing enough to witness – to watch a woman so regal and dominant turn into a blathering recluse overnight – but the most disturbing part was that she stitched with her eyes closed. Every day and night, every stitch of needle and thread was done by touch. As if to illustrate this, Bella's thin fingers set the bone needle down on her lap and searched for a nearly invisible scrap of black thread lying on the table beside the candle. The strand was as thin as the filament of a spider web, yet the woman still guided it through the eye of her bone needle and resumed her stitching – all with her eyes closed. Her chanting resumed:

Keeper of truth. Warden of lies. Turn away light. Darken the skies.
Absence. Periphery. Shadow and shade. Smoke and vapour. What is unmade, is made.
Bone of my bone. Shadow of me. Blood of my blood. Shadow of thee.
Absence. Periphery. Walk and be free.
Warden of truth. Keeper of lies. Strengthen this shadow. Sharpen its eyes.

Absence. Periphery. Shadow and shade. Smoke and vapour. What is made, is unmade.

Bone of my bone. Shadow of me. Blood of my blood. Shadow of thee.

Absence. Periphery. Walk and be free.

Sodja stayed as the woman began the litany again from the start, then respectfully backed out of the room, chamber pot in hand. Using one arm, she stealthily climbed back down the trellis, emptied the night soil in the cherry orchard and returned the vessel to Bella's room. When she returned, the old woman was sitting quietly in the corner, her hands folded in her lap, her eyes still closed. Sodja looked between her grandmother and the sewing project that had so obsessed her. She crossed the room and softly placed one hand atop Bella's open palms. Using her other hand, she picked up the nearest cup of water and held it to the woman's parched lips.

For a while the cup sat there, moistening the woman's dry skin without a drop being drunk. A minute passed then two. Finally, Bella's lips parted and the lukewarm water trickled into her mouth. She swallowed, coughed. Swallowed some more. Sodja filled her mouth twice more before the woman turned her head aside. Sodja slid a brown piece of apple between the woman's lips, but the fruit hung there for a second and fell to the floor.

'Not hungry today?' Sodja whispered, her heart aching, wondering how long the woman could survive like this.

Bella said nothing, did not even open her eyes. It was as though she had fallen asleep in her chair, though Sodja suspected she was still awake. Listening. Waiting. Perhaps she enjoyed the company. Perhaps she knew it was Sodja who took care of her, who kept her alive when others had left her to die. If that was true, though, her grandmother gave no indication of it. She sat in silence, her knobby hands clutching Sodja's for several minutes, and then the old woman squeezed Sodja's hand, picked her sewing needle back up and resumed her chant.

'Keeper of Truth. Warden of Lies. Turn away light. Darken the skies.'

Sodja carried the dishes down to the servants' quarters, then crept back upstairs and stealthily moved towards her original objective: the bedchamber of Matron Tiana. Outside the temple vault, it was the safest and most secure location in the mansion, and while it was possible Tiana kept her financial ledgers in the vault itself, Sodja knew her mother well enough to guess she would keep the record book on her person at all times. It was the only way she could promise the Slavers Guild their records were kept safe, and thus the only way Tiana could keep using the Rocas family's temple as the banking house for the foreign slavers of Innistiul.

It was also the only evidence Sodja had to prove Tiana had killed her husband and Sodja's father, Vintan Rocas.

An accidental peek at the woman's financial ledgers some months ago was the first thing that had tipped Sodja off. She hadn't understood what she was seeing at first, but as she'd flipped through the pages and read her mother's notes, the reality of the situation had become clear: Tiana Rocas and the Slavers Guild had come to a mutual agreement to permanently remove Vintan and the Thieves Guild from Luquran politics. Vintan had already stepped down as the Guild's master thief – relinquishing that position to his first lieutenant, Tymmit Blank – but that didn't matter to Matron Rocas or the Slavers; Tiana had made certain that Vintan's death was included in the arrangement, Blank and his other lieutenants were murdered, and the Guild was driven out of the city – and Sodja's mother had been paid for arranging all of it.

It was all there in the ledgers – a record of their communications, an accounting of payments made and debts owed, receipts and depository notes. Tiana had kept track of all of it, her merchant instincts strong as ever, and she'd been handsomely rewarded for her work. The vault inside the Temple of Dorchnok was full to bursting, and the Slavers Guild had virtually taken control of the city. With King Lenka's health in decline and no heir apparent, it seemed likely Tiana was positioning herself to make a bid for the throne of Greater Luqura.

But not if Sodja got hold of that ledger – the ledger she had stupidly left behind when her mother caught her reading the damnable thing. Tiana had been quick to reclaim the book, and Sodja had been just as quick to flee the mansion. They had both made a mistake in letting the other go. Now Tiana sought to silence Sodja, and Sodja sought to reclaim the ledger so she could publish the truth of the Rocas family's dealings – legal and illegal – with Innistiul. Doing so would cast a shadow on her family's ambitions for the crown and, with luck, it might even turn the tide against the foreign powers hoping to control the Luquran throne.

Sodja approached her mother's bedchamber, her heart thudding in her chest. As she reached for the lock, though, she felt a chill pass over her and turned to see Ketrit standing behind her in the hallway.

'Hello, sister.'

Sodja waited a breath. Then another. 'Aren't you going to call the guards?'

'I suspect you would be long gone before they arrived.'

'Not if you caught me first.'

'True enough.' He gestured at the door. 'It's not in there, you know – and she's expecting you to come looking for it.'

'Traps?'

Ketrit nodded. 'Why do you keep coming back?'

'Why haven't you stopped me?'

'For our grandmother. I know you've been visiting her – even if the rest are too stupid to realise it. I've even covered for you a few times.'

'But why? Why not have Rista waiting to ambush me? Why not end this?'

'I told you. For Bella. She seems to do better after your visits – at least she used to. These past few weeks I haven't noticed much of a difference. I think ... maybe it's her way of letting us know she's ready to move on.'

'You don't really think—?'

'I *do* think. I love Grandma Bella, Sodja. Not as much as you, maybe ... but I've cared for her. Cared enough to sit while she ate, to check on her a few times a day ... but that's my limit. I can't empty her chamber pots or be her full-time caretaker – and I certainly can't stand between her and Mother.' He sniffed, studied

Sodja from head to toe. 'Tiana wanted me to marry you, you know. Just like Aunt Daunia and Uncle Pyodr.'

Sodja turned her eyes to the floor, knowing Ketrit was only half right. Like the rest of the Saevors, Tiana placed high value on maintaining a pure Kroseran bloodline – but Sodja had never been intended for Ketrit. He was supposed to be the noble sacrifice, the one who married into the royal family and secured ultimate power in Luqura.

'Don't worry,' Ketrit added, sensing Sodja's unease, 'you're not my type.'

Sodja snorted. 'Don't fancy your sister?'

'I don't fancy *women*.'

Sodja paused at that. She had known her brother was picky when it came to love interests, and she had guessed at his preferences, but he'd never confided them to her – not in her whole life at the estate. She wondered what made him tell her now.

'Have you told Mother?'

This time Ketrit snorted. 'Wouldn't matter if I did. She's got her eye on a crown, and she will keep putting noble women in my bed till I seed one of them.'

Ketrit was right about that. And clearly knew what Tiana planned for her youngest two children.

'You should come with me,' Sodja protested, hoping she could convince him. 'Fight back.'

'No,' Ketrit said, resigned. 'We both know how that will end. Tiana gets what she wants, and she destroys anyone who stands in her way.' There was a warning there – possibly a threat. 'Besides,' he continued, 'there are perks to sitting on a throne. After a decade or three, Mother might even pass into shadow and shade, and I could rule.'

'Unless you die early and Rista takes your place.'

'Perhaps,' Ketrit said. 'I'll take my chances, though.'

Sodja huffed and turned away, thinking that was all to be said. Ketrit had chosen his side, and while his position was tenuous, he had also chosen to dig himself in. She glanced back at her mother's bedchamber, still wanting to try for the ledger, but she knew Ketrit would stop her. He probably wasn't lying about the

345

traps, or it not being there, either, which made her wonder again why he cared enough to stop and talk to her.

'Sodja ...'

She turned, surprised by the intensity of her brother's voice.

'Don't come back here – not ever again.'

Sodja studied the pain on her brother's face. What must it have cost him to say that? And yet, as she glanced back at her grandmother's room, she knew what her answer would be. Unfortunately, they both did.

'You know I can't do that,' she whispered, her gaze returning to her brother. 'Bella needs me, and I need that ledger.'

'Then be prepared for an ambush the next time you climb the trellis. Mother doesn't know about your nightly visits ... but she'll figure it out soon, and I can't cover for you for ever. In fact, this is the *last* time I cover for you. You're on your own.'

'And so are you.'

'So it would seem.'

She turned towards her grandmother's room, prepared to leave the same way she had entered – but she stopped with her back turned, her hand on the doorknob. 'And what about Bella? What will happen to her when I leave?'

'Just like us – on her own, too.'

Sodja turned back, her true emotions breaking through her facade of stoicism. 'Ketrit ... please. She'll die without someone looking after her.'

'Then she'd bloody well better remember how to look after herself!' His usually pale cheeks were flushed red now – angry, finally. Sodja had wondered how long it would take. '*She* left *us*, Sodja. Just like Dad and Grandpa, only her body is still here. She used to defend us – to fight for us – but now she's left us to fend for ourselves. It's time we both stood up and did that.'

'She'll die,' Sodja repeated, not knowing what else to say.

'Then let her die – let the *past* die with her. I'm focusing on the future, and I suggest you do the same.' His cheeks had regained their pale colour and he turned his back on her, walking away. 'Don't come back again, Sodja – or I'll bury you along with the past.'

Chapter Thirty-Four

Farthinand Caldaren proved to be a solid ally to Sraon and his friends, sailing them straight to Quiri without any additional stops or acceptance of payment. 'Sraon Cheng has saved my life more than once,' he explained, twirling his thick, black moustache. 'I count myself lucky to be able to repay that favour.'

Despite the man's geniality, Titus and Therin spent most of their time below deck, away from the deckhands and other Innistiulmen. Annev stayed with them, helping them recover from the torture they had endured. He didn't press them about it, and during one of their long silences, Annev bought a deck of playing cards from one of the Innistiul sailors and asked his friends to teach him to play. Thereafter they spent their time playing cards and worrying over Sraon, who regained consciousness twice during their two-day trip, but who seemed unaware of them each time.

When they finally docked in Quiri, Annev climbed to the deck and was greeted by the salty tang of seawater and a humidity that made him all too aware he needed a bath. All told, they had travelled nearly sixty leagues to reach Quiri, and though they'd made good time with the wind in their favour for the entire trip, it might not have been enough to save Sraon. The whites of the man's eyes were almost entirely yellow now, and his injuries had turned from purple to black; even the veins beneath his skin were starting to darken. Annev knew the man would have died a dozen times over if Reeve hadn't tended to him constantly, but the effects of the Dionach's magic had also waned with each passing day.

But now they were in Quiri, a city state that was smaller but centuries older than Luqura. Sodar had called it the religious capital of the Darite Empire and the Holy Seat of its Pontiff Prime. The Enclave of the Dionachs Tobar was based here, too; its members and their forbidden magic hidden from the eyes of the Church and its fanatical leaders.

In many ways, the Kingdom of Odarnea was a macrocosm of Chaenbalu, with farmers and peasants tilling the open land at its borders and the voice of rule coming directly from the capital and its Pontiff Prime, whose structure matched that of Chaenbalu's former Academy and deceased headmaster. Sodar's heretical teachings and secret use of magic likewise paralleled the Dionachs and their Enclave. Even the familiar lines and details of the Academy's architecture had been reflected in Quiri's many domed cathedrals, with their ribbed vaults and flying buttresses. It was as if the entire village had been expanded to fill a kingdom – and Annev was ambivalent about it. He had left Chaenbalu seeking help, looking for answers and hoping to walk his own path. Yet it seemed the answers would only come if he walked the path Sodar had laid out for him.

'I will not be ruled by these people,' Annev whispered, reminding himself why he had come. 'I won't get caught up in their politics or their prophecies. I'm here to heal Sraon and get rid of the Hand of Keos ... and that's it.'

Even as he spoke the words, though, Annev couldn't help but remember Jian's ominous words: *The High Priest of Odar can remove the Hand of Keos, but only if the Vessel aids him first.*

'So this is Quiri,' Therin said, joining Annev at the prow.

'Yeah.' He turned to look at his companion whose eyes filled with wonder as he took in the city. 'Still think you want to live here?'

'Eh, it can't be as bad as the Academy.' He paused. 'Then again, I thought the same thing about Luqura – until that madman hacked off my nipple.'

Annev grimaced. 'Yeah, I'm sorry about that.'

'It's fine,' Therin said, cheery as ever. 'I wasn't getting any use out of them, and you healed me up pretty fast with that magic

348

bandana thing.' He chuckled. 'If it's all the same to you, though, I'd like to keep my remaining body parts.'

Titus joined them. 'Is Sraon ready?'

'Yep. Just finished loading him onto the mare. Master Reeve is talking with Captain Frani, and then we'll head into the city.'

'I'm so glad he saved the horse. We should really give her a name now that she's been with us for so long, though. Maybe Willow?'

'I like Willow,' Therin said.

'Let's go get Willow then – every minute we spend here is a minute Sraon could be getting healed.'

Even with Annev's admonitions, it took another ten minutes before the sailors had the boat tied off and the gangplank extended. They said their goodbyes to Captain Frani, and then Reeve led them past the wharf and into the heart of the city. Annev was shocked by how much taller the buildings were here, with most matching the height of those in Banok or Luqura but many others rising as high as three or four storeys. That, combined with the winding paths of the old city, made it difficult to see what lay beyond the buildings immediately surrounding them. It made Annev claustrophobic in a way he hadn't been in either Chaenbalu or Luqura. Even in Banok, where the houses were so close together you could step from one roof to the next, there had still been thoroughfares and plazas – vistas where you could stand and see the rest of the town. There was none of that here, and Annev quickly became lost in the twists and turns of Quiri's cobblestone streets and its towering gothic structures.

'So,' Annev said, speaking quietly to the high priest, 'where exactly is this Enclave?'

'Shhh,' Reeve said, holding a finger to his lips. 'We don't speak of it inside the city. There is a path, but its secret is closely kept.'

'Are we going to have to wear blindfolds?'

The priest chuckled. 'Nothing so mundane as that. You've seen me wield skywater, yes? Well, to preserve our secrets, I will use *quaire*.'

'I thought they were the same – just different names.'

'They are the same, and they are not.'

'Okay,' Annev said, losing his patience. 'What does all this have to do with finding the ... uh, place that we are going?'

'Skywater,' Reeve explained, his tone taking on that of an instructor, 'refers to the physical elements of ice, water and air. For the metaphysical, though – for the *mind* and the *will* – we usually reserve the term *quaire*, which can be manipulated to read another person's thoughts. It can also be used to *siphon* those thoughts – to make you forget what you have seen, or persuade you you've seen nothing at all.'

Annev immediately thought of the Rod of Compulsion, which allowed the user to impose their will on another. But that had been a dark rod, a foul thing that had been used to enslave others. Was Reeve saying the Dionachs possessed the same ability, not limited by an artifact? Annev shuddered at the implications.

'It's vitally important,' Reeve continued, 'because our path isn't hidden by secret tunnels or magic mists. It hides in plain sight, right under the nose of those most desirous to find it.' They stopped walking and Reeve gestured to a magnificent multi-tiered cathedral topped with looming spires and grinning gargoyles. 'This is the Holy Seat of the Church of Odar,' Reeve said, eyes glinting in the morning sun. 'Pontiff Prime Medur lives there along with his fanatical bishops, high priests, and Inquisitors.'

'Inquisitors?' Annev asked, his pulse quickening. 'I thought they were Terran mages?'

Reeve nodded. 'There are four Terrans types: Bloodlords, Inquisitors, Earthshapers and Artificers. The Inquisitors that live here are called Seekers, and they have no magical blood-talents to aid them in their questioning, so they must use darker tools to extract their confessions and find their answers. It is not a pretty thing. Pray you never meet them.'

Annev looked back at his trailing friends, supporting Sraon to keep the blacksmith in Willow's saddle. It sounded as though he was leading them into danger, not into safety.

As if seeing his concern, Reeve gestured at the building behind them. They had stopped in front of a flat wall built from uniform blocks of carved granite – but now Annev looked at it again there was an iron door in the wall, the arch surrounding it laden with glyphs and unfamiliar arcane runes.

'How?' Annev asked, astonished.

'With glyph-speaking and *quaire*,' Reeve said, knocking on the portal. 'Anyone that looks at this door will see the symbols carved above its arch and forget it. Instead of an iron door, they see granite blocks. Instead of an entrance, they see an impasse. The magic prevents the uninitiated from finding our home and keeps our brethren safe.'

'But I can see it now?'

'Because I've allowed you to do so – because I've removed the scales of unsight from your eyes. Even so, you won't retain a memory of this door or these runes without our assistance.'

Annev grunted, his thoughts returning to the Rod of Compulsion and how it functioned. 'So, now we can enter – what happens when we leave? Can we find this door again?'

'Not without my help. Finding the door means remembering the Runes of Forgetting – something you won't be taught unless you become a full Dionach.'

'So the runes act like a sort of key – a *mental* key – which you only give to members of the Order.'

'Precisely. You have an excellent mind, Ainnevog.'

Annev took the compliment as Reeve opened the iron door and a bald-headed monk welcomed them to the Enclave.

Chapter Thirty-Five

'This is Dionach Leskal,' Reeve said, introducing the monk while untying Sraon from the black mare. 'I've already spoken with him regarding our need for haste, and you've all been introduced to him.'

'What?' Therin said, voice squeaking. 'How? When?'

Reeve tapped his temple, a sardonic look on his face. 'We spoke with *quaire,* my boy – with telepathy.' He turned to the bald Dionach, a muscular man with round shoulders, a severe face and a thickly braided beard. 'Brother Leskal, is everything prepared for Sraon?'

'We are ready, Brother Reeve. We will take excellent care of him.' Leskal stepped forward to retrieve Sraon, but instead of cradling the unconscious blacksmith or slinging him over his shoulder, the priest withdrew a stoppered wooden tube from the folds of his robes. One end of the bamboo cylinder was topped with a thick, horsehair brush and, as Annev watched, Leskal stooped to paint a glyph on the floor. A trace of water flowed behind the head of the brush, outlining a rune. Leskal whispered a few words of Old Darite and the glyph evaporated, transforming into a translucent disc of air. Leskal quickly lifted Sraon onto it and floated the man down the arched hallway, away from Reeve and the rest of the group.

Titus and Therin stared, open-mouthed. 'Did you *see* that?' Therin asked, eyes wide. 'That was ... incredible!'

'Wow,' Titus breathed, almost reverent. 'Is that the sort of magic we'll be learning, Master Reeve?' Another robed priest emerged from one of the side chambers and silently took Willow's reins, leading the mare away into a side passage.

'Perhaps. But please, call me Dionach Reeve – or just Brother Reeve. We don't call ourselves masters here, for the only true master is the All-father.'

Annev silently wondered how much theology would be mixed with the Dionach's lessons on magic and glyph-speaking. Sodar had already taught him the major tenets of the Darite faith, and he knew hundreds of Old Darite glyphs and runes. If Annev did choose to stay and learn with the Order, it would almost certainly put him in a class ahead of his friends. He clenched his golden hand into a fist. Not that he was here to learn, of course.

'Where is Brother Leskal taking Sraon?' Annev asked, as he and his friends followed Reeve down a long hallway.

'Brother Leskal leads the Shieldbearers. He and the leaders of the Breathbreaker and Mindwalker castes – Dionachs Honeycutt and Holyoak – are gathered to help Sraon. With Honeycutt's help, Leskal should be able to neutralise the poison and flush it from Sraon's system. Holyoak will monitor Sraon's mental state and make certain no lasting damage has been done to his brain.'

'You think that's a possibility?' Annev asked, anxious.

'In truth, I think it more than likely.' Reeve's expression turned grim. 'Saltair's venom has affected Sraon's capacity for thought and memory. When I probed his mind on our journey, Sraon didn't remember who he was. He certainly doesn't remember us. Don't be too alarmed, though. We've seen this sort of thing before, and we've become quite good at healing damage done to the brain. When it comes to mental healing, you could say it's our specialty.'

'You sound very familiar with the venom,' Annev said, slowing his pace and thinking of the missing members of the Dionachs Tobar. 'Has Saltair attacked the Order before?'

'Not the Order, but our allies – our connections in Luqura and Quiri. Those we've treated experienced similar fugues, though they were less severely bitten. Sraon took a lethal dose of venom, which is why I've been so eager to get him here. We'll flush the poison first and then Dionach Holyoak can assess whether Sraon's *quaire* has been permanently affected.'

'And if it has?'

'Then Sraon won't remember any of his past and possibly won't be able to form new memories. In the most extreme case, he could even lose control of his mental faculties and bodily functions. He'd become a child – lacking any capacity for self-care or higher thought.'

'That's terrible,' Titus said, horrified.

'It is,' Reeve agreed. 'I'm optimistic that it won't come to that but ... well, we'll see. In other cases, Dionach McClanahan has been able to repair the victim's injuries and help them recover most of what was forgotten. McClanahan is the leader of our Stormcallers, a very talented woman.' When Annev gave Reeve a puzzled look, the high priest stopped in the middle of the hallway. 'Sodar *has* taught you the four castes of Darite magic?' Annev shook his head and Reeve puffed out his cheeks in agitation. 'Unbelievable! Two decades with the man and he couldn't be bothered to cover the basics.'

'That's not true,' Annev said, suddenly defensive. 'Sodar taught me a lot about magic, but I only learned how to access it this past week.'

'Perhaps some more *orthodox* teaching methods would have helped speed that process along.'

'He also taught me to read and write,' Annev pressed, his cheeks reddening. 'And how to fight. He taught me theology and the *Book of Odar* and—'

'How to mend your clothes and cook your own meals and lace your boots. Yes. When it comes to the principles of magic, though, he did you a disservice. You don't understand the distinction between *quaire* and skywater. You don't know the four Darite castes or what they do. Did Sodar even teach you glyph-speaking?'

'Yes,' Annev said, a little too quickly.

'I suppose we'll see.' He nodded at Therin and Titus who had hung back and were trying to look inconspicuous. 'What about you two? Did you pick up anything useful in that Academy?'

'How to pick locks?' Therin offered, uncertain.

'What about you, Titus? Anything about magic?'

'They taught us it was evil.'

Reeve snorted. 'You'll be starting with the basics then. Once Sraon is stable, you'll be tested for the talent – not much point teaching you if you don't have it.'

'And what if they don't?' Annev asked, freshly worried for his friends. 'Would you turn them out? Have their memories erased?'

Reeve stared at him, a hard edge to his face. 'You think that's what we do here? Did we do that to Sraon when Sodar brought him to us? Or Tukas or Keezel? No! We taught them the principles, same as all our brothers and sisters, and we gave them a home. Most have since become our eyes and ears across the Empire – a valuable thing, in these times.'

'And dangerous work, too.'

'Aye,' Reeve said, holding Annev's gaze. 'There are risks in every profession, but no cause is more noble or more needed than our own.'

Annev held his tongue this time, but he saw too many uncomfortable similarities between the philosophy of the Dionachs Tobar and the Order of Ancients in Chaenbalu; old men filled with hypocrisy and convinced of the importance of their missions. Such people were prone to sacrifice others to achieve their goals, as Annev had seen first-hand with Elder Tosan, and even with Sodar to a certain extent. He wasn't about to repeat past mistakes.

'What's the test?' Annev asked, thinking of the tests Sodar had administered – practising with artifacts like the bottomless bag, drawing glyphs and trying to activate them. He imagined Reeve would be doing something similar, though he'd said Sodar's methods were unorthodox. Perhaps the Enclave's tests would help Annev understand himself and his magic better. Perhaps they'd even reveal why he'd had so much difficulty using Darite magic?

'There are three factors that determine one's ability to use the talent: blood, art and craft. You are born with the blood, which may be one gift from a single parent, or a hybrid talent from both. We can't test your blood directly, though, since that would require Terran magic – so we'll be observing your affinities for art and craft.'

'Aren't those the same thing?'

'Not exactly. Art is your innate ability to use the talent. The

Ilumites say you can't properly teach art. It's not a list of rules or a set of facts – it comes from your spirit, your intuition, and your creativity. We may not be able to teach that here, but we can still test it, and it's why we call it a blood-*talent*. The "talent" part refers to your personality and creative spirit. That, combined with your ancestry, is usually enough to determine whether you can become a successful Dionach.

'Craft, on the other hand, refers to something you can learn or something that can be taught. You may have the blood-talent, for example, but I doubt you know how to use it fully. Instruction can fix that, and hone your skills, and it's one of the primary goals of our Order: the pursuit of knowledge and its application.'

Titus and Therin marvelled at Reeve's explanation as the man led them into a great hall filled with tables and chairs. A scattering of blue-robed priests sat at the tables – some reading, some writing – though none sat together, nor did they converse. The result was an atmosphere of almost eerie silence that Annev felt uncomfortable breaking.

'Why were Sodar's teachings so different?' he half-whispered, feeling self-conscious.

'Several reasons, I should think. He already knew your parentage – he knew your entire bloodline – so there was no question of blood.'

'From my father, perhaps. My mother was an Ilumite, though, so why didn't he teach me any Ilumite magic?'

Reeve quirked an eyebrow. 'I'm surprised he didn't. It's possible that's the one area where Sodar actually listened to me.'

'You mean ... you told him *not* to?'

Reeve nodded, leading them through the hall and out of the foyer. 'Studying multiple magics tends to dilute your talent, especially when the fields aren't closely related. Sodar knows this: he studied broadly but never accumulated the same power as other Dionachs. I have an aptitude for all four Darite castes, but I chose to focus my studies on shieldbearing. That means I can compress skywater – form shields of air, blades of ice, that sort of thing. It's primarily a martial school. The other castes are harder for me.'

'Darite castes? You mean ... the Mindwalkers, the Breath-breakers, the Shieldbearers and the Stormcallers?'

Reeve led them up a set of stairs. 'Correct. Sodar was a Breathbreaker, as was Arnor. Both good at stealth and subterfuge – but they were capable of so much more. Arnor became one of our best Breathbreakers. Sodar ...' Reeve shrugged. 'He focused on a variety tasks, not the least of which was protecting your bloodline, but despite his several centuries head-start he never developed the same level of talent as Arnor. Sodar was versatile, I'll grant him that, but not especially talented – not in the traditional sense, anyway.'

'So you asked him to keep my studies focused on Darite magic.'

'Yes. It seems that backfired, though, because he never gave you the proper theoretical foundation.' Reeve stopped in front of a wooden door, knocked twice, then opened the portal.

'Welcome back, Brother Reeve,' a cheery voice said, its owner stepping out from behind a wooden lectern set in front of a slate chalkboard. Opposite the lectern was a neat row of five desks. It looked very like the Academy in Chaenbalu.

'Thank you, Brother McClanahan,' Reeve said, stepping into the room. 'It's good to be home.'

'McClanahan?' Therin said, approaching one of the desks cautiously. 'I thought you said she was a ... she.'

The new Dionach laughed, set down his stick of chalk and wiped his hands on his robes. 'You mean my wife, Misty. A very talented Dionach. And yes, Therin, Dionachs *can* get married.'

The boy stared at the man in surprise, and Reeve dropped a hand on Brother McClanahan's shoulder. 'Tym is just showing off – he's a Mindwalker, who has a bad habit of reading other people's thoughts without meaning to do so.'

'Well, I wouldn't say that I don't *mean* to – I have to exert a little effort, after all – but it's a habit. I like to hear what's going on around me, and some people's thoughts are louder than others.' He winked at Therin, grinning broadly. 'Like your blonde friend from Chaenbalu – Faith, is it?' He chuckled. 'Don't worry, I'm good at keeping secrets.'

'He's *terrible* at it,' Reeve whispered, leaning over to Annev.

'I am *not*!' But the man was still smiling as he said it and Annev sensed the whole thing was some sort of joke. 'Anyhow,' he continued, 'it's always good practice to keep your thoughts quiet while you're here.'

'Quiet?' Annev asked.

'Yes. Some thoughts are whispers, some are shouts, just like talking, and we do most of our talking up here.' He tapped his temple, suddenly thoughtful. 'Is your girlfriend a *ghost*?'

'She's not my girlfriend!' Therin said, blushing. 'And she's ... gone is what she is.'

'Oh, my dear boy. I'm so sorry.' He hesitated. 'Odd to be thinking about *that,* though ...'

Reeve cleared his throat and reclaimed their attention, saving Therin from further embarrassment. 'Brother McClanahan will be administering your blood-talent tests,' he declared, 'and once the four caste leaders are free, each of them will assess you personally.'

'And then you can meet Misty!' Tym said, smiling once more. 'Oh, I'm so excited. We haven't had new recruits in *years*. Excellent, excellent.' He looked over the trio of boys, a mischievous glimmer in his eyes. 'I'll bet you're a Stormcaller,' he said, pointing at Therin. 'Lots of loud thoughts. Makes it easy to push them into other people's heads.' He looked at Titus. 'And you ... so quiet and observant. I'd bet my teeth you're a Mindwalker.'

'But *you're* a Mindwalker,' Annev said, a smile quirking his mouth, 'and you don't seem very quiet.'

Tym guffawed, slapping Annev on the back and leaving a chalk imprint on his cloak. 'He's got a sharp wit, doesn't he? Bit of a martial look to him, too, with that bloody scarf and red cloak. A Shieldbearer, for sure.' He clapped his hands together, chalk dust puffing into the air. 'This is all conjecture, of course. I'm right less than half the time, but I do like to make a sport of it before the tests start. Keeps it fun – and it's been so *long* since I've tested anyone!' He shook his head. 'Well, come on then. Take a seat and we'll get started.'

Chapter Thirty-Six

The boys fidgeted in their seats while Brother Tym finished drawing. Annev studied the pictures. They were runes, or perhaps pictographs, none of which looked familiar to him; instead of sharp lines and geometric angles, Tym shaded symmetric circles with looping blobs of overlapping chalk dust. When he was done, he set the chalk down and looked at the boys.

'Well,' he said, hands clasped together, 'what do you see?'

'It's ... chalk?'

'A very literal mind, Brother Annev. Now what does the chalk look like?'

'A stain,' Therin said, half-raising his hand. 'Like something I might have spilled on my shirt.'

'Good. Dig deeper now. What pictures do you see within that stain? What's the story behind the marks?'

Titus raised a timid hand. 'It looks like two people talking – a woman and a man.'

'Good! Very good, Brother Titus. Anything else?' Titus glanced at Reeve, who stood at the back of the room, then at Annev. Tym waved a finger. 'Don't look to them. Look to yourself. There are no wrong answers. Tell me what *you* see.'

Titus concentrated on the chalk smudges. 'The man is angry ... and the woman is crying. There's something between them – a liquid, maybe a drink. Tea, I think. They aren't arguing about it, but they're both holding the cup. There's steam rising between them.'

'Where is the steam coming from?'

Annev expected Titus to say it came from the tea, but Titus surprised them all. 'It's coming from *them* – the woman's tears and the man's anger. It's floating between them ... like a cloud.'

Tym and Reeve shared the briefest glance, and Annev could tell something significant passed between them. 'Very good, Brother Titus. What about you, Therin? What do *you* see?'

Therin laughed. 'Well I don't see *any* of that – except maybe the smoke, the mist.'

'And where is it coming from?'

Therin stared at the chalkboard, his expression thoughtful. 'I'm not sure. Maybe something behind the mist ... something hidden.'

'Can you guess what's making it?'

Therin shook his head. 'A person maybe? I dunno.'

'That's just fine. What about you, Annev?'

Annev studied the chalkboard, trying to make sense of its patterns, its symmetry and its shapes. He saw beauty there, but it was abstract. He saw variations in the chalk shading and density, but he didn't see a story there. He just saw ... chalk. He stared at the board until the silence became uncomfortable, and he considered making up a story like Titus', but he guessed Brother Tym would see through his subterfuge, so instead he spoke the truth.

'It's just chalk.'

Tym hmmed to himself, thoughtful. 'Just chalk. Interesting.'

Annev squirmed in his seat, feeling foolish as the seconds ticked past. Brother Tym folded his arms, his thumb tapping his bottom lip. 'Very interesting,' he said again, then he turned and erased the images with his bare hand. When the board was nearly clean, he turned back to Annev. 'And now?'

Annev looked, seeing symmetry eroded, the lines blurred. There was nothing there, only a ghost of the original image, yet Annev did see something this time, something he hadn't noticed when the lines had been crisp and the shades perfect.

'I see ...' He stopped with the word on the tip of his tongue. A glance at Reeve and Brother Tym showed they had heard his thought without him saying it.

'What do you see?' Therin asked.

'Blood,' he said, seeing no reason to lie. 'I see a dark pool of blood.' Annev thought of Cenif, the mutilated animal that he and Crag had found in the Brakewood. He thought of the *feurog* that had fallen beneath his sword as he tried to save Sodar. He thought of the dead guards he had fought in Janak's palace and the slavers he had killed in Luqura while trying to save Therin and Titus.

'Blood ... and ashes,' he said, both a curse and the truth of what he saw. To Annev's left, Therin sputtered, unable to hide his mirth while Titus looked stunned.

'Interesting,' Tym repeated. 'Very, *very* interesting.' He looked over at Reeve, a silent conversation happening between the two Dionachs. The latter nodded and Tym turned back to Annev. 'Brother Reeve is going to continue testing Therin and Titus in here, Annev. We're going to go to another part of the Enclave to continue your testing.'

Annev was unable to shake the feeling his friends had passed but he had failed somehow. It was absurd – Annev had studied with Sodar for years, and Therin and Titus didn't know the first thing about magic – but maybe that was the problem. Sodar had taught him the *craft*, while Therin and Titus might have simply possessed the art. If they both had an innate and intuitive sense for magic, then they might succeed where Annev always failed.

I've never actually used Darite magic, Annev thought, remembering his encounters with the artifacts and attempts at glyph-speaking. *I know all the runes and the words of power ... but I've never got them to work together. I've always used an artifact.* The thought sent a chill up Annev's spine.

Maybe he *wouldn't* be in a class ahead of his friends. Maybe their abilities would exceed his own – maybe they already did.

'Come, Brother Annev. There are many ways to test a talent.'

Annev stared down into the well, feeling claustrophobic within the rough-hewn walls. He and Brother Tym had descended two flights of stairs and passed through another long tunnel before reaching the small chamber containing the Enclave's primary source of water.

'There's a cistern on the roof that gives us cleaning and washing water,' Tym explained, opening the door. 'The well gives us drinking water, and an untainted source of skywater.' Annev had taken an uncomfortable look into the well and seen his reflection a dozen or so feet down.

'What am I supposed to do?'

Brother Tym pulled a bamboo water brush tube from his tunic, identical to Brother Leskal's, then he walked around the perimeter of the room drawing glyphs for *quaire*, air, ice and water at the edge of the stone well.

'Stand next to the wall and hold your hand over the water. Tell me what you feel.'

Annev did so, walking slowly around the well first, feeling foolish for allowing himself to be tested for magic. It was just like the tests he had done with Sodar in Chaenbalu – the same expectations, followed by the same failures and disappointments.

Things would be different this time, he told himself. Annev *knew* he had magic now; he possessed the talent, he just didn't know which one.

Annev held his arm out until the muscles ached and the blood in his fingertips felt cold.

'Well?'

'My hand went numb,' Annev said, apologising as he lowered his arm. 'I didn't feel anything.'

'Not so,' Tym said, smiling. 'You said your hand was numb – your skin was chilled? That could be the sign of a Shieldbearer, who can shape ice.' He paused. 'But you don't believe me. You think your hand went numb because you stood in a cold basement with your hand out until the blood drained from your fingers.'

Annev grimaced, surprised by how closely Tym's words echoed his thoughts. Even Tosan hadn't been able to do that, and he'd had a magic ring that told him when people were lying.

Like the copper ring I took from the Vault, Annev thought.

'A Ring of Inquisition?' Tym said, interrupting Annev's wandering thoughts. 'Very interesting. And you managed to *use* it?' He stopped, holding up a hand. 'Sorry, you didn't *say* that, but ... well.' He tutted his tongue against his teeth. 'I should like to see it sometime. We see so few artifacts in Odarnea, what with the Church destroying any magic they can find. To stand in a vault

362

filled with artifacts ... Simply incredible.' He looked down into the well, his reflection looking at Annev.

'Still nothing, eh? Well, that's fine.' He pointed at the base of the well. 'Any reason you chose to stand in that spot?'

Annev glanced around. 'No,' he said, trying to remember which glyph Tym had painted on that portion of the waist-high wall. 'Which glyph did you paint here?'

'None,' Tym said, tapping the wall in four different places. 'I wrote the glyphs *here*. Nothing was written on that side of the wall.'

Annev's shoulders slumped. 'So I haven't given you anything useful.'

'On the contrary,' Tym said, waggling an excited finger. 'Sometimes nothing *is* something. You walked around the well before holding out your hand. You moved to stand *between* the glyphs, as far away from them as possible.'

'I did?'

Tym nodded. 'If you'd just walked up to the wall, you'd have stood in front of the *quaire* glyph. But standing over there? It's as if you intentionally avoided them.'

Had he? Annev couldn't remember, but it seemed possible. He hadn't paid too much attention to Brother Tym painting them, and they'd evaporated by the time he held out his hand. He hadn't known where any of the glyphs were.

So was it an accident ... or had he done it on purpose?

'Let's go back upstairs,' Tym said, brushing back his messy brown hair. 'We'll go to the roof and see what happens when you jump off.'

'When I *what*?'

The Dionach gave him a grin and Annev knew that the expression was genuine. 'A joke,' he said by way of apology. 'We're not all as stodgy as Brother Reeve. Come along. I want to introduce you to Misty. The other brothers haven't called for her, so she can help me test your *quaire*.'

'Does that mean Sraon is doing okay?'

Tym tilted his head as if listening to someone. 'Leskal and Honeycutt have extracted the poison, and Brother Holyoak says there is no permanent damage. He may not be himself when you see him, but he should retain control of his faculties and his memories.'

Annev gave an audible sigh of relief. He had been so worried for his friend that he hadn't really wanted to participate in Tym's tests. Now that he knew the blacksmith was all right, he might have a better chance of focusing. It would be nice, he decided, to get some resolution on whether he could actually do any glyph-speaking.

'When can I see him?'

'After we speak with Misty. Reeve is with Sraon right now, and the other caste leaders are meeting Titus and Therin. Once we've finished with Misty, Sraon should be ready to talk to you.'

'Thank you,' Annev said, once again overwhelmed by relief. 'I'm ready.'

Annev stared into the woman's pale green eyes, trying not to let their colour remind him of Myjun.

'Focus on what she's trying to tell you,' Tym said, 'not on how pretty my wife looks.'

Annev's cheeks flushed with embarrassment as Misty elbowed Tym in the ribs. 'Stop it! You're distracting him.' She smiled at Annev. 'It's nice of you to say, though.'

'But I didn't—'

'You didn't *say* it, but thinking it aloud amounts to the same thing. Once you've been here a while, we can teach you how to keep your thoughts quieter. I could hear you without even trying to eavesdrop.' She glanced at Tym. 'Unlike *some* people.' Misty shooed her husband to the other side of the room.

'Annev, I'm going to send my thoughts around you now – right past you. It will be as if they're floating in the air, waiting to be plucked out. Concentrate; close your eyes if you need to, and see what you feel. What thoughts enter your mind?'

Annev closed his eyes and tried to concentrate, but visions of Myjun's death still flooded his mind, and he found himself unable to think of anything else. He opened his eyes and found Tym and Misty staring at him, each with a look of profound sympathy and sadness.

364

'It's fine,' Annev said, uncomfortable beneath their twin gazes. 'She wasn't ... she didn't even like me – not really. She nearly got me killed, and Sodar died because ...'

Because of me, he thought. *He died because I was too stupid to listen to him – because I cared for someone who didn't care at all about me.* Annev bit his lip, cursing himself for thinking aloud. He looked down at his hands, unable to meet the gaze of either Dionach.

'I'm so sorry, Annev,' Misty said. 'Maybe we should try this another time – when your mind is clearer.'

Annev nodded, grateful for the reprieve. 'Yeah. Maybe later.'

'Come on,' Tym said, patting Annev on the shoulder. 'Titus and Therin are just upstairs. You can talk to them while Reeve and the other Dionachs move Sraon to his room.'

'A natural Breathbreaker,' Honeycutt said, a look of pride stamped across his narrow face. 'Uncanny instincts. As soon as we teach him the glyphs and the words, I expect him to rocket through the ranks. He'll be a Dionach before the end of the year.' Therin beamed silently, unaccustomed to praise.

'And young Titus!' Holyoak said, equally enthused. 'The boy is a natural – and not just at mindwalking! Fantastic instincts. I expect we have a hybrid blood-talent here. Haven't seen one of those in ages – and now, to think we might have another dualist in our ranks! Outstanding. Where did Reeve find these boys? Are there any *more* of them?'

Annev forced a painful smile, his inability to perform Darite magic somehow made worse by his friends' successes.

'I moved a coin across a table!' Therin said suddenly. 'Annev, it was ... amazing! Brother Honeycutt drew this symbol and told me what to say, and I just ... I just *pushed* it. It was incredible!'

'Brother Holyoak was talking to me,' Titus interrupted, 'but not with words. I could hear him, could *feel* him in my head. He said he wasn't even *trying* to talk to me. I was drawing out his thoughts all on my own.' He shook his head, practically crying with joy. 'Annev, this place is *amazing*.' He paused, his expression changing. 'It didn't go so well for you, did it?'

Blood and burning ashes, Annev thought. *Is he going to start reading my thoughts now, too? Is every godsdamned one of my friends a burning prodigy?* Annev kept the smile on his face, but the Dionachs in the room turned to stare at him, most looking pained. Brother Tym seemed to be wincing, hands half-raised to cover his ears, and Dionach Holyoak was frowning.

'Well,' Reeve said, clearing his throat. 'This might be a good time to visit Brother Sraon.'

'If it's all the same to you, I'd like to continue testing Novice Titus,' Holyoak said, the smile slowly returning to his face. 'He has a real talent – blessed with the art and the blood – and I'd like to see if it extends to the craft.'

'That's fine,' Reeve said. 'Fewer visitors might be better for Brother Sraon anyway. Just restrict yourself to telepathy and mind-reading. No *actual* mindwalking yet. I know Titus is talented, but we'll need to build up his defences before he does anything dangerous.' He glanced at Honeycutt. 'Do you want to keep working with Novice Therin?'

'Of course, Brother Reeve.' Honeycutt tugged on his pointed chin. 'Do you think Brother Leskal will want to see Therin again?'

'No. Neither of the boys seem to be Shieldbearers, though we're hopeful about Annev – he's got the feel of a fighter to him. He's keen to see Sraon first, though.' He nodded to Brother Tym and Dionach McClanahan. 'Thank you both for working with Annev. There will be further opportunities tomorrow, I am sure.'

The red-headed woman and her round-faced husband bowed, neither looking at Annev as Reeve escorted him away.

Chapter Thirty-Seven

The Dionachs had moved Sraon to a room at the opposite side of the Enclave, with a window facing the city and the lands to the north. According to Reeve, the injured blacksmith had stayed in that room when he began his novitiate, decades ago.

'He was about your age when he first came to the Order. Fresh from Innistiul and fed up with the slave trade. Eager to start a new life and cultivate a new faith.' Reeve sighed. 'Strange to think of him now as a grown man. We probably look the same age now, but to me he'll always be that wide-eyed boy from Innistiul.'

Since Sraon's cell was on the top floor, they had to climb a third set of stairs to reach the long corridor of the novitiate's cells. Annev suddenly feared running into Titus and Therin there, but they were still below, continuing their training. He felt conflicted about that. On the one hand, he was happy that his friends were excelling at something, especially after years of struggle under the masters in Chaenbalu. It was a great change to finally be treated not simply as adequate or fair, but as superior – as prodigies even – but that superiority also stung Annev. He wasn't accustomed to being the least talented of the three. It made him feel small and inconsequential when he'd fought tooth and nail at the Academy to prove he wasn't, and had taken pride in being a deacon for Sodar as well as an acolyte. Now the world had been turned on its head: Annev was at the bottom, and Titus and Therin were swiftly climbing to the top.

This is stupid, Annev tried to remind himself. *I'm not here to study with the Dionachs. I'm here for Sraon, and to get help removing this damn hand. Once that's done, I'm getting out of here.*

It was a fair plan, but Annev worried about his companions. Should he leave them behind? Or bring them back to Banok to reunite with Brayan? Annev didn't know. He hadn't wanted to take them to Luqura with Reeve, predicting they would be a liability. Here in Quiri it seemed they might flourish ... though the Order would inevitably enlist them in its intrigues and politics. That seemed an especially bad idea given how many members of the Order had gone missing these past years.

Their lives aren't my responsibility, Annev reminded himself. This wasn't Chaenbalu and all of them were being treated as adults. If Titus and Therin wanted to join the Order, Annev couldn't stop them nor would he try. Doing so would have made him no better than Sodar and the Dionachs Tobar – and Annev intended to do better than that.

Reeve swung a door open and the first thing Annev noticed was the old embrasure and narrow loophole overlooking the street below. From what Annev had seen of the Enclave, he guessed it had been a fortress at some point, maybe even a castle. Rooms had been repurposed since then, and it seemed even the city had forgotten its existence. So close to the Holy Seat, yet still hidden in plain sight. The door swung open further, revealing the bed and the swarthy, sweat-soaked man lying atop it.

'Annev,' Sraon croaked, forcing himself to sit up. 'I'm glad to see you, lad.'

Annev rushed forward to hug the man, squeezing him until the blacksmith gave a groan.

'I'm sorry,' he said, embarrassed.

'No, no,' Sraon said with a cough. 'It's fine, lad. Just mind the shoulder, eh? Bastard keokum had some sharp teeth. Wouldn't be surprised if he'd left a few in there.'

There was an awkward moment of silence and Reeve cleared his throat. 'I'll give you two a chance to talk. Not too long, though. Sraon needs his rest and Dionach Leskal will be waiting for us.' The Arch-Dionach stepped back into the hallway and closed the door.

"The others all right?' Sraon asked. 'The brothers didn't want to say much while they were gettin' me patched up.'

'They're all fine. Therin lost a little skin to that slaver, Elar Kranak, and Fyn decided to stay behind in Luqura. Titus and Therin came north. They're testing with the other Dionachs now.'

Sraon grunted, his expression sour. 'Never did like the look o' that Elar fellow. Knew he was mixed up in somethin' rotten, the way he hounded us in that plaza. And that albino chap – the soothsayer?'

'Jian Nikloss,' Annev said, a pang of guilt washing over him as he realised he'd already forgotten the Yomad's sacrifice. Granted, he hadn't known the man long, but Jian *had* sacrificed himself to save them – and Annev had liked the man besides. It seemed a betrayal to have forgotten him so soon.

'He, uh ... didn't make it.'

'Ah,' Sraon said. Annev found himself itching to say more – to admit that, if not for the soothsayer, he might have levelled the entire Ash Quarter and killed everyone in it, Sraon and his companions included. Instead he bit his tongue – coward that he was – and let the man's memory stand half in shadow, half-remembered.

Sraon tsked. 'I'm sorry, lad. If that creature hadn't jumped me – if I'd lifted my halberd ...' He raised an upturned hand, as if in supplication. 'I let you boys down. I'm sorry about that.'

'No,' Annev said, stepping back to the edge of the bed. 'You got us all the way to Luqura, past soldiers and bandits, city gates and guards. We wouldn't have gotten anywhere near the city if not for you.'

Sraon grunted. 'That's true enough, I s'pose. Probably would've been scooped up by that Alcoran fellow and carted off to join the war in Borderlund.' He forced a smile. 'I dare say you would have done all right, even then. But you're here at the Enclave now, and Brother Reeve and the other Dionachs will take good care of you lads. I kept my promise to Sodar.'

Annev gave the barest nod, acknowledging Sraon's words but unable to agree with them. The blacksmith seemed to think that, by coming to Quiri, Annev had joined the Order – and he didn't have the heart to dispel the man's delusions.

'I see you've still got that golden hand.'

Annev raised the smithing glove, his surrogate fingers flexing beneath the surface. 'Yeah. Seems everyone's been busy keeping some old blacksmith alive?'

Sraon sputtered. 'Old? You should take a look around, boy. Half the people here have grey hair – and the ones that don't could still be older than your great-great-grandfather. Just look at Reeve – he's older than *Sodar*. Did you know that?'

'No,' Annev said, surprised. 'I mean, he said he'd seen the Hand of Keos before – thousands of years ago at the Battle of Vosgar – but I assumed he was younger than Sodar. He *looks* younger.'

'You wouldn't be the first to think that. Seems that when you make the ageless covenant, your body *stops* ageing, but you don't get any younger. Sodar was one o' the last to make the covenant, and he was old. Reeve was one o' the first, and he's older than old. If you can believe it, he's been around since the First Age.'

Annev tried to calculate how old that made him – several centuries more than Sodar, maybe as old as four or five thousand years – but he supposed that after a while, one or two centuries didn't matter that much.

'Do they just never die?' Annev asked, realising the foolishness of his question. 'Of course, they can *die* – Sodar died – but, I mean … it seems almost impossible that anyone can be that old. What with all the wars and battles, you'd think he would have been killed long ago.'

'Aye, most of the Ageless *were* killed. Not many left now. I guess Reeve didn't get to be so old without being a cautious bastard.'

Annev nodded in agreement, thinking again how Reeve had abandoned them at the first sign of trouble. True, he'd saved Sraon's life – and he had come back for them – but it didn't change that he'd looked to his own safety first. Annev needed to remember that, and to not rely on the Arch-Dionach's assistance. More than likely, if they were in trouble, he'd be on his own again.

There was a knock on the door, as if the man had been summoned by his thoughts. When the portal opened, though, Dionach Leskal peered in.

'Brother Sraon, you should get some rest. They're bringing up some food for you now, and then you should try to sleep.' The bald-headed Dionach tilted his square jaw at Annev. 'You can come with me. We can talk while you eat. You need to drink plenty of water so we can practise your glyph-speaking.'

Annev was already dreading another repeat of his failures that morning, but he put on a brave face for the blacksmith. 'Rest up, Sraon. I'll try to visit later.'

'I'll be fine, lad. Go on and join your friends – show them that magic you got buried inside. Ain't no need to be hidin' it here.' He smiled as though his confidence might help, but it made Annev's stomach churn with more anxiety. He swallowed, raised a hand in farewell, and then followed the leader of the Shieldbearers out into the corridor.

Dionach Leskal tugged his braided beard, his frown framed by his thick moustache.

'You've got to *will* it. Imagine what you want to happen and then manifest that will through your words. Focus on a point then imagine the skywater contracting around it. Pressing together, condensing into a plane of air or a blade of water.'

'Which am I imagining – air or water?'

'Either one. The element doesn't matter so much as the action.'

'It would help me,' Annev said, dancing from one foot to the other, 'to think of what I'm compressing it into.'

'Think that way if you like, but you'll be better served just thinking of it as skywater – something amorphous that can become *any* of those things. If you're a Shieldbearer, you might discover you possess an affinity for one over another – ice, air or water – but they're all skywater. If you become a Breathbreaker, you may have better luck forming mists or fog, but that's an *expanding* motion – you'll practise that with Brother Honeycutt.'

Annev frowned. 'So is it pushing and pulling, or pressing?'

Leskal slowly wiped the moisture from his mouth and moustache. They had spent the better part of an hour standing atop the open roof of the Enclave. Sweat stained the Dionach's armpits and Quiri's oppressive heat and humidity continued to bear down on them.

'You can think in terms of pushing and pulling if you like, but *you* are not the centre.' He gestured at the air and sky, at the clouds and the invisible moisture that clung to their bodies. 'Collect the skywater around you and then compress it into something tight and sharp. It could be a blade or a ball, a plane or a sphere. Whatever shape it takes, hold that image in your mind and then pair it with the glyph we drew. Speak the word and release your will.'

Annev inhaled, filling his lungs with air, preparing to speak – then he paused, uncertainty creeping in. 'Shouldn't we use a more specific rune? I mean, this is just the symbol for *quaire*. I feel like I'd be more successful if I drew a shield glyph or a wall glyph. Or maybe if I drew the symbol for air or water – or maybe ice?' He gestured at the swooping ellipse they had drawn together using the Dionach's bamboo brush. The symbol had already begun to fade, the water quickly evaporating under the bright sun and oppressive heat.

'No,' Leskal said, his tone a mask of patience. 'That's not necessary at this stage. Developing your will and the proper frame of mind – *that* is what's important.'

Annev stared at the remaining drops of water, the glyph almost completely disappeared now. 'What if we used blood or saliva? Those wouldn't evaporate so fast – especially the blood – and then we wouldn't have to keep painting the glyph on the ground.'

Leskal's broad shoulders slumped. He stared hard at Annev, eyes fixed, then, with careful precision, he stepped forward and erased the glyph with his foot.

'*Brúigh!*'

The air around them suddenly became dry as the moisture in the air pressed together, compressing itself into a tight ball of liquid. Annev felt the hairs on his arms rise as the sweat from his skin evaporated, disappearing into the ball of water now floating in front of them. The sphere hovered at the height of Annev's eyes, floating, spinning.

'*Brúigh!*'

The ball of water suddenly flattened, transforming into a sheet about two handspans in width and length.

'*Brúigh!*'

The sheet of water rolled together like a scroll, suddenly translucent. The spear of water rotated, and Annev saw the Dionach had transformed it into a spike of ice.

'*Brúigh!*'

The ice cracked into shards, which were again compressed into a sheet of shimmering water. No, not water – air. With a single command, Leskal had transformed the dagger of ice into a wall of air. Annev reached out, pressing against the wall, and was surprised how solid it was. He leaned against it, pushing. Leskal raised an eyebrow, and then Annev's hand suddenly slipped through, the wall disappearing as he nearly fell on his face.

The leader of the Shieldbearers steadied him, his patience having evaporated along with the skywater wall. 'We're done for today, boy. I need to rehydrate before I can do much more – and I'm not sure it will make any difference.'

He dismissed Annev with a wave of his hand.

Chapter Thirty-Eight

Myjun glared at the hazy grey circle that floated high above the horizon. Though its centre was black as night, the perimeter of the ring glowed with an eerie incandescence that reminded her of starlight. When it rose, the ring cast everything in a muted grey light, erasing some shadows and softening most others.

'What is that?'

She and the assassin had been travelling across a featureless grey stone landscape for what felt like days, and Myjun had begun to notice some repeated features. The grey ring was the most obvious. There was also a recurring change in the texture of the stone, and a nearly imperceptible incline that rose on their right before disappearing into fog and mist.

Oyru did not bother to look up. 'It is the Eye of Dorchnok, a reflection of the sun in the Shadowrealm. It marks the passage of time in this world.'

'So we have been travelling for three days without rest or food?'

'You can think of them as *days* if you want, but they are not the same.'

'What do you call them then?'

Oyru raised a hand to point at the light grey ring hovering in the starless sky. 'Dorchnok's Eye marks the antumbra – what you would call day, though it is more like the waning of the shadows. When the eye is absent from the sky, that is the umbra – the night. Five umbras will pass here for a single day in your world. In three more umbra we will arrive at the first of the wastes. That is where we will begin our hunt.'

Myjun looked at the dull, shadow-lit landscape and sneered. 'You speak of wastes, but this whole world is a wasteland. No dirt. No plants or animals. How do you even know where we're going?'

'By following the Eye of Dorchnok. It descends behind us now, so we are moving east.'

'And even though the landscape is unchanged, we're getting closer to Alltara?'

Oyru nodded. 'In your world, the shadows lack real dimension. The shadow world is only a little different. Things appear to have depth because shadows have depth, but their shapes are still flat – mostly. Even so, this world is a mere echo of life. A barren parallel to the physical world.'

'Then there is nothing here to hunt, and we are going *nowhere*.'

Something shifted in Oyru's expression. A look of annoyance? Amusement? It was as if he also wore a mask, though Myjun was getting better at deciphering its subtleties. 'The wastes serve as landmarks, and those are real enough. They are like the shade-pools in the Brakewood, except they lead to the *next* world – to the World of Dreams.'

Myjun squinted at the colourless landscape. She tried to im-agine a dark pit where monsters might hide. In this featureless void though, the idea seemed impossible.

'There is nothing out there.'

'There is, and in four blinks of Dorchnok's Eye you will see it for yourself. Terrors made flesh. Nightmares brought to life.'

'Shadow demons,' Myjun hissed.

Oyru grunted. 'Their true name is eidola – eidolons. They lurk in the cracks of this world and feast on the dreams of men and women in order to gain somnumbra, the life-force that sustains us in these wastes – but preying on another's dreams is unsavoury and dangerous. Much better to meditate.'

'Meditation.' Myjun's tone curdled at the word. 'Why not simply feed the way these monsters do?'

'Because it is not so simple and because we are not monsters. The eidola feed on the dreams of the living because they are not living themselves. We *have* lived. We can form our own dreams. We do not need to prey on the shadows of others' thoughts. Would you eat another human's faeces? Would you breathe another's breath? It is life to them since they have no life of their own, but to us it is poison.'

Myjun scoffed. 'Fine. When do we meditate then, in this land full of monsters?'

Oyru looked back at the grey ring, which had started to dip below the horizon. 'Soon.'

They continued their long walk, but barely a few minutes had passed before Oyru broke the silence himself.

'The Shadowrealm has a way of muting one's spirit. Do you feel its effect on you and your powers?'

Myjun considered it. 'I think so. I'm still full of anger, but it is different. The pain is not as sharp as it was. I feel less ... impulsive?' Oyru nodded as if this made sense to him and Myjun continued. 'The mask feels no different – at least, not the artifact itself. Do you think that will affect my powers?'

'We will find out when we reach the waste.'

Myjun pursed her lips then stroked the side of her golden cheek. 'I suppose we will.'

They walked for perhaps another hour then, though it was difficult to tell exactly how much time had passed in this dream-like place. When Dorchnok's Eye finally disappeared and the darkness around them grew more intense, the assassin turned back and called for a halt. 'Sit, tabibito. We will begin your meditations now.'

They spent an indeterminate period of time sitting with their legs crossed and their eyes closed. Every few minutes, Oyru prodded her with an instruction to clear her mind, to summon the void inside herself or some other spiritual nonsense. Each time, Myjun tried to do as he instructed. Each time, Myjun forced herself to close her eyes and sit in silence. Time seemed to crawl by. She listened to the rhythms of Oyru's breathing and tried to slow her own to match his. Instead, her breathing quickened. She felt agitated. Restless. She tried not to dwell on the time they were wasting just sitting in the Shadowrealm. Breathing. Sitting. Meditating. Doing *nothing*.

A bloody waste of time.

'Clear your mind, tabibito. Become the nexus for the Dream World and allow the somnumbra to saturate you.'

Pointless. Useless.

Myjun's thoughts swirled around her … yet she felt herself growing tired. Her body felt heavy, and she seemed on the precipice of falling asleep.

'Do not sleep,' Oyru warned, his voice stealing the drowsiness from her thoughts. 'Sleeping is a path to the Dream World. Only *meditate*. That is all your body requires.'

'I'm *trying*. It just feels so …'

Pointless. Useless.

'Become the void,' Oyru repeated for perhaps the hundredth time. 'Your aura betrays you. Your mind is disquieted.'

'Of *course* it's disquieted,' she hissed, her eyes popping open. 'Instead of hunting Annev, we're sitting in one of the Five Hells, and I have a flaming *demon* whispering in my ear.'

Oyru stood, impassive. 'Come,' he said. 'The umbra is waning and Dorchnok's Eye begins to open. We will try again when you are less distracted.'

It was like that for three days – three *antumbras* – and on the eve of the third umbra, Myjun's patience was at an end.

'I can't!' she shouted. 'The mask … it keeps interfering!'

'You *must* do it,' Oyru said, not bothering to open his eyes. 'If you cannot learn to achieve a meditative state, you will not absorb enough somnumbra and your body and mind will wither and die.'

'*Somnumbra*.' The word tasted bitter on her tongue. 'I can't see it. I can't smell it or taste it. How do you know I haven't already absorbed it?'

'You have.'

'Then why the *hell* are we still doing this?'

Oyru exhaled. Not a sigh, never that much emotion, but it felt much the same out here where every movement, every action, seemed to echo with intent and purpose. 'Because,' the assassin said, 'you haven't received *enough* of it. Your body will constantly absorb somnumbra while you are in the Shadowrealm, but it will not be enough to sustain you. That is why you must rest. It is why you must learn to meditate.'

Myjun closed her eyes and tried to find her centre – whatever *that* was. She found anger there, a coil of hatred and venom twisted into flame and fire. Her instinct was to hold onto that flame – to nurture it, to let it grow – but Oyru said she must discard it. To acknowledge those emotions ... and set them aside.

'My pain makes me stronger. I should just embrace it!'

'No. Then *it* controls *you*, and that is the opposite of strength.'

Myjun growled and forced her eyes to remain closed. It was always the same. Every umbra, Oyru forced them to stop and meditate when the shadows were at their peak and when, as now, the grey ring of Dorchnok's Eye had passed beyond the horizon. Instead of sleeping, they stilled their bodies and relaxed their minds, allowing the somnumbra to penetrate them – or attempting to.

Why can't I do it? Myjun wondered. *Why can't I overcome the mask?* She'd grown to loathe the nights in the Shadowrealm, so frustrated with her ineffectiveness at absorbing the elusive vitality that allowed them to survive in this dreary place.

'I'm relaxing,' she said, consciously making her teeth unclench and her muscles loosen. 'I'm quieting my mind, body and spirit.'

'You are not,' Oyru said, sitting opposite her with his eyes also closed, 'but it is an admirable attempt.'

Myjun sniffed, her eyes opening into slits. 'How would you even know?'

'Because I am in tune with the shadows and their energies. Because when my own spirit is quiet, I can feel the fire raging in yours. Your mind is full of doubt and indecision. It is the opposite of the void. It is chaos.'

In spite of her anger, Myjun saw and acknowledged the truth in his words. 'I did not doubt myself in the physical world,' she said, annoyed that it felt so different here.

'You *did* doubt yourself,' Oyru said, eyes still closed, 'but those doubts were being drowned out by your anger and the magic of the mask. Now that its power is weaker, you can hear your own doubts. They have always been there, but now you must acknowledge them.'

'And discard them.'

'Yes.'

Myjun glared at the demon sitting opposite her in his ragged black clothes, nearly invisible in the half-light. 'You want me to find the void inside myself,' she muttered, 'but I don't feel it – I barely *understand* it. Perhaps if I had some instruction ...'

Oyru's eyes popped open. 'I can see this is causing you some disquietude. So I'll explain: your soul is composed of spirit, mind and body, all of which must be fed to keep you alive. The spirit feeds on the choices you present it with – it must be *challenged*. Without a challenge, your spirit atrophies. Likewise, your mind will wither if it's unable to create or consider new ideas. Afterwards, your soul needs time to rest and digest what you've consumed. Meditation and sleep both serve this purpose, and that generates somnumbra – cognitive energy. Your body gets its energy from consuming food ... but your soul also needs somnumbra.'

'But why meditate? Why can't we just sleep?'

'Because sleep brings us too close to the Cognitive Realm – to the World of Dreams. Our powers are weaker there. We might even be incapable of returning.'

'Hence the meditation.'

'Yes.'

Myjun closed her eyes and tried to focus again, one fist clenching and unclenching as she tried to relax. Her brow furrowed, and when she opened her eyes again she saw a hint of a smile tug at Oyru's mouth. Just a hint, but it was uncommon enough that it might as well have been a laugh.

'It's *difficult*, conjuror – I'm not a half-demon like you. If I were in the physical world, I'd do better.'

'I doubt that,' Oyru said, still watching her. 'We recuperate somnumbra more quickly here – almost five times as fast, just as time in the physical world passes slower than it does here.'

'Five times,' Myjun said, considering. 'Are those ratios always the same?'

Oyru shook his head. 'In some parts of the Shadowrealm, like Reocht na Skah, the disparity is greater – it increases the closer you get to the Heart of the Void. At its centre, a thousand years can pass within the span of a single day's rotation.'

Myjun's voice dripped with scorn. 'That's impossible. You would die.'

'In a sense, you do. Death is a transition to the Spirit World, and that world touches the centre of Reocht na Skah. It is a place of passing, where time as we know it ceases to exist and things become ... eternal. That is also why the Heart of the Void touches all realms. It functions as a crossroads between the Lands of the Gods. In the physical world, it manifests as a pool of physical light – a well of liquid luminescence.'

'Liquid light? That's ... what the *feurog* poured on my face!'

Oyru nodded. '*Aqlumera*. That fountain is an extension of the Heart of the Void. It manifests differently in each world – and it is very, very dangerous.'

'How does it manifest here?'

Oyru shrugged. 'This is the World of Shadows. What is light to a shadow?'

'Death?'

'Yes. It is a fountain of life, a well spring of magic, but its essence is so pure that a shade cannot endure it. That is why the centre of Reocht na Skah is called the Heart of the Void. Nothing lives there. Nothing walks or hunts there. Even the inescapable clutches of time cannot endure there. Only spirits can pass through, for they are part of its stream, and by that passage they enter the World of Spirits.'

'Then I'm *so* glad we have to pass through Reocht na Skah to reach Alltara,' Myjun snapped.

'We will only pass adjacent to it,' Oyru countered mildly. 'Reocht na Skah is in Takarania, near the mountain trolls' home in Alltara – where the ironwood grows, and where you will forge your armour – but by travelling along its border in the Shadowrealm, you can gain years of experience. You could spend a lifetime there and only a few months or weeks would pass in the physical world. In that time, I can truly make you my equal. Perhaps with your new talents you could even surpass me.'

'I do not wish to spend another *day* in your company, much less a lifetime. You would see my anger cooled. You would seek to deny me what you have promised.'

Oyru held up a finger. 'I deny you nothing and your anger will not cool so easily. Your passions are weaker here, true, but the Mask of Gevul's Mistress will not let you forget your hatred. And I won't allow your hatred to rule you. *You* must learn to *control* your passions. To harness them. Gaining that mastery here will make you stronger there. Do you see?'

Myjun saw, but she was not certain she agreed. Her emotions had fuelled her before and she worried about letting that anger cool too much here in the shadow world. She had given up everything when she'd made her pact with this devil. Her hatred and the promise of revenge were all she had left. If they, too, were taken from her ... she'd have nothing. Her beauty gone. Her father dead. Her soul indentured to a demonic servant of Keos. And for what?

Oyru's words gnawed at her like a death sentence. A lifetime? Myjun refused to suffer this half-man for so long. She would flee or kill him long before then.

But Myjun found she could be patient, too – more so, with Oyru teaching her to control her powers. She needn't tell him her decision. She only needed to glean what he could teach her, and then she could hunt and kill Annev herself.

'How much time will actually pass in the physical world while we are travelling?'

'If my plans are not frustrated it will take a month and more to reach Alltara. Perhaps a three-month round trip. Much of that depends on how swiftly we reach Reocht na Skah and how often we need to return you to the physical world.'

'Why would we return?'

'Your physical body needs more than somnumbra alone. You will need to slake your thirst by shedding the blood of your enemies and sate your hunger with the destruction of life, and there is neither life nor blood here. Returning will also allow me to gauge your progress – and determine in which areas your training is still lacking.'

Myjun set her mouth in a grim line. 'Fine. As it seems I have no choice, we will do it your way. Do not think to deceive me, though. Before six months have passed in the physical world, I *will* sup on Annev's blood. His life is mine and you have promised to help me destroy him.'

'I have and you will. You have my word. Now, set your body and emotions aside. Centre yourself amidst the chaos surrounding you, but do not let it touch you.' He fixed his cold, black eyes on hers. 'Do it now – and don't forget: we must gather all our strength for the next umbra ... and the hunt that comes when we reach the waste.'

Myjun closed her eyes. *The hunt*. That was something she understood, something she could focus on. She turned her gaze inward and meditated on the battle that was to come.

Chapter Thirty-Nine

It had been two days, and the Dionachs had mostly given up on Annev managing any glyph-speaking. Brother Tym and Dionach McClanahan were the only exceptions. Annev had met with Misty again and, while he hadn't had any luck performing telepathy, both she and Tym felt it was important to help him quiet his thoughts and protect his mind from the intrusion of others.

'You don't need to be a Dionach to protect your mind,' Misty had explained after another glyph-speaking failure. 'Your mind is your own, and people trying to implant their thoughts in your head are like peasants trying to storm your castle. They can overwhelm you if you let them, but the walls and defences are yours. No one is getting in unless you're complacent, or you *choose* to invite them in. Even then, you can eject them whenever you like.'

Annev toyed with a crusty bread bun, spinning its round edges between his fingers. 'I'm not sure that analogy helps.'

'No?'

'People's thoughts wander,' Annev said, watching as Tym crunched noisily into his apple. 'They don't stand still – you can't station them at a post – and you can only think one thought at a time. That's just one guard, one person protecting an entire castle.'

'He's right, Misty,' Tym said, swallowing. 'You're teaching this like a Stormcaller who's trying to break into someone's mind palace, but it's more like ...' He waved his apple in front of him. 'Like ... plucking a drunk bird out of the air.'

'That's worse, Tym. Much worse.'

Tym smiled, eyes wide with false innocence, then he opened

383

his mouth to take another bite of fruit, but instead Misty snatched it from his hands.

'Better analogy,' she said, holding the apple out to Annev. 'Think of this as an idea – a thought – which my husband is chewing very loudly, some might say *impolitely*.' She eyed Tym, who wiped his wet mouth and shrugged, eyes bright with mischief. 'Now, if Tym wanted to, he could probably eat this apple without causing such a spectacle. We can still hear him since we're standing so close, but if he were quieter, he might escape notice.'

Misty handed the apple back to Tym, who inclined his head, acknowledging the superior lesson.

'So ... protecting my thoughts is like chewing with my mouth closed.' Annev tore off a piece of bread and popped it into his mouth, softly chewing. Tym nodded.

'There's one more way,' Tym said, casually wiping the sticky juice from his fingers. 'Imagine you're at a banquet. Everyone is talking and shouting. Eating and drinking. Very noisy. You'll be lucky to hear yourself talking, let alone the person asking you to pass the salt. Your mind can be the same way. Keep a whirl of mindless thoughts and ideas spinning around you – maybe even contradicting ideas – and it all becomes a jumbled mess to anyone listening.'

'If you can't tell,' Misty said, 'that's Tym's favourite way to mind-wall people. It's not enough that he keeps his thoughts to himself – he enjoys confusing others with the thoughts spinning around in his head.'

Tym grinned as he tossed the apple core over his shoulder. 'Guilty.'

Annev felt he was beginning to understand. He tore off another hunk of bread and chewed with his mouth shut, trying to do the same with his mind.

'Good!' Misty said, her green eyes sparkling. 'I can barely hear your thoughts now. Tym?' She laid an arm around her husband's shoulders.

'I can hear him,' Tym said, squinting, 'but it's hard to understand.' He turned to his wife. 'I think he's worried you're going to stick something in his ear.'

384

'No!' Annev felt his cheeks flush hot as he glanced between Misty and her husband. 'I was wondering how I can know my thoughts are my own. How do I know someone isn't tampering with them or manipulating them?'

Tym grunted and looked to Misty. 'He asks good questions.'

'Yes, he does.' Dionach McClanahan glanced sidelong at her husband, then at his discarded apple core. 'Forcing someone else to do your will is difficult. Just as in real life, you're more likely to change someone's mind if they're already well disposed towards the idea you're trying to implant.' She nodded her head at Tym, and he suddenly frowned at the apple core he had tossed and went to pick it up.

Annev lifted an eyebrow. 'Did Misty make you do that?'

Tym scoffed. 'Misty? No, I just realised someone would have to clean it up, so I might as well . . .' He looked at his wife, his mouth falling open. 'You *did* do that! You sneaky little siren.' He raised the apple core to his mouth, getting halfway before he stopped. 'You're trying to make me *eat* it now?' He groaned in disgust then hurled the apple core away.

Misty grinned. 'You see? A little nudge and someone will think it was their own idea – partially because it was – but if you push too hard too fast, they'll resist the idea. And once someone knows you're trying to invade their thoughts, it's *much* more challenging. You could try a blunt force attack, but it would need to be over-whelming. You'll be more successful if you distract them with something inconsequential first . . .'

Annev glanced at Tym, whose nose had begun to twitch. He brushed at it, twitched again, then rubbed at both nostrils.

'. . . then go for the punch.'

Tym's hand flew up and he slapped himself in the face. The man cried out, nearly fell out of his chair and then stumbled from the table.

'Misty!' Tym rubbed his stinging cheek. 'That's really not fair.' Annev laughed in spite of himself, watching the exchange. 'I thought a *bug* had crawled up my nose!' Misty grinned too and a moment later all three of them were laughing.

'Okay,' Annev said, having caught his breath. 'But how could

Tym have stopped you? What happened to all this talk about castles and soldiers patrolling the walls?'

'Eh,' Tym said, shrugging. 'I'm an easy target because I'm used to inviting other people's thoughts into my head – and Misty is a bully who's accustomed to entering my head.'

'Am not.'

'You are, too.' He stuck his tongue out at her then scratched his nose again. 'Misty, you're proving my point.' The scratching stopped almost instantly. 'It's simple, Annev. Keep your thoughts to yourself and wall yourself off from sympathies that feel out of place. Examine each thought as it comes to you and decide if it's yours. If you trust it. If you know your own mind, no one can get through your defences.'

Annev chewed this over, remembering how it had felt when Janak used the Rod of Compulsion on him and his friends. It had been so subtle, so easy to be lured into thinking things that weren't his own thoughts.

'Quieter, Annev.' Tym said, tapping his temple.

Annev frowned, realising he had been projecting his thoughts, and Tym continued. 'To keep your thoughts private, step *away* from them. Hold them too close and people will see you're protecting something – you'll draw their attention. Keep everything at a distance, though, and it becomes hard to see the trees through the forest. You understand?'

Annev nodded, distancing himself from the emotions and memories linked to Janak's keep. Instead, he thought of the Rod of Compulsion, and then the rods contained in the Vault of Damnation. He thought of the unidentified wooden wand in his pocket, and his breathing slowed. He felt himself ride the wave of thoughts, thinking of all the artifacts, rods and wands he had seen over the past few weeks.

'That's excellent,' Tym said, smiling. 'Just a lot of noise. I can't hear a thing.'

Annev returned the smile right as the hellfire wand Elder Tosan had used came to mind. The rod Tosan had used to kill Sodar.

'Oh boy,' Tym said, his smile suddenly falling. Misty laid one freckled hand over his.

'I think it's time we gave him some space, dear.' They both stood up and Tym gave him a sympathetic look.

'We'll see you tomorrow, Annev. Keep practising.'

Annev watched them go, seeing the sympathy on their faces. When they had left the dining hall, though, Annev crunched the bread roll in his fist and flung it across the room. It sailed high overhead, arcing as it approached the opposite entrance to the hall. As it fell, the door swung open and Titus and Therin entered, the bread bun thudding into Therin's chest.

'Who the hell—? Annev! Did you throw that?' He smiled, rubbing his chest. 'Nice shot!'

Annev sighed, resigned to being outshone by his friends in another frustrating conversation about magic. 'Hey. How are your classes going?'

'Good,' Titus said, arms folded behind his back.

'Fine,' Therin said at almost the same time. 'Things are fine.'

Annev clucked his tongue. 'Just fine?'

'Yep.'

The silence was uncomfortable. He hadn't seen either of them since his angry mental outburst, and now it hung in the room between them. They didn't even have rooms close to each other – Therin and Titus were on the novitiate's floor with Sraon while Annev's room was below ground level. A guest room, because none of the Dionachs had come forward to sponsor him. His days had already fallen into an uncomfortable rhythm of having nowhere to go and his friends being too busy to see him.

'Right,' Annev said at last, turning to go. 'Well, I guess I'll see you later.'

'Wait, Annev.' Titus grabbed his sleeve. 'I'm sorry we've not seen you. With all our classes we've barely had time to sleep.'

'Huh,' Annev said, feeling envious of the attention they were getting and embarrassed of that envy at the same time. 'That's ... great. You must be doing really well.'

'Eh, our progress has slowed down,' Therin said, rolling his shoulders. 'They've gone from being delighted with our tests to trying to *teach* us something – with the caste leaders now, not just

387

our sponsors – and it's become a lot harder to do anything with *quaire*.'

Titus grinned ruefully. 'I can't do a thing with skywater. Not a puff of wind nor a drop of water – nothing.'

'Huh,' Annev said again, feeling a little better. 'Well, I can relate to *that*.' He smiled, and this time he meant it. 'You're still doing well with Brother Holyoak, though, right, Titus?' The boy nodded enthusiastically. 'What about with Dionach McClanahan and the Stormcallers? She seems really nice – and I would think it'd be easier for you to push *quaire* instead of skywater.'

Titus shook his head. 'I can pull thoughts and sense what others are thinking. No luck pushing thoughts or trying to influence others.'

Annev felt another surge of relief. 'Therin? Any luck with Dionach Leskal?'

'A little. Condensing skywater feels really different from expanding it. Right now, I'm working on floating a drop of water in the air by compressing all the skywater around it. Most of the time I just end up spraying us both with mist, but I did get it floating for half a second this morning.'

'That's great,' Annev said, genuinely impressed. 'Any luck with ice?'

Therin snickered. 'Hells, no. Honestly, I don't even think I'll be able to work with water – just the air around it. I much prefer my classes with Brother Honeycutt. Annev, we've been making sound bubbles using pockets of voided air! It's *incredible*. They make these little popping explosions when the air rushes back in.'

'Explosions?' Annev asked, suddenly wary of the magic his friend could wield.

'Yeah! Watch this.' He spit on the nearest table and began drawing a glyph.

'Therin!' Titus admonished. 'We're not supposed to practise outside of classes. It's dangerous. If the Dionachs catch you, they won't teach you a thing for a week.'

Therin hesitated, then shrugged and wiped the spit off the table. 'Well you get the idea. Later this week he's going to teach me to cast the bubbles around my shoes so I can walk in complete silence. Can you imagine knowing how to do that back at the Academy? All those stealth classes with Master Der?' He chuckled. 'Magic makes things so much easier.'

'In my experience, it makes life harder.' His friends' smiles suddenly fell away, and Annev realised he'd said the wrong thing again. 'That's great, though,' he added, trying to restore the mood. 'I'm really glad you're both doing so well.'

'Yeah,' Therin said. 'And you're ... doing okay, too?'

'Yeah. Reeve's busy researching about my prosthetic, so we haven't made any progress there yet. Once he's ready, though, he'll get the other Dionachs to help him try to remove it.' That's what the man had said, anyway, but Annev suspected the Arch-Dionach was busy with other tasks and letting Annev cool his heels, hoping that he'd find a glyph-speaking talent, earn a sponsor of his own, and decide to stay. They'd both been disappointed by Annev's lack of progress, though, and hadn't really spoken since that first failure-filled day.

Therin nodded. 'Good. Well ... we'll see you around.'

'Yeah.'

'Bye, Annev.'

He left them in the dining hall, not wanting to linger, and soon found himself standing in the corridor with nowhere to go. He'd seen Sraon just before lunch, then run into Dionach McClanahan and her husband. With nowhere to be, Annev turned and began walking back to his room on the lower level, which took him through the library – the large room filled with tables that he'd seen on first entering the Enclave. At present, a handful of Dionachs sat at each one, each silently reading a tome or copying a manuscript. It still seemed odd that it was so quiet, but Annev now suspected some of the brethren were holding silent, telepathic conversations.

As Annev walked through the great hall, he began counting the faces he recognised. Outside of Reeve, Brother Tym and the four caste leaders, Annev saw perhaps a dozen other Dionachs living at the Enclave and maybe half as many Journeymen Dionachs. The building was very large, though – almost as big as the Academy – with many empty rooms on its various levels. It made him wonder if the rest of the Dionachs were travelling, or if this was all that remained of the Order. Arnor had told Sodar a few hundred Dionachs remained, approximately fifty of whom were supposed to be ageless ones. Those numbers didn't match what Annev had seen here, though. He made a note to himself to ask Reeve about it.

When Annev arrived at his cell he paused, seeing the door was ajar when he was certain he had closed it. Suddenly wary, Annev cautiously edged the door open and peered into his dark room. Nothing seemed immediately out of place, but he slid the glove from his left hand and used its supernatural glow to faintly illuminate the room.

Everything was just as he had left it. Nothing strange or unusual. Annev grunted, still suspicious, and checked the artifacts he'd brought from the Vault. The dragon-whelp cloak lay bundled in one corner of the room, its muted red scales flat and unremarkable in the glow from his hand. He checked Sodar's bottomless bag, removing items until he felt certain the contents had gone untouched. Reassured, he began dropping everything back into the sack, then stopped at the unidentified wooden rod. Annev held it, wondering at its magic, then remembered he still wore the Ring of Good Luck. Could it help identify the wand? Annev doubted that ... but perhaps it could give him some hint about how it was supposed to be used?

Annev clutched the wand in his right palm, allowing it to touch the silver-gold codavora ring, hoping it might improve his chances of identifying the artifact. He imagined summoning its magic.

Nothing.

Annev opened his hand and imagined the rod spinning in his palm, pointing towards ... something. Towards himself?

The rod didn't move.

Annev sighed, his failures at glyph-speaking still razor sharp – but this wasn't the same. Annev *knew* how to use artifacts. It was the one thing he seemed to be good at. So why couldn't he use this one? What was different?

As he considered it, Annev's attention drifted to his glowing hand. Since Luqura, he'd been unable to properly relax or let go of his emotions – he'd been too worried what might happen if he accidentally lost control of the Hand of Keos – but perhaps that same worry had prevented him from accessing his magic. What if he relaxed just a little? Just enough to use the codavora ring's magic ... and maybe identify the wand? He could do that without letting his emotions take control, couldn't he?

Annev took a deep breath, closed his hand again and imagined leaving his room, retracing his steps to the dining hall. Titus and Therin would still be there, eating their lunches. He saw the rod pointed at Therin and the boy's nose suddenly gushed with blood. In his vision, Therin sprang up, staunching the blood and swearing at Annev.

But Annev's emotions were disengaged from the imagined scenario. Instead of reacting, he swept the Hand of Keos over his friend's fallen blood and collected a few of the red drops. Annev raised it to his lips ... to taste it? No. The thought disgusted him. Annev didn't want the blood ... but the *rod* did. The artifact wanted to taste Therin's blood – to taste *anyone's* blood, if they carried the blood-talent. The stronger the better.

Annev blinked, his concentration broken, ending the vision, and sat in the near-darkness of his cell staring at the plain wooden rod in his hand – a magic wand that craved the blood of people with a talent for magic.

The truth of the artifact suddenly dawned on Annev and he gasped, nearly dropping it. With blinding clarity, he now knew the rod's purpose, its name and its function. A prickling sensation crept up from the base of his prosthetic arm and made his left elbow and forearm tingle. He licked his lips and carefully placed the Rod of Artificing atop his pillow.

I'm a failure at Darite magic, Annev thought, quietly locking his bedroom door, *and no one here has been able to help me remove my prosthetic. But maybe ...* he picked up the rod, turning it over in his hands ... *maybe I can help myself.*

Dolyn and Reeve had both said Annev's best chance of re-moving the Hand of Keos was finding an Artificer like Urran, but that wasn't an option at the Enclave – perhaps it wasn't an option anywhere. Using an Artificer's wand, though? Surely the effects would be the same. And if Annev could learn to use it – if he could discover its powers and learn to control them – then maybe he could use the Rod of Artificing to solve his own problems.

It needs blood, he thought, remembering his premonition, *but not my blood*. In his vision, the rod had been drawn to the blood of an artisan – *any* artisan. Why? Was it to remove his cursed hand … or to forge a new artifact?

Annev didn't know. The notion of creating an original artifact appealed to him, particularly after his friends' successes at performing magic, but his primary concern was removing the Hand of Keos. If he had to steal someone else's blood to make that happen, he would do it … but maybe that wasn't necessary.

Dolyn had said a person's blood was analogous to aqlumera because it contained quaire, lumen, and t'rasang. That's why it's necessary for artificing. Annev frowned, considering. *I'll have to experiment. If I can use the rod without involving another person's blood-talent, so much the better. But if not …*

If not, he would have to get creative about acquiring someone else's blood.

Chapter Forty

The way Fyn saw it, he needed three things. First, he had to convince the Ashes crew he would fight for what he wanted, and that he'd try to be fair if they followed him. That was basic gang leader stuff, and already accomplished by taking out Fisher and making his case to be their new chief. Promising *mostly* even shares allowed him to put off being fair until they completed a job together, at which point he'd already be chief. A tidy way of pushing off his debts to the future. It might come back to haunt him somewhere down the road, but for now it was a debt he was happy to acquire.

The second thing Fyn needed was a clever plan to handle Saltair and avoid or eliminate any interference by the Slavers Guild. This was probably the most difficult of the three, and Fyn still didn't have a clue what he was going to do – but he had another day to figure it out, and he assumed an idea would come to him.

The third thing Fyn needed was a win. His accomplishments at the Academy meant nothing here, so he needed to establish a strong reputation – and fast. Telling the crew he had been responsible for Saltair's injuries had definitely impressed them, as had putting down the Fisher King, but Fyn needed more than a body count to prove he could lead. He needed to bring funds to the table – something tangible besides weapons and murder – and he needed to find a base of operations.

Ideally he could satisfy both conditions by finding a pre-existing hideout that was already guarding a sizeable amount of cash. It also had to be well hidden and relatively safe from intruders, otherwise there was little point in claiming it. As if that weren't challenge enough, he'd have to take it from whichever gang held it without drawing Saltair or the Slavers Guild's attention.

The more Fyn thought about it, the more impossible it seemed. He'd need to do the research, perform some reconnaissance, and assemble a team to help him seize whichever hideout he picked.

But the whole reason for doing this was so that Fyn could *get* a team. He needed a hideout to convince Fisher's former gang he would be a worthy leader ... but he needed a gang to help him seize a suitable hideout.

And so it went, around and around in circles. With no reasonable solution, Fyn's head had begun to hurt, but by the second day, Fyn realised the answer was staring him in the face: Fyn *had* a team, but only if he presented a good enough plan. Then, if they helped him seize the hideout he'd chosen, he would achieve all his goals in one blow. Best of all, Fyn knew who owned the hideout he wanted ... he just didn't know exactly where their hideout was located. For that last bit, Fyn needed intel; about the city and its leaders, its politics and its connection to the Slavers Guild. Being new to the city, Fyn didn't have any friends that could help him in that area ... but he did have an enemy – a former adversary to whom he owed a visit.

So it was, after almost two days of fretting and fussing, Fyn was wandering the rooftops of the Ash Quarter searching for the woman that had eluded him in Banok. He doubted he'd find her, but he had a hunch she might find him if he returned to the last place they'd seen each other. He'd been standing there for a few hours, watching evening turn to dusk and dusk to night, when a familiar voice greeted him from the shadows of the neighbouring rooftop.

'Hello again.'

'Lady Rocas.' Fyn turned to greet the masked woman. 'I was hoping to see you. Are you taking good care of my artifact?'

Sodja slipped off her raven mask, a sly smile tugging her lips. 'I'm sure I don't know what you mean.'

'Damn near blew my head off trying to retrieve that thing,' Fyn said, enjoying the banter.

'And then you went and lost it.' She tsked. 'Probably safer if it stays with me.'

'I'm not here about getting it back.'

The woman's forehead wrinkled, her eyes suspicious. 'You're not?'

'Nope.'

'Then why have you been looking for me? Why did you visit my home?'

'Your *former* home. You haven't been there for months – and your family seemed eager to find you.'

'That's my affair.'

Fyn supposed it probably was. 'And that lizard monster who followed us?'

'He's not connected to me.'

'You sure? Because he attacked us shortly after we left your estate – and I could have sworn I saw him following us through your orchard.'

'I told you, he's nothing to do with me.'

'But he *is* connected to your family.'

Sodja's eyes narrowed. 'Where's all this leading, boy?'

'The name is Fyn.' He took a deep breath, prepared to say something, then slowly let it out. 'Look, I don't mean to get off on the wrong foot. I just ... I need your help.'

Sodja stared at him, confused, then her head tilted back and she laughed – a rich, vibrant sound, throaty and full of promise. 'I *steal* from you,' she said, still chuckling, 'you insult me, and then you ask for my help? That's terrific.'

Fyn was unfazed. 'What do you know about the Slavers Guild?'

Sodja sobered, her eyes narrowing once more. 'Why? Are you working for them?'

'The opposite. I need to avoid them – *neutralise* them – only I don't know the city or its politics ... and I figure you do.'

'Good guess. There might only be four people in all of Luqura who know more about them than I do.'

'So ...?'

'Ah-ah. First tell me what this is about.'

Fyn hesitated, wondering how much to share. 'You know I

395

came from an academy in the Brakewood?' Sodja nodded. 'Well it's gone now. Nothing left. No people, no buildings – nothing.'

The woman's smile slipped from her face. 'Was it Janak? I didn't ... I'm sorry.'

Fyn watched Sodja shift her feet, apparently anxious. There was something she wasn't telling him. Almost as if she felt responsible – but that was impossible; Annev and those monsters had destroyed the village. What would make Sodja think it was her fault?

'No,' he said at last. 'Janak was preparing to attack the village, but when he died, the people he had enchanted were released from the compulsion. He wasn't involved in the destruction.'

'Right,' Sodja said, looking relieved. 'Who then?'

'Not really sure. It was linked to one of my companions, though – the one you chained to the corpse and left for dead.'

There it was – that look of remorse again. 'I saw what happened to his hand,' she said quietly. 'For what it's worth ... I'm sorry.'

Fyn studied the woman, trying to decide what to make of her. She was an assassin – a cold-blooded killer – but she was apologising for Annev's lost hand, an injury she hadn't even caused. Why? What was it to her?

'Why did you come to Janak's keep in the first place? Was it just for the rod?'

Sodja looked down into the streets below. 'I stole the rod because I knew it was powerful, and my family had helped Janak acquire it.' She took a deep breath, then held it, as if uncertain whether to say more. Fyn waited her out, patiently listening.

'Do you know much about Janak Harth?'

'Next to nothing,' Fyn admitted. 'I only know he was a merchant – an important one – and that he had an artifact the Academy wanted.'

Sodja nodded, seeming satisfied. 'Baron Harth was also an influential member of the Slavers Guild and allied with my family – which made him *my* enemy. I knew hurting him would hurt them all. He was their primary contact in Banok and the key to any trade with Borderlund or Lochland. My family had put him in touch with ... someone powerful ... and they were going to use him to get to your village and its treasures.'

'Silver staves,' Fyn swore. 'That's more complicated than I guessed.'

'That complication is what made it easy to unravel. Whoever took the rod would have stopped Janak from destroying your village, which would hurt my family and the Guild.'

'Bloody bones,' he swore again. 'We all thought ... we just assumed we were safe there. We thought no one knew about Chaenbalu.'

'It was only rumours at first – something about thieves and religious zealots in the Brakewood – but then Janak said he could find a way to the village. That's why I assumed he'd destroyed your home.'

'He wasn't directly involved – but now I think the truth may be more complicated than what I originally thought.'

'Something to do with your friend's new hand?' she asked, surprising Fyn.

'What do you know about that?'

'I'm right, aren't I? That arm with the glowing light ... it's connected.'

Fyn nodded. 'When did you see it?'

'I followed Saltair to the warehouse and saw it just before those *nechraict* woke up and started killing everyone.' She shuddered. 'What was all *that* about?'

'We picked up a friend in Banok,' Fyn admitted. 'A necromancer. He didn't make it out of there, though.' He still wasn't sure what to make of the strange albino. 'I assume you saw how that ended. Saltair is still out there, and I don't have my crew any more. If I'm going to survive here, I need to know what I'm up against.' He matched Sodja's gaze. 'If you want to help yourself, start by helping me. I'm an enemy of Janak ... and of your family and the Guild. Tell me what I need to know, and maybe we can help each other.'

Sodja looked out over the bleak landscape of the Ash Quarter, her eyes distant. 'Four people control the Slavers Guild. There's Dante Turano, the Ringmaster. He controls most of Luqura's underworld, including the gladiator pits. A lot of money goes through them – all of it illegal. The Thieves Guild used to keep him in check, but the Slavers Guild drove the thieves out of Luqura.'

'The Pits,' Fyn repeated. 'I've heard people in the Ash Quarter talking about them.'

'Dante gets a lot of his fighters from the Ashes – beggars, street urchins, poor folk who get tangled up with the Watchers and can't defend themselves. They all get hauled off to the Pits. The city watch allows it because they're on the take, and they claim it thins out the vermin in the Low Quarter. Keeps it from getting too crowded.'

'That's disgusting.'

'Yes, it is. Then there's Braddock Whalen. Chief Guildmaster. He controls the Guild's interests in Luqura, and is unofficially under the thumb of Consul Phoeba Ondina Anabo.'

'Who?'

'King Cheng's ambassador. Consul Anabo speaks on his behalf, and is obeyed as if she were King Cheng himself.'

'The Ringmaster. The Guildmaster. Consul Anabo.' Fyn ticked the names off on his fingers. 'Who's the fourth?'

'The financier for all of Innistiul's operations in Greater Luqura – Matron Marchioness Tiana Rocas.'

'Rocas? You mean ...?'

'My mother.'

'Odar's balls. That's ... complicated.' He paused to think. 'Why does the Slavers Guild use your family instead of a traditional banking house?'

'Because Luquran banking houses charge outrageous fees for everything: loans, deposits, promissory notes, currency exchanges. They take a bite out of it all – every coin and clip – so the surest way to conserve your coin is to find a foreign banking house licensed to operate in Greater Luqura. To be approved for that, your family must have mostly foreign blood and control a legitimate business that operates beyond the Darite Empire; they must also be one of the peerage *and* they must have lived in Luqura for the last two hundred years or more.'

'That's ... oddly specific.'

'It's intentional. Many noble families fulfil the first or second condition, but fulfilling the first and *third* is difficult since they tend to exclude each other. There aren't many old nobility in Luqura with mostly foreign blood – and only one has been here for more than two hundred years.'

'The Noble House of Rocas.'

Sodja nodded. 'We're the only foreign banking house allowed to operate in Greater Luqura, so King Cheng and the Slavers Guild deal directly with my mother. Tiana gives them the rates they want, and they give her heaps of gold. And that's not even the best part.'

'Enlighten me.'

'The Rocas family has the full political backing of the Slavers Guild—'

'Which is also foreign?'

'No. The Innistiulmen are foreigners, but the Guild itself is under the protection of the peerage.'

'And since the Rocas family is one of the old nobility, they're both helping each other out.' He paused. 'Wait a second. I think I figured out what you were going to say. King Lenka is sick, right?'

'He's been sick for ages – but yes.'

'And he doesn't have an heir, which means the nobility expect one of them to be handed the throne – only most don't realise it's already been bought.'

'And the ones that *have* realised ...'

'Are lining up to kiss your mother's arse.'

'Exactly. That's why I targeted Janak. Losing his household along with the Rod of Compulsion sets them back on their heels.'

'In what way?'

'Janak was supposed to consolidate influence in the eastern half of Greater Luqura – in remote places like Corlin or Hentingsfort, most of which stay out of capital city politics – but then your village got tangled up in things ... and I guess Janak had some plans of his own.' She shook her head. 'It's a bit of a mess, I admit, but killing Janak and stealing the rod won't stop my mother and her allies from making a run at the throne – it only slows them down.' Sodja's expression softened. 'So, what's your issue with the Guild?'

Fyn snorted. 'My issue is everyone in Luqura is pissing their pants trying to please these bastards. Apparently I can't lift a finger to feed myself without getting their say-so.' He lifted an eyebrow. 'That sound about right to you?'

'More or less.'

'Well I don't do things that way. I'm forming a gang to start peeling off some of that money and power for myself.'

A look of withering sympathy spread across Sodja's face, its depths equally profound and patronising. 'Did you not hear a word I've been saying?' She jumped the gap to his rooftop, her gaze pinning him in place as she stalked towards him. 'The Guild has ingratiated itself into *every aspect* of life here in the capital, and it's reaching for other parts of the kingdom. The nobles are dependent on slave labour. The citizens rely on the gladiatorial bouts for their entertainment. The city guards require the Guild kickbacks to supplement their poor pay and stop them turning into bandits. Piece by piece, they've been cutting away Luqura's identity and turning it into a mirror image of Innistiul. The only thing left to do is install a new monarch when Lenka dies. You can't fight them like that. If you try, the Watchers will take you down.'

'I've heard of the Watchers. Who are they – *what* are they?'

'They're the eyes of the Guild – and they can be anyone. They don't typically wear uniforms and they could as easily pose as a noble at court as a beggar on the street. Some of them are from Innistiul. Some are local. Some are ... something else.'

'Like Saltair?'

Sodja nodded. 'He's a mercenary with several employers – including King Cheng, my mother and the Guild – who use him to punish anyone who crosses them.'

'I suppose that makes sense.' He chewed his lip. 'So, if I'm going to fight the Guild, it would make sense to take out this lizardman, right?'

'Probably.'

'And he must have some kind of hideout – somewhere to sleep, where he stashes all that mercenary money?'

'A lot of that money is tied up in the banking house ... but yes. I'm sure he has a place, and plenty of cash stored there.'

'And would you know where this place is?'

'I have some guesses ... some good ones, I think.'

'Perfect. Welcome to the crew.'

Sodja snorted. 'First of all, *you* should be the one asking to join *my* crew. Second, I'm not *looking* for a crew – neither to lead one nor to join one.'

'Why not? You're clearly at odds with your family, and they're sending a murdering lizardman to hunt you down. The same lizardman who's been hunting me and my friends. That sounds like an excellent reason to team up.'

Sodja's grey eyes sparkled and she stepped closer. 'An alliance of convenience?'

'Why not?'

'You're sure there's no other reason you want my help?'

Fyn smiled, his heart thudding in his chest. 'Could be a few other reasons.'

'Such as?' She licked her lips, teasing him.

Fyn closed the distance between them – and something poked him in the stomach. He looked down and saw a knife pressed to his ribs. 'Ooh. Now that's not nice.'

'I never said I was nice.'

He leaned down and kissed her anyway, the tip of the knife sliding through his shirt and nicking his belly. She bit his lip and he tasted blood, but she didn't slide the knife in any deeper and she didn't break the kiss.

'I'm not nice either,' he whispered into her ear, 'but sometimes you gotta take your chances.'

'Yeah,' she breathed, trying to find her words. 'I guess so.'

'We gotta find a room.'

Sodja stepped back, blinking. 'What, now?'

'Some place private – big enough for six or seven people.'

'I don't ...' She stopped, her hand tightening around the knife. 'Ah. You want me to find a place for your gang to meet. I thought ... never mind.'

Fyn smiled, teeth flashing. 'I *told* you I wasn't nice.'

Chapter Forty-One

'You're insane.' Neldon stood up, head shaking, hands wringing. 'You want to track Saltair to his hideout ... and *kill* him? That's insane!'

'Why?' Fyn protested. 'How is that any less sane than giving away three-quarters of your take to the Guild each week? How is it any different to what you five have been doing since you started preying on the Ashes?'

The seven of them were standing in a derelict building that used to be a bakery – not very defensible, but suitable for a meeting of their size. Fyn had chosen the location because it was on Tumbledown Street, which would be non-threatening territory for the gang members he was hoping to recruit. Sodja had then approved the place, but only after scouting to make certain no Watchers were camped nearby – and it was a good thing they weren't, because Neldon had a difficult time lowering his voice once he became agitated.

'*Why?*' The crew's medic paced the room, scoffing. 'Because he's a flaming seven-foot-tall *keokum* who can smell us coming from a mile away. Because he has poison spit, razor teeth, and can crush our skulls with his bare hands. Keos! They told me you were a smart one, but there's nothing smart about this. You're a bloody lunatic!'

'We know where he lives,' Fyn said, unfazed by Neldon's diatribe. 'We know how often he goes there, and we know how secure it is. He doesn't have any guards. We can take him while he's sleeping. Maybe poison his food and water before he arrives, then finish the job when he takes ill.'

'Aren't you listening to me? He's a *keokum*, you idiot. He doesn't need to sleep. Poisons can't kill him – hells, his body *makes* poison. We can't take him!'

'You're scared.' Sodja said from her place in the shadows. 'It's okay to be scared – but you don't know what you're talking about. You're describing a legend – a fantasy, a myth. Saltair is a monster, not a god.'

'*He's a broken piece of the Hand of Keos,*' Neldon replied, head still shaking. 'He's the closest thing to a god you'll ever see made flesh. All claws and venom and death. You track him to his lair, you'll be dead, and I won't be there to patch you up.'

'You don't know what you're talking about,' Sodja repeated, rising to her feet.

'Excuse me,' Poli said, raising her hand. 'Who is she and why is she here?'

'Yeah,' Siege said, taking a bite out of a large leathery fruit. 'Did we miss the introductions?'

'Right,' Fyn said. 'This is S—'

'Raven,' Sodja cut him off. 'You can call me Raven – and I've worked with Saltair before. I know he can be taken out because we've done jobs together, fought together. I've seen him get hurt. Seen him *bleed*. He's mortal like the rest of us – and I can take you to his lair.'

The rest of the crew fell silent, considering. Even Neldon seemed to be weighing her words.

'You said he could regrow his limbs,' Way said, arranging a puzzle of wooden tiles stacked in front of him. 'How long does that take?'

Fyn tried to remember what Annev had said. 'It took them about an hour to grow back, after my last crew cut off his arm and his tail.'

'And what happened to them?' Neldon asked. 'Did Saltair kill them?'

'No, they all survived, but they took off for Quiri. Decided Luqura wasn't for them.'

Way grunted. 'If it takes us more than an hour to try killing Saltair – well, then we're probably dead anyway.' He pointed to

Sodja. 'And you think we can trap him in his hole? That all seven of us can work in there after we take it over?'

'It's not a hole. People assume he's got some cave he lives in – something properly monstrous – but it's just the basement of a burned-out tenement. He's got a few floors to himself and tunnels that connect to other buildings in the Ash Quarter. Most of them are caved in, but he keeps a few open so he can come and go as he pleases.'

'So,' Fyn picked up the narrative, 'we can wait till he's inside the lair and then block the other tunnel entrances. He'll be trapped, with no high ground or open spaces for running or jumping. In the tunnels, his height and size will even be a disadvantage to him.'

'Do we really need to fight him then?' Siege asked. 'I mean, poison might not work, but couldn't we just ... starve him out or something?'

'I'm fairly certain he's got food there,' Sodja said, 'and he's definitely got access to water. It'd be a long wait, and we'd have to watch every tunnel to make sure Saltair didn't escape. Too risky.'

'It's a good idea, though,' Fyn said, pointing at Siege. 'We talked about the options and we think the best solution is to seal the tunnels and then smoke him out.'

'Smoke?' Siege said. 'You mean light a fire and ... just sit back and wait?'

'More or less.'

'Hold up,' Quinn spoke for the first time. 'It's not that easy. You can't just blow smoke down a hole.'

'Why not?' Siege asked, taking another bite of his fruit.

'Because smoke *rises*, you idiot. You'd have to get underneath him – find a tunnel beneath his lair and let the smoke drift up from there – and that means you'd need to leave at least one entrance open so that the smoke has somewhere to go.'

'Correct,' Fyn said, nodding at the dark-haired young woman. Now that they were in the same room, Fyn saw how different she and Sodja looked. Still similar – both had pale skin, dark hair, and a spare, dangerous frame – but the similarities stopped there.

'We'll actually want to open two tunnel entrances,' Sodja said, taking up a charred stick of wood. She tested it on the nearest wall then began sketching the plan she and Fyn had discussed. 'We seal everything off except for the upper and lower tunnels – the front and back entrances. We light the fire in the lower tunnel, and let the smoke be drawn into Saltair's lair.'

'Like a smokestack,' Siege said, perking up. 'Or a chimney flue.'

'Exactly. Once the team at the upper entrance smells smoke, they can seal their end and trap Saltair inside. Once the smoke is thick enough, the team at the bottom can seal their tunnel and wait for Saltair to suffocate.' She looked around at the rest of the crew. 'That's it.'

'How many tunnels are there?' Way asked, still busy with his wooden tiles.

'Seven,' Sodja answered, drawing a second sketch on the wall. 'Four are already blocked from Saltair's side, so we'll need to make sure they're doubly sealed on our end. The other three are more or less as I described. A front entrance descending from the surface, a back entrance that connects to the Undercity and an emergency exit.'

'Where's that?' Way asked.

'It lets out into the North Tocra. Damn near impossible to get into Saltair's lair that way, given the way the current flows, but it makes for a quick escape if you can hold your breath long enough to pop out the other side.'

'And how exactly do you plan to seal these tunnels?' Neldon asked, his tone still sceptical. 'We're not engineers. If you try to collapse the tunnels, you might bury us all – or drown us.'

'We'll do it the same way you would build any wall – brick by brick.' Fyn grabbed a second charcoal stick and began shading in the exits Sodja had sketched. 'We'll carry stones down to the tunnels and use cement to seal them up. The first four tunnels will be easy because we can take our time.'

'What about the other three?'

'We'll use a cave-in for the upper level. Gravity will be on our side there, and we can stay above the tunnel when it collapses. The lower level will be blocked by a blazing fire filling the length of the tunnel, and we can coat it in tar and other flammable materials. We figure Saltair isn't likely to try to exit that way, but if he does, he'll be slow, choking on toxic fumes, and half-burned. If he runs that way, we can finish him off real quick.'

'What about the river?' Quinn asked. 'What's to stop him from just swimming away?'

Fyn looked at Siege and Poli. 'Do you two know how to weave a fishing net?'

Poli smiled. 'I do – but don't trust Siege to make one alone. He'll foul it up.'

'Not true!' the large man protested. 'Well … it *is* true, but it's impolite to say it.'

'Great,' Fyn said. 'You can help Poli. We're going to get some metal chains and some cables, and then you're going to weave a net heavy enough to trap a lizardman. If we don't drown him or burn him, we'll catch him and cut off his head.'

Poli exchanged a wicked look with Siege. 'I think we can manage that.'

'Good. While you're making the net, the rest of us will get to work sealing tunnels.'

'Hold on,' Neldon said, raising a hand to object. 'Let's say this crazy plan works out just like you say. Let's say we kill Saltair and take his hideout – and let's go a step further and assume the place is still liveable. What then?'

'Then we'll have a base of operations that the Slavers Guild doesn't control, plus Saltair's funds. We'll be rich, protected, and well hidden.'

Neldon still looked unconvinced, but Siege slapped the dour doctor on the back. 'You see, Ned? I *told* you he was smart!'

'They'll find us,' Neldon protested, shaking off his friend's hand. 'The Watchers *will* find us. Even if we get away with killing Saltair and taking over his lair, the Guild will start looking for us – they'll send their Prime Watchers if they have to – and when they find us, that'll be it. The fish will feed on our bones and life will go on like normal for everyone else.'

'Always the pessimist,' Siege clucked, wrapping a beefy arm around the scholar-doctor. 'You gotta take some chances, Ned, else we'll be paying dues to the Guild when we're fifty.'

'I *am* fifty.'

'My point exactly!'

Neldon took a deep breath. 'I'm certain I'm going to regret this,' he said, head shaking, 'but I guess you can count me in.'

'Good,' Fyn said, tapping the drawing on the wall. 'Then let's start building some walls and weaving some nets. We've got a lizardman to catch.'

Chapter Forty-Two

Myjun stood on the precipice and stared into a vortex of chaos. Below her, she watched a sea of shadows act out an endless play of life and death, murder and mayhem, sex and seduction. Its players were primarily men and women, but she also saw children and animals, monsters and other sentient beings for which she had no name.

If ever hell had a gate, this was it.

'This is what people *dream* of? This rape and murder and violence?'

'Yes. You see now why I called it a poison.'

Myjun shook with an emotion she had not felt since putting on her mask. Shame? Disgust? Embarrassment? Such feelings seemed foreign to her now, as if all her previous emotions had been funnelled into her hatred – and perhaps it had. Her stomach tightened into a knot and she felt as though she would be sick.

'This is not humanity. This is not life.'

'Correct. This is a *shadow* of life. They are not real – they are only thoughts and dreams, impressions and memories – though the ones that are capable of leaving the Dream World are more akin to nightmares. Only dreams that focus on life and death can bridge the gap between the Dream World and the Shadowrealm, where the eidola are drawn to their potency.'

'You mean, they feed on our nightmares ... on our fears and emotion.'

Oyru nodded. 'Not just nightmares. Secret desires, forbidden impulses, dark thoughts and darker deeds. They are drawn here from the World of Dreams and the eidola are drawn to *them*. They seek life so desperately they will suck the marrow from the worst parts of it. Fill themselves with pain, and re-enact nightmares, to taste a fraction of the life they've been denied.'

'And we have come here to kill them.'

'Yes.'

'Good. How?'

Oyru pointed into the chasm. 'You see how they are formed from the nether, yet they kill one another with teeth, talon and claw?' Oyru raised a hand and a spear of black vapour coalesced in his palm, its shape solidifying into a cruel weapon with an obsidian edge, the black blade nearly half as long as the shaft. 'This qiang is nether, too,' Oyru continued, 'as is my armour.' He tapped his shadow armour with the tip of his spear. 'They are shards of the void. Shadows made into substance. Like the eidola, they can rend and pierce and cut. They are smoke and steel, void and vapour. They are not real, but they are echoes of the real world – and *these* shadows have bite. In this world, the nether blades drink the life of any living thing they touch – and they are as sharp as any blade forged in the physical world.' To illustrate his point, Oyru dragged the tip of his qiang across his chest, raking a deep gouge in his void plate.

Myjun nodded. 'How do I fight them then? Can you give me one of your blades?'

'No. I can in the physical world, at the cost of my somnumbra. Here, your constructs belong to you and you alone. They must come from your own mind – or, perhaps in your case, your soul. Try summoning your soulfire blades. They may not work here, or they may work differently ... *if* you can conjure them.'

Myjun shifted her focus away from the scampering eidolons and turned it inward: her anger was still there, as was her pain, but neither emotion demanded her full concentration as they once had. She wrapped herself in those emotions now though, embracing them and then channelling them into her hands.

A dim light flickered in her palms ... then died.

Oyru shook his head. 'You are a Soulscreamer, tabibito. The key to unlocking your power lies within your spirit and your *voice*.'

409

'Go to hell.'

'Is this not close enough?' Oyru asked, gesturing at the pit.

Myjun looked at the monsters circling the ever-widening crevasse. The pit was vaguely ovular with slopes that descended like terraces into the darkness. The ground immediately surrounding the pit was likewise raised so that from a distance it would be impossible to spot the dark scar in the otherwise grey landscape. Still, there were signs: the grey eidolons flitting in and around the pit, the wordless screams that seemed to echo from it. Oyru had led them there straight as an arrow, unerring and undeviating, as if he himself had been drawn there ... just like the eidolons. Myjun stared at the roiling mass of shades and shadows, their inhumanity uncomfortably familiar. She felt her body tremble; her chest shook, and then she opened her mouth in a wail that channelled all of her frustration and anger, her pain and disgust. Something flickered in front of her face – a spark or a flame – and then it was gone.

'Interesting,' Oyru said. 'You have the potential for Lightslinging too, it seems, though your ability to shape the light will be limited here.' He looked down into the pit then back at Myjun. 'The eidola do not have souls for you to ride, so you cannot augment your powers by feeding on their emotions here. You must channel your magic without the benefit of soulriding.'

'How?' Myjun asked, the question bitter on her tongue.

'The same way you fought the blood drake.'

Myjun thought back a lifetime ago to her battle with the draken in the Vosgar. She had been weaponless and injured, but when it had clamped its jaws around her – when her life had been all but forfeit – she had found her power and channelled it into her blades.

'It nearly killed me,' she said, her voice low and ragged, remembering the pain. 'I was half dead. I hurt so badly ... felt so desperate – and I was so *angry*. Angry at myself – angry at life, at being unable to punish my father for all that he took from me.'

'Your father?'

Myjun started at her error. 'Annev! I meant *Annev*. He killed my father. He lied to me ... *embarrassed* me and destroyed my life.'

Oyru nodded. 'Your battle with the draken brought out your

desperation: panic, fear, pain. These are your weapons. Above all, though, you must use your pain. Every strike against you makes you stronger. Every blow makes you bolder. Accept it. Embrace it. You struggle to summon your soulfire blades outside the dangers of the pit. To *kindle* your flame, you must hurl yourself into the fire.'

Myjun didn't hesitate this time. At Oyru's suggestion, she sprang over the ledge, heedlessly throwing herself into the violent whirl of grey and black. Something snatched at her and she spun in the air, glancing off a stone as the world tilted around her. When she finally crashed to a halt, it was to discover she had fallen fully halfway down the slopes of the terraced pit. Myjun's eyes swivelled between the gnashing, clashing maw of eidolons at the bottom level and the thousands of other shades that now blocked her return to the uppermost ledge.

'I can't summon my blades!' she screamed, her fingers sparking with light.

'Improvise!' The assassin gestured at the eidolons beginning to surround her, their lithe shapes capering just beyond her meagre soulfire. Myjun tried to shape the flame into blades, to condense it into something that would cut and maim and kill. Instead the flame sputtered, growing brighter for an instant and then dimming.

One of the nearest eidolons – a strange, shambling thing with impossibly long arms, a flat face and night-black eyes – reached for her. Myjun held up the flame, intending to menace it, but instead the eidolon's slender fingers snatched at the fire. The shadow demon immediately cried out in pain, its fingers withdrawing, but then it swung for her a second later, its sharp claws digging into Myjun's wrist. She shrieked, jumping back, and her flame brightened once more. Sensing her weakness, and being drawn to the light, the other eidolons began to swarm.

'You're soulfire will attract more of them,' Oyru shouted cheerfully from the ledge above. 'And so will your blood!'

'HELP ME!' Myjun screamed as more teeth and nails bit into her flesh. Grey hands and translucent limbs wrapped tight around her chest and neck. Choking her. Killing her.

'Help yourself,' Oyru said, standing pitiless on the precipice. 'Use that spark. Find your flame.'

Myjun screamed as an eidolon's mouth clamped down on her mask, its teeth grinding against the golden metal that protected her face. Glittering shadows swirled around her like pale stars in a drunken sky and she felt her hot blood dripping from a dozen cuts. Another monster tore into her thigh, its fingers prising open her flesh.

More teeth. More claws. More panic. She was going to die. She was going to *die*.

A primal scream tore from Myjun's throat and a bright cone of fire crashed into the eidolon atop her. The demon flew back, the wreckage of its face streaming smoke and mist. Myjun's fingers tightened, her bloody hands clutching at the creatures around her. She flexed, screaming, and a bright burst of soulfire ignited in her hands, the white flames collapsing the crumbling jaws of her demonic attacker. When she closed her fingers, she felt the now-familiar soulfire blades coalesce in her palms. Acting on instinct, she slid and slashed, twisted and cut. The white knives slid into the shadows, separating them, burning them ... consuming them. Distantly, Myjun felt her mask trying to heal her, but the injuries she sustained were outmatching the speed of her magic.

Myjun didn't care. She peeled the eidolons from her, stabbing and cutting, slashing and spinning. As she killed, the eidolons slumped into shadowy slag, their pieces disintegrating into smoke, silt and ash.

An enormous eidolon with the body of a spider and the face of a little girl jumped atop Myjun, its legs pinning her hands and arms to her body. Shadowy webs spun about her like silk and steel, trapping her, restraining her. The spider-girl blinked at her with eidolon eyes – cold, black and empty – and then her mouth opened to reveal two long fangs dripping with venom. It tried to bite her but Myjun screamed into its face, melting its spectral flesh into grey gristle and bubbling tar. She fell from the spider's grasp and tumbled down another ledge, caromed off a shadowy boulder that sprouted arms and tried to grapple her, and fell past it. She toppled down two more terraces and then rolled to the edge of a third, her arms still bound tight to her sides.

She couldn't move – she could barely breathe – yet still more demons were surrounding her. She sensed that she had reached the bottom of the pit, or was near enough to it that she couldn't see beyond the swarming mass of black and grey bodies. She was battered and bruised, bloodied and broken. She tried to angle her soulblades to cut the shadow silk binding her arms to her body, but it was impossible. She screamed again, a beam of light sweeping from her mouth, obliterating two more of the rampaging monsters.

But it was too much. There were too many and she couldn't free herself. An armoured pincer clamped down around her throat, crushing her windpipe. The white blades in her hands sparked then guttered out. More monsters rushed in.

A pair of boots landed silently beside her, their shape and dimension seeming otherworldy in the sea of flat greys and muted blacks. An obsidian spear slashed in front of her face and the heavy pincers fell away in a haze of sooty bone and smoking chitin. The qiang flashed again and she felt the black blade slice across her ribs, its edge parting the cords that had bound her. Oyru's arm slid beneath her, then hoisted her to her feet and in the same moment Myjun wanted to both embrace her companion and stab him in the face.

'Summon your blades,' the Shadow Reborn commanded, his qiang already biting into the neck of another eidolon.

Myjun tried. She shouted into the enveloping darkness, imagining another blast that would throw back the horde of shadows – but her broken voice died in the dark. Black tentacles emerged as if from nowhere and wrapped around the assassin's wrists and ankles. An enormous creature with bat wings and the armoured body of a bear snapped its fist across Oyru's spear and the weapon broke into pieces. Its fist slammed into Oyru's face and black smoke and red gore leaked from the Shadow Reborn's crushed eye socket.

Blood. Actual blood. It seemed Oyru wasn't invincible after all.

More hands grappled Myjun's waist and arms – some human, some feral, all demonic. Too many, too strong to fight. She saw Oyru fall beneath the black wings of his attacker and then she stood alone at the centre of the pit, the shadowy forces of hell marshalled against her.

Myjun did not scream.

She did not move.

She focused on the blood dripping from her body, felt its warmth as it pulsed from her heart and flowed into her bleeding limbs. She felt the spark within her, the fiery aura that consumed her soul – that *was* her soul. She held the fire close until it filled her, until something *bloomed* within her.

She did not shriek. She did not shout. Instead, Myjun gave a single whimper – a muted cry of failure, longing and loss ... and defiance. At its core, at the centre of her frustration and pain, was a thread that refused to be broken. A knowledge that, though she may die here, she had not resigned herself to her fate. She would let her fire consume her before she gave up.

As if in response, Myjun lit up from within. A flash of white lightning sprang from her chest, its forked tongue igniting her blood and driving into the hundred hands that held her. Another fork and the tongues of white fire multiplied, electrifying the grey eidolons. The monsters holding her exploded. Their gaunt faces contorted, their inhuman figures twisting, writhing and then fluttering away into grey-black ash. Lightning forked again, its arcs flashing out in a ripple around her, touching each level of the terraced pit, consuming the next circle of eidolons. The lightfire chained and arced, with her at the heart of it, and the eidolons around her screamed ... and were silenced.

Ash and vapour hovered in the air and the grey ring of Dorchnok's Eye began to rise above the horizon. Myjun slumped to the floor of the pit, her energy spent, and laid her head against Oyru's plated torso. As the antumbra dawned, she slipped into a meditative trance, ignoring her wounds and focusing on the regular rise and fall of the Shadow Reborn's chest.

Chapter Forty-Three

Dionach Honeycutt stroked the short beard that traced his jawline as he studied Annev from behind a pair of round spectacles. 'The water glyphs aren't meant to be permanent,' he said, eyes shifting between Annev's face and the gloved Hand of Keos. 'They are a point of focus – a tool to help direct one's will – but for you, they may be a source of distraction.'

'A distraction?' Annev shifted in the chair opposite Honeycutt. They sat in the man's private chambers, his collection of old books and scrolls covering three of the room's four walls. 'I thought the glyphs were an essential part of the spell.'

'Not so! It is a helpful tool for focusing one's will and invoking Odar's blessing – but it is not essential. Haven't you seen the others glyph-speak without drawing runes?'

Annev realised he had. Just last week, during his failed lesson with Leskal, he had seen the caste leader erase his glyph before compressing skywater into air, water and ice. Leskal hadn't stopped to draw a new glyph, and Annev had been too disappointed by his own failures to wonder how Leskal had managed it.

'You know more Old Darite than half our current Dionachs,' Honeycutt continued, still stroking his chin, 'but that knowledge hasn't aided you. More likely it's *hindered* you.'

Annev stared at the lines of water he had so carefully painted on the stone table sitting between them, the arcane symbol for air still visible. 'So this isn't important – I don't *need* to draw the symbols.'

'Most Dionachs discover their abilities well before they learn a full range of glyphs. We start with a general glyph, relying on our intent to shape a specific outcome until we learn new, precise runes to enhance our magic – which can be further honed by our intent. But you are a special case.' He held up a finger. 'You've got a head full of Old Darite already, but without having strengthened your mind and will, it distracts you – it's weighing you down instead of lifting you up.' Honeycutt erased the glyph, leaving the table's surface scattered with beads of water. 'Just concentrate on what you want. Imagine the water separating and expanding. Imagine it filling the room with mist or vapour. Can you visualise that?'

'I think so.' Annev hesitated. 'What do I do now, though? Do I still speak the glyph?'

This time it was Honeycutt's turn to pause. 'Not just yet. Keep concentrating on what you want – but focus your mind and your thoughts into something small and precise. Sharp as a needle. A needle of focus, pushing your *quaire* into this room, imposing your will on the world.'

Annev kept the idea tight in his mind. He ignored the words of power and the glyphs and imagined his will as an extension of himself, the way he'd first succeeded in using Mercy to cut the corner of Sodar's kitchen table. He focused that will, then carefully pushed it into the moisture glistening on the wooden tabletop. Annev felt a deep *boom* in his chest and the room shuddered, making Honeycutt jump from his chair.

'Gods be damned,' the Dionach swore, brushing his robes and patting his chest. 'What did you *do*?'

'I don't know!' Annev said, raising his hands in defence. 'I thought *you* would tell *me*.'

Honeycutt ran a finger through the water still glistening on the table. 'Nothing has changed here in any discernible way.' He rubbed his mouth and cheeks with one hand. 'It felt like ...' He looked from the table to Annev's face. 'What were you imagining?'

Annev shrugged. 'You said to make the skywater inside the room expand – so I imagined I was standing in the centre of the room, trapped inside a bubble. I was pushing on its walls. Only they resisted me. Every time I pushed, they pushed back. No matter how hard I tried, they stayed in place.'

'What changed?'

Annev thought about it. 'I don't know. I was still pushing when the bubble just ... popped. Everything rushed out – the air, the strength I was pushing against the wall – it all just ... went. That's when the room shook.' Annev looked up at Honeycutt. 'Did I glyph-speak?'

'Honestly ... I don't know. What you say sounds more like will-speaking, which is technically a branch of glyph-speaking.' He paused. 'You say your strength leaked out of you?'

'Sort of. I was pushing on the bubble with all this pent-up force. When it popped, it was like someone pulled the rug out from under me. All that energy I was pushing outward just ... left.'

'Do you feel spent? Tired or thirsty?'

Annev considered it. 'No. I felt disorientated and a little frustrated ... but it wasn't like you or the masters described it. I don't feel like I've lost something – my *quaire* feels the same.'

Honeycutt grunted. 'What *did* it feel like?'

Annev answered slowly. 'It was like ... turning a key in a lock. Something shifted – something changed – and then it suddenly clicked into place.' The feeling reminded Annev of using artifacts in the past – and of his current attempts to use the Rod of Artificing – but as he didn't want to reveal that secret to the Dionach, Annev refocused his attention on the moment.

'Do *you* feel changed?'

Annev thought about it. He touched his chest, flexed his hands and arms, looked around the room and slowly nodded. 'Do you know that feeling after you've been sparring, when your muscles are tired but they also feel stronger?'

'Yes.'

'It's like that,' Annev said, 'but more subtle. I don't hurt, but something feels ... different.'

'Good or bad?'

'Good, I think.'

The Dionach grunted again. 'Annev, what you've just described is very unusual – very unlike glyph-speaking, or will-speaking for that matter.'

'Different ... in a good way?'

'To be honest, I'm not sure. If it's related to that Terran prosthetic, it might not be – but it also sounds like ...'

'Like what?'

Honeycutt ran his tongue along his teeth. 'You know, I've studied Terran magic quite a bit – it's not something most Dionachs will admit to, so I wouldn't go sharing it with the rest of the brothers.' He smiled. 'Anyway, *your* talent ... it feels a bit Terran, which doesn't make sense since you have no Terran blood.'

'So, what does that mean?'

'Annev ... you could be a keokum. I don't mean you are spawned from the Hand of Keos, but the same magical rules might apply.'

Annev stood up from the table. 'I'm *not* keokum.'

The Dionach raised both his hands in defence. 'And I didn't say you are – not *exactly*. What I meant was: your magic doesn't seem to function in the orthodox manner, and that distinction *technically* makes you keokum. It's not a bad thing either. It just means the typical rules for magic might not apply to you.' He frowned. 'It's probably wise not to mention this to the other Dionachs – not yet anyway. Leskal and Holyoak aren't as open-minded as me – or McClanahan, or even Arch-Dionach Reeve.' He tutted. 'Probably best not to tell your friends, either. Novice Therin isn't good at keeping secrets, and I wouldn't want this one to get out.'

Annev nodded, though he wasn't sure he agreed. As a rule, he didn't like keeping secrets – from his experience at the Academy, the longer he kept one, the harder it became to tell the truth – but he was already hiding his experiments with the Rod of Artificing. Compared to that, this second secret was insignificant. Harmless. It wouldn't help anyone if they thought he was some kind of keokum, so it made sense to keep quiet about it. Likewise, Annev knew the Dionachs would get the wrong idea if they discovered he was trying to acquire their blood, so all around discretion seemed the best course of action.

'I won't tell anyone what happened ... but I need you to teach me more about it. Help me understand what I did.'

'Not much to tell. You imposed your will on the world, Annev – but not using *quaire*. In fact ... I think you used *t'rasang*.' Annev opened his mouth to protest, but the caste leader cut him off. 'I have a lunch appointment with Dionach Leskal now, but I'd like to continue our discussion tomorrow, if that's all right.'

'Sure,' Annev said, swallowing his disappointment as Honeycutt rose to his feet. 'Would you like me to walk with you?'

'No, I'm supposed to meet him in his quarters. You run on ahead, though. Get yourself something to eat.'

Annev bowed, then made his way down to the kitchens, mulling over Honeycutt's words. Once there, he absentmindedly collected a bowl of soup from Dionach Webb, an older Shieldbearer whose physique was as imposing as Dionach Leskal's. He then went to eat in the large dining hall and discovered Therin and Titus were already there, the latter waving him over.

'It's not as good as Master Sage's, is it?' Titus said, dipping his bread into the tepid stew.

'Or as good as Sodar's pottage,' Annev agreed, poking at something grey floating in his broth.

'But,' Therin said, chewing, 'it *is* food, and we didn't have to pay for it – we don't even have to wash the dishes afterwards! That's an improvement over the Academy.'

'Who washes, then?'

'Dionach Webb,' Titus said. 'He does some glyph-speaking and magics the dishes clean with skywater.'

Annev took another bite of the grey mush, chewed and decided the vegetable was *not* a potato – it might not even have been a vegetable. 'How are your classes going?' he asked.

'Great,' Titus said, finally smiling. 'I've memorised all the basic glyphs and command words, and the caste leaders all say I'm doing really well managing my *quaire*.'

Therin laughed at this. 'That's just their way of saying you're not very powerful. You go too slow – you're too *careful*.' Therin tapped his chest with his thumb. 'I made the water float today – not just a drop either, but a whole cup of it!'

'How?' Annev asked, thinking about his class with Honeycutt. 'How do you keep the pressure focused enough to make anything float, let alone water?'

'It's pretty difficult,' Therin said, chewing on something tough. 'Leskal can do it almost indefinitely, but that's because Shield-bearers can condense the skywater into whatever they want and it'll hold its shape till they release it. As a Breathbreaker, I'm constantly expanding the skywater, so I have to keep the pressure up the whole time – kind of like holding a saucer filled with water above my head and trying not to spill a drop.'

Annev meditated on the poor analogy, guessing at Therin's meaning and wondering if there was a better solution. 'What if you pressed the water against something else – like a wall?'

Therin picked at his teeth, thinking. 'That'd be easier, but I'd also spatter the water everywhere.'

'And if you tried to shape the way the air expands – like a bowl or a cone … instead of a plate? By pushing air in two directions, you could contain the water without letting it spray everywhere.'

'Yeah,' Therin said, nodding, 'that's a good idea, actually.' He took a bite of his bread, crusty flakes spewing from his mouth as he spoke. 'I'm surprised you haven't made any progress with the Dionachs, Annev. You catch on to the principles really quick.'

'And you already know the words and symbols,' Titus added. 'I've been studying them every night so I can start mindwalking with Brother Holyoak.'

'I thought you were already mindwalking?'

'No, just mind-reading. Mindwalking is a lot harder – more dangerous, too. Dionach Holyoak says it's like opening the door to someone's mind and walking inside. You can't force people to do things like a Stormcaller might, but you can look at their old memories – even ones they might have forgotten.' Titus glanced around the room then leaned closer. 'Brother Honeycutt says you can even take those memories with you when you leave.'

Annev glanced at Therin, who seemed equally aghast. '*Take* them? Take them how?'

Titus made a sweeping motion like he was plucking something out of the air and putting it in his pocket.

'Wait,' Annev said, holding up a finger. 'You could take someone's memories and make them your own? You could make them forget something?'

Titus shrugged, his eyes still darting around the room. 'I *think* so? That's the way Dionach Holyoak described it – it all has to do with manipulating *quaire*.'

Annev shuddered. 'Why would anyone do that – and why would he *tell* you about it?'

'He said it might come up during my Test of Ascendancy, for journeyman status.'

'They're going to *promote* you?' Annev said, his head spinning. 'But ... we've only been here a week!'

Therin grimaced, avoiding Annev's gaze. 'They're going to test me, too. We only found out yesterday evening.'

'So you won't be novices any more – you'll be journeymen?'

Titus nodded.

'But ... your *magic*,' Annev spluttered. 'It's not developed enough yet. You only just started!'

'Yeah,' Therin admitted, 'but it doesn't take that long to memorise a few glyphs and words, and we've already learned the basics. Besides, if we don't pass the test, they can just keep us as novices for another month. Then we can test again.'

'One month,' Annev repeated, his head shaking. 'And we've only been here a week.' He looked up at his friends, suddenly suspicious. 'Have they said what you need to do to become a Dionach?'

'Well ...' Titus said, hesitating.

'Yep,' Therin said, answering for both of them. He slurped a mouthful of soup then grimaced and dropped his spoon. 'Titus needs to do some mindwalking, that's the gist of it. And I need to demonstrate all four breathbreaking skills. If I can master one of those and just demonstrate another two, I'll become a journeyman.'

'What are the four skills you have to learn?'

'Water-to-mist,' Therin said, counting them off, 'sound bubbles, air bubbles, and void bubbles.' He smiled. '*Lots* of bubbles. They're not always round, but they're still called bubbles.'

'What's a void bubble?' Titus asked.

'A sphere with no air or water inside it.'

'Isn't that just a sound bubble?'

'No, because you can still hear *inside* a sound bubble – and you can breathe. A void bubble doesn't have *any* air, though, so it's completely silent inside and out. Also, once you've pushed all the skywater out, things stick to each other.'

'They stick?'

'Yeah! Honeycutt demonstrated for me with a block of wood. When he wrapped it in a sound bubble and dropped it on the floor, I didn't hear a thing – but when he held it against the wall and made a void bubble, it just ... stuck there. Like it was floating, except I couldn't budge it.' He grinned. 'I've been practising that one, but I can't get it quite right. Something about the shape of the bubble.'

'And you learned all of that ... in a week?'

'Yep. I get the impression me and Titus are something special. Brother Zayas said he's been a journeyman Stormcaller for almost two years – and he was a novice for *five* years before that.' Therin grimaced. 'I'd go mad if I had to study glyph-speaking for that long.'

'I'm sure you'd do fine,' Titus said, placing his own bowl aside. 'We studied to be avatars for a decade and a half. A few years studying magic doesn't seem long at all.'

'So you'll both probably take your tests ... when? Three months from now? A year?'

'Two weeks. That's what Leskal said, anyway.' Therin stood up. 'I can already do three of the four Breathbreaker skills, but I still need to master at least one to become a journeyman. Void bubbles are kind of tricky, so I think I'll focus on either sound or mist.'

'You should do mist,' Titus said. 'You're getting good at that.'

'He is?' Annev looked at Therin. 'You are?'

The wiry boy grinned then dipped his finger in the discarded soup.

'Therin ...' Titus said, dragging his name out into a whisper. 'We're not supposed to do that outside of class.'

'It's fine,' Therin said, drawing a glyph on the table. 'There's no one else here, and even if there were I bet they wouldn't tell anyone.'

Titus bit his lip, fretting, but he didn't argue. Therin leaned over his soup, one hand hovering over the murky water and the other hovering over the glyph.

'*Ceò*,' he whispered, his eyes half-lidded in concentration.

As Annev watched, a thick mist began to churn up from the bowl of grey soup, its tendrils spiralling outward as it expanded to fill the space around their table. Annev's eyes widened. He could feel the vapour in the air as the fog thickened and obscured his friends on the other side of the table. He leaned backwards, his head popping out of the bubble, and saw the limits of the sphere that contained the swirling white mists. A moment later, the bubble popped and the mists dissipated.

'See,' Titus said, wiping at the moisture clinging to his nose and cheeks. 'He's good, right?' Annev nodded, too shocked to speak.

In all his years living and training with Sodar, Annev had never seen the priest do anything like what Therin had just done. Which seemed especially strange now Annev knew Sodar had been a Breathbreaker – like Therin.

What did that mean? Had Sodar kept the extent of his magic secret, even from Annev? Or was it as Reeve had said: Sodar hadn't been a very powerful Dionach, but he had commanded a wide variety of magics, perhaps including some Ilumite spell-singing? Annev didn't understand how that was possible without Ilumite blood, but then he remembered Sodar using his magic to light lamps and warm his food – which was a skill none of the Dionachs at the Enclave had shown. Annev supposed that, in his own quiet way, Sodar had been both the least and the greatest of his brethren.

As Annev pondered this, he looked up and saw a trickle of blood coming from Therin's left nostril. Annev snatched up a cloth from the table and pressed it to his friend's nose.

'What's this for?' Therin asked, holding the rag up for inspection. 'Oh ... damn it. Dried out my nose again.'

'Pushed too hard,' Titus said, tutting. 'I *told* you. We shouldn't be practising without supervision.'

'It's fine,' Therin said, swatting Annev and Titus's concerns aside. 'It's not like I didn't get nosebleeds when we were sparring at the Academy. This is better, actually. I don't have a headache to go with it.'

'Here,' Annev said, handing Therin a fresh napkin. 'I'll take care of that.' He took the bloody rag from Therin and quietly pocketed it. At the same instant, he glanced up to see Arch-Dionach Reeve duck out of the dining hall.

'Excuse me.' Annev bolted up from his chair. 'I've been trying to talk to Reeve for days and he keeps avoiding me.' Titus and Therin waved Annev off as he sprinted after the head of the Order.

'Dionach Reeve!' Annev shouted, rushing down the hall. 'Please wait! Brother Reeve!'

The Arch-Dionach reached the end of the corridor and seemed to have every intention of rounding the corner and making a run for it. Instead, Annev's magic boots sped him fast enough to catch up with the high priest and grasp his elbow. Reeve jerked to a stop and seemed surprised to have been caught.

'Brother Annev! What an ... unexpected surprise. Was there something you needed?'

'I've been trying to speak with you for days!' Annev said. 'Every time I visit your quarters, you seem to be absent; every time I find you in the halls you're rushing off for some meeting or other. I don't like being given the run around.'

'Annev,' Reeve said, sounding long-suffering, 'I'm a busy man, and running the Enclave requires a great deal of my attention. If this is about removing your hand, you should know I am still researching it, and will not attempt anything until I'm certain it will pose no danger to you or the Order.'

'And what about the danger you're all in while I'm still wearing it?'

Reeve quirked an eyebrow. 'What do you mean?'

'I mean that Jian Nikloss sacrificed himself so that I wouldn't destroy my friends and raze Luqura's Ash Quarter. I mean that two nights ago I woke up in a room full of smoke because I'd forgotten to wear my glove to bed, and the heat from my hand set the pallet on fire. I mean that every minute I'm still wearing this hand is a minute your people are in danger. We don't know how this prosthetic works – and I'm terrified I might level this entire building, burn everyone in it and destroy half of Quiri by accident.'

Reeve stared at Annev, his face ashen. 'You might have mentioned this earlier, Brother Annev. I thought these episodes ended after you left Banok – once you'd had time to adjust to your circumstances. This is ... most concerning.'

'Yes,' Annev said, practically hissing the word. 'I've tried to be patient, and I've tried to speak to you in private, but you've—'

'I've been avoiding you,' Reeve finished, harrumphing. 'No, it's fine – and it's my fault. I've had little news, though, and so I've had little to share.'

'But there has been *some* news?'

The high priest nodded. 'It mostly concerns Bron Gloir and the location of the Oracle. It seems Bron was travelling east of Luqura when he disappeared.'

Annev's eyes narrowed. 'What does this have to do with my hand?'

'It concerns the entire Order,' Reeve said, matching Annev's glare. 'It's essential that we find Bron and get the Oracle back – but it's more urgent for you.'

'Why?'

'Because I think the Oracle will speak to you. As I've said before, I think you are the Vessel mentioned in the prophecy. If the Oracle *will* talk to you, it might tell you how to remove the Hand of Keos.'

Annev studied the high priest, feeling as though Reeve were keeping something from him ... something about Bron Gloir and the Oracle.

Then again, Annev thought, if his suspicions were correct, he knew something the high priest did not: he knew Janak Harth had most likely stolen the Oracle from Bron, and he knew the lamp containing the Oracle was probably buried beneath the Academy's ruins in Chaenbalu.

As Annev considered how much to share with Reeve, the priest's eyes narrowed. 'You know something about this, don't you?'

Annev hesitated, wondering if it would be wise to hold something back or if doing so would actually hinder his own goals. Before he could speak, another Dionach entered the corridor on his way to the dining hall. Annev glanced at the man's back then cleared his throat. 'Maybe this is something we should talk about in your quarters?'

'Agreed,' Reeve said, leading the way.

Chapter Forty-Four

'I can't believe you didn't share this sooner.' Reeve paced around his small windowless study.

'To be fair, I didn't know for certain that it was the Oracle.' Annev paced the austere room too, examining Reeve's personal affects. 'Sodar never described the Oracle in detail, and Janak didn't call the lamp the Oracle until his face was mangled and he was half dead.'

'Janak must have been the Crippled Warrior. One of the five the Oracle said it would speak with.' Reeve ran his fingers through his hair, as if in denial. 'I *cannot* believe it – would never have thought it possible. Harth must have had help, if he was able to capture Bron and take the Oracle for himself – hell, *whole armies* have been unable to stop Bron!' He collapsed into a chair beside the cold hearth and looked up at Annev.

'You'll need to come with me back to Chaenbalu.'

Annev shook his head vehemently. 'I'm only *guessing* that it's still there—'

'Where else could it be?'

'And I do *not* want to go back.'

'But we need it to remove your hand! Annev, you *must* come with me. You're one of the very few still alive who can circumvent the circle of protection around Chaenbalu.'

'Titus and Therin could take you – and Fyn and Brayan. Hell, so far as I know, Brayan is still waiting for us in Banok.'

'We can collect him! You can meet him on our way south,

when we stop in Banok to search Janak Harth's palace for clues about Bron.'

'And what if Bron is dead? Have you thought of that? Also, I'm pretty sure Janak's palace was burned to the ground.'

A sly smile crept onto Reeve's face. 'I can assure you, Bron is not dead. Much as he may wish otherwise, that man is very much alive.'

'So the legends are true? About his shapeshifting and his thousand lives?'

The priest gave a dry laugh. 'If anything, the stories are too tame – though I suspect that's mostly Bron's doing. He doesn't like being talked about as if he's a monster – a demon that consumes your soul and possesses your corpse – so he's made an effort to change the stories, at least a little. Make them less haunting and more heroic.'

'Really? How?'

A faint smile tugged at the corner of Reeve's mouth. 'You've heard the Thousand Lives of Bron Gloir?'

'Of course. That's Titus's favourite story.'

'Well, Bron wrote it.'

Annev scoffed. 'No, Gerhalt Stern wrote that over two hundred years ago – along with some of the best poetry from this Age.'

Reeve's smile broadened. 'I shall pass your compliments along to Gerhalt when we see him then.'

Annev stared. 'Bron Gloir *is* Gerhalt Stern?' He shook his head in disbelief. 'Is he anyone else I should know about? Chade Thornbriar, maybe?'

Reeve's smile faded. 'What do you know of Thornbriar?'

'Odar's *balls!*' Annev swore. 'You're joking? Are they really the same person?'

Reeve made a face. 'They are *not* the same. If Bron Gloir's story is an endless tragedy, then Chade Thornbriar's is an unending joke – one that I find both tasteless and humourless.'

Annev grunted, making a mental note to find out more about this Thornbriar. 'Reeve, I told you my only reason to aid you was to remove the Hand of Keos ... but if you can't help me, perhaps I should leave before I endanger anyone.'

427

The high priest jumped to his feet. 'But that is precisely my point, Annev. I need the Oracle *before* I can help you. I need to be *certain* no harm will come to you or the Enclave before we attempt anything dangerous.'

'But that's not good enough!' Annev said, struggling not to shout. 'I don't need magic to see you want the Oracle for yourself, not to help me. Hell, you haven't even *tried* to remove the hand – none of you have.'

'It's only been a week.'

'A very *long* week, and now Titus and Therin are preparing to pass the journeymen Dionachs test? It all seems very fast – very convenient.'

'What are you suggesting? You think we're trying to bind your friends to the Order so that ... what? So you feel obligated to stay and help us?'

Annev shrugged. 'You said it. It's certainly starting to feel that way – and it certainly *looks* that way.' Reeve started to argue but Annev raised a finger. 'I'm not saying you haven't been helpful, or that the other Dionachs haven't been kind.'

'What *are* you saying?'

'That I don't like to be coerced – or feeling compelled to help you for my friends.'

'Fair enough,' Reeve said, marching towards his door. He opened it. 'I would have thought your obligations to Sodar were enough, but it seems you've already forgotten those.'

'My obligations to Sodar,' Annev growled, 'have nothing to do with you.'

'Then the Order of the Dionachs Tobar has no obligation to you either.' He nodded at the doorway. 'Good day, Brother Annev. Let me know if you decide to stay with us any longer. If you do, I can have you moved to the Enclave's lowest levels – my understanding is the beds there are less likely to ignite.' He gestured again at the door.

Annev started to leave, his temper rising, but then he felt the familiar flush of heat coming from the Hand of Keos and froze in place. Reeve stared at him, then he too glanced down at the smithing glove.

'I'll go back to Chaenbalu.'

'What?' Reeve looked up, shocked.

'I said ... I'll go back. I'll retrieve the Oracle. I'll help you put your house in order. We can stop in Banok and look for Bron Gloir, too.'

'Really?' Reeve said, half incredulous. 'Why the sudden change in attitude?'

'Because,' Annev said quietly, 'I can't live a normal life with this weapon attached to me. I can't go on hoping that what happened in Chaenbalu won't repeat itself – because it *will* happen again. Without your help ... I'm sure it will.' As he spoke, a tendril of smoke wafted up from his hand. Reeve sniffed the air, noticed the smoke and stifled a curse.

'Yes,' he said, his tone more subdued. 'I understand – and thank you for agreeing.'

'Know this, though,' Annev said, finally meeting the high priest's eyes. 'You could have *tried* to help me – you could try today, right now – but you've chosen to wait until we find the Oracle. You have given me no choice in that matter, so if any accidents happen while I'm waiting for you, they're on *your* head.'

'Then I will be doubly certain your belongings are moved to the lowest level of the Enclave,' Reeve said, his tone cold once more, 'and that no one else shares the floor with you.' He nodded at the door and Annev left in a huff, slamming the portal shut behind him.

'Bastard,' Annev swore, marching down the hall, fuming and already second-guessing his decision to stay. Remembering Jian's prophecy was a cold comfort – the Seer had told him Reeve would only aid him if he first helped Reeve – so Annev recommitted himself to the task. He would help the high priest find the Oracle, and then they would use it to find a way to remove the Hand of Keos. That was all Annev could do, and cursing his fate wouldn't change it.

Annev reached the stairwell and found his feet carrying him upward to Sraon's bedroom, his anger gradually coming under control. He knocked hard on the blacksmith's door, took a breath, then knocked again more softly.

'Who is it?' Sraon answered from the other side.

'Your favourite one-armed freak.'

'My what now?'

Annev pushed open the door to see Sraon, bare-chested, sitting in a chair beside the loophole. He leaned back from the embrasure and squinted at Annev. 'Who are you?'

'Very funny,' Annev said, plopping himself down on Sraon's bed. 'I just came from Dionach Reeve's study.' He swore under his breath. 'That man irritates me to no end.'

Sraon stared at him, his face clouded in confusion. 'Dionach Reeve?'

'Yeah,' Annev said. 'He's been avoiding me — and then when I finally cornered him, he tried to guilt me into helping him find Bron Gloir and the Oracle.'

'Bron Gloir ...' Sraon mumbled, sounding distracted. 'You'll be searching for Lord Gloir then?'

'What?' Annev said. 'No! Weren't you listening? He has no intention of helping me remove my hand. He's just waiting me out, hoping I'll get attached to—'

'Why in the five hells would you want to remove your hand, lad?'

Annev stated at Sraon, noticing for the first time that the man's eyes were bloodshot and his expression haggard. 'Sraon, are you all right?'

The scarred blacksmith shook his head. 'Havin' the damnedest time remembering where I put my shirt.' He looked at Annev. 'Who are you again?'

Annev's blood ran cold as his heart began to hammer in his chest. 'It's me ... Annev.'

The blacksmith tutted, his eyes watery. 'Honestly, lad, I don't even recognise the name.'

'Annev ... or Sraon?'

'Neither.' He turned his attention back to the loophole. 'Feelin' awful parched, though. You know where I can get some water?'

Annev nodded, backing away from the room. 'I'll get some immediately.'

The smith smiled. 'Good lad.'

Chapter Forty-Five

'Regressions like this are alarming, but fairly common.' Misty laid a hand on Annev's shoulder, reassuring him.

They were in the library now, a full day after Annev found Sraon in his fugue state. The blacksmith had since been returned to the Enclave's sanatorium, and Arch-Dionach Reeve was personally ministering to him. Having no magic of his own to help the man, Annev had offered to help Misty and Tym research what little the Order knew about the lizardman and his poison.

'She's right,' Tym said, pulling a worn tome from the library shelf. 'Well, she's right when you're talking about people who've been bitten by Saltair. There's something about his venom that arrests the body's natural responses. It paralyses you at first – your mind and your body – but then it penetrates deeper. The poison numbs your pain and keeps the wound from festering, so most people leave it alone and think they're healing.' He set the book down in front of Annev. 'But that's what Saltair wants you to do. Then his poison starts playing on your mind. Makes you forgetful, open to suggestion.' He turned the pages then tapped one written in artful handwriting. 'One of our Dionachs, Heida Topolski, was infiltrating the royal family of Innistiul when Saltair bit her. We were fortunate that one of our novices had accompanied her and made certain to record the effects of the injury and its poison.'

'What happened?' Annev asked, scanning the page.

'Nothing at first,' Tym said. 'Topolski seemed unwell, but then she got better. She continued attending the balls and banquets, but she started forgetting who she was. The novice tried to remind her, but Heida had forgotten too many of her old memories – she believed she was a House Matron from Eastern Odarnea.'

'And if the novice tried to remind her of her true mission,' Misty said, 'Heida got angry. She didn't remember the mission or how to perform magic – she didn't remember the Enclave at all. The whispers at court and the intrigue with the Cheng family became her world.'

'What happened to her novice?'

'She tried to help – tried to heal her mind with Stormcaller magic while Heida slept. She was caught, though, and Topolski accused her own novice of witchcraft. The girl had to flee back to the Enclave without her mentor.'

'And she's still there? At King Cheng's court?'

Dionach McClanahan nodded. 'Last time I checked, yes. The noble family sometimes brings her out for banquets. They have her sit and eat with them like a pet – an open secret that everyone laughs at.' She shook her head in disgust.

Annev studied the page again, then looked up. '*You* were the novice! *You* wrote this.'

Misty smiled. 'It was almost a decade ago.' She tapped the page thoughtfully. 'Fortunately for Sraon, the poison *has* been flushed from his system. With Dionach Topolski, my Stormcaller healing was undone by the poison still in her body. I couldn't cure her without bringing her back to the Enclave, and I couldn't do that without her cooperation.' She looked down at the book, then closed it with finality. 'I couldn't save Heida, but I promise you we can save Sraon. He *will* remember who he is, even if it takes a few extra weeks to stabilise him.'

A few extra weeks, Annev thought, remembering his plans to search for the Oracle in order to remove the Hand of Keos. Since Reeve was tending to Sraon personally, that would further delay their mission. *Which means I'll still be here when Titus and Therin take their Tests of Ascendancy*. It wasn't the worst thing that could happen – Annev was curious to know how his friends would do, and he really did want to cheer them on despite his own failures – but he didn't relish the thought of more delays, or of feeling further indebted to Reeve and his Order.

On the other hand, Annev thought, clutching the artifact in his pocket, *having a few more weeks would let me keep testing the Rod of Artificing – and collect some additional blood samples.* He had two already – one from Dionach Leskal after inviting the man to spar, and another from Therin when the boy had bloodied his nose at lunch the previous day. Annev had experimented with both since then, but hadn't made any progress unlocking the secrets of the Artificer's rod.

I've got Shieldbearer and Breathbreaker blood, he thought, *but those only manipulate skywater.* Maybe that's why he kept failing? Maybe to be successful he needed a different *kind* of blood. After his conversation with Honeycutt, Annev speculated that Terran blood might be easier to manipulate with the Rod of Artificing – but there were no Terrans at the Enclave. That meant he had to focus his studies on Artificing with Darite blood and Darite magic.

Annev sighed, feeling frustrated. Maybe, to get the rod to do anything, he needed a connection to all four callings, *including* the metaphysical. If that were true, he'd have to get a blood sample from someone who could manipulate *quaire*. Annev eyed his two companions, the Mindwalker and the Stormcaller, and tried to imagine a tactful way of requesting their blood.

Tym stared at him.

Damn it, Annev thought, belatedly remembering his mental barriers. He tried to quiet his thoughts, to think of something other than his perverse need to acquire their bodily fluids. 'I should go,' Annev said, suddenly standing up.

'Hold up.' Brother Tym laid a hand on his arm. 'Annev, do you need something?'

'I ...' He looked at his companions, the only two people who had befriended him since coming to the Enclave. 'It's nothing,' he said, cheeks reddening.

'What does he need, Tym?' Misty was replacing the book on the library shelf. 'Is it something that might help Sraon?'

Annev hesitated. *Could* his project help Sraon? He hadn't decided on a specific artifact to make – he'd begun by trying to remove his arm, and when that had failed, he had started to experiment more generally, but he'd been stymied by both the need

433

to obtain someone else's blood, and knowing what to do once he had it. The more he experimented, the more he felt certain the rod needed blood to function.

Now that Annev considered it, though, his failures at forging an original artifact might have been due to a lack of focus; he'd been *extremely* focused when trying to remove the Hand of Keos ... but not when he had tried to artifice something new. Maybe, using Tym and Misty's blood, he could forge something that would help Sraon. The blacksmith's remaining injury was predominantly psychological, after all, so if Annev wanted to help him, he'd need some way to access his memories and remind him who he was.

'Yes,' Annev said, before he had a chance to reconsider. 'I think it could help Sraon.'

'What is it then? How can we help?'

Annev looked between the two of them, his cheeks reddening. 'I ... need some of your blood.'

Misty frowned, taken aback. 'You need our—'

'He's telling the truth,' Brother Tym interrupted, studying Annev. 'I'm not sure how our blood could help Sraon, but if you really think it might ...' He looked at Misty who seemed uncertain, then he shrugged, grinning. 'It's not like it's a limited resource.'

He turned back to Annev. 'How much do you need?'

Annev retired to his room on the basement floor only to remember that Reeve had followed through with yesterday's threats by asking Dionach Webb to move Annev's belongings one level down, to the very bottom of the Enclave's building. Annev had been angry about the idea at first but had quickly discovered that he liked the increased privacy of the sub-basement level. None of the Dionachs or novices seemed to go down there, and nothing else of importance was on that floor – just a half-dozen empty rooms that were too cold, too dark and too damp for anyone to want them. Reeve had demonstrated a hidden sense of humour, too, having seen fit to furnish the room with various extravagances taken from other parts of the Enclave. Chief among these were a full-length mirror, a chest of drawers, a woven tapestry, a stuffed mattress and wool blankets, a brass washbasin and matching candelabra, and an impressive bathtub. Annev shook his head at this last, wondering where the Arch-Dionach thought he would get enough hot water to fill the tub – let alone what he was supposed to do with the dirty water when he finished. But he supposed that was the point. It was a statement – part apology and part insult. Whatever the high priest's intention had been, though, the sight of the wash tub made Annev feel unexpectedly valued, and he decided, since he was staying, to try to use it. Before he did, though, he had something else in mind ...

Once he was sure all his belongings were in place, Annev lit the tallows in the candelabra and shut the door. Then he opened his bottomless sack and retrieved the two scraps of cloth holding Leskal and Therin's blood samples. The rags had been wet with blood when Annev had used them to daub the Dionach's and Therin's injuries, and when he pulled them from the bottomless sack he was pleased to see the blood was still fresh – cold but still damp. He placed both scraps atop the side table holding his washbasin, and then he withdrew the vials of blood taken from the McClanahans – their contents still warm.

Once Tym had convinced Misty to help, the leader of the Stormcallers had decided the blood had to be properly drawn, bottled and sealed, and found a syringe and an appropriate collection of vials ... and secured Annev's promise to return everything when he was finished.

In the light of his candles, Annev stripped the glove from his cursed prosthetic, reached into his tunic and extracted the Rod of Artificing. As he had done the previous night, he touched the rod to the wet scraps of cloth containing Leskal and Therin's blood. As expected, nothing happened and Annev moved on to the fresh vials.

As he dipped the tip of the rod into the first vial, Annev imagined the artifact absorbing Tym's blood and then starting to glow, its essence somehow filled with Tym's blood-talent.

Nothing happened.

Annev stared at the rod, disheartened by his continual lack of success. Even the Ring of Good Luck had been unable to show him how to unlock the rod's secrets.

Thinking what else he could try, Annev dropped his hand into the bottomless sack and pulled out the copper Ring of Inquisition. After a moment he slipped the heavy copper band onto his thumb, and the room flared to life with the crimson mists he associated with the ring's magic. At the same time, Annev sensed a distinctive pulse coming from the bloody rags lying on the table and a much stronger one emanating from the two vials.

For the second time, Annev approached Tym's vial and dipped the narrow end of the Rod of Artificing inside. He tilted the vial, allowing the blood to wash over the tip of the rod – and then he waited.

Still nothing.

Annev withdrew the wand and switched it to his left hand while he re-stoppered the vial. As soon as the Rod of Artificing touched the Hand of Keos, the blood coating the end of the rod began to evaporate, its essence being absorbed into the rod itself.

Annev stared, awestruck, then watched as the rod began to glow with scarlet light.

Keos, Annev swore, *now what am I supposed to do?* As Annev considered it, the rod's glowing aura began to pulse, shifting slowly between dark maroon and bright crimson. His heart began to race and his mouth grew dry. *Damn, damn, damn.* He looked around the room for somewhere – anywhere – to discharge the magic. On instinct, he reached his right hand into the bottomless sack and pulled out a silver coin. He stared at it, uncertain, then felt his heart leap as the pulsing rod began to blink faster and faster, shifting in brightness and intensity.

Acting purely on instinct, Annev jammed the tip of the rod against the face of the silver moon and imagined the power inside the rod transferring to the metal coin. The room flashed with light – fierce and brilliant – and Annev felt a burning pain in his right hand. He flung the coin across the room, cursing as he clutched his injured fingers and palm. The open vial of Tym's blood toppled off the side table and shattered on the stone floor, making Annev swear again. Then, in his haste to clean up the mess and collect the glass shards, he cut his hand open.

With a roar of disgust, Annev swept the rags and the vial of Dionach McClanahan's blood back into the bottomless sack and, between the light from the candelabra and that of his golden hand, he picked up the tiny glass shards littering the floor and carefully placed them next to the washbasin. He checked his hand for further injuries but, aside from the cut he'd just received, he appeared unharmed. Sighing, he washed both hands in the basin, cleaning them thoroughly as he tugged off the two magic rings. Belatedly, he remembered the coin he had hurled across the room and stooped to look for it beneath his bed. He found it in the corner, pressed against the wall, and took a moment to examine the silver moon.

Aside from a spot of blood staining the face of the coin, the moon seemed unchanged. Annev turned it over in his hand, straining for any pulse of magic coming from the silver disc ... but there was nothing.

Annev dumped both the Rod of Artificing and the silver coin back into the bottomless bag. He dropped the Inquisitor ring into the sack as well, but when he picked up the silver-gold codavora ring, he stopped.

Something was different – something *felt* different.

Cautiously, Annev slid the ring back on, his breath held as he tried to sense the artifact's magic. As usual, he felt the twin blood-talents intertwined within the ring ... and now a third one accompanied the pair.

A blood-talent, Annev realised, that had strong echoes of Brother Tym's magic.

Chapter Forty-Six

Edra sat in silence in a copse of pine just within the treeline that bordered the East Road. The latter connected the wealthy capital of Luqura to the neighbouring kingdom of Borderlund and its own capital, Paldron. Edra had been there twice on artifact retrieval missions, and what he'd seen gave him little taste for returning: castles, towers and fortresses on every hill, river and crossroads. There wasn't much that amounted to a trading post or town square, no great market or bazaars as they had in Luqura. No, the country of Borderlund was a patchwork of duchies and smaller estates, with each landowner acting like a king – and warring with one another when they should have been defending the Kuar River against potential invasion from the Terrans.

Not that Edra minded. Men who were constantly fighting had no time to plant and harvest crops. And when armies in Borderlund didn't have enough to eat, they had two choices: steal from one another, or pay the wagon trains of Luqura to bring them food and rations. The latter meant sending money and goods for trade from Paldron to Luqura – and that meant travelling the East Road.

The very road Edra and the other former masters were now camped beside.

'Is Aog coming?' Der asked, his figure lost amidst a swirl of smoke and shadows.

'Hell if I know,' Edra said, flexing his magic gauntlets. Handy things those – thin and supple as anything, but stout as steel plate. For all his initial reluctance about using artifacts stolen from the Vault, Edra was beginning to think it was foolish to have sat on these wonders. That was over now, though, and they were all adapting to their new roles – some more easily than others.

'The Lord of Damnation's probably got him working the tunnels again,' Denithal wheezed from behind his flat white mask, its surface devoid of any features save two mirror-black eye lenses.

'So what if he does?' Edra said, still flexing his gloves. 'If Aog prefers manual labour over robbing coaches and caravans, that's his choice. He's always had a thing for solitude and building muscle. Maybe tunnel work agrees with him.'

'Might be,' said Der, his voice soft as silk amidst the black mists, 'except Aog also enjoys killing, and he has little chance of murdering anything in that rabbit warren Kenton's put him in.'

'Well,' Edra said, stroking his red leather armour, 'did anyone think to invite him?'

Silence.

Denithal's white mask turned to look at Der's smoky figure, though how either of them could see the other's expression was beyond Edra. The black mists around Der wavered and a gloved hand appeared in the fog, dissipating the magic smoke. The former Master of Stealth had taken off his mask – a black face wrap that completely moulded to his skin, similar to the fabric that wrapped the rest of his lean, muscled body – and he squinted meaningfully at Denithal, who perched the rigid white shell of his own mask atop his wizened head. The elderly alchemist looked pointedly at Edra.

'Ather said not to invite him,' the former ancient rasped. 'He didn't say why. I didn't ask.'

'He said the same to me – and to leave our amulets behind.' Edra frowned. 'What's that about?'

Der shrugged. 'I left mine, too ... but it seems odd not wearing it. I mean, it's supposed to protect us. So why leave them?'

'I left mine by accident once,' Edra said, distracted by Murlach's distant figure dragging traps into place, preparing for another ambush. Even from that distance, he could hear the soft whir and click of the contraptions covering the man's body – more like some monstrous insect than a human, his limbs and torso covered in wire tentacles, spindly metal arms and clacking pincers. 'I forgot it,' Edra continued, 'and didn't think anything of it. A few hours later Kenton found me and handed it back. Told me I should always keep it on me – so it could protect me. Damned if I know how he knew I wasn't wearing it.'

'But you left it today, didn't you?'

The trio turned to see Ather, the former Master of Lies, step out nimbly from behind a gnarled oak. 'You each left your amulets in Chaenbalu as I instructed, did you not?'

Edra slowly nodded and, to his relief, so did Der and Denithal. 'I can't imagine why we'd listen to a serpent like you,' Denithal croaked, wiping saliva from his lips, 'but here we are.'

Ather waggled the fingers of his powder-blue Gloves of Persuasion.

'Blood and filth,' Edra swore. 'You tricked us. Why?'

'The same reason I asked you all to meet me here – and not to invite Aog.' Ather brushed back his trimmed coif of hair. 'I'm afraid our dear Master Kenton has been manipulating us. *Spying* on us.'

'How's that?' Der crossed his arms. Edra knew that look – and the stance, too. If the former Master of Stealth didn't like Ather's answer, he might follow up with a throwing star to the man's throat.

'I have suspected it for some time,' Ather drawled, unintimidated, 'and I spent the last few weeks testing my theory. Whenever we're wearing the amulets, Kenton knows where we are and, I believe, he can hear our thoughts. Unless he's with Kiara in the Vault of Damnation. Whatever demon magic protects that place also interferes with the amulets. Kenton's there right now with that witch, scrying or screwing or whatever the hell it is they do down there. That's why he hasn't come looking for us ... yet.'

'Damn me,' Denithal burped, his hands patting his chest for a blue vial that he quickly uncorked and chugged. 'Sorry,' he said. 'The yellow ones do wonders for my energy, but they give me some frightful indigestion.'

'How did you learn this?' Edra asked, pointedly ignoring Denithal.

Ather raised an eyebrow. 'Did none of you think to try to

identify the properties of the talismans? You simply took Kenton at his word?' The predatory popinjay snorted. 'And I suppose none of you thought it odd those amulets were a matched set? The first thing I did was sit down and properly identify each artifact – but you were all too eager to play with your new toys. You didn't stop to think that young Master Kenton might be trying to control us?'

Neither Der nor Denithal could meet his gaze. Edra at least had enough steel not to look sheepish, but Ather's words rang painfully true. How long had he spent admiring his new leather armour and marvelling at his new weapons? He'd never once in that time thought to second-guess their properties. *Let the boy identify the artifacts and assign them*, he had thought, *and I'll make use of them*. The former Master of Arms met Ather's eyes.

'Aye,' Edra said. 'Seems we were a bit hasty in trusting the boy. What should we do then? We can't put the amulets back on or he'll know we've figured out his secret.'

'I mean to get out of here,' Ather said, nodding towards the road. 'To leave Chaenbalu for good. Even if Kenton were being straight with us, you saw what Annev did to Elder Tosan – how he blew up the Academy and damn near killed us all. If we're smart, we'll stay far, far away from that.'

'But where can we go?' Der asked, looking pensive. 'The Academy ... the Vault and the magic?' He looked between the others. 'What else is there for us?'

Ather gave a dramatic sigh, dusted off a fallen tree, then sat down. 'We should call Murlach over. If you haven't guessed yet, we aren't ambushing any caravans today. I just needed an excuse to get us all together.'

'And Aog?' Edra asked. 'Why didn't you invite him?'

Ather peeled off one of his magic gloves and waved the garment at him. 'These don't work on Aog. I thought it was because of his armour, but he didn't even respond to when I touched his face. It's like he's ... not there.'

'That's nothing new,' Denithal said, snorting.

'No,' Ather objected. 'This was different. Kenton's done something to him, I think. Got him wrapped tighter than the rest of us, I'd wager. Haven't you noticed? He keeps the Master of

441

Punishment like some sort of pet. Has him digging those tunnels beneath the Academy's ruins or running an errand of some sort. Aog's never really been the sycophantic type, and this reeks of magic.' He tapped Der on the shoulder with his gloved hand. 'Go fetch Murlach?' Der nodded and sped away to collect the monstrous Master of Engineering.

Edra gave him a pointed look. 'You just manipulated Der,' he accused. 'How is that any different than what Kenton's doing?'

'Because,' Ather said, smiling wickedly, 'I'm me and he's not.'

Edra sniffed but didn't argue the point. Murlach and Der were back a minute later, the former frowning from within the nest of cables and wires surrounding his face and neck.

'What's all this about Kenton?'

'He's been spying on us,' Edra said, before Ather could offer a more garrulous explanation – Keos, but that man could *talk*. 'Ather figured out the amulets were involved somehow,' he continued. 'You still wearing yours?'

A tentacled arm sprang to life at Murlach's side, the pronged tip slithering into his armour. There was a loud hissing sound and then his exoskeleton split open. 'So,' he said, 'you finally figured it out.'

'Figured what out?' Edra said, a moment before Der.

'The talismans.' Murlach's tentacle retreated from his armour, its pincers drawing the amulet over his head before displaying the artifact for all to see. 'I wondered how long it would take. Which of you was it?'

Down the road, one of Murlach's twiddlesnap contraptions clanked shut, eliciting a squeal as some poor animal was snapped and snared – but the rest of them gave it no mind.

Edra pointed to Ather, head shaking as he said to Murlach, 'If you've known this whole time, why would you wear it?'

Murlach spun the talisman in front of Edra's face so that he saw a peculiar drop of silver clinging to the amulet's ruby.

'What's that?' Der asked, stepping forward to examine the artifact. 'Some kind of ... metal spider?'

Edra grunted in agreement. The addition to the amulet *did* look like some sort of metallic arachnid, with eight tiny legs and a blood-red thorax that matched the ruby beneath it.

Murlach let each man see it in turn. 'When we were down in the Vault, I saw another half-dozen of these talismans sitting on a shelf at the back of the chamber – all with these metal spiders attached to them. That got me wondering, so I started poking around and found six unattached spiders sitting on the lower shelf. Didn't take a genius to figure Kenton had modified ours, so I snatched one of the spider-amulets and gave it a closer look. Tried to figure out what kind of tricks our Cursed Leader was trying to pull on us.'

'And?'

Murlach's silvery tentacle dropped the amulet back over his neck. 'The spiders alter the magic a bit. Instead of allowing Kenton to always hear my thoughts, they let me choose which ones to share and which to keep to myself.'

'Why not tell the rest of us?' Der asked, his brow furrowed.

Murlach shrugged. 'I wanted to see how things played out – and I didn't trust you lot to keep my secret.' He gestured at Ather with his pincers. 'That's all moot now that Ather's played our hands for us, though . . . so what's the new plan?' He eyed the Master of Lies with unmasked contempt. 'You going to confront him?'

'After what he did to Master Carbad?' Ather said, his eyes widening with just a hint of terror. 'Hells no. I thought we could just leave – but first I wanted to collect some insurance.'

'Which is?'

'*Aqlumera*,' Ather said, his grin returning as he smoothed the thin line of his moustache. 'Tosan didn't like us entering the Vault because he didn't want people knowing we were sitting on an emperor's ransom. Just a bottle of that stuff would make us rich as kings – and I know folks who'd be more than eager to buy it. So imagine this: we hurry back to Chaenbalu before Kenton realises we've discovered his secret. Murlach stays up here and uses his amulet to convince Kenton we're all still with him. When Kenton comes to investigate – and to see why we've taken off our amulets – the rest of us will break into the Vault. We can grab some more artifacts, steal a few bottles of *aqlumera* and meet up with Murlach at the old mill. We circle south to the Brake Road and then we go east, away from Luqura and Banok and anywhere else Kenton

443

might think to look for us. If we go to Port Caer, we'll have mountains of gold before the end of the month and can live out our lives in peace. Or we can turn mercenary and sell our services to the highest bidder. The point is we'll have options.'

The others watched Murlach, who seemed to have become the de facto alternative to Ather's leadership. 'I don't think there's any reason for me to wait here,' Murlach said. 'I can choose which thoughts Kenton sees, and I can do that as easily with you in Chaenbalu. And no need to regroup at the mill. We can just grab the *aqlumera* and get the hell out of these woods.'

Der and Denithal glanced at Edra then, surprising him with their deference. The former Master of Arms waited just long enough to acknowledge their unasked question. 'It has a certain attractiveness to it. Much better than waiting for Kenton to figure out what to do with us. I'm in.'

Der and Denithal nodded – and that was that. One last theft, one final betrayal, and they would be free of Chaenbalu for ever. Murlach went to retrieve the trap he'd left on the road, and Der and Denithal replaced their masks, the former disappearing into an amorphous cloud of black smoke.

'Hey, fellas!' Murlach called back to them a minute later, his voice projected by some ingenious artifact inside his suit. 'You need to come and look at this!'

'What is it?' Ather shouted back, his nimble knee-high boots dancing him out of the treeline and down the slope leading onto the road.

'You remember those metal monsters that attacked the Academy?' Murlach asked, a tremor in his voice. 'The twisted ones that ran off into the forest?'

'Yes,' Edra said, feeling a cold prickle of fear creep up his neck. 'Why? Did you find one?'

'Not sure,' Murlach said, his speaker clicking off as the group approached him from behind. 'It looks a lot like one ... but also not.'

Edra finally saw the beast caught in the jaws of Murlach's enormous twiddlesnap: unlike the feral, mutated monsters that had attacked Chaenbalu, this creature seemed ... well, not like a creature at all; more like a man wearing full plate armour, his body segmented by overlapping metal plates. *Metal and stone,* Edra amended, slowing. Then he realised.

That's not armour ... that's the creature's flesh!

'Gods,' Denithal rasped from behind his white mask. 'It *is* one of them!'

Ather's slender rapier hissed from its scabbard and Edra drew his own leaf-bladed long sword. Denithal dipped his hands under his bandolier and popped a red vial from his pocket, and while Edra couldn't see Der's figure amidst the cloud of smoke, he assumed the Master of Stealth was similarly preparing for battle.

'You can put your pricks away, boys,' Murlach shouted back. 'It's dead.'

'From the twiddlesnap?' Der asked amidst his cloud of smoke. 'Those aren't lethal.'

'They are when they're big enough to crush a wagon wheel.' Murlach used his pincers to prod the metal man's iron head and neck. 'How in the name of the Gods does this magic work?' he wondered aloud. 'Made of metal and stone ... but not a machine. Is it a man ... or a golem?' He shook his head, apparently more impressed by the artificery than concerned by the dark omen of the creature's presence.

'Should we be worried that it was skulking about the East Road?' Edra asked.

'No,' Ather said, any fear in his tone concealed beneath his usual veneer of vanity. 'This changes nothing. We go back to Chaenbalu, get the *aqlumera,* and head to Port Caer.'

Murlach dropped the creature's iron head and stood straight, his mechanised body nearly a foot taller than without his suit. 'We should keep an eye out for more of these buggers, though. If this *ferruman* is anything like the ones we saw in Chaenbalu, there'll be more – lots more.'

Edra was suddenly anxious to get back to the questionable safety of Chaenbalu's familiar ruins.

'Let's move.'

Chapter Forty-Seven

'Does she live?' Kenton asked, leaning dangerously close to the edge of the *aqlumera* pool. 'Show me again. I have to know if she survived.'

'She lives, Cursed One. She lives and will yet live. As I promised, her life is only truly in peril when she returns here. You should not trouble yourself with these visions.'

'Show me *again*, Kiara! I need to know what has happened to her.'

The witmistress rubbed her temples then clasped her hands together. 'Magic is not free, Kenton. Even when we use the *aqlumera* instead of the shadepools, there is a cost for scrying and I do not spend it lightly.'

'But those demons nearly *killed* her!'

'Those demons failed – as I foretold.'

The Master of Curses ripped his blindfold away and stared into Kiara's eyes, his own flaring with demonic fire, their light flickering at the edge of his vision. 'Show. Her. Again.'

'No.'

Kenton's cheek twitched and his hands shook as if he were about to strangle the woman. Instead, he spun away from the *aqlumera* cistern and smashed his fist against the nearest shelf of artifacts. Magic flared from his Glove of Indomitability and the wood exploded into splinters. A heartbeat later, a catalogue of magic stones toppled to the floor, the rocks and pebbles scattering in all directions.

Kiara frowned. 'Tantrums do not persuade or inspire obedience.

They are a sign of weakness. A demonstration that you are incapable of leading.' She tucked a lock of hair behind her ear, the rest firmly secured in a neat bun. Since the Academy's collapse, the other masters and ancients had started to relax, not seeking to impress one another, much less Kenton. Kiara had gone the opposite way, though, becoming even more formal, acting like a teacher in the midst of lecturing a student; her skirts were always clean and ironed, her face was always washed, her hair was always neat.

Kenton, by contrast, was a haggard shadow of his former self who cared little for the company of others. The only exceptions were Kiara, whose magic allowed him to watch Myjun in the Shadowrealm, and Master Aog, whose will he had entirely dominated. At the moment, the former Master of Punishment was digging a new tunnel from Chaenbalu's lowest dungeon to the abandoned bakery at the perimeter of the village square – a secret tunnel, in case Kenton was ever trapped beneath the Academy again. Kenton had not yet admitted to anyone, not even himself, that he no longer wished to leave the Academy's ruins. Its tunnels and its magic had become familiar to him, and he was becoming obsessed with the *aqlumera* pool and watching Myjun. He had no reason or desire to leave – not to wash, not to sleep, not even to eat – and the Vault's artifacts meant he never had to.

'I could make you show me,' he growled. 'I could *force* you.'

'You can't and you won't. Harming me will ensure you never see Myjun again. So you will let me rest. You will see the visions again when I am ready, not when you command. Is that clear?'

Kenton's lips puckered, his skin tightening as he felt his scarred face struggle to contain his scowl. 'Quite clear,' he whispered, his voice so low it was almost impossible to hear.

'She is not dead, Kenton. She is resting, and it will take time for her wounds to heal.'

'How long?'

'Hours. Days. Not long, I suspect. Time passes more swiftly there, but while she is resting, *we* should rest.'

Kenton stroked his scraggly beard. 'I don't like that half-man. What he does ... what he's *doing* to her. He's killing her. Maybe not her body, but her spirit.'

447

'I'm not certain that girl ever really had a spirit.'

Kenton's eyes flashed, their brilliance almost blinding, their light swelling to throw back the shadows in the corners of the room. 'You know nothing of Myjun.'

'Don't I? She was best friends with my apprentice, and the daughter of the headmaster. I knew her all too well. Her little schemes, her vanity. I knew her mother, too, before she died. Hells, I practically raised that girl with the other witwomen. If the Academy had lasted a few more years and her father hadn't been an obstacle, we would have indoctrinated her into the Brides of Fate.'

'Did you know she had magic?'

'I did.'

'How?'

Kiara raised an eyebrow, her cool grey eyes inspecting him. 'Come with me.'

The witmistress's bedchamber lay two floors above the Vault, completely undisturbed by either the Academy's collapse or the *feurog* attack, save for the narrow tunnel hidden behind Kiara's bed. She had already explained how that single tunnel had allowed the *feurog* to enter the Academy, but she had been less forthcoming about why. 'A clean slate,' she'd told him. 'No witnesses to pursue us when we left with Annev. No survivors to guide any others to the village.' It had all seemed very cold to Kenton.

'What did you want to show me?' he asked, sitting down in a padded rocking chair.

'This.' Kiara handed him a small black book and Kenton riffled through its pages. He saw dates, names and numbers – a chart of some kind – and a short description beside each name. In most cases, it also mentioned the parents' names, or potential strains of magic.

'This is a logbook,' he said, flipping to the end. 'A log of … stolen children?'

'It was our job to locate and monitor infants who might become the Vessel. We abducted them from all over Greater Luqura and brought them here to be trained. One-armed infants were our first priority, but none of them ever possessed the talent – none until

Annev – so instead we kidnapped those likely to inherit the talent, thinking one might lose an arm during their training or an artifact retrieval mission ... but it never happened. It was very vexing.'

'What's this?' Kenton asked, showing her an asterisk next to one boy's name and the bright red letters *NM*. 'Sage Lenka. Is this the Academy's cook?'

'Yes. "NM" means non-magical. Not every child had magic. Some were taken for political reasons.'

'Hold on. "Lenka." Is that supposed to be *King* Lenka? As in the King of Greater Luqura.'

Kiara nodded. 'He had three children. The youngest boy was supposedly stillborn, but he's actually been cooking the Academy's meals for the past decade or more.'

'You stole a *prince*?' he breathed. 'Damn me. What for?'

'Politics, mostly. We had our reasons.'

Kenton flipped forward a few more pages and saw his reap mates. 'Fyunai Harth ... son of *Janak Harth*?' He looked up. 'That's the merchant we killed in Banok!'

'Just a strain of Ironborn in that one – nothing major – but Janak's mercenary exploits let him amass too much power too quickly. Taking his son was meant to keep the bastard in line ... but something went wrong at the reaping. Janak fought back. His wife was killed and he was crippled – but we still managed to steal his son.'

'Fyn,' Kenton breathed, head shaking in disbelief. 'He killed his own father. That prick of a headmaster sent him to kill his own bloody *father*.'

'It was no accident. Tosan was aware of his students' parental lineage.'

Kenton flipped to another page and found his own name. 'Reotan NM,' he read beside his nameless father – and beside his unnamed mother ... 'Terran Artificer?' He looked up. 'I'm bloody *Terran*?'

'Of course, you are. All Artificers are Terran.'

'But ... I don't look Terran.'

'You have your father's looks – like a Tir Reotan pirate – and your mother's magic. She was an Artificer.'

'There are no names written here.'

'No. We tended not to record the rapists, pirates or whores.'

Kenton's mouth twitched, but he held his anger in check. 'And I was stolen?'

'You? No. Your father didn't want a brat on his ship. Witwoman Kelga purchased you from your mother on the streets of Luqura.'

Kenton wanted to ask more but his throat closed up. His finger drifted down the page until he found Annev's name. 'Ainnevog ... but no number. No origin, no parentage.' He looked up. 'Why not?'

'Infants have their heels inked with numbers – to help us keep track of you all. Annev had no such number. My best guess is Sodar smuggled him into your reap.'

Kenton snorted, finding some dark humour in it all. 'So why show me this?'

Kiara took the book and flipped to a group of pages he had missed. 'These are our notes on the wit-apprentices. Only a few are stolen each year, though sometimes a witwoman will get pregnant – in the case of us Brides, we select a mate with an affinity for prophetic magic. Myjun and her mother were both witchildren, but Myjun's grandmother was a proper Bride of Fate ... who married *this* man.' Kiara flipped to another page and tapped a spidery inscription next to an infant from the thirty-seventh reap.

'Edwin,' Kenton read, taking back the book. 'Son of Donald the Bard. Strong affinity for Ilumite magic.' He looked up. 'This is how you knew. You had your prophecies and the Academy's training ... and this.'

'Yes. That's how we knew Myjun would probably have the talent, though it was impossible to guess which strands would become dominant. Terran, Ilumite, Yomad. We never know until you reach an age where the magic is potent. We try to bring the girls into the Brides of Fate around then. For the young men ... well, there's usually no harm in having a little of the talent, particularly if they're never taught to use it. It makes them better avatars. And if some stumble upon how to use their magic ... well, avatars have such a high mortality rate.'

450

'Did Duvarek have it?' Kenton asked, his voice sounding hollow. 'Is that why he was killed?'

'Duvarek had it and I think he knew – it's probably why he drank so much. But we didn't kill him. That was all Janak's fault.'

'But Tosan had me kill him ... because he got caught. That wasn't your doing?'

'No.'

Kenton relaxed, suddenly aware he'd been on the point of violence. 'That's good,' he said, his heart thudding heavily in his chest. He passed the logbook back. 'I need to check in on Aog and the other masters.'

'Are they giving you trouble?'

'Not Aog. The slave ring keeps him completely docile – though he needs new commands every few hours or he's liable to sit down in one of the tunnels and wait to be told what to do next.'

'And the others?' Kiara asked, her tone implying something she knew that he did not.

Kenton frowned. 'Ather's being a pain. He may have figured out the amulets.'

'And if he has?'

'Then I'll kill him.'

Kiara nodded as though she'd expected as much. 'You're sure this isn't motivated by your history with him?'

'My history?' Kenton asked, tense once again.

'Your scar,' she said, gesturing to the band of mottled flesh that was now almost entirely hidden by the leathery, calloused skin surrounding his lidless eyes. 'No lingering resentments for that?'

'Oh, of course,' Kenton said, his gloved hand gently scratching the small patch of scarred flesh, 'but Ather has some subtlety that the others lack, so I'll overlook our past – so long as he stays in line. He recently stopped wearing his amulet, though, and I don't think that's an accident.'

'He's testing you,' Kiara said, her eyes glinting.

'I think so, yes. And he keeps asking about the Vault – keeps lingering whenever I enter or leave.'

'Then make an example of him.'

'I think he wants the *aqlumera*.'

Kiara's coy smile transformed into a frown. 'He can't take any of it. In the wrong hands, that magic could be catastrophic ... not to mention you've trapped a demon down there.'

'He's not trapped,' Kenton said, his lips pressed into a firm line. 'He's waiting for another chance to escape.'

'Then why hasn't he tried to possess me?'

Kenton smiled. 'That pin you wear in your hair. Did you not guess its enchantment?'

Kiara's frown deepened. 'Identifying enchantments is not one of my strengths, Master Kenton.'

Kenton filed that information away for the future. 'It protects the wearer from spectral possession. So long as you wear it, Elder Tosan can't use you as a conduit.'

'And do you wear a similar artifact?'

'I do,' Kenton said, tapping the cuffs of his Gloves of Indomitability. 'These protect my hands *and* my soul.'

Kiara nodded, seeming impressed. 'You really are a marvel with artifacts. I doubt anyone in the Academy's history was so well suited to be their keeper.'

Kenton's smile slipped and he turned from her then, choosing to busy himself checking on the masters. His eyes grew distant, and he located Aog in the dark tunnels of the Academy's lowest levels. The brute was sluggishly carving away at the soil, his enchanted shovel simultaneously softening and hardening the earth that he cut away. He didn't even need to cart away the dirt he excavated – it was simply vaporised. Kenton mentally told the man to dig for another hour and then come and eat, and then he checked on the other Sons of Damnation.

'Something's wrong,' he said, his brow furrowing. 'They've taken off their amulets – all except Murlach.'

'And where is he?'

Kenton tried to glean the master's location. 'The East Road ... I think. But it doesn't feel right. His thoughts are ... chatty. He never thinks aloud this much.'

'What's he thinking?'

'Something about robbing a caravan. It sounds like the others are with him.' He concentrated. 'Oh, shit.'

'What?' Kiara asked, a touch of dread creeping into her voice.

'They found something on the road. One of those *feurog*.'

'Oh,' Kiara said, visibly relaxing. 'You needn't worry about them. Without someone to drive them, they're little more than animals. That's why Cruithear's priests cast them out – and why we snatched them up. I admit they make hardy soldiers, but they prefer to hide from men. Besides, there aren't many of them left. I've tried to recall the survivors but none have responded.'

'No,' Kenton said, frowning. 'This one isn't like your monsters – not exactly. Murlach ... he's calling it a *ferruman*. It's not mutated like those others – not half-human, half-monster. It looks ... Well, damn. It looks like Janak Harth, after he drank that vial of magic.'

Kiara's nonchalance suddenly vanished. 'Where did Murlach spot this *ferruman*?'

'On the East Road. The golem got caught in one of his traps.'

'It's not a golem,' Kiara said, scowling. 'If it looks like Janak Harth, then it's human. A real man or woman, not a construct.'

Kenton studied her, his magic revealing the aura of fear she fought to hide. 'What aren't you telling me?'

The witmistress pursed her lips. 'The *feurog* were monsters – failed experiments of Cruithear – but the God of Minerals had *some* successes. Cruithear made those lucky enough not to become monsters into his elite soldiers – his Ironborn warriors. I suspect one of those is the *ferruman* Murlach saw.'

'Why would one of those be here?'

'Without scrying, I can only guess – but Cruithear is jealous of his elites. He hoards them like a miser with his coins ... so if one is here, he means to attack someone, or something.'

'What would be worth it, to him?'

Kiara swore. 'I haven't asked the spirits ... but Cruithear needs *aqlumera* to forge his warriors. The only reason he hasn't made an army of them is because *aqlumera* is expensive, extremely limited, and difficult to locate – especially untainted.'

'Except here,' Kenton finished. 'In the Vault of Damnation.'

Kiara nodded. 'Most of the *feurog* are mutants because the *aqlumera* that formed them was tainted – but if Cruithear discovered the existence of our fountain, and if he found one of

453

Chaenbalu's survivors and persuaded them to act as his guide ...'

'Then he'd bring his best soldiers here,' Kenton finished. 'An army of *ferrumen* could be on their way to Chaenbalu now. They could be just outside the village. Surrounding us. Looking for a way into the tunnels.'

'That is a possibility.'

'And the masters are all north of the Brake. All except Aog.' Kenton felt his adrenaline rising. 'Blood and filth. How can we be sure?' The answer suddenly came to him and he let his eyes unfocus, sweeping his vision beyond Kiara's bedroom and across the landscape around the Academy. He turned in a full circle, his magic eyes piercing rock and stone, air and earth, and saw nothing alarming within the bounds of the village. He gave up after a minute of searching. 'It seems we're safe from ... wait.' Kenton stopped, his eyes locking on to four warm bodies skulking near the edge of the village. Not *ferrumen*, but actual men.

'I don't think the masters are north of the Brake.'

'What? Where are they?'

'Just south of the village, near the old mill.' Kenton paused. 'Why is Murlach thinking about robbing a caravan when he isn't anywhere near the East Road?' he wondered aloud. 'Something isn't right.'

Kiara tutted. 'Focus on the *ferrumen*. If you must question your Sons of Damnation, do so – after they've helped you scout the Brake for more of Cruithear's creatures.'

Kenton quirked an eyebrow. 'Is that advice ... or a command?'

Kiara snorted. 'My days of commanding others died when the Brides of Fate perished. You are the Cursed Leader, Kenton of Chaenbalu. I only advise.'

'So long as that advice benefits you.'

'So long as it benefits us both.'

'Very well. I'll go round up the masters and scout the woods.'

'And I will return to the Vault and scry from there – which will take time, not to mention magic.'

Kiara scratched her wrist and Kenton saw a patch of her skin had begun to turn ash-white, the cost of using her powers.

'This is important, Kenton,' she continued. 'If Cruithear has sent any of his *ferrumen* to the surface, then they are coming for the *aqlumera*. He can't be allowed to take possession of it.'

'Because he'd use it to create more monsters?'

'No! Because it would disrupt the lines of fate – Annev's quest, Myjun's arrival. It hinges on the *aqlumera* being here. I'd prefer that Cruithear not gain the power of Chaenbalu's secrets ... but that is nothing compared to it ruining the prophecies.'

'And then,' Kenton continued, piecing together the logic, 'I might never see Myjun ... might never save her.'

Kiara nodded. 'It could create a chain of events that leads to Myjun killing Annev ... and to her being killed in turn.'

Kenton stood straight, his eyes flaring with a dark red light that made it seem as though Kiara's bedroom were being consumed by demonic flames. 'Then we shall throw them back,' he growled. 'No mages or *ferrumen* shall enter the Vault. None will trespass here.'

Kiara fretted, still anxious. 'It may not be so simple. If Cruithear has sent his elites, he may have sent his *entire army*. Worse, these *ferrumen* aren't like the *feurog*. They'll be as cunning as regular men and as strong as golems. Keos take me! If Cruithear has sent his elite guards, he might even come himself.'

'Would he really do that?'

Kiara shrugged. 'He has done similar things in the past. He is never content with what he has gained. Always expanding. Always searching. If he comes here with scores of mages and *ferrumen* ... I don't think there's any way we can stop him.'

'We must focus our energies on repelling any possible assaults,' Kenton said. 'Go and scry for soldiers in the Brake.' He pulled a ruby amulet from his cloak – one adorned with a silver spider – and passed it to the witmistress. 'Wear this. If an army is camped on our doorstep, leave the Vault and tell me exactly what you've seen. The artifact will allow us to communicate using our thoughts.'

'And what will you be doing?'

'I want to travel to the East Road and see this monster for myself. Murlach's description is vague, but he keeps returning to it. Obsessing over it. I'll scout for more *ferrumen*, or Cruithear's approach, along the way – but I won't engage him. If we really are about to be attacked, I want to prepare some defences. Matter of fact, I think I'll start Aog on some adjustments to our tunnel system before I head out. Do me a favour, though, and keep an eye on the masters. They're camped just north of the swollen stream and east of the old mill. Which I'll worry about later.'

'Perhaps you should test your Cloak of Secrets? The speed you gain by bridging the distance between two points in space could be invaluable.'

Kenton considered it. 'True,' he said, touching the hem of his night-black garment, 'but I think not. I don't dare tempt it with my safety – not yet.'

'Yet you still choose to wear it.'

'How can I not when its magic is so invaluable?'

Kiara pursed her lips, humming thoughtfully. 'Perhaps you are wise. Not all powers are worth the price we pay to use them.'

'Did it work?' Denithal asked, wiping his dripping nose.

Ather held up the bandolier of vials he'd borrowed from the elderly alchemist, each one glowing with a rainbow-hued liquid light. 'The fool boy never sealed the second entrance to the Vault.'

'Gods be praised,' Denithal wheezed. 'We're rich! No more of this camping out in the woods or sleeping in tunnels. Slaving for a whelp that's young enough to be my grandson.'

'Grandson?' Der teased, dispelling his cloud of smoke. 'Can you imagine a woman willing to bear your spawn?'

'Might be I spawned *you*,' Denithal huffed. 'I was quite the philanderer in my day.'

'Aye, I'm sure you were, pater.'

'Stow it, you two,' Edra growled, his hand resting on the hilt of his enchanted sword. 'We're not out of the woods yet. We still need to get to Port Caer and contact Ather's buyers. We won't see a bloody gleam of gold for some weeks yet.'

'Actually,' Ather crooned, his lean figure stepping from the shadows, 'there's been a slight change of plans.'

'What's this?' Murlach barked, his pincers clacking beside him. 'We're sticking to the plan, Ather. Port Caer or bust. No changing your mind mid-scheme.'

'Oh, but I've had a distinct change of heart, Master Murlach. And mind ... and soul.' The former Master of Lies glared at his companions, his eyes glittering in the darkness of the Brakewood, his face illuminated by the liquid light he held.

'What are you on about, Ather?' Edra asked, his tone suddenly wary.

'Having been trapped in the Vault of Damnation for these past few months, Master Edra, I'm not content to sit idly by and let you lot squander the magic Kenton has so kindly armed you with.'

Trapped ... in the Vault? Edra stared at his companion, not liking his change in tone.

'What's this?' Denithal burped, his lips flecked with vomit. 'I didn't agree to follow *you*, Ather. Screw off and give us our share of the loot. Or better yet – give us the whole damn bandolier and go sod yourself.'

Quick as a snake, Ather backhanded the old alchemist in the face. Denithal crumpled like a broken rag doll, spluttering saliva and blood.

'Wait!' Edra shouted, his sword half drawn – and then he recognised the eyes he was staring into. 'Gods ... you *can't* be. You're dead. We saw you ...'

Ather stroked his chin as if he wore a goatee – and smiled. 'I *was* dead – some form of death anyway – but I'm back now, Master Edra, and everything can go back as it was.'

'As it ... was?' Der repeated, looking dumbstruck. 'I don't understand, Ather.'

'Ather is gone, Derek. I exorcised his spirit and he is no more. I inhabit this body now.'

Edra's body shook with realisation. 'El–Elder Tosan?'

The former headmaster smiled from behind a face that was not his. 'In the flesh – so to speak. I'll say this, though. Young Master Kenton had a good idea about migrating our operations to Banok. He seems to have abandoned his plan ... but I think it has some merit. So we will be changing course. We're not heading to Port Caer. We're not going to sell the *aqlumera* and none of us are getting that vacation so deliciously described by our dear departed Master Ather – if it's any consolation, he was going to stiff you anyway. No, my brothers, we're going to Banok just as Kenton first suggested – and we're going to hunt down Annev.' He glowered at the other Sons of Damnation, his face dark and hollow. 'But first, you are going to recognise that I am your lord, liege and headmaster ... and you are my servants. Understood?'

No one spoke, and the silence spoke volumes.

'Excellent,' Tosan said.

Part Four

Stormcaller was the first known caste among the Order of the Dionachs Tobar. It contained all forms of Darite magic, elemental and metaphysical, inward and outward. As such, the Stormcaller was considered a master of all aspects of *quaire*, including the powers of the mind and the elemental forces of air and water.

Over time, a distinction was made between those who could practise the physical arts and those who were masters of thought and will. To reflect these distinctions, the Mindwalker caste was created for passive telepaths – able to hear the thoughts of others but not manipulate them.

In the Second Age, the separate campaigns of Brother Dahveedan Shen and Sister Micah Wixom led to the foundation of two new castes within the Dionachs Tobar, namely the Shieldbearer and Breathbreaker castes. Entirely elemental, these two groups gave voice to those whose powers lay exclusively in physical skywater magic, with little-to-no metaphysical powers, and acknowledged the binary of outer-expanding magic and inner-condensing magic. Like the Mindwalkers, the Shieldbearers came to be associated with those who could draw *quaire* to themselves or collect it in a finite location, while Stormcallers' and Breathbreakers' strengths lay in expanding their access to *quaire*. For Stormcallers, this meant manipulating others' thoughts or impressing one's own thoughts on another; for Breathbreakers, it meant manipulating skywater itself by evaporating or expanding its physical properties.

Over time, this binary method of magical instruction has spread from the Dionachs Tobar to the priesthoods of Lumea and Keos, creating a clear distinction between the elemental and metaphysical prime magics, as well as their inward and outward binaries. The crystallisation of these castes came towards the end of the Second Age, and among the Order of the Dionachs Tobar they are described as follows:

STORMCALLERS:
Component: Metaphysical *Quaire*
Focus: Outward, Pushing, Extending, Expanding
Elemental Manipulation: Psyche, Mind, Identity

MINDWALKERS:
Component: Metaphysical *Quaire*
Focus: Inward, Pulling, Contracting, Condensing
Elemental Manipulation: Psyche, Mind, Identity

BREATHBREAKERS:
Component: Physical Skywater
Focus: Outward, Pushing, Extending, Expanding
Elemental Manipulation: Air, Sound, Water, Mist, Fog, Vapor

SHIELDBEARERS:
Component: Physical Skywater
Focus: Inward, Pulling, Contracting, Condensing
Elemental Manipulation: Air, Water, Ice

Though our present Stormcallers do not possess the ability to call down storms as our ancestors once did, they are nevertheless proficient at summoning 'mental storms', creating disorientation, confusion, or even compulsion among their targets. The same evolution can be seen within the other three castes; namely, as Dionachs become more proficient at wielding some kinds of magic, their ability with *other* forms of magic often fades or becomes muted. Over generations, this can result in entirely new strains of magic (as has happened with the New Terrans), which leads this author to speculate that perhaps our own static Darite castes will need to evolve once again to recognise new evolutions in our magical chemistry. What those might be, one can only guess,

462

though it might be a valuable school of research. If one could predict the evolution of our magical abilities, might it not also be possible to manipulate or redirect those strains?

— Dionach Jerrod Smith, Stormcaller of the First Order;
Fourth Age of Luquatra
'On the Origin of Castes', *Darite Magical Theory*, A History of Magic
Enclave Library, Quiri, Odarnea

Chapter Forty-Eight

'I don't understand,' Annev said for the third time. 'Why can't I see him?'

'Because Sraon's condition is very delicate. Your presence could make his trauma permanent.'

Annev scrutinised the high priest using the magic of his enhanced codavora ring, but he was soundly rebuffed by the strength of the man's mental walls. *He's hiding something*, Annev thought, *but what?*

'Have Titus and Therin been in to see him?'

Reeve sighed, his expression dour. 'Annev, can we talk about this another time? I'm really very busy.'

'I've noticed. In fact, you've become so busy that you've completely forgotten about our agreement.'

'And what agreement is that?'

Annev snorted. 'I agreed to help you find Bron Gloir and the Oracle of Odar, and you agreed to use the Oracle to help me remove the Hand of Keos.'

'And?' Reeve said. 'That agreement has not changed.'

Annev felt his frustration creeping in, threatening to seize control of his emotions. 'It's been two weeks. You haven't said a word to me. You haven't bothered to update me about Sraon's health, and you haven't discussed our journey to Banok or Chaenbalu once.'

'That's because you can't do anything to aid your friend, and I never said I would accompany you south. We talked about the possibility of an expedition and you offered your assistance in locating the Oracle. The rest takes planning and preparation.'

Annev groaned aloud. He felt like he was going mad. Reeve's responses felt like a repeat of the conversation they had shared two weeks ago – and the man didn't seem in any hurry to change the status quo. It was almost as if the high priest wanted Annev to stay, but not to do anything. He didn't ask Annev to help the Order or perform any services, nor did he hasten Annev's departure. He didn't even ask about the Hand of Keos, despite Annev having explained the dangers of keeping it at the Enclave.

'Fine,' Annev said, forcing his tone to remain civil. 'When do you think I might leave?'

'So hasty, Annev – so quick to rush into danger, to start experimenting. I understand your desires—'

'How long?'

Reeve look at him flatly. 'I don't know. There are many factors to consider – not least that there are assassins out there hunting down the members of our Order. I can't send you to any of our safehouses, so you'll need supplies for food and lodging. I need to determine which of my Dionachs to send with you and—'

'Tym and Misty. They've both befriended me, and I'd enjoy their company.'

'Misty must remain here to steward the Stormcallers—'

'Just Tym then.'

'—and Brother Tym is helping me heal Sraon's memories,' Reeve said firmly. 'I need them both here.'

'Send me with Dionach Webb then – or alone, I don't care.'

The Arch-Dionach sighed. 'The most useful thing you can do is stay here – and stay out of trouble.'

Annev swore in frustration and tried to use the codavora ring again to probe Reeve's thoughts, but it was like clawing at a mirrored wall. He felt as though he were treading water, unable to make any progress towards his goals.

Reeve reached for the door to his private study. 'You should go and see your friends, Annev. They'll be taking their Tests of Ascendancy soon, and I imagine you want to be here to support them when they do.'

Annev did want to support his friends … but seeing them move forward while he was stuck in place ate at him. He couldn't argue the point, though, for the high priest had already retreated into his study.

'There's a testing room for each of us,' Titus said, as they left the library. 'It's down on the lower levels – not far from your new room.'

'But they won't tell us what will happen until we get there,' Therin interjected, 'which is stupid. How are we supposed to prepare?'

'It's not that stupid,' Titus argued. 'We were never told what to expect in the Tests of Judgement. Figuring it out was part of the test.'

'But it should have something to do with our training. That should be obvious, right? I mean, they aren't going to try to get me to do any mindwalking, are they? Because I'm rubbish at that mental stuff – and they've barely mentioned a word of theology, so they better not be testing us on all that rotting priestcraft.'

'Don't you find that strange?' Annev said, finally speaking up.

'What?'

'That we've been here for over a month and they haven't spoken a word of doctrine to us. Nothing about the purpose of the Order, or our relationship to Odar.'

'I'm fine with that,' Therin said, wiping a bogey on his sleeve. 'I hated all those classes. Modern and Ancient History. Mathematics and Agronomy. Boring stuff that was never useful. Give me stealth classes with Master Der any day.'

'I liked those classes!' Titus protested. 'Ancient Benifew was my favourite – and besides, you always hated combat training.'

'Not all of it. I liked knife-throwing and the like. I just didn't care for the parts where people were beating me up.'

'That's not what I'm talking about,' Annev said, interrupting. 'I'm talking about religion ... philosophy. Why we're here – not just in this room, but why we exist at all.'

Therin shrugged. 'Sounds like something Sodar would have taught.'

'Exactly!' Annev said, his voice lowered. 'These men are all priests, of the same Order as Sodar ... but have you heard a single one of them explain their doctrine, their tenets or anything besides how to use magic? It all feels so ... hollow.'

'That is strange, I suppose,' Titus conceded, 'but maybe it's something they teach you once you've become a member of the Order.'

'Shouldn't it be the opposite?' Annev pressed. 'Shouldn't they start with their doctrine, before we learn any magic, rather than after we've become magically dangerous?'

'I don't know,' Therin said, raising both his hands as if in defence or even apathy. 'And so long as it's not part of the Test of Ascendancy, I don't much care.'

'It just doesn't feel right,' Annev said, dropping the topic. His friends clearly felt no need to learn more about the religion they were supposedly on the precipice of joining. Perhaps, in their minds, they had always belonged to it – or perhaps they had no faith to speak of – but it all felt wrong to Annev. All this focus on training the boys' powers with skywater and *quaire*. What was the point of it? The implication was that they were creating new members for the Order and strengthening its dwindling membership, but if that were the case a spiritual conversion should be essential. Instead, the Dionachs seemed focused solely on the physical survival of their Order, on acquiring power for themselves and their caste members, rather than the preservation of any central doctrine. Sodar had mentioned this, though Annev had assumed he referred to a lack of faith at the Academy. Now, he wondered ... had Sodar meant the men and women of his own Order? And if Annev had even a modicum of talent manipulating *quaire*, would he have been so engrossed in his training that he didn't notice? Aside from his secret attempts at artificing, he had little else to think about. Perhaps it was natural that he began to see the cracks in the facade, while his friends were swept up in an entirely different experience.

'You'll both do great on your tests, I'm sure,' he said, trying to be supportive. 'It's not like the Academy, where it was a competition. You only have to contend with yourselves – and they wouldn't test you if they thought you would fail.'

Therin's mood seemed to brighten at this. 'Yeah, that's a good point. They keep saying we're really talented and all, so the test is probably something simple, like pushing some rocks across a table or some mind-reading, you know? Just a rite of passage.'

'Right,' Annev said, slapping his friends on the back. 'I'm sure you'll both do great – and I'll be waiting right here at the end of it.'

'I wish you could watch,' Titus said, wringing his hands a bit. 'Only full Dionachs are allowed to – otherwise it might give someone else an unfair advantage in their test.' He chewed his lip. 'You probably won't take the test, though? Maybe they could make an exception.'

Annev swallowed the bile that rose at the thought of his failures. Worse, it seemed, his friends had given up on him ever learning to manipulate *quaire*. He had privately accepted his failure, but it hurt to have his friends speak so plainly about it. Once again he questioned his motives for coming to the Enclave and thought of Jian's prophecy: *You will learn the truth if you go to Quiri – but it will not make you happy, and you will not join the Dionachs Tobar.*

Annev had chosen to come anyway – to defy Fate and claim his own destiny – only the longer he stayed here, the more out of place he felt. He knew it to be a strange and irrational feeling, yet it persisted.

Perhaps I should just go, he thought. *Just leave in the middle of the night – the middle of the day, even. Titus and Therin don't need looking after. Reeve is no help ... and now he won't even let me see Sraon. I have no reason to stay.*

'It's fine,' Annev said, realising he'd let the silence stretch too long. 'I'll be just down the hall. When you've finished your tests, we can celebrate together.'

'You're sure?' Titus asked with a faint look of concern.

'Absolutely – now go and earn your robes.'

The two boys split away towards the rooms where they would be tested, and Annev watched them go, still feeling melancholy.

I'll give Reeve one last chance. Tomorrow morning, first thing. And if he won't send me to reclaim the Oracle, I'll pack my things and go anyway. I can search for it without his aid – or I can return to Luqura and conclude my business with Saltair. Maybe reconnect with Fyn. The more

Annev thought about it, the more he liked that idea. *I'll pack now*, he decided, *while Therin and Titus take their tests. There's no reason to wait.* That felt right. The Enclave might manage to ensnare its novices with promises of power and the lure of magic, but it had no hold over him – only promises they had failed to keep. Even Sraon's unstable condition no longer compelled him to stay; he had no way to help his old friend, and no better reasons to stay if or when he recovered. Annev was the master of his own fate, and he'd be damned if he was going to let a cursed golden hand, a lost Oracle, or a book of old prophecies dictate his path.

He glanced after his friends once more, now silently wishing them well, and then he hurried towards his rooms to prepare for the journey he expected to make on the morrow.

Chapter Forty-Nine

Titus stood in a lamplit room facing both of the Dionach McClanahans, Misty and Tym, Dionach Holyoak, and Arch-Dionach Reeve. The latter stood with his arms folded, analysing Titus. Titus stared back, then began studying the odd assortment of junk that filled the corners of the room. Tarnished candelabras and cracked wooden chests, chipped figurines and rust-pitted weapons, sticky cups and dusty bowls, a heap of moth-eaten clothes and a rack of purplish bottles, their contents empty or else crusty and black.

'Hello,' Titus said timidly. Not one of them replied – in fact, other than Arch-Dionach Reeve, they seemed unwilling to make eye contact with him. Titus cleared his throat.

'So ... what am I supposed to do?'

Silence.

'This is my Test of Ascendancy, right?'

More silence.

'Are you not allowed to talk?' Titus asked, his suspicions aroused by the prolonged and uncomfortable quiet. An inkling of an idea came to him. 'Ah. I'm supposed to read your minds, aren't I?'

Silence.

So, it was a puzzle. They wanted him to read their thoughts – to mindwalk – for instructions. He reached out, tentative at first and then with greater confidence. His mind brushed Reeve's and was met by a mental wall that seemed erected specifically to keep *him* out. Titus moved on to Dionach McClanahan and found the woman was singing a silent tune to herself to stop Titus tugging

470

on her thoughts. He moved on to Brother Tym and found his answer. The man was repeating a litany in his mind:

Hello, Titus. This is your Test of Ascendancy, the purpose of which is to determine your readiness to become a journeyman Mindwalker. To succeed in this test, use your mindwalking skills to extract key pieces of information from the Dionachs in this room. Their clues will lead you through the test, of which Arch-Dionach Reeve is the arbiter. He will ensure no one purposefully or accidentally reveals the answers. Your first clue is that you are searching this room for a specific item, which you will present to Arch-Dionach Reeve. May Odar bless and protect you . . .

Hello, Titus. This is your Test of Ascendancy, the purpose of which is to determine . . .

Titus smiled.

He walked closer to the group of priests and studied Dionach Holyoak, the Mindwalkers' caste leader. The priest would not meet his gaze, which Titus understood now. Meeting his eyes would let Titus peer into the man's soul – and see what he was trying to keep hidden. Titus reached out with his mindwalking powers and found that instead of walling his thoughts away, the man was flitting between several hundred thoughts, a noise of nonsense designed to disguise one piece of information. Titus tried to grab a flying thought, but it was like trying to catch rats in the dark – he felt them skitter past, brushing the edges of his mind, but they were gone before he could catch and examine one.

Titus returned to Misty, knowing her strength as a Stormcaller should make her the most susceptible to his mindwalking skills. She was still humming a silent tune to herself, but this time Titus attuned himself to her thoughts. Instead of battling her wordless song, he tried to quiet his own thoughts so that they matched hers and listened attentively for several minutes until he could start humming the same tune. As he did, he seemed to pierce the veil covering the woman's mind and glimpsed the image she held fixed behind that curtain of noise: a wooden chest, its lid battered yet secured by a rusty iron lock. Titus inclined his head in thanks, then circled the room until he spotted what he was looking for.

Titus pulled the small locked chest into the centre of the room, placing it squarely in front of the four Dionachs. No one moved, though Titus thought he glimpsed a smile tug the corner of Brother Tym's mouth. Still, no one said anything.

Okay, Titus thought. *I need the key, and it's going to be in here somewhere.* He glanced around the room, seeing the mounds of junk piled in the corners. He'd never find a single key buried in so much rubbish – and there was no guarantee there was only one key in here. He could try picking the lock ... but he was fairly sure that wasn't part of this test.

He reached out to Dionach Reeve's mind again, and again he was rebuffed by the strength of the man's mental wall. It felt like mirrored steel – flawless, impervious. Perhaps if he were a stronger Mindwalker he'd have found a way through the man's defences, but given his limited experience he had a better chance of beating Fyn or Annev in unarmed combat – which was to say no chance at all. He turned back to Brother Tym, listening to his thoughts once more, but again he only heard the droning, unthinking wall of recited words:

> *... use your mindwalking skills to extract key pieces of information from the Dionachs in this room. Their clues will lead you through the test, of which Arch-Dionach Reeve is the arbiter ...*

Was the word 'key' a clue? Was there a riddle in Tym's words at all, or were they simple instructions? For a moment, Titus wished Annev were there to help him piece it together – he had always been so good at solving puzzles – but then Titus reminded himself he had a skill Annev did not possess: Titus could mindwalk, and that was precisely the skill he needed to pull his threads from the Dionachs and assemble the answer he sought.

Titus sat down on the floor beside the chest and pondered Dionach Holyoak, a stout man in dark blue robes with grey-streaked black hair, spectacles and a black goatee. He started listening to the man's skittering thoughts, and began to detect a pattern. A list of unconnected words:

Water. Sky. Horsehair. Key. Wood. Swirl. Bone. Sponge. Paint. Dry. Cork. Table. Pine cone. Chestnut. Feather. Black. Rock. Worm. Bottle.

And then it repeated again. *Water. Sky. Horsehair. Key ...* There was that word again. Titus fixated on it, drawing on it in his mind – the key that would unlock the chest – and when Holyoak cycled through his word list again, Titus waited for the word 'horsehair' and then, in the instant that Holyoak thought of a key, *pulled* on the thought, tugging it from the spinning shield of nonsense words. As he pulled, others thoughts came with it:

Bottle. Black. Cork. Water.

The blond boy got to his feet and approached the rack of dirty bottles, searching through them. At the back of a shelf was a corked black bottle half-filled with a watery liquid. Titus took the bottle down, uncorked it and poured the contents out onto a nearby coat. Something jangled inside the dark glass and, as the liquid streamed out, a small key fell into Titus's hand. The boy set the bottle down and hastened back to the chest. To his delight the key fit! Titus grinned broadly as he twisted it and the lock clicked open. The lid of the chest popped open to reveal—

It was empty.

Titus stared at the chest, unable to fathom where his deductions had gone wrong. The four Dionachs were as impassive as ever, gazing at the floor or staring into space.

Except for Arch-Dionach Reeve, Titus thought, seeing the man's penetrating gaze. *He isn't looking away. Is that because he's the arbiter ... or is he challenging me to meet his eyes?*

Titus decided to try it. He stared into Reeve's eyes, half-distracted by the man's stolid expression, then focused on his irises – the windows to his soul. As he did so, Titus sought out the *quaire* tied to the high priest's soul and tried to tug on its threads. As expected, Reeve resisted and Titus had to dive deeper, immersing himself in the icy waters of the man's steely psyche. Swimming amidst the thoughts that resisted him, Titus felt as if he were adrift in an ocean of blackness, his own psyche floating in a void of starless night. He simply could not find a thought upon which to anchor himself. No tether to cling to or exert force upon.

He retreated, feeling as though he had somehow failed. Could they really expect him to penetrate the high priest's mind? Titus studied the box and key again then listened once more to Tym's instructions, Misty's soundless tune and Holyoak's list of nonsense words. He had missed something – some clue or hint to solve the puzzle – yet he couldn't fathom what.

He examined each Dionach's mind again ... the message, the words, the tune, humming it to himself as he approached Reeve. And this time he felt something altogether different from the high priest. Not the icy ocean of words or thoughts, but the warm intuition of the high priest's feelings. He could feel the man working to remain indifferent, yet sensed a subtle warmth from him whenever Titus meditated on the Test of Ascendancy. The aura felt altogether different from the *quaire* the Dionachs had taught him to manipulate, yet for that it felt no less real. Titus probed it with his spirit and felt the warmth of the man's soul, distilling an echo of whatever he was feeling.

Titus withdrew his mind and spirit from the Arch-Dionach, then attempted a two-pronged approach, first brushing his own thoughts against the ocean of the priest's psyche, then drawing on the aura of his spirit. It felt almost as if he had found a backdoor into the high priest's mind, for as he allowed his thoughts to be heard, he was able to siphon off Reeve's reactions – not any conscious thoughts, but as a *feeling* – an intuition. Titus considered the puzzle of the chest and felt Reeve's interest increase.

The item I'm supposed to find ... it's connected to the chest. But how, when the box is empty? Titus felt a pulse of approval as if, upon hearing his thoughts, the Arch-Dionach's spirit had reacted.

Not wanting to reveal this secret tactic, Titus continued to hum, masking his own thoughts behind it. As he started to hum aloud, Reeve's feelings suddenly became crystal clear.

The item used to be inside the box, but it has been moved.

The meaning formed in his mind as though translated from an impression; Reeve had not consciously spoken those words in his mind, yet Titus had felt them all the same.

Disorientated for a moment, Titus stopped humming and his connection to Reeve's spirit suddenly dissolved.

I have to keep humming, Titus thought. *That's the secret! I can hear him when—*

Reeve glanced sharply at Titus, his brow furrowed in suspicion. Titus blinked, realised his error, and immediately erased all conscious thoughts from his mind, presenting a blank slate to the Arch-Dionach's scrutiny.

A heartbeat passed, then three, and Titus felt the Dionach's attention slowly retreat.

Titus went back to humming and Reeve's scrutiny seemed to fall away entirely, unable to penetrate the gauze of music, intuition and emotion.

Where are the contents of the box now? Titus thought, slowly letting that question seep through the web of music and into his consciousness, then allowing it to brush the icy ocean of Reeve's mind. The high priest did not consciously respond, yet his aura seemed to pulse. Titus was on the right path.

Is it hidden amidst the junk? Titus tested, again allowing the conscious thought to penetrate his web of music. This time Reeve's emotions seemed to cool.

Okay, Titus thought, *so someone took it out.* He hadn't meant it as a question but Reeve's emotions spiked. Titus was on the right track ... and he got an impression of the stout Dionach with the black goatee.

Dionach Holyoak.

Still humming, Titus drifted away from Arch-Dionach Reeve and used the same mental trick on Dionach Holyoak. The man's mind was still dancing between the words on his list, always moving, impossible to grasp. Titus imagined the box sitting in the centre of the room, then tried to bring its original contents into focus ... something important ... something vital to solving the Test of Ascendancy. Immediately, Titus got the impression he sought – complete with thoughts pulled from Holyoak's litany of nonsense: *Wood. Horsehair. Swirl. Paint. Sky. Water.*

Titus was looking for a bamboo water brush – the same instruments the Dionachs used to paint impromptu water glyphs. Titus smiled. Now he knew what he was looking for ... but where to find it? Titus tried to tempt Holyoak with the question, but it was Brother Tym's emotions that lit up.

Titus stepped back and thought he detected an ill-concealed smile on Tym's face. The Dionach not only knew where it was ... he had it. He looked closer at Tym's clothing, saw a slight bulge beneath the man's tunic and felt Tym's emotions quicken once more. This time, however, Titus sensed anticipation from all four Dionachs.

Titus stopped humming then slowly extended his hand, allowing his fingers to slip beneath the collar of Brother Tym's tunic. He felt a familiar wooden cylinder there, pinched it between his fingers and withdrew the horsehair brush from Brother Tym's inner pocket. Flushed with elation, Titus returned to the centre of the room and held the item aloft to Arch-Dionach Reeve. Then, dropping his mental barriers, Titus shouted the thought: *Gotcha!*

Tym laughed aloud and Misty's song faded. Holyoak looked satisfied and Reeve raised his eyes to stare at the bamboo water brush. Then he smiled.

'It's yours,' Reeve said, his mental walls suddenly falling away. 'You have earned it, Titus – it's a badge of your journeyman status within the Order.'

Dionach Holyoak clapped Titus on the back. 'Remarkable!' he exclaimed, his stoic face alight with emotion. 'Many novices find the chest but struggle to locate the key. I dare say only three of our brethren have ever solved the puzzle of the water brush – the rest give up!'

'So ... I've passed?' Brother Tym began to laugh. 'What?' Titus asked, feeling off-balance. 'What did I do?'

'Yes, you passed,' Misty said, delighted. 'We just hadn't expected you to find the water brush. That's ... like extra points.' She glanced at Reeve then at Dionach Holyoak. The former shook his head while the latter nodded enthusiastically.

On instinct, Titus reverted to his mindwalking trance and caught snippets of the silent conversation the four priests were having.

He's passed all four tests! Dionach Holyoak seemed to shout. *He's allowed full Dionach status.*

He's too young. Reeve's thoughts were cool and impractical.

He may be young, McClanahan rejoined, *but he still passed the test. If the others found out he passed and we denied him full status—*

You can't change the rules just because he's the youngest member of our Order, Brother Tym said, joining the argument. *He found the water brush. He's entitled to a full—*

No, Reeve said, his thoughts implacable. *Too much too soon. It's dangerous.*

What's dangerous? Titus asked, unconsciously joining the silent conversation. The four priests turned to him, three of them grinning in amusement. Reeve blinked, and his face flushed with embarrassment. He coughed, then cleared his throat.

'That was a private conversation,' he said, clicking his tongue. 'You weren't meant to hear that.'

'But he did,' Brother Tym said, raising his finger, 'which further proves he's ready.'

'We shouldn't put up barriers to his advancement,' Holyoak said, nodding in agreement. 'Besides,' he said, glancing sharply at Reeve, 'once we've elevated him as a journeyman Mindwalker, his next level of advancement is decided by his caste leader – which is *me.*'

'I could veto his advancement to journeyman,' Reeve said, meeting Holyoak's gaze. 'There were ... irregularities during the test. I'd like to ask Titus about them.'

'If you tried to veto,' Holyoak countered, 'the three of us could overrule you.' He looked at Misty and Tym who both gave their agreement. 'So it's up to you, Brother Reeve. You can object to his advancement now and we can overrule you – and advance him to Dionach status anyway – or you can agree with us and we can make the decision unanimous.'

The high priest pursed his lips, his face unexpectedly stony. He glanced at Titus then back to the caste leader of the Mindwalkers. 'So be it,' he said. 'Novice Titus, you are hereby elevated ... to full Dionach status.'

Holyoak nodded in satisfaction and clapped Titus on the back again. 'Welcome to the Mindwalkers, my boy!'

Chapter Fifty

Annev started packing. In the back of his mind, he knew Sraon might still need his help or that Reeve might still aid him in his quest to remove the Hand of Keos ... but he didn't believe it. The high priest could have helped Annev at any point in the past month. Instead he had delayed and demurred, always finding one excuse or another to postpone. Annev had tried to be patient, but his last conversation with the Arch-Dionach had left no doubt that the man was stalling. It was as Jian Nikloss had foretold: the high priest would only aid Annev if he first helped Reeve reclaim the Oracle and set his own house in order – and now Reeve wouldn't even do that.

I could have left weeks ago, he thought, annoyed. *If I had just listened to the soothsayer, I could have stayed in Luqura with Fyn.*

But Sraon had needed help after their confrontation with Saltair – that was the real reason Annev had come to Quiri. He had told himself it was also to remove the Hand of Keos, but after Jian's prophecy he'd had little faith Reeve would actually help him.

Annev stared at his pack, its load lightened by the near-weightless bottomless bag he still carried. Was he really going to abandon Sraon, Titus and Therin? He wanted to. He wanted to leave it all behind, to sever his ties of obligation and friendship and pursue a path that was *truly* his. He just wasn't sure he could. Staying at the Enclave, supporting his friends, making certain Sraon had fully recovered ... it was as Elder Tosan had said: he was helping others at a cost to himself.

But Tosan had been wrong, hadn't he? The old headmaster's

world view didn't permit compassion or selflessness – he had been *wrong* ... which left Annev languishing in a city that held no love for him, and all because of a perceived commitment to old friends and dead mentors. It was frustrating. Paralysing. Suffocating.

Annev sat down on his bed and tried to draw breath. The room suddenly felt stifling, as if he were choking.

No, Annev *was* choking. The air was thinner somehow. Annev stared at the lamplit walls, his lungs straining. He rushed to his door, tried to open it, and found that while the handle turned, the portal would not open. He wanted to scream but didn't dare. He tried to force the door open but failed to move it even an inch, not even with the Hand of Keos. He pulled out his dagger and tried to pry at the door's frame, but the blade slid across an invisible barrier – a wall of air that perfectly sealed his room.

I'm going to suffocate in here, he thought, uncertain whether to take shallow breaths and conserve the remaining oxygen, or to breathe deeply and claim the portion that remained.

And then he saw the painting.

Therin stepped into the bare room designated for his Test of Ascendancy and stopped, uncertain whether he'd entered the right space. The chamber was completely empty, about thirty feet in length and half as wide. The ceiling above him stood higher than expected – almost twenty feet – and a door with a sliding peephole stood at the opposite end of the room.

And that was it.

No, Therin realised. There *was* something else in the room. At the far end of the dimly lit chamber, he could see a block of something white and translucent resting on the floor. Ice? He stepped closer and the door swung shut behind him, leaving him in darkness. At the same instant, Therin felt a solid pressure nudge him from behind, sliding him towards the centre of the room. He turned, confused by the invisible wall that had suddenly manifested, and realised three more walls of air were now pressing on him from the front and sides. He was stuck, unable to move forward or backward, unable to reach any of the room's extremities.

Something shifted beneath him, and Therin felt a barrier solidify beneath his feet. He knelt down and touched another wall of air, and then he felt himself being lifted towards the ceiling by the unseen platform ... and Therin had no way to stop it.

Gods ... I'm going to be crushed!

The oil painting was a new addition to his room. It was non-descript and unassuming – a portrait of two men in black robes sitting at a table, conversing with one another – but an oddity caught Annev's attention: a series of faint grey glyphs denoting the words for compressed air, painted onto their robes.

Feeling light-headed, Annev slashed the hidden glyphs apart, his blade cutting two triangles of fabric from the painting. The air inside the room seemed to shudder and Annev tried to take a breath.

But there was none to be had.

The walls surrounding Therin held him tight, their pressure forcing him inexorably closer to the chamber ceiling. He stretched and found he could touch it, its stones uncomfortably close ... and moving closer still.

'Blood and ashes!' Therin swore, practically screaming. 'What kind of test *is* this?' He reached out into the dark, his hands patting the invisible barriers that held him.

'I can do this,' he told himself, dispelling images of his body being crushed against the ceiling. 'I just need to keep my head. The walls are air ... I can push them back. I can move them. This is a *Breathbreaker* test.' He took a deep breath, concentrated his will, and spoke the command word.

'*Ceò!*'

The walls pressing against Therin popped, crashing him to the floor. He rolled on the stones, groaning. At the opposite end of the chamber, the peephole slid open and a tiny square of light illuminated the room once more.

Therin struggled to his feet and staggered to the door, only to find it was locked. He peeked through the peephole and saw a room beyond, similar to the one he stood in – and similarly empty.

His avatar instincts kicked in and he reached for his lockpicking tools – but they were gone.

The hell . . . ? Someone stole my flaming lockpicks!

Therin spat in disgust – and then glimpsed the block of ice. He'd forgotten about it while pushing back the walls but now he spun on his heel and went back to it, seeing a small key embedded in the giant cube of frozen water.

Ice, he thought. *Water-to-mist will expand the skywater, which would turn the ice into . . . water.*

He knew what he had to do.

Placing his hand atop the block, Therin used his body heat to slick the surface of the ice. With water dripping from his fingertips, he traced the glyph for skywater on the stones and marked it with the diacritic accents for expansion and evaporation. Holding the symbol in his mind, he said firmly: '*Gal-gal-galú.*'

The glyph evaporated in front of him – but the ice block and frozen key remained.

I can't breathe! Annev was beginning to panic.

Why hadn't destroying the glyph disrupted the spell? Where had he gone wrong? Amidst the dizzying haze, Honeycutt's words resurfaced: *The glyphs are only a tool. The critical piece of glyph-speaking is focusing one's will.*

Somebody had placed the glyph in Annev's room as a point of focus . . . and they were still holding it together with their will. To break the spell, Annev had to disrupt that connection.

But first he needed to breathe. Otherwise, in another minute, he'd be unconscious . . . and then he'd be dead.

Acting on instinct, Annev grabbed his bottomless bag and shoved his hand inside, thinking of all the artifacts he had recently collected or acquired. He pulled out his rings, the handkerchief, the Rod of Artificing. He tossed them all on the bed, sliding the rings on so they might actually aid him. His vision blurred as the world shaded in red mist, and the air in his lungs seemed to slip away entirely. The room grew even more red and hazy.

I need air, he thought. *I need . . . to breathe . . .*

He sat heavily on the bed, looking down at the scented

handkerchief, and blinked in disbelief: the symbols for air, water, and *quaire* were stitched into its surface.

That's right, he thought, snatching the artifact from his bed. *This handkerchief makes air* – scented *air!* Annev slammed the lacy cloth against his mouth and sucked greedily at the fabric. A blissful breath of floral-scented air filled his lungs.

Praise Odar!

He inhaled deeply for what felt like the first time in an eternity. Even as he breathed, though, Annev could sense the oxygen inside the artifact was being rapidly depleted. The handkerchief wouldn't last long without any air to fuel its magic.

It needs quaire ... *skywater.*

Air ... or water.

Annev ripped the bottomless sack open again, shoved his hand inside and summoned his waterskin. After Sodar's death, he had become relentless in always keeping the skin stocked and stored in his bottomless bag. Now that preparation proved Annev's salvation. He peeled the handkerchief away from his face, already feeling light-headed without it. Using his teeth, he jerked the cork from the skin and poured half the cow bladder's contents over the lacy handkerchief, dousing the fabric in cool, clear water. It evaporated, as though the thin cloth were some kind of magic sponge, and then Annev slapped the handkerchief back over his mouth. The effect was immediate: the handkerchief's *quaire* was restored and, with it, air began flowing once more.

Praise Odar, he said silently again.

But the waterskin would eventually run out ... and then so would the handkerchief's *quaire*. At best, Annev had only bought himself a little time. To truly save himself, he had to escape the room or restore the air before the handkerchief's magic wore off.

'Cracking hells!' Therin swore, thumping the frozen block. Why hadn't the ice evaporated? What had he missed? He'd established a physical connection between the thing he was trying to melt and the glyph he'd drawn, so ...

Oh, right. Therin silently berated himself. *I didn't mentally reinforce the connection when I activated the glyph. I just diffused the magic into the air.*

Focused once more, Therin drew the glyph on the stones again, but when it came to speaking the command words, he turned his mental focus on the block of frozen water and imagined the two handspans of ice melting into water and then evaporating into steam.

'*Gal,*' he said. '*Gal-galú.*'

Water immediately began to shed from the ice block, a portion of it dissipating into steam. He kept the image of melting ice in his mind, and half a minute later he could see the key poking out of the frozen block.

Okay, Therin thought, pulling it free from its frozen prison. *That's two of the four breathbreaking skills: air bubbles and water-to-mist. They'll still want to test me on sound bubbles and void bubbles, though.* Therin inserted the key, turned it, and pushed the portal open. He half expected to see someone standing on the other side, but whoever had opened the peephole had retreated to the next room. What he did find was perhaps more perplexing: oil paintings covered the walls … and tiny brass bells littered the floor. On the other side of the room was another locked door.

It didn't take long for him to puzzle out what the Dionachs expected him to do.

Therin retreated to the corner of the first room, picked up the remaining ice and returned to the threshold of the second room, where he drew the symbols for sound and silence. He envisioned a space of voided air around his feet – two spheres that would silence all sounds – then he spoke the command word. With measured steps, he began walking across the bell-strewn floor. Even with the precautions of his sound bubbles, he took care to not let the brass bells roll away after brushing them aside with his feet. Slowly, he forged a path across the room, the only sound that of his heartbeat and breathing. At the far end of the room, he used the same key to unlock the door and open the final testing chamber.

Beyond the threshold of the room was a pit, the floor over ten feet down and extending the entire length and breadth of the chamber, which was itself about thirty feet across. In an even more disorientating twist, the other door wasn't aligned with the one he had entered, nor with the bottom of the pit – it wasn't even fixed on the opposite wall; instead, a trapdoor had been cut into the ceiling in the centre of the room, the opening more than five feet from any of the sheer walls. To reach it, he'd have to fly ... and his Breathbreaker magic wasn't anywhere near strong enough for that.

Therin studied the bottom of the pit, half expecting some spikes or other trap to be at the bottom, but it was simply a deep hole with sheer walls and no obvious way of climbing back out if he fell to the bottom. He sat down, flummoxed.

How in the five hells was he supposed to reach that door?

The seal around Annev's mouth was imperfect, and he felt the vacuum trying to siphon away his fresh air.

He was running out of time.

Using his waterskin and the command words the Dionachs had taught him, Annev tried to draw glyphs that would enable him to break the spell threatening to kill him. He tried pushing with skywater, first forming the air into a bludgeon, and then honing it into a sharp knife, but he failed to compress the *quaire*. He tried pulling at the invisible walls, expanding and stretching them until they became so thin he might tear a hole through them – but Annev's connection to the *quaire* remained intangible and the magic walls held.

He couldn't perform Darite magic, that much was clear. He had been able to use the handkerchief, though, and its magic was tied to an artifact ... so maybe if he pressed the handkerchief against the invisible walls, he could siphon off the skywater that had been used to form them?

Exulting that he might have a way to escape the void bubble, Annev took a deep breath then slapped the cloth against the solid wall of air that prevented him from opening his door and leaving his chamber. He waited, imagining the handkerchief siphoning off the skywater that had been used to form the invisible barriers. When his lungs began to demand he take another breath, he tore the handkerchief away and prodded the wall of air forming the perimeter of the void bubble.

Nothing. The barrier was solid. Annev tried forcing the door open but, again, nothing budged.

Annev moved the handkerchief back to his mouth, inhaling again, only to find the wall of compressed air had siphoned the magic from the handkerchief – it was devoid of *quaire*.

Panicking, Annev squeezed liquid from his waterskin, splashing the handkerchief once more with the precious liquid. Feeling dizzy, he breathed the floral-scented air again.

That didn't work, he chastised himself. *What else can I do?*

Annev turned his attention back to the bed and picked up the Rod of Artificing. Its mechanics were still mostly a mystery to him, but he had gleaned a little bit of knowledge by experimenting with it. To be of any use, the rod needed blood to interact with. With his left hand still holding the handkerchief to his face, Annev placed his belt knife between his knees and prepared to slash his right hand – and then he stopped.

Through the magic of the Inquisitor ring, Annev spotted a faint life-force tied to his room – not quite blood, but similar. Stranger yet, it was tied to the cryptic painting.

Taking another deep breath from his handkerchief, Annev shuffled over to the oil painting and studied the faint red glow emanating from the hem of the second man's black robes: a thread of the blood-talent seemed to be tied there, connected somehow to the glyphs Annev had physically destroyed.

It's connected to the person who activated the glyph, Annev realised, a reassuring hum from the codavora ring confirming his instincts. He stared at the threads of magic, their vaporous connection pink and tenuous. Could he use the Rod of Artificing to untangle those threads and dismantle the glyph? There was only one way to know.

Switching the handkerchief to his right hand and holding the rod in his left, Annev threaded the tip of the rod through the hole he had sliced in the canvas. Something thrummed at the tip of the wand, as if he could feel the pulse of magic coming from the person at the other end of the thread.

Annev ... *pulled.* He wasn't sure how else to describe it, except as a kind of grasping motion. The thread of blood-magic resisted him, its fibres strong, its magic potent. Annev grasped them again, but this time he *pushed* at the magic – and this time his touch scattered it.

In an instant, the wall of air surrounding his room seemed to pop, collapsing as air rushed in to fill it. Annev breathed and his lungs filled with the comforting taste of damp stone and stale basement air.

Annev dashed to his door and flung it open, casting about for some sign of the person who had tried to kill him, but there was none: the hallway was empty.

Spitting curses, Annev rushed back to his room, jerked the painting from the wall and carried it out into the hallway. Using the magic of his copper Inquisitor ring, Annev delved deep into the threads of *quaire* he'd so recently severed, searching for the faint pink glow that might alert him to the assassin's lingering presence.

There *was* something there – something faint and fading – yet as Annev gripped it with the Rod of Artificing, the whisper of magic seemed to grow more substantial, its thread as fragile as the filament of a spiderweb. Moving cautiously, with the painting in one hand and the rod in the other, Annev followed the thread of magic down the hallway and towards his would-be assassin.

This is a void bubble test, Therin thought, *so maybe I can use void bubbles to suction myself to the walls* ... He doubted his magic was strong enough to carry him all the way to the trapdoor, though. Even if they held, his chest and arms would still be fighting the pull of gravity – and with the magic depleting his reserves of *quaire,* he'd quickly tire ... and drop like a stone.

But maybe there was a way to compensate for that.

Using the last of the melting ice, Therin stooped to the floor and drew the glyphs that would expel the air surrounding his palms and knees, enabling them to suction to the stone walls. He then created a second pair of slightly modified glyphs that would anchor to his feet. Finally, he consciously tied the spells to his limbs and held the first set of glyphs in his mind. He carefully edged his fingers and toes against the wall then spoke the word of power.

'*Folús.*'

Therin felt the voided air push away from him and smiled. With the same caution he had learned at the Academy during his stealth classes with Der and Duvarek, he carefully slid out over the threshold and pressed his palms and knees against the wall, suctioning them to the perpendicular precipice. As his feet lifted off the ground, he activated the second pair of glyphs and directed the air away from his feet, pushing his body upward. He felt a moment of elation as his body become almost weightless, and then he immediately tipped forward, his head and chest crashing into the wall. Were it not for his hands and knees still maintaining their suction, he would have certainly fallen – and then he had his feet under him again, his balance restored.

It's working, he thought. *It's actually working!*

Still thrusting the air away from his feet, he began to move hand over hand, pulling himself along the wall with the support of his void bubbles. He had crossed nearly half the distance to the trapdoor when he suddenly felt winded, not from the physical exertion, but from the *quaire* his spells had already depleted.

Damn, he thought, picking up his pace and reaching the ceiling where he fumbled to reorientate himself, knowing he would have to dispel at least one pair of glyphs to move forward. He dispelled the void bubbles around his knees, and his legs immediately swung away from the wall. Instead of falling, though, he kept his palms suctioned to the ceiling overhead and allowed the air bubbles beneath his feet to support his weight. Therin's arms trembled, his muscles straining to pull himself upward as he fought to maintain his vacuum grip on the ceiling; he shuffled along, drawing himself closer to the trapdoor and farther away from the wall. His feet dangled, floating in the air, and he struggled to maintain his mental connection to the skywater.

With a burst of strength, Therin swiped for the door handle, suctioning it to his palm, and then he twisted, pulling himself upward as he did so. Only the portal didn't open.

It was locked – of course.

Spitting curses, Therin carefully freed his hand from the trapdoor and withdrew the key from his pocket, his feet wobbling crazily beneath him. He felt dizzy, attached by only one hand, and struggled to take a breath. His mouth suddenly felt parched as he jammed the key into the lock, turned it, then felt his air bubbles collapse beneath him. Suddenly, all of his weight hung from the tenuous grip of his single suctioned hand.

The trapdoor above Therin sprang open, surprising him, and his palm popped free of the stone. Before he plummeted into the pit, a hand grabbed the collar of his tunic, jerking him to safety.

'Don't worry, Journeyman Therin. You only need to pass *three* of the four tests.' Dionach Leskal set Therin down carefully, his feet firmly on the floor.

'He would have passed the fourth test, too,' Dionach Honeycutt objected, 'had you not startled him by swinging that door open!'

'He was going to fall anyway, Jayar – and besides, he already passed.' The leader of the Shieldbearers thrust a cup of water into Therin's shaking hands. 'Drink this,' he said, 'for the *quaire* burn.'

Therin drank greedily, his mind still fuzzy, as Honeycutt grinned broadly at him. 'Welcome to the Breathbreakers, Journeyman Therin! I'm delighted to have you – and what an exceptional job you did.'

'Oh,' Therin said, still breathing heavily, 'it wasn't that difficult. Got myself worked up a bit by the moving walls at the start – seemed like you were trying to kill me!' He laughed with only a hint of his doubt creeping through, and was relieved when the other priests chuckled.

'It's a mean trick, I know, but a good Dionach can perform his spells under immense pressure.' Leskal clapped a meaty palm on the boy's back. 'And you certainly did that today!'

'I should say so,' Honeycutt said, his own arm weaving around Leskal to rest on Therin's shoulders. 'How exactly *did* you dispel that void bubble? Neither of us saw how it was done without a glyph or a command word. Quite remarkable for someone of your age to have that level of focus.'

'Oh,' Therin said, taken aback. 'Well ... I *did* use a command word in that first room. Maybe you just didn't hear me?'

Leskal and Honeycutt stared at him as in confusion. 'First room?' Leskal asked, tugging his chin and braided beard. 'No, those were air bubbles – I made those. Honeycutt is talking about the void bubbles in the second room.'

Therin watched the pair, his expression dubious. 'The room with the paintings and the bells?'

Honeycutt nodded. 'Exactly. The air … there was a vacuum in that room, yet you conquered it so swiftly, and then immediately set about silencing the bells. It's more common for novices to panic and fall unconscious.'

'Or they manage to dispel the vacuum,' Leskal added, his teeth white and fierce behind his beard, 'and ring the bells in the process. But you managed both tasks in silence – and with remarkable speed.'

'Vacuum?' Therin repeated, bewildered. 'The other novices … fell unconscious?' He stared at them, still not quite understanding the conversation.

'Yes,' Honeycutt said. 'The vacuum in the bell room.'

'Although, there was that time Sister Rachel—'

'Leskal, you don't need to repeat your wife's achievements for Journeyman Therin. No one needs to hear that story again.'

'She held her breath!' the caste leader for the Shieldbearers shouted, his voice full of pride. 'She skipped the glyphs altogether, raced through the bell room and unlocked the door without making so much as a jingle, a tinkle or a peal.'

'Because there's no air in a vacuum,' Therin said, speaking slowly, 'and without air … there is no sound.'

'Exactly!' Leskal said, grinning. 'Bit of a cheat, I admit, but she used her void bubbles to climb the walls in the third room – same as you – so it was all square in the end.'

'I half-think you married her for her mischief,' Honeycutt said, his expression droll.

Leskal grinned. 'That's all beside the point. Therin – what a performance!'

Therin hesitated to return either the smile or the enthusiasm but in the end he settled on the former. He forced himself to curve the corner of his mouth, just enough to bare his teeth, in acknowledgement of the caste leader's praise. It was quite possible he even deserved it, though the uncomfortable feeling in the pit of his stomach suggested otherwise. A vacuum in the bell room? Therin recalled no such thing, and he was certain he'd have noticed being unable to breathe. Perhaps he'd caught a lucky break, though – and, if so, he was in no hurry to reveal it.

'Come on, lad. We'll see if Titus has finished his test.'

Annev followed the thread of blood-magic as it wound its way through the corridors. When he heard voices approaching, he stopped, ducked around the corner, and pressed himself into a small alcove.

'We'll be lucky to have that one join the Order.'

That sounded like Dionach Honeycutt. Could he be the assassin? A traitor to the Order?

'Don't act so serene and pious, Jayar,' said the second voice – Dionach Leskal. 'That's gloating if I ever heard it!'

'New members should be celebrated,' Honeycutt objected, his wiry form gliding past the alcove where Annev hid.

'Especially the ones for your caste, eh? No, don't deny it. You've got plenty to celebrate. Another member gives you another vote in the Council, after all.'

'Only after he's been made a Dionach,' Honeycutt protested mildly, 'and that could be months yet.'

'Doubtful,' Leskal said, passing Annev in the gloomy hallway. 'Holyoak and McClanahan already got Titus elevated to Dionach status, which will upset the balance if left unchecked. They'll have to raise Therin soon in response.'

As the two men walked away, Annev felt a slight tug on the gossamer thread of blood-magic he'd been following. The thread snapped, fading into nothingness – and as it broke, he spied Dionach Honeycutt look sharply over his shoulder, his eyes narrowed as if to pierce the darkness of the alcove where Annev was hiding.

Chapter Fifty-One

Sealing the tunnels proved more of a chore than Fyn had guessed, mostly because he'd underestimated the sheer labour involved in transporting so much stone. Fortunately, the Ash Quarter had loose stone in abundance – which Sodja had counted on when they'd made their plan – and having a team of seven working together made the work go much faster.

'We should get larger shares of the loot,' Siege had complained, 'since Poli and I are doing the heavy lifting.' He hadn't been wrong either. The two former dock workers were at least as strong as Fyn, though they seemed to tire easier.

'You get the share you agreed to when I took leadership of the crew,' Fyn countered, seeing this as an opportunity to assert his leadership. 'Way and Neldon are doing most of the cement work, but you don't see them complaining or asking for larger shares.'

'Maybe we should *all* get larger shares,' Poli countered. 'If we're contributing more than the rest.'

'Fine,' Fyn said, seeing where the hustle was going. 'Way and Neldon get more because we're relying on their expertise to seal the tunnels. Me, you, and Siege get more because we're hauling more stone than the rest. Raven and Quinn get more because they had to scour the Ash Quarter for enough chains to block the river exit. We're all getting more, so we should all be happy.' That seemed to please the dock workers, though Way and Quinn were snickering.

'They'll be ornery,' Way whispered, 'when they realise everyone getting extra shares means that no one does.'

'We're all doing our part,' Fyn said, smiling, 'and we're going to get our shares.'

The four alternate tunnel exits were quietly fortified and sealed within the week, but it took another three days to scavenge enough chain and weave it into a reasonable net. Installing it proved the most exhausting task of all, since it required building a small raft to ferry sections of the heavy chains across the river and then carefully haul them up into the mouth of the river tunnel. Few of the Ashes crew were strong enough to manage that task, for they either couldn't swim – like Quinn – or they were exhausted trying to install the chains while keeping their heads above water. In the end, only Fyn, Sodja, and Way were capable of performing the task, and Way almost drowned on his first attempt to bolt the chain to the rock. The metal chains had tangled him as they slid from the raft, and Fyn had to fight to untangle him before the heavy metal links sank to the river bottom. More time had to be spent scavenging additional chains, and then only Sodja and Fyn were allowed to bolt it to the rock.

Fyn ended up ferrying the final section of chain across the river, and it proved to be the most difficult. By the time he drove in the final eye-bolt, his teeth were chattering from the cold, his muscles were aching from trying to stay afloat while lifting the heavy metal links, and his lungs were burning from repeatedly diving underwater to weave the chain through the improvised netting. He had to take regular breathers between the links of chain, and then resume screwing in the last bolt, being careful not to make so much noise that he might accidentally draw out the lizardman from his basement burrow. Fortunately for him, Sodja had used her connections to obtain some magical assistance: a dozen plugs of clay that would temporarily soften the stone it was pressed into. Sodja called them 'sandhogs' – an essential part of any thief's kit – and Fyn was grateful for them, for even with their aid, the work was exhausting. When he finally swam back to the riverbank, the others had to haul him from the water, and he spent the next day recuperating. Once he felt up to his full strength, they planned the final details of their assault on the lizardman's hideout.

'On Sixth- and Seventhday,' Sodja said, 'Saltair usually travels to the High Quarter.'

'He boards with the Rocas family,' Quinn volunteered. 'And he works for them, tracking down runaways and the like for the Guild.'

'Yes,' Sodja said, her gaze drifting from Quinn over to Fyn. 'That's correct.'

Fyn met the noblewoman's grey eyes, her strained expression indicating she didn't want her identity known by the crew. Ever.

'So,' Fyn continued, picking up the narrative, 'Saltair won't return to his lair till after the weekend – and during the week he's nocturnal.'

'That's good,' Neldon interjected. 'We can smoke him out in full daylight. That'll make it easier to spot him if he surfaces near the river.'

'And I'm supposed to cover the underwater tunnel with my harpoon?' Poli asked. 'Just me?'

'That's right,' Fyn said.

'But what if he breaks through the chains? Or tears out the bolts? What do I do if he reaches the river?'

'You *harpoon* him. That's why you're there.'

'But ... just me?'

'It'll be fine, Poli.' Sodja tried to sound reassuring. 'The smoke and fire will spread fast, and Saltair will probably try the upper tunnel before he makes for the river exit. With the sandhogs, we drove those bolts in deep, so he's not likely to break through; he's more likely to get tangled and drown himself. Even if he does somehow make it, he'll be an easy target for your harpoons.'

Poli fidgeted with her gaff, still uncertain. 'I don't like being alone.'

'You won't be alone for long, Poli,' Siege said, patting her on the shoulder. 'Once Neldon and I drop the rocks and seal the upper tunnel, we can head your way.'

'We could always swap places,' Neldon said to the worried dock worker. 'I can cover the river exit with my manuballista, and you can help Siege drop those rocks into the upper tunnel.'

'I was hoping you'd supervise Siege,' Fyn said, seeing the

round-shouldered baker was happily munching a skewer of salted mud carp. 'That cave-in has to be thorough – not a single chance Saltair could dig his way out before the smoke gets to him. Airtight would be ideal.'

'Hey,' Siege said, wiping his mouth and holding a hand to his massive barrel-chest. 'It doesn't take a genius to drop rocks on someone's head. You want us to seal the upper tunnel? It'll be sealed. Trust me – and Poli will be a bigger help than ol' Nedders.'

'Thank you for that vote of confidence,' Neldon said, brushing a speck of dust from his coat. 'Ford is right, though. I think Poli's speed and strength will be more helpful than my simple oversight. Besides . . .' He tapped the miniature crossbow strapped to his hip. 'My manuballista will be more effective if Saltair surfaces near the river mouth. Poli would only get one or two good shots with her harpoon, and then she'd have to swim in with her gaff. I can get off ten or more bolts in the same time.'

'Silver staves,' Fyn swore. 'Can you really crank and load it that fast?'

Neldon smiled. 'It's a prototype that Way and I designed. My manuballista has a hand pump and a cartridge that carries the bolts. I don't have to load. I just pump it and fire.'

'And you're a good shot? Better than Way and his short bow?'

The rest of the crew shared a laugh at that. 'Let's just say,' Way said, still chuckling, 'that you were lucky when you took Neldon out first during our brawl in the alley. If you'd saved him for last, he'd have pumped you so full of arrows you'd have looked like a flaming prickleback.'

The others had a second laugh and even Sodja cracked a smile. Fyn cleared his throat uncomfortably and began again. 'Hitting someone in an alley is different to shooting someone floating in a river – even if that someone is an eight-foot lizardman.'

'Yes, yes,' Neldon said, sobering. 'I assure you, I can hit the target if it comes to that.'

'Fine,' Fyn said, steering the conversation back to their plan. 'Neldon covers the river while Siege and Poli start the cave-in. Quinn and Way stay with us' – he gestured to himself and Sodja – 'and us four will make sure the lower tunnel is tarred and oiled.

We'll haul out the dry wood and light it up. If Saltair comes to investigate, he'll have fire and throwing knives to deal with – not to mention the smoke and fumes.'

'That blaze will be hot as hell,' Sodja added, 'and the tar will make it impossible to attempt the tunnel. If he wakes up before the fumes get to him, I expect he'll run for one of the other exits, but he won't have long before the smoke fills the place.'

'Which means he'll be coming for our tunnel,' Poli said, her hands clenching the haft of her gaff pole. 'I still don't like it.'

'It'll be fine, Vaiolini,' Siege said, his meaty hand leaving greasy fingerprints on her shoulder. 'Neldon and Fyn and Raven have it all worked out.

'How will we time it?' Quinn asked, breaking her silence.

'Oh yeah,' Siege said, swallowing. 'Is someone keeping count or ...?'

'Candles,' Fyn said, hefting a bag of candlesticks Sodja had purchased from the lower market. 'Tallow candles cut to the same length. They should give us three or four hours to get into position. We'll drop you and Poli off first, light everyone's candle, and you can start lugging stones to the tunnel mouth in preparation for the cave-in. Once the wax burns down and the wick is smoking, start the avalanche.'

'What if ... ah, what if he hears us?'

Fyn studied Siege and Poli, starting to second-guess his decision to have them work together. Despite being the crew's muscle, they were both clearly frightened. If Saltair discovered them while they were still moving stone, he expected them both to run ... and Saltair would tear them to pieces. The plan would be ruined.

'I'll go with them,' Quinn said, her eyes piercing, her expression dark. 'We'll be quiet as the dead – *quieter* – and if Saltair comes to investigate, we will murder him with shadow fire.'

Poli flicked her fingers in the sign of Odar and Siege muttered a dark curse of his own. Even Way and Neldon seemed to pale at the woman's suggestion.

'What's shadow fire?' Fyn asked.

'Flames that you can't put out by any normal means,' Way said, his expression souring. 'Odar's beard, Quinn. I thought you said you wouldn't mess with that stuff any more.'

'I will to kill the lizardman.'

Fyn studied the Kroseran woman, understanding she harboured her own grievances against Saltair. 'What did he do to you?' he asked, sensing he already knew the answer. It was confirmed when Quinn lowered the shoulder of her tunic, revealing a slave brand.

'Not Saltair alone, but his employers, too – the whole Rocas family.'

Fyn glanced to Sodja but she did not look away from Quinn. 'And what did *they* do to you?' she asked, her face a mask.

'They stole the ocean trade from my ancestors, captured our trading vessels and turned them into pirate ships, and enslaved my family ...' Quinn's eyes were bright with unshed tears. 'When I was still a child,' she continued, 'my parents and I ran away from that life. We fled to the Low Quarter and they sent Saltair to hunt us down. My parents hid me ... but he found them. He killed them both ... and took their heads back to satisfy Marchioness Saevor.'

'Saevor?' Fyn said. 'I thought we were talking about the Rocas family.'

'Yes,' Quinn said, watching Sodja closely. 'I was eight when the Saevors became the House of Rocas – when Tiana Saevor married Vintan Rocas. That was almost three decades ago, and they've done everything possible to make the other noble houses forget their origins – except *I* have not forgotten. Not what Saltair did to my parents ... or the debt the Rocas family owes us.'

'I'm sorry for your loss,' Sodja said, her face betraying nothing. 'I, too, have been hurt by the Rocas family.'

Quinn nodded once in acknowledgement. She would not let Saltair return to the upper tunnels, Fyn decided. She would stop him, or she would die trying.

'Quinn ... why didn't you mention this before? Why are we smoking Saltair out of his lair if you can just burn him with magic?'

The sombre woman glared at him, and Way replied on her behalf. 'It takes a lot out of her, Fyn. Makes her tired – *really* tired.'

'I didn't know magic did that.'

'Shadow magic does,' Sodja said. 'And the weaker your magical skill, the more it takes from you.'

'How do *you* know that?' Quinn asked.

'How do you think?' Sodja snapped her fingers and a thin mist of shadows appeared in the palm of her hand. 'I've never conjured shadow fire ... but I can do other things.'

'I figured you might.' Quinn paused. 'Is Raven your real name?'

'As real as Quinn is.'

'You ever fight in the Pits with that raven mask?' Neldon asked, thoughtful.

'Maybe,' Sodja said, evasive.

Neldon grunted. 'Then I know you by reputation.'

'She any good?' Poli asked.

'Yeah. One of the better ones, I'd say. Though it's been ... what? Three years now?'

'About that.'

'Never seen you without your mask before.'

'I only wear it for public appearances.'

'Back to shadow fire,' Fyn said, trying to refocus the conversation. 'Why don't we use it to smoke Saltair out?'

'Because it doesn't create smoke,' Poli said, her face pale. 'It just ... burns. It clings to you like your shadow and it just keeps burning. You can't put it out and it never lets go of you. It doesn't burn anything *except* you.'

'Well,' Fyn said, clearing his throat. 'If that is true ... that's pretty terrifying. But if we light up Saltair with shadow fire, we could just seal him in his lair and wait for the flames to consume him. Come back when there's nothing left but ashes, right?'

'It doesn't work that way,' Quinn said, her tone sharp. 'Even if I could summon the fire without becoming exhausted, it's not what you are imagining. It's not the sort of flame that can light a torch or cook your food. You call it fire but ... it's something else. Trust me.'

Fyn gave up. 'Fine. I'll trust you to supervise the main entrance. You're in charge. Siege and Poli, you follow her orders. Got it?'

The two hulking dock workers nodded, and Fyn turned to

Way and Sodja. The latter held up her hand. 'The three of us light the fires and kill Saltair if he comes anywhere near the lower tunnels. We know what we're doing, Fyn – and I'm sure Way doesn't have any questions.'

Fyn looked at Way. '*Do* you have any questions?'

'Ah,' Way said, his expression neutral. 'Just two.'

'Which are?'

Way held up the wooden tiles Fyn had seen him fiddling with over the last two weeks. 'Will we have any downtime while we're waiting for those candles to burn down, and do you know how to play blood-stones?'

Chapter Fifty-Two

'I'm still not sure I understand,' Fyn said, staring at the modular maze that had been constructed from the carved wooden tiles.

'I'm sure you don't,' Way said, plucking the last of the red stones from the game board. 'I feel dirty after that – and coming from a backstabbing sneak thief, that's saying something.'

'That was embarrassing,' Sodja said, shaking her head. 'I've never played before, and even I thought that was a beating.'

Fyn eyed the squat candle, his cheeks reddening. 'We should probably get ready to light the oil, yeah? That candle is getting low.'

'We've got an hour or more before it gutters out,' Sodja said. 'You should play him again.'

'Why don't *you* play him?'

'Fine. I will.' She sat down cross-legged in front of the olive-skinned thief. 'Do we need to reconfigure the board?'

'We don't have to.'

Sodja smiled. 'It seems like setting it up is a third of the game. Another third is selecting the right champions based on the terrain and the units your opponent chooses to field.'

Way gave a sly smile. 'You're not wrong.'

'Well, I don't want to touch that mess Fyn helped you build. Let's reset it.' They gathered up the tiles, divided them in half and slowly took turns laying blocks of wood adjacent to one another. When they had finished, the game board resembled a lopsided maze.

'Why'd you build it that way?' Fyn asked. 'It's not symmetrical now. He's got the advantage.'

'No,' Sodja said, tapping the tiles. 'Mirroring every tile placement he makes is the same as letting him pick the terrain and gives him the advantage. Instead, I've sacrificed optimal positioning in one area for advantages in other areas.'

'Where?' Fyn asked, studying the board. 'Here?'

Sodja scowled up at him from her place on the floor. 'If I point it out to you, it's not much of an advantage.'

'Oh,' Fyn said, lowering his hand to his side. 'Sorry.'

Sodja lifted her eyes from the wooden tiles. 'Did you hear that?'

'What?' Fyn asked, checking the still-burning candle as he heard a dull rumble echoing from somewhere deep inside the tunnel entrance. A moment later, he heard a low growl from the heart of Saltair's lair.

'Keos,' Way swore, scooping up his game pieces.

'That came from the upper tunnel,' Sodja said, her eyes wide in the half-darkness.

Fyn grabbed the candle and tossed it into the tar-covered tunnel. There was a *whoosh* as the oil caught fire and smoke began to billow and pour from the tunnel entrance. The trio coughed, caught in the sudden brightness of the bonfire, and then the natural ventilation of the tunnel took hold and the smoke and fumes were drawn away into Saltair's lair and the upper tunnels. A minute passed, then two. The flames crackled merrily, consuming the oil, tar and dry wood piled in the tunnel mouth as the trio stood in silence, straining to hear what was happening at the opposite end of the tunnel.

Way swallowed, his face covered in soot. 'Did they collapse the tunnel early?'

A loud crash and tumble of stone echoed far away in the dark, its force magnified by the sudden explosion of hot air blown back into their faces. A feral roar followed, its rage almost palpable.

Fyn stepped back from the smoky tunnel entrance, the fumes beginning to billow back in their direction. 'Saltair must have been alerted to them sealing the upper tunnel. He tried to escape – or maybe attack them – and they collapsed it on him.'

'Gods be good,' Way prayed, his voice almost a whisper. 'If he didn't escape, and if they didn't kill or cripple him, that monster will be headed this way.'

As if in confirmation, they heard the whooping, gnashing roar of the lizardman's rapid approach and a monstrous figure appeared at the end of the tunnel, its head and shoulders hunched beneath the low ceiling. Saltair ran full speed towards them, now a dozen strides from the fiery tar.

Fyn snatched up his throwing knives and hurled them just as Way lifted his short bow. The arrows took Saltair in the chest and shoulder but skipped off the monster's reptilian scales. Fyn's knives followed, one sinking into the creature's softer abdomen while the other two blades skittered off his black plating and were lost in the smoke and darkness.

Unfazed by the knife sticking from his gut, the lizardman reached the brink of the flames and threw himself across the gap, his body leaning forward, angling so as not to brush the sticky tar or flaming oil. As he sailed towards them, Fyn spied a flicker of grey shadow dancing across the lizardman's left arm, face and flank.

Shadow fire, Fyn thought.

The lizardman touched down just three strides shy of clearing the flaming gauntlet, his long three-toed feet sinking into the hot tar and fire. Saltair howled, bent his legs and prepared to leap forward again to clear the last of the smoke and flames.

Sodja's arms whipped forward and a flurry of five-pointed stars thudded into the beast, their dark-grey metal somehow piercing the monster's armoured chest, each one driving him back. The lizardman stumbled, fell back into the fiery oil and landed in the burning, sticky black goo. He tried to rise, but the length of his tail was stuck to the floor, afire from base to tip.

Saltair roared, forced himself onto his hands and feet, then leapt from the muck, launching himself towards the trio and tearing his serpentine tail free of his body as he flew.

In an instant, Fyn's maces cleared their sheaths and slammed into the flaming monster, their fluted edges crunching into Saltair's shoulder and smashing his black plates. Saltair reeled from the blow, knocked the maces free and swiped his claws at Fyn's face. Fyn dodged and swung his maces a second time, cracking both weapons into the lizardman's right leg. This time he felt the bones crunch beneath the black plating and Saltair's knee buckled. The keokum turned, either to flee or to attempt a second attack, but Sodja's chain-whip lashed out first, wrapping itself around his good leg. The beast staggered forward and Sodja pulled, throwing the lizardman off-balance.

Fyn saw his opening. He stepped forward, swung out with both arms and crunched his maces into the opposite sides of the lizardman's skull. The flanged maces stuck there, embedded in the monster's scales, and Fyn drew his falchion. Sodja pulled her chain taut, dragging Saltair's good leg from beneath him and sending him sprawling onto his back leg. Fyn swung his sword with all his strength, his blade cutting into the last leg still supporting the keokum. The falchion severed the lizardman's left leg at the knee joint and Saltair crashed into the ground, his elongated head smacking into the stones while black blood spewed from his open wound. Fyn's maces clattered to the floor beside him and the monster screamed in pain, a mere foot from the flaming tar.

'Nooo!' he roared. 'Foul humansh! I will break your bonesh and feed on your flesh!'

Fyn lifted his falchion a second time, preparing to chop his heavy sword through the creature's lightly armoured neck. As the blade descended, Saltair rolled backward, dodging the weapon and throwing himself back into the fiery, tar-covered tunnel whence he'd first come. In spite of his injuries, the keokum rolled through the sticky flames, his arms, hips and broad shoulders cartwheeling to carry his broken body down the tunnel and into the smoke-filled darkness.

'He's headed for the river,' Fyn said, mesmerised by Saltair's severed leg and tail, their charred masses still wriggling in the flaming mire.

Way nodded, his shaking hands returning his short bow and arrows to his quiver. 'We can't chase him – not unless we want to be burned. Possibly suffocated, too.'

'No,' Fyn said. 'If he stays in there he'll die. We don't need to follow him for that.'

'So do we wait here?' Way asked, covering his eyes and mouth. 'I don't want that smoke to take us as well.'

'Fall back to the first branch in the tunnel,' Fyn said, his gaze flinty. 'We keep ahead of the smoke. When the tunnel splits, we'll split, too, and prevent him from doubling back.'

'I can investigate the lair,' Sodja offered, her eyes assessing the flames.

'No, it's too risky. I don't care how many clever somersaults you can do – it won't get you past that fire, let alone all the smoke.'

'I've got tricks for handling that.' Sodja replied.

'Let me guess, you can shadow walk or some nonsense like that.'

'Something like that, yes.'

'Damn sorcerers,' Fyn grumbled. 'Fine. Do your magic and check on Saltair. If you need help—'

'You'll come running to save me?' Sodja's eyes flashed with amusement.

'No,' Fyn said, his face a sober contrast to Sodja's. 'You'll be on your own.'

Sodja's lips turned down into a sulky pout. 'Not even a pretence of gallantry?'

'No,' Fyn answered, eyes flat. 'You want to use your magic to scout around, that's your choice. I can't risk myself or the others if things go sour. If you run into trouble, you come back here. Understood?'

'Got it. Should take me less than twenty minutes to scope out the river entrance and get back here.'

'And if you're gone longer than that?'

Sodja smiled. 'I guess you'll have to come and fetch me.'

Fyn glowered at her, but before he could think of a rebuttal, Sodja had faded into the smoke and shadows, her grey silhouette dancing over the tar-covered floor and disappearing after Saltair.

Fyn wiped the sooty sweat from his brow and studied the entrance to the underground pool, its black surface undisturbed in the torchlight. At the edge of the water, three of the eight bolts still clung to the bedrock, their eyelets twisted by the weight of the cable netting and the violence of Saltair's escape; the others had been torn completely free and were probably lying at the bottom of the North Tocra river.

'I should have secured it better,' Fyn muttered. 'This is my fault.'

Sodja huffed. 'Will you stop blaming yourself and start listening to me? When Saltair ripped this thing free he would still have been burning, bleeding out and missing a tail and a leg. Once he was trapped in that net, he couldn't swim. He couldn't *survive*. He sank to the bottom of the river – and that's that.'

Fyn wiped his hands on his stained trousers and stood. 'I'm sure you're right, but I'll feel better once we've heard from Neldon.'

Even with Sodja's assurances it was safe, the crew had waited a full hour after the smoke and flames had died down before venturing into the lizardman's lair. It had taken almost that long for Quinn, Poli, and Siege to circle around to the lower tunnel entrance, and Fyn had immediately sent the stout fisherwoman back to the river mouth to fetch Neldon. Way and Siege had set about unblocking one of the sealed side passages in order to improve the air flow in the hideout, which now stank of naphtha, faeces, and rancid meat. Exhausted after her magical expenditures, Quinn had retired to take a nap, which had left Fyn to study the details of Saltair's improbable escape.

'We found his strong-box,' Sodja said, obviously trying to change the subject. 'Want to take a look?'

'I assume you've already counted its contents?'

'Yes,' Sodja admitted.

Fyn grunted. 'Divvy it up, including half of whatever you stole. You can keep the rest as a finder's fee.'

'I did not—'

'We're thieves, Raven. It's our nature. Let's not waste time denying it.'

Sodja sniffed. 'I should have stolen more.' She paused. 'Don't you even want to know how much was in there?'

'Honestly, I'm more interested in talking to Neldon and then cleaning this place up. Did you see what that keokum was eating?'

Sodja grimaced. 'I'm familiar with his diet. I don't need to see the evidence.'

'They were people,' Fyn continued, as if she hadn't spoken. 'I think ... one might have been a kid.'

'Probably taken from the Ash Quarter,' Sodja said, her expression neutral. 'Most of his captives are given to the slavers, but a few don't make it that far.'

'The slavers ... it always comes back to them, doesn't it?'

'The slavers and my family, yes. They're a cancer, eating away at Luqura.'

'Tiana Rocas, Dante Turano, Elar Kranak, Phoeba Anabo, and Braddock Whalen.' He ticked the names off on his fingers. 'The five we have to take out – the ones running this city and spreading this filth.'

'You still want to help me take them down?'

'It's not about who's helping who.' Fyn stood, his eyes fierce as he locked gazes with the noblewoman. 'We're the Ashes crew now – and the seven of us are going to clean this city up together.'

Chapter Fifty-Three

For Annev's part, it was all he could do not to spoil his friends' triumphs with the details of his brush with death during their Tests of Ascendancy. He couldn't leave the Enclave as he'd originally planned – not with knowing there was a traitor-assassin hidden amongst the Dionachs Tobar – and he couldn't tell Titus and Therin about the attempt on his life, or share his suspicions about Jayar Honeycutt. He would have been accusing Therin's mentor of attempted murder, and that seemed unwise without being sure. Even so, Annev had still wanted to share his secret with Titus and Therin, but that opportunity was quickly stolen from him. He had barely made it back to his chambers when his friends started pounding on the door.

'Annev!' Therin bellowed. 'We've got news!'

'We passed!' Titus shouted, not so loudly as his companion. 'We *both* passed! Come on. We're going to the kitchens to celebrate.'

Annev cracked the door open, searching for an excuse to stay behind. It seemed unwise to join his friends so soon after the attack, when he was worried about putting them in danger. 'You're going to the kitchens? At this hour?'

'Rot that,' Therin spat. 'Titus is a *full Dionach* now! He can get us outside the Enclave – we can explore the city!'

Annev's eyebrows shot up at that and he tried to recall the restrictions that had kept them cloistered in the Enclave, sensing there was a problem with Therin's logic.

'He's speechless!' Therin laughed, misunderstanding Annev's

open-mouthed confusion. 'Our Master of Sorrows can't believe Titus became a Dionach first!'

Titus blushed, his eyes unwilling to meet Annev's. 'It's no big deal.'

'Congratulations,' Annev said, forcing a smile onto his face. 'It's good that someone has finally recognised your talents. Tosan and the Academy never gave you enough credit.'

The blond boy's cheeks reddened further. 'So you'll celebrate with us?'

'Will they really let us go? I mean, isn't there a ceremony or something?'

Therin waved away the objection. 'They won't keep us inside over something like that – and anyway, I'm sure we can get Brother Tym or the caste leaders to agree.'

'What about the Runes of Forgetting?' Annev said, remembering his concern. 'Have the Dionachs taught them to either of you? If they haven't, we won't be able to find our way back to the Enclave.'

Titus's excitement waned. 'I might learn them this week – now I'm a Dionach, I mean.'

Therin snapped his fingers. 'We can get Brother Tym to join us! He knows the runes. He could show us the sights and we could have some fun.' He snickered. 'If Misty will let him.'

Annev chewed his lip and glanced back into his room, his gaze lingering on the shredded painting that had nearly killed him. He wanted to search the cursed portrait for clues to his would-be attacker – but he had been too efficient at stopping the attack: all remnants of the glyph, whether physical or supernatural, had been stripped away when Annev had used the Rod of Artificing to dismantle the ward. He suppressed a sigh and, with obvious reluctance, stepped out and locked his door behind him. 'We shouldn't stay out late,' he said, a final protest.

'Nonsense,' Therin said, clapping him on the back. 'This will be our first free night since ... well, since *ever*! None of us got to explore Banok, and we were too busy running for our lives in Luqura. We can finally enjoy a real city – and I *mean* to.'

This time Annev smiled for real. His friend was right, of course, though it was hard to admit it. They'd spent their entire lives in Chaenbalu, and all they'd done since leaving the village was Sraon or Reeve's bidding. His friends craved freedom just as much as he did, and Annev wouldn't deny it to them tonight, not even at the risk of his own life.

So they all went to find Brother Tym, and Misty surprised them by agreeing he could be their chaperone, but only if *she* were permitted to chaperone *him*. The caste leader bundled them off to the kitchens to grab some cold meat and stale cake, and then the couple took them out for a night of modest celebrations.

'We can't take you into any of the bars or pubs,' Misty cautioned. 'It's too dangerous for the Brotherhood to be seen there. One loose tongue can cause a world of trouble.' The group reluctantly agreed, though Tym convinced his wife to let them bring along a bottle of honeywine, and they headed to Quiri's botanical gardens where Therin surprised them all by producing a small cask of maple beer – pilfered from Dionach Webb's private stores. It became a merry gathering, though Annev abstained from the alcohol, worried about how it might affect his control over the Hand of Keos. Therin initially took offence, insisting his friend join in the merriment, but when Annev explained his concerns Therin changed his tune and would not permit Annev even a sip of the liquor.

Midway through their revel, Annev felt a strong premonition of dread from his codavora ring. That impression was followed by the distinct need to return to his room, but when he expressed that desire no one else wanted to cut the celebration short. Annev fretted as the pulsing from the ring-snake artifact grew more intense, and he decided to try the second ability of his codavora ring.

Staring down at the silver and gold entwined serpents, Annev shifted his focus from the Seer blood in the silver snake to the Auramancer blood trapped in its golden twin. His initial feeling of dread receded, and he felt more confident he was doing the right thing. Calling upon the Ilumite magic, Annev suggested returning to the Enclave again, sharing and amplifying his sense of dread. This time the premonitions gave the group a collective shudder.

'We should go back,' Tym said, corking the bottle he carried under his arm. 'Gets dangerous out here at night.'

'And we should all get some sleep,' Misty added, nodding in agreement. 'It's been a fun evening.'

Titus voiced his agreement while Therin protested, if mildly, that they should celebrate a while longer.

'You can celebrate again another night,' Tym said, urging them onward. 'Better, now, to head to your beds. Now that you're Dionachs and journeymen, you'll be asked to carry out other tasks for the Order, and it's best to be rested for them.'

Therin groaned, but his maple beer was gone and his heart wasn't in it. 'Fine.'

Back inside the Enclave, Annev bid farewell to his friends and hastened to his chambers, his dread growing. When he reached the door to his quarters, he mentally prepared himself for another attack, either mundane or magical, but he discovered no assassins, nor any traps waiting to be triggered. A moment's observation revealed what had changed: the cursed painting, which Annev had left on his bed, had vanished. Annev searched for any sign of theft or forced entry, but he found nothing. The painting had simply disappeared. All that remained were the two triangles of fabric he'd slashed from the canvas, and only then because he'd stored them inside his bottomless sack.

'Rot and ashes,' he swore under his breath.

Chapter Fifty-Four

'Well done!' Neldon shouted, after another successful night of skulduggery. 'That's three slaver houses toppled in as many days. The Guild would have our eye teeth if they could get their hands on us!'

'If they even knew where to *find* us!' Siege gloated, drinking heavily from his tankard. 'I swear, if I'd known robbing slavers was this profitable, I'd have given up the Ash Quarter years ago.'

Sodja smiled, content to watch the crew enjoy themselves. She'd had few friends after the Thieves Guild had been driven from Luqura – and none at all after her father's death – and she'd forgotten what it felt like to have companions. Sodja studied each in turn, her eyes lingering on Fyn's broad shoulders. She felt proud of them – proud of their accomplishments, their unique strengths and their ability to work together – and she wondered if this would become her new normal. A crew ... a family. It felt good to be part of something, to trust that others were watching her back.

'The River District suits you, Siege,' Way said, his own eyes glassy with drink. 'Less ashes make you less ashen.' The thief giggled at his joke, then burped.

'It's nice and all,' Poli said, over the rim of her cup. 'I mean, I like having a base to come back to instead of foraging for river trash down at the docks ... but I don't feel comfortable shacking up here either. We never found his body, right? How can we be sure he's dead?'

'He's deader than dead,' Way said, taking another slurp. 'Skull bashed in. Burned to a crisp. Covered in tar. Legs broken – hell,

Fyn done chopped a *whole leg* off! Plus, he lost his tail and all the rest. Crust and crap, Poli, what more could you want?'

'I don't like it.' Poli's hands slid from her tankard and fidgeted with the gaff hook beside her. 'What if the river put the fire out?' she worried. 'What if his limbs grow back and he comes looking for revenge?'

'Number one,' Way said, raising a wobbling finger. 'That chain net was gone. Stands to reason that ol' Saltair hopped into his water hole and got tangled in it. Chains dragged him to the river bottom.'

'Yes, but—'

'Number two,' Way continued, gaining momentum. 'Neldon watched those waters like a hawk and never saw a bubble or a bobble or a breath. So unless Saltair learned how to breathe underwater, he never resurfaced.'

'Right, but—'

'Number three,' he said, stepping forward to tweak Poli's nose. 'Quinn burned his whole left side with shadow fire – and you seen what that stuff does. The river wouldn't have put it out, so if he *did* suddenly learn to breathe underwater, he's been crippled by blade and fire, chained to the bottom of the riverbed, and left to burn there till his soul expires.' He smacked his lips. 'Now I say that deserves another drink.'

Neldon saluted him and Way snatched his mug to take another long quaff. This time when Way belched, he blew the fumes into Poli's face. That got her swearing and she thrust him away, the drunk rogue still laughing.

'It's not funny!' she protested. 'This place gives me chills. I don't like thinking that creature lived here all this time and now we're camping out in his hole. The stink of him still lingers.'

'He's not coming back, Poli,' Sodja said, her tone light and reassuring. 'Way's right. If Saltair were still alive, we'd know by now. It's been two weeks and not a single person's come snooping around. That tells me no one else knew where this hole is.'

'*We* found it,' Poli protested. 'Why can't they?'

Siege rumbled his agreement, a fat beef sausage waggling in his fist. 'Poli's got a point, you know.' He took a bite. 'How *did* you find Saltair's hideout, Raven?'

Sodja looked at Fyn who gave a small shrug, his face betraying nothing. If she wanted to tell the crew about her family, Fyn wouldn't stop her. Nor would he tell them for her. She still felt, though, that sharing was too great a risk, especially with Quinn's vendetta against her family – even if it was a vendetta they both shared.

'I found Saltair,' Sodja said, her gaze drifting back to Siege, 'because I'm the best godsdamned thief this side of the River Kuar. Give me a hint of any treasure, any secret, any hideout, and I will ferret it out, claim that secret and take it as my own. The God of Shadows likes to share others' secrets with me, and I'm of a mind to listen to him.'

Sodja picked up her tankard of Black Gambit and took a long, slow sip, allowing the others to digest that. She wasn't lying – she really did have a gift for finding things others wanted to keep hidden, and she'd honed that gift while thieving with her father. Her brothers had their own unique talents – Ketrit with his keen mind and ability to intuit what others were thinking or feeling, and Rista with his love for sadism and his perverse talent for inflicting pain on other human beings.

Could the Guild or her family find Saltair's former lair? Possibly, if the crew got sloppy and made mistakes. Barring that, she felt they'd taken sufficient precautions to keep themselves safe from the Slavers Guild. Traps were set. Nightly watches were posted. They weren't going to be surprised or ambushed the way they had Saltair, and this was their home now. This crew Fyn had cobbled together was beginning to feel like family. It put an unexpected kink in her plans, this need to look out for one another – to *trust* one another. These people were still strangers. They owed her nothing and she owed them even less.

And yet she was growing fond of them – Fyn in particular. The young man hadn't made any amorous advances since his surprising kiss on the rooftop of that derelict building, and she was beginning to resent his general lack of interest. He responded to her prods and taunts with jibes of his own, sure enough, but he hadn't looked at her the way he'd done on that rooftop. He hadn't tried to hold her or made any attempt to repeat that single lusty kiss they'd shared almost a month past. It was almost enough to make her cross, despite not knowing her own feelings about him.

'At the rate we're going,' Sodja said, setting aside her mug, 'the Slavers Guild is going to spot the pattern of our attacks and either try to bait and ambush us with a juicy target or hole up entirely and prepare for a sustained Guild war. We're not a large enough threat for them to suspend operations altogether – not yet – so I'm guessing they'll try an ambush.'

'Well, that doesn't sound good,' Siege said, his jolly demeanour sobering.

'We're not going to let that happen,' Fyn said, stepping in to take control of the conversation's direction. He always seemed to know just how to give her the space to say her piece and influence the conversation, but not leave her to drive things entirely. He wanted the leadership – he needed it, and he instinctively reached for it whenever he felt it slipping. Sodja liked that; she liked a man who knew what he wanted. Though she wished she knew if he wanted her.

'Instead of taking out another base of operations or a trading house, we're going to think bigger, and neutralise its five leaders.'

'Ooh,' Way said, his speech slurred. 'Sounds downright villainous. We've moved straight from theft and arson to kidnapping and extortion.'

'And probably murder, too,' Sodja said, her face grim. 'None of these people are saints, not when they're up to their elbows in blood and Innistiul gold.'

'Ringmaster Dante Turano rules the Undercity. He abducts people from the Low Quarter for the fighting pits.' Fyn looked at Way. 'Sanhueza. You lost your family to those pits, yes?'

All of Way's drunken mirth suddenly dissolved into a dark cloud of despair. 'They were so young. What could they want with boys that young?' He shook his head.

'Well, now's your chance for revenge,' Fyn said, unmoved by the man's silent tears. 'If we take out the Ringmaster, that's one less linchpin holding the Guild together.' He turned his attention to Quinn. 'You already know about Tiana Rocas's connection to the Guild. Saltair was just the start of it. If we take out Tiana and destroy her banking house, we can bankrupt her family and the Guild in one blow.'

'I'm in for that,' Quinn whispered, quiet and intent.

'Good. Elar Kranak handles most of the slave trade in and out of the Luqura. He's our target in the River District, and I have a personal debt to settle with him.'

'Tiana Rocas in the High Quarter,' Neldon repeated. 'Elar Kranak in the River District. Dante Turano in the Undercity and the Low Quarter. That's three. I assume Braddock Whalen factors into this somewhere, as the Guild's chief slavemaster.'

Fyn nodded. 'He has a mansion in the Merchant Quarter that's the Guild's public face. He's the nexus for all the information, money and slaves that exchange hands in Luqura.'

'That's four. Who's the fifth?'

'Phoeba Ondina Anabo – the chief consul between Luqura and Innistiul.'

Neldon hissed through his teeth. 'Keos, but that's a tough list of targets – and now you add a consul to the list? That's as good as asking us to assassinate King Cheng.'

'It may come to that,' Sodja said, her eyes sparkling in the lamplight. Neldon grimaced.

Fyn cleared his throat. 'This woman, Consul Anabo, meets with Guildmaster Whalen and conveys the will of King Cheng to him. She's authorised to respond to any problems with the slave trade between Innistiul and Luqura, on King Cheng's behalf.'

'And when she's in Innistiul?'

'Authority reverts to Whalen,' Sodja said. Fyn had explained it well, remembering most of what she had taught him earlier that week. He was a fast learner.

'So,' Neldon continued, 'if we're going to disrupt communication between the Guild leaders, we should target either Anabo or Whalen next – but those are high-profile targets.'

'Guildmaster Whalen. Anabo is out of the city at the moment. If we can take him out before he has a chance to debrief her, there's a good chance we can pick off the Guild leaders before they wise up to our plans.'

'So are we kidnapping them or … ?'

'We're killing them, Siege,' Fyn said, his tone matter-of-fact. He glanced at Sodja, checking that she planned to kill her own mother, despite knowing this was what they'd agreed. She nodded in response and he seemed satisfied. 'Does everyone understand that? You're not thieves and street thugs now. You're assassins. Can you handle that?'

Way shrugged as if the distinction made no difference to him. Quinn stared at him as if he were stating the obvious, while Poli and Siege slowly nodded. They had done their share of killing before, though Sodja suspected the deaths had always been incidental. As with their attack on Saltair, though, their objective this time was blood. The Slavers Guild was a five-headed hydra, and they were planning to execute each one.

Now Neldon cleared his throat. 'Executing those five leaders will only create a temporary power vacuum here in Luqura. King Cheng and the Guild will fill those positions, and then it will be business as usual. All our work, all that risk ... for nothing.'

'Not if we fill the vacuum ourselves,' Sodja replied.

'What? With the seven of us?' Neldon snorted. 'You think Siege would make a good Ringmaster? Or did you imagine Quinn as the next matron of House Rocas?'

'We're not going to take control of the Guild. We're going to *replace* it.'

'With what?'

Sodja waited to see if any of them could guess where a new power might come from. Finally, Way snapped his fingers.

'You cunning little minx,' the thief said, his eyes bright with excitement. 'You want to bring them back, don't you? The whole rotting Guild – you know where they *are*.'

Sodja smiled. 'I do. They're still in the kingdom, and with the right impetus, I think we can get them to come back. Possibly even help us.'

'Wait,' Siege swallowed another mouthful of sausage. 'Who are we talking about now?'

'She means to bring back the Thieves Guild,' Neldon said, his face brightening too. 'That's it, isn't it? You want to lop off the heads of the Slavers Guild so you can bring back the old masters of the Undercity.'

'Why not?' Sodja asked. 'It was theirs before the Innistiulmen stole it from them – before the merchants and nobility sold it from under them.'

'And you know where they are? It's been several months since I've heard anyone so much as whisper their names.'

'I told you I'm good with secrets,' Sodja said, letting a small smile tug at her mouth. 'I know where they've gone, and I know they won't come back unless we make a hole for them to fill.'

'And what do we get out of it?' Poli asked. 'You think once we've brought them in, they'll just give us a place at their table?'

'The Thieves Guild steals money from people,' Quinn said, surprising them all. 'The Slavers Guild steals *people* from people. They claim its legal, like they're selling criminals or slaves purchased from their previous owners – but they are *stealing people*. My people. Way's people. Your people.' Quinn slipped a knife from her boot and slammed it into the barrel of Black Gambit they were using as a table. Poli stared at her. Swallowed. Nodded.

'We don't need the Thieves Guild to pat us on the head and give us a bone,' Quinn growled. 'We do this because it's worth doing – because it *needs* doing. And we need them, when it is done, so it does not happen again.' She jerked her knife from the barrelhead and resheathed it. 'If you want to go back to robbing your cousins at the docks for clips and coppers, that's your choice. Me, I'll do this for free. Every one of those scabby Nishers deserves to die – and I'll do the cutting.'

'And I,' Way said, raising his mug.

'Me, too,' said Siege, followed by Poli and Neldon.

'Right then,' Fyn said, clapping his hands together. 'Now that you know what we're planning, let's talk about how we're going to take out Guildmaster Whalen.'

'Can't we just sneak up and fire one of Neldon's bolts through his head?'

Neldon smiled sardonically at his enormous companion. 'We *could* do that, Siege. But then we would have to leave the city – very fast, because these bolts are custom-made by me, and they're known to the Guild. I could have shot Saltair at the river because no one would have recovered his body. Plugging one into Guildmaster Whalen would be entirely different.' Neldon looked over at Fyn. 'I assume you have something more elaborate in mind? Sneaking into the Guild Hall and poisoning Master Whalen's cups?'

'Actually,' Fyn said, 'the plan is much simpler.' He flashed a wolfish grin. 'We're going to walk right up to him ... and stab him in the face.'

Siege spluttered, spraying sausage across the table. Next to him, Poli was having difficulty swallowing her ale. She coughed, pounding the improvised table, her eyes watering. Neldon and Quinn stared at Fyn, waiting for him to reveal the punchline.

'You can't stab him in the face,' Way said, his speech slurred. 'You get him in the cheek, he lives. Put out an eye, he lives. No, no, no. In the chest – right in the heart.' He scratched at the stubble growing on his cheeks. ''Course, getting that close might be a bit ... tricky. Assuming you want to live, that is.'

'That's the best part,' Fyn said, still grinning. 'None of us are going to get within a hundred feet of him.'

Chapter Fifty-Five

In the end, it was nearly as bad as Kiara and Kenton feared.

The Sons of Damnation had completely vanished, from both Chaenbalu and the Brake, and no amount of searching revealed the masters to either Kenton's magic vision or Kiara's scrying. The men had not died. They were not hiding in the Brakewood or anywhere along the East Road. The five masters had simply vanished.

'It's as if they found a way to hide from my magic,' she said, vexed. 'I don't understand it.'

Worse than their disappearance, though, was the confirmation that the *ferrumen* had indeed infested the woods northwest of Chaenbalu – and had spent the last few days surrounding the village. This would have been catastrophic, had the army not been smaller than Kiara had originally projected. Better still, Cruithear was not part of the invasion party, sparing them a confrontation with the Younger God of Earth, Stone and Metal ... though his vanguard was not without consequence. In addition to a platoon of well-armed *ferrumen* – nearly fifty elites in all – Cruithear had sent a dozen mage-priests, from Stonesmiths and Ironborn, to the dualist Forgemasters. It wasn't the whole Orvanish clan, but it was still a daunting force.

'What are they doing?' Kenton asked. 'Have any of them reached the standing stones?'

'Not yet, but I think I've identified their guide.' They stood inside the Vault, and Kiara raised her hands over the luminous waters, moving as if she were weaving something intricate in the air and the light. Gradually, the translucent golden water transformed into a glowing glass surface, its reflection showing Kenton two people: a lean woman with powerful arms and shoulders, who stood beside a litter bearing the Academy's former quartermaster.

'Brayan?' Kenton said, disbelieving. 'Why would he aid Cruithear's army?'

Kiara spun her hands in a winding motion and the scrying pool magnified the quartermaster's pallid face and sickly complexion. 'He's bed-ridden,' Kiara said, holding the vision on his face. 'Who's the woman?'

'I don't know.' Kenton frowned. 'I've never seen her before. She seems quite fond of Brayan, though.' As he spoke, the woman from the vision lifted a waterskin to Brayan's lips and the supine man drank it greedily.

'Perhaps they've come seeking aid,' Kiara offered. 'Brayan could have told them how to get here, and since he's been blessed with *aqlumera* – the same as you and all the infants taken from outside the village – that blessing would allow him to bring others inside Chaenbalu's circle of protection.'

'Perhaps,' Kenton said, his expression dubious, 'but why bring soldiers? Why bring mages and *ferrumen* if he needs medical assistance?'

'You think he's been coerced?'

'I think your first instinct was right. Brayan's been forced to bring these people to Chaenbalu, and Cruithear intends to use him to seize the Vault and its contents. Why else would he be on a litter?'

'We can't let that happen, Kenton.' The witmistress spun her hands in the opposite direction. As she did so, the vision in the *aqlumera* pool shimmered then displayed the village and surrounding forest. 'Groups of mages and *ferrumen* are covering the main roads and the watchtowers. The rest seem to be waiting atop the hill beyond the west tower.'

'Waiting for the others to get in place, you mean.'

'Yes. It seems this woman intends to surround the village before bringing the rest of her soldiers into Chaenbalu.'

'Sensible,' Kenton said, remembering his lessons on warcraft with Masters Edra and Duvarek. 'They're anticipating resistance – or trying to prevent us from escaping. Are there any near the windmill or the southern river?'

Another shift of Kiara's hands and they could see the swollen stream running east to west, just south of the village. 'One patrol,' she said, squinting. 'It's the weakest part of their noose. Probably because they don't expect us to try to cross the stream.'

'Nor will we. I have no intention of running.'

'Well, what do you intend to do? And where's Aog?'

'He's nearly finished sealing the tunnels. After that, he'll await my instructions.'

Kiara dismissed the scrying vision with a final wave of her hands. 'Please tell me you don't plan to collapse the tunnels.'

'What if I do?'

'Then you're a fool. These mages are priests of Cruithear. Most of them spend their whole lives underground, and the Stonesmiths and Forgemasters can shape the earth with their hands. Dropping a ton of rock on their heads would do precisely nothing.'

'Are their heads made of metal, too?'

'The *ferrumen*'s are. The mages ... I doubt it. Maybe the Ironborn?'

'So the Stonesmiths and the Forgemasters can dig their way out, but only if they haven't been concussed or had their skulls crushed.'

The witmistress pursed her lips. 'You're playing a dangerous game, Kenton.'

'No, I don't play games, Kiara. That's the difference between me and the others from Chaenbalu. For me, this has never been a game. I've always known the stakes.'

She studied him. 'I can't get word to you from the scrying pool. The Vault's magic prevents our amulets from communicating.'

'I won't need your scrying out there, witmistress. I've got these.' He indicated his blindfolded eyes. 'Once I'm outside the Vault, I can see to the ends of the village ... maybe farther. Still, I can only look in one place at one time, and it's not instant. If you scry something, duck over to that trapdoor and crawl into the lower chamber. The amulet should work there – just stay clear of my traps.'

The witmistress gave him a look that suggested the words 'duck' and 'crawl' were some kind of obscenity, though she did acknowledge his words. 'If it comes to that, perhaps I shall. Though I think it unlikely I will leave the Vault unless I am in immediate danger.'

'Can't you peer into the future and see what will happen?' he mocked.

'Sometimes Fate blesses me with glimpses ... intuitions similar to the one you shared regarding Myjun's ability to kill Annev, but that is not true prophecy. *That* requires a blood sacrifice, and unless you or Aog are willing to volunteer for that sacrifice, the answer is no. I cannot peer into the future and tell you what will happen in the next few hours, much less the final outcome of this invasion.'

Her words gave Kenton pause. 'Then ... how did you know Myjun would return here? You spoke of that as if it were prophecy.' Kiara stared at him, waiting for him to come to the correct conclusion.

'In the grand scheme of things,' Kiara said, 'lives are one of our cheapest and most plentiful resources – and when the need is greatest, they can be spent like copper clips at a market fair.'

'May I ask who you *spent*?'

'It is impolite to do so,' She said, her grey eyes as cold as mid-winter snow. 'Suffice to say, when the schism between the witwomen finally erupted, there were bodies to spare for divinations.'

'Ah,' Kenton said, stroking the remnant of the scar on the side of his face. 'And you feel that all those witwomen ... the witgirls and the infants. The acolytes and avatars. The masters and ancients. All the people of Chaenbalu. They were worth sacrificing ... just to find Annev?'

'They were.'

'And then you failed to claim him. Despite all your prophecies, your sacrifices bought you nothing.'

'They cost me nothing, too. Annev will return to this village and ask for my help forging a sword – and I will give it ... in exchange for his promise to accompany me to Takarania and Terra Majora.'

Kenton scoffed. 'And you think he will agree?'

'The prophecies say that he shall.'

'Well prophecy can have its way with Annev, so long as it brings Myjun to our doorstep ... though I'd still prefer he died into the bargain.'

Kiara gave him an enigmatic smile. 'In the end, you may still get your wish.'

Kenton met the woman's gaze and their wills seemed to align once more. Perhaps, Kenton thought, they had never actually been at odds.

'Watch for the *ferrumen*,' he said, pulling the ironwood artifact key from his cloak. 'Watch the tunnels especially. If any survive, I need to know where they go so Aog and I can hunt them down.'

'What makes you think Aog can kill a monster made wholly of stone and metal?'

'He's spent the last month digging with a spade that vaporises earth and rock. I'm sure he'll manage.'

Kiara snorted. 'You can't defeat the armies of Cruithear with a magic shovel and a few collapsed tunnels.'

Kenton had his hand raised towards the keyhole of the great ironwood portal. 'I'd be far less confident if Cruithear himself had come, or if he'd sent his entire clan instead of a vanguard. His lack of commitment will be his undoing.'

'So confident,' the witmistress muttered, a wry smile on her face.

'Mm?'

'You remind me of Carestin Estes-Hansen,' Kiara said. 'A poet from the Second Age. "And with such ease doth man defy the Gods by hoarding pow'r in golden rings and rods. Then turning 'gainst the Gods he cries: I rule myself and see with opened eyes."'

Kenton quirked his head, the artifact key still raised to open the great door. '"With opened eyes",' he said, half-smiling. 'Almost sounds like she's talking about me.'

'It's not impossible,' Kiara said, turning back to glare at the pool. 'Some say Carestin was a prophet as well as a poet. Who can say when her words were meant for?'

Kenton grunted. 'I don't care one way or another for prophecy.'

'Even when they involve you? There are some that do, you know.'

'Yes,' Kenton said, his smile wilting into a frown. 'Like you, Janak Harth called me the Cursed Leader ... and some kind of heron? Or maybe I was the Doomed Cripple and Annev was the leader. I'm not sure, and I don't think it matters.'

'It could matter quite a lot in the end.'

Kenton sniffed then slid the artifact key into the door. 'We can worry about it when the end comes.'

As the portal closed behind him, Kenton heard the witmistress ask, 'And what if our end comes today?'

As soon as he was clear of the Vault, Kenton searched the tunnels around and beneath him. Within a moment he had located Aog's hulking form through the rock and earth, and communicated instructions to the man.

'Kill any who approach you,' he said, speaking aloud though his master-slave bond with Aog did not require it. 'Kill them if they approach, but do not abandon your post. When I give the signal, collapse the tunnels.' He waited for the Master of Punishment to respond. A heartbeat passed. Then two. Finally, he felt a voiceless 'yes' echo through the bond. Kenton sighed with relief. One part of his plan, at least, would be ready. If he was lucky, it could wipe out more than half the mages and elites that were, even now, tightening their noose around the village. He felt a tingling sense of anticipation at the imminent violence, then stilled his thoughts and focused his energies. His right hand grasped Mercy, and the weapon felt comfortable in his hands, its magic alive and familiar.

I am the air and the ice, it whispered. *I am the edge that sheathes the blade.*

Yes, Kenton whispered back. *Today we will test your edge against stone and metal.*

I have carved these things before, it replied, surprising Kenton with the thought, until he remembered using the blade to dig himself out of the caved-in tunnel.

You are right, he said. *Today we battle the earth once more ... and this time it will fight back.*

523

Mercy replied with a single image: the moment after he had discovered the sword's magic. He had been standing in Janak Harth's burning study, about to confront Annev, and had carved a single sinuous line in the stone floor with Mercy's magic blade. Kenton blinked, startled by the vividness of the memory.

You ... remember that?

The sword hummed in his hand, its magic throbbing like a heartbeat, its pulse matching his own: *I am the wind and the water. The mind and the memory. I am* quaire *and I am yours. Wield me but do not waste me.* Kenton consciously let go of the sword's hilt. The throbbing stopped, as did the weapon's whispered words, though he felt them echo in his mind.

'Time to hunt some mages.'

Chapter Fifty-Six

Ord Captain Elaur Coppersmith wiped her brow and glared into the winding tunnel. Something had been glimmering at the far end, though the darkness now reflected nothing but shadows and earth.

What was it about tunnelling that made her anxious? Not claustrophobia – that sickness had been bred out of the Orvanes long ago – and not the darkness itself. She doubted it was the fear of a cave-in, either, though they were always a possibility. She just preferred working outside. Shaping stone and metal with her hands, creating tools and crafts the way her father had taught her. That was satisfying work. Comforting. Worthy of her illustrious heritage, and not all Stonesmiths were gifted at it.

Crafting tunnels was grunt work, though. Anyone could do it, but it required a heavy dose of the talent to move more than a handful of dirt at a time. She had gained her captaincy, in fact, almost entirely based on her ability to move large quantities of earth. That she could do so while maintaining the structural integrity of those tunnels for her fellow soldiers made her something of a marvel – a prodigy that was valued higher even than the master craftswomen back in Orvania.

'And that's why I'm here,' she muttered to herself. 'So they can use me as a bleeding shovel.'

'What was that, Captain Coppersmith?'

Elaur looked up to see the Ironborn lieutenant watching her. Isabelle's topaz eyes gleamed with amber fire in the torchlight, and her ivory skin had the flawless appearance of water-worn river rock. At her hip, she carried the heavy crossbow common to Ironborn officers, though she had yet to draw its string, let alone arm it.

'Just lamenting my life choices, lieutenant.'

Isabelle gave her a warm smile full of perfect ivory teeth. 'Nothing new then. Shall I tell the elites to proceed?'

'Not yet. Has your sister returned from delivering those messages to the file captains?'

Isabelle shook her head. 'She'll be back soon, I'd wager.'

'And the high priestess?'

'No new orders. We're to hold our positions till the tremors start.'

Elaur was uncertain how she felt about that. She didn't like going in unprepared, but she also hated all this waiting. With all the stealth, the campaign had been slow to start, compounded by needing to wait for their invalid guide to get each captain past the village's protective circle. That might have been tolerable, had they not been delayed a full day by one of the older elites getting himself killed on the East Road.

Where did that damn trap come from? Elaur wondered for perhaps the dozenth time. *Was it a warning? Who put it there and why?*

Ingenious as the trap was, it could have been a random accident. Riche had been among the oldest living Ironborn, more than a hundred and score years, and while his metal body did not decay as quickly as flesh, his mind was another matter; dementia had claimed most of Riche's faculties over the past decade, and though his body was still primed for battle, his mind was not truly fit for anything more than a march.

And now he was dead. The first military casualty in almost five hundred years, and it had happened under her command. It didn't seem fair, but there it was: her watch, her command, her failure. Caution had been essential from then on, but it made every hour drag by.

Elaur bit off a curse and returned her attention to the darkness at the end of the tunnel. She *had* seen something there … hadn't she?

★

Kenton stalked the forest just outside the village, the border marked by the faded standing stones spaced evenly along Chaenbalu's perimeter. Even with his eyes bandaged he saw as clearly as a man might see at noon – better, perhaps, since his supernatural vision was not impeded by the trees or deepening shadows.

Half a league ahead of him, Kenton watched the first group of intruders mill about in the falling darkness. Torches were being lit and passed among the *ferrumen*, which meant the monsters likely held no advantages in the gloom of night. That was good, especially as the firelight would negate their night vision. So long as he stuck to the shadows, he would be nearly impossible to detect.

Kenton gave a sad smile, reminded of the long hours he had spent training in the dark with Duvarek, the Academy's deceased Master of Shadows. Dove had trained Kenton to move without being seen or heard, to use the environment to his advantage and, if necessary, to kill without raising an alarm. Kenton had always imagined he'd rely on his own skill, not any cursed artifacts or infernal talismans, but Duvarek had also taught him to use every advantage he had: 'Never give less than your best, and you will never be disappointed by the results. Never give an opponent an advantage you might take for your own. Never show mercy nor expect any in return.'

Until fate and circumstances had forced him to kill his mentor, the wine-soaked Master of Shadows had been the closest thing Kenton had to a friend, or a father. Kenton was still angry about his part in Duvarek's death, and he reached for that anger as he watched the intruders preparing to attack his home again: these *ferrumen* were invaders, hostile forces come to seize the only home he and Duvarek had ever known. They did not come in peace, and their presence threatened Kenton's chances of saving Myjun from her prophetic death. Bringing Brayan here and forcing him to serve as their guide was confirmation of their inhumanity, and crossing the marker stones had been nothing less than a declaration of war.

Kenton flipped back the folds of his Cloak of Secrets and withdrew the Shadow Bow, an impossibly lightweight weapon that fired bolts of nether. Kenton had no idea if the nethereal arrows would puncture the *ferrumen*'s fortified flesh, but they would not break against metal or stone, and the bow loosed with the strength of a hundred men. His plan involved killing the human mage assigned to the party of warriors, and then to use other tactics to eliminate the remaining monsters.

Kenton drew the bowstring to his ear, sighted along the arrow that materialised there, and loosed.

Two thunderous cracks echoed in the darkness, startling both Kenton and the *ferrumen* soldiers. After a moment of confusion, it seemed Kenton had missed, for the human mage still stood amidst the crowd. As his eyes refocused, he saw that noise had come from his arrow piercing the two trees that stood between him and his target. With the use of his supernatural vision, he had failed to notice either one and had accidentally shot through them both, their trunks exploding when hit. A heartbeat later he saw the mage crumple to the ground with a thumb-sized hole punched through his chest.

So much for stealth, he thought, replacing the bow in his cloak and drawing forth the bottles of acid that would rapidly eat through the *ferrumen*'s mineralised flesh. After activating his Boots of Silence and Shroud of Shadows, he raced through the dark and hurled two of the magic bottles at the nearest soldiers. Glass shattered and screams rose into the night as Kenton sprinted forward, darting among the *ferrumen* like a shadow-spawned demon, Mercy carving through the stone and metal flesh of the remaining *ferrumen*. Not killing so much as blinding and crippling them. When all eight of the remaining monsters had been felled, he made quick work of the survivors with Mercy's magically honed edge, cleaving limbs, severing spines and decapitating heads. When he came to the last monstrous warrior, Kenton drove the point of his sword through the creature's gemstone eye, punching through as if its skull were a husk of rotten fruit. The screams had fallen silent, and while Kenton cleaned and sheathed Mercy, he opened a line of communication with Aog, who was still skulking about in the southern tunnels.

★

'Something wrong, Ord Captain?'

Elaur tugged her long braid – a mark of distinction among so many bald-headed elites – and sighed. *Was* anything wrong? Had she seen movement or was it a shadow? The flicker of torchlight?

'It's probably nothing – some iron ore or damp rocks reflecting the light. We're close enough to that river that it's bound to be damp down here. Best check it out, though.'

The senior lieutenant nodded then whistled for the elites to form up. At the same instant, a breathless young woman with the same flawless river-rock skin dashed up. Unlike her older sister, the messenger had glittering pink stones in the place of her eyes and carried a short spear instead of a crossbow.

'Ho, Captain Coppersmith!' She saluted Elaur then winked at the senior lieutenant. 'Orders have been delivered. Did I miss anything?'

'Not yet. There may be something at the end of the tunnel, though. Want to check it out?'

The quartz-eyed messenger grinned. 'Nothing would please me more.'

'Need a breather?'

The two Ironborn women broke into laughter. 'Good one,' Katerin said, pounding her sister on the back with a clacking stone fist. The sound was dulled by Isabelle's padded uniform, but it still drew a hiss and a glare from their captain.

'Keep it down,' Elaur scolded. 'Just because we haven't seen anyone doesn't mean we're alone. Follow protocol: ranks of two, weapons drawn, silent march.' She jerked her head meaningfully at Katerin. 'That means couriers to the rear and away from combat.'

Katerin's groan was cut short by a glare from Elaur. There was a full heartbeat of hesitation then the pink-eyed woman saluted smartly and moved to the back of the queue. Elaur indicated a veteran elite with black metal skin.

'Toorch. Pair up with the lieutenant and scout ahead. We'll follow.'

The iron-skinned elite scratched at a patch of rust on his bald pate then saluted and took his place beside Isabelle.

'Hey there, lovely.'

'It's Lieutenant Lovely to you. Now shut up and ready your weapon.' Matching actions to words, she drew the braided wire string of her crossbow and began to load it with a steel-tipped brass bolt.

'Easy there, Belle. Just making conversation.' Toorch drew his heavy bladed gladius and grinned around a mouthful of pitted iron teeth. He took a budle of greased rushes from one of the other elites and lit it from the torch carried by Lieutenant Isabelle.

Elaur watched the two scouts go, thinking she'd have to promote the lieutenant to file captain soon. She did most of a captain's duties already, but because she served directly beneath Elaur she did not have direct authority over the file they currently led. Perhaps that would change soon. If the high priestess had more expeditions like this one in mind, there would be more opportunities for promotions and, hopefully, more elites to command.

'I don't see anything,' Toorch said when the pair reached the far end of the tunnel. 'The tunnel branches left and right. Looks all clear.'

'No, hold on,' Isabelle said, raising a rocky finger. 'Look down there.'

Toorch followed where the lieutenant pointed and idly scratched the rust spot on his scalp again. 'Just a shallow crack in the wall. Nothing to—'

A flash of metal shot out of the darkness and suddenly half the veteran's face was gone. Not smashed. Not dented or crushed. *Gone.* Liquid metal burbled out of the remaining half of the elite's face and he crashed to the ground. Dead.

Isabelle fired her crossbow into the shadows just as metal glinted in the darkness. There was no plink of the metal bolt hitting its target. The projectile simply vanished. Isabelle took a step back towards Elaur and the remaining elites, but before she could take another, a dark metal spade crashed into her neck and shoulders. The young woman's mouth opened in a voiceless 'O' and then her stone head rolled away from her torso, her topaz eyes still gleaming. They seemed to reflect the gleam of the torchlight and then guttered out, her body clattering to the floor.

Kenton jogged south to the swollen stream marking the southern boundary of the village, his path taking him close to Aog's current position. It seemed the old Master of Punishment had been forced to engage a group of *ferrumen*, and if Aog were crippled or killed it might jeopardise other parts of Kenton's plan. As he ran, he tried to check in with Kiara, but the old witmistress did not respond. Hopefully that meant she was still inside the Vault of Damnation, not that the *ferrumen* had already penetrated their defences and were plundering the Vault. Kenton trusted that the witmistress was too cunning to let herself be taken unawares, though, and she also had access to the Vault's myriad treasures. He guessed anyone attacking the Vault would pay a heavy price to breach the ironwood door – and an even greater one if they approached through the Academy's dungeons. Kenton had personally seen to the defence of that hidden entrance, and he would know the instant anyone entered the room where he had nearly been buried alive.

Ten ferrumen dead, he thought, vaulting a fallen tree and sprinting into the open fields of Chaenbalu's fallow farms. *Ten ferrumen and one mage ... and another ten and a mage are with Aog. Three more groups are in the tunnels, and there are mages patrolling the village.* Kenton allowed his eyes to unfocus as he scanned the ruined farmsteads and burned-out shops. Half a dozen buildings held an equal number of hidden figures, and he drew the Bow of Shadows back out from the folds of his cloak.

Let's see if we can thin their numbers a bit along the way.

Kenton sped through the dark, firing as a young mage unwittingly stepped out from behind the cover of a collapsed shed. The shadow bolt passed through the mage's chest with barely a sound and then thudded hard into the earth, sending up clods of dirt and stone. Kenton remembered how easily the shadow bolts had destroyed the trees in the Brakewood, and re-evaluated the damage the magic bow might do to the *ferrumen*'s stony skin. Even if it didn't kill them, he had no doubt that it would cripple the creatures.

As if in invitation, a *ferruman* and an Ironborn mage stepped out from the building where they'd been hiding, and Kenton drew his Shadow Bow again. Nether bolts flew without light or sound and thudded into both targets, exploding the chest of the first and blowing a fist-sized hole through the pelvis of the second.

Neither got back up.

'Fall back!' Elaur ordered, her voice ragged with a sudden wave of fear and anger. 'Back down the tunnels – now!'

'Isabelle!' Katerin roared, rushing up from the back of the line. 'Isabelle! Isabelle!'

'GET BACK!' The captain threw out her hand to stop the young woman, but Katerin passed Elaur in two long strides, heedless of the danger.

'It killed my sister!' she roared, her quartz eyes glimmering with sparkling fire. 'I'll kill it!'

'NO!' Elaur shoved her fist into the tunnel wall and called on her stonesmithing magic. Tremors shook the ground and the ceiling farther down the tunnel mouth collapsed, burying the armoured spade-wielder. Elaur dug deeper and pressed the rock tight around their assailant, then she opened up the earth and dropped the attacker into a pit filled with razor-sharp mineral spikes. It took a lot out of her – she felt fatigue and weakness seep through her body as she was suddenly depleted of her vital minerals – but the spade-wielder was gone. Buried and vanquished.

'No!' Katerin wailed, her short spear cast aside as she reached for her sister. 'NO!'

'It's over!' Elaur shouted, trying to grapple the young woman's stone shoulder. 'She's gone. Let her go.'

'No!' She gathered up Isabelle's broken head and pressed it against her breast, sobbing, though there were no tears that could ease her grief.

'Should we still fall back, Captain?'

Elaur looked up and saw the question came from Slate, her junior lieutenant. 'I ... yes. We should be safe now – whatever that thing was, it's dead – but there could be more of them. Fall back and secure the tunnel entrance. I'll follow with the courier.'

The junior lieutenant saluted and turned to leave, but before he did, Elaur placed a trembling hand on the elite's marbled shoulder. 'Isabelle and Toorch are both gone, Slate. You're the new senior lieutenant – so keep our elites safe.'

The middle-aged soldier blinked lapis-blue eyes flecked with gold. 'Yes, Captain.'

Elaur's hand fell away and the lieutenant led the seven remaining elites down the corridor. Beside her, Katerin continued to wail.

Kenton dashed into the tunnel hidden near the broken water wheel and had barely a moment to refocus his vision before a squad of *ferrumen* marched around the corner. He took a knee and fired point-blank into the group, blasting limbs and heads from torsos. The cold metal fingers of one of the *ferrumen* dug into his shoulder and then slashed at his left bicep. The Shadow Bow went flying and he fell to the earth in a shock of pain. He reached for Mercy just as another of the *ferrumen* jumped him, and then the bones of his right arm cracked beneath the heavy weight.

'Damn you!' Kenton swore, pressing back as the power of his magic amulet quickly healed his flesh and broken bones. 'Damn you all to the hell from which you spawned!' With his enhanced magical strength, he threw off the *ferruman* who had pinned him and brought Mercy's enchanted blade to bear, slashing the eyes and throat of two nearby soldiers. The first went down clutching the shattered remnants of his lapis eyes, and the second tumbled backward into her companions, her bronze throat leaking steam and molten metal blood.

Before the soldiers could regroup and press their attack, Kenton grabbed an enchanted mixture from his cloak and threw it at the nearest group of *ferrumen*. The green glass shattered, and something erupted into the air, spraying them with damp green spores and viscous slime. Kenton jumped back as the cloud of fungus spread like a living fog, covering stone and metal skin. One of the soldiers screamed then choked as the spores lodged in his throat. Another tried to run but found herself glued to the body of the first *ferruman*. Kenton stepped forward and freed her with a sweep of his magic sword, first by severing her trapped arm and then by chopping both knees out from under her. He snatched the Shadow Bow back up, sheathing Mercy in favour of the enchanted arrows. His fingers found the string, pulled and nocked an arrow. *Thwum.* A stone head shattered into pieces. *Thwum.* A metal chest exploded, knocking one *ferruman* back into those huddled behind it. *Thwum. Thwum. Thwum.* Kenton did not wait for them to get up. He didn't wait to see who was dead and who was merely injured. He simply aimed and fired. *Thwum-thwum. Thwum.* Metal shrieked and stone exploded. *Thwum.*

'Stop! Please!' The cry came from the blinded *ferruman* with the shattered blue eyes. He stared sightlessly at Kenton, evidently not realising his comrades were already dead.

'Never show mercy nor expect any in return,' Kenton said, lifting the bow and nocking a nethereal arrow.

Thwum. Broken slate and shattered skull exploded into rock dust.

Elaur rose to her feet as soon as the screams of the elites echoed down the tunnel.

'Stay here!' she commanded as Katerin rose to go with her.

'I will kill them!' the young messenger screamed, her eyes glittering in Toorch's fallen light. 'They will pay for this.'

'No! You will stay here – you will survive because you're smarter than the rest of them. And faster. And stronger. Like your sister. Stay here, and *survive.*'

More screams. And then thunder echoed through the collapsed tunnels, followed by a shriek of twisted metal and broken rock.

'What is down there?' Katerin whispered, her eyes wide with fear.

Before Elaur could form an answer, the ground beneath their feet began to rumble and crack, dropping the pair to their knees. A moment later, a hole opened up behind them – cutting off their escape – and the armoured behemoth with the black spade rose from the darkness, his dark figure tall and impassive. The hulk's armour had giant bleeding rents and holes from the stone spikes, which had driven into its flesh … but the beast seemed unharmed. It raised the shovel like a massive battle axe and grinned with fiendish delight.

'Run,' the captain whispered to Katerin's ear. 'Go and tell the others what has happened. Tell them how we fell.'

The courier shook her head. 'We're trapped. Your magic is gone. We can't—'

'Tell the others,' Elaur whispered, her warm hand brushing the young woman's bare scalp. 'Do not let our sacrifice be in vain.' Then she plunged her hand into the yielding earth and called upon its powers. At the same instant, she thrust Katerin backwards into the sloping tunnel she had formed and the elite rolled like a boulder down a chute, and into a wider tunnel beneath their current position.

The armoured monster advanced on her, his sharp spade held high overhead. Elaur ignored him as she sealed Katerin into the tunnel below and fell limp, her magic having leeched her bones of all their minerals. She could practically feel them snap beneath her bodyweight. The pain was excruciating, and her only comfort lay in knowing her death would be quick.

The spade-wielder brought down his weapon and buried it beside her skull, vaporising the rock there. Elaur blinked, her eyes unfocused in the flickering torchlight, and saw a second figure stand beside the first: this one had bandaged eyes, shaggy black hair and a cruel smile.

'She's exhausted her magic,' the newcomer said, sheathing his sword and tucking a black onyx bow beneath the folds of his cloak. 'Perhaps that means she'll answer my questions.'

'Cruithear bury you,' Elaur gasped, her teeth clenched so hard she felt them cracking under the pressure.

'On second thought,' the stranger said, resting his boot on her skull, 'let's not take any prisoners.' He stomped down once, hard – and Ord Captain Elaur Coppersmith was no more.

'Dig here,' Kenton said, tapping the spot where the obstinate mage had sealed away the last of her soldiers. 'One *ferruman* escaped. If you open this part of the tunnel, she'll drown when we flood the rest of the warren.'

Aog nodded in mute understanding, raised his shovel, and began carving his way into the connecting tunnel below.

'Wait ten minutes,' Kenton continued, wiping his boots on the dead woman's uniform, 'then open the flood gates. The other Ironborn are already in the tunnels, so let's give them time to worm their way closer to the Academy's dungeons. I don't want any of them trying to flee.' Aog nodded again, and Kenton wondered why he bothered explaining his plan to someone who was essentially an automaton.

'Just collapse the tunnel in ten minutes,' he snapped, then he strode back the way he'd come, his magic vision searching for signs of any survivors. When he reached the surface, he saw that some of the mages had made their way to the ruined Academy, and as Kenton began to jog towards them, he felt the amulet around his neck begin to glow with power.

'Kenton?' the talisman crackled, reflecting Kiara's thoughts.

'Yes, Kiara – you needn't speak your thoughts aloud. Once you've opened a connection to me, I can hear what you're thinking.'

'Is that so?' Kiara said, her thoughts reflecting her utter distaste at the notion. 'I think I'll stick to speaking aloud.'

'There are mages outside the Academy,' Kenton said, sensing Kiara's thoughts reflected his own. 'They'll use Stonesmiths and Forgemasters to break into the ruins and search for the Vault.'

'Yes,' Kiara said, picking up the thread of his thoughts, 'and Brayan is with them. This high priestess seems to want to keep him close.'

'Can they breach the Vault?'

'Yes. Brayan knows the way inside, even if the hallways have been collapsed, and I suspect he knows of the trapdoor as well.'

'He does,' Kenton agreed, remembering a conversation between Elder Tosan and the former quartermaster. 'He could point them to either entrance, and their Stonesmiths could bore a tunnel straight to the *aqlumera* pool. You should leave the Vault. Get to higher ground.'

'Higher ... Kenton, what do you have planned?'

'There are another thirty *ferrumen* down in the tunnels,' Kenton said, sprinting to the surface and flying like a bowshot towards the centre of town, 'and the mages are all converging on the Vault, so you should get out. Let them all get underground. Hell, they can even try to breach the Vault and steal the *aqlumera*. Long before they get there, Aog is going to open the tunnels beneath the mill pond.'

'And all the water from it and the southern stream will come crashing down on their heads,' Kiara finished. 'That ... might work. But it will almost certainly flood the Vault and the Academy's lower levels.'

'I'm counting on it.'

'You mean to bury them beneath a lake of water ... and lose the *aqlumera* with it?'

'Yes.' There was only silence from the other end of the talisman. 'Witmistress?' he asked, fearing the connection had been broken.

'Aog will likely be killed in the flood,' Kiara finally said, though her thoughts were anywhere but on the man's safety. 'You're willing to sacrifice him, and all of Chaenbalu's treasures, to win this battle?'

'Why reserve our strength for the next battle if we can't survive this one?'

'That's not an answer,' Kiara said, her tone flat.

'It is,' Kenton said, pulling up short beside the village courtyard. 'I will sacrifice everything – every friend, every treasure – to get one step closer to my goal.'

'I suppose that answers my next question. You would have let me drown in the Vault?'

'Yes.'

The bluntness of his answer seemed to give the witmistress pause. 'You're not even going to pretend you would have saved me?'

'No. I expected you to save yourself – or to contact me earlier.'

'Mm. Very touching.'

The thoughts and feelings that reverberated back to Kenton through the amulet were the opposite of what he felt in the woman's tone. Was she ... proud of him? Had his decision to sacrifice the witmistress paradoxically made her more fond of him?

'You are strange,' Kenton whispered through the bond of the amulet. 'My decision to sacrifice your life should not engender such pride.'

'I did the same when I sacrificed all of Chaenbalu's inhabitants to find Annev.'

They were both silent then, and Kenton felt he understood the cunning old witwoman better. 'They are coming,' he said, sweeping the ruins with his vision. 'The mages are inside the ruins – and the *ferrumen* are approaching from the other tunnels.'

'Yes,' Kiara said, her tone preoccupied. 'I need to collect some things from the Vault before it floods. I'll meet you outside ... if I can.'

The connection broke off abruptly and Kenton assumed she had re-entered the Vault. With measured movements, Kenton removed his blindfold and set it on the ground. He stared into the dark and watched the *ferrumen* in the tunnels beneath his feet. Nearly all of them and their mages were accounted for. This was good. They'd tightened the noose, and then hanged themselves with it.

Suddenly the ground beneath his feet shook and Kenton saw the whoosh of air and water push through the catacombs beneath Chaenbalu. He felt the connection to Aog's amulet grow faint as the man suffocated beneath a ton of earth and water, and then their connection disappeared entirely. He watched the water roar through the tunnels beneath his feet and witnessed each life as it was drowned out. Two mages tried to open new tunnels – tried to find a way to escape – but they were too slow. The current took their bodies and their spirits.

With barely a thought, Kenton withdrew his Shadow Bow and nocked an arrow, expecting to see at least one of them claw their way back to the surface. Some came close, but not before the water claimed them. The pink-eyed messenger who had escaped Mercy's blade and Aog's spade lasted the longest, holding out for several minutes in an air pocket inside the underground arena formerly used for Tests of Judgement. In the end, though, she too was drowned.

He saw no sign of the witmistress, nor did he know how he felt about that absence.

'Kenton.'

The witwoman's voice crackled at the other end of his talisman and he smiled. 'You're alive,' he said, surprised by the warmth he felt for her and her unconquerable spirit. 'Where did you wash up?'

'The Brakewood,' she said, sounding exhausted. 'You forgot to seal the tunnel in my private chamber – the one I used to bring the *feurog* into Chaenbalu.'

'Ah,' Kenton said. 'Of course.'

'You didn't forget, did you?' Silence. 'You left it open on purpose.'

'I still need you, Kiara,' Kenton said, tucking the Shadow Bow back into his cloak without a hint of remorse. 'You're the only one who can show me Myjun's progress in the Shadowrealm ... and I'd miss your mentorship.'

'Is that sentiment, young Master Kenton? And here I thought you were willing to sacrifice everything to achieve your goals.'

'Oh, I am. But only a fool sacrifices something he does not need to lose.'

'Wise words, Master Kenton. Meet me in the Brakewood then, near the old shadepool where we watched Myjun enter the Shadowrealm. Perhaps there we can continue your apprentice-ship.'

Kenton broke his mind-link with the witmistress and turned one last gaze on the ruins of the Academy and the surrounding village. He felt a queer sense of nostalgia for the old village, which was quickly dispelled by his subsequent vision of the dead mages and monsters drowned in the flooded tunnels.

Not one stirred there – not one had escaped the destruction – and that seemed good to him. Perhaps it meant the Academy's ghosts had finally been laid to rest. Perhaps it might even lay his own ghosts to rest.

With ritualistic slowness, Kenton picked up the black bandage and covered his lidless eyes – then he strode into the darkness of the night, and the deeper darkness of the Brakewood.

Chapter Fifty-Seven

Myjun danced between the lines of Yomad warriors laying siege to the great wall. Arrows flew like rain behind her, their fine Terran broadheads punching through chainmail and crashing into the exposed arms, loins, and faces of the men clustered about her. The shattered remnants of one arrow deflected off the breastplate of the man behind her and shot through her calf, shooting pain up her leg and spiking her body with a rush of adrenaline and magical strength. She slapped a hand to her leg and ripped the shaft from her flesh, causing a second flash of pain and a rush of strength as her magic stitched her ruptured skin and muscle back together.

A swarthy Yomad in a filthy beige tunic stepped ahead of his companions and stabbed the point of his spear towards Myjun's side. She dodged, allowing its edge to nick her as she stepped in close. The weapon bounced off her hip and her soulblades plunged into the man's chest. In the space of a heartbeat, his eyes burned to ash and his corpse dropped to the sand.

A heavy long sword swung for Myjun's neck. She sensed its weight as it moved through space, felt the air pushed ahead of the blade. She smelled the tang of forged steel and the musk of the soldier's sweat as he brought the weapon down to meet the base of her skull.

Myjun rolled forward, her momentum following the direction of the sword. As she fell, she dispelled her first knife and extended the length of the second. Her empty left hand hit the ground, catching her fall just as the Yomad's sword passed overhead. She flexed, pushed herself back to her feet and spun. The soulfire sword in her right hand clove through her attacker's bracer and forearm and then she swept it backwards to decapitate him.

More arrows pounded the earth beside her feet and the Yomads clustered nearby began to scatter, their ragged battalion retreating to the tall ivory towers that dotted the length and breadth of the Neck. Myjun watched them go then allowed her sword to disappear in a flash of light. Arrows chased the soldiers till they pulled out of range, but an insulting number still pattered down around her, their feathered butts popping up from the soil like strange flowers in a mud-churned garden of death and blood.

Myjun wiped her blood-spattered face, leaving long streaks of crimson along her golden cheeks, delicate brow and shining jaw bone. Another arrow flew past, this time grazing her shoulder. She merely gritted her teeth.

'They flee from you.' The voice came from the shadows of the trench the Yomads had abandoned.

'As they should,' Myjun growled. She licked her cracked lips behind the mask and imagined the coppery taste of the blood on her face and the texture of the soldiers' flesh between her teeth. She was so hungry ... yet her body felt full. As always, their deaths had strengthened her.

Oyru looked to the looming Harwall behind them, its length disappearing leagues into the distance, its ancient stones protecting the southeastern corner of the Terran Empire. 'We should go. The archers will keep firing so long as we stay in range. They do not know you fight for them, even though you've killed a hundred of the Yomads.'

As if to emphasise his point, an arrow plunged through the half-man's chest, and exited more slowly from his back. A plume of black vapour trailed the injury and the assassin's flesh knitted itself back together. He climbed from the shadows then beckoned Myjun to follow, and they moved away from the Terran soldiers on the great wall, strolling towards the fleeing Yomads.

'I do *not* fight for them,' Myjun snapped, nodding back at the towering wall that blocked the other end of the isthmus. 'I fight for myself. I would kill them, too, if you would let me.'

Oyru's finger rose to trace the black scar that marked his missing eye. 'Those soldiers belong to the Legions of Keos, which makes them our allies.'

'I have no allies.'

'Not even me? Not after I risked my own life and sacrificed this for you?' Oyru tapped the withered eye socket, its flesh puckered tight in contrast to the wide, unblinking eye pinning her with its soulless glare.

'That was *months* ago – and I didn't ask you to save me, you half-demon bastard.' The words hissed from her like steam from a kettle. 'You're not a saviour or a rotting martyr. You're a con-juror, a killer, and a bloody liar. All you do is torture me and tell me to kill, and delay fulfilling your promises.'

Oyru shrugged as if her words meant nothing, which only enraged Myjun further.

'I will fulfil my promises,' the Shadow Reborn said, resuming their walk. 'We have made good progress these past few weeks.'

'Months,' Myjun corrected. 'It's been five *months*.'

'Only if you reckon time by the blinks of Dorchnok's Eye. Barely three weeks of travelling in the Physical Realm, and we have already reached the last leg of our journey.' The assassin gestured to the field of ivory towers dotting the narrow isthmus of Lubree, a no man's land that separated the continents of New and Old Terra. 'Terra Minora lies just beyond the Neck, protected by the endless towers and the Spear of Tacharan. Once you are sated, we will cross back into the Shadowrealm here in Lubree – at the Noose of the Neck – and from here pass into Takarania and Terra Minora.' He pointed to a speck on the horizon that could barely be seen above the heads of the innumerable towers ahead of them. 'You see that lone tower? It is the Spear of Tacharan. It marks the end of the Neck of Lubree and the beginning of Takarania. Powerful magics protect it and the land surrounding it, preventing entry. Even sailors must avoid the isthmus and its shores and travel to Alltara in the south or Krosera in the north. We will avoid its curse, though, by crossing the Neck in the Shadowrealm.'

'And how much further to Alltara?' Myjun asked, unable to conceal the venom in her tone.

'Terra Minora is the home of three peoples: the Shalgarns of

Alltara, the Yomads of Takarania, and my people in Krosera.'
Oyru gestured past the isthmus. 'Takarania lies at the centre of
Terra Minora and borders the Neck. It is a buffer between the
shadowlands of Krosera and wildlands of Alltara, which we must
pass through to reach the Iron Mountains and the troll clans. Doing
so will also bring us close to the obelisks that guard the House of
Brass at the centre of Takarania – perilous in either realm.'

'So we must still avoid them? Even after travelling into the
Shadowrealm?'

'We must, but for separate reasons. In this world, the Brazen
Towers mark the borders of Takarania and are abutted by the
mountains of Alltara. East of the mountains is the House of
Brass, home to the priests who worship the God of Death. In the
Shadowrealm, their temple overlaps the Heart of the Void – the
centre of Reocht na Skah.'

'I thought you said that it's dangerous to go to Reocht na Skah
– that we could get trapped there for eternity.'

'Just so. To avoid both, we will enter the shadows and cross
beyond the Neck. That will take us beyond the reach of the Spear
of Tacharan. We will then remain in the Shadorealm and skirt the
edge of Takarania to avoid entangling ourselves with the magic of
Reocht na Skah. If we turn immediately southwest, that will take
us directly into the Alltaran mountains and troll territory.'

'To get my rotting armour.'

'Yes.'

'And then you will take me back to the Empire to kill Annev.'

'Yes.'

'Fine. Let's go.'

Oyru gestured at the soldiers who had finally reached the safety
of their ivory towers. 'You have satisfied your bloodlust?' He
asked the question as though he were offering her a nibble of a
scone instead of the lives of a half-dozen men and women. 'We
will not return to the physical world again – not till we reach
Alltara – so you should take your fill now.'

'My hunger is never satisfied,' Myjun said, not bothering to
hide her bitterness, 'but I will survive the trip.'

Oyru nodded. 'The distance between here and Alltara would

take a week to traverse over land – assuming we were unmolested by the Yomads and their magics. In the Shadowrealm it will take a month or more ... but time will distort even more as we cross into Takarania. The greatest eidola also concentrate there, near the borders of Reocht na Skah, and that will slow our pace further. That means it will likely take us considerably longer than five weeks to reach the troll mountains – at least, so long as we are travelling in the Shadowrealm.'

'How much time will all of this take in the Physical Realm?'

'Still a week by standard time, but we will be stuck in the shadows for two months at least. And if we choose to venture nearer to southern Takarania – towards the heart of Reocht na Skah – it could be even longer.'

'So why not return to the physical world once we are past the dangers of the Spear of Tacharan?'

Oyru eyed her with his remaining black eye, its stare penetrating her to the core. 'Because I believe the extra time and training would benefit you. You have grown much over these past five months, but you still lack full control of your powers. You have not learned to bend or reflect the light as Bladesingers and Lightslingers do. You've learned to channel its baser elements – to summon your soulblades and channel the lightfire – but it seems the subtler arts are beyond you.'

'And what do you know of the light, half-man? You're a master of the shadows. You couldn't even teach me to summon the light, much less shape it. I learned that myself.'

'Only because I forced you to.' He raised a hand to scratch the corner of his empty eye socket.

Myjun sniffed. Perhaps he regretted his decision to save her, though if he did, Oyru never expressed it – and the omission hurt her more than any accusation.

'I will not delay my vengeance for ever,' she asserted. 'We should go west, straight into the mountains of Alltara. Reocht na Skah can keep its monsters and its secrets – and I would prefer we keep our current pace. If we stay in the Shadowrealm but keep close to the shoreline, that could be the fastest route of all.'

Oyru said nothing, looking east – past the towers along the

isthmus and towards a green coast that was almost entirely shrouded in mist. 'We are close to Krosera now. If we crossed the Neck and went northeast instead of southwest, we would be in my homeland.' He looked wistful – and then he raised his face scarf and it was hidden.

Myjun stared at him as if she'd just been slapped across the face. The man had been frowning – actually *frowning*.

'You don't fear the death priests or the eidolons,' she said, accusing. 'You're not even afraid of spending a thousand years in the shadow of Reocht na Skah ... but you *are* afraid of going home – and even then you tease yourself with it. Your words imply we might go there, yet you clearly wish to stay away. Why? What terrors do Krosera's shadowlands hold for you?'

Oyru turned to face her, his scarf falling away, his normally stoic demeanour replaced by one of hatred and fear.

'The Kroserans and their impotent Shadow God can go to hell,' Oyru said, his words colder than they had ever been. 'We are bound for Alltara. I will hasten our journey as you've requested – and you will not speak of my homeland again.' As he said these last words, he covered his mouth and nose more completely, though the black fabric could not hide the tiny tear that trickled from the corner of the assassin's eye. He dabbed it with his scarf, erasing the proof that he did indeed have a soul – but not before Myjun saw it.

Chapter Fifty-Eight

'Why do you serve Keos instead of Dorchnok?'

They were back in the Shadowrealm and long past the Neck of Lubree. In their crossing, she had seen no evidence of the endless ivory towers that protected the isthmus, nor any shadow of the lone and awful Spear of Tacharan. She had instead seen black waves of smoke that filled the depths of the Sauthron and Estron Seas. When she had later asked what happened to those that tried to sail those dark waters in the Shadowrealm, Oyru snorted, shook his head, and muttered something unintelligible about Voidweavers. The reaction seemed entirely out of character for the usually stoic assassin, and the adjustment in her relationship with the Shadow Reborn left Myjun feeling adrift. At the same time, the assassin's odd mood seemed to invite a more personal connection – something Myjun felt open to now they had left the physical world and the perpetual rage of her mask had been dimmed and dulled.

'I do not serve Keos,' Oyru said, morose. 'I serve Dortafola and *he* serves Keos.'

'Which is the same thing – and you did not answer my question. Why did you abandon your worship of Dorchnok?'

'Are you not equally impious? Did you not abandon your worship of Odar to follow me?'

'That's different. I was damned – marked by Keos – and I had no choice. Not if I want to kill Annev.'

Oyru said nothing for a long, long time. When he finally did speak, it was with the measured words of someone who was unused to speech – as if the person behind the mask were speaking to her for the first time.

'I was betrayed once. Like you, I loved someone and was betrayed by them. She wasn't Kroseran. She came from an Ilumite clan in Faer Fen and sailed across the Estron Sea to Northern Krosera. She pledged herself to me and then she wooed another Kroseran warrior – a warlord named Gevul the Terrible – and helped him destroy my house and my family. I killed Gevul, but not before he killed her ... the woman I still loved.' Oyru stared at the black waters, his face unreadable. 'I tried to save her, I tried to bring her back – but Dorchnok would not heed my prayers. He did not save my family, he did not save her, and he could not save me.' The assassin turned south and pointed to the smoky horizon. 'I ventured into Reocht na Skah. I thought that if I could reach into the Spirit World, I might persuade Oraqui to come back to me.' He fixed his eye on Myjun. 'She was a dualist – an Auramancer and a Lightslinger – but she could only do two things with her magic: she could manipulate others' emotions and she could project illusions – reflections of the people and things near her. You have similar powers ... sometimes you remind me of her.' He looked back to the horizon.

'You entered Reocht na Skah,' Myjun said, her voice quiet.

'I did.'

'To the Heart of the Void.'

'To the very centre, yes.'

Myjun swallowed. 'How long were you gone? How long did you search for her?'

'A week or two.'

'A week or ... in the Heart of the Void? When a day here is a thousand years there?' Oyru's single eye shifted back to her, his usual stoic look back in place. 'What made you leave? Or did you just give up?' She hadn't meant it as a jab, though it came out that way. Still, if Oyru was offended he did not show it.

'Dortafola came looking for me. Gevul had been one of his Siänar and when the man was killed ... well, he needed a replacement. Who better than the man who killed Gevul? He tracked me through the Shadowrealm to Reocht na Skah and promised that if I served him – that if I forsook my worship of Dorchnok and followed him – he would return Oraqui to me.'

'And did he?'

Oyru stared at her, his face a mask. 'Maybe,' he said – and a chill went up her spine.

'So you learned about Ilumite magic from her?'

Oyru said nothing. He hadn't spoken since their last conversation, two antumbras ago. Not a word. They had turned southwest towards Alltara, keeping the black mists of the Sauthron Sea to their right and the endless grey plains to their left, and Myjun was tired of the shared silence.

'She taught you about her magic, maybe even her people, and in return you taught her about Krosera and your magic.'

Silence.

'What made you think your master could bring her back?'

More silence.

'This was hers, wasn't it? This mask.' She tapped her gilded temple and forehead. 'Did Gevul give it to her?'

'Do not speak his name,' Oyru breathed, his voice as cold as ice – as cold as death.

'Or what?' Myjun demanded, both relieved he had broken his silence and angry he had kept it for so long. 'Will you beat me? I will drink the pain. Kill me? I don't think so.'

'I would leave you here,' Oyru said, his tone still apathetic, though Myjun wondered if even his apathy was a mask. 'I would leave you in the shadows, trapped here for ever, and return to the physical world without you. You may have grown stronger, but you cannot traverse the planes of existence. You would be doomed to waste away until all life had left you and you became an eidolon.'

'Is that what happened to you?' Myjun demanded. 'Because you stayed so long in Reocht na Skah?'

'Yes.'

Myjun was satisfied. 'Then I will not speak that name again.'

Oyru focused on a black fixture that blanketed the horizon. 'We are approaching the shadows of the Alltaran mountains,' he said. 'We are almost to our final destination.'

'We made good time, then.' Myjun stepped beside him, sharing the view. Though it seemed the land had been flat for these many miles, she saw now that they had been climbing a long, gently rising hill. All around them the ground gradually fell away, the decline slow and steady behind them, almost imperceptible. Ahead, the slope grew more abrupt, first falling and then rising again with greater height and severity. This pattern continued until the ground erupted in the black wall of mountains that stained the distant horizon.

'How can these exist here?' Myjun asked, her eyes fixed on the mountain range.

'Near as I can tell, it reflects their proximity to Reocht na Skah. The power of the Shadowrealm lies thick on the mountains in the physical world, so their reflection in this world is more solid. It is the reason Alltara's ironwood trees can be seen here and why another species grows in the hills of Krosera – and why they cannot be cultivated anywhere else.'

'Ironwood?' Myjun sniffed. 'We have bushes of the stuff in Western Daroea.'

'A mongrel subspecies, no doubt transplanted by the Druids in Fertil Hedge. They are not the same. Even the ironwood trees in Krosera are different from those here. Not worse – not mutated like your own shrubs – but different.'

Myjun rolled her eyes and let it drop, ready to move on.

Oyru wasn't. He pointed at the grey ring above their heads. 'It is time to meditate. Also ...' He tilted his head. 'Something is hunting us.'

Myjun spun, her eyes searching the horizon in every direction. From her vantage point, though, the plains looked empty. 'Is there another waste nearby? I would have spotted—'

'No waste. What hunts us is not so easily seen, nor is it attracted to the dreams and nightmares that bubble up from the Cognitive Realm.'

'What is it then? An eidolon?'

Oyru stood in silence for a long while, his eyes still locked on the mountain range ahead of them. 'You recall I said someone who was trapped here in the Shadowrealm would waste away and become eidola?'

'Yes.'

'That was an oversimplification. People do not become shadow demons – not truly – they become something worse.'

'Worse than shadow demons?'

'Flesh wraiths … and witherkin.'

'Wraiths and witherkin,' Myjun said, tasting the words. 'Some kind of ghost? Something that eats our flesh?'

'Yes … and yes.'

'And what hunts us?'

'It is too soon to tell.'

Myjun's skin prickled with fear, and she found herself responding with anger. 'So what the hell does *it* want? Why is it hunting us?'

'Because,' Oyru said, his eye turning to face her, 'I sent it here. I trapped it in the Shadowrealm when I attacked your village.'

Myjun met Oyru's gaze and the blood slowly drained from her face. 'You mean a ghost is trying to kill us, and it's somebody from Chaenbalu?'

Oyru nodded. 'It could not have followed us here without my noticing, but it might have used the *aqlumera* as a dimensional gate to Reocht na Skah.'

'We can do that?'

Oyru shook his head. 'Not us. A Voidweaver or a Dark Lord could, but I am only a Shadowcaster.'

'Then how … '

'I don't know, tabibito. I only know it is someone from your village. A man, I think, or he was a man once.'

'How long has he been following us?'

'Since the last umbra.'

'And where is he now?'

'Hiding. He seems to favour the deeper darkness of the umbra, so he stays out of sight of Dorchnok's Eye. That is why we should meditate now, before the antumbra passes. Because when the umbra is here, I think we will have a visitor – one that might crave our flesh in addition to our spirits.'

550

Myjun stared up at the black sky and wondered how any kind of light existed in this endless world of shadows. There were no stars overhead, yet she felt as if she stood beneath the starlight of a moonless sky. And when the grey ring of Dorchnok's Eye rose on the horizon, that starlight became more akin to moonlight. At the peak of the antumbra, when the eye stood directly above their heads, it was almost as bright as dawn or dusk in the physical world – yet there was no sun, moon or star: the light simply *was*.

Myjun had come to think of it as shadowlight, which softened the darkness of the Shadowrealm's deeper blackness. Now, with Dorchnok's Eye absent from the sky and the shadowlight faded to darkness, the umbral night possessed an alien intensity. Strangely, though, the black smoke of the Sauthron Sea seemed to sparkle more brightly during the umbra, as if its own luminescence increased when it did not have to compete with shadowlight or the Dorchnok's antumbral eye. They were camped near those shimmering waters now, its black vapours lapping at the grey land. Yet as Myjun turned her gaze across the wide, nethereal sea, it seemed more like a veil of stars.

'He is coming,' Oyru said, rising from his meditative trance.

'The flesh wraith?' Myjun asked.

'Or the witherkin, yes. I glimpsed his form at the last umbra. I meant to kill him then, before he could hunt us, but he disappeared.' He pointed into the black vapours of the ocean. 'And now he has returned.'

Myjun stared into the night-black vapours and saw that where most of the waters still sparkled with light, a space near the shore had lost its luminescence. Not long after that, she realised the darkness had the shape of a man and was coming towards them.

'Do you know ... before he was taken ...'

'Who he was?' Oyru shook his head. 'I do not know the names nor do I recall the faces of the people the eidola stole from your village. I only wanted Annev.'

The darkness drew closer and, as it did, Myjun saw more of the shade's features revealed by the shadowlight: the broad forehead, the long nose and narrow eyes. It took her another moment, but then she knew the wraith's identity for herself.

'That's Yohan ... the village chandler.'

'A candlemaker. Interesting. His will must have been strong to survive all this time.'

Myjun remembered the chandler's forceful personality, her anxiety rising. 'Have you determined what he wants?'

Oyru stared at the shade, his single eye squinting into the darkness. 'Flesh wraiths crave life and take it in the form of flesh. Witherkin want vengeance. They have unfinished business and won't rest till it is fulfilled.' Oyru summoned his twin flyssas and stepped purposefully forward.

'And this one is ... ?' Myjun took a step back as the chandler's ghost drew nearer.

Oyru's twin swords passed through the chandler's shade, cutting the ghost neatly through the neck and chest. The blades passed through Yohan's body without any resistance and then emerged out the other side. Then the ghost's eyes opened wide and shifted from night-black to pure white.

'Witherkin!' Oyru said, dispelling the blades. 'Run!'

Matching words to actions, the assassin bolted from their camp by the waters and flew straight as an arrow towards the dark mountains on the horizon. Myjun followed a heartbeat later, her soulblades screaming into existence in her hands.

'Why are we running from a chandler's ghost!' she shouted, not looking back to see if the witherkin was following them.

'That is a spirit trapped in the Cognitive Realm,' Oyru bellowed. 'They are to the Shadowrealm what the eidola are to the physical world: abominations. Nightmares. Void blades do not harm them, and they will devour your mind *and* your somnumbra. They are the wandering death of this land!'

'You could have told me this before!'

'Flesh wraiths are rare. *Witherkin* are almost non-existent.'

'Well, this one seems pretty damn existent!'

They ran on in silence, their fleet pace carrying them swiftly over the rolling hills towards the mountains.

'Will my soulblades kill it?'

'Not likely. This stupid candlemaker is only partially here. This is an echo of him; the rest has perished or moved on to the Spirit World.'

'So how do we kill him?'

'We don't. He is dead already – but his mind will not relent. If we give him what he wants, he may pass over.'

Myjun ventured a glance back and saw the black ocean shore recede into the distance. There was no sign of the witherkin.

'Can we stop? I can't see him.'

'No. Witherkin are not tethered to this space, just as we are not temporally tethered to space in the Physical Realm.'

'Speak sense!'

'He is not *behind* us because he is not actually *here*.'

'I said sense!'

Oyru stopped abruptly and Myjun had to pivot to avoid crashing into him. He gestured at the rolling hills ahead of them and the sloping shores at their backs. 'He is a shadow of the Cognitive Realm. His will is causing him to manifest here, but he is not actually here.'

'Then why are we *running* from him!' Myjun shouted, her temper flaring.

As if in response to her question, a black shadow began to coalesce beside them, its glaring white eyes burning like the wrath of the sun.

'Because of that,' Oyru said, and then he resumed his sprint.

'How in the five hells can he *do* that!'

'Nine Hells,' Oyru said, not breaking stride. 'But your question is still valid. He's not tethered to this plane, so as soon as we stop moving, he can shift to wherever we've run to.'

'So,' Myjun said, gulping for breath, 'we have to keep moving indefinitely?'

'Until Dorchnok's Eye rises and antumbra dawns ... yes.'

'Shit.'

They ran on in silence, neither one daring to look back, until Myjun slowed to a walk. Oyru ran on for a dozen paces, then turned.

'What are you doing?'

'If all we have to do is keep moving, we can walk. We don't *need* to run.'

Oyru stared at her blank-faced. Then, as if realising he had stopped moving, he jogged to catch up with Myjun and then kept pace beside her. They walked in silence for a hundred paces, then Myjun snorted aloud.

'I can't *believe* you never thought to walk.'

'They are not something I encounter often,' Oyru said, his voice strained.

'What did you do last time? Run like an idiot?'

The assassin peered sideways at her. 'I am not usually toting around a tabibito, much less one who cannot shift themselves to the physical world.'

'So you run away … to another plane. You go to the physical world and hope it forgets about you?'

Oyru exhaled. 'Basically.'

Myjun laughed, her tone full of spite. 'You're pathetic. You're supposed to be this terrible, undying killer who can pop out of the shadows and murder you – and here you are running from the ghost of a candlemaker.'

'Witherkin,' Oyru said, his tone just shy of sullen. 'He is not just a ghost. He is witherkin.'

Myjun slowed her pace even further then stopped. Oyru walked two more steps then stopped, too. 'What are you doing?' he asked.

'Testing something.' She concentrated and summoned her soulblades.

A moment later, the chandler's shade appeared beside them, his black mouth yawning open in a silent scream. Myjun took a cautious step towards the spectre and then rammed her daggers of light into the ghost's eyes.

The witherkin's face contorted into a look of shock, then rage. His eyes flared, growing wider, brighter, and the chandler's black hands reached out for her.

Myjun stepped away, out of reach, then started walking. Oyru was just a step behind and, behind them, the witherkin's eyes grew dim and his black form faded into the shadowlight.

'I had to try,' Myjun said, dispelling her soulfire blades.

554

'Obviously – and now you see why witherkin are not so easily vanquished.'

Myjun grunted. 'So are *you* witherkin?'

'No. Maybe. Perhaps if I allowed one of the eidola to consume my soul, I would become one.'

'Or a flesh wraith?'

'No. My body has grown too accustomed to somnumbra. I can survive on that alone … but that means I cannot stay in the physical world for too long. I am dependent on this world. I have become one of its denizens.'

Myjun nodded, piecing it all together. 'You had unfinished business with Oraqui. You searched Reocht na Skah for her, for seven thousand years. Time warped and stretched and you became dependent on somnumbra … and you became a half shadow, half man.'

Oyru kept pace beside her. 'Annumbra,' he said. 'Years in the Shadowrealm are called annumbra … and I spent ten or twelve thousand of them in Reocht na Skah. Waiting. Searching. Praying for her to return to me.'

'Do you regret it?' Myjun asked.

'Sometimes,' he said, that single eye fixed on the horizon, 'I regret that I did not wait longer.'

Chapter Fifty-Nine

Having passed their Tests of Ascendancy, Therin and Titus established new routines with the journeymen and Dionachs from their respective castes. The most notable of these was Titus receiving instruction on the more nuanced arts of mindwalking, including how to enter an unguarded person's mind and browse their dormant memories. The former steward was innately better at it than every journeyman in his caste, and that talent affirmed Dionach Holyoak's decision to elevate him to full Dionach. With that promotion, Brother Tym also began teaching Titus the principles of mind-leeching: drawing on another person's thoughts and absorbing them, as if one's own. Mind-leeching could also erase memories from a subject's mind, but Dionach Holyoak and Brother Tym both agreed it would be prudent to master one aspect of the skill at a time.

For Therin, life at the Enclave had become far more interesting as a journeyman Breathbreaker. The skills he practised with Dionach Honeycutt and his fellow journeymen weren't altogether new, but their application required a new level of complexity, nuance and creativity. He used vacuum bubbles to scale sheer walls, cling to ceilings and run up vertical surfaces. With the application of air and sound bubbles, he learned how to silence himself and those around him, how to create explosions with displaced air and how to propel himself with almost no friction or loss of momentum. He described his training in detail to Titus and Annev, thrilled by each new discovery and excited about combining them with the martial skills he'd learned at the Academy.

For Annev's part, life at the Enclave had changed just as drastically since the theft of the booby-trapped painting. Before the attack, he'd been determined to leave – to do anything except wait for Reeve to decide his future. But now he had a purpose again. He had a suspect, and he was tired of running from people who meant him harm. He'd tried to hide in Chaenbalu and they had sent the *feurog* and the Shadow Reborn. He'd gone to Banok and an assassin with a crossbow had tried to murder him. He'd fled to Luqura and been chased in turn by Elar Kranak and Saltair.

Enough running.

No longer content with simply leaving Quiri and returning to Luqura, Annev decided to go on the offensive and begin hunting the people who were secretly hunting him. He told himself it would be cowardly to run and leave his friends to fend for themselves, and he had no intention of making them targets to save himself.

Yet Annev held no illusions about what that meant for his own safety. Every day he took additional precautions against future attacks, and against any attempts to interfere with his belongings or his quarters. When his friends invited him to lunch, he was careful to eat food he had prepared himself. When he entered a new room or walked down a corridor, he slowed to study the walls and furniture for subtle glyphs or wards. At night, he stopped sleeping in his room and instead rotated between the many empty chambers of the Enclave's lowest floor.

And then there were his experiments with the Rod of Artificing. Once he had discovered that the Inquisitor ring allowed him to see the hundreds of invisible glyphs covering the walls of the Enclave, Annev began to experiment, dismantling them. When he saw a rune or ward that looked potentially threatening, he took out his rod and tried to uncover which Dionach or journeyman had cast it. Sometimes the threads fell apart in his hands, but more often he was able to follow the ribbon of magic back to the caster. Sometimes Annev would then interrogate those Dionachs, using his codavora and Inquisitor rings, but his questions never yielded the answers he sought.

That vigilance came with a cost, too, for as the days turned into weeks, he became increasingly morose, sleep-deprived and paranoid. On the rare occasion that members of the Order came to speak with him, Annev refused to see them until he'd donned his entire arsenal of artifacts – including his dragonscale cloak and his flamberge. He took the same precautions when walking around the Enclave, leading to some Dionachs whispering behind his back. He overheard himself described as Sodar's unfortunate project – an oddity, a curio. Some brothers seemed to be afraid of him and his glowing golden hand – a fact confirmed by the auramancy of his codavora ring – which only pushed Annev further into depression. He struggled to be interested when his friends shared the exciting magics they were performing, and he convinced himself he couldn't tell his friends what had happened. Gradually, his silence transformed it into a secret.

And Annev continued to search for his attacker.

He recalled Arnor warning Sodar about traitors amidst the brotherhood, and Annev became suspicious of every member of the Order save Therin and Titus. Donning his Inquisitor ring, he endured the sanguine-red cloud that permanently misted his vision and counted it a small sacrifice for having constant access to its magic, in particular its ability to sense the pulse of those nearest him. He became adept at discerning when someone was lying or, more often, when they were anxious or excited about something. The codavora ring likewise proved invaluable, as Brother Tym's blood had layered a third ability atop the two magics already stored in the serpent-shaped artifact. Now he could catch glimpses of the thoughts of whomever he scried. He had to be close for it to work, and he had to concentrate to activate the magic, but it let Annev hear whatever words or thoughts were running through that person's mind. It's also how he knew what the Dionachs whispered about him behind his back – and what had precipitated his depressive, downward spiral.

During most of his investigations, Honeycutt was his primary target, and Annev frequently tried to talk to the man about his movements on the night of the attack. Each time he found Honeycutt alone, though, something interrupted their conversation. First Holyoak needed an urgent word with the caste leader;

then Dionach Leskal did. On his third try, Honeycutt simply said he was too busy to chat. Insights from the Inquisitor ring showed him the man was agitated, perhaps even angry, but he got no confirmation of Honeycutt's guilt. Even the mindwalking powers of the codavora ring were strangely silent, as if the man were deliberately shielding his thoughts. It might have seemed suspicious, but the other Dionachs took similar precautions around him. The same had not been true during his first week using the codavora ring's mindwalking powers, but something had changed since then. The mages had grown wary of him ... colder and more suspicious. Leskal had indefinitely postponed their sparring sessions, and Holyoak had become mentally and emotionally closed off, his mind perpetually guarded by an impenetrable psychic wall. Even Dionach McClanahan had begun to distance herself, though she tended to greet him warmly in the Enclave's corridors.

It was two weeks since the attack, including eight days of being treated like a pariah, when Annev had an unexpected encounter with Jayar Honeycutt. The caste leader had been approaching Annev in a corridor, and Annev had fully expected the man to turn and walk the other way, but instead Honeycutt looked up from his musings, his eyes brightened and he waved Annev towards him.

'Brother Annev! Might I have a private word with you?'

Annev was completely taken aback by Honeycutt's friendly demeanour. Then he nodded, slow and uncertain. 'Yes, Dionach Honeycutt.' He paused. 'Is now convenient?'

'Now would be perfect. In my chambers?'

Annev fought to keep his expression neutral. 'Lead the way,' he said, not trusting himself to say more. The caste leader did and soon Annev was walking beside him, erecting his own mental barriers and wondering why Honeycutt wanted to talk. He suspected a trap, and he began surreptitiously checking his artifacts. Honeycutt surprised him by taking Annev through the Breathbreakers' wing and directly to his personal chambers.

The room was unremarkable, as nondescript and impersonal as the many unoccupied rooms on Annev's basement level, though when Honeycutt closed the door, Annev noticed a single glyph charred on its inside face – the ward for silence. Then he saw the familiar cursed portrait, propped against the far wall.

'*You* took it!' Annev exclaimed, staring wide-eyed at the damaged painting.

Honeycutt showed neither guilt nor regret. 'When I saw it was missing from the Breathbreaker testing room,' he said, 'I tracked it to your bedchamber. I couldn't fathom how it had got there, much less why you had defaced it. My initial guess was that you had taken it to help your friend Therin ... but that did not explain why you destroyed the painting or dispelled its charm.' He eyed Annev closely, looking concerned. 'You didn't steal this painting. Someone put it in your room.'

Annev nodded.

'If I don't miss my guess,' Honeycutt continued, 'you were in there when the glyph was activated. All the air was suddenly expelled from your room, yes?' Annev nodded again and Honeycutt's expression darkened. 'I'm sorry, lad. I placed and activated those glyphs as part of the final Breathbreaker trial. I had no idea someone had moved it to your quarters, and it must have been a shock when I activated the ward for Therin's test. I'm not sure who moved it, but it seems they did it with the intention of harming you.'

Annev couldn't believe what he was hearing. 'So you've known about this since the test ... and you didn't tell me?'

Honeycutt shrugged. 'At first I thought you took the painting to help Therin. Then I foolishly hoped you were absent when the ward was activated ... though the damage to the painting implied otherwise. Your behaviour convinced me, too. You *were* present when the glyph was activated, and I fear it frightened you into thinking someone was trying to harm you. Perhaps you even realised I set the ward, and decided I was trying to scare you.'

'Scare me?' Annev said, his voice rising. 'It damn near *killed* me!'

Honeycutt frowned. 'The air would have been pushed from your room, of course, and that's frightening. But all you had to do was leave its sphere of influence.'

Annev's temper was rising, though he began to see the puzzle pieces fitting together. 'I *couldn't* leave, Jayar, because someone had sealed my room from the outside. I assumed ...'

'You assumed it was me.' Honeycutt's face grew pale. 'Someone tried to kill you, and they tried to make it look like I was the one responsible.' He frowned, his eyes growing misty with concern. 'My boy ... I'm so sorry. That must have been dreadful.'

Annev slowly nodded, uncertain how to process this new revelation. As he watched, he saw Honeycutt's eyes grow distant. The man tutted his tongue, his head shaking. 'It must be one of our Dionachs, most likely a brother who lacks the skill for breathbreaking.'

'What makes you think that?'

'Because if they possessed the skill, your attacker could have conjured the shield wall and the vacuum sphere themselves. They'd have no reason for this subterfuge with the painting.'

'Or,' Annev said, picking up the direction of Honeycutt's thoughts, 'the attacker *has* the skill ... but they needed an alibi. They needed someone else to cast the spell so they could prove they had been elsewhere during the attack.'

'Perhaps,' Honeycutt said, his thumb and forefinger stroking his beard. 'But the attacker would still need to stay close so they could lock you in your room and seal the chamber. That suggests we are looking for a Shieldbearer – or, at the very least, someone who possesses a talent for condensing skywater.'

Annev could hardly believe he was finally making some headway with the man he had most suspected of being his attacker. It took him a moment to adjust.

'You don't seem surprised that someone is trying to kill me.'

'I'm not – at least, not entirely. Arnor was sent to check in with Sodar, in part to ensure your safety.'

'You know Arnor?'

The Dionach nodded. 'He was my second. A natural Breathbreaker and a skilled spy.'

'Was?'

'Yes,' Honeycutt said, looking distraught. 'You see, he still hasn't returned from his mission ... and you have. The implication is not good.'

Annev vaguely remembered dreaming about Arnor's death the night before his Test of Judgement. He had held his tongue because he couldn't remember the details beyond its gruesome nature, and he had hoped nothing terrible had befallen the man, but on hearing Honeycutt's words his hopes quietly died. He swallowed, feeling uncomfortable.

'Arnor believed there were traitors within the Order. Do you?'

Honeycutt nodded once, his eyes flicking to his closed door. '*Sàmhchair*,' he said, gesturing with his hand. The glyph on the door flared white then cooled to a sombre blue. 'Does that answer your question? I am certain there are traitors in the Order, though I don't know their motives. Some may be grasping for power, not realising it further destabilises the Order. Others may be working for a foreign power – perhaps more than one.'

'But you have barely thirty brothers lodged here. You speak as if more than a third of them can't be trusted.'

'More like half, though I think most Dionachs remain uncorrupted by foreign powers.' He shook his head, his expression dour. 'But I speak as if this is something new. Politics has always been rife within the Order, despite Reeve's attempts to govern with neutrality. This attack on your life is a new development. Given Sodar's unique mission and your golden hand, I can see two motives: either your attacker perceives you as a threat to the Order and plans to do us a service by eliminating you ... or your attacker has allied themselves with the Terran God-king, Neruacanta.'

'Neruacanta?' Annev asked, recognising the name from Sodar's notes on the Siänar. 'You think the ruler of the Terrans has infiltrated the Order?'

'More than likely, yes.'

Annev fretted at this new revelation but set it aside for later reflection. 'How many Dionachs or journeymen would be capable of sealing my room and trying to suffocate me?'

'Speaking strictly of shieldbearing, where I am qualified to judge, I'd say at least half the brethren have enough skill to conjure an air wall, but not sufficient skill to form an airtight seal. Probably half a dozen of those – maybe a few more when you include the journeymen.'

'All Shieldbearers?'

'All except myself, Dionach Holyoak and Arch-Dionach Reeve.'

'Holyoak. But ... he's a Mindwalker? He manipulates *quaire*, not skywater.'

'He's a dualist, like me. His primary talent is mindwalking, which exerts an inward pull on *quaire*, but the adjacent skills are stormcalling and shieldbearing, the former because it uses the same physical form of magic and the latter because it uses the same inward-pulling force. Holyoak can condense the air almost as well as Leskal, whose only talent is shieldbearing, but he's also the best Mindwalker at the Enclave.'

'And Brother Tym is his second.'

'Yes.'

Annev nodded, believing he understood. 'And your own talents ... you're a Breathbreaker – you can push and expand the skywater – so your twin talent would either be pushing *quaire* as a Stormcaller or pulling skywater as a Shieldbearer.'

Honeycutt smiled. 'As it happens, I have *both* those skills.'

'You mean ... you have *three* blood-talents?'

'One primary and two secondary, yes.'

Annev digested this new information. 'Were both your parents dualists?'

'Yes,' Honeycutt said, still smiling.

'Then two of your grandparents were Mindwalkers,' Annev said, taking a guess, 'and the other two were a Stormcaller and a Shieldbearer.'

'My grandmothers,' Honeycutt said, nodding with enthusiasm. 'You're a bright young man, Annev.' His smile faded. 'Bright ... and in terrible danger. If we accept that a Shieldbearer tried to kill you, we should talk to Leskal. He knows the heart of every Dionach in his caste. He'll know if any of them have been acting suspiciously.'

'Shouldn't we take this to Reeve?'

'If you trust him.'

Annev's already considerable paranoia spiked further. 'Should I *not* trust him?'

Honeycutt's eyes shifted between the door, the painting and then back to Annev. 'Reeve is blessed with a talent in all four of the Darite arts,' he said slowly, 'but he's always favoured the Shieldbearer caste. If Reeve is above question, Leskal is not. He has a blunt martial mindset – always more likely to use a hammer when a chisel or a spade might be better. He's a good Shieldbearer, and I doubt he would willingly betray the Order, but he'd also do dark things to protect it. If you ask Reeve, though, he'll tell you the man is above reproach.'

'So Leskal might attack me, if he thought he was protecting the Order,' Annev said, piecing together the Dionach's meaning, 'That means he'll do anything Reeve asks of him ... and Reeve will protect him in turn.' Honeycutt said nothing but tapped the side of his nose, his eyes bright with intrigue. Annev continued his train of thought. 'Then I can't trust Leskal ... but you think I should still talk to him?'

Honeycutt nodded. 'He *might* have been behind the attack, but I think it more likely one of his Shieldbearers has acted independently.'

'What about Reeve and Holyoak? Or could someone else have tried to kill me?'

'Any of the Stormcallers could have done it, I suppose.' Honeycutt tapped his skull. 'Not everyone keeps their thoughts guarded from mindwalking and stormcalling. A sufficiently powerful Stormcaller could have manipulated an equally powerful Shieldbearer into sealing your room ... and *anyone* could have stolen the painting, so it becomes less likely that one of my Breathbreakers was involved.'

'And more likely that it's one of the Shieldbearers ... or one of the Stormcallers. Odar's balls, that doesn't eliminate many people, does it?'

'Not when you consider that many of the Breathbreakers and Mindwalkers are also dualists. Though they'd have to possess a powerful secondary talent if they were involved in your attempted murder.'

'Damn,' Annev swore. 'Who can I trust, then?'

'Trust?' Honeycutt said, a pained smile twisting his face. 'My dear boy, I thought I made it clear: no one – not even me. If McClanahan or Holyoak were involved, they could have persuaded me to do something I would never rationally do, and then make me forget I'd done it.' He met Annev's eyes, his expression intense. 'Trust *no one*.'

Annev nodded, feeling better about Honeycutt's relative innocence but also realising he was no closer to discovering his assailant. 'I guess I don't have any leads, then. With the right preparation, anyone could have been part of the attack.'

Honeycutt chewed his lip. 'Truth be told, I doubt any of the caste leaders were involved.'

'What makes you say that?'

'Because if one of us had tried to kill you, you'd be dead.'

'Perhaps,' Annev rejoined, 'or perhaps you're not giving me enough credit.'

Honeycutt inclined his head, a small gesture of respect. 'For your sake, young man, I hope I'm right. Any one of the caste leaders would be a dangerous enemy. I do not envy your predicament.'

'Dionach Leskal seems to be avoiding me – *all* of the Dionachs seem to be avoiding me, but Leskal seems especially agitated. He suspended our weekly sparring sessions and hasn't spoken to me since.'

The caste leader grunted. 'Let me talk to him. I'm no Mindwalker, but I fancy myself a good judge of character. Folk around here tend to underestimate that, once they've learned how to peek into someone's thoughts.'

Annev wondered if he'd fallen into that trap himself. He'd been so focused on the mindwalking powers of his codavora ring that he'd been less alert to others' behaviour.

'Thank you,' Annev said – and he meant it. Honeycutt had brought him one step closer to finding the answers he sought.

Chapter Sixty

'Can I speak with you, Annev?'

The question came from Brother Tym just two days after the conversation with Dionach Honeycutt. The monk had been waiting outside Annev's bedchamber and appeared ill at ease.

'Of course,' Annev said, his mind leaping to conclusions. *Does he know I've been spying on him and Misty?*

Tym gestured at Annev's door. 'In private, please?'

Annev noted that Tym's heartbeat was steadily rising. He tried to read the man's thoughts but could only glimpse a churn of emotions. 'Sure' he said, unlocking the door and gesturing for Tym to enter ahead of him. Annev finally relaxed when he saw Tym's pulse didn't spike as he entered. *He's not here to ambush me. What then?*

'What do you need?' Annev asked after closing the door.

'To confess.'

This time it was Annev's pulse that spiked. He kept his emotions in check, though, his face a mask. 'Oh?' he said, his voice squeaking in spite of himself.

'Yes, I've ... I'm afraid Misty and I have betrayed you.'

Annev was so taken aback by the admission that he wasn't immediately angry. He had been telling himself to suspect everyone, but he hadn't honestly thought Tym and Misty would attack him. Or admit it.

'It was an accident,' Tym went on, nervously filling the silence. 'Misty hadn't meant to tell anyone – neither of us had – but she's

566

terrible at keeping in her secrets. She's so open, it's difficult to keep things guarded, and she let it slip during a stormcalling lesson.'

'Let what slip?' Annev asked, suddenly unsure what the Dionach was talking about.

Tym's face was downcast. 'You remember when we accidentally learned that you needed our blood? We didn't ask why because we trusted you, in part because Sodar had trusted you, but also because you *didn't* ask us for our blood, or intend to share that secret with us, so it certainly wasn't ours to share with others.'

Annev was half waiting for Tym to accuse him of adding the Mindwalker's blood to his codavora ring – but then the truth came to him in a rush.

'Misty told them … you told them I wanted their *blood*?'

Tym's eyes were bright with moisture. 'We didn't really say it out loud, you know? We were taking turns defending and attacking and the journeymen Mindwalkers and Stormcallers and … well, Misty slipped up and then Journeyman Zayas blurted out what he'd heard and suddenly it was like trying to get smoke back into a bottle. When I realised what they were talking about, my own thoughts jumped to that conversation and … well, I made things worse. And now we realise you've been ostracised as a result. Annev, we're so sorry.'

'How long ago?' Annev asked, his heart almost beating out of his chest. 'How long ago was this?'

Tym's brow furrowed. 'I should have come to you about it sooner, Annev. I'm so sorry.'

The codavora ring hummed with the answer Brother Tym was too embarrassed to voice. 'Two weeks! It's been two *weeks*?' This was why everyone had been so skittish around him, why the Dionachs had all been so guarded. He'd been so focused on finding the person who had tried to kill him, so wrapped up in his paranoia and depression, that he hadn't stopped to consider *why* he had suddenly become the Enclave's pariah. His fears certainly hadn't helped, but there had been far more going on behind the scenes.

'Journeyman Rochelle and Dionach Pennington think I'm a Terran spy … or keokum.'

'You heard that, did you?' Tym exhaled, the air hissing through his clenched teeth. 'Silver staves, Annev, no one really thinks that. It's just whispers, you know? They all know you're Sodar's pupil and a mix of Darite and Ilumite. It's well known Sodar never let a drop of Terran mix with that bloodline – didn't want to dilute the magic, he said – so everyone *knows* you can't be Terran, much less a Bloodlord or anything dark like that.'

'A Bloodlord?' Annev's anger abruptly turned into a smile at the thought, and the irony. 'I ran from Chaenbalu because I have magic – I was called a keokum there, too, you know – and I come here, the one place I should be safe, only for the whispers to start all over again. I can't escape it ...' His tone darkened again. 'The fear and the hatred. It just keeps following me.'

Tym's eyes suddenly went wide as he stared at Annev's left hand. Annev glanced down just as he caught the whiff of burning leather and saw his blacksmith glove was smouldering. Small holes appeared in the charred leather, their gaps revealing the fiery golden light beneath.

'Dammit!' Annev swore, tearing the black glove off and throwing the smoking, tattered thing to the ground. He stomped on it, extinguishing its flames. Beside him, the Hand of Keos grew hotter – a dark smouldering red.

Tym was backing away.

'It's fine, it's fine!' Annev said, trying not to panic as much for his own sake as for Tym's. He attempted to calm himself and the glowing artifact by forcing his breathing to slow. Even so, his heart thudded heavily in his chest, and the terror he'd felt in the Boneyard in Luqura suddenly rose to claim him. He remembered Elar Kranak and the Innistiul slavers surrounding them, threatening to kill him and his friends, and his readiness to burn it all down. He remembered how he'd felt just before killing Tosan and Myjun in Chaenbalu ... how they too had called him a monster and a Son of Keos. His friends had magic and no one was calling *them* keokum – and at that, all his buried jealously rose as well. The deep frustration of knowing he could never be part of this group of brothers and sisters – that he would never truly belong anywhere.

A damnable ball of fire began to grow in Annev's hand.

Tym shouted a curse, flung the door open and bolted down the hall, shouting something unintelligible. More calls of alarm rang out.

Don't do this. He fought to control his emotions. *You don't want this. Your friends are here ... Sraon and Titus and Therin. All these people, these* good *people. They trusted you, brought you into their home. Don't do this.*

But part of him *wanted* to do it. Some deep, unacknowledged part of his soul wanted to burn it all to the five hells, to wipe all the traitors and hypocrites from the face of Luquatra. His friends had moved on without him. Sraon had forgotten him. Even Tym and Misty had betrayed him. But he could purify the Order in one blast – all the lies and the intrigues and the whispering would all just disappear. A snap of his fingers, a flick of his wrist and *FOOM*.

The Order of the Dionachs Tobar destroyed in fire and damnation.

Quiri, the Empire's religious capital and oldest city – broken, burning, ruined.

It would be as easy as destroying Chaenbalu – as easy as destroying Luqura would have been. And so many more people would die because of him. Because he couldn't control his own damnable fears and hatred. Because he couldn't free himself of his accursed hand.

Annev felt the orb of fire and death begin to slip from his fingers, growing even brighter and hotter, and the smouldering pieces of furniture around him lit up in flame. Next the floor would begin to melt, just as the stones beneath him had melted into slag and molten rock in Chaenbalu ... after Tosan killed Sodar.

I'm a very poor replacement for your father.

Annev gasped, the words coming unbidden to his mind, barely more than a whisper.

I've done my best to fill that void in your life, and not out of duty or obligation. I do it because I believe in you, Annev – more than you believe in yourself – and every action I take, every day of my life, reaffirms that belief.

Sodar's words, spoken to him the day before his Test of Judgement – the day before Annev's world began to spin out of control. It had never stopped spinning. That had been the last day that made sense to him – the last day of his childhood. The room burning brightly around him, Annev felt the tears fall as he remembered the small things, the bittersweet memories of sparring with Sodar in the woods and learning new lessons while earning new bruises. He remembered Sodar keeping count every day while Annev raced back with water from the village well. Sodar's faith, his hard work, his dry jokes and stoic sense of morality. The ageless old man had been a guardian, a caretaker, a surrogate father. He'd acted as a grandfather to an adopted family as, in turn, they grew up, grew old and died. Sodar had endured for centuries, watching over Annev's ancestors, bearing the burden of a prophecy no one else believed. Even among his brethren – the Enclave he had known for millennia – Sodar had been alone.

And now Annev was alone . . .

. . . and that meant, perhaps, neither of them was alone.

At that unexpectedly comforting thought, Annev took a breath, blinked away his tears, and saw the glowing ball of light in his hand began to dissipate. As it did so, the heat from the flames and molten rock suddenly reached him. With a start, he sprinted into the hall, barely escaping the conflagration now consuming his non-magical possessions. Anything he'd been wearing had been protected by the Hand of Keos. Everything else was on fire.

Damn, he thought, backing away from the flickering flames and smoke that continued to billow from his room. Choking now, he sprinted along the corridor and up the stairs. He had barely climbed two steps before crashing into Leskal, Honeycutt and two other Dionachs.

'Where is it?' Leskal demanded, barely glancing at Annev.

'My room,' Annev stammered, his body shaking.

The four Dionachs ran towards it, glyph wands held aloft, drawing wards while they ran. Working together, the Breathbreakers sucked the oxygen from the room while the Shieldbearers used water and ice to cool the burning wood and melted stone. Honeycutt spared a glance at Annev as Leskal and his fellow

Shieldbearer continued their work, and his thoughts were clear as a bell to Annev through the codavora ring.

Damn near killed us all.

He was right. Annev *had* nearly killed them all – and likely a good chunk of Quiri, too. Given his proximity to the Pontiff Prime's palace, he could have laid waste to the upper echelons of the Darite Church's clergy.

I'm a monster, Annev thought. *I'm a danger to these people.* It didn't matter that someone at the Order had tried to kill him – if Annev was really this dangerous, if he really had so little control over himself and his magic, perhaps they had even been right to try. Perhaps he was better off far away from anyone he loved.

Just then Reeve came hurtling down the steps, his robes flapping behind him as he took the stairs two or three at a time. When he saw Annev and the faintly glowing Hand of Keos, he stopped, his eyes drawn to the corridor behind Annev.

'The fire is out,' he said, unable to meet the high priest's eyes.

Reeve's expression was dour. 'Good ... good.' His frown deepened. 'Come with me, boy.'

The magic of the codavora ring revealed what the Arch-Dionach was thinking. The high priest didn't even try to hide it. He was practically screaming: *I have to get rid of him. He's too dangerous.*

Annev found himself agreeing, though Reeve's next thought nearly broke him.

Sodar would be devastated to see this.

Chapter Sixty-One

The Arch-Dionach gestured to the pair of wicker chairs set beside the low table.

'Take a seat, Annev.'

Annev did, unnerved by the high priest's silence. Even using the power of his codavora ring, he had been unable to glean a hint of the man's thoughts after his first outburst, which Annev took to signify Reeve had slammed down his mental defences again. He wondered if this meant the high priest had realised Annev could mindwalk – if only in a limited capacity.

If Reeve knew of his new powers, though, he did not mention them. Instead he slumped into the chair opposite Annev.

'You've been busy these past few weeks,' the man said, rubbing his temples. 'Unoccupied with lessons, yet busy all the same.'

Annev's sense of déjà vu assaulted him as he recalled similar conversations with Elder Tosan. Fortunately for Annev, the Arch-Dionach had less interest in hearing himself talk and a greater desire to get to the point.

'You've been causing a stir at the Enclave ever since your friends were promoted into the Brotherhood.' Reeve held up a thumb and began counting on his fingers. 'Wearing that dragon cloak and sword, as if you're preparing for war. Waving that magic wand about as if it might protect you from some evil – or maybe conjure some. I don't know how, but you've been dismantling just about every idle glyph you've found in the Enclave. You damn near froze the west wing last week.' He shook his head. 'The damnedest thing is I don't think you even realise what you're doing. It's not malicious ... but it's not reassuring, either.'

Annev was surprised ... and Reeve was right; in the past few weeks, Annev had become neurotic about using his Rod of Artificing to check his surroundings for activated glyphs and abandoned artifacts. It had accelerated his proficiency with the item, but his familiarity had also led to experimentation. He'd been trying to study the residual magic in abandoned wards left by absent Dionachs and had discovered the threads binding each mage's *quaire* to his activated glyph. Annev couldn't see those threads without the benefit of his Inquisitor ring, and he couldn't touch them without the Artificing rod, but when he used the artifacts in tandem, Annev had found he could manipulate the strands of blood-magic and track them to the mages who cast them. In the most innocuous cases he had used his rod to sever the links to the absent mages, and each time he'd watched the magic unravel as the spell's *quaire* dissipated into the air. It had given him a notion of how glyph-speaking was supposed to work – how the Dionach's *quaire* could power each ward – yet he'd been unable to replicate any of the wards he'd dismantled. He had told himself he wasn't hurting anyone and that his tinkering would go unnoticed ... but it seemed he'd been wrong.

Annev folded his arms, his right hand clutching the Rod of Artificing beneath his robes. 'I don't deny it,' he said unabashed. 'It was ... necessary.'

'Why?'

Annev bit his lip, uncertain. *'Trust no one'* echoed in Annev's mind, but Reeve had protected them back in Quiri, and Sodar had trusted him. Even Honeycutt had grudgingly admitted the man would look after Annev's interests ... and he had to trust someone, at least a little.

'On the night of the Tests of Ascendancy,' Annev said, his voice growing stronger as he spoke, 'someone tried to kill me.'

'What?' Reeve's brow furrowed. 'Why am I only hearing this now?'

'Because I don't know who to trust, so I've been trying to untangle who did it on my own ... and it's been difficult.'

Reeve stroked his goatee, his mental walls back in place. 'I see.'

Annev waited but the high priest said nothing else. 'Well?' he asked, feeling flummoxed. 'What should I have done?'

'I believe you,' Reeve said, his face a mask, 'and you should have come to me sooner.'

'So what can we do?'

'Nothing.'

Annev's head cocked to the side. 'Nothing? You mean, exactly what you've done *without* knowing? Are you just waiting for the assassin to try again?'

'More or less,' Reeve said, his cool demeanour hiding his actual thoughts. 'With some precautions to protect you, but acting strangely might deter the traitors from revealing themselves. Perhaps it already has.'

Annev stared, his mouth agape as realisation dawned. 'You *knew*. I mean, you've known there's a traitor here ... and you didn't do anything.'

Reeve sighed. 'We talked about this before you came to the Enclave, remember? You worried whether the Order would be safe for you and your friends.'

'And you said it *was*!' Annev cried, furious.

'There are degrees of safety,' Reeve said, not bothering to explain further. 'You were safer here than you would have been walking the streets of Luqura.'

'And now?' Annev asked, his cheeks hot with anger.

'And now ... now *we* are not safe with you here.'

And there it was.

Annev realised he was standing. He tried not to look at the golden hand hanging from his left arm, but its power seemed to attract both their gazes. Reeve inclined his head, seeing they both understood.

'You've been collecting the blood of our Dionachs,' Reeve said, his expression grim. 'I don't know why, but I can only suspect it is as potentially destructive as your experiments with our wards. I might have accepted this all stemmed from the attempt on your life ... but it doesn't matter now. Whatever good might have been done by keeping you at the Enclave, it's now outweighed by the danger you *pose* to the Order.'

Annev understood, of course. In Reeve's position, he'd have come to the same conclusion. Annev would hate leaving Therin and Titus behind, but they were better off without him – and in less danger, for sure. They had outgrown him at the Enclave. He moved towards the door but the high priest stopped him.

'Hold on, now. Where are you going?'

'I'm leaving.'

Reeve grimaced. 'You're too valuable to send away – and too dangerous to keep here.'

Annev's gaze pinned the Arch-Dionach. 'You can't have it both ways ... can you?'

Reeve glanced at Annev's hand once more. 'How long would it take you to find the assassin, if you had some help?'

'What?'

'How long? Could you solve the mystery if I gave you twenty-four hours?'

Annev choked back a laugh. 'You're not serious.'

'I am.'

'I've been searching for weeks. I've come up with nothing – *nothing*.'

'But you have your suspicions, and your investigations have had to be covert. What if Dionach Leskal aided you? I believe you've already developed a rapport with him, and he's one of the few Dionachs I fully trust.'

Trust no one. Annev began to shake his head then checked the instinct. He hadn't found an opportunity to interrogate Leskal yet. Perhaps this would work.

'If you trust him, then I'd be happy to have his help.'

'Good.' Reeve stood, his expression softening. 'I'll let it be known that you're going on a mission for the Order – something suitable for Sodar's chosen one – and you can say your goodbyes. Use that time to investigate – and be alert. If the assassin really wants to kill you, they'll have to make their move quickly, and we'll be ready.'

'Wait, *that's* your plan? I pretend I'm leaving, and you wait for someone to kill me?'

'You *are* leaving,' Reeve said, his face hardening once again. 'And you *are* going on a mission.' He stroked his moustache, his eyes darting to the door and back to Annev. 'Yesterday I received a letter inviting Sraon to Innistiul to parley with his cousin, King Cheng. Sraon's condition remains unchanged, though, so I need to send someone on his behalf.'

'His cousin? King Cheng is ... hold on. Are you suggesting I go to *Innistiul*?'

'Yes.' Reeve stared at him, his eyes cold. 'You're a bomb waiting to explode, Annev de Breth. No matter where I send you, no matter what mission I give you, there's a chance that bomb will go off ... and I don't want it anywhere near me or my people.'

'You want – you think ...' Annev was unable to force the words out.

'You're a weapon, Annev. Sodar was right about that, though I doubt you've been sent here to kill a dead god.' He gestured at the Hand of Keos. 'I've seen what it can do. You were screaming about the destruction it could cause so loudly I suspect every Dionach with a drop of Mindwalker blood heard you. And I saw you struggle with the same impulse in Luqura.'

'You *knew* about that?'

'Of course. How did you think I *found* you?' Reeve gave a deep, shuddering breath. 'Gods be good, boy. If you can do that just by losing control for a few seconds, imagine what you might do if you tried to harness it – to direct it towards something or someone that *ought* to be destroyed.'

'But why go to Cheng? He's part of the Empire – a *king*. I would think ... I mean, if I were to destroy anyone, wouldn't it be the Terrans?'

Reeve turned his hands upward. 'Would you send an untested weapon into the midst of your enemies? Knowing they might gain control of it?' Reeve frowned. 'Cheng is a worthy mission for you. His kingdom derives its power from enslaving others – including other Darites – and we've long suspected him of colluding with the Terran high priest, Neruacanta. He has connections to Saltair, and there's a good chance he's part of the machine that's been trying to kill you. Killing him might end your problem at the root.'

'But you have no evidence.'

'No. Just my suspicions, the same as you.'

Annev found he was considering it. Could he summon the destructive power of the Hand of Keos, and channel it to cold-bloodedly kill someone? Could he become an assassin, not just of a king, but an entire kingdom? He hadn't been able to in Chaenbalu, when Tosan asked him to kill a single stranger. What made him think he could when innocent lives were at stake?

Before he could even begin to shake his head, Reeve laid a hand on his shoulder. 'Annev, you *can't* stay here, and wherever you go you'll be endangering the lives of those around you. Best that you choose someplace ... expendable. A place where, if the worst happens, you can make a difference. Innistiul is a good choice. Not so far as New Terra or as dangerous as the pits of Daogort. It's an island, removed from the heart of civilisation, built on wickedness.'

Annev didn't know what to say – didn't know if there was anything he *could* say. Still, he tried. 'I could go somewhere far away from everyone. I can live like a hermit, in the desert or the forest. Maybe I could go back to Chaenbalu and look for the Oracle. At least Chaenbalu's circle of protection would—'

'That circle is no guarantee of safety, Annev. Your village was found once. They can find it again. As for remote parts of the Empire ... well, Innistiul is close enough to Quiri that we could still send for you. But if you tried to go into hiding, there's a chance your enemy would find you before we did – and turn you against us.'

'I would never.'

'Never say never, Annev. I've seen stranger things, and you're still confused about your place in the world. A skilled Stormcaller could push dangerous thoughts into your mind. Plant a few seeds, then reap the destruction.' He leaned forward. 'This is why I've kept you from leaving the Enclave. Much as I would like to, I can't risk sending you to look for Bron Gloir or the Oracle. You're simply too dangerous.'

Annev's head shook in denial, even as he felt Reeve's words resonate within him. He couldn't stay, that was true, but nor did he need to become a killer. He had enough blood on his hands for a thousand lifetimes.

'I'll leave,' he said at last, his fist clenched at his side, 'but I'm no tool. I'm not part of your Order and I'm not your assassin. I'll go where I please.'

'Then I hope you go to Innistiul.'

Annev frowned. 'What business does Sraon have with his cousin?'

Reeve clasped his hands together in front of his chest, his eyes shrewd. 'A member of the royal line has been killed – making Sraon second-in-line to inherit.'

'Who is first?'

'Cheng's only son. Barely more than an infant.'

Annev's brow furrowed. 'So you wanted me to kill Cheng and his son.'

'I didn't say that.'

'You didn't need to. If I brought the Hand of Keos to Innistiul, it would destroy the whole palace – maybe the whole *island*. All for what? So Sraon could inherit the ruins? So you could have another piece to manipulate on the chessboard? Odar's balls, the man doesn't even remember who he is!'

'Because someone at the Enclave leeched his memories, Annev! *That* is why Sraon can't remember things. It's not Saltair's poison – that was removed from his system soon after arriving here – but someone in the Order wants us to *think* it is. Someone has been tampering with Brother Sraon's memories. He knows something – about you, I think – and someone wanted that information badly enough that they leeched all of his memories about you and your time together in Chaenbalu.'

'They *what*?' Annev eyes were burning, the tears starting to well up behind his eyes. 'Why didn't you tell me?'

'Because I'm not sure he'll ever recover – and I wanted to spare you both from the pain of that loss.'

'You say that … but you also want to send me to Innistiul so Sraon can become its next king. You don't care about helping him recover. You just want to use him ... like you want to use me.'

Reeve spread his hands again, his face a mask. 'For the greater good, Annev. We are all tools in the hands of Odar. Perhaps this is the reason Sodar protected your family line.'

'No,' Annev said, his temper flaring again. 'Sodar protected the line of Breathanas so that one of my family would kill Keos – or Neruacanta, or whoever is possessed with the spirit of the Fallen God – *not* to commit genocide. Sodar would be *disgusted* if he knew what you're asking.'

'He would be disgusted by what happened *today*!' Reeve retorted, his voice rising. 'Your hands aren't clean, Ainnevog de Breth – *no one's* are. Not even Sodar's. The sooner you realise that – the sooner you see we can't fix the world without breaking it first – the sooner you'll finally do some good.'

Annev's heart thudded in his chest and he felt the blood rising to his face. He didn't dare look down at the Hand of Keos for fear of what he might see. He had to calm himself, but he couldn't walk away either. Not now that Reeve had finally shed his mask.

'Tell me the truth,' Annev said, the coolness of his voice belying his anger. 'Was everything about this hand a lie? Was this your goal all along?'

Reeve faltered and he licked his lips. 'I ... have a notion – a theory about it.'

'Then why not tell me?' Annev said, calling on the powers of his codavora and Inquisitor rings. 'Why not try it? Why have you *kept* it from me?'

'Because you wouldn't like it,' Reeve said.

'And?' Annev asked, knowing there was more.

'And I hoped you might help us. The Hand of Keos has powers we don't fully understand, and I thought it might be useful.'

'As a weapon,' Annev said, his anger rising to the surface.

'No!' Reeve said. 'Not initially. I hoped you would lead us to Bron Gloir and the Oracle. That was true. The prophecies ... if you really are the Vessel then I think it could take you to the Staff of Odar – or maybe to Odar himself.'

Annev's anger blew away like smoke in a gust of wind. 'You ... want to find Odar?'

'And Lumea,' Reeve said. 'I thought that with the diamagi we might have a chance to find the Gods and bring them back. Maybe we could *end* the Silence of the Gods.'

Annev stared at the high priest and realised the man was blushing, having said it out loud. Reeve saw Annev as a tool, but hoped he was a compass, not a knife. One which would allow him to re-establish communion with his God, silent for two thousand years. The high priest's intentions had been good ... but Annev had failed. He had failed to manifest any talent at glyph-speaking, he was endangering the Order, and it was too dangerous to go to Chaenbalu. Annev didn't have to check his rings to know Reeve was telling the truth; Reeve had finally realised Annev couldn't help him.

'I'll go,' Annev said, his anger spent, his hand glowing faintly in the dim light of the Arch-Dionach's study. 'I might even go to Innistiul, but not at your behest.'

Reeve sank down, his back bent in resignation. He nodded.

'You said you'd give me twenty-four hours? If during that time I can find the traitors hidden in the Order, I'll take care of them myself. Can you agree to that, too?'

Reeve shrugged. 'Can I stop you?'

'Not likely.' He paused. 'And I want to know your theory about removing the Hand.'

Reeve's face paled and he shook his head. 'You won't like it.'

'It couldn't be worse than nearly destroying the entire Enclave,' Annev retorted.

'No,' Reeve said, 'perhaps not for us, anyway. For you, though ... the solution to a problem can sometimes be more painful than enduring it.'

Annev studied the Arch-Dionach. 'Fine. You keep your secrets and I'll keep mine – but I'm going to take Leskal and find those traitors. When I find them, you will not interfere. Not even if the traitor was a friend – *especially* not then. I'll handle the interrogations and decide what's to be done with them.'

'You're proposing a witch hunt – in which you'll do anything in pursuit of your killers.'

'Yes.'

'And if you accuse the wrong person? If you endanger innocents?'

'What makes the lives of your Dionachs any more precious than all of the innocents in Innistiul you're happy to sacrifice?'

'Because they are *mine*, dammit! Because they are my friends – people I've trusted for centuries.'

'And at least one of them is a traitor.'

Reeve pursed his lips. 'Then know in turn: if you hurt someone unjustly, I will hold you accountable for it. Being Sodar's chosen one won't save you from my wrath.'

Annev met the man's gaze, his expression hard. Neither moved, neither flinched. Annev nodded. 'We understand each other then.'

'Yes.'

Annev hesitated on the threshold, his brow knit in consternation. 'You called me Sodar's chosen one ... from the line of Breathanas.'

'Yes.'

'It seems strange, impossible even, that I could be the only surviving member of that line. Surely there are others – other branches and other children – after two millennia.'

'Did Sodar ever say there were no others?'

'No ...'

'Then there's your answer.'

'But why me? Why my line?'

Reeve shrugged. 'Ask Sodar. *He* believed in that prophecy. He decided the rules – whom to follow and protect ... and whom to set aside. I believe his preference went to children born with the talent. After that, it was usually the first-born males – patriarchal crap. Half a dozen times he had to "make do" with untalented girls, to my amusement.'

'Then there's no rhyme or reason to it. It was ... arbitrary.'

Reeve inclined his head. 'And now you see why so few of us put weight in his mission. Twice the line he was following *died out* and Sodar had to search out one of the surviving branches.'

Annev couldn't believe it. Sodar and his prophecies ... it was all a lie. Deep down, Annev had suspected this – he had *known* it, yet he'd still chosen to honour the dead man's wishes. Hearing Reeve's cold explanation felt as if someone had pulled back the heavens and shown him there were no gods – no order, no prophecy, no fate or magic. Things were simply what they were: bleak and chaotic, cold and hard. You built what you could from it and prayed it would last long enough to make a difference. It was a painful realisation, and the sharpness of it gave Annev the determination to do whatever came next.

'I'm heading to my quarters on the bottom level. If Leskal is still down there, he may not wish to work with me. Could you draft a letter requesting his aid?'

'I'll tell him myself – right now.' Reeve took a moment, his eyes staring blankly into space. 'He'll meet you in front of your chambers.'

Annev nodded his thanks and walked away.

'Twenty-four hours!' Reeve called after him.

Chapter Sixty-Two

Dionach Leskal was waiting for Annev, pacing the lowest level of the Enclave, tugging the twin tails of his braided beard. On seeing Annev, he inclined his head towards the melted corridor where Annev's former bedchamber lay.

'Everyone else has cleared out. Just us on this floor now.'

'Good,' Annev said, clearing the last step. He wore the codavora and Inquisitor rings on his right hand, while his ungloved prosthetic held the Rod of Artificing. Leskal eyed it with undisguised hostility.

'What's that for?'

'Unravelling the truth.'

Leskal's brow furrowed. 'You made this mess, boy – you and that damn hand. You don't need any magic staves or rods to reveal that truth.'

'There may be something else to discover down here.' Annev watched Leskal closely through the scarlet mists of his Inquisitor ring. 'Did Reeve tell you I'm leaving tomorrow?'

Leskal's heartbeat seemed to slow. 'I ... hadn't heard.'

'I'm going north on a special mission.'

'Mission? You'll be coming back?' Leskal's pulse began to rise.

'I think that, wherever I go, I'm leaving Quiri and the Enclave for good – maybe even leaving Odarnea.'

Leskal's heartbeat slowed again. 'Well, I'm sure wherever Reeve is sending you, it's important.'

Annev had to suppress a cynical smile at hearing that. Assassinating King Cheng and destroying the city state of Innistiul was unnecessary, tragic, and foolhardy. 'Important' was not the word he would have used – if anything, it was the opposite: Innistiul had been deemed expendable ... and so had Annev. So had Sraon.

Leskal seemed to believe him. He would be relieved to see Annev gone, but he harboured no ill will towards him – certainly not the kind that involved elaborate assassination attempts.

If Leskal wanted me dead, he'd be concerned about my leaving the Enclave. He'd be agitated, not calm. I should be able to trust him with my investigation.

Annev nodded towards the remains of his bedchamber. 'I need your help. I think I'm missing something.'

Leskal studied the hallway and the remains of the room. 'What are we looking for exactly?' He stepped through the stone archway that had been the door to Annev's bedroom, the wooden portal and timber frame having been burned to a dark smudge staining the ground.

'I think there's a shield glyph tethered nearby,' Annev explained. 'Its power was disrupted about three weeks ago, but it may still be linked to the Dionach that formed it.'

'Linked?' Leskal shook his head. 'Glyph-speaking is just the Ward and the Will – an intention or a thought made manifest.'

'But it consumes the caster's *quaire*, yes? It leaves a mark on the world ... an impression or link to the person who made it.'

The Shieldbearer slowly cocked his head to the side. 'I suppose that's one way of describing it. And you say it's inactive?'

'Yes.'

Leskal grunted. 'Well, that's it, then. There's nothing else connecting that ward to the person who formed it – the ward is gone.'

'No,' Annev said, shaking his head. 'I can't explain it, but I'm sure. I just can't see the remnants of the glyph.'

'If it was inside your room, you probably destroyed it.'

'No ... look out here in the hallway. Somewhere close to the door.'

Leskal began to check the melted stones forming the sagging archway. 'Why would you have a wall of air placed near your door anyway? Did you mean to lock it?'

'*I* didn't place it there. Someone else did.'

Leskal scowled, his hands caressing the stone. 'Why would someone do that?'

'Because they were trying to kill me. First, they trapped me inside, then they forced out the air by stealing part of Therin's Test of Ascendancy.'

'What are you talking about? When did this happen?' Leskal's hands slid to his sides as he faced Annev in alarm.

'Nearly three weeks ago,' Annev said, watching as Leskal's heart began to race.

'We have traitors ... among the brotherhood?' Leskal shook his head, the braids of his beard swinging fiercely. 'The castes have had their differences in the past, sure, but the men and women you see here at the Enclave are among the best to enter our Order. All the chaff was burned away—'

'During the Faction Wars?'

'Yes.' Leskal hesitated. 'Arnor explained all that to Sodar, did he?'

'He did.'

'And Sodar shared it with you?'

'Not exactly. I was eavesdropping.'

'Mm. That makes more sense. Sodar was so tight-lipped, you'd have thought his mouth was painted on. Didn't like anyone but Reeve knowing he was alive, let alone where he was.'

'Maybe he had a reason for that?'

'Oh, he was always worried about spies or traitors, long before the Faction Wars. But a broken water clock still tells the right time twice a day, eh? Can't keep the Order spotless for millennia without a few rotten apples making their way into the barrel.'

'And that rot can spread,' Annev said. 'You think you cleaned it out during the Faction Wars, but one of your brethren is not who you think.'

Leskal snorted. 'I've known most of this lot for *centuries*, lad. I've trusted them with more than my life.'

'Well, whoever formed the ward I'm looking for tried to use Darite magic to kill me.'

Leskal scratched his chest, his expression souring. 'If a

585

Shieldbearer were trying to kill you, they'd crush you with a wall of air or scythe your head from your body with a blade of ice. This attempt, though ... I don't know. If it's true, then I doubt you're looking for a Shieldbearer or a Breathbreaker.'

'I know. Honeycutt and I discussed it. I have some theories but ... I *need* to find that glyph. It's the key to the whole puzzle.'

'But you said the glyph was destroyed?'

'I think it just became untethered from its magic. Someone formed the ward and activated it, but I managed to disrupt the *quaire* flowing to it. It's inactive now, but not destroyed. So it's still here ... somewhere.'

'If it's still intact and I could imbue it with my own *quaire*, could you see it?'

'Probably, but then its magic might just lead back to you.'

The caste leader sucked his teeth. 'No way to know till we try.' He turned towards the wall, filled his lungs with air and began to chant, his eyes half-lidded. '*Balla.*' He looked up and down the corridor then shrugged. '*Sgiath. Bacadh.*' He frowned and waited once more. 'I don't feel anything, Annev. I'm sorry.'

'Wait,' Annev said, his brow furrowed. 'Intent is important when forming glyphs. What if instead of "shield" or "wall" you try something more specific. Maybe "seal" or "trap". Something that could imprison me in there and seal out the air?'

Leskal grunted, rolled his shoulders, and turned towards the open doorway. '*Seuladh. Príosún. Gaiste.*' After the third command, three small glyphs flared in the stones at the base of the wall and Leskal blinked, taken aback. 'Odar bless and keep me. You were right, boy.' He stooped to squint at the tiny runes that were already beginning to dim. He looked amazed. 'Damn small glyphs – they blend in almost perfectly with the stone. Not chiselled or painted.' He stood, growling thoughtfully to himself. 'Someone must have forged an air blade and used it to carve the stones. Delicate work, even for a skilled Shieldbearer. Less than a handful of our Dionachs could manage it.'

Annev crouched to examine the three small runes. 'Let me see if I can distinguish your *quaire* from the Dionach who inscribed the glyph.' After concentrating on the magic of his Inquisitor ring, Annev saw three glowing threads of magic appear in the air before him, their threads connecting Leskal's *quaire* to the triangle of wards. As before, Annev could see faint traces of glowing magic flowing up and down the lengths of each thread, their diaphanous strands lightly connected to Dionach Leskal's chest. Annev probed the threads with his Rod of Artificing and felt them thrum beneath his touch.

'Did you feel that?'

'Feel what?'

'I guess not,' Annev said, his wand beginning to untangle the three twisting threads of magic. He kept probing till his rod had a firm grip on the three strands of magic – and then he tugged.

Leskal gasped as he flung a hand to his chest, his eyes wide with shock. 'What in Odar's name was that?'

'Magic,' Annev said, fighting to keep the smile from his mouth. 'Why? How did it feel?'

'Like the wind got kicked out of me ... but worse. It wasn't good, I'll tell you that much.'

'Sorry. Your magic was hiding the threads that carried it. Now I've found them, I had to sever your link to examine them.' Annev slowly ran the tip of his wand across the vaporous pink threads. He felt them thrum in response but noticed their pitch had changed. Interesting. He plucked them again and felt the thread twang in response, its pulse coming from Leskal's direction. Annev frowned but checked all the way along the magic bond, stopping when his hands came to a halt in front of Leskal's chest. 'It's still connected to you,' Annev said, shaking his head. 'I was hoping it would lead me to the person who formed the glyph, but I think activating the glyph overrode the original bond.'

'Sorry, lad. It was a good effort.'

Annev sighed, prepared to give up, but as he turned away from Leskal, his magic vision showed him a faint trail of not just one or three but six individual links.

'Silver staves,' Annev breathed, shifting to view the threads from multiple angles. 'How did I miss this?'

'What?'

'Could you draw a different glyph? It can be anything. Just draw and activate it.'

The caste leader raised an eyebrow, but he drew out his bamboo water brush and painted a rune on the stones between them. '*Ardán.*' The air between them pulsed for just a moment and then Leskal casually stepped onto the floating platform of condensed air.

'How's that?' he asked, his feet hovering just two inches above the ground.

'Great,' Annev said, reaching out with his wand and cutting the magic to Leskal's ward. The platform disappeared with an audible *pop* and Leskal dropped back to the ground. He grabbed Annev's shoulder, half to steady himself and half to scold the boy, but before the Dionach could say a word, Annev stooped beneath his grasp and examined the inactive ward. He nodded in satisfaction. 'Just as I thought. Only one thread.'

'Is that a good thing?'

'We'll see.' He pointed at the floor. 'Could you reactivate it now?'

Leskal huffed. 'So you can cut my strings a second time?'

'Yes,' Annev said, 'but if I see two strings after I sever your magic, I'll know a new thread is forged every time someone activates the glyph. If I see only one thread, that means ... well, something else.'

The leader of the Shieldbearers shook his head but did as he was asked, though this time he didn't step onto the floating platform but gestured at the faintly glowing platform of air. 'Go for it.' He winced as Annev severed the magic to the glyph and stood in silence as Annev checked the link a second time.

'Staves,' Annev swore. He looked up at Leskal. 'I see two threads.'

The caste leader grunted. 'Is that good?'

'It confirms my suspicions,' Annev said. 'A new link *is* formed each time you activate the ward ... which means you've activated these wards before.' Annev tapped a finger on the three runes inscribed near the base of the doorframe.

Leskal tugged his beard, not understanding. Then he did. 'You think *I* etched those runes into the stone? You think I attacked you? Annev, I swear to you, I would never—'

'Never knowingly attack me,' Annev finished. 'I know – I believe you.'

'Well— You do?'

Annev nodded, not wanting to explain he could see the truth in the man's unguarded thoughts. 'Leskal,' he said, 'I think someone's been tampering with your mind.'

'There's definitely a hole there,' Tym said, once he'd mindwalked through Leskal's memories. 'There are portions during the Tests of Ascendancy that have been taken by another Dionach.'

'Another Mindwalker,' Misty said, her fists clenching. 'Gods, Tym. This is exactly why it's so hard for the other castes to trust us.'

'I'm not convinced it is a Mindwalker – or if it is, they're working with a Stormcaller. From what I could see, it looks like someone tried to fill the gaps in Leskal's mind with new memories in place of the ones that were stolen, but they didn't do a great job. They've left gaps where something large was stolen and something smaller took its place. Even the memories themselves don't feel real. Like a copy of a copy.'

'What does that mean?' Annev asked, seeing Leskal's ashen face.

'That it was someone Leskal trusts – someone with whom he had his defences down, so they could get a foothold on his mind. After that, though, they'd be able to use one form of magic to cover up another. They could have used Stormcaller magic to convince you to place those wards outside of Annev's room, and then the Mindwalker magic could have erased your memory of ever having done it.'

'Damn,' Leskal cursed, pounding the small table where the three of them were sitting. Annev stood apart from the trio, silently using his codavora and Inquisitor rings to determine whether Tym and Misty had been a part of the subterfuge. It didn't take long to determine that his friends were uninvolved.

'A friend,' Leskal repeated. 'Someone I trust implicitly.' He looked up, his eyes shining with moisture. 'You don't think ...'

His voice trailed off, unable to finish the question they were all asking themselves.

'It wasn't Reeve,' Annev said, certain. 'He wants me to find the assassin, and he's been trying to help me since before I arrived here. If he wanted to kill me, he could have left me to die back in Luqura.'

Misty nodded. 'Who else could it be?'

Their minds simultaneously jumped to the same conclusion, but Leskal spoke the name.

'Holyoak's the only bastard with the talent to pull this off.'

'Yes,' Misty agreed. 'He could manage both the stormcalling and the mindwalking without the aid of another Dionach ...'

'It makes sense,' Tym said. 'He could have used his magic to ensnare Leskal while his defences were down. Then he'd have made Leskal take the painting to Annev's room and draw the Shieldbearer wards. Honeycutt would have activated the void bubble wards as part of Therin's Test of Ascendancy, and that must have triggered a second command for you to activate the barrier outside Annev's room.'

'A second command?'

'It's difficult to do,' Misty said, 'but it's possible to nest thoughts and suggestions within other commands. It's difficult, since the target usually recognises they're being tampered with and breaks the spell. Unless you erase the memory of the tampering.'

'That's terrifying.' Annev looked between Dionach McClanahan, Tym and Leskal. 'He could have tampered with all of us then – with *anyone* here at the Enclave.'

'Not really.' Tym raised his hand. 'Most Dionachs, particularly those with metaphysical talents, are too practised at exercising our minds. Breathbreakers and Shieldbearers focus on the martial uses for skywater, though, so they're more susceptible. Even then, your mind would—' He cut off as Misty elbowed him sharply in the ribs. 'Why did you—?' He grunted as she elbowed him again.

Annev stared in surprise at the pair before Leskal cleared his throat. 'I think Brother Tym is trying to say you need to be especially gullible. Maybe even stupid.'

'I was going to say open-minded,' Tym offered.

'No need to sugar coat it,' Leskal said. 'I focus on fighting with my body, not my mind.' He looked at Annev. 'I'm surprised he wasn't able to influence you, though, Annev. You don't seem to have any talent with *quaire*.'

Annev wondered if Tym's Mindwalker blood had somehow protected him from Holyoak's malignant intentions. If it had, though, he'd have been vulnerable up until then.

'Annev has a strong will,' Tym said, smiling faintly. 'He trained with Sodar for almost two decades – and he spent his whole life hiding in Chaenbalu. That sort of thing strengthens the mind and the will far more than any blood-talent.'

Leskal grunted. 'Sodar always preferred breadth over depth. I suppose he was right in this case.' He nodded at Annev. 'We should take our discoveries to Reeve and start a formal investigation. We can arrest Holyoak then and begin a proper interrogation.'

'How long will that take?'

'Not too long. A few days, perhaps a week.'

'That's not fast enough. I have to leave the Enclave tomorrow, with my answers. If Holyoak tried to kill me, then I'm not waiting for the Order to investigate. I'm going after him *now*.'

'Are we certain it's Holyoak?' Misty asked. 'He's been here longer than Tym and I – and he's an ageless one! If he's a traitor, how long has he been working against us? A year? A century? A *millennium*?'

'How old *is* Holyoak?' Annev asked.

'Reeve is the eldest – he beat Sodar by several centuries – but Honeycutt and Holyoak aren't far behind. The first joined the Order in the middle of the Second Age. The second joined at the end, shortly after the Battle of Vosgar.'

'Over two millennia then,' Annev said, his voice barely above a whisper.

'It's one of the reasons I would never guess at Holyoak being a traitor – but Dionach McClanahan has a point. We're jumping to conclusions. We need something concrete before we accuse Holyoak. This could be the work of some other Dionach, perhaps multiple people working in concert.'

'You really think there could be so many traitors left in the

Order?' Misty said, her voice trembling. 'Gods, I don't think I could survive another Faction War.'

'Holyoak was with Misty during Titus's test,' Tym said, holding up a hand. 'He has an alibi.'

'But we've already established the assassin used Honeycutt and Leskal to attack me. We no longer need to prove he *performed* the attack, just that he orchestrated it.' The rest agreed and then an idea struck Annev. 'Brother Tym. Dionach McClanahan. When someone erases and replaces memories, do they leave anything behind? A mental fingerprint or a trace of magic?'

'I know of nothing like that,' Tym said.

'Me neither,' Misty said. 'With skywater it's easier to leave those kinds of traces, but with *quaire* things are less physical.'

'And what if I could see the metaphysical,' Annev continued, undeterred. 'What if there was a way I could view the *quaire*'s influence?'

Tym frowned. 'Is that even possible?'

Annev nodded. 'Your glyphs ... when the glow of magic is pulled away, I see a residue of energy.'

The Dionachs exchanged a look. 'That sounds like what Amhran told us,' Tym said, turning to his wife.

Misty turned back to Annev. 'This residue,' she said, 'how would you describe it?'

'Like ... glowing lines of magic?'

'Describe it for me?'

'The lines are sort of pink – cloudy, like mud kicked up in a pond – but more warm than cold. They feel almost alive.'

Misty frowned. 'Amhran described it as light shining through a pane of glass – like motes of dust in a sunbeam. Does that resonate with what you felt?'

'No, this feels less abstract ... more connected, like the thread is still part of the person who made it. Almost like I can feel their heart beating at the other end.' He paused. 'Who is Amhran?'

'A Dionach Lasair,' Tym said. 'An Ilumite spellsinger.' He shook his head. 'This doesn't sound like an Ilumite blood-talent, though.'

'It's not a blood-talent,' Annev said. 'I'm using two different artifacts to see and manipulate the threads.' Tym didn't seem convinced. 'Look, it doesn't matter *how* I do it. What's important is that I can track down whoever tampered with Leskal's mind. I've done it already with Honeycutt and Leskal.'

'Yes, but that was with skywater – elemental magic. *Quaire* is metaphysical so it will be harder to manipulate ... and more dangerous.'

'I'll take the risk.'

'Not dangerous for you,' Tym corrected. 'Dangerous for Leskal. If you're tampering with his brain and something goes wrong, you could kill him – or worse.'

They all turned to look at the leader of the Shieldbearers, who shrugged. 'Tym has a point. You have no experience with *quaire*, Annev. Why take that risk when we could simply wait for an investigation?'

'Because I don't trust the Order,' Annev interrupted. 'Frankly, I'm surprised any of you still do. What if other Dionachs have been compromised? What if Holyoak has tampered with whoever conducts the investigation? Hell, what if an investigation has already started but nobody can remember it?'

Misty gave another outright refusal, but Brother Tym nodded bleakly. 'It's not without precedent,' he said. 'Something like that happened almost a millennia ago. I doubt it is the case now, but we can't discount it.'

Annev offered a grim smile of gratitude. 'I have an idea,' he said, looking between the three Dionachs. 'Tym, are you certain which memories were implanted in Leskal's mind?'

'Fairly certain, yes.'

'What would happen if you leeched one of them from Leskal and pulled it into your own mind? If you kept it intact and held it in the forefront of your mind, I could use my artifact magic to trace its origin and discover who formed it.'

Tym tapped his chin, considering. 'That ... might work. Isolating one memory from the others would ensure you don't tamper with the rest of Leskal's mind, and I have plenty of experience protecting myself. I could hold that memory up for you and seal off everything else. Metaphysically speaking, it'd be a safe

593

place for you to try experimenting with threads of *quaire*. And, since it's not *my* memory, nothing would happen if you disrupted or destroyed it. There's a chance you might hurt the person who forged it, but that could be a benefit in this case. I think we should try.' They all turned to Leskal and the Shieldbearer nodded in consent.

'Shouldn't we talk to Arch-Dionach Reeve about this?' Misty asked. 'If something goes wrong, we may need his help.'

'Yes,' Leskal said. 'And it may be prudent to quarantine the Enclave. If we discover a conspiracy, we don't want them escaping. This may be our one chance to fix what the Faction Wars couldn't – without further bloodshed.'

Misty squeezed her husband's shoulder. 'I'll talk to Reeve. Be careful.'

Tym smiled, his lopsided grin belying the drama of the moment. 'You know me.'

'Yes, I do – so *be careful*. Don't try anything till I come back with Reeve. Promise?'

'Sure.'

Misty studied her husband, her eyes fierce. '*Promise* me.'

'All right! I promise we won't attempt anything dangerous till you return with Reeve. There, are you happy?'

'I will be once this is sorted out. Good luck,' she said to Annev, and dashed from the room.

Leskal looked between Tym and Annev, then failed to suppress his smile. '*Now* who's the gullible one?'

Annev glanced between the two Dionachs, his suspicions confirmed. 'We're going to do this, aren't we? We're not waiting.'

Tym gave a helpless smile, though his eyes were full of gleeful mischief. 'I promised we wouldn't do anything *dangerous* ... so we'll be careful. Leskal will be fine, as will I – and you know all the safeguards that I mentioned. You'll be safe, too. Plus, you said you're in a bit of a hurry ... ?'

Annev nodded. He was tired of waiting on others, *especially* Reeve.

'Let's do it.'

Chapter Sixty-Three

'I've got it,' Tym said, leaning back while Leskal sat opposite him. The other Dionach blinked.

'Is it really that easy? I didn't feel a thing.'

'That's sort of the idea,' Tym said, his smile returning. 'I took the memory that seemed the most obvious implant.' He looked at Annev who sat at the foot of the bed in Misty and Tym's adjoining chamber. 'Are you ready?'

Annev nodded, his fingers twisting the codavora ring on his finger. He forced himself to stop and then grasped the Rod of Artificing in his left hand. He wasn't sure the rod would be helpful, but he had used it to manipulate skywater glyphs in the past and assumed he'd need it now. Between the codavora and Inquisitor rings, Annev felt confident he would see whatever magic had been tethered to the falsified memory and from there find a link to whoever had forged it.

'I'm ready.'

Tym's eyes grew distant. 'I have it. See if you can access it.'

Annev reached out with his magics, his mind questing to sense Tym's thoughts. It wasn't like being a passive observer, and this time, as he brushed his mind against Tym's, Annev tried to actively engage. As he did, he sensed Tym's *quaire* as a rush of disconnected speech, a stream of half-articulated words and ideas that blurred into flashing letters, worbling sounds and distorted images.

At the same time, Annev's own thoughts became hazy, scattered, and unfocused. His sense of identity slowly drifted away from him, and Tym's thoughts became indistinguishable from his own. When

Annev realised his thoughts about Misty were actually coming from Tym, he immediately drew back and tried to centre himself.

'Everything okay?' Tym asked.

'Yeah,' Annev said, blushing. 'I just ... that surprised me.' Tym quirked an eyebrow and Annev threw up his own mental barriers. As soon as he did, his sense of identity mercifully reasserted itself. Feeling more confident, he blinked away his disorientation and refocused on Tym and Leskal's faces. 'Let me try again. See if I can get a firm grasp on the memory.'

'I should have given you more instruction before you attempted to mindwalk. Even if you're using an artifact, certain principles will still be the same.'

'Such as maintaining a firm grip on my identity?'

Tym smiled. 'That would be one, yes. Also, since you're investigating Leskal's memory, it helps if you hold a mental image of him in your mind. It gives the implanted memory something to latch onto.'

'I think I can do that. Anything else?'

'*Quaire* doesn't work the same way as skywater. Whatever you've done in the past ... it may not work here.'

'Could you be more specific?'

'No, unfortunately. I'm not especially talented with skywater, so I can't really tell you the differences. Holyoak could, but we can't really call on him just now.'

'Got it. I'll try again.'

Tym laid a hand on Annev's shoulder then, his voice dropping to a whisper. 'Sorry about swallowing you up in my thoughts. I thought I'd fortified myself against any mind melding, and I expected your mindwalking abilities to be weak. I won't underestimate you this time.' He nodded at the Rod of Artificing. 'I'm not sure how that wand lets you access my mind, but its magic is strong.'

'It's not the rod,' Annev said, then realised he might have said too much. He bit his lip then decided to push on anyway. 'One of the rings is a Mindwalker artifact. It has some other abilities, too, but ... yeah. That's what does it. I'm using Mindwalker magic and the rod is enhancing the power of the artifact.'

Tym grunted. 'It seems powerful. I promise to stay more focused this time.'

'And I'll keep a firmer grip on my identity.'

'Go slow,' Tym said, his hand falling from Annev's shoulder, 'and keep your walls up. Focus on a mental image of Leskal.'

'All right,' Annev said, nodding. 'Let's try again.' Once more, Annev sent his mind questing to engage with Tym's, though this time he'd fortified his own mental walls. Even so, as Annev formed a mental image of Leskal he found himself drawn towards Tym's thoughts – or what seemed to be his thoughts – and was once more assaulted by a maelstrom of words and images. As they swarmed around him, embedding themselves in his metaphysical flesh, Annev fought to keep a firm grip on his self-identity.

He was a boy from Chaenbalu, a son of murdered parents, the ward of Sodar Weir and heir to a fate he neither understood nor embraced. He was Ainnevog the phoenix, risen from the ashes of Chaenbalu's destruction. He was Annev the magpie, forged of both the darkness and the light. He was the Master of Sorrows, survivor of destruction and bringer of desolation. He was a danger to himself and his friends, and yet he could not bring himself to part with them. He was a hypocrite and a teenager, a warrior and a thief, a keokum and a dalta. He was full of contradictions, yet he burned with the fierce determination to forge his own path – to never become another's tool or take another's life unless both necessity and his conscience required it.

The onslaught of images threatening to engulf him gradually slowed, and the storm against his mental walls petered off to something more like the crash of distant waves against the barbican of his psychic fortress. When he realised he was still intact and that no part of him had bled away, Annev ventured to open himself to those lapping waves, as if his foot were tentatively touching their waters or as though he were gradually peeking out from the lids of his metaphysical eyes. What he saw shocked him.

Annev saw the Enclave before him. Not the room where he had left Tym and Leskal, but a corridor deep in the Enclave's bowels; ensconced torches lit the walls and a braided beard itched his chin as it swung heavy beneath his jaw. With a jolt, Annev realised he was seeing the world through Leskal's eyes, his own mental perspective now eclipsed by that of the Shieldbearer.

Distantly, Annev watched as the man moved about the Enclave, ate his lunch then – discomfortingly – took a trip to the privy. Thereafter, Leskal took his time passing through the Enclaves' hallways then climbed the steps leading to its rooftop to train. He worked through a set of exercises identical to the ones he had tried to teach Annev, and then the Shieldbearer retired to his bedchamber. Throughout it all, Annev noticed that Leskal often heard the voices of passing Dionachs, but never saw any person's face. No one stopped to speak with the Shieldbearer, and Leskal never turned to see anyone in his peripheral vision. Once he realised that, the whole experience suddenly felt surreal, as if Leskal walked in a haze ... which might be precisely how Tym had identified this group of memories as counterfeit.

It all feels so disconnected, Annev thought. *Even the walls and floor seem indistinct, like I'm walking in a dream.* He focused again and tried to concentrate on the details of Tym's stolen memory: somewhere in this vision there should be threads of *quaire* binding the imagined world into a metaphysical forgery. If those threads were here, though, Annev couldn't distinguish them from the rest of the vision.

They're here somewhere, Annev told himself. *I just have to open my eyes to them. To see them for what they are here, not what they might be in the physical world.* The thought made sense to Annev, whether it was his own or some stray intuition leeched from Tym.

Stay focused, Annev thought, banishing his doubt and clinging to his sense of what felt right or wrong. He had only found the pink trails of blood-magic when he had focused his attention on the Old Darite glyphs and then dispelled them. Before that, the near-invisible blood-talent tendrils had been hidden beneath the glowing nimbus of the blue-white skywater glyphs – but there was none of that here. No glyphs. No wards. No mystic runes of power. So how to make the pink threads of blood-talent manifest themselves?

I'm working with quaire *now,* he reminded himself, *not skywater ... and the Dionachs said* quaire *was just a metaphysical manifestation of skywater. Since everything in this vision is already metaphysical, maybe they* don't *look different.*

The thought resonated with Annev, so he retraced his steps from the beginning of the stolen memory and moved forward in time, once more observing the world through Leskal's eyes and looking for anything that looked like Old Darite – anything that remotely resembled a glyph or a ward – but he found nothing. He tried a second time, but still saw no glyphs. He had just finished watching Leskal go through his training on the rooftop for the third time when a new thought prickled his mind. He latched onto it and concentrated, forcing the subconscious premonition into his conscious thought.

The patterns of Leskal's arms and hands looked familiar. They reminded Annev of something Sodar had taught him … one of the many times Sodar had tried to test Annev's Darite magic.

The patterns of his hands. They're glyphs. *He's using his arms to draw glyphs in the air.* The insight struck Annev like a bolt of lightning, nearly knocking him from his mindwalking trance. He hadn't noticed the patterns because they weren't anchored in traditional space; within the confines of Leskal's memory, these runes had been inscribed across the currents of time, with every motion of Leskal's hands drawing threads of *quaire* together and weaving them into unique glyphs of power.

Acting on instinct, Annev tried to compress the observed memory into a smaller scale. He sped through the training on the rooftop, watching as Leskal's arms blurred into a frantic weave of hands and air. Such was their speed, the Dionach's arms became nearly invisible, while the glyphs they wove solidified into a pair of blue-white runes hovering in mid-air.

Annev held that moment in his mind as if time itself were something he could manipulate, and the twin runes glowed brighter, their *quaire* buzzing in front of him. Annev hesitated and then, as he had done in the past, he *pushed* against the magic bound to the Darite glyphs. At first something resisted him, but then he felt the Rod of Artificing grow warm in his prosthetic hand and the magic gave way. As the glyphs unravelled and their nimbus of *quaire* dissipated, Annev saw the familiar pink strands of blood-talent which, unlike the Darite glyphs, seemed to hum with a life of their own. Annev reached out, tentative, and grasped the first of the two ephemeral fibres.

Annev reeled as his psyche contacted the metaphysical thread of magic. He felt his mental grasp slip and his mind almost broke free, his consciousness threatening to fly back to the Physical Realm. The thread itself snapped and Annev slammed back to the Enclave's rooftop, shaken and bruised.

But the forgery held. Annev still watched from Leskal's eyes, and the second thread of blood-talent still glowed faintly pink in front of him. Steadying himself, Annev concentrated and reached out slowly a second time, knowing this was his last chance. He felt as if he were holding his breath, and then his conscious mind touched the second thread. His vision blurred, but Annev hung on, his grip on himself and the world around him both firm and gentle.

He was plunged deeper still into the forged memory, and a new world unfolded in front of him.

Chapter Sixty-Four

In the past month, Annev had used blood-talent threads to trace old wards back to their creators, his body crossing physical space to locate the Dionach at the other end of the trail. This time it felt as if he were racing across some astral plane, one that echoed the reality of the physical world, but which held none of its concreteness. And he didn't travel alone: the forged memory – the very world that he had been inhabiting – travelled with him, its cognitive presence trailing and preceding him.

In the instant Annev made this connection, he felt the bubble around him crash into another reality that seemed both more and less real, its setting both foreign and native. The Enclave's rooftop was still beneath his feet, but instead of Quiri's ancient buildings and the looming spires of the Holy Seat, Annev saw an imitation of the Pontiff Prime's palace, its glittering granite stones replaced by black basalt and polished obsidian. Gone were the Darite nobles, merchants and priests who filled its streets in the Physical Realm, replaced by hulking golems of iron and steel, stone and bone. The abominations patrolled Quiri's abandoned streets in twos and threes, the former shops and homes left in ruins, their structures even worse than the burned and broken buildings of Luqura's Ash Quarter.

What is this? Annev wondered. *What nightmare have I entered?* Beyond the Holy Seat, Annev saw more of the city's ruins and then a horizon thick with wave upon wave of black-armoured, red-painted soldiers. Squadrons of flying gargols and more hulking golems supported each legion, which were in turn led by fists of men and women garbed in scarlet silks, crimson capes and carmine tunics. As Annev trained his gaze on the unarmoured soldiers, he found the scene rushing up towards him – or perhaps his vision was rushing down to meet them – for he could suddenly see the pulsing veins and arteries standing stark upon the flesh of grim-faced mages.

Bloodlords, Annev thought, his heart hammering in his chest, *and the Legions of Keos*.

The first mage was male, his skin dark as hammered bronze, the veins on his face and neck crawling like black vines across his skin. A petite woman with ivory flesh stood beside him, her prominent veins dark red and rusty brown. Opposite them, Annev spotted a second, taller woman, her skin dark as coal – though the veins on her face glowed with the warmth and colour of burning embers. Her gaze shifted abruptly, as if she were looking back at Annev, and he felt his vision retract sharply, his empowered sight reeling and returning to the roof of the Enclave.

He shuddered. Was this some vision of the future? Some sadistic nightmare?

Annev's gut told him it was neither, for if the future held some far-flung reality where the Sons of Keos conquered Quiri, then surely the Enclave itself would have been destroyed. Everywhere Annev looked, though, the Dionachs' keep remained uncorrupted, its grey stones intact. The immediate scene was at a dissonance with what lay beyond the Enclave's walls, as if the building itself had been plucked from another world.

This is where the implanted memory was forged, Annev realised. *It must have been constructed here and then transplanted into Leskal's consciousness.* He turned, once more glancing over the parapets, and spotted a vaporous, pink strand hanging in the air in front of him, its length trailing down to his closed hand.

The blood-talent thread, Annev thought, remembering that he'd been holding it when he'd shifted here. He still had the delicate filament pinched lightly between his fingers, its power so refined, so quiet, that he hadn't realised he still held it. Annev felt the thrum and hum of the blood-talent within the ribbon of magic and turned to sense the opposite direction of that floating thread, its trail of light flowing towards the lightless walls of the transformed Holy Seat.

The Pontiff Prime's palace. Was that significant? Had the head of the Darite Church somehow been involved in the attempt on Annev's life? That made no sense. Annev shook his head as if to clear it, and the answers fell into place in front of him: the black stone palace was not the true Holy Seat, just as this nightmare dream was not the real world; both had been constructed to suit the mind and temperament of whoever had imagined them. Just like Leskal's counterfeit memory, these were false thoughts – psychic fabrications inside someone else's mind.

The assassin, Annev realised, his heart racing. Gods, why hadn't he seen it before? Leskal's memory had been *forged* here. The traitor, the person who had tried to kill him ... *I'm inside his mind. I'm inside the rotting traitor's mind.*

The realisation was a chilling one: somehow, with the aid of his artifacts, Annev had stumbled upon a back door into the assassin's psyche ... but it made sense. In the physical world, he had followed the threads of blood-talent to a person. In this cognitive realm, the threads had instead led him into the mind of the Dionach who'd forged the psychic connection with Leskal. It all made sense.

But who is the traitor? Where are their mental defences? Annev's gaze swept over the ruined landscape beyond the Enclave, and he had his answer.

The soldiers – the Bloodlords and the monsters – they're part *of the defences. And they're protecting ...* The pink thread in his hand led unerringly towards the corrupted Holy Seat. *That's the heart of it. I haven't slipped past the traitor's defences – I'm standing at the brink of them. I have to break into the Pontiff Prime's palace. The Holy Seat itself.*

Or the Unholy Seat. Annev studied the black basalt rock, its flat surfaces seeming to drink in the light just as the gleaming plates of obsidian reflected it back.

I need to get in there. The traitor – Holyoak – his consciousness is in there. Whatever I'm looking for ... it must be in there.

Annev exhaled, scratched his chin, and found that Leskal's itchy beard was gone. *That's one positive thing, at least.* He checked and found this mental image of himself contained not only the artifacts he carried in the Physical Realm, but also the ones he had lost in Chaenbalu and Banok: Mercy hung at one hip, and the magic flamberge, Retribution, was sheathed on the other. Even Sraon's hand axe was back, its gleaming steel haft protruding from a breakaway holster on his back.

That's how I know none of this is real, Annev thought. *Mercy and Sraon's axe are gone, so the rules of the real world don't apply here. Maybe I can shape this world into whatever I want it to be ... whatever I need it to be.* Annev looked down at the slender thread of magic clutched in his fist. With a start, he realised that his fist, too, was different: gone was the glowing Hand of Keos, replaced by the camouflaging artifact he had worn since he was a baby – the magical prosthetic he had lost in Janak's burning keep.

Annev inhaled sharply at the familiarity of his old hand and at the relief he felt on being rid, however temporarily, of the Hand of Keos.

And yet there was a pang of regret there, too, as if by losing the cursed golden hand he had lost something he had only just begun to understand. It was an irony, particularly as his chief goal was to rid himself of the monstrous artifact. Its absence struck him more keenly than he could have imagined, and he found himself wishing he still had the legendary artifact for this upcoming confrontation.

As if in response, the mundane prosthetic began to shift, its pink and olive skin morphing into golden metal and beginning to glow with an unholy luminescence. The hand itself grew larger, too, until the Hand of Keos once more dwarfed its fleshy twin. A familiar stone of unease settled into Annev's stomach.

I'll be all right, he told himself. *This isn't the real world. I can control it here, and I may need its power.* Yet even as he sought to reassure himself, he had doubts. Would using the Hand of Keos in the metaphysical realm affect things in the physical world? Could he actually control the Hand if it existed as an idea instead of a genuine artifact? He wasn't sure, but he also wasn't willing to face Holyoak without it.

But first I need a plan ...

Annev returned his gaze to the Unholy Seat, supposing he might climb down to the ground and try to enter the front door, but that felt simultaneously too easy and too dangerous: if the patrols of roaming golems didn't catch him, it seemed likely the Unholy Seat would have other defences. So how else might he reach the other end of the blood-talent thread?

As if on cue, the metaphysical world responded; the space around Annev began to flex and distort as the very fabric of reality shifted to accommodate his imagination. Within seconds, the dark clouds above his head and the grey stones beneath his feet had stretched and warped, their horizons twisting to converge on a finite point of space just beyond Annev's reach. He stared at it, uncertain what he was seeing, and felt an overwhelming sense of vertigo. He could no longer say what was up or down, nor what lay ahead or behind him, but the black walls of the Pontiff Prime's palace were indisputably closer – and a long strip of twisted space seem to connect the two buildings.

It's a bridge forged from space itself.

Annev took a hesitant step towards what should have been the edge of the roof and the space around him warped further, twisting into a platform that stretched to cover the distance between him and the Unholy Seat. A second step sent Annev hurtling onto the bridge as the space behind him warped and unwrapped into a vague impression of what it had once been. Ahead, the black palace wall had seemingly unravelled, its sheer obsidian stones blossoming like a flower and then spiralling outward, opening a portal into the sanctum of the Unholy Seat. And at the centre, Annev glimpsed the vaporous ribbon of blood-talent, its fine thread still taut between his fingers and the as-yet-unseen anchor on the other end. Emboldened by his progress, Annev took a deep breath and stepped again, his metaphysical body shifting to enter the heart of the palace.

Annev blinked. The bridge had vanished, the walls closed up behind him. He stood before the imposing Pontiff Prime's throne and was struck by two things: this could not be the Pontiff Prime's true throne, for it bore none of the Darite art that would set it apart as a seat for Odar's high cleric; instead of the arcane glyphs or artistic conscriptions, this throne was carved from calcified bones, stony skulls and bloodless sinew – an homage, no doubt, to the Fallen Lord of Earthblood. And sitting on that damnable throne, in jet-black, earth-brown and vermilion robes ... was the caste leader of the Mindwalkers.

Blood and ashes ... I was right. I found him.

'Hello, Dionach Holyoak.'

Holyoak seemed to twitch on his throne, his eyes glancing sharply down to Annev, who stood before him.

'*You*,' he breathed, his sunken eyes gleaming with an intensity Annev had never seen in the Physical Realm. 'How did you come here?' The Dionach seemed genuinely surprised and angry at Annev's presence.

Did he not guess I was coming? Annev wondered. *Did he not notice me enter?* Annev knew next to nothing about mindwalking. Perhaps he truly had bypassed the man's mental defences and approached unnoticed.

'You tried to kill me,' Annev said, cutting to the heart of it. 'You brainwashed Leskal and used him and Honeycutt to attack me.'

Holyoak's face seemed to wither, his mouth twisting into a puckered sneer. 'And you survived, with no talent for magic, you cockroach. You surprised me when I swore I would not be surprised again – that I would not make a move against you until I was certain it would end in your death – yet here you are, *surprising* me once again.' His eyes narrowed, his fingers tapping the tibia that formed one arm of his throne. 'You cannot be here. You should *not* be here when you have no talent for this.'

'I'm just full of surprises,' Annev said, his hands twitching for either of his swords, though so long as Holyoak made no move against him, he needed to let the man talk. He had come here for answers, and it seemed the Mindwalker would provide them.

'Why have you been trying to kill me?' And there it was. The heart of it all. The question he'd wanted to ask ever since the attack in the Brakewood.

The caste leader sniffed. 'You've seen my vision for the world.' Holyoak gestured beyond the walls. 'And you're a threat to that. Your very existence jeopardises it.'

Annev felt his hatred for the man well up. 'You're a servant of Keos.'

'And I have been for centuries – long before you were born. Don't take any of this personally.'

'Take it personally?' Annev scoffed. 'You tried to *murder* me! Was it all you? The attack on my village? Those monsters who came to destroy the Academy?'

Holyoak's mouth opened, then his face twisted in confusion. 'The what?'

'The *feurog*,' Annev snapped. 'The eidolons. The shadow demons. All of that was you.'

Holyoak looked uncertain, then gave the barest shake of his head. 'No, I started to work against you when you entered the Enclave. Any forces you encountered outside Quiri were not of my design.'

'Liar,' Annev breathed, his anger boiling to the surface. 'You *knew*. *You* sent them to Chaenbalu. You killed my friends. You killed *Sodar*.'

There was a pang of sorrow on Holyoak's face. 'No. I ... liked Sodar – we all did. I can't imagine anyone at the Enclave wishing him harm.'

'But you're not part of the Enclave,' Annev said. 'You serve the Fallen God of Earthblood. All of this—' Annev gestured at the palace, at the unseen monsters and Legions of Keos marching beyond its walls. 'You *want* this. You want to destroy the Order and all it stands for. You're not part of the Enclave – you're a traitor.'

'I'm a realist who has studied the hearts of men and seen how their thoughts betray them. I've watched them fight and fall and fail. The God-king has already won! Odar is gone. Lumea is silenced. The Younger Gods are but poor imitations of their father – fragments of a larger whole. And the Order is dead. It has been dying for centuries and these fools refuse to see it.'

'You're a traitor who lost his faith and went searching for a new god. You sacrificed your own brethren out of fear – out of *cowardice*.'

Holyoak's lip twitched. 'You know nothing of fear, boy. I've seen what the God-king can do. I've been to the mines of Daogort and stood at the very heart of Keokumot. You speak of fear and cowardice.' He sneered. 'You are a child.'

'A child who survived your traps and defeated your assassins, who wormed his way into your mind. A child who wields the hand of a *god*.' Annev allowed his anger to flow into his fist, to let it glow fierce with the hatred he felt for this man. He wanted Holyoak to see it – wanted him to *know*. He felt his lip curl and then he growled: 'Kneel.'

'What?'

Acting purely on instinct, Annev approached the bottom of the dais and slowly began to climb the steps. 'I said, *kneel*.'

Holyoak stared at him, his eyes widening as Annev drew closer to the necrotic throne. Fear twisted his lips. 'This is *my* palace. My fortress. You cannot harm me here.'

Holyoak raised his hand and a dozen bright steel chains shot out of the walls, their barbed ends ready to pierce Annev's chest. Annev glanced up, not bothering to dodge, and the metal links suddenly transformed into coiled serpents, their bodies dropping limp to the ground.

'No!' Holyoak crowed, cringing on his throne. 'This is *my* refuge. How are you doing this?'

Annev glanced at the snakes writhing at his feet – ring-snakes. Codavora. Ouroboros. As one, the serpents raised their heads and began to slither towards the dais.

'Kneel,' Annev commanded, taking another step. Holyoak rose from his chair.

'Wrong direction.' Annev allowed his fist to flare and the ring-snakes slithered over the man's limbs, binding him. Annev took another step, close enough that he could reach out and seize the traitorous Dionach. His voice grew cold and he fixed the full weight of his gaze on Holyoak's sunken eyes.

'*Kneel*.'

The Mindwalker fell to his knees, terrified. 'Don't,' Holyoak breathed, his voice barely a whisper. 'Please, don't.'

Annev's magical intuition had been screaming at him as he'd climbed the steps. Instead of thinking or planning, he'd listened to his emotions, acting purely on instinct – but on hearing Holyoak's pleas, his intuition clarified into certainty: *He's lived a life of petty darkness and fear. He's used his magic to spy on the hearts of his friends and traded away their secrets.* Annev saw it all with perfect clarity now, understanding that both the codavora and Inquisitor rings were enhancing his vision of Holyoak's deeds, motives, and in-tentions. He saw the man as a victim of his own ambition, his magic slowly corrupting him, enticing him to delve deeper into the hearts and minds of his unsuspecting friends and brethren. He had betrayed their trust – first by spying on their private thoughts and fears, and then by sharing those secrets. He'd debased himself, and by so doing become an unwitting agent of the Terran God-king – a spy among the Brotherhood.

'Did you steal Sraon's memories?'

Holyoak hesitated and Annev drew Retribution from its sheath, its undulating edge bursting into flames.

'I did!' Holyoak shrieked. 'They are here – all of them. Take them, please!'

A tiny golden chest appeared on the floor at Annev's feet, no bigger than his fist. Annev picked it up, his eyes never leaving Holyoak's, and he slipped it in his pocket.

'Now confess,' Annev ordered, sheathing his sword. 'Tell me how you were corrupted. Tell me *why*.'

'I don't ... I *can't*.'

Annev's fist flared again – blindingly bright – and the man quailed. The ring-snakes tightened their grip around his arms, legs, and chest, and his eyes began to bulge. 'Please!' he shouted. 'Wait! I'll tell you!'

And so, he began. It had started as Annev had foreseen: Holyoak had used his magic to spy on his brethren and then sold those secrets to the Terrans. He'd been greedy. He'd been weak. And once he'd dug himself a hole so deep he believed himself beyond redemption, the God-king had his agents bring Holyoak to Keokumot, to the very heart of the Terran domain.

'I wasn't always a traitor,' he said, more to himself than Annev. 'I believed in the Order ... but after the Silence of the Gods – when Odar stopped speaking to us and the Brotherhood became reviled – I saw how foolish it all was. Neruacanta is real ... and the God of Skywater is dead.'

Part of Annev quaked on hearing the name of the Terran

God-king spoken aloud … yet something greater also stirred. Anger? Resentment?

'You worship false gods, Holyoak. Keos was destroyed during the Battle of Vosgar. You know this. Reeve and Sodar were there – they *saw* it.'

'And yet Sodar did not believe he had fallen! He believed, as I do, that the spirit of Keos could not be vanquished by a mortal man.'

'So where is your God of Earthblood now? If he is so powerful, how can he be threatened by my birth?'

'Because you are the *Vessel*! You are the key that unlocks the power of Keos – the power that was stolen when his body was consumed!'

'If that is true,' Annev said, 'then I am *part* of Keos. I am holding his power right here … in front of you.' He raised the glowing hand and sparks of flame jumped from his fist, burning holes in the thick carpets leading to the dais.

Holyoak's eyes widened. 'You … you're just a pretender! A tool for the God-king. A stupid boy who—'

Annev called on the fire filling his palm and commanded it to wash over his skin and clothes, his whole body suddenly wreathed in flames that did not consume him. Holyoak gasped, and Annev could feel his thoughts and emotions churning in a sea of self-doubt. He saw that fear and instinctively seized on it. With barely a thought, the fiery wings of a great phoenix sprouted from his back and spread out behind him, their flames darkening, their feathers smouldering with ash, soot, and smoke.

'Bow before your God, Mikael Holyoak.'

'No!' the Dionach wailed, though he fell prostrate before him. 'You cannot be *him* … you are only the Vessel!'

Again, Annev felt his instincts rule him. He reached out his left hand to Holyoak and slowly closed his fist, imagining the palace beginning to crumple, its shape twisting to match his vision. He heard Holyoak scream as if from a distance, as the walls of the palace cracked and tumbled down around them. Without seeing, Annev felt the stone slabs of basalt roll in upon themselves like simple sheets of parchment.

As Annev had imagined, so it became. The only surprise was how easily he had done it, how little control Holyoak had over his own mind – but the wailing Dionach only blubbered at Annev's feet, a wrecked shell of a man, beaten before he'd barely begun to fight.

The light in the room flickered and Annev paused his destruction of the Unholy Seat. A tremor shook the floor, the vibrations echoing up from the deep heart of the world and resonating throughout the black tower – and Holyoak looked at Annev, his eyes wide with fear.

'What have you done?'

The blood-talent thread began to pulse between Annev's fingers. All around him, the trembling grew deeper. Louder. More resonant. Annev cast out with his mind, attempting to bend the world to his will once more ... but this time he failed. His wings extinguished themselves, the ring-snakes binding Holyoak shrivelled into ash, and Annev stepped backward from the trembling dais. A crack appeared in the necrotic throne and drops of garnet bled from its seat, flooding the floor.

'What have you done?' Holyoak shouted, convulsing on the bloody carpet. Annev turned his attention to the man to see a crimson mist spraying from his nose, leaking from his ears, running from his eyes. He watched in horror as the Mindwalker screamed once more, his voice a wet croak of madness. 'WHAT HAVE YOU—'

Bile, blood and vapour exploded from the man's face and his head flew backwards, a pulpy mess of gore and brain matter. Annev fought the urge to vomit, his eyes turning from the violence to the pink thread clutched in his golden hand. He felt his conscious mind being pulled deep into the ribbon of magic, his mental barriers shuddering and cracking as the metaphysical world around him continued its collapse. The palace didn't buckle or break, so much as it disintegrated into nothingness. The black shards of the floor fell away, dropping Annev into a void without depth or substance. His metaphysical body fell so fast he knew he must be plummeting into an endless void, even though his feet remained solid beneath him, and his mental barriers collapsed around him with a heavy thud.

He was falling – it *felt* like he was falling – in a vacuum. He stamped his feet on the floor and felt them make contact, yet he knew with certainty he was still rushing downward. His senses screamed at him, knowing that at any moment he would slam into a second unmovable force and be obliterated by it.

Before the end could come, though, Annev felt a new force tighten around his waist and shoulders – a harness, a sheltering presence that he recognised as Brother Tym. His descent slowed, his metaphysical body angling away from whatever was rushing to meet him, and Annev's sense of vertigo lifted along with it. The darkness of the void slowly transitioned into the brightness of moonlit snow. He blinked, shuffled his feet, and felt the crunch of ice crystals beneath them. In the distance, he saw towering walls of sheer ice, so immense that they had to be far, far from where they stood. The walls surrounded him, not to trap but to protect, their four corners resolving into a perfect square. A circle stood inside that square, and Annev stood inside the circle.

A river, Annev thought, watching the water flow in a wide arc around him. *A circular river?*

And then Annev understood: he was inside the walls of Tym's mind, his consciousness protected by a mental fortress that manifested as impenetrable walls of ice, windswept barriers of snow, and rushing waters of thought. He stood in a courtyard of sorts; the river of water prevented Annev from approaching the walls, and the walls prevented Tym's wild thoughts from approaching Annev.

He made this space for me, he realised, *a safe place for my mind within his own conscious identity – very clever.* Drained by the confrontation with Holyoak, he stood at the centre of that wilderness, protected, untouched by wind, held within a practical, organised mind; it was the cool presence of logical thoughts, untouched by feeling or warmth. Yet even there, surrounded by the frozen walls of Tym's thoughts, Annev felt the jovial character and emotion of the man shine like bright rays of sun beating down on the courtyard. Without precisely knowing how, Annev felt Tym's presence beside him and turned to see the cheery Dionach standing beside him.

'That was a close one,' Tym said, smiling and anxious at the same time. 'I almost lost you there.'

'Yes,' Annev said.

Tym nodded, leaving it at that. 'We've been trying to wake you for hours. You need to come back.'

'Hours? But ... how is that possible?'

'It's like you're sleeping, Annev. Caught in a dream.' He laid a hand on Annev's shoulder. 'You *need* to wake up.'

'Dionach Holyoak!' Annev said, suddenly remembering his original purpose in entering Tym's mind. 'He's the traitor. We have to find him. He tried to kill me!'

'We know. He's been taken care of.'

'Taken care of?' Annev repeated. 'How do you know? What have you done?'

'I'll explain, but you need to wake up now.'

Annev turned back to the frozen landscape. 'How do I do that?'

'I'm not sure. You've been unreachable for so long – as if you were shielded from us. The moment that changed, I swept you up and brought you here, but you still haven't woken. It's as if something is anchoring you in the Cognitive Realm, and it won't let you go.'

Annev remembered the golden chest in his pocket. He pulled it out and handed it to Tym. 'These are the memories Holyoak stole from Sraon. Could this have been anchoring me to this world?'

Tym's eyes lit with unabashed delight. 'Annev,' he said, taking the chest in both hands. 'I don't know how you got these ... but you've just saved your friend's life.' He patted the tiny chest with a look of astonishment then carefully tucked it into his tunic.

'Can you wake me now?'

Tym shook his head. 'That wasn't it. Could it be something else? Some other anchor you're still holding onto?'

Annev looked down at his golden fist, thinking, and gave a dry laugh as he held up the pink filament of blood-talent. 'It's still there,' he said. 'It's so light I didn't realise.'

Tym's face quirked into a frown. 'What is?'

Annev held up the thread of blood-talent. 'It's hard to see,' he said, turning it between his fingers. 'But it connects to Holyoak. That's how I tracked him down. It tethered him to Leskal's implanted memory.'

'What am I looking at?'

'You don't see it?' Annev asked, raising the translucent fibre until it shimmered in front of Tym's eyes. 'It's a thread of blood-talent.'

The Mindwalker stared at Annev's fingers, blinked once, then looked at Annev. 'I don't see anything.'

Annev prepared to argue, but he saw no point in it. For some reason he couldn't fathom, Tym couldn't see the thread. 'It's there,' he said, his own gaze returning to the filament as if to confirm he was not going mad. 'This is how I found Holyoak.' A subtle change came over Tym's face. Anxiety? Trepidation? Annev couldn't place it.

'I believe you, Annev, but I can't see it for myself. Can you let it go?'

Annev hesitated then sheepishly let the ribbon of magic slip from his fingers, its thread still humming with the promise of magic. 'There,' he said. 'It's done.'

Tym cocked his head to one side then nodded. 'You're waking now. I'll see you on the other side.'

Annev wanted to ask more questions – about mindwalking, about what had happened to Holyoak and what would happen to Sraon – but the light and the landscape were already growing hazy and indistinct. He tried to speak, but when he breathed in, he felt his lungs fill with air – his *actual* lungs. He could feel his physical body once more and the reality of the metaphysical world fell away, its strangeness swallowed in a rush of white light.

Part Five

To the Guardians of the Well and their High Priest,

On behalf of the High Keeper of the Flame, allow me to transmit my best wishes and fondest greetings. My name is Kryss Jakasen – merrymaker, treasure-hunter extraordinaire, Dionach Lasair, and betimes adventurer – and I require your assistance on a mission of the utmost importance. I am in the midst of constructing a team of uniquely talented individuals who can help me construct an item of vast magical consequence – a Sword of Seeking. It is my belief that with such an artifact, we might finally restore Lumea's Voice, recover Odar's Mind, and bring an end to the Silence of the Gods. For my gambit to succeed though, I require an insignificant portion of your time and an infinite measure of your trust.

More to the point – I need your magic.

If I have piqued your interest, I hope you will meet me in the townshire of Banok, Greater Luqura, on midsummer's day. My sister Luathas will be waiting there to greet you, and it is my hope I will also be present. For the nonce, I am travelling to Luqura to investigate the delay of certain members of our party – an albino necromancer by the name of Jian Nikloss, and a Kroseran noblewoman named Sodja Rocas. Once I have recovered those imperative to our cause, I shall return post-haste to Banok to complete the ritual and forge the Sword of Seeking (no doubt with your invaluable assistance).

Which brings me to my final request. I believe a young man named Annev may have joined your company recently, or else he is due to arrive soon, and his presence may be instrumental to our cause. If it is possible, I wish you to urge him to join you on your journey southward so that he can participate in this quest. I have a notion that his skills will be ... handy.

Yours truly,
Kryss "Red-thumb" Jakasen

Chapter Sixty-Five

'We play blood-stones among the nobles, too,' Neldon said, setting his pieces atop the board. 'But the champions have other names – military ones, usually – and we play with all eight pieces, not just three.'

'All eight? It's a lot to remember what each piece does, let alone what they can do once they've collected the blood-stones.'

'Not so hard as you may think. All games have rules. All wars have soldiers. You must learn the strengths of your men and the rules of engagement.'

'Right,' Fyn said, looking dubiously at the pieces on the board. 'So, what do you call this one? The Demon.'

'That's the Spymaster.'

Fyn grunted. 'And the Thief?'

'Scout.'

'The powers are the same, though, right? The abilities ... everything is identical?'

'Yes, identical. If you play with three pieces, it is not a true game of blood-stones – just a skirmish – but playing with all eight is the full game.'

'Well, I'll stick with my appetiser, thank you. I can barely follow the rules when there's only three tokens. You put out all eight and start using different names, you may as well give me a concussion.'

'We'll stick with three for now, then. One day, though, we must play the full game.' Neldon slid his troll forward three squares.

In response, Fyn skipped his thief token around a two-dimensional wall and plucked the blood-stone from beneath his champion.

Nelson nodded in concession, and Fyn turned to see if Way was returning yet from his errand in the Undercity. They played in an alcove adjacent to one of the many ladders that climbed towards the surface of the Old Low Quarter and Ashes district. Below, he could see the churning mass of slavers and slaves, labourers and tradesmen, all funnelling in and out of the Undercity's narrow tunnels and expansive chambers. Way claimed there were even some enslaved giants labouring in the larger tunnels, though Fyn had yet to see such creatures.

'Distract me from losing to you,' Fyn said. 'What's your story? How did you end up with Fisher and his gang?'

'Mm. It is ... complicated.' Neldon picked up a red glass counter and set it atop the placard denoting which of their champions had collected a stone. 'The others call me a doctor, but I consider myself a scholar of the human body more than a healer of its ailments. There's a university in Quiri, you see. One that teaches men about the bones and muscles that make up our flesh. My family didn't approve of my studies, though, so after a few years, I was told to come home and dispense with all that rubbish. I declined, so my father contacted the banking houses and removed my name from his line of credit. The University could no longer house me, which left me beggared.'

'So you came crawling back to Daddy?' Fyn fidgeted with his champion placards then set a thin plate of wood atop the caricature of his demon – putting him to bed, as it were. It was probably the wrong move, but he cared less for the game and was becoming more interested in Neldon's tale.

'I eventually came back, yes ... after a detour of sorts. I met Poli and Siege on a riverboat – neither of them were beggars or criminals at that time – but we didn't realise our past acquaintance until fate and circumstance brought us separately to the Ash Quarter.'

Fyn grunted. 'This is sounding more like a story about how the original gang was formed.'

'Maybe it is,' Neldon said, smiling. 'It was almost a year before I returned to my father's house. By then I'd spent a good deal of time on the streets ... not to mention a few dark months living in the Boneyard.' He gave a wistful smile. 'All those corpses. I just

620

couldn't pass up the chance to do some more scholarly work.'

Fyn grimaced at this and Neldon's smile deepened. 'That re-action is not atypical – but I saw an opportunity to advance my research and I took it. That's how I met Way, and he introduced me to Fisher – I never liked the man, by the way. Sanhueza ex-plained I was a doctor of sorts and Fisher said they could use my skills in the Ash Quarter. Lots of gangs need patching up, you see, and that was another opportunity to continue my research – and all for free. I amputated limbs, performed surgeries, repaired bodies. Good work, I think, but dangerous. Fisher offered me protection and I became friends with Way after I'd learned his story – it's a tragic one, that.' He sniffed and shook his head. 'Quinn was already working for Fisher back then, and it wasn't long before Poli and Siege joined the crew. They'd been ferrying folk across the river but those operating the toll bridges didn't like losing business to riff-raff, so they scuttled their boat and gave them a beating besides. Left them for dead till Fisher brought them to me. I patched them up and they joined his crew.'

'Small world,' Fyn said, moving another game piece and trying to stave off his inevitable defeat.

'It is.'

'So, what happened when you saw your father?'

'Ah. He'd heard about the Boneyard Butcher and had put one and two together. I showed up on his doorstep looking like a beggar and he said I could go back to my fornicating corpses. Didn't want anything to do with me. Cursed ever sending me away to school and wished a pox on me for not heeding him more closely.'

'Sounds like a right wanker.'

'Yes, I suppose he is – or was.'

'Dead?'

'Caught an infection that winter and the rot seeped into his bones. Probably could have healed him if he'd sent for me ... but he didn't.'

'And his fortune? Your family?'

'My mother died of consumption before I was sent off to school, and my only other sibling was too young to remember me. She fell into my aunt and uncle's care and our inheritance became their fortune.'

'Well,' Fyn said, his face souring. 'I don't know heads or tails about how all that works, but I reckon you're lucky for knowing your family. I never knew mine – never had any, unless I count you lot, and I'd have to be pretty desperate to do that.'

Neldon returned the smile. 'Desperate indeed.' He looked over the scaffolding they perched on. 'Speaking of desperate, that's Way coming back from the Pits now. Time to pack up.' At a nod from Fyn, they scooped up the borrowed blood-stone tokens and dismantled the game board, tucking the pieces back into Way's drawstring sack.

Fyn nodded towards Way. 'How often does he come down here, anyway?'

'To look for his boys? Every week. I don't think he's missed one since they were taken.'

'And he hasn't seen either since?'

'Not a glimpse, a word or a rumour.' Neldon grasped the rungs of the ladder and climbed down to the floor of the Undercity's open market.

'So why does he keep coming back?' Fyn dropped down beside him, silent in spite of the weapons he was bristling with. 'Way seems smart. He must know they're gone for good.'

Neldon shook his head. 'Hope, my young friend. He continues to hope, and that is a strong thing. It cannot be bartered, bargained, or reasoned with. He will search for those boys until he finds them, or death claims him.'

Fyn wasn't sure what to make of that. He didn't care for anyone or anything to the degree that Way cared about finding his stolen kids ... and he wasn't sure whether that was good or bad. As he pondered it, Way sidled up to them, his eyes less watery but no less bloodshot.

'I found him,' Way said, scratching the sides of his mouth. 'Well, actually it's a *her* – but you know what I mean.'

'You're sure she carries messages between Dante Turano and Braddock Whalen?'

'I'm sure. She's got the silver messenger pin fastened to her

622

collar, right next to Turano's black sigil and Whalen's blue one. She's the one Raven wants.'

'Right. We'll tail her together. Find out where she lives. Once Raven finishes at the docks, we'll circle back and have Raven snare her, too.'

Way chewed his lip. 'Sounds good, chief.'

'Something wrong?'

'I ... I don't trust this magic idea. You say Raven has it under control, and that's well and good, but it don't calm my nerves none. You read me?'

'Yes, I get it. I can tell you from experience, though: this should work. The Rod of Compulsion can get people do the damnedest things. It just needs time to sink its hooks into them.'

'How do you know? You've used the cursed thing before?'

'No, someone else tried to use it on me. Didn't turn out so well for them, though, because I'm a hard-headed jackass.'

'Well, let's hope this messenger has a softer head than you then.' He nodded at a soot-stained market stall where a black-clad, slender woman had slipped from a tent and was scurrying away down one of the side tunnels adjoining the underground marketplace. 'That's her,' he said, thumbing his nose. 'Keep your distance – don't want to spook her.'

Sodja emerged from the riverboat cabin with a subtle smile on her lips. Waiting for her on the dock were Quinn, Siege and Poli.

'Did it work?' Siege asked, his eyes bright. 'Did you snare him?'

'Tight as a noose. Took some time to figure out how to use the blasted thing, but I've got the rod figured out now – and that messenger Zane is wrapped around my finger. He'll do what needs doing.'

'And the Guildmasters will think Elar Kranak has turned against Whalen. Very clever.'

'Elar Kranak, Tiana Rocas and Dante Turano. If we turn each of their messengers, it will look like all three conspired against Braddock.' Sodja smiled, taking in the northern entrance to Luqura's underground lock and the line of boats waiting to use it. 'Amazing what modern engineering can do, eh?'

623

Poli nodded with enthusiasm. 'I always liked the locks. Best part of the trip, I thought. Passing through the sluice. Watching the water levels rise and fall – and seeing those great cathedral ceilings overhead. Like getting swallowed by some great whale and passing out the other side.'

'Smelled like it, too,' Siege said, stretching his great arms over his head. 'I never liked the canal myself. Stinks too much down here. Always worried about the mast scraping against the ceiling, or that our smaller boat might get crushed in the press.' He grimaced. 'Nah, my favourite was always the open part of the voyage – when we'd sail between Quiri and Luqura, or south to—'

'Rot and dreck!' Quinn swore. 'That's our boat – that's my *family's* boat!' Everyone turned to look at the boat anchored beside them. 'Right there!' she yelled, her face red with anger as she slapped the ship's hull. 'That's the scar of my family's symbol showing through the paint. Those marks – that's a leaping rabbit. That's the *Lapin!*'

'Shhh.' Sodja stepped up to hush the older woman. 'It hasn't been your family's for years. You said it was stolen from you – taken by pirates.'

'By the Rocas family,' Quinn said, spitting at the flying black bird. 'They stole it from my grandparents. The *Lapin* belongs to *me*. It belongs to my family – to the Gwyins.'

'You don't even know how to sail it,' Sodja said, smoothly leading the woman away from the water's edge and back towards the River District. 'You don't even know how to *swim*.'

'Only because they stole it from me – they stole my heritage. My *life*.'

'Oh, Quinn,' Siege said, attempting to lighten the mood. 'I thought *we* were your life – the sun and stars and everything below. That three-masted galleon, though, it's just wood and rot. Even if you were of a mind to take it back, it's not likely to fit in your pocket.'

'I *will* take it back,' Quinn said, her eyes smouldering with uncharacteristic passion. 'I'll steal it and I'll learn to sail her back to Krosera.'

'Why? So the Rocas family can take it from you again?' This from Poli, her face hard as stone. 'You know you won't be able to keep it, not till that whole family is in the ground.'

'Then that's what I'll do. After this business with the Slavers Guild, we should use the Thieves Guild to destroy the Rocas family. Take back everything they've stolen.'

'Come on,' Sodja said, tugging her elbow. 'If everyone went around killing folks for offending their parents and grandparents, this city would look like the Boneyard.'

'They *beheaded* them, Raven! I watched Saltair do it. That whole family deserves to die.'

Sodja slowly let out a breath. She glanced at Siege for help, but the big man shook his head, knowing enough to stay well out of this argument. 'Tiana Rocas ordered my father's death, Quinn. I hear your pleas for vengeance. You can have it – enough blood to swim in – but we do it as a team, on our terms. Agreed?'

Quinn stared hard at Sodja then nodded, mollified. 'Where are we going now?'

Sodja gritted her teeth. '*We* aren't going anywhere. I can handle the next messenger on my own.'

'You're going to their estate, aren't you?' Quinn asked, her eyes full of knowing. 'You think I'll do something foolish if I come with you.'

'Won't you?'

Quinn's cheeks reddened, and Sodja had her answer.

'Go back with Siege and Poli. Fyn and the rest should be back by now. As soon as I snare Tiana's messenger, I'll join you.' She paused, considering her next words. 'The messenger belongs to the old Kroseran blood – one of the original Saevors and a brother of Tiana – so when our scheme is finished, you will already have a portion of your revenge.'

Quinn gave a slight nod of approval. 'We'll see you in a few hours then.'

Braddock Whalen, Chief Guildmaster for Luqura's Slavers Guild, was in high spirits after a meeting with King Lenka, the wizened and ailing leader of the Empire's richest and most prosperous city.

The king was in better health than usual – he hadn't soiled himself once during their hour-long conversation – and not having to endure the royal stench always put Whalen in a good mood.

He was especially happy that Consul Phoeba Ondina Anabo had gone back to Innistiul for a month, which more or less gave Whalen the run of the capital. The nobles fawned over him, the merchants paid their dues – and then some – and the city feared him. He bowed to no man or woman – not while Anabo and Cheng were in Innistiul – and he was free to do as he pleased. Yields from the Low and Ash Quarters were up, and a new caravan of Ilumite whores would be arriving that evening, fresh from their training in Innistiul. He might even stop by the Guild Hall to greet them and select a few to join his harem. First, though, Braddock Whalen would celebrate by taking in a show at the Pits. Dante Turano had invited him numerous times over the winter, but Whalen had been unable to escape the consul's scrupulous eye. Now that spring was here, Whalen planned to visit the Pits as often as possible to enjoy the Ringmaster's games before the summer stench filled the Undercity's tunnels.

Yes, that would do nicely. A round of death games followed by a warm bath and a good whoring. King Lenka had given Whalen the perfect start, for the perfect day.

'Guildmaster Whalen!'

Whalen turned as he stepped off his palanquin, irritated to be interrupted. 'Pyodr Saevor. To what do I owe the—' He cut off the pleasantries, realising he was addressing one of his lessers, and sighed haughtily. 'What does Tiana want? If it's to discuss our interest rates again, tell her—'

'Chief Guildmaster.'

Whalen turned again, flanked by the young woman who served as Dante's go-between – Mazala something-or-other. He sensed his evening was about to be ruined. 'My dear, if the Ringmaster has a message, tell him I will be—'

'Braddock Whalen?' a quavering voice asked from the opposite side of the palanquin.

Whalen's faltering smile slipped completely and he focused all his terrible attention on the last messenger to address him, an older man from Innistiul – distant cousin to Archon Kranak. He growled, baring teeth. 'Zane, this is not a good time. If Elar wants to speak with me, he'll have to—'

Zane plunged his dirk into Whalen's eye, then yanked it out with a stomach-twisting *thwop*. The blade descended again, stabbing him in the cheek and jaw and simultaneously stifling his cries. He tried to draw breath – to scream and shout murder, vengeance, death—

Thump.

Thulp.

Mazala and Pyodr drove their own blades into his back and kidneys. Again, they withdrew the daggers. Again they stabbed. *Thunk. Thwelch.* Whalen coughed blood and bile, and looked up to see Zane's dirk plunging straight for his temple.

Thop. Thump. Shunk.

The cries of alarm sounded, raised by the palanquin bearers, but by then Braddock Whalen had descended in a heap to earth, his night of extravagances thoroughly ruined.

And he'd been having such a good day.

Chapter Sixty-Six

'Did you see the look on his face?' Way shouted, laughing as they filed back into their lair. 'He looked so surprised before he pissed himself!'

Siege grinned. Beside him, Poli was clutching her sides, her dark face streaked with tears as much from laughter as from nervousness, exhaustion, and adrenaline.

'And that,' Sodja said, flipping the Rod of Compulsion and snatching it from the air, 'is how you get the Guild to cannibalise itself.' She felt good – she felt *great*. The plan had succeeded perfectly, and the slavers and her family were finally getting what they deserved.

Neldon clapped, slow and steady, then growing in intensity and enthusiasm. 'Bravo and brava – a toast to Fatal Fyn and the Raven!'

Fyn grinned and raised a mug with the others, their tankards crashing together. 'So,' he said, once they'd drunk, 'what happened to the messengers? I half expected the palanquin bearers to run them through.'

'No,' Neldon said, sucking at his teeth. 'The bearers were all slaves; there's no love lost between them and the deceased Guildmaster. I wager they would have cheered the assassins on, if not for a concern they might get blamed for the crime.'

'So what happened to the messengers?' Fyn repeated, sitting at their new makeshift table – an old door they'd reclaimed from the Ash Quarter and propped atop three barrels of Black Gambit, a syrupy liquor Saltair had clearly been fond of.

'Seized by the Golden Guard,' Way said, clucking his tongue.

'And once you're in their hands, you're a half-step away from being given to the Watchers.'

'For some light torture,' said Poli.

'Or not so light,' Quinn said, flipping up the corner of her shirt to reveal several ugly scars puckering her narrow waist. Poli winced to see them. Sodja controlled her own reaction, though she felt no less uncomfortable.

My family did that, she thought. *Maybe I was even the one who reported Quinn to the Watchers. I never considered the repercussions – it would have been impossible to know. Impossible that I'd remember.* Her heart shrank at the thought, to think she'd so callously served her mother, to think she might *still* serve her mother if it weren't for her father's death. She felt like a hypocrite – she *was* a hypocrite. She took another pull from her mug of Black Gambit.

'So this Golden Guard,' Fyn asked, still trying to familiarise himself with Luquran politics, 'do they work for the Guild?'

'Yes and no,' Neldon said. 'They're technically King Cheng's standing royal guard, but whenever Cheng and Anabo are gone they report to Guildmaster Whalen. I suppose, now, they report to Archon Kranak.'

'He's next in line to become Guildmaster?'

'He'll be the interim Guildmaster, though I expect he'll line enough purses to secure the formal title. Since the Golden Guard is stationed in the River District as part of a treaty with King Lenka, they're nominally under his jurisdiction.'

Fyn tapped his lips, brow furrowed. 'So, for the moment, Elar Kranak controls the Golden Guard, the River District and most of the slave trade in Luqura?'

'Correct.'

'And the Watchers?'

'No,' Sodja said, interrupting. 'The Watchers aren't technically part of the Guild. They just look after the Guild's interests.'

'So ... the Guild serves the Watchers?' Fyn asked, still not understanding.

'It's more of a partnership. Neither is the master.'

'How do you know this?' Neldon asked, his voice low, almost accusatory.

'So who *is* in charge of the Watchers?' Siege asked at almost the same time. 'Who commands the Primes?'

Sodja bit her lip, realising she'd said too much. The Black Gambit was getting to her, and the old rules of engagement didn't exactly apply here. She could tell the crew all of her family's secrets so long as they didn't connect Raven to Sodja – and that was seeming more and more likely.

They're going to find out eventually, Sodja chided herself. *Hells, they should have guessed the moment I told them my nickname.* She glanced at Quinn, and saw the woman was scrutinising her closely. Her eyes widened.

And here it comes . . .

'The Rocas family,' Quinn breathed. '*Tiana* controls them!'

Sodja exhaled. Quinn had uncovered a different secret. Relieved, she took another swallow from her tankard.

'And the Prime Watchers,' Quinn continued. 'The mage, the torturer, the spy . . . they're her *children*.'

Sodja nodded again, a little pale, and took another drink.

'Are you saying you know who the prime trinity is?' Way said, his eyes darting between Quinn and Sodja.

'Wait,' Fyn interrupted, raising his hands. 'What trinity is this? Who are the Primes?'

'The Prime Watchers,' Neldon explained. 'They're a powerful trio who answer to the Guildmaster and direct the Watchers – except Raven is saying they *don't* report to the Guildmaster. They're known as the mage, the torturer and the spy.'

'Ketrit,' Quinn said, 'Rista and Sodja. *They're* the trinity?'

Shit. Sodja set her tankard down, her head swimming. This was it. This was when they would all figure it out, when her short spell of freedom would come crashing down around her – and it would start with Quinn. The woman was too perceptive.

Across the table, Quinn's expression remained tight, her voice quavering. 'How do you know all this?'

Sodja's mouth was dry. She glanced at Fyn, who shrugged unhelpfully, though he did take a step towards Quinn. It seemed he still had her back, at least. She felt a flush of gratitude followed by the sudden urge to vomit. She checked her chain-whip and realised she had left it on a barrel at the back of the room. *Damn it.* She tried to calm her nerves and made sure she had a firm grip on her shadow powers, knowing whatever she said next would probably end in a fight – maybe even her death.

'Have you heard any other names for the Primes?' she asked, her voice strained. 'Any strange names?'

'Sure,' Siege said, failing to read the room. 'There's the Squid, the Spider ... and the Raven.' He said this last bit with sudden lilt to his voice.

'You ...' Quinn said, her face turning bright red. '*You!*' A dagger in her hands, she lunged across the table at Sodja. Fyn grabbed her wrist, but Quinn smashed an elbow in his face and slithered out of his grasp. She lunged again, knocked the battered table aside and landed in front of Sodja just as she finished weaving her fingers in front of her chest. An inky pool of shadows spread across the floor under Quinn's feet. Her knife was swinging as dark spindly arms and clawed fingers shot up from the blackness, seizing Quinn's ankles and tripping her. More demonic hands shot out of the shadepool and latched on to Quinn's arms and wrists.

'I'm not like them!' Sodja cried, snatching up her whip and backing towards the nearest tunnel exit. 'I've been helping you *fight* them!'

'Have you?' Neldon asked, stepping between Quinn and Sodja. 'Or did we just kill Guildmaster Whalen for your mother?'

'Why would Raven want to kill Saltair?' Poli asked, looking dumbstruck.

'We still don't know he died, remember? *She* checked the tunnels. How do we know she didn't help him escape?'

'But why?'

'To gain our trust!' Quinn shouted, still fighting her supernatural bonds. 'So we'd eliminate her family's rivals for her. *That's* how she knew where Saltair's lair was – that's how he *escaped*. It all adds up.'

'No,' Fyn objected, moving to stand opposite Neldon. 'Her own uncle Pyodr was one of the messengers sent to kill Whalen. He's in the Golden Guard's custody now. You said yourself that's as good as a death sentence.'

Sodja stood at the back of the room, in the shadows of the tunnel mouth. She didn't want to run, but she didn't want to fight her friends either. Her body shaking like a leaf, not with fear but with rage – full of anger at herself – and her quiet words were ones of bitterness and self-reproach. 'Blood and shadows,' she swore, 'I shouldn't have said anything.'

'Why would she tell us about the Prime Watchers unless she was no longer with them?' Fyn said, seizing on Sodja's mutterings. He stepped closer to her, putting his back between her and the rest of the crew. It was stupid. It jeopardised his leadership with the crew, yet Sodja found she loved him for it.

'Why would she volunteer her secret?' he continued. 'If she is here to manipulate us, then she had no reason to tell the truth.'

Neldon shared a glance with Way. 'That's a fair point.'

'No!' Quinn screamed, her fingers suddenly alight with flickering black flame. 'She's trying to trick us! She will *betray* us.' She spun her wrists, grasped the demonic hands that bound her, and set the shadow flame to consuming their intangible skin, the grey fire dancing, slicking and slithering as though it were alive. Some of the hands retreated into the shadepool, the black fires quenching as they fled, but more shot out to replace them. Quinn was grasped by the throat, chin and shoulders and pulled towards the inky darkness. By degrees, the whole of Quinn's body began to sink into the mirk.

'Enough of this!' Neldon shouted, his manuballista appearing from his robes. He pointed it at Sodja and Fyn stepped between them, once more risking his life for her. 'If you truly mean us no harm,' Neldon pleaded, 'release Quinn and dispel your shadows.'

'She's trying to *kill* me!' Sodja yelled back, though she stopped the hands from dragging Quinn into the darkness.

'I *will* kill you!' Quinn screamed, still struggling against her bonds, her face inches from the black pool.

Fyn turned, his face red with anger. 'Both of you *stop*!' he roared. 'Sodja, release Quinn. Quinn, dispel your shadow fire.'

Quinn hissed with hate and fury, but some of that anger slipped out of her as, with Fyn standing between them, Sodja began to dispel the demonic hands holding her captive. Quinn's body was expelled from the darkness and then, out of nowhere, her eyes seemed to roll back, her knees folded, and she toppled onto her side as though stunned from a blow. The shadow fire winked out and, an instant later, so did the shadepool and the shadow hands. Siege and Poli were quick to help their friend.

'She's asleep,' Poli said, her scarred hands stroking Quinn's brow and black hair. 'Drained herself to the dregs trying to hold onto that shadow fire.' The fisherwoman passed Quinn's limp body to Siege, who carefully placed the sleeping woman in her hammock.

'All right,' Way said, clearing his throat, 'now that we aren't all trying to kill each other, how 'bout we discuss this like adults.' He looked at Sodja. 'Raven isn't your real name, is it?'

'I never said it was.'

'Didn't say your name was Sodja Rocas, Prime Watcher, of one of the most powerful houses in Luqura, either. Gods be good, which one of the trinity are you? The mage? The spy?'

'The spy. I told you: I'm good at discovering secrets – it's my gift. My oldest brother, Ketrit, is the mage, though he's no better with shadow magic than me.'

'Well, so long as you're not the rotting torturer. Then I'd have run you through myself.'

'Rista is the sadist – and if I could, I'd slit his throat myself.' She grimaced. 'He's dangerous, you know ... but it's worse than that. Something is wrong with him. He likes the torture, and my mother encourages it.'

'You mean she uses it,' Neldon said, his tone combative. 'She sends him to prey on anyone who opposes the Guild, to torture them till she gets what she wants.'

'You think that's the worst of it?' Sodja said, shuddering. 'Tiana gives Rista slaves to practise on – innocent people to interrogate.'

'To torture, you mean.'

'Yes ... and to kill. She enjoys it, I think – the thrill of the power. She watches him do it.'

'So why tell us this?' Way asked, interrupting. 'And why now? What do you want?'

'I need you to know who the monsters really are. To see why I have to fight them.'

Way nodded at that, though Neldon seemed less sure, and Siege and Poli were clearly sceptical – their eyes wide with trepidation and fear.

'But you're one of them. You've helped them do these things,' Neldon said, his tone still accusative but also paired with a new earnestness. 'What changed?'

Sodja slowly met each person's eyes in turn. 'Tiana murdered my father because she thought his interests – his good heart and unorthodox values – conflicted with her own. He was a noble-man ...' She gave Neldon a knowing look. 'But he was also a thief.' She glanced at Way, Siege and Poli. 'Only my mother wanted to do more than pick Luqura's pockets. She wanted to *rule*, she wanted *power* – and the Slavers Guild was the quickest way to achieving that goal.'

'So that much at least was true,' Neldon said, taking a step closer. 'The Rocas family really did kill your father – you just didn't mention he was also the Rocas family *patriarch*.'

'Do you blame me?'

Neldon stroked his chin, his expression thoughtful. 'I suppose not.' He looked to Quinn's hammock and shook his head. 'You probably shouldn't be here when she wakes up.'

'How long will she be out?' Fyn asked.

'Usually most of the day, after something like this. Give it at least twenty-four hours. We'll talk to her. See if we can convince her not to kill you. Might be she'll even stick with the crew if she believes you're after the same thing.'

'And the rest of you?' Fyn asked, looking from Way to Siege and Poli. 'You'll stick?'

'You still planning on killing Dante Turano and upending the slave trade in the Undercity?' asked Way.

'Yes.'

'Then I'm still in. Though, truth be told, I'd like to get to that sooner rather than later. My boys ... my boys are still *down* there ... somewhere.'

'You're sure, Way?' Neldon said, his manuballista still held in his hands. 'She could be lying – could still be working for Tiana Rocas. You still want to get involved?'

'As long as we take out the men who stole my wife and children, I don't much care about her motives.'

'Fair enough.' Neldon looked to Siege and Poli. 'What about you two?'

Siege looked at Poli. 'I'm not saying I want to leave the crew, but I need to think it through. Poli and I should talk ... and I want to hear from Quinn.'

'I think we could all use a little space,' Neldon said, 'some time to reflect on what we've accomplished, and want to do next.' He looked to Fyn and Sodja. 'Maybe you should both give us a day or two.'

Sodja swallowed back an emotional outburst and simply nodded. Fyn added his assent, and they both retreated to the upper tunnels.

'Why did you tell them?' Fyn asked when they were safely away, just a few miles above and north of the Undercity.

'I don't know.' And the odd thing was, she really didn't. 'They started talking about the Watchers and I just ... I didn't want that reputation following me any more. I didn't want to carry that burden any longer. I know what my family did to Quinn and her parents. Every time she looked at me, I felt like she had already guessed the truth but couldn't voice it – and I couldn't bear it any longer.'

'Well, your secret is out now.'

'You knew the whole time, though,' she said, studying him out of the corner of her eye. 'Every time they spoke about my family – every dirty story Quinn whispered about them – you kept silent. Why?'

'Why not? They're your secrets, not mine.' He led the way, now confident with his familiarity of the upper tunnels.

'And you're not afraid I'm secretly working for my mother?' she persisted. 'That I persuaded you to form this crew and hunt down these people because it's what *she* wants?'

'Oh, I'm sure you've manipulated me, but you forget – *I* was the one who approached *you*.'

'And what if I said I'd planned that? What if all of this is a scheme, using you, just to get back at my family?'

635

'I'd say you're telling me things I already know.'

Sodja looked at him then, her eyes intense. 'Then why go along with it?'

'Because we want the same thing, Sodja.'

'Which is?'

'To turn the world upside down and place ourselves atop it.'

Sodja smirked at that. 'I think my reasons are a bit more nuanced.'

'Sure,' Fyn laughed, then climbed a rusted metal ladder into the basement of an old warehouse in the Low Quarter, midway between the Ash Quarter and the Lower River District. 'You want to murder your whole evil family because you've had enough of them – and because they killed your father – and you want to kill their allies because when you've got vengeance on your mind, you want the whole world to burn.'

'Maybe not the whole world,' Sodja said with a slight smile, her hands reaching for the first rung, 'and not *everyone* in my family is terrible. I mean, we're all thieves and murderers, but we're not all like Rista and Tiana either. My grandmother Bella is the kindest, wisest woman I've ever known.' She stopped at the top of the ladder. 'Well, she used to be. She's not herself these days.'

Fyn helped her up the last step. 'You don't have to explain yourself to me. I told you before, I'm not a nice person and my hands are no cleaner than yours.'

'I doubt that.'

Fyn huffed. 'We can compare body counts if you want ... but I'm telling you, none of that stuff matters to me. If the rest of the Ashes crew abandons us, that's fine. I'm not going anywhere.'

Sodja looked at him intently in the murky darkness of the warehouse, her eyes shining as if with unshed tears – and then she leaned over and kissed him. It was a fierce thing, more raw than the kiss they had shared on the rooftop a month ago, and it left them both wanting more. When they finally broke apart, their breaths were heavy.

Fyn licked his lips, uncertain. 'You, uh ...'

'Shhh.' She pressed a finger to his lips and pulled him down into the dark recesses of the forgotten building.

Chapter Sixty-Seven

'Why are you able to heal here but not in the Shadowrealm?'

'You mean my eye,' Oyru said, squinting at the trolls camped just beyond the treeline. 'I do heal there, but it is more natural than supernatural. Here in the physical world, the shadows are more ... substantial. I can't feed myself as easily on the somnumbra here, but the shadows are more potent. I suspect it is also related to the passage of time. Things happen more slowly here, but my essence is also tied to the Shadowrealm, so my healing is exponentially faster in the physical world. That is only true in the shadows, though. My healing is more normal in the darkness and completely negated when in the sunlight.'

'Is that why you prefer coming here at dawn and dusk?'

'Yes.'

Myjun sat down beside the assassin. The mask was rioting her emotions once again, and it took some self-control not to run into the clearing and murder the family of shaggy brown creatures camped there. The ironwood trolls they'd been searching for were taking turns shuffling between the light of the fire and the darkness of the forest, their long arms gathering armloads of gnarled roots, fallen limbs and tree bark, then shovelling them into the bright yellow flames.

'Do you think ...' She tried to force the malice from her voice. 'Do you think that's why I can't lightsling here ... but I can there?'

Oyru considered, then slowly shook his head. 'I think it's related to your mask. The artifact augments your healing in the physical world, at the expense of your Ilumite magic. It draws on the power of your emotions to fuel its own magic. When you are in the Shadowrealm, though, emotional auras are dampened. That weakens the mask and – paradoxically – allows you to draw on more of your Ilumite magic.'

'That makes no sense,' she hissed, this time unable to keep the scorn from her voice.

'As I said, paradoxical.'

Myjun sniffed. 'Do you think the witherkin will be waiting for us when we return?'

'Most likely, yes.'

'Then why return at all?'

Oyru gestured beyond the trees to where the Sauthron Sea – the *real* Sauthron Sea – sparkled in the light of the rising moon and stars. 'We will have to pass through the Neck on our return journey west and enter the Shadowrealm again to bypass the Spear of Tacharan's protective magic. It is impossible to survive the shadow of the Spear without the Death God's blessing.'

'Then we take a ship,' Myjun pressed, still fighting the emotions of her mask. 'You said it yourself: we could circumvent the tower's curse if we avoid Takarania altogether and simply book passage from Alltara back to the Empire.'

'That would work for you,' Oyru said. 'But I would have to return to the Shadowrealm before we reached land, and since the ship does not exist in the Shadowrealm I would be plunged into the starry void of the endless sea.'

Myjun remembered Oyru's previous reticence about the ocean and his inability to traverse it in the Shadowrealm. 'We'll keep travelling during the umbras and spend more time meditating during the antumbras, then. There isn't much difference between the two anyway, and we don't actually sleep in either.' She paused. 'I still can't believe we're running from a rotting ghost – Yohan the *chandler's* ghost. He was so scared of bees and blood that he bought his wax from the mead-maker and traded for tallow from the butcher.' She sniffed, disgusted by both their inability to kill the candlemaker's spirit and their joint cowardice at being unable to confront his spectre.

'I assume his unfinished business involves some vengeance

against me,' Oyru said, finally looking away from the fire. 'I can think of no other reason why he would pursue us. Not unless ...' He turned his single eye on Myjun. 'What was your relationship to this chandler?'

'Relationship?' Myjun laughed bitterly. 'He was a mean old bastard with an eye for anyone younger than his wife. Never tried anything with the witgirls – he wasn't stupid enough to do *that* – but he got away with preying on plenty of village girls.'

'Mm. So it must be vengeance against me for summoning the eidola and his being trapped in the shadows.'

Mynun sniffed. 'In his defence, that was a rotten thing to do. You damned some of my friends to the shadows, too.'

Oyru shrugged. 'Assassins aren't in the business of making friends – or keeping them. You are better off without them.'

'Then why are you training me? Why bring me here? Aren't I a *burden* to you?'

The assassin hesitated. 'Yes.'

'So why are we doing this? Why are we hunting trolls in these woods to steal ashes from their campfires? Why are you making armour and training me to be your apprentice?'

Silence. Myjun felt the urge to prompt him again – to poke and prod and evoke some kind of angry response – but she held her tongue and watched as the largest trolls took turns sinking their sharp black nails into an ironwood tree the group had felled just before dusk. Until that point, the fires had been fed by natural lumber, but now the trolls began peeling the impossibly tough ironwood into splinters of kindling and strips of tinder. She marvelled at it, knowing from experience that ironwood bark was as hard and inflexible as its namesake, and its heartwood was harder still – closer to steel than iron. Yet the trolls of Alltara seemed to possess the strength to rip it into firewood.

'They eat the ashes,' Oyru said, ignoring her questions. 'That's why they make the fires. When the coals die down, the trolls eat the ironwood ashes. It's what makes their bones so dense and their teeth and nails so sharp. They're more than trolls. They're *iron* trolls. More, the magic of the Shadowrealm penetrates these old mountains and their dark forests. The trolls do not only eat ash, they consume their magic.'

'I didn't think trolls ate trees, much less ash.'

'The ones in Alltara do. They're omnivores, though. They prefer meat – just as we might prefer a rich pastry or dessert – but it's an indulgence. This' – he gestured at the old Alltaran forest – 'is their real food.'

'And you brought me here to ... what? Eat ashes?' she scoffed. 'Even without the mask, there is no rotting way you'd make me eat that dreck.'

'You're not going to eat it,' Oyru said.

'Then what the hell—'

'Hush and prepare your weapons,' Oyru said, summoning his flyssas. 'Once they have finished gathering the ironwood, we will slaughter the tribe. Take care, though. Their hide and bones are tough, even to my void shards and your soulfire blades, so we will have to attack strategically.'

'Our magic doesn't work on them?'

'Not well, no. It is part of the enchantment of the ironwood. In addition to its mythical strength and flexibility, it repels all but the most persistent magical attacks.'

Myjun let loose a series of expletives, each more foul than the last. 'You tell me this *now*? Seconds before we attack them?'

'Try to avoid their claws and teeth, and focus your attacks on their eyes and mouth. If you see a chance to separate their head from their necks, you can try it ... but don't overcommit. Chances are high that your weapons won't work on their hides – not even their necks – so stick to soft tissue and organs, like their mouths and eyes.'

'Noted,' Myjun said, her anger beginning to rise. With battle imminent and the mask already working, she was eager to feel pain and cause pain. Eager to kill and feed on the lives of these monsters. It would be a challenge, if Oyru was to be believed, and Myjun desired a challenge. She *hungered* for it.

Back in the clearing, the largest troll dumped his final armload of dense ironwood amidst the embers of the smoking fire. A moment later, some of the smaller strips of ironwood already lying there

640

began to smoke and sizzle, its strange branches belching black soot and then popping like shots of thunder in the night.

'Now?' Myjun asked, struggling not to race into the clearing and slash the throat of anything vaguely humanoid.

'Now,' Oyru said, sliding into the shadows and stalking towards the nearest beast.

Myjun let the rage pour into her. She inhaled deeply and tasted the smoky scent of ironwood resin on her tongue, almost syrupy sweet with a mellow charcoal overtone. She smelled the trolls' feral musk. She stalked nearer and realised the one she had scented – a male – sat with his companion just outside the firelight. He roared something Myjun did not understand, then rolled his mate over and began to mount her.

The magic of the mask awakened painful memories of Kenton ... and Annev. She had tried to forget her seductions, her clumsy attempts to woo both boys, for it shamed her to think what they had later become. Now, with the fumes of the ironwood filling her nostrils and the magic of the mask heightening her passions, Myun felt the memories flood her thoughts. Closeted kisses. Secret trysts that had failed to come to fruition. Carnal thoughts she'd fought to suppress and later sought to forget. She'd been betrayed by them both, first by her attraction to Kenton and then by her fascination with Annev. It filled her with shame and anger, but also with a sense of longing and loss – with regret at what might have been if things had been different. Those reflections then fed back into her anger, and the tight control Myjun kept over her emotions threatened to slip free. She strengthened her grip, though, and rode the wave of her emotions – not allowing them to control her, nor fighting against them as she had in the past; instead, she bridled them, harnessing their strength and allowing their power to fuel her attacks.

With a predatory snarl, Myjun leapt atop the two trolls, her twin blades slicing as she fought back the tears of hatred stinging her eyes, blinding her to the carnage she inflicted. All around her, Myjun could hear shouts of pain and the guttural cries of the frenzied troll clan. She became frenzied herself, her emotions further fuelling her magic, speeding her beyond the reach of tooth and claw. She saw the anger in Kenton's gaze and fought to dominate it. She saw the betrayal in Annev's eyes after she'd discovered his missing limb, and she sought to blind him.

All around her, the trolls were falling, sprawling backwards with their eyes burned out. One beast leapt atop her, surprising her as it wrestled her to the earth like an angry bear. It raked its claws down her back and she howled with both pleasure and pain. She twisted in his grasp, her fists slamming his armoured skin, forcing the soulfire blades into his chest. The iron troll convulsed ... and died.

Myjun gasped, crushed by the weight of the shaggy beast. With an effort, she rolled out from under the dead troll's bulk and blinked away the blood that stained her vision. There were scores of monstrous corpses scattered about the clearing, and her body was already healing from the few wounds the trolls had inflicted. She'd grown faster and stronger during their many months hunting eidolons – and though these trolls were fast, she was faster.

Oyru stood over a troll that was still moaning in the shadows. His flyssas flicked down, piercing its skull, and the thing shuddered and fell silent. With a grunt, the assassin yanked his narrow sword from the troll's eyes. The Shadow Reborn looked at her curiously. 'You fought differently tonight. Less angry. More ... focused. It was almost a dance. Very beautiful.' He dispelled his swords and walked close enough to her that Myjun could smell the hot blood on his clothes.

'Have you gained control of your emotions, then?' he asked. 'Have you discovered how to use the powers of the mask without letting it master you?'

Myjun's mind returned to her waking vision: she had never lain with Annev or Kenton, though she had come close with the latter, and the mask had centred her anger on that. She had been attracted to Kenton until the fool boy had been scarred. She'd never been able to look at him the same way after that. And then Annev had been worse. The deceptive one-armed bastard had been marked by Keos the whole time – and he'd kept it secret from her. He'd made her fall in love with him and then ...

What is wrong with me that everyone I love or care for is damaged

642

or corrupted? Even my father. Even me. Everything I touch turns to
ashes ... and I am drawn to the darkness.

She looked up and saw Oyru studying her, his pupils like wide
pools of inky blackness. He saw something in her, and nodded his
approval.

'You are ready to face the test of ashes. Come with me to the
fire.'

Myjun complied, feeling dazed and angry, only vaguely aware
that she'd dispelled her soulblades. She studied Oyru in turn, and
when he beckoned her to sit, she did.

Oyru extended his hand and wisps of smoke trailed behind
his fingers. She half expected him to summon one of his flyssas,
but instead a pair of shadow-black tongs appeared in his hand.
He stretched the tool into the fire and plucked out one of the
crumbling orange embers that glowed there.

'Ironwood embers,' Oyru said, bringing the coal in front of
him, 'will cool to resin and ash when they make contact with
organic matter. The trolls eat them when there is only a touch of
warmth remaining. To make your armour, though, the embers
must be hot. Your blood will cool them, and the mask will heal
your burns before they can scar ... but it will still be painful.'

Myjun nodded.

'The resin will take about an hour to harden into plate armour.
It will be thin – like wearing a second skin – but it will be as tough
as steel. Where you need more flexibility, we will use the residue
from the ashes, which will still be stronger than any chainmail or
leather you might wear – and protect you against magic, but it
won't be as strong as the resin. Even so, this is the most powerful
and versatile armour in existence, and the best kept secret of my
long-dead family clan.'

'Why do you not wear it then?'

'The magic does not bond with half-men.'

'Then why didn't you obtain it before you became a half-man?'
Myjun asked bluntly.

Oyru hesitated, then placed the coal back in the fire. 'My father
swore to bring me here and perform the ritual, but when he was

killed that duty passed to my mother. She refused – for many years – because she disapproved of my choice of mate.'

'Oraqui.'

He nodded. 'In the end, she won my mother over by offering to take the test of ashes herself. She knew what it meant – both the pain, and that it would for ever mark her as one of our clan. So my mother brought us both here, to these mountains. To the troll lairs. First she made me watch as she burned Oraqui's flesh ... and then she made me help.'

Oyru fell silent, no sign of emotion, or weakness as he looked into the fire.

'I burned her with the ironwood resin and its ashes,' he continued, 'but when it was my turn to take the test, there weren't enough embers left. We swore to come back together – she would perform the ritual for me as I had for her – but then Oraqui betrayed me and brought Gevul down upon my household.'

Myjun couldn't hold her peace. 'Why did you wait for her, after that? Why would you still think she cared for you?'

Oyru gestured to the fire with his tongs. 'Because Oraqui knew my family's secret. She could have brought Gevul and his clan here and given our magic to them ... but she never did. She kept her word. She helped Gevul kill my family, but she kept our greatest secret.'

'Why would she do that?'

Oyru shrugged. 'If I ever see her again, perhaps I will ask.'

'It makes no sense. She helped *kill* your family – why not betray that one secret?'

Oyru hesitated. 'Perhaps when we have hurt someone we love, it is natural to hold something in reserve, something to show we are not wholly monsters. Perhaps it is a cry for help or redemption.' The assassin plucked a fresh coal from its embers. 'Or perhaps in a mad world, we cling to a single virtue so we can excuse the other atrocities we allow ourselves to commit.'

'I think it's the latter.'

The Shadow Reborn shrugged. 'People are complicated.'

'But you still love her. Even though she killed your family, you still love her.'

'If you must ask that, you did not understand my story. Oraqui joined my family when I burned her with these coals. She became part of my clan.' He extended the ironwood ember towards Myjun. 'I offer you the same.'

Myjun stared at the orange coal then looked back to Oyru's single eye. Without a word, she shed her clothes and stood, fierce, before him.

'I am ready.'

'Then I will bathe you in embers and ashes,' he whispered, and pressed the hot coal to her skin.

Myjun hissed, just as the coal against her skin hissed, the latter glowing red with fire and blood. The pain was bright and brilliant, almost overwhelming, and as it cooled it gave her clarity amidst the hazy vapours of charred ironwood. Oyru rolled the ember over her and the pain flared anew, but when she looked down at her flesh, she saw not bubbling burns, but a beautiful blue-black chitinous layer covering her flesh.

'This will transform me into a monster,' Myjun growled through gritted teeth. 'I will never be free of this – just like my mask.'

'We are already monsters,' the assassin breathed in her ear, continuing the ritual, 'and now our bodies match our hearts.'

Chapter Sixty-Eight

Annev stared at Tym's round face.

'Dead?' he whispered. 'But ... I just saw him. He was alive.'

Brother Tym's eyebrows narrowed. 'You mean ... you saw him while mindwalking?' Annev nodded, earning a frown and a contemplative grunt from Misty and Tym respectively. 'What did you see?' Tym asked, his expression neutral.

Annev opened his mouth to answer, then he recalled how his vision had ended: how blood had sprayed from Holyoak's eyes, ears and mouth. He remembered the mist. The *gore*. How it seemed he could taste the man's blood on his lips.

But none of that was real, Annev thought. *We were mindwalking – we were in Holyoak's mind, and I didn't attack him.*

But was that true? Annev had used the Hand of Keos to break down Holyoak's mind palace. Was that also an attack on the man's literal mind? Had Annev's actions inadvertently caused his death?

'How did it happen?' Annev asked, reinforcing his own mental walls.

'You'd been under for a few hours,' Misty said, laying a hand on Tym's shoulder. 'Tym was monitoring you from outside the implanted memory and we were considering waking you but then something happened. You had ... some kind of breakthrough?'

'You found the *quaire* glyphs!' Tym interjected, unable to keep the excitement from his face. 'It was brilliant. I never would have found them.' He turned to Annev. 'But then you did something strange. You made the glyphs disappear ... and then *you* disappeared.'

'I dispelled the *quaire* glyphs to see the trail of blood-talent and follow it to the traitor. Holyoak was at the other end – the forged memory must have led me into his mind. I spoke to him … and he admitted betraying the Enclave.'

'We gathered that,' Misty said, her eyes full of sympathy. 'Tym couldn't reach you, but you were mumbling. We caught pieces of what you were saying.'

'I was talking in my sleep?'

'Mindwalking is not sleep,' Tym corrected.

'It looks near enough from the outside, though,' Misty said. 'We heard enough of your accusations against Holyoak for Reeve to send some brothers to take him into custody.'

'Did he fight back?'

'He wasn't even awake,' said Misty. Tym seemed about to say something, but a glare from her stifled whatever objections he'd been about to raise. 'There's a time and a place for teaching mindwalking technique, dear.' Misty returned her gaze to Annev. 'Holyoak was in a trance, like you, and nothing we did woke him. We worried that forcibly waking either of you might cause some mental or psychic damage, so we agreed not to wake either of you unless you became distressed. Holyoak was placed under close guard in a warded cell and you were kept in our bedroom.'

Annev abruptly realised they were not currently in Misty and Tym's bedchamber. The room was much smaller, and clearly unoccupied. He tensed when he noticed the tiny glyphs carved into the walls.

'This is … one of the warded cells?' Annev said, stating the obvious.

Misty nodded then glanced sidelong at her husband. 'Do you want to tell him?'

'Might be better to show him,' Tym said, his hand gently falling on Annev's shoulder. 'Come on.'

Not much was left in Tym and Misty's bedroom: a badly charred bedspread, a soot-stained clothes chest, and scraps of smoky linens.

The rest was gone – the bed, the books, the table and chairs – all burned to ash and cinders. Annev stood in the centre of the room and swallowed, his throat dry from the lingering smoke and the bile that burned the back of his throat. His feet traced the curve of the melted stones beneath his feet and then he bowed his head in shame.

'I'm sorry.'

'It wasn't your fault,' Misty said, immediately at Annev's side. 'You didn't know what you were doing. You had no idea what was happening in the physical world.'

'It's *my* fault,' Tym said, his own head bowed with regret. 'I should have moved you the moment you made contact with Holyoak – *before* then maybe – but I wanted to keep a close eye on you. I thought this was a good place, but ... well, it was my fault. I'm sorry.' The apology seemed as much for Misty as Annev.

'It's *nobody's* fault,' Dionach McClanahan replied, her long arms draping over Tym's shoulders. 'It was an accident. No one could have predicted this.'

Annev was less certain. He had willed the Hand of Keos to appear during his mindwalking trance: he had wanted it, summoned it – and then he had conjured its magic. He had brought the destructive flames into the Cognitive Realm, supposing they wouldn't reach the physical world ... and he'd been wrong.

'How—' he croaked, his voice dry. He swallowed and tried again. 'How did you stop it? How did you move me?'

'As soon as the hand started glowing, we had some of the brothers come and try to contain the fire with a shield spell,' Tym said. 'That worked for a bit, until the flames ... well, they pushed the shield outward. I'm not sure how. I mean, it shouldn't have been possible. But they couldn't contain the fire, and I couldn't wake you, and the bed caught fire and things were all a merry blaze for a bit. Reeve left Brother Honeycutt to watch Holyoak and dashed down here to help – he vented some of the fire into that corner of the room, that's how the bookcase caught flame – and things were stable enough that we were able to float you down to the cells. Got you tucked away nice and neat. Well, mostly neat.' He looked around his ruined bedroom and shrugged. 'It's nothing that can't be replaced. There are copies of most of these books in the library – and the rest I can replace myself.' He tapped the side of his skull. 'I've a pretty good memory.'

Annev nodded, reminded of the chest of memories he'd recovered from Holyoak. 'Did you get those memories back to Sraon? Will he be okay?'

'He'll be fine,' Misty said. 'Tym passed me the stolen memories and I handled the transplant personally. Reeve supervised. Sraon should make a full recovery, but it will still take a few days before he feels like his old self.'

Annev felt relieved until he returned his attention to the room's destruction. 'All of this ... How was I not injured?'

'Good question,' Tym said. 'Near as we can tell, the flames don't harm you. Don't understand why, but they don't. Made our job a sight easier, in any case. We shielded you in a ball of skywater – ice, air, water – and that made the transport possible.' He chuckled. 'Funny thing was, as soon as we got you to your cell, things began to quiet down. Turned the fire off yourself, I think ... but that's when the trouble started up with Holyoak.'

Annev studied the Mindwalker's wary face. 'What *did* happen to Holyoak?'

Tym cleared his throat. 'You remember how Honeycutt was left to watch Holyoak – when Reeve came dashing to help you?'

'Yes,' Annev said, his eyebrows narrowing. 'What happened?'

'Honeycutt killed him.'

Annev wasn't sure he understood – then his eyes shot wide open. '*Honeycutt* killed Holyoak?'

'Near as we can tell, yes.'

'The manner of death was consistent with a Breathbreaker attack,' Misty added. 'And Brother Honeycutt has since fled the Enclave.'

'But ... why?'

'We don't know,' Misty said as Tym splayed his hands in the air. 'There's been some speculation that they were working together ... and unfortunately that makes sense.'

'If Honeycutt suspected Holyoak was talking to you,' Tym added, 'he might have decided to eliminate him before he could be interrogated.'

Annev nodded, imagining the Mindwalkers and Stormcallers prying into Holyoak's memories, sorting through his thoughts and exposing his secrets. 'Has anyone else fled?'

'No. Just him.'

'Could there be other traitors hiding at the Enclave?'

Tym sighed. 'I had hoped you could answer that for us. I assume Holyoak didn't tell you very much.'

'No.' He gave a brief summary of what had transpired between him and Holyoak. When he had finished, both Tym and Misty seemed to be studying him with new eyes. 'What is it?'

Misty glanced at Tym, her eyes averted. 'You pretended to be Keos?'

'Well ... no, not exactly. I just intimidated him with the Hand and let him come to his own conclusions.'

'So you *pretended* to be Keos,' she repeated, more forcefully.

Annev winced. 'I guess.'

'And you told him to kneel?' This time there was no mistaking the look of disgust she tried to hide.

'It seemed appropriate,' Annev said, wishing he'd omitted that detail.

Tym's eyes were twinkling. Misty shot him a look and he threw up his hands, defensive. 'What? It was clever! He had to be convincing, didn't he?'

Dionach McClanahan sniffed then rolled her eyes. 'Men. Always quick to use the bluntest instrument in the room.' She turned back to Annev. 'Did you get any inkling as to whether he had acted alone? Whether Honeycutt or anyone else had assisted him?'

Annev thought about it. 'He seemed surprised when I accused him of instigating the attack on my village and said he had only tried to kill me after I came to Quiri. But that can't be true ... can it?'

'I don't know, Annev. Why would he lie about that but admit being a servant of Keos? Why admit trying to kill you but deny the rest?'

Annev thought for a long while. Finally, Tym broke the silence: 'I worked closely with Holyoak, Annev – close enough to know when he left the Enclave. He was a bit of a recluse. He relied on messengers to communicate with distant members of our caste, and he rarely left Quiri.'

'What about Saltair? Did Holyoak ever communicate with him?'

'Not that I know of,' Tym said, chewing his lip, 'but I doubt anyone at the Enclave would admit to communicating with one of the Siänar.'

'What about a merchant named Janak Harth?'

'Janak who?'

'Harth. He had a reputation for collecting artifacts. Lived in Banok.'

'I've heard of him,' Misty volunteered, 'but how is he connected to the attack on your village?'

'Honestly, I'm still not sure, but he had planned to attack Chaenbalu. The *feurog* that finally did destroy the village ...' Annev shuddered, remembering them and the phantasmic shadow demons. 'Maybe they weren't connected – or maybe it was me. They were all trying to get to *me*.'

'That may be true,' Tym said, 'but so far as I know, Holyoak never had any contact with Janak Harth. In fact, the only suspicious thing I can identify is that he dispatched two of our Mindwalkers to visit the more distant Dionach chapter houses.'

'Why is that suspicious?'

'Because of those Dionachs who have travelled in the last year, all of them have been lost or killed, except for those two Dionachs – Chan and Davies, both Mindwalkers.'

'And close associates of Brother Holyoak,' Misty said, her lips pursed. 'That does seem suspicious.'

'Teiksim Chan and Rockford Davies? I can't really imagine any two Dionachs less suspicious. They're both dualists, like Holyoak, actually.' Tym looked at Misty. 'Do you think that's significant?'

She furrowed her brow. 'Maybe ... but we should be wary of prejudice. Mindcallers and Stormpsychics have a history of being profiled as deviants. We can't just assume their guilt, not even with Holyoak's betrayal. And, I doubt Rockford's dualist nature is relevant. He's a condenser, right?'

'A Mindshear,' Tym supplied. 'Half Mindwalker, half Shield-bearer.'

Misty sniffed. 'I can never keep those titles straight. Too many dualist names by half.'

'One hundred and thirty-two among the prime mages,' Tym said, smiling, 'and if you include the New Terran hybrids, you can have as many as—'

'Please don't.'

'Four hundred and sixty-two,' he finished, still grinning.

'Makes my head hurt just thinking about it,' Misty said, pinching the bridge of her nose. 'Anyway, I doubt it's relevant. If Dionachs Chan and Davies are traitors, it will be due to their proximity to Holyoak and his influence, not because they are Mindwalker hybrids.'

'So Chan and Davies are the only ones who survived recent trips abroad,' Annev pressed, not wanting to lose the thread of their discussion. 'They're both Mindwalkers with connections to Holyoak. That's more than enough to investigate them.'

'Dionach Chan's proximity to the Empire's border, on her mission, would have made her a perfect messenger, especially since she and Holyoak were both Mindcallers,' Misty added. 'They could have passed messages freely between one another, and then Dionach Chan could have passed those messages on to their Terran allies. She had the ability and the means to be invaluable to a spy network.'

'What about Davies?' Annev asked. 'Where was he stationed?'

'His territory covered the southern half of the Empire,' Tym said, his expression darkening. 'I don't want to jump to any conclusions, but if Holyoak was orchestrating the assassinations of our missing members, Davies would have been perfect for the job. Mindwalking would have allowed him to spy on others, and his talents with skywater could make him a skilled assassin.' He pursed his lips. 'Blood and bile, I hope we're wrong. Davies has always been a good friend to me. I can't imagine him killing all those people. Dionach Kadmon, Brother Witherspoon, Sisters Rugebregt and Morgenstone ... so many deaths, so many missing.'

He clutched a hand to his mouth and muttered a quick apology before ducking out of the room.

Annev and Misty both looked after him in sympathy, but when Misty turned back to Annev, he could see her steel. 'We've tried to keep Holyoak's death quiet, but with Honeycutt's disappearance, rumours are going to spread. They probably already have. If we're going to track down Chan and Davies, we'll need to move fast.'

'Agreed,' Annev said, grateful for the change in Misty's attitude. 'I don't have much time to hunt down the traitors, and this recent debacle won't encourage Reeve to extend my stay.'

'Indeed not,' said a deep voice from the other end of the room. Annev turned and saw it was the Arch-Dionach himself, who entered with Brother Tym under his arm and a thunderous expression. 'You will leave the Enclave tomorrow.'

'I hoped that—'

'I am grateful for your work – but it doesn't change *this*.' He gestured at the melted stones and charred furniture. 'It's too dangerous for you to stay here. That hasn't changed, Annev. Holyoak is dead, so we have no one to question. Honeycutt is gone, and I can't spare anyone to hunt him down with the threat of additional traitors hiding within the Order.'

'We've been talking about that,' Annev said. 'Dionachs Chan and Davies might be connected to Holyoak's betrayal. Or even assisted him. If you quarantined them—'

'Quarantined?' Reeve sniffed. 'Boy, how many Dionachs do you think we have here at the Enclave? About two dozen. How many of those do you think I can trust? Odar's beard, you think I'm worried about people running? I *want* them to run. I'm worried about whether I can keep control of the bloody place.'

Annev blinked. 'You're worried about a coup?' Reeve nodded. 'So ... you're not going to track him down? You're going to let Honeycutt go?'

'I don't have a choice, Annev. The Order is in danger. The Enclave isn't safe. I need to put my house in order before I start chasing down traitors and heretics. Frankly, I think we might have been overwhelmed already except we received some troubling

news from the south just as this business with Holyoak happened.'
He pulled a creased letter from his robes, its seal broken.

'Troubling news?' Annev said, his eyes briefly drawn to the
letter. 'Reeve, what could be more troubling than this? We need
to act fast if we're going to catch Honeycutt!'

'You're right ... so take this.' He extended the letter to Annev.
'Read it when you have the chance, and decide what you'd like
to do.' Annev took it apprehensively.

'What is it?'

'For now, it's just a distraction. Reports about a besieged city
and a request from some travelling dreamers, when we need to
focus on the traitors in our midst.' He nodded to the others.
'Misty and Tym will help me interrogate Davies and Chan, after
we've questioned a few others of our brethren and confirmed
their allegiance remains with Odar and the Dionachs Tobar.'

'I could help, though,' Annev offered, his fist tightening. 'I
need to help. These people ... Reeve, this conspiracy may have
been responsible for the attacks on my village. For Sodar's death.
I won't just leave this investigation now.'

'What makes you think they're responsible, Annev? Holyoak
knew nothing about Chaenbalu or Sodar's mission. I alone knew
Sodar's location, and I only shared it with Brother Arnor.' He
paused. 'And he's dead.'

Annev considered this. 'Would Arnor have told anyone else?'

'Only his caste leader.' The group was silent as Reeve's indig-
nant, instinctive words slowly sank in. 'Dammit,' Reeve swore.
'Honeycutt knew.' The Arch-Dionach tugged his goatee. 'Damn,
this is all my fault.'

Annev felt his fist clench tighter. 'No,' he said, his voice icy.
'This is *Honeycutt's* fault. You made a mistake, but he profited
from it. He's definitely part of this.'

'Probably. But I can't send anyone after him, Annev.'

Annev's wandering compass suddenly pointed resolutely in
one direction, and he knew what he had to do. He could finally
leave the Enclave and continue his pursuit of the people who had
attacked him and the villagers of Chaenbalu. The certainty of it
felt good – it felt *right*. Like he'd finally found his purpose.

'*I'll* go. You want me to leave anyway, so I may as well hunt Honeycutt down and get answers out of him.'

Reeve tutted his tongue against his teeth, his eyes shifting between the two silent Dionachs at his side. 'I don't like it ... but you're right. I can't keep you here, and I can't stop you.' He glanced meaningfully at Annev's golden hand, which had begun to glow with a dull red luminescence.

'Blood and ashes,' Annev swore, tucking the hand behind his back and trying to calm his emotions. 'I'm sorry.'

Reeve nodded, accepting the apology without drawing attention to it. 'I had this made for you.' He tossed a black felt glove to Annev, its cuff stitched with silver thread and its palm and fingers padded with ... something. Annev slipped it on to his left hand and was immediately impressed by its fit.

'It's got a few *quaire* glyphs woven into the lining – shields of air and water, something that might help quench an unintentional flame ...'

'It's great,' Annev said, grateful to Reeve for saving the moment. 'Thank you.'

He nodded again. 'Gather your things and go after Honeycutt if you must ... but be careful. You're resourceful and brave – you've been trained as an assassin and a thief – but you're going up against a full Dionach with over a thousand years of experience, and that puts you at a serious disadvantage. He might kill you or you might kill him, but you're just as likely to blow up half the city. I hope that, if it comes down to letting Honeycutt go or destroying Quiri, you'll do the smart thing and save your revenge for another day. Another time and place.'

'I'm not looking for revenge,' Annev protested, his cheeks flushed with anger and embarrassment.

Reeve was unconvinced. 'I know that look, Annev. I've worn it myself. You think you're looking for answers – and you might find them – but consider the cost before you do anything you may regret.'

Annev remembered how close he had come to destroying Quiri and nodded.

'Good.' Reeve patted Tym on the back. 'Brother McClanahan,

I'm sorry you are becoming the Mindwalkers' leader under such sad circumstances – but I need your help. I'd be pleased if you and Misty would help me root out any remaining heretics. It's time we finally rid ourselves of the rot that's been hiding under our noses. May Odar protect us ... and may the Order survive our investigation.'

Chapter Sixty-Nine

Annev's goodbyes with Tym and Misty were quick, and accompanied with a promise to reconnect once their missions were complete. Even as he said the words, though, Annev doubted he'd return to the Order. There was nothing for him here – he'd come to that conclusion long ago – and his presence endangered not only the Enclave, but his friends. He hastened to Titus and Therin's quarters to say his goodbyes but didn't see either boy in their rooms, so he headed back down to collect his few unburned possessions in preparation for his departure. Just as he reached the basement, he found them.

'Annev, we've been looking for you!'

'Titus, Therin! I was—'

'You heard the news about Dolyn and Brayan?' Titus continued.

'Dolyn and ...' Annev's heart fell into the pit of his stomach. Was this related to the letter Reeve had given him? Annev had completely forgotten about the Orvanish blacksmith and the burly quartermaster. He hadn't even sent word to Banok to let Brayan know the party had moved on from Luqura to Quiri.

And I promised to return for them. Blood and ashes, I'm a horrible friend.

That wasn't all he had promised and forgotten. With painful clarity, Annev remembered swearing to Red-thumb that he would introduce Jian Nikloss to Sodja Rocas in Luqura and look after the albino necromancer. Annev hadn't kept a single promise: he hadn't returned to Banok, he had never found Sodja, and Jian had died to save him.

Annev smothered his wave of guilt and made himself ask: 'What news?'

'The whole damn town has been taken hostage!' Therin said, his tone near hysterical. 'We've been searching for you ever since we heard.'

'Sorry, I've been a bit occupied.' He stopped. 'Wait ... so Brayan has been taken *hostage*?'

Titus nodded. 'Annev, I'm worried. They aren't letting anyone out.'

Annev had an uneasy feeling sinking in his gut. 'This is in Banok?' They nodded. 'Do you know who's doing it?'

'A group called the Sons of Damnation,' Titus said, looking concerned.

'They aren't Terran,' Therin added. 'That's been confirmed by the few who escaped before the gates were sealed.'

Annev swallowed back bile, beginning to fear what was coming next. 'How many?'

'Just a handful, Reeve heard. Annev ...' Titus wetted his lips. 'Annev, they used *artifacts*. They used magic to control the towns-folk, but they've also been saying horrible things about anyone who might have a talent for magic – even a little. And I think ... well, I think they may be looking for you.'

Rotting blood and ashes. Annev's knees suddenly felt weak and his mouth had gone dry at this confirmation of his fears. 'Why do you think they want me?'

The boys shared a look and Therin spoke. 'They've made it clear they're looking for someone with one arm or someone with a giant golden hand.'

That sealed it then. The few masters left alive at Chaenbalu were the only group whose agenda might match Titus and Therin's description. Annev let out a long, slow breath and shook his head. 'They didn't seem like a threat. I thought they'd leave us alone ... but they must have found a way to plunder the Vault and come after us. Dammit. We should have killed them – made a clean slate of things. We were merciful, and now this is happening.' Annev looked up to see Therin looking thoughtful and Titus horrified.

'Killed them?' Titus said, practically whispering. 'You don't mean that, Annev. Master Edra was with them – and Master Der and Master Carbad!'

'Ather would've been no loss, though,' Therin said. 'Sweet as a viper, that one.'

'Aye, and Master Aog was a brute killer. Who does that leave? Denithal and Murlach? The alchemist and the engineer?' Annev almost scoffed. 'Those men loved their arts more than anything else. None of them deserved to survive when the rest had died.'

'But Edra . . .' Titus protested weakly. 'He wasn't so bad? Rough as he was, he was still fair.'

Annev had to nod at that, remembering how the weapons master had chosen not to disqualify him from the Test of Judgement after nearly throwing Lemwich off the roof. 'The past is the past . . . why in the hells did they decide to take over Banok? Even if they are looking for me, it makes no sense.'

'It's been almost a month since they seized the town,' Titus croaked. 'Word was slow to get here.'

'A *month*? Why hasn't Lenka stopped them? Banok is the cross-road to the eastern kingdoms and he's got a hostile force in control of his second largest city.'

'I don't know,' Therin said, 'but bandits have started to cluster around the town now it's clear no aid is coming. Trade with the eastern kingdoms has slowed to a trickle, and merchants are avoiding Banok.'

Annev reached the door to his latest room and, out of habit, checked for traps. 'I hope Brayan and Dolyn made it out. The masters aren't apt to treat a priestess of Cruithear kindly if they discover her.' He opened the door, satisfied it was safe.

'Annev, we need to help them.'

He laughed then – not because it was funny, but because it was all too much. He'd nearly destroyed the Enclave, which he had to leave anyway. Reeve was interrogating the remains of the Order in search of traitors – and now this business in Banok. It was all too absurd to feel real.

'What are you going to do?' Annev said, stifling another laugh. 'The godsdamned King of Greater Luqura can't help Banok . . . and you want to rescue Brayan and Dolyn?' He began scooping up his possessions. Most could be squeezed into his green hiding sack, the rest he tossed into a small but sturdy rucksack.

'We can't just leave them there, Annev.'

'Why can't we, Titus? No one else is in a hurry to help. Why is it our responsibility?'

'*Because* no one else will help, Annev. That's why it *has* to be us. I can't leave Brayan there, he took care of me when they made me a steward. He stood up for you when Tosan and the rest wanted to kill you – and now he needs our help. Dolyn was injured, trying to help you, and now she's trapped.'

Titus's words twisted his gut. It was true, of course. Every word of it. Brayan had fought alongside them when the *feurog* attacked. He had defended Annev when Tosan had tried to have him executed. And now he was in danger because Annev had let the Sons of Damnation live. Being merciful and letting those men work out their own fates was coming back to haunt him.

'Dammit,' he breathed. He didn't want this, the burden of responsibility; he wanted vengeance. He wanted to hunt Honeycutt down and drag answers from him. He wanted to punish those responsible for destroying the village and killing Sodar. He wanted to stop reacting to someone else's plots and start making his own. He did *not* want this hopeless quest to Banok.

Annev turned from the blank wall he'd been facing. 'Maybe you haven't heard yet, but ... during your Tests of Ascendancy, Holyoak tried to kill me. I didn't want to spoil your promotions by telling you about the attack at the time.'

'Holyoak?' Titus breathed. 'But ... but he was so helpful with my training. I would have sensed something. At least, I think I would have.'

'How did he try to kill you?' Therin asked.

'It doesn't matter,' Annev said, waving his hand. 'The important thing is ...' He wasn't sure how much he should say, but decided his friends deserved the truth. 'Holyoak was killed, probably by Dionach Honeycutt. They may have been working together, and now Honeycutt has fled and Reeve, Leskal and the Dionachs McClanahan are searching for other traitors hidden amongst the Order. I have to leave, but no one is being allowed in or out of the Enclave – did you know that?' The two boys shook their heads in silence.

'I know you both want to help. I know we owe a debt to Brayan and Dolyn ... but this isn't the right time to be a hero. You should stay here and help the Order – they *need* your help. You're among the few they can trust to put things in order here – and once things have quieted down, you can ask Reeve to send some Dionachs to Banok to toss out Aog, Ather and the rest.'

'What about you?' Therin asked, his eyes suspicious. 'Where are you going?'

'I'm going after Honeycutt.'

The wiry boy snorted. 'That's funny. Weren't you just saying to stay here and help – to not run off and be a hero?'

'I'm not a hero. I'm too dangerous for that, and what I'm doing won't be heroic.'

Both boys paused at that, but in the end neither was swayed. 'You should come with us,' Titus said. 'We'd have a better chance of making it to Banok if you came along.'

'Hold on,' Therin interrupted. 'Why are you leaving the Enclave when the rest of us are held here?'

A sad smile tugged at Annev's mouth. 'Reeve asked me to leave.'

'What! Why?'

Annev removed the new glove from his hand, then willed the latter to brighten into a fierce glow. 'This hand is dangerous,' he said. '*I'm* too dangerous to stay.'

'And you think leaving will make it any safer?' Therin snorted. 'Rot and dreck, Annev. Don't you think you're better off with people who can help you? Or do you think it's wise to go running off into a crowded city with a cursed hand that glows like the flaming sun? Blood and hell. You *do* remember what happened back in Chaenbalu, don't you?'

Before Annev knew what he was doing, he cuffed his friend across the face with the back of his right hand, the rings clawing into Therin's flesh. Therin stumbled backward into Titus, his hand clutching his bloody cheek, his eyes wide with shock.

'I haven't forgotten,' Annev growled, his temper hot, his blood pumping in his ears. 'I *can't* forget. While you're practising your little spells with the Dionachs, I'm down here *remembering* what it was like to burn down a building filled with friends, women and children.' He took a step forward, the narrow confines of the room forcing his friends to step back.

'When you're upstairs enjoying your views of the city,' he continued, 'I'm down here in the dark, because staying underground is the only place I'm fit to live.' Another step. 'When you're joking, enjoying your new life and your new magic, I'm hiding from assassins.' He slammed his metal fist against the doorframe, causing his friends to jump backward into the hallway. 'And now you tell me to stay here, where people can help, when those same people have told me to leave.'

'Annev,' Titus began, his voice pleading though it came out like a whine. 'He didn't mean—'

'I know what he meant, Titus, don't keep apologising for him.' He sniffed and fought off the sneer that tugged at his lips. 'You two want to leave? Fine. Leave. Break your oaths to the Order and pretend to be heroes – but when it all goes to hell, when you get captured or raped or killed, I can't come and save you. I'm fighting my own demons. Ones that don't go away.' He waved his golden hand at them. 'Ones I can't get rid of ... or forget.' He spun away then, his eyes barely registering the smouldering imprint his hand had left in the wood. Behind him, his friends were small and frightened.

I shouldn't have said that, Annev thought, immediately regretful. *They didn't deserve to have my frustrations taken out on them.*

Only he couldn't take back the words – and he couldn't deny that he had meant them. Titus and Therin really were safer here at the Enclave, and he had no more desire to run off to save Banok than he did to stay here at the Enclave. He had a lead on who was responsible for the attack on Chaenbalu and he meant to follow it. Every minute he spent here was another minute Honeycutt might elude him.

'Fine,' Therin said. 'We *will* go. We don't need you, and we can take care of ourselves.' Annev heard him turn to go, but then the footsteps halted halfway down the corridor. A moment later, he was back. 'One more thing,' he said, his tone icy. '*You're* the one leaving *us*. You've decided we're a burden.' He waited for Annev to respond, but he had nothing to say. Therin's words reflected what lay in his heart: Annev had outgrown his friends, and he was determined to find his own path, not be fettered by others' expectations.

Annev didn't say any of it. He didn't have to. He was sure Titus could hear his thoughts – Annev wasn't shielding them – and Therin could see it in his face.

'Figures.' Therin spat at his feet. 'You and Kenton are the exact same. As soon as you think you can get by without us, you drop us like so much rubbish. But we don't need you, you know that? We've grown here – without you, *despite* you – and I bet that burns you up inside.'

Annev spun and Therin flinched, hand raised to block another blow to his face – but Annev didn't strike him. Instead, he pulled his dragonscale cloak over his pack and shoulders, nodded to them, and pushed past into the hallway. Therin watched him go in silence, and Titus reached out a hand to slow him.

But Annev did not stop. He couldn't, because if he did, they might see the tears staining his cheeks. They might see the uncertainty in his eyes or realise how much Therin's words had stung him.

He pushed on, not allowing himself to look back, no goodbyes or farewells. It didn't feel right, but Annev told himself this was how it had to be. It had to be a clean break. No ambiguity. No promises to see one another again. He told himself he was doing it for them – to keep his friends safe – but some quiet part of him was glad of the separation, and that same part knew his motives weren't entirely altruistic.

Annev wiped his cheeks, set his jaw and calmed his emotions. 'I'm coming for you, Honeycutt,' he whispered, climbing the steps towards Honeycutt's chambers. 'I'm coming for you, and you're going to tell me every secret you know – every single thing that led to the attack on Chaenbalu – and then you're going to pay for Sodar's death ... and the deaths of every man, woman and child taken by Oyru, his eidolons and the *feurog*.'

Annev stopped in front of Honeycutt's door then rested his fingertips on the wood: he felt the magic from the man's Ward of Silence there, the glyph burned into the opposite side of the wood planks. He focused on it, gritted his teeth, and used the Rod of Artificing to unmake it. When he was finished, his fingers clutched the ephemeral threads of blood-talent left behind by Honeycutt's ward; at its opposite end, he felt the familiar hum and thrum of life.

'I'm coming for you.'

Chapter Seventy

Using the amplified power of the Inquisitor ring, Annev found he could illuminate the faint ribbons of blood-talent until their woven strands of pink light glowed as fierce as a scarlet sunrise, a red streak that stood bright against the coppery mists filling his vision. Annev had grown so accustomed to those mists that navigating them had become second nature. He followed the trail of blood-talent into the darkness, its strand humming with Honeycutt's pulse, and when he reached a shuttered window that led out into the night, he knew Honeycutt had used it to make his unseen exit from the Enclave. A glance at the walls outside told him much of what he needed to know.

He used his Breathbreaker magic to float down from here, Annev thought, searching for another glyph. He didn't see any symbols at the window's ledge, so he supposed it lay at the other end of the drop. To find out, Annev would have to climb down – no small task given the height of the Enclave's walls. The brickwork wasn't sheer or well maintained, which at least gave Annev's clever hands a chance to find purchase amidst the mortar, stones and ledges. Though the Hand of Keos might be a hindrance. It was strong, but its fingers might be too large to fit into the cracks and crevices.

Only one way to find out. Annev wound the corded threads of blood-talent around his golden fingers, then eased himself over the window ledge. *This is crazy,* he thought, glancing down at the cobblestone street far below. *I have no safety rope and I have no experience climbing with this prosthetic. I should leave through the front door, circle the building, and find the place where Honeycutt landed.*

But he suspected the Enclave's magical defences wouldn't allow him to find its eastern wall, and the Dionachs guarding the front door might not know they were supposed to let Annev leave.

It'll be fine, he thought, trying not to think about slipping. *If I need to, maybe I can use the Hand of Keos to create handholds in the stone.*

Fortunately, it never came to that. After his right hand found purchase amidst the uneven stones, Annev eased his left hand down the wall and found it clung to the rocks with almost no effort. He hadn't melted the stones or reshaped the bricks to fit his massive hand, yet he felt certain magic was somehow at play.

Devilry, he thought. But he was grateful for it and used it to descend swiftly from the upper floors of the Enclave.

The trouble came when he was halfway down the building. The brickwork there was much tighter, and Annev found himself relying more and more on the magical strength and dexterity of his left hand ... and worrying that relying on it too much might break the delicate blood-talent threads leading to Honeycutt.

As if in response to that fear, as Annev reached for another handhold he felt the tension on the magic thread tighten un-expectedly around his fingers. He stopped, feeling it ease, then reached again. The thread of blood-magic strained further ... and then they snapped. Annev cursed, lunging for the falling filaments as they began to disintegrate, and felt his right hand slip from the weather-worn stones ...

He tumbled backwards to the street below. He twisted in the air, clawing desperately to sink his magic hand into the stone, to slow his fall or assert any measure of control over his descent, and only managed to move so his face would hit the ground first. He barely managed to get his hands beneath him before smashing into the stones.

Bones broke on impact.

He heard as well as felt the sickening crunch and the wet thump of soft meat against cobblestones. It would have been worse – far worse, by his estimation – without the sudden *woosh* of air he'd felt just before hitting the street. It spread out beneath him like a mattress of straw and feathers, saving him from the worst of the fall, but his head still rang like a bell on Seventhday.

'Keos,' he coughed, winded, sputtering the curse he'd been unable to scream. He spat, dribbling saliva onto the street, and was relieved to see it did not contain his blood. He struggled to right himself, moving carefully in case his neck or spine had been injured. They seemed intact, though – and even his hands and wrists were unbroken, despite being the first to strike the cobblestones – but his right arm had snapped, the bone protruding from his skin at the elbow. 'Blood and bones,' he moaned. Then he gritted his teeth, clutched his arm and forced himself to his feet.

Annev glared up at the window he'd fallen from and then back down at the stones that had caught him. How far had he fallen? He'd thought two storeys, but now he wasn't so sure. And what had broken his fall? Had his magic prosthetic tried to save him? It wouldn't have been the first time, but he didn't see how the Hand of Keos could have formed the shield that saved him from a worse fall.

Shield. He stared at the ground again. *It was a shield, wasn't it? Some burst of wind . . . some pad of air?* He might have wondered for longer, but then he glimpsed the blue-white glow coming from his codavora ring, saw a dark stain beneath the haze of magic and cautiously rubbed the wet smear away. As he did, the glow of magic disappeared and Annev's golden fingers came away flaked with blood. But not *his* blood.

And then it came to him.

This is Therin's . . . from when I slapped his face. This is Breathbreaker *blood*. A chill ran through Annev; remorse for injuring his friend, and elation that he might have accidentally performed Darite magic without possessing the skill himself. He had accidentally bonded Brother Tym's Mindwalker blood to the silver-gold codavora ring, and this seemed similar, though Therin's blood did not appear to have permanently bonded with the artifact.

He had still exploited his friend's blood-magic, though. How? Not by making a glyph or speaking a word of power . . .

Had Annev simply burned out the magic in his friend's blood? If so, that would explain why it was dry instead of wet or sticky: the *quaire* had been leeched from the liquid.

The pain of his broken arm screamed for attention, and Annev realised he'd have to save that mystery for another time. He moved with the practised caution of someone who had grown used to tending his own injuries. Sodar had once helped him, but those days seemed a distant memory now. The priest's teachings remained, though, and Annev had one other artifact to assist his ministrations. The fingers of his left hand brushed his neck, the golden skin somehow warm to the touch, and Annev carefully untied the bloody rag he'd grown accustomed to wearing as a grisly neckerchief.

The Shirt of Regeneration had definitely seen better days. In its current state, no one would see anything more than a sweat-soaked, bloodstained rag – but it was still potent. Once he'd un-wound the scarf from his neck, he carefully tied the cloth around his bicep. He was about to shift the rag so it covered his broken bone and ruptured elbow, but then he hesitated. Would the arti-fact try to seal his flesh with the bone still protruding? The shirt had healed broken bones before, back in Chaenbalu when he had fought the *feurog* ... but those bones hadn't broken his skin – and hadn't Reeve counselled him *not* to heal Sraon while the venom was still in his body?

Blood and piss.

Annev braced himself against the wall of the alley, held his right arm in the grip of the Hand of Keos ... and pulled. With a grinding *pop*, the broken bones shift back into place and an intense wave of agony threatened to wash over Annev. Before he could black out or the bones could shift again, he dragged the healing cloth over his injury and pulled it tight.

The magic took hold of Annev's flesh before he'd prepared himself, and he felt the twist and pop of bones resetting and then mending. He screamed a second time at the sudden agony then choked back a cry as his skin burned hot beneath the rag, the flesh fusing together and completing the healing process – six weeks of healing in one go. He felt sore and drained, and the light of his glowing left hand revealed that a pink scar now laced his skin, but the pain was greatly diminished. Annev flexed his elbow and, aside from a last muted *pop*, nothing seemed amiss. He was whole again.

Should have taken the damn stairs, he thought, looping the rag back around his neck and catching his breath. He looked around for the blood-talent thread and only then remembered the link had broken mid-fall – disintegrating in his fingers. He swore aloud, then kicked a copper coin at his feet. The clip flew across the darkened alley and plinked as it hit the shadowed wall of the Enclave.

There's got to be another one of Honeycutt's glyphs nearby, he told himself. *Probably one he used to float down from that window.* In fact, the more Annev thought about it, the more he suspected his miraculous puff of air had probably come from Therin's blood combined with Honeycutt's discarded rune. *That* made sense. Assuming he was correct, Annev attuned his senses to the magic of the Inquisitor ring he wore and began to scour the street, his eyes searching for any sign of glowing glyphs. A moment later, he spotted the telltale glow of magic coming from the opposite side of the street.

The coin. Honeycutt must have anchored his magic to it and thrown it down ahead of him. Annev snatched it up and turned the copper rectangle over in his palm. Sure enough, one side had been painted with a skywater glyph – the symbols for air and water, but with some modifications common among the Breathbreakers. The magic would have acted as a shield, repelling whatever hit it but without inflicting any violence on the thing it pushed away.

Clever. Very clever.

Feeling more certain of his theory that the copper clip had saved him from colliding with the cobblestones, Annev scanned the coin for traces of Therin's blood magic. He expected to see threads of his friend's blood-talent leading back into the Enclave … but the only trace of magic Annev found belonged to Dionach Honeycutt.

So what had generated the miraculous puff of air that had saved him at the last second? Annev didn't know, but suspected it was still connected to Therin's blood.

I'll have to experiment with that later, Annev thought, pulling the Rod of Artificing from his pocket. With the wand's aid, he dispelled the coin's active Breathbreaker glyph and sifted through the remnants of skywater vapour. He found Honeycutt's thin ribbon of blood-talent, but instead of tracing its length with his fingers, Annev dropped the coin into his pocket, effectively anchoring the thread to his person. This left his hands free, and made it much less likely he'd accidentally break the connection; in fact, so long as he didn't touch the thread with his prosthetic or the Rod of Artificing, it seemed to be fine. He could still see the thread with his Inquisitor ring, but not interact with it – and that suited Annev perfectly. He concentrated on the pink filament of light and watched it brighten once more to a fiery red, its trail easily discernible in the soft glow of moonlight.

'It's time to pay for your crimes, Jayar Honeycutt,' Annev whispered to the night air.

Chapter Seventy-One

Annev walked a few miles north and east, away from the docks and towards the city's most northern gate. The streets were quiet and surprisingly well lit, given the lateness of the evening, the cobbles worn smooth from centuries of foot traffic, wagons and horse hooves. As the city's northern gate came into view, Honeycutt's trail veered sharply east then terminated at the end of a quiet street where a nondescript, single-storey home stood silent amidst an overgrown garden. Honeycutt's trail led inside, and Annev's avatar training allowed him to break in with relative ease. From there he followed the fugitive's glowing blood-talent thread straight to a trapdoor cleverly concealing the building's secret basement. As Annev approached, his enhanced vision spotted the glyph Honeycutt had set to warn of intruders, and it was a simple affair to dismantle it. The Dionach had set few other defences – mostly wards that Annev also dismantled, but also some artifacts that were quickly confiscated – and so he caught the man sleeping, half naked and entirely unprepared for his arrival.

'Why did you kill Dionach Holyoak?'

Honeycutt woke with a start, blinded by the brightness of the flaming sword hovering in front of his face.

'What in the hells is the meaning of this?'

'Answer the question,' Annev said, bringing the sword close enough to singe the man's beard and forcing him to jerk his head back to his pillow.

'Wh-what do you mean?' he sputtered.

'You killed Holyoak. I want to know why – and don't lie to me. I'll know if you do, and it won't end well.'

The Breathbreaker blinked, squinting against the fire that threatened to blind and burn him. '*Ainnevog*? Is that you?'

'Answer the rotting question!' He pressed the tip of the flamberge against the man's skin and Honeycutt jerked his head backward once more.

'Odar's beard! Annev, what's this about?'

'Stop messing me about!' Annev slashed Honeycutt's hand. The fiery blade slammed into his fingers and severed the two smallest digits with a meaty thunk.

'Rot and hell!' The priest screamed, his cauterised flesh still sizzling. 'Why did you . . . ? I didn't *do* anything!' In truth, Honeycutt hadn't – but he'd been about to. The Inquisitor ring had showed the man's pulse spiking, and the mixed magics of the codavora ring had showed Annev the man's mood, emotions and thoughts: Honeycutt had been preparing to cast a spell.

'Piss me about again, it's another finger – and if I see so much as a muscle twitch, I will plunge this sword through your rotting face. Do you understand me?'

'I . . . yes,' Honeycutt whispered, his voice dry. 'I understand.'

'And if you breathe a word of Old Darite,' Annev continued, his temper high, 'I will cut out your tongue and feed it to you.'

'Yes, of course. I understand. No tricks.'

'The same goes for any artifacts,' Annev warned, guessing that would be Honeycutt's next move. The artifacts and prepared glyphs that Annev seized or dismantled were secreted among the caste leader's possessions and clothing. He also found a sizeable sack of gold and silver among Honeycutt's belongings and that, too, disappeared into Annev's bottomless sack. But Annev still felt he had to be cautious: if he had missed any sigils, Honeycutt would simply need to invoke his will and speak a command word, and the Dionach would have the upper hand. The tables could turn fast and hard. 'No glyphs,' Annev repeated. 'No spells. No magic of any kind.'

'I have no—'

'*Enough*. I know when you're lying and I know when you're

672

pretending, so stop faking it. I can feel your anger – your contempt – so drop the mask.'

'And then what?' Honeycutt said, his tone shifting from simpering to sneering. 'You'll let me go? Or do you plan to hand me over to the Order?' He sniffed. 'I didn't kill those messengers, you know. That was Holyoak's doing – him and his little accomplices. If you're hunting for justice, you should look for them.'

'What *little accomplices*?'

'Dionach Chan.'

'And Dionach Davies?'

'Possibly. I don't know.'

That was true, Annev thought. *That's good. That gives me a baseline.*

'You should be thanking me for ending his life,' Honeycutt said, clutching his wounded fingers. 'He would have killed you if I hadn't intervened.'

'What are you talking about?' Annev asked, remembering the incident with the painting in his bedchamber. 'I saved myself!'

'You think Holyoak only tried to kill you *once*?' he scoffed derisively. 'You were lucky I was there to prevent the other attempts. Reeve would have *happily* sacrificed you, so long as it meant finding the assassins within his own order.'

'So, he *was* using me as bait.'

Honeycutt looked smug. 'Of course. Reeve would sacrifice anything to save his precious religion, to discover the traitors in his midst – even you.'

'Even me,' Annev repeated, knowing with a cold and undeniable certainty that Honeycutt spoke the truth. The Arch-Dionach had never held much affection for him or shown any interest in Annev beyond determining how he might benefit the Order. Before now, Annev had assumed his role as bait for the assassins was incidental – that it was a necessary risk or a tertiary benefit of some greater plan the Arch-Dionach had in mind – but now Annev wondered if he'd had it backwards.

'Think about it,' Honeycutt continued, implacable. 'Reeve's spent years trying to uncover those traitors ... and suddenly he had a target for them. Someone he knew they'd already tried to kill in Chaenbalu, and again in Luqura.' He leaned forward, his eyes bright with malice. 'So, Reeve brought you and your friends to Quiri, put you under his protection and made sure everyone saw you. He *wanted* you in plain sight of those traitors. And then he sat back, pretended to be disinterested and waited.' Honeycutt cackled. 'But they were too cunning. Holyoak had been above suspicion, and he could make others act on his behalf.'

'Like Dionach Leskal,' Annev said.

'And me,' Honeycutt continued. 'He didn't brainwash me, but he still used me. He stole that damn painting and would have framed me. If he had succeeded, Reeve would have turned his suspicions on me instead. Another distraction so he could continue to plot against you.'

'There were other attempts then.'

'Half a dozen, so far as I know. Some more serious than others. You dismantled quite a few on your glyph-hunts.'

The rings indicated the man was speaking the truth.

'I never knew.'

'You weren't supposed to know. My orders were to remain hidden – to collect information, to observe.'

'Orders? Whose orders?'

Honeycutt smiled – thin lips exposing his teeth, more unsettling than reassuring. At the same time, he began to ease himself into a more comfortable sitting position. On instinct, Annev flicked the flamberge towards the man's neck and Honeycutt gave him an exasperated look. 'Must I really spend this interrogation lying on my back?'

Annev studied the man's aura but saw no signs of subterfuge. He nodded, if reluctantly, and allowed the man to sit up.

'Thank the gods,' Honeycutt groaned after propping himself up on the narrow bed and mattress. 'Can I dress this wound?' He shook the stumps of his pinky and ring finger at Annev, both clutched in his other hand.

'Not until you convince me you're worth saving.'

'Fine,' Honeycutt puffed, his eyes burning with disdain. 'Mikael Holyoak served Neruacanta, the Terran God-king, on a two-fold

674

mission: to exterminate the Order of the Dionachs Tobar ... and to kill you.'

'I know,' Annev said, his voice cold. 'I asked who *you* work for.'

Honeycutt went silent, his eyes darting around the room as if searching for something – someone? – amidst the darkness. He was so earnest that Annev almost began to look, too. He caught himself at the last instant, and instead shifted his grip on the flamberge. If this was a trick, he'd be ready for it. Honeycutt seemed unaffected by the implied threat, though, and as the silence dragged on, Annev tried a different question. 'Holyoak said he'd been waiting centuries to find me,' he said at last. 'To *kill* me. Do you know anything about that?'

'Yes. More than you, it seems.' He smiled, a touch smug.

'Would you care to share?'

'Given that you cut off my fingers? No, not especially.'

Annev frowned. 'I could torture you, you know. I could force you to tell me.'

Honeycutt's gaze flicked to the tip of Annev's sword and back. 'I doubt it. You're not the torturing type.'

Annev glanced at the severed fingers laying beside the bed. 'There's a first time for everything,' he said, trying to make his voice sound hard.

Honeycutt laughed – he actually *laughed*. 'No,' he said, wiping tears from his eyes. 'I don't think so. Those capable of torture simply do it – no posturing, no talk – because they *like* it or because they have learned to endure it. The ones who don't? *They* threaten. If you were capable of torturing me, you'd have done it already.'

The tip of Annev's sword wavered then dipped towards the ground, and he chewed his cheek, fearing Honeycutt was right. Sensing Annev's hesitation, Honeycutt grew bold and eased his legs over the edge of the bed. 'I see you don't mean me any harm, and you should have guessed that my goal has been to protect you. So why not let me go? Better yet, why don't you come *with* me, and you can meet my master? Let him convince you of our mutual sincerity.'

Annev considered it, not out of any trust or mercy towards Honeycutt, but because it would take him to one of his hunters.

He could ask his questions, and he might finally get answers. Alternatively, he could use the Hand of Keos to rain fire and death down on his pursuers while they were together.

Don't be an idiot, he told himself. *You know how this will go if you agree. He will betray you, just like Kenton and Myjun did. He will use you, just like Reeve ... and Sodar. He is a liar and a traitor, and he is definitely not your friend.* Annev felt his temper rise and he tightened his grip on his sword. *He just wants to control me and my Keos-be-damned hand, and he protected me because his master needs me alive. He is not my friend ... and that means he is my enemy.*

'Arch-Dionach Reeve said Sodar's location was secret from everyone except Arnor,' Annev said, studying Honeycutt's aura even as he tried to read his mind. 'And that he would not have shared that information with anyone but his caste leader.' He raised the flamberge and pointed it at Honeycutt. 'Did you or your master send assassins to my village?'

Honeycutt's aura flared with a colour and brightness Annev did not recognise, yet he caught a word break through the man's mental defences: a single damning name.

Oyru.

'Arnor didn't tell me,' Honeycutt said, evasive, his aura flooded with anxiety. 'I did not know ... did not send anyone.'

A half lie.

'But you knew *who* he was visiting,' Annev said, filling in the blanks, 'and you shared that information with someone else. *They* sent the assassin.'

Oyru, Honeycutt's thoughts pulsed again, visible to Annev's magic scrying. 'I didn't.'

He was lying. Annev could read it in his aura, could see it in the pulse of his blood.

'Someone was sent, yes,' Honeycutt tried again, 'but you were not to be harmed.'

'*I* was not to be harmed ... but no such protections were afforded my friends. Your master sent *Oyru* to abduct me, which means *Dortafola* is your master. You answer to the First Vampyr, beloved of Keos ... and that makes you a member of the Siänar.'

Annev's eyes widened as the truth of it dawned on him. '*You* ... I know who you are. Who you *really* are.'

Honeycutt's eyes darted towards the exit then back to Annev's face. He would try to run, but not before attempting an incantation. Some hidden glyph or ward that he intended to activate. Now Annev knew, he could spot it. Hidden behind the bed and against the wall, its lines etched into the stone and then painted over with a sticky mixture of water and pine resin.

'Your name – your *real* name – is Valdemar Kranak. You're the ageless one who betrayed Neven nan Su'ul to the Terrans.'

Honeycutt shook his head, but both of Annev's rings told him he had the right of it. This man – this Dionach Tobar – was one of the first traitors to pledge himself to Dortafola and join the Siänar. Sodar's notes had a complete sketch of the man ... and he'd been hiding right under Arch-Dionach Reeve's nose. No wonder they hadn't seen it. No wonder they could never quite clean the rot from their Order. It had been so deep, had stretched back so far ...

'I didn't know Oyru would kill so many of your people,' Honeycutt repeated, hoping to distract Annev from his revelation. 'If Arnor had brought you out of the village—'

'Then Oyru would have abducted me after killing Arnor and Sodar.'

The Siänar's aura flashed with fear and guilt, and he moved at the same time, raising his hand as Annev brought his flamberge down hard. The blade sunk deep, severing Honeycutt's forearm near his elbow. At the same time, Annev smashed the golden fist of Keos into the man's jaw, shattering bone and spraying teeth and blood across the room.

Honeycutt fell in a heap on his mattress, gargling blood. Annev stepped over him, leaned close and smashed the glyph on the wall, destroying both the sigil and its magic.

'We're going to have a talk now,' Annev said, untying the rag around his neck. 'I'm going to use magic to keep you alive ... and we'll see just how good I am at this torture thing.'

Chapter Seventy-Two

Myjun ran her scaly fingers over her shorn scalp, caressed the blue-black chitin that covered her body – and smiled, not because it pleased her, though it did, but because the pain had been so deliciously sweet and unending. The ironwood armour now covered her in a tapestry of tight-fitting plates, each no bigger than a piece of coal. As promised, Oyru had completed the ritual by painting every joint, crack and crevice of her body with the ironwood ashes, turning the more supple parts of her a toughened grey-white. The result left her completely immune to cuts, scrapes and slashes while simultaneously leaving her movements unhindered. Heavy piercing and bludgeoning weapons could still harm her, though Oyru promised their lethality would be mostly mitigated by the armour, and the magic of her mask would still heal her – though its magic would be fuelled in less obvious ways.

And his promises held true.

For her, the trolls' teeth had lost their bite and the eidolons' claws held no sting. This angered her at first, for without the pain it was difficult to soulscream, though she could still channel the physical pain of her hunger into the mask, allowing her to heal and fight with supernatural stamina. It also meant that in the Shadowrealm, she would have to fuel her magics entirely with emotional pain, a task made harder by the shadows' innate ability to dampen her emotions. In most instances, she'd been able to summon soulfire sparks, but these were more akin to claws or talons than blades; and while they would injure the eidolons, she rarely conjured enough lightfire to burn out their eyes.

In the physical world, Myjun found her Ilumite magic even less reliable, with her emotional aura frequently drained to fuel her mask's Terran magic. To compensate for her lack of soulscreaming, Myjun leaned more heavily on the mask's magic to augment her strength, speed, and endurance. She became more feral, more cunning, and more confident in her battle instincts.

They spent several days in the mountains of Alltara, avoiding the umbras of the Shadowrealm and the witherkin that lurked there. Upon discovering a second, smaller herd of iron trolls, Oyru offered Myjun his void shards as weapons, but she declined them in favour of manipulating the beasts into smashing one another with their heavy ironwood clubs. At the assassin's instruction, she used Oyru's nether to shape the long bones of the trolls' forearms into a pair of wickedly curved blades, and the trolls' clubs into a pair of short ironwood staves. Using Myjun's blood as a binding agent, the pieces formed a pair of grisly sickles – foreign weapons that Oyru referred to as kamas.

'These weapons are the second secret of my clan,' the assassin said, 'though it is one shared with several other Kroseran families. Such tools were forged for every member of my household, but the women used kama in particular, to harvest grain and to battle other clans. I will teach you the katas, so you can adapt them to your own fighting style.'

'Will they work against the eidola?'

'They will, though not as effectively as your soulblades. More like my flyssas,' he said, summoning the two thin swords, 'able to injure the incorporeal eidola as well as more mundane creatures from the physical world.'

'Why do you not carry such weapons then?'

'I *do* carry them,' Oyru said, his twin swords waving indelicately in front of her nose. They vanished and were replaced by the assassin's broad-bladed short spear. 'But allow my own weapons to serve as a caution to you: when you have killed enough eidola with them, the Shadowrealm will start to reclaim the ironwood magic. My qiang and flyssas were once as solid as your kamas, but over time they've become more nethereal than real. I can summon and dispel them at will, and their forms are still potent in both realms ... but you may not be so fortunate. If your kamas ever begin to fade – if they seem to be more shade than steel – then their usefulness to you is at an end. It won't be long before they are reclaimed by the Shadowrealm.'

'Will they last until our return to Chaenbalu?'

'They will – and probably a score of years beyond that.'

'Then they will serve me fine. My only goal is to kill Annev.'

Oyru nodded, his qiang vanishing into smoke and mist. 'And when you have fulfilled your vendetta, what then? When your vengeance is satisfied ... will you stay with me? Will you become a companion among the Siänar?'

Myjun stared at the assassin, then at the grisly weapons in her hands. 'I do not wish to serve anyone – no man or half-man, no demon or vampyr, no god or demi-god. When Annev is dead, I will decide then where I go and what I do.'

'I do not ask you to *serve* me,' the Shadow Reborn persisted. 'I am offering you a purpose. And a home. As my equal.'

Myjun was unable and unwilling to hide the contempt in her voice. 'You serve Dortafola and he serves Keos. I will not serve *any* of you.'

Something shifted, deep in Oyru's gaze, but he kept any emotion from his voice, for his tone was all ice and apathy: 'Very well. When Annev is dead, I will release you from your servitude. When you have killed him, you may forge your own path.'

Myjun had not expected Oyru to concede the point so quickly.

'Come,' he said, gesturing to the rotting troll hides. 'I will show you how to make a belt for your weapons. You will not need sheaths since your skin is protected. I can also make garments to conceal your ironwood armour.'

'The belt is enough,' Myjun said, standing straight as a spear in the pre-dawn light. 'My new flesh scorns both the heat and the cold. When my enemies see me, they will hesitate. And if they believe I am vulnerable, they will underestimate me.'

'You speak the truth, but without the wisdom of experience. There are times you must pass among the sheep without alerting them to the wolf among the fold – and since you have not learned to bend the light into illusory clothing or shadows of invisibility, you must garb yourself in something more ... innocuous.'

Myjun suddenly realised what he was suggesting. 'I will not demean myself by wearing those troll hides. They smell like piss and dung, and that was before they started rotting.'

'True enough, but the hides are still special. They are saturated in the magics of the Shadowrealm, which makes them pliable to my magic.'

Myjun raised an eyebrow at this, realised the expression was lost behind her mask, and tilted her head in an exaggeration of emotion. 'If you can remove their stench and stitch something that is actually flattering, I might agree. Tell me, though. In addition to being a conjuror, are you also a tailor?'

Oyru bowed his head. 'An assassin must learn many skills, and while dealing death is my primary talent, it is not my only one.' He gestured to the hides. 'The clothes will be tasteful, you will see. Now, help me rend these.'

Myjun tried to maintain her meditative trance, but the knowledge of the coming umbra was too distracting. She finally popped open her eyes and stared into the darkness, waiting for the witherkin that she knew would come.

'You did well,' she said, grudgingly, stroking the velvety fabric she wore. 'I could not say it when we were in the Physical Realm – the mask ... makes saying such things difficult – but you did do well.'

Oyru's single eye slid open, his gaze piercing her to the soul. 'You are welcome, tabibito. You should resume your meditations, though. The witherkin will be here soon and then we will need to continue our walk to Takarania.'

'I was thinking,' Myjun said, rising from the ground. 'We should find a way to kill it. You said yourself: he is an echo from the Cognitive Realm – from the World of Dreams. So why not face him in the Dream World? Why not carry ourselves there in sleep, kill him and rid ourselves of this walking curse?'

Oyru's head was shaking before she had finished speaking. 'The Dream World is too dangerous, too difficult to navigate. I might never return us to Shadowrealm, much less the physical world.'

'So you will let this spectre chase us all the way back to Western Daroea? You will let him follow you across time and space?'

'I will outlast him,' the assassin said, unmoved by her tone. 'His spirit will tire of pursuing me and he will go of his own volition to the World of Spirits.'

'Why would he give up? *You* did not give up in Reocht na Skah.'

'My will is stronger than his. A chandler's ghost from a tiny village in the Brakewood? I will defeat him by outlasting him.'

'Then why not just kill him?'

'Because of the danger—'

'That's not it. I have never known you to shy from danger. Admit it. What prevents you from entering the Dream World?'

Oyru paused, his shoulders slumping half an inch. 'If I dream ... I will dream of *her*. I can fight the demons of this realm, but I cannot withstand those I summon from within.'

'But I will be with you,' Myjun said, stepping up and pulling him to his feet. 'I will be there – and if there are demons we cannot face alone, we will face them together.'

Oyru studied her, his single eye intent on the eyes behind her expressionless mask. 'We would go together? We would face her and the witherkin ... together.'

'Yes.'

'And what of your own demons? You will encounter your own nightmares there.'

'And you will help me kill them.'

Something softened in the assassin's expression. 'On the next umbra, we will go.'

'Why not now?'

Oyru gestured to the mist coalescing behind her. 'Because the witherkin is already here.'

Chapter Seventy-Three

'Absolutely not.'

The hefty Shieldbearer placed her hands on her hips and stared daggers at whichever boy dared to look at her. 'Arch-Dionach Reeve has given strict instructions. No one is to leave the Enclave under any circumstances.' She scowled at both of them. 'You'll be here until this whole mess has been sorted out.'

'But we have permission from Arch-Dionach Reeve!' Therin protested, pulling the forged slip of paper from his travel pack. It had been Therin's own idea, one of which he was especially proud. He'd guessed – quite correctly, as it happened – that forgery wasn't one of the skills taught at an Enclave where telepathy was so prevalent, and so he had obliged himself by breaking into the Arch-Dionach's study, unlocking his desk and pilfering a few samples from the high priest's writing drawer. In another stroke of luck, one piece of parchment had even held the Arch-Dionach's signature. In the end, though, it had been Titus and not Therin who had successfully copied the Arch-Dionach's scrawl. Shortly thereafter, they had drafted the letter of permission that Therin now held out to Sister Agatha.

The pair watched the Dionach take the folded piece of parchment and scrutinise its contents, her expression dubious. As she did so, Titus felt his insides twist into a knot.

'Now why would the High Priest be sending children with notes when he could just as easily send me a mental note with a bit of stormcalling, hmm?'

'Ah …' Therin swallowed, stalling for time. 'He, uh …'

'Said he'd have his mental walls up,' Titus jumped in. 'During his interrogations. He didn't want to be interrupted repeatedly for this.' And the truth was, that slip of paper had already got them past two Dionachs. Sister Agatha was the toughest yet, though. She spent another full minute reading and rereading the scrawled note before fixing her bloodshot eyes on the two youths.

'You must understand, *Brother*,' she hissed, making her sentiments about Titus's elevation clear, 'the repercussions of letting you go without first consulting the High Priest.' She snorted. 'Arch-Dionach Reeve is already on the war path. He'll skewer anyone for even a hint of treason. If I let you and your friend here walk away *now*, in the middle of his interrogations, I'd be stripped of my rank and condemned as a traitor.' She sniffed and ripped the forgery into pieces in front of them.

'No!' Therin wailed.

'My orders are to keep you and the rest of the Order *here*. Inside the Enclave.' Agatha folded her arms, her immense bulk blocking the passage. Therin tried to peek around her wide figure, but the Dionach just shook her head. 'Those doors are shielded, boys. No one is sneaking out, so if you want to leave this way, Reeve himself will have to vouchsafe for you – in person.' She jerked her double chin at them. 'Now go on. Back to your studies.'

Titus clutched his pack and spun on his heel, his round cheeks already bright with embarrassment. Therin was slower to follow, earning himself a hard glare from Sister Agatha.

'What now?' Titus squeaked once they were out of earshot. 'This place is locked up tighter than a wine barrel ever since Annev escaped. The windows and doors are sealed. There are guards on every floor ... I don't see a way out of it!'

'Do you still want to go to Banok?'

Titus nodded. 'Brayan's trapped there because we never went back for him or sent him word ... it's our fault he's there.'

Therin frowned. 'We don't *know* he's still there. He could have escaped that siege altogether.'

'You don't know Brayan like I do. He keeps his word – plus, he promised to help Mistress Dolyn.'

'It's been months now. Surely her hands have healed, and

Brayan would have decided he's better off coming to Luqura to look for us?'

Titus hesitated and Therin slapped a hand on his shoulder, his suspicions raised. 'Hold on there. What aren't you telling me?'

Titus's pink cheeks flushed to bright red. 'I ... um ... I've been keeping an eye on him.'

'On Brayan? You've been mindwalking?' Therin's eyes went wide. 'All the way to Banok?' Titus nodded and Therin's eyes went wider still. 'Holy hells, Titus! I didn't think it was possible at that kind of distance.'

Titus smiled weakly. 'I don't think it's supposed to be. Brother Tym said he can pull thoughts from people outside of Quiri if he knows them well enough and has a fair idea of where they are, but Banok is way outside his range. If both people are Mindwalkers it's a bit easier, but ... yeah.'

'I'll be damned. You're full of surprises, aren't you?'

Titus shrugged. 'I don't see how it helps. Brayan is still in trouble, and we still can't help him.'

'What kind of trouble? What have you seen?'

'We'd been here for about a month when I realised I could hear Brayan's thoughts. It was an accident. He was reading a letter from Arch-Dionach Reeve saying we'd been taken to Quiri and that everything was fine. He was so relieved, and thinking about us just as I was thinking about him and ... well, we connected. I knew his thoughts like they were my own. Didn't realise what I was doing at first, but I was mindwalking ... by mistake.'

'Without any glyph work?' Therin scoffed. 'You're sure you didn't imagine it?'

Titus gave the older boy a withering look. 'Have you ever mindwalked?'

'Er ... no.'

'Then don't assume I'm stupid. I hate it when you do that.'

'Right.' Therin looked chagrined. 'Sorry.'

'It's fine. Now believe me when I say I heard Brayan's thoughts.'

'But without glyph work – and from Banok!' He shook his head but stopped just short of questioning Titus again. 'Wish I could do that. I'm rubbish without a good glyph to focus on.' He paused. 'What's that like then? Like you hear his thoughts or what?'

Titus wobbled his head. 'It's not always the same – and it's not as simple as breathbreaking.' Therin snorted at this, but Titus continued. 'Just think about it: when you breathbreak, you're working with air and water. They might resist you, but their resistance will always be the same. Not so with mindwalking. It always depends on whether the person is open to your influence or not. If they're resistant, I'll have a bear of a time. But if they don't care – or don't know what I'm about, or if they're thinking about me – it's like an invitation to listen in. *This* connection was different, though. It was like ... like I was physically transported into his mind. Like I was right there in the room with him.'

Therin whistled, impressed. 'So what did you see?'

'Brayan had just sat down to supper with Mistress Dolyn and they were talking about the letter, which got Brayan thinking about us. Dolyn started asking him about the village and the Academy, and he was talking about me and my apprenticeship and ... I don't know. He seemed *well*. Happy even.'

'So ... that's good isn't it?'

'It was. But the next time was different. I think he was sick because Mistress Dolyn was tending to him, not the other way around. He was deep in a fever dream, which made it hard to connect with him anyway. I'd been practising my mindwalking and the connection sort of sucked me in.'

'Silver staves,' Therin swore. 'Still without any glyph work?'

'That time I did have a glyph. I was supposed to practise attacking Dionach Honeycutt's mental fortress, but then I felt Brayan and I just sort of ...' He passed his hand through the air and made a whooshing sound. 'I got pulled in – or I pulled *him* in.'

'And you think that aligns with the invasion of Banok?'

Titus nodded. 'He was in a bad way, Therin. He ... he might have been dying.'

'Keos, Titus! Why didn't you tell me?'

'Would it have made a difference?' Titus asked, feeling both defensive and guilty. 'I wanted to tell you – and Annev – but we'd

686

just sworn our oaths to the Brotherhood and everything was so complicated. Annev started acting strangely, and we were both busy with our training.' He took a deep breath then exhaled. 'I did tell Dionach Holyoak about it, and he said he'd tell Reeve.'

'Oh,' Therin said, the one word speaking volumes.

'Yeah.' They were both silent, each thinking through the depth and ramifications of Dionach Holyoak's betrayal.

'Anyway,' Titus said, 'I had trouble reaching Brayan after that, so I didn't have any news to share. I assumed Reeve had taken care of it – that he'd asked someone to look into it – but now I don't think Holyoak ever spoke to him.' He chewed his bottom lip, frowning. 'This is all my fault. If Brayan is dying – if he's dead – then it's because I didn't make sure help was sent.'

'Come on, Titus,' Therin chided. 'You can't think like that. Being able to read the thoughts of someone in another kingdom doesn't make you responsible for them.'

Titus chewed his thumb, unconvinced. 'I just … I feel guilty that we left him there, you know?'

Therin nodded slowly. 'I know what you mean.'

'You do?'

'Well, not about Brayan but … you remember when we saw Faith's ghost?'

The younger boy's eyes went wide. 'I try not to. It was so … strange.'

'Exactly! It was so real – in the woods and then again in Banok – but we haven't seen her since. It's like … I don't know. While we've been here in Quiri, I keep thinking of her. Wondering if maybe we should have stayed.'

They had stopped in a corridor on an upper floor and were just a few doors down from Sraon's bedchamber. Without thinking, Therin stopped in front of the blacksmith's door and knocked.

'What are you doing?' Titus asked.

Therin waited. Silence. He knocked again. When there was no answer, he tried the door handle. Locked.

'What are you doing?' Titus repeated, looking over his shoulder to see if anyone else was in the hall. 'Sraon's in the sanatorium.'

687

'I know. Just wanted to make sure he wasn't back yet.' Therin removed a set of lock-picking tools from his tunic and set to work on the door. 'The Shieldbearers have sealed all the doors and windows, but maybe they forgot about the one in Sraon's room.'

'Suppose they did. How would we get down?'

Therin held up a pair of carved rune stones he wore around his neck. 'I can use these to push us off the walls and the ground.'

Titus looked dubious. 'But ... that's how Annev escaped. The Brothers will have thought of a way to prevent that.'

'Do you have a better idea?' The door clicked open and Therin tucked his tools away. 'Let's be quick.'

They ducked inside and Titus shut the door behind them, re-locking the door. At the other side of the room, Therin had passed the neatly made bed and hustled over to the shuttered window. He tried to throw the shutters open. 'Dammit.'

'What?' Titus asked, sidling up next to him.

'It's shielded.' He reached out and placed his fingers on the wood, only to lower them a moment later. He spat. 'Wall of air.'

'So that's it then,' Titus said, his shoulders slumping. 'We can't get out.'

'Not necessarily.' Therin's gaze shifted to the side and he grinned with mischief. 'No one is physically guarding this way out of the Enclave, so this is still our best chance of escaping.'

'What about the ward?'

'I can use my magic to counteract it.'

'You mean ... dispel the shield?'

Therin nodded. 'They painted the glyph on the other side of the shutters, closed them, then activated it. That's clever, since I can't just deface the glyph, but I can still use the expanding force of my Breathbreaker magic to counteract the condensing force of the Shieldbearer's glyph.'

'Maybe,' Titus said, his gaze alternating between the closed door and the shielded window, 'but the Dionach who prepared that spell will know if it fails. They'll send someone to investigate.'

'So we'll have to be quick. Get out the window before they get here.'

'And if they send someone down to the ground at the same time?' Titus shook his head. 'This isn't a good plan, Therin. These people know their magic. They've *thought* of this. If they don't want us to escape, we aren't going to find a way out.'

'Annev got out,' Therin said, his tone taking a dark turn. 'He got out without a lick of Darite magic.'

'He had his artifacts, though – and he left before they tightened security on the—'

'Odar's balls! Do you want to get to Banok or not, Titus?'

His jaw clenched and his lips pursed into a frown. 'Yes. I'm going to find out what happened to Brayan. I promised I'd help him. We're going.'

'Good.' The other boy reached into his pack, withdrew a brush, and uncorked a small bottle of ink. He dipped the bristles into the black liquid, then deftly painted the counter glyph onto the interior shutters. When he was finished, he replaced the glyph-making tools in his pack and whispered the activation word. The shutters pulsed and Titus felt a blast of wind rush over his skin. Therin stepped over to the window, touched the shutters and swung them wide open. 'See?' he said, hefting his pack and climbing onto the windowsill. 'Simple.'

Titus's eyes were distant. 'Someone's coming,' he whispered. 'Running up the stairs right now!'

'Blood and ashes. Come on!' Therin licked the surface of one rune stone hanging around his neck then tipped over the window ledge and dropped out of sight.

Titus leaned out the window to see Therin speed towards the ground, then slow before gently touching down to the earth. He looked up and beckoned for his friend to join him.

Titus took a deep breath and worked up the nerve to climb onto the window ledge, then was startled when the Dionach reached Sraon's locked door. The priest twisted the handle, swore, then pounded on the door. 'I know you're in there!' he shouted. 'Stop right now! We have brothers waiting below your window!'

Titus glanced back outside and saw Therin was still alone on the street below. The others hadn't reached the street ... but they would soon.

Titus clutched his possessions tight and leapt, praying to Odar and any other god that might hear him as the ground rushed up to meet him – and he realised he'd made the biggest and final mistake of his life.

A rush of wind thrust up from the ground, abruptly slowing his descent. *Praise Odar!* Titus thought – and then he slammed into the earth, the air suddenly knocked from his lungs.

'Sorry!' Therin shouted, clambering to help the stocky boy to his feet. 'I didn't account for how solid you are. My weight's spread out and you're … more compact.'

Titus rose to his hands and knees then stood on wobbly feet. 'I'm alive, at least,' he wheezed, still catching his breath. 'We need to go … they're coming.'

Therin gave a wolfish grin. 'They'll have to catch us then – and we've got an advantage.'

'How's that?'

'Because they're just mages – and *we* are avatars.'

'Steward,' Titus mumbled, tapping a thumb to his chest. 'But never mind. Lead the way.'

'I will, but first …' Therin spat on the other rune stone hanging from his neck then whispered a few words of Old Darite. The boy seemed to rise an inch above the ground, then Titus felt his own bulk floating above the earth.

'Use the tips of your shoes to push off the ground and the walls. It's a bit like ice skating on the mill pond. We won't leave any tracks and we'll move a lot faster.' Without another word, Therin skated off into one of the alleys surrounding the Enclave.

Titus took a moment to gather his bearings then took a hesitant, sliding step towards his fleeing companion, and then another. As he darted around the corner, he heard the shout of the Dionach Tobar who had finally burst into Sraon's room. Before the anonymous brother could glimpse Titus, though, he had already skated ahead and caught up with his companion.

Chapter Seventy-Four

Therin gestured to the narrow sloop tied to the dock, its captain studying them from beneath the shadow of his main sail. 'We can afford this one,' Therin said, keeping his voice low. 'He says he can leave right now, too.'

'And he'll sail us all the way to Luqura?'

Therin nodded. 'I say we take it. I've got the coppers and we don't have time to haggle.'

Titus's expression was dubious. 'I don't like it, Therin. It ... just feels wrong.'

'What would you have us do instead? Swim all the way to Banok? The river doesn't go that far, anyway – and I'm sure as hell not walking. Blood of Odar, Titus! It's screamin' hot out here and we don't have a lot of options.'

Titus glanced at the riverboat captain. He tried to glean his thoughts – to mindwalk with him – but something was off. Then he tried his trick with Arch-Dionach Reeve – the one where he hummed a bit to get a sense of the man's feelings – and Titus felt as though his spirit were brushing up against a storm cloud.

'It feels wrong,' he repeated.

Therin sniffed. 'Feelings? You're not mindwalking right now. You're just antsy because we're being chased – and I'm telling you this is our best chance of getting to Banok in one piece.'

Titus chewed his lip and glanced over his shoulder, looking east towards the Enclave. They *did* need to hurry – the brothers would be there soon, and they couldn't afford to delay their departure any longer. Maybe a compromise?

'Fine. We can take the boat, but not all the way to Luqura. We'll get off at the next port – just far enough to outrun the Brotherhood – and then we'll find a new route. A different ship or a caravan wagon or something.'

Therin groaned, clearly wanting to argue the point yet choosing to hold his tongue. 'Whatever you *want*. Just get on the bloody sloop!'

Titus took a step towards the gangplank, locked eyes with the ship's pale captain and raised a hand in greeting. 'Ahoy! Permission to come aboard, Captain ...?'

'Norton,' the stout sailor answered. 'Rondeth Norton, but Norton's good enough. Or captain.' He gestured to Therin. 'This one says you've the coin for it and you're fixing to leave soon.' He peered over Titus's shoulder, first at Therin and then back towards the city – towards the Enclave. 'This all of you?'

'It is,' Therin said, stepping up to join Titus on the gangplank. 'Is that a problem?'

The captain seemed to chew the question over in his mouth. Finally, he gave a slow turn of his head. 'Not a problem. Just ... thought you might have another one with you.'

Titus glanced at Therin, feeling even more on edge, but his friend purposefully ignored him.

'Just us, Captain Norton.' Therin looked up and down the boat. 'Any other crew with you?'

The pirate – for that's how he seemed to Titus – sucked his teeth and glanced sidelong at the ship's cabin. 'Might do, might do – but I can sail this ship myself if needs be. She's only a forty-footer. I could do sixty in a pinch, though I might need an extra hand when it comes to docking.' He chuckled as if he'd just shared some private joke then ambled over to the opposite side of the ship.

'So ... he *does* have more crew with him?'

Therin watched the captain go, glanced back at Titus and shrugged. 'I think so? Seemed a bit evasive, though.'

'Yes.' Titus watched as the captain began to crank the windlass, his broad shoulders heaving with each turn of the crank. 'Listen, Therin—'

'I know, I know. You don't feel good about this.' He sucked in a deep breath then let it out, looking flustered. 'We don't really have a choice, Titus. Not unless you're fine with the Brotherhood dragging us back to the Enclave.' He glanced back at the dock as though he were expecting the Dionachs to suddenly appear behind them.

'I haven't got all day!' the captain shouted, 'and you boys aren't paying me enough to sit around and wait for you.'

Therin stepped onto the ship and Titus grudgingly followed. 'Titus,' Therin said, once they'd stepped clear of the gangplank and the bustling captain. 'Could you mindwalk with him a bit? Just to be safe?'

Titus raised an eyebrow, a tiny smile tugging at the corner of his mouth. 'Having second thoughts?'

Therin snorted. 'You're the one who said this didn't feel right. Don't pin this on me.'

Titus's smile vanished. 'Truth is I've been trying to read him since you pointed him out. His mind seems a bit muddled, though. Not a lot of coherence.'

'Is that normal?'

'Not exactly,' Titus said, already regretting their decision to board the boat. 'I usually see it with non-adepts who are trying to keep me from reading them – like the brothers at the Enclave.' He frowned then turned his attention to the cabin, exploring with his mind to see if he sensed others below deck. 'There *are* people down there, Therin – more than one. They're thinking about ...' He paused, uncertain. Was that right? Were they really thinking about *Annev*?

Titus dropped to the deck, snatched the bamboo water brush from his tunic and began to trace the glyph for mindwalking. When he was finished, he focused his attention on the glyph, spoke the activation word and redirected his mental focus towards the men below ship. It took a moment to focus, not having seen the men in person nor knowing anything personal about them, but their proximity made it easier for Titus to sense their intentions, and they weren't making any attempt to hide their thoughts.

... understand why they won't let us kill ...

... bet that golden hand would ...

... only need to keep the one. The others can ...

... all this business with Terrans. We ought to ...

'Therin!' Titus whispered, though it felt more like a shout. 'We have to get off this ship. Right. Now.'

'What!' Therin hissed, also whispering. 'Why?'

They both turned at the sound of Captain Norton hauling up the gangplank. The stout man turned and gave them a sinister grin. 'Get comfortable, boys. We've got a long journey ahead. You should pop down to that cabin and get yourselves some shut eye.'

Titus suddenly felt as though he'd been stung by a stumble-stick. 'This is ... I mean, we're fine up here.'

The pirate's eyes narrowed. 'Oh, I insist. Much easier to navigate without you two in the way. Just head down those steps there and we'll push out.' The barrel-chested man slipped behind the wheel without taking his eyes off them.

Therin swallowed. 'What's below?'

'Men. Who want to kill us, I think.'

'Keos,' Therin breathed. 'I should have listened to you. Let's jump ship then.'

'Not the time,' he whispered. 'Can you reach the dock from here?'

Therin nodded. 'We only just pulled away. I can ... oh, hells.'

'What?' Titus followed Therin's gaze and saw four Dionachs Tobar trying to blend in with the crowd, scanning the dock workers and ships' decks.

'We can't jump ship now,' Therin whispered, his eyes darting between the Dionachs at the docks and Captain Norton behind the ship's wheel. 'They'll see us. We have to stay here.'

Titus shook his head vigorously. 'Those men below deck ... Therin, they'll *kill* us!'

A hard look settled over Therin's usually insouciant features. 'Then we'll have to attack them first. They'll find they can't surprise us, and we're going to cheat.' He forced a grin and wiggled his fingers. 'We've got magic now, right? And we're no slouches when it come to a fight.'

Titus wasn't so sure about that last part, but he kept his doubts to himself. 'There's four of them down there, I think. Can you take that many?'

Therin hesitated. 'I might be able to push the air from the cabin – make a void where they can't breath – but I'd need to hold it long enough for them to pass out, and that would use up most of my *quaire*. I used a lot of it getting us away from the Brotherhood.'

'Yeah, that's what I was afraid of.' Titus paused, neither one willing to admit that they weren't confident in their own martial abilities. 'I, uh . . . I might be able to do something. Dionach Holyoak and Brother Tym were teaching me some advanced mindwalking techniques. The ones where we pull so hard people's thoughts can actually be ripped free of their minds – mind-leeching. Makes them forget things – at least for a little while.'

'That's . . . well, that's downright frightening. How does it help us, though?'

A plan was forming in Titus's mind. 'The better question might be what we do once we've subdued the men.'

'You don't want to kill them?'

Titus was taken aback. 'No! I mean . . . why? Did you want to?'

'Not if we can avoid it. So . . . what do we do?'

Titus looked back at the fat pirate who was still eyeing them suspiciously. 'If I can glean some information from Captain Norton, I might be able to get us farther downriver.'

'Ah, hold on. You want to *sail* the ship? By yourself?'

'I'd have your help.'

'That's not really an advantage,' Therin said, his face turning a sickly shade of green. 'Keos, it's like when those slavers held us in Luqura.'

Titus shared the feeling. 'We need to stall long enough to leave the bay and begin sailing upriver. If we can do that, we might be able to subdue the men below deck and take over the ship ourselves.'

'Corruption of Keos. You really think we can do it?' The dock was now pulling comfortably away from them.

'Well . . . worst-case scenario, you can float us back to the shore, right?'

Therin shrugged. 'Maybe? If I can do that, though, I may as well try to suffocate the men below deck.'

'It might come to that,' Titus said, handing Therin a canteen from his pack. 'We'd still need to sail the ship, though, and I'm not sure I can get all I need from Captain Norton in time.' He stifled a whimper. 'Just tell me you can get us to shore if we need to jump ship in a hurry.'

Therin took a long swig then nodded. 'I can probably do that. We'll probably get wet along the way, but I can draw *quaire* from the ocean if I have to.'

'Boys?' The pair turned to see Captain Norton fiddling with the mainsail, his head cocked as if he'd been listening in on their conversation. 'You should get below deck before we reach the river mouth. Gets a bit treacherous there.'

'Don't you want our coin first?' Therin asked, jingling his purse.

The captain raised an eyebrow. 'Aye, I suppose I would. Why don't you bring me those coppers now?'

Therin had taken a step towards Norton when the cabin door swung open and two men climbed up to the deck. The first had the swarthy skin of an Innistiul slaver and a long moustache that dropped over his upper lip and merged with his sideburns, leaving his chin and jaw clean-shaven. The second man was paler than the captain, with two long scars on his face – one that swept over his nose and twisted his upper lip, and a second that creased his forehead and left eyebrow. He squinted at Therin, and Titus realised he wore a painted glass eye in his left socket.

'Mates,' the captain growled. 'You were to stay below deck till we reached the river.'

'Aye,' the scarred man said, his tongue tracing the tips of his yellow teeth. 'Got a bit stuffy down there. Came up for some air.'

Norton grunted. 'Stow that coin for now, lad. I'll collect it later.'

Therin hurried back to Titus, keeping a careful distance from the two sailors on deck. 'What are they thinking now?'

'The one with the moustache wants to take us below deck. Tie us up. Maybe try to sell us in Luqura. The other one ...' Titus paled, tears welling in his eyes. 'We need to go *now*, Therin. Before we get too far away from the docks.' He shuddered, glancing back at the scarred pirate. 'We can't stay here.'

Therin swore again, looked at his rune stones, and squinted at the shore they were rapidly sailing away from. 'We should go now then. If we land there' – he pointed at the shore between the seaside docks and where the mouth of the Tocra emptied into the ocean – 'we'll be far enough away from the Brotherhood that they aren't likely to see us jump ship.'

Titus nodded, his expression fierce. 'Float us about halfway. We can swim the rest.'

'You sure?'

'Yes. If you use up your *quaire*, you won't have the stamina to swim yourself the rest of the way. Halfway is good enough – and you don't need to keep us above the water. We'll be getting wet no matter what.'

'Right,' Therin said, his eyes a bit wild. 'You ready?'

'Hey! Get away from that rail!' Captain Norton stepped in their direction and the other toughs leapt to follow him.

'Now!' They launched themselves from the deck, their arms windmilling as they plummeted towards the surf. Titus hit the water with a tremendous crash a second before Therin and was sucked under by the ocean current. He coughed, spinning beneath the churning waves, then felt something push him back towards the surface. He rose from the depths, choking out saltwater, and spotted Therin hovering just beside him.

'Come on!' Therin said, reaching out his hand. 'It's easier if I'm only moving one mass.'

'You little shits!' Someone was shouting from the stern of the sloop, which was speeding away. 'You're dead! You hear me, boys? You're *dead*!'

Neither boy looked back. Instead, Titus grasped Therin's forearm and pulled himself upward. He rose halfway and Therin sank to meet him, their legs dangling below the surf as they cut through the water.

Therin grimaced. 'You need to lose some weight, Titmouse.'

'I'm working on it,' Titus barked, still clutching tight to his

697

friend. 'And if you call me that again, I swear I'll punch you in the kidney.'

Therin snorted but didn't push his luck. 'Sorry, Titus.'

'I mean it, Therin. No more.'

'All right.'

'And when we get to shore, *I'm* picking the ride to Banok. I'll use my Mindwalker magic. Either way, you're not in charge any more. Got it?'

Therin squinted at Titus, one hand clutching his friend, the other shielding his eyes from the spray of the surf. Finally, he nodded. 'You got it, Titan.'

Titus scoffed at the new nickname, but this time he didn't correct his friend.

Chapter Seventy-Five

It was three days before Fyn and Sodja returned to the Ashes lair, having acquired an intimate knowledge of one another, from the physical scars they hid from the world to the emotional scars they hid from themselves. Neither could define what they had now, but they both knew it was precious, and worth protecting. Neither dared say as much, for fear that doing so might shatter their delicate and evolving relationship.

So, when they finally returned to the lair, it was with some underlying anxiety that their companions might somehow perceive their new relationship and force them to talk about something neither had the power or desire to articulate.

But they needn't have worried. Only Sanhueza was there to greet them.

'Way?' Fyn said as they emerged unchallenged from the upper tunnels. 'Where is everyone?'

The sneakthief sat at the battered table nursing a cup of thick dark liquid, its scent so potent Fyn knew it had to be Black Gambit, a spicy sweet nobleman's drink that singed the hair off one's nostrils. Fyn hadn't much cared for it – the taste of molasses was too strong, and he preferred drinks that were less likely to kill him – but Way, Sodja and Neldon had developed a taste for the stuff after trying the barrels Saltair had left behind.

'They're all gone,' Way said, taking another sip.

'Gone where?' Sodja asked.

'Gone all places,' Way said, his speech just a tiny bit slurred. 'Quinn woke about two days ago. Started on about how we let you go. Me and Ned told her to lay off and she boxed his ears.' He sniggered at that and took another nip. 'She cooled down yesterday – and by that, I mean she wasn't swearing to drink your blood – but she still didn't want nothin' to do with you or any o' your plans. Said she was done playin' at politics an' told me and Ned to bugger off.'

'Where did she go?' Fyn asked. 'And where are Neldon, Siege and Poli?'

'Quinn got it in her head she needed to steal back her family's boat. Got Siege and Poli to help after she promised to make them chief mate or boatswain or some rot like that. Tried to get Neldon an' me to come, too, but I said I was waitin' for you to go after the slavers in the Pits. Neldon wouldn't reply – said he needed to take a walk. That was last night, I think. Woke up this morning and Neldon was still gone. Quinn said she weren't waiting no longer and took off with the rest of the crew, and that left me alone with ol' Gambit here.' He slapped the nearest barrel and a tot of the syrupy stuff sloshed out of his mug onto the table.

'Kraik and Keos,' Sodja whispered, 'she's already gone to steal the *Lapin!*'

'That was about sunrise, though,' Way said, taking another nip from his mug, 'so they've either stolen it and are sailin' around Helmstook by now – or they're dead.' He drained his cup to the dregs and, with a loud belch, slapped it atop the battered door they used for a table. 'I, for one, am entertaining both notions, which means they've either stolen the boat and died or they died *then* stole the boat, which makes them kind of ghost pirates.'

'Way,' Fyn said, 'you're drunk.'

'I've been drunk before, and this feels different.'

'You're *very* drunk.'

'That could be it.'

Sodja cursed again. 'We need to find them before they do something stupid.'

'And him?' Fyn asked, jerking a thumb at Way. 'He's not safe to be alone right now.'

'Ballocks,' Way spat. 'I'm better off than them ghost pirates.'

'He comes with us,' Sodja said. 'We might need his help.'

Fyn frowned at the drunken thief. 'What kind of help would he be?'

'A lot, once I cleanse the poison from his body.'

'Cleanse?' Way slurred. 'I don't need a bath.' He sniffed his armpit then grimaced, a groan slipping from his molasses-stained lips. 'Might be I do.'

'Step back,' Sodja said to Fyn. He did so and she spun her hands in front of her chest, black threads of shadow appearing as she did. Within a few seconds, the shadows had surrounded her hands and arms, their colour and shape gradually shifting until her limbs seemed almost two-dimensional. More shadows flocked to her hands and fingers, their threads like thin streams of smoke, and then she began to weave them into a large net of tightly packed ash and charcoal. She approached Way and lifted the weave over his head. The thief stared up at it, goggle-eyed, as she brought it down over his body, its ephemeral fibres passing through him as easily as fingers sifting through sand. Way's expression changed as she passed over his head, chest and stomach. Sodja didn't stop there though, her arms continuing past Way's legs until they moved into the rock floor and she tugged the shadow weave through the soles of his feet.

Way gasped in surprise, the colour draining from his cheeks. 'Gods be good! What is that?' He blinked, panting, and Fyn saw his glassy look was gone.

Sodja carefully folded the black shade up into a ball. As she did so, her arms began to regain their three-dimensional shape and flesh tones. After a few more seconds, the ball of shadow was smaller than her fist, a dark grey sponge in her ghostly white hands. A final squeeze forced a sticky stream of coal-black syrup over her hands to dribble onto the floor. Sodja peeled this residue from her skin like a pair of thin oily gloves and then tossed the shrivelled black things to the floor.

'How do you feel?' she asked, dusting her hands on her trousers.

'Unpleasantly sober.'

'Good. Grab your things. If we're lucky, we'll find Quinn and the others before they make a huge mistake.'

'What about Neldon?' Fyn asked. 'Shouldn't we wait for him?'

'Who says he's coming back?'

'He will,' Way said, rubbing his temples. 'Neldon's not the type to cut and run.'

'Be that as it may, we don't have time to wait if we're to help Quinn, Siege and Poli.' She pointed to Way. 'Drink some water and I'll give you something for that headache. Let's move.'

It was late evening by the time Way, Sodja and Fyn reached the northern lock where they had last seen the *Lapin*. The ship was gone, but some quick work with the Rod of Compulsion revealed it had sailed east upriver, towards the Artisan Quarter. They searched the docks on both sides of the Tocra as dusk fell. The waning light made their hunt more difficult, but Sodja continued on as though her eyes were unaffected. This was confirmed when they entered the long-term docks just as twilight receded and full dark fell, for Fyn had stood squinting in the darkness until Sodja led them, straight as a bowshot, to the three-masted vessel. Only when they were closer could Fyn see the whitewashed image of a leaping rabbit seared into the boat's hull, overlapped by the painted silhouette of a flying crow. He moved closer but Sodja laid a hand atop his shoulder.

'Stop. There are four soldiers on deck, with crossbows.'

Fyn looked back at the vessel, squinting, then stepped back into the shadows of the nearest galleon. 'I didn't see the guards. You must have incredible eyesight – or are you using shadow magic?'

Sodja gestured at the galleon behind them, with the same flying crow painted on its hull. 'Most of the ships anchored here are owned by my family – and yes, there may have been a little magic involved.'

'This a good thing, right?' Way asked. 'I mean, if there are guards on deck, Quinn probably hasn't found the ship.'

'It seems that way,' Fyn said, 'but think about it. We found the boat in a few hours – in the dark, no less – and Quinn's had the whole day to search. So either she gave up and decided not to go back to the lair or ...'

'Or she found it and everything went to hell.' Way stared at the starlit image of the whitewashed rabbit and swore. 'So what do we do? Search the *Lapin*?'

'I don't think so,' Sodja said, still studying the guards. 'Whatever trouble they ran into, it probably happened hours ago.'

'So where would she be?'

'My guess,' Sodja said, her lips pursed, 'is that they were captured or killed. If they're dead, the sailors would've tied stones to their ankles and dropped them in the river. If they're alive, the dockmaster would've brought them to the master of the River District.'

'You mean Archon Kranak,' Way said, his expression grim. 'Rot and dreck – he'll skin them alive!'

'Only if they're lucky,' Sodja said, no less sombre. 'He might bring in the Watchers.'

'Cracking hells,' Fyn swore. 'Are you saying your brother, Rista, might have them?'

'I don't know ... maybe we're worrying for nothing. I don't know Quinn that well. If there's a chance she'd abandon—'

'They've got her,' Way said, his tone adamant. 'Siege and Poli, too. They'll have followed her – and she's never been the type to back down from a challenge, or forgive a debt, or make a plan. She likes to run headlong into things.'

'Let's assume the worst,' Fyn said, his hands itching to draw steel. 'If Elar has them, where would he take them? Somewhere in the River District?'

'No,' Sodja answered. 'Too many eyes at the docks – too many witnesses *anywhere* along the river. Even if half the city guard is in the Guild's pocket, there are officials who would love to put Elar's head on a pike given the faintest proof. If it's work Rista can't take home with him, there's only one place he'd go to torture someone, and no one will ask questions.'

'The Boneyard,' Fyn said, remembering his last encounter with the slave merchant.

'Exactly.'

'Rot my bones, Sodja. We have to go there *now*?' Way shivered. 'I can barely face the Boneyard in the daylight. It's straight out of a nightmare – and it only gets worse after sundown!'

'I know,' Sodja said, her expression calm. 'That's why Elar will take Quinn, Siege and Poli there. And it's where we'll find Rista.'

Way looked at Fyn. 'You gonna do this?'

'I've done it before, against Elar no less, and I'm still standing.' He didn't think it wise to mention that, had it not been for Jian Nikloss's intervention, he likely wouldn't be here to tell of it. Instead, he put on a brave face and tried to mask his fear. 'Quinn is your friend, right? Siege and Poli, too.' He looked at Sodja. 'They're family.' She met his gaze and he felt something pass between them. Something that resonated with the thing they didn't dare articulate – except maybe he just had. Fyn looked at Way and saw he had also struck a chord with the old thief.

'Silver staves, but I'll be damned if I leave family behind. Let's *go*! We need to hoof it back to the Ashes if we're going to be any help to them.'

'Too slow by half,' Sodja said. 'We'll take the river. We'll save our strength that way, and we'll still get there faster.'

'The river?' Way frowned. 'You have a sloop hidden in your pocket?'

'No.' She pointed at the Gwyin family's old galleon. 'I've got a vessel floating in the water, though.'

'We can't *steal* that, much less sail it.'

'We don't need to sail it.' She pointed up at the soldiers on deck. '*They* will.'

'How? Why?'

Sodja smiled, her face grim. 'One of the men with the crossbows is wearing purple and grey – the old livery of the House of Saevor – which means he's actually a Watcher, and he's on duty.'

'Keos,' Way breathed. 'That probably confirms what happened to Quinn and the others.' He paused. 'But I thought you left the Watchers. Why would they listen to you?'

'Because they followed my orders once, and that makes it easy to use *this*.' She withdrew the golden Rod of Compulsion from the folds of her tunic, winked at them, then strode out of the darkness and up the gangplank to the *Lapin*.

Chapter Seventy-Six

The *Lapin*'s crew docked the trading vessel at the north end of the city, as near to the Ash Quarter and the Boneyard as the galleon could possibly sail. From there, Sodja led Fyn and Way across the Low Quarter's rooftops, through the ruins of the Ash Quarter, and into the heart of the Boneyard. As before, the deeper they travelled into the northwest corner of the city, the more desolate and forsaken the homes and populace became. Lacking the light of the new moon, the district lay almost entirely in darkness, its occupants too afraid to light a candle in case they drew unwanted attention. In the few places they did encounter lights, they were unattended bonfires, their fuel either mundane or grotesque. With every step they took, the smell of human waste and rotten meat mixed with the scents of cold ash and charred flesh.

'I hate this place,' Way said, his eyes shifting between the shadows of the ruined buildings and their narrow, trash-filled alleys.

'Don't you come here once a week?' Fyn asked, his hand resting uneasily on the falchion sheathed at his hip.

'In the daylight, searching for my children. Even if it's just to find their corpses ... I need to know they're not languishing somewhere, in pain. That they aren't being tortured while calling out for a father who never came.'

Fyn fell silent at that. He'd never known his own parents or cried out for them. He'd wondered who they were and whether he'd been stolen from them, or simply been given up, but he hadn't let the question consume him. Instead, the masters and ancients had become his parents, and his own goals had reflected those of the Academy. Now all of that was gone, and in their absence Fyn had begun to wonder if his mother or father were still out there searching for him. It was not a comfortable thought – he preferred the certainty of knowing his place in the world, even if it meant being alone – and he sympathised with Way's need for closure.

'Does Rista have a place to work down here?' Fyn asked Sodja.

'A few. It depends what he's doing. The nearest one is a more intimate setting – just big enough for himself, his tools and his prisoner – so I doubt he'd go there. With Siege, Poli and Quinn, he'd need some help, likely a few Watchers plus a handful of Elar's slavers. That means a larger space, and a few rooms.'

'So?'

'So he'll be in a collapsing tenement near the north side of the district.'

'Any notion what to expect when we get there?'

'Beyond the Watchers, Rista likes traps – to dissuade other Boneyard tenants from claiming the building – so watch your step, check for tripwires and contact poisons. Try not to open or close anything.'

'He doesn't have a safe route to get inside?' Fyn asked.

'I'm sure he does, but he never shared it.'

'I thought you worked together.'

'I told you: Rista is a sadist. Any pain he can cause – any excuse to demonstrate he is in control – he'll take it, over Ketrit and I or anyone else.'

'But you would have worked better as a team. Hurting you would have just ... hurt himself.'

She shrugged. 'You've never known anyone like that?'

Fyn opened his mouth to answer and found he had no reply – not because he couldn't think of a response, but because *he* had been that person ... and he no longer liked admitting it. He'd repeatedly sabotaged his friends just to prove he could – to show he was still in charge – and he'd caused unnecessary pain to make himself feel powerful. In a place where the ancients and masters had the final say over their lives, he'd needed to feel any scrap of power he could. It had been different in Luqura, though, particularly without Annev. For perhaps the first time in his life, Fyn had felt in control of his destiny … and it had terrified him.

He understood that now. He saw his decision to usurp the Fisher King for what it truly was: an act of panic, a desperate need to control something familiar. It had given him that momentary thrill of power – that intoxicating sense of control, of being superior – but it had also shown him he was completely out of his element; he hadn't known about the Slavers Guild or Saltair or the Watchers or any of Luqura's politics, which had convinced him to seek Sodja and ask for help – something he'd never done before. It was astonishing that she'd chosen to help him, and not only because it aligned with her interests. By degrees, her quest had become his quest, and the Ashes crew had become more than a means to an end. He didn't want to admit how he'd changed, because that also meant admitting he'd once been like Rista.

'Yeah,' he said at last. 'I knew someone like that.' Sodja studied him in the darkness, and he feared she knew exactly who that person was.

'People aren't always rational,' she said. 'We hurt ourselves all the time – and we hurt those we love, the people we're supposed to rely on or who rely on us. If you put your entire trust in someone, even yourself, you'll be disappointed.'

Fyn chewed on that as they continued their journey. Beside him, Way walked in a determined silence, peering into the darkness for unseen predators. As they passed a block of charred tenements that had collapsed into the underground tunnels, Fyn cleared his throat.

'How's your headache?'

'Nearly gone. Whatever Raven did … er, Sodja, I mean – whatever it was, it must be some powerful stuff.'

'It's poison,' Sodja said, without missing a beat. 'A low enough dose clears your body of toxins. Expurgates the alcohol and leaves the inoffensive bits behind.'

'Oh,' Way said, his steps faltering. 'What, er … what does it do in higher doses?'

'Strips your stomach lining till the acid in your gut eats through your bowels. Bloody horrible way to die – and when I say bloody,

I mean it literally. A large enough dose would have you pooping your intestines out with your breakfast.'

Way clutched his guts, horrified. Fyn smiled and prodded him with his elbow.

'At least your headache's gone, though, eh?'

The tenement Sodja led them to was taller than Fyn expected – exactly five storeys high, with another three floors below ground. Rista regularly shifted his workspace within the tenement, she explained, and there were a hundred other spaces likely to be trapped. They were discussing how to navigate the warren and find their friends when one of the doors on the main floor opened and two dozen masked figures flowed out into the night.

'Purple and grey ... more of the Watchers,' Fyn said as the group passed the alley they were crouched in, beside a heap of dry bones and skulls.

Sodja stood, looking grim. 'But why are they leaving?'

Fyn and Way stood, too, neither one wanting to voice their thoughts. 'Could be they've finished what they started?' Fyn said, sour. 'Could be we're too late.'

'Silver staves,' Way swore. 'We *can't* be. Not again.'

Sodja ignored him. 'You still want to go in, or should we follow the Watchers?'

'You're thinking they're headed to our lair?' Fyn spat his own curses. 'If Neldon's back there and they find him ...'

'We don't know they're headed there,' Way said, head shaking. 'Might be they're going home. It's late, you know? Might be they're not needed any more and Rista is in there alone. We got no reason to think they're headed to the lair.'

'But if they are?' Fyn asked. 'What then?'

'Neldon's a smart one.' Way sucked at his teeth. 'He doesn't get caught out that easy.'

'I caught him out when I ambushed the Fisher King in that alley.'

'Yeah, well ... look, we don't *know* they're headed there, but we have a pretty good idea Quinn and the rest are in *there*.' He pointed to the tenement. 'We gotta pull 'em out. Can't abandon them for dead now. Please, boss. We can't give up on them yet.'

Fyn looked to Sodja, uncertain, but her face was a mask.

'It's up to you, Fyn. We can run in there and hope it's not too late for Siege, Poli and Quinn ... or we can try to beat the Watchers, run back to the lair and make a stand if Neldon's waiting for us. Maybe set a trap.'

Fyn weighed his options. This was the burden he'd accepted when he'd made himself crew leader. Damn, but it didn't seem right. No matter what he chose, he was leaving someone on the hook. 'We're going in,' he said at last, praying that Neldon stayed away from the lair for just one more night. 'We'll try to follow the Watchers' tracks and hope we don't run into any traps. Hopefully Quinn and the others will be at the end of it.'

'Hopefully they're not in there at all,' Way said, his eyes worried and wet, 'but I think they are.'

The side entrance was neither guarded nor trapped, but a sizeable number of fresh corpses had been nailed to the walls, discouraging would-be squatters and explorers.

'Gods,' Way breathed. 'Will the whole building be like this?'

'Some of it's worse.'

'If it gets much darker, I won't be able to see anything,' Fyn said, his hand slipping to cover his mouth and nose.

'If it smells any worse, I won't be able to breathe,' Way said, trying not to retch.

'Sodja,' Fyn said, ignoring the man's gagging noises, 'how much can you see right now?' In the near-darkness, Sodja's grey eyes seemed to grow wholly black, their edges tinged by a lighter circle of grey that almost seemed to glow.

'I can see enough. You?'

'My night vision is near useless,' he said, surveying the room and the door at the opposite end. 'In a room without starlight, I'll be blind.'

'The windows will all be boarded up.' She drew close to the door, her nimble fingers checking for traps and testing the lock. After a moment, she swung it inward, revealing a pitch-dark corridor. She poked her head inside, then looked back, her grey eyes barely visible. 'I won't be blind in there, but I won't see much better than you either.' She pulled a squat grey lamp from the folds of her cloak, touched the wick, and the lantern glowed with an otherworldly grey light.

'Damn,' Way said, his eyes drawn to the artifact. 'I almost prefer being in the dark.'

'It's shadowlight,' she said, shining the hooded lantern into the dark corridor. 'It has some unique, mostly advantageous, properties.' She directed the light onto the floor. 'Like revealing the footsteps of anyone who recently used shadow magic.'

Fyn studied the ghostly beam and saw a pattern of black footprints painting the floor, their flow moving through the corridor, into the room and out the door from which they'd entered. 'Those are the Watchers,' he said, his eyes squinting at the flickering silhouettes. 'Do they all have shadow magic?'

'Yes. It's essential to becoming a true Watcher − not just a common spy − but almost none of them have more than a strain. Their bloodlines are too diluted to do more than perform a simple cantrip or two.'

'Like Quinn's shadow fire?' Way asked, drawing closer to the portal and black lantern.

'Yes. I've never seen a mage with that talent, but I've heard of it. I could probably do it if she showed me how, but I doubt she'd be willing to teach me anything.' A wry smile spread across her face, her eyes sad. 'Might be I could teach her a few things, too. She's got a strong bloodline and likely more than a touch of magic, even if it's untaught.'

'Seeing in the dark. Siphoning poisons. Summoning shadows.' Way chuckled. 'Yeah, I expect she'd enjoy an apprenticeship − assuming she doesn't cut your throat first.'

'Assuming she's still alive,' Fyn said. He stepped up to the door, stuck his head through and sniffed the air. A faint charcoal smell overrode that of maggot-ridden flesh. 'Come on,' he said, stepping through the doorway. 'We'll use the lantern to follow the footsteps.'

'Hold up,' Way said, edging through the door just behind Sodja. 'You said the shadowlight is *mostly* advantageous. What's, er, the disadvantage?'

'Only two,' she said, overtaking Fyn. 'It makes everything look flat and washed out, so it can be hard to judge depth. Everything becomes varying degrees of grey; details don't stand out.'

'Yeah,' Fyn said, studying the light. 'The lamp isn't casting a shadow, either.'

'The shadows cast their own light back at the lamp. We call it the nether: the reflected light of the Shadowrealm, which is itself a reflection of the absence of light in the physical world.'

'Let's pretend I understood that,' Fyn said, hearing a strained chuckle from Way. 'What's the second disadvantage?'

'Spectral shadows,' Sodja said, leading them down a side passage.

'What? Like ghosts?'

'You could call them that. Sometimes the light reveals a glimpse of the shadows inhabiting the other world. Most of the time, they're eidolons – living shadows, demons – but sometimes it goes deeper than that.' She paused. 'Just take my advice and stay away from them, okay?'

'Fair enough.'

'They went up these steps,' Sodja said after half a minute of following the footprints. 'Looks like they came through that door.' She led them up a creaking flight of stairs to the next threshold. Fyn checked it and came up with a razor wire.

'There's at least one trap here,' he said, snipping the wire with a tiny pair of shears. He slipped the latter into his chest pocket before pulling out his lockpicking tools. 'Could be they're on the other side of this door,' he said, tapping the tumblers until he felt the lock turn.

'Let's hope so,' Way said, watching as Fyn eased the door open and Sodja's lantern lit the gruesome spectacle inside.

Chapter Seventy-Seven

A quick glance into the room showed Sodja everything she needed to know. There was only one body inside, hung in mid-air by half a dozen gaff hooks that were pierced through her arms, shoulders and hands. The final fishing gaff belonged to Poli herself and had been hooked into her jaw, its handle nailed into the ceiling, leaving her suspended like a fish on a hook. Her dark skin had been flayed from her body, making it hard to immediately recognise her.

'Keos,' Fyn breathed, as Way retched a stomach full of watery Black Gambit into the hallway.

Sodja didn't blink. She had expected this – Rista had always had his favourites. As she'd suspected, Rista's tools had been cleared away and moved to another room, probably reserved for his next victim. He liked to work that way, each subject taking his full time and attention. She looked for any bloody boot prints or other signs of her brother's passing but, as expected, there were none – nothing except the faint glimmer of shadowdark painting footprints on the floor in the wan light of the shadow lamp. It was impossible to spot Rista's in the chaos of weaving boot prints, but it was clear where they had come from and where they were going.

'There's another door just behind her body,' Sodja said, masking her emotions as she carefully sidestepped the pools of blood. She practically had to walk the perimeter of the room to avoid it all. 'Rista went through there.'

'Went through or came from?' Fyn asked, his eyes darting between the door they'd come through and Poli's skinless corpse.

'Can't say.'

'Do y'all hear that?' Way asked, wiping vomit from his mouth. 'It sounds like ... clanging?'

'Yeah,' Fyn said after pausing to listen. 'From somewhere above us, I think.'

'That means someone is still here,' Sodja said. 'Someone is still *alive*.'

'Gods be good. Let's go!'

Fyn gestured to the hanging corpse. 'What about Poli?'

'We'll come back for her. Scatter her ashes at sea or something – I'm sure she'd like that. There's no way we're leaving her here.'

'Right,' Sodja said, finding the door unlocked. 'Let's go.'

The thumping, clanging sound grew first loud then faint as they navigated the corridors. As she approached the next stairwell, Sodja examined its steps and discovered several holes punctuating its planks, beneath which an array of syringes stood poised to inject their deadly contents. She pointed these out to her comrades then lithely danced up the stairs, avoiding the trap and proceeding swiftly towards the banging metal.

'Careful,' Fyn said, catching up to her. 'That sound might be bait.'

'I'm sure it is,' Sodja replied, not slowing her pace, 'but Quinn and Siege need us. We can't second-guess ourselves; we must be committed to helping them.'

'Sure,' Fyn said, marching beside her. 'But all these traps and no one here to stop us – no guards, no one to challenge our entry. It feels ...'

'Like a trap,' Sodja said, knowing exactly how he felt. 'I've been thinking the same thing.'

'And?'

'And we keep going.'

'Hey,' Way said from the back. 'You hear that? Not clanging – someone's yelling. That's ... that's *Siege*!' The smaller thief pushed past them and began sprinting down the corridor.

'Way, stop! You can't—'

A soft twang echoed down the corridor and Sodja and Fyn instinctively dropped to the floor. A thud echoed through the hall and then Way dropped down beside them.

'That sounded like a crossbow,' Fyn whispered.

Sodja slowly lifted her head. 'A pair of them.' She nodded at the two finger-thick bolts sprouting from Way's chest, then pointed to the broken tripwire. The swarthy thief gasped, his chest and lungs heaving in wet raspy breaths. Fyn knelt beside him, his and Way's eyes wet with tears.

'Tell my boys,' he said, blood gurgling from his mouth as he propped himself on his elbow. 'Tell them I never stopped lookin' for them. And give 'em these.' He fumbled at his hip, then handed Fyn the pouch containing his blood-stone tiles. 'Made it for 'em. Tell Dar—' He coughed, spraying blood across his chest. With painful slowness, he eased himself back to the floor. 'Tell 'em I loved them,' he croaked.

'You'll tell them yourself,' Fyn said, grasping the man's hand. 'We just need to get these quarrels out of you and Neldon will patch you up. Give it a few days and you'll be ...' He trailed off as Way's hand went slack, his limb falling to his side.

'Damn,' Fyn said, releasing his grip and laying Way's hand back on his chest. 'Didn't even get to ask his boys' names.'

'Darvin and Graeme,' Sodja said. 'The oldest should be about sixteen now. He was sent off to serve some rich lord in Borderlund. Page boy or similar. Graeme ... nearest I could determine, he died the year he was taken. Way was right about that. They shouldn't be taking them so young.'

Fyn's mouth dropped open. 'You *knew*?'

'Yes,' she said. 'I do my research.'

'But ... how?'

'The Watchers have eyes everywhere, and my family keeps detailed records of all financial transactions for the Guild. I used the Rod of Compulsion to ask the questions that needed asking and I got my answers. I knew about Quinn's boat, too.'

'Why didn't you say anything?'

'Because of *this*.' She gestured at Way's corpse, at the tenement's bloody walls and the darkness hovering beyond the grey light of her shadow lamp. 'Neldon aside, the crew was held together by their hatred for the Guild. It was clear as soon as I met them. You start giving them something else to live for, they fall apart. The *crew* falls apart.'

Fyn stared at her, blinking in the dim shadowlight. 'I suppose,' though he didn't seem certain. He looked back at Way and his expression hardened. 'He went to the Undercity and the Boneyard every week ... and we just let him go. We never helped.'

'Look, we can't change the past. Way's dead, but Siege and Quinn might still be alive.'

Fyn's gaze seemed to unfocus. 'Yeah, I guess. Just do me a favour: don't leave me in the dark next time.' He shuffled off towards the banging noise, and Sodja wondered if perhaps she'd misjudged him. He seemed to let nothing faze him, but she had clearly unnerved him. Perhaps there was more depth to him than she realised. If so, she couldn't decide whether that was a good or bad thing.

Sodja followed Fyn as the banging quieted. The young man stopped at a juncture in the hallway and listened, his head cocked, his eyes alert.

'If Neldon wasn't motivated by hatred of the Guild, why did he stay with them – with us?' he asked, without turning towards her.

Sodja peered into the dark, her expression thoughtful. 'He liked feeling wanted, that he was making a difference somehow. When you're a noble living in the shadow of your parents' legacy, it's easy to feel like you're spinning in circles – like nothing you do really matters.'

'Are you speaking from experience?'

She shrugged. 'In Luqura, everyone is a piece on the royal game board – we can all be sacrificed. I learned that when my father died.'

Fyn spun at the sound of a muffled scream. 'That's Siege!' he said, preparing to sprint down the corridor.

'STOP!'

Fyn froze, his leg suspended in the air, then slowly lowered his foot to the ground. A half-dozen paces ahead of him, just at the edge of the shadowlight, they could both see the dull reflection of something flat and metallic stretching from floor to ceiling, its edge practically invisible when approached head on.

'What in the hells is that?' Fyn asked, sliding sideways to peer at the eight-foot blade of nether hovering in front of him.

'It's a void blade – a shard of nether. That thing would cleave you from toes to temple.'

'Damn,' Fyn breathed, sidestepping past the shadow construct. 'I thought razor wire and false floor plates would be the worst of it.'

'You don't understand Rista.' Sodja slid past the void blade, her lamplight barely reflecting off its black edge.

Just ahead of them, behind a closed door, they could hear Siege's hoarse screams, his muffled shouts seeming both close and distant. Sodja stopped at the door, checked for traps and slowly turned the lock. The portal eased open with a wailing creak and a wave of heat washed over them.

'What is that?' Fyn asked, shouldering past her. At the centre of the room stood an enormous black kiln, its mouth large enough to admit a full-grown man. They could hear Seige's frantic, wordless screams from a vent at the top.

'Flaming hells – they're cooking him *alive*!' Fyn took a step towards the door then stopped, his body tense as he searched for unseen traps. The floor was covered in ash rising almost to his ankles, with bits of bone and charred wood scattered amidst the grey powder.

'There,' Sodja said, pointing to a wire attached to the kiln's door handle.

'And there. Damn, but I hate not being able to rush in!' Fyn nudged a camouflaged jaw trap with his toe, its metal teeth half buried in the ash. He picked up a dry leg bone and used it to trip the device, the metal jaws slamming shut and shattering the bone. He pushed both aside then carefully waded into the ash, his feet sliding across the floor. A few seconds later he reached the kiln, clipped the tripwire and used the hem of his tunic to throw the lever and open the furnace door.

'Gods,' Sodja whispered, her hand rising to cover her mouth.

Inside the kiln, Siege was blackened, blistered and screaming. Fyn reached inside, heedless of the smoke and heat, and tore the large man from the furnace, his body dropping heavily to the ground. Ash billowed up from the floor and the man's skin seemed to crackle beneath Fyn's touch. Sodja stepped back, coughing, then waved away the cloud of smoke and soot obscuring her lamp's shadowlight. Fyn knelt over Siege's body, his ear pressed close to the burned man's lips.

'Trap,' he croaked, his voice cracking like dry leaves. 'Told them the plan. They know—' He wheezed as he tried to say more. 'Quinn ... Hurry.' His body shook, and he fell still.

Fyn muttered a curse then looked up at Sodja. 'If we'd been faster, we might have saved him. We need to hurry to save Quinn.'

'Rista keeps his captives alive as long as possible, but if they've run out of things to tell him he'll move straight to mutilation and murder.'

'Right – let's move fast but stay alert.' He spared one more glance for Siege then eased himself up from the floor. 'You think Rista will still be with her?'

'Yes. Are you prepared for that?'

'More than prepared,' he said, drawing his maces from the holsters on his back. 'We owe him for Siege and Poli and Way – and I mean to collect on that debt.'

'Just watch out for his magic. Rista isn't as skilled as either me or Ketrit, but he can still conjure void blades and turn the shadows against you.'

Fyn moved towards the door at the back of the room. 'I've fought a shadow mage,' he said. 'The shadows kept healing him, so we had to use light and fire to disrupt his magic. After that, regular weapons could hurt him. Is Rista the same?'

Sodja slowly shook her head. 'Rista is flesh and blood, just like us. Even when he steps into the Shadowrealm, he's still flesh. He's just stepped halfway between this world and the next.'

Fyn's hands tightened on his maces. 'So if Rista turned into a shadow, I could still kill him – I could smash him with these and hurt him?'

'Yes. The damage would be lessened, but you'd hurt him. Be aware he could take a full step into the shadows and dodge your attack, though.'

'Okay,' he said, chewing his lip. 'So how do I stop that? How do I gain the upper hand?'

'Two ways. You either disperse the shadows with fire or you pull them to you and keep him from grabbing them. The last one is how I would usually fight him, but you won't be able to do that.'

'Will that shadow lamp help?'

'No – the opposite, actually. Maybe the best thing would be for me to grab the shadows and keep him from pulling on their magic. I won't be able to summon any myself, though, so you'd have to fight him in the dark with just your weapons.'

'That all?' he said, sniffing. 'I'm not worried. I've trained for that.'

Now it was Sodja's turn to scoff. 'Don't get cocky. Rista can see in the dark as well as I can, so you'll be at a disadvantage. He may also have Watchers with him. If he does, I won't be able to help. I'll need to focus all my energy on preventing them from touching the Shadowrealm.'

Fyn rolled his shoulders, his bravado bleeding away. 'Okay, then. Now that I know what we're getting into ... let's save our friend.'

Chapter Seventy-Eight

They reached the top floor of the tenement and had disarmed half a dozen more traps before finally finding Quinn, whose screams had echoed through the maze of corridors and stairwells, and eventually led them to the final torture chamber. Inside, Quinn had been bound to a table beneath an elaborate water clock that slowly dripped acid onto the Kroseran woman's face. The device was designed to draw out her pain as the corrosive substance gradually dissolved her flesh. When they reached her, the woman's nose had already been eaten away and her cheeks were a mottled, smoking mess.

'Bloody hell!' Fyn swore, dashing to Quinn's aid. With no thought for himself, he started untying the bonds securing her to the table. Sodja searched frantically for traps to keep them both safe, and as he hastened to untie the last buckle, nothing was triggered. Quinn slid from table and escaped another large spit of acid that would almost certainly have hit her in the eyes. As it was, her face was a grotesque mask of horror. Her nose was the worst of it – a bubbling, gaping hole of blood and bone – but it seemed that sacrifice had allowed Quinn to protect her eyes and mouth from the rest of the acid. Rista and the Watchers were nowhere to be seen.

'Oh Gods,' Quinn rasped, her voice nasal and pinched. 'It burns!' She raised a hand to her face but didn't dare touch the wet, red flesh.

'At least you're alive,' Fyn said.

'I have a salve.' Sodja reached into the folds of her tunic and produced a small vial. Without asking permission, she uncorked the bottle and began splashing its dark contents across Quinn's face.

'Son of *blood*! That burns as much as the acid!'

'That's because it's healing you. Now hold still.' She reached into her tunic again for bandages, which she wrapped around the woman's face.

'Shit! Could you at least be gentle about it?'

'I could,' Sodja said, wrapping the bandage tighter, 'but I won't.'

Quinn visibly forced herself to remain still while Sodja worked, her laboured breath hissing between gritted teeth. 'You think I rotting deserved this, don't you?'

'No,' Sodja said, her tone even. 'I'd have preferred none of this to have happened.'

'Where are the others?' Quinn asked.

'We ... didn't get to them in time,' Fyn said.

'I figured. They made us watch what they did to Poli. By the time they started on Seige, she'd already told them everything. And you saw ...' Her voice broke. 'You saw what they did to Seige.'

'Yes.' Fyn slowly exhaled, uncertain what to say.

'He was a good one, too,' Quinn added. 'Not vicious or bitter like the rest of us. Never really carried a grudge. Just liked being part of the crew.'

Sodja laid a hand on Quinn's shoulder. 'Way is dead too. He heard Seige calling for help and ran to save him. Caught a pair of bolts in the chest.'

Quinn ran her fingers over the bandage covering her face. 'We're caught in a rotting spider's nest,' she whispered, head shaking. 'This whole place ... it's just one big trap laid by your brother.'

Sodja nodded, her eyes meeting Quinn's. 'He takes pleasure in it. Always has.'

Quinn lowered her hand from her face. 'At least I'm alive. More than I can say for the rest of the crew.' She paused. 'What happened to Neldon? Did he not come?'

'Couldn't find him,' Fyn said. 'He still hadn't come back when we returned.'

'Poli told them our plan to dismantle the Guild,' Quinn said, her breath quickening. 'They know about the lair and the Rod of Compulsion. All of it. If Neldon goes back...'

'Then they'll kill him,' Fyn said. 'Yes. We chose to come for you first.'

'And I appreciate that – really, I do.' She frowned, her eyes intense. 'Now let's save Ned before my stupidity gets him killed, too.'

They'd guessed what they would find inside the moment Sodja spotted the first slaver's body. A crossbow quarrel had punctured the man's left eye and a second bolt was buried in his chest close to his heart. A few more steps brought them to another dead Innistiulman, and a dozen more, before they found Neldon's ravaged corpse.

'This is all my fault,' Quinn said, her eyes glassy as she studied the dead nobleman.

'No,' Fyn said. 'Neldon knew what he'd signed up for. You all did. You even tried to warn me off it, but I was too stubborn to listen.'

'Stop whipping yourselves,' Sodja said, her eyes hard. 'You're doing the Guild's work for them. They want us to think we can't fight them, that it's our fault if we fail – but it's a lie. We blame *them* – Elar and his agents. They're the ones holding the knife and giving the orders. We are not to blame for fighting back.'

Fyn grunted in agreement, his expression still full of remorse. 'At least Neldon took some of the bastards with him.' There were half a dozen corpses littering the main salon. Several had bolts in their eyes or chests, and at least two had been pricked by Neldon's rapier. The slender sword lay on the floor, its blade snapped in half. They had searched for Neldon's manuballista as well, but the slavers had obviously stolen the weapon after murdering its owner.

'At least they didn't torture him,' Sodja said, eyeing the corpse.

'No, instead he was hacked and slashed to bits. You can barely even recognise him.' Quinn sniffed then cried out in pain, her hands clutching her ruined face. 'This was never his fight,' she said, her eyes wet with tears. 'He only stayed because of us – because he thought he could make a difference.'

'He did make a difference,' Fyn said. 'So did Siege and Poli and Way ... they made their own choices. We are not responsible for their deaths.'

'I know,' Quinn said. 'I just ... Neldon did more good than the rest of us, even back when he was doing experiments in the Boneyard. Folks called him a monster, but ... he tried. He wanted to help people and he didn't let cretins like his father or the Guild dictate who or what he was.' She knelt down in front of the dead man and laid a hand across his chest.

'You're right,' Fyn said, 'and we're going to make them pay for his death.'

'How?' Quinn asked, blinking back the tears. 'They know where the lair is. They can come back here anytime and finish us off. They know our plan – who we planned to attack, and how. They'll be waiting for us.'

'So we use that against them,' Fyn said, forcing Quinn to turn her bandaged face and meet his gaze. 'We'll abandon the lair – let's burn it to the ground so no one ever comes back here. Or set a trap for anyone that does.'

'And then what?' She wheezed. 'They'll be expecting us to seek revenge, and they know we're going after Rista and Tiana Rocas – or Elar Kranak and the rest of the Guild. Either way, they'll be *waiting* for us.'

'Exactly. They'll expect us to attack Tiana or Elar, because they're the ones who killed our friends – so we'll attack someone else.'

Quinn's eyes were full of pain. 'You mean Dante Turano,' she said after a short silence. 'The Ringmaster. You think he'll be vulnerable?'

'Not exactly. They still know he's a target so security will be tight. They aren't likely to let us or anyone else near him, either – not knowing we have the Rod of Compulsion.'

'So we can't reach him.'

'No,' Sodja said, catching on. 'We can't reach *him*, but we can reach his people. They control the Undercity, but they can't be everywhere at once and they can't watch their own backs. If we use the Rod of Compulsion on a few key people, we can turn the whole thing against them.'

'What use is it to corrupt a few of his cohort?' Quinn demanded.

'Because we're not just going to sneak in and assassinate the Ringmaster,' Fyn explained. 'We're going to turn his whole operation against him – all his slaves, the gladiators in the Pits, the underminers, and all the other bastards who've been forced to work down there and serve him. We'll turn it all against him. We'll start a flaming revolt – and then we'll barge into Turano's sanctum and cut his rotting head from his shoulders.'

Quinn nodded. 'Way would have liked that. That's what he wanted to do from the start. I just—' She choked on the tears, forced them down then waited till her voice steadied. 'We'll do it for Way, then. And for Neldon. For Poli and Siege.'

'And for Way's kids,' Fyn added.

'And for you, and your parents,' Sodja said, drawing Quinn's gaze. 'And for my father. We'll do it for all of them.'

'How? With the rod, yeah, but you can't corrupt a hundred people.' Quinn paused. 'Can you?'

'I'm not sure,' Sodja said slowly. 'The artifact isn't like shadow magic. I don't really know its limitations.'

'I might,' Fyn said, tugging his dreadlocks. 'We learned a lot about artifacts at the Academy, and I've seen first-hand what the Rod of Compulsion can do.'

'Academy?' Quinn asked.

'It's a long story,' Fyn said. 'The main thing is: a man named Janak used the rod to control over a hundred people – but it has its limitations. You've got to coax them a bit; you can't force people. You have to lure them into lowering their defences. Once you've done that, you can slowly bind their will to your own. Corrupting them requires a lot of concentration, but maintaining the compulsion is much easier once it's been established.'

'Really?' Sodja asked. 'That's strange. When we corrupted Whalen's messengers, it became harder to maintain control each time we added a new person. Four was difficult. I don't think I could have done more than five or six.'

723

'That's ... interesting.' Fyn strained to recall every boring lesson he'd had with Ancient Dorstal. 'It's more effective when you're close to your target. We had you running all over Luqura using the rod. Maybe you were spread too thin?'

'Maybe that's part of it,' Sodja said, looking dubious. 'It felt more substantive than that.'

'What do you mean?'

'When we were waiting for Whalen, all of the messengers were close. I felt one kind of pressure decrease – you could say my concentration wasn't spread so thin – but there was a second pressure, one that spiked just before they attacked Whalen.'

'What did it feel like?'

'Like the messengers were fighting the compulsion. An internal pressure, whereas the first felt more external.' She studied Fyn. 'What about if *you* tried using the rod? That might make a difference.'

Fyn remembered battling Janak Harth's compulsion in Banok. He'd resisted the wily merchant's control, but only barely, and the struggle had nearly cost him and his companions their lives. Janak had been controlling hundreds of other townsfolk and even members of his own household at the time. Had that affected his ability to corrupt Fyn? Had he only failed to because he'd stretched himself so far ... or had there been another reason?

'Some folks have an affinity for using powerful artifacts or other kinds of magic. I can't use any of that – just common artifacts and the like.'

Sodja quirked an eyebrow. 'Really? I could have sworn you had a bit of Terran blood in you.'

'What makes you think that?'

'Seeing into the Shadowrealm reveals a reflection of people's auras. Ilumites can see and even manipulate that light, but shadow mages see their inverse – their absence. Yours is familiar but foreign, which I usually associate with Old Terran blood or people descended from one of the New Terran tribes. You've got a strain, at least. I'm certain of it.'

Fyn wasn't sure what to make of this revelation. 'So you think I'm a bloody keokum?'

724

Sodja stared at him, her face unreadable, then she slapped him. Her hand moved so fast he didn't have to time to react. He stared at her in shock, his face red and stinging. 'What—'

'Don't be an ignorant arsehole, Fyn. I can deal with one or the other, but not both.'

'But what did I—'

'Do you think *I'm* keokum? Do you think everyone born with the blood-talent is a flaming fragment of the Hand of Keos? Please tell me you're not that stupid.'

'I ... no, of course not. I just—'

'You were just being an arsehole.'

'Yes ... I mean, no! Honestly, I thought everyone with magic was ... you know. That's what you call them.' He hesitated, glancing first to Quinn and then back to Sodja. Neither seemed apt to offer support. In fact, Quinn seemed angrier than Sodja.

'Where the hell did you grow up?' Quinn shook her head in disgust. 'Ignorant. Rotting. Flesh-sucker.'

'Hey!'

'It's not his fault,' Sodja said, her anger cooling. 'The folks that raised him taught him magic was evil, or some crap like that.'

'Didn't they train him to *steal* magic?'

'Yes – so they could *hide* it. Locked it in an underground vault or some nonsense.'

'Wow,' Quinn said, eyes studying him as though he were the one with the horrific, bandaged face. 'Did they tell you we drink blood and have sex with animals, too?'

Fyn's cheeks reddened. 'You don't really do that.' He meant it as a statement, but he had to fight to keep the question from his voice.

Sodja exchanged a look with Quinn then laughed. He suspected Quinn would have laughed, too, had it not been for the bandages covering her injured face.

'We do, though,' Quinn added, her eyes still full of mirth. 'I mean, *we* don't, but other Terrans do.'

'Just Inquisitors and Seers,' Sodja said, 'who do *not* have sex with animals.'

'I've heard the Shalgarns do,' said Quinn. Sodja was clearly

725

surprised by this admission, but Quinn continued. 'Skinchangers can take the shape of other animals. Get two of them together and ... well, both of them are still technically human. Maybe it doesn't count.'

'That's disgusting.'

Quinn shrugged, ambivalent. 'Who am I to judge?'

Sodja turned to Fyn, her expression softening. 'Okay, I guess we're both a little ignorant. Still, don't call people keokum. Saltair is a keokum – a *real* one – and so are the five magic races – dragons, giants, dryads, eidolons and faeries – but it's an insult to call a human a keokum.'

'Why?'

'Because you're saying they're less than human.'

'But ... isn't that offensive to the actual keokum?'

'What? I don't follow.'

'Well, if calling a human "keokum" is an insult, wouldn't that also be offensive to the non-humans? Shouldn't we just call them dragons and giants and what not?'

Sodja stared at him, her face unreadable until Quinn burst into a short bout of laughter, cut short as the injured woman cursed and clutched her burned face.

'Something funny?'

'He's got you there, Lady Rocas,' Quinn said, suppressing another chuckle. 'When you get right down to it, we're all a bit prejudiced – just a matter of perspective. Different flavours of the same hatred, you know?' She eyed Sodja, her expression knowing. 'My family's magic is diluted because we mixed with other races. Yours is strong, though, even out here far away from Krosera. If I had to guess how that was possible, I might come up with some prejudices of my own.'

Sodja glared at her. 'I don't do that – I don't practise that.'

'*You* might not, but your family does.'

'What's she saying?' Fyn asked, though he suspected he knew.

'Nothing,' Sodja said, her usually pale face turning a bright pink. She turned back to Fyn. 'My earlier point still stands: you've got a touch of magic to you, Fyn. My guess is you're Ironborn – an Orvane. There's a strong strain of Orvanish blood in Banok, so

726

there's a good chance you were taken from there. Rumour was Janak Harth was also an Ironborn.'

'What would it mean if I was one?'

'You'd be stronger than the average person, tougher in body and spirit. Some Ironborn – the rare ones – even have metal bones or skin that's hard as boiled leather.' She poked him in the gut and gave him a wry smile. 'From what I've seen, you're not *that* kind of Ironborn. You're strong, though – and you've got good stamina.'

She winked and then it was Fyn's turn to blush.

Quinn rolled her eyes. 'Is there a point to this?' she asked.

'Just thinking out loud,' Sodja said, her smile fading. 'Fyn said Janak could use the rod on many people. If he is Ironborn, he might be able to do the same thing.'

'You think I might be able to control more people with the rod,' Fyn said, understanding her point.

Sodja nodded. 'If you can control more than me, even if it's just ten or twenty, that will give us the leverage to start a coup in the Undercity.'

Fyn stroked his chin, considering it. He wasn't exactly comfortable with the notion of using magic, but he'd been content to let his friends use it for his benefit. If he used that rod, though, he'd suddenly be like them – he'd be *one* of them: a keokum, a flaming Son of Keos. Yet as Fyn weighed his feelings, he found his prejudice no longer made sense to him. And if he could perform magic – if he'd been unknowingly using it his whole life – what difference did it make? He'd still be the same person, just more powerful. He pursed his lips.

'Okay. We can try it.' He looked around the lair, his eyes settling on the barrels of Black Gambit. 'Let's try it somewhere else, though.'

'I was thinking we should head to the Undercity. Start small and work our way up.'

'I'll need to hide my face,' Quinn said, her fingers brushing the damp gauze. 'This is too distinctive.'

'You can wear my raven mask,' Sodja said, her hand lightly brushing the other woman's shoulder. 'Just until your face has healed.'

'Heh. Come on now, Lady Rocas. We both know that won't happen. I'm not a rotting Inquisitor. What's done is done.'

Sodja met her eyes then slowly nodded. 'You're right, but the offer still stands.'

'All right.' Quinn pointed at the barrels of dark liquor. 'Now let's burn this place to the ground.'

Chapter Seventy-Nine

'Once more, from the beginning,' Annev said, wringing out the blood-soaked cloth he'd been using to heal Honeycutt's wounds. 'Your name?'

'Jayar ... Honey—'

'No, no. Your *real* name. As one of the Siänar.'

'Valdemar. Kranak ... the Shadow.'

'Good. And where are you from?' Annev said, dripping the last drops of blood onto his dragonscale cloak.

'Gorm Corsa,' the broken man croaked around broken teeth.

Annev nodded, then strolled back to the table where Honeycutt lay restrained. He checked for injuries and put away the magic cloth when he found none in need of immediate attention. The stump of his forearm was also healing well, though Annev had been unable to reattach the severed limb. 'Gorm Corsa,' he repeated. 'You were born in an ancient Darite kingdom, which you later betrayed to the Terrans.'

Silence.

'Come on, we've been over this. It won't hurt to say it again – not unless you want it to.'

'Yes. After the kingdom fell,' Honeycutt said, his words now spilling out, 'after Neven nan Su'ul was destroyed, my master sent me to join the Dionachs Tobar ... as his spy.'

'See? It's so much easier when we string it all together like this.'

'I am ... your ally. You do not need to—'

'No. Your companion Oyru killed my fellow students in Chaenbalu. He would have killed Sodar and he probably killed

Arnor. You are not my ally. You serve your *master*. And who is that?'

'Dortafola,' Honeycutt said, forcing out the words as though he were reciting a painful litany. 'First Vampyr. Beloved of Keos. I serve him. I serve Keos.'

'Good. You're learning.'

It had taken Annev nearly three days to get everything he'd wanted from Honeycutt – the man was as stubborn as a mule, as dangerous as a viper and as pompous as an arse – but the traitor had eventually answered Annev's questions. During that time, Annev had repeatedly healed most of Honeycutt's wounds using the remains of the Shirt of Regeneration. With its aid he had also inflicted a multitude of pains on the priest without fear of killing him – from breaking bones to flaying skin. He had not liked it – in truth, it sickened him – but he had separated himself from the work, assuaging his guilt by reminding himself it had to be done: he needed answers and Honeycutt had them.

Still, the traitor couldn't answer all of Annev's questions. Honeycutt knew nothing about Kelga or the *feurog*, and he could only speculate about Janak Harth's connection to Cruithear and reasons to attack the village. Though what he did know – about Holyoak and Neruacanta, about Saltair and Oyru and their service to Dortafola – had filled in many blank spaces.

'Tell me again about the God-king,' he said, for perhaps the twelfth time. 'What are Neruacanta's goals and why does your master oppose him?'

Annev had discovered the tunnel leading to this second safe-room after subduing Honeycutt and healing his wounds. The priest had been in no position to fight back and Annev had used that advantage to strip him and bind him to the table. This didn't prevent Honeycutt from casting spells by drawing directly on his body's *quaire*, though, and he'd made another attempt at using magic to escape Annev's bonds. A void bubble had appeared around Annev's head, depriving him of oxygen, and a second wall of air attempted to crush his skull. The magic of this second spell was too weak, though, and Annev had quickly disabled both spells with his Rod of Artificing.

After that, Annev deliberately kept the man dehydrated so he could not fully replenish his stores of elemental magic – an act that effectively denied him access to his Breathbreaker and Shieldbearer powers. Honeycutt then tried to affect Annev with his stormcalling abilities, but Tym and Misty's training sessions afforded Annev sufficient protection from those weakened mental attacks. Bleeding the Dionach had further deprived Honeycutt of both his strength and his remaining *quaire*, and left him white as a sheet besides. Annev knew how precious that blood was, though, so he'd saved it, experimenting with it whenever the priest fell unconscious. Sometimes Annev smeared that blood on his dragonscale cloak – one of his current experiments; other times, he wrung it into a bucket – one of two he had found in the warehouse. At present, the first pail was half full of Honeycutt's blood, its macabre contents still lukewarm. The second was mostly full of water, though Annev was careful to keep that far from the dehydrated Dionach.

'I have already told you,' Honeycutt protested, his lips parched.

'Tell me again,' Annev said, relentless, 'and then you may drink.'

The promise of water had the desired effect. Honeycutt licked his lips, tried to adjust himself on the table and then recited the words he had spoken barely an hour before. 'The God-king Neruacanta wants to kill you because you are the Vessel. Your existence gives proof to the lie he lives every day.'

'Which is?'

'That he may be the king of New Terra, but he is *not* a god. That is why Dortafola secretly opposes him. That is why he will not allow Neruacanta to destroy you – because *you* are the Vessel.'

Annev nodded, no longer surprised by the man's answer, though it had caught him off-guard the first time he'd heard it. Annev had thought the God-king wanted to kill him because of his lineage – being a descendant of Breathanas, prophesied to kill Keos, as Sodar had thought – but Honeycutt's testimony had shown the fallacy in the old priest's beliefs. What's more, his words meshed with the prophecies of Jian Nikloss and Kelga the wood-witch. Even Witmistress Kiara had named Annev as the Vessel.

'Tell me the prophecy again,' Annev commanded. 'Recite the words of The Shattered Hand and the Broken Vessel.'

The priest groaned, his spirit broken. 'Yet he is not lost, for only a God can destroy another God. Yea, his spirit shall survive, and his Vessel shall be reborn – a God-king, a saviour and destroyer – for just as the broken cruse holds no oil, neither can the Broken Vessel hold his spirit. Yea, its pieces must be found, consumed, and reforged. Only in that death can there be life. Only in the cleansing fire of purification can the taint be removed. Only by embracing destruction can he be reborn.' Honeycutt stopped, wetting his lips.

'I must memorise all of it. Continue.'

Honeycutt shuddered in what might have passed for a nod. 'And from the Shattered Hand proceed the fragments of the Broken Vessel,' he lisped. 'Seven endowed with power, heirs to his magic. Six born of flesh, heirs to their father. Five claimed by clans, heirs to his children. Three bound to Earthblood, stewards of what is. Two tied to Entropy, heirs of what is not and what may be. The seventh bears the mark of Keos and the Last Hope of Lumea, and whoso possesses his spirit at the last day shall rule the seven parts.

'And these fragments shall war with one another, consuming each other until a new God of Earthblood rises from the ashes of their conflict. And his power shall exceed that of Odar and Lumea. And his worshippers shall be as numerous as the sands of the sea and shall sweep the Darites and Ilumites from the earth. Then shall Keos Reborn rule over every land, and every creature born of Earth and Blood will submit to his will or die.'

Honeycutt's words echoed inside the cavernous room. Annev stared at the floor, a bloody rag in his right hand and a knife in the other. 'The seventh bears the mark of Keos,' he repeated, looking up. 'That's me.' He raised his golden hand. 'This is the mark.'

'I think so. I ... do not know.'

'And whoso possesses his spirit at the last day shall rule the seven parts,' Annev repeated, echoing the prophecy. 'Keos,' he swore, fists shaking. 'It's all so much worse than I thought. So much darker than Sodar imagined.'

'Water?' Honeycutt croaked, his eyes hopeful, his tone desperate.

Annev looked at the scarred Dionach and felt a pang of sympathy for the man in spite of his betrayals. So far as Annev could tell, Honeycutt hadn't personally murdered anyone, though he had been complicit in hundreds of deaths perpetrated by Dortafola and his Siänar. Most of those crimes were centuries old, but the attack on Chaenbalu was recent.

He did not murder the innocents of Chaenbalu, Annev thought, *but he facilitated it. Does he deserve mercy?* Annev didn't think so, and even if he did, he doubted his ability to return Honeycutt to the Enclave for judgement; the man would try to escape, and then Annev would have to kill him anyway. Assuming he did deliver Honeycutt to the Dionachs Tobar, Annev wasn't sure he trusted Reeve and his priests to get justice done – not with traitors in their midst – and if Reeve entangled Annev in the Order's schemes again, he might never escape the Order's manipulations.

Annev walked over to the pail resting beside his blood-slick cloak and scooped out a ladle of water for the weary priest. The man drank greedily, half its contents spilling down his face and naked chest.

'Thank you,' Honeycutt whispered.

Annev waited to see if the priest would use this ration of sky-water to cast any spells – an act that would kill him if he spent too much *quaire* – but he merely smacked his lips. 'Another?'

'Answer my questions first.'

'Questions!' Honeycutt barked, a shadow of his former obstinacy returning. 'Questions, questions. You've asked all your questions! I've *answered* them. Now ... please ... let me go.'

'Just a few more questions,' Annev repeated, 'and then I will decide if I trust you enough to let you go.'

The priest heaved a deep, hollow sigh. 'Ask your questions, Son of Seven.'

Annev was distracted by Honeycutt's choice of words. 'Why did you call me that?'

'Because that is ...' Honeycutt stopped. 'Nothing. I misspoke.'

Annev studied his prisoner, his curiosity piqued by Honeycutt's sudden reticence. 'The prophecy says the gods will war with one another,' he continued, picking up his previous thought, 'and that they are hunting me because they want to resurrect Keos. So they can *become* Keos?'

'I ... think so. The Younger Gods are likely to interpret it that way.'

Annev nodded, another piece of the puzzle clicking into place. 'And how does Dortafola interpret the prophecy?'

As expected, Honeycutt froze, the tension in his aura showing he was choosing his words carefully. 'I cannot speculate. The Beloved has commanded that he alone explain it to you.'

'So you don't know?'

'I do not.'

'But you suspect.' It was not a question, nor did Honeycutt interpret it as such. Instead, the priest bit his lip and held his silence. Annev watched him, waiting. Finally, he lifted his belt knife.

'Our time together has been educational,' Annev said conversationally. 'I've been learning a lot about the human body. What it is ... and what it is not.' His words sounded chilling even to himself, but speaking this way removed him from the immediacy of the moment, making him feel like an observer instead of a participant. It had allowed him to hurt the priest when he would have otherwise been too horrified to continue.

Like I'm playing the villain in one of Master Ather's mummery classes, he thought, *except this is real ...*

'Don't,' Honeycutt whimpered. 'Please ... don't.'

'We've explored the muscles and bones,' Annev continued, his actions dissonant with his thoughts, 'but we haven't explored what's in here' – he tapped Honeycutt's chest – 'or here.' He rested the blade on the Breathbreaker's forehead.

'Keos take me,' Honeycutt sobbed. 'You're a *monster!*'

You're not wrong, Annev thought. *I left Kenton in that prison cell in Chaenbalu and never went back for him. I destroyed the Academy and everyone in it. I killed Kelga and Janak and Tosan ... and Myjun.* Annev had acted in the heat of the moment, by accident or with good intentions. He could not say the same of the torture over the past three days; it had been calculated and cold, and while he

734

might claim his motives were well intentioned, his methods had been unapologetically monstrous.

'I am what I need to be,' Annev said, and drew his knife across the man's brow, a red line blossoming where his blade parted the flesh.

The man on the table screamed but Annev ignored him, for Honeycutt had been right: threats of violence might motivate men, but monsters were only moved by action. He had learned that lesson well, and in absorbing it had moved beyond posturing. He did what needed to be done, and the results spoke for themselves.

'I don't *know*!' Honeycutt shouted. 'I can only guess, and Dortafola said I should never – aaugh!' The traitor screamed as the knife bit deeper into his skull, the blade scraping the bone.

Annev paused to adjust his grip on the knife and the man's bloody scalp. 'I understand you don't want to break your promise,' Annev said, his voice cool and even, 'but that promise prevents me from trusting you.'

'I can't!' Honeycutt shouted, his blood running over his face and trickling down the corners of his eyes. 'Dortafola will kill me! He will *know*.'

'You seem so certain ... but if the vampyr were all-knowing, he would have come to save you by now. Either he does not know, or he does not care what happens to you.'

Honeycutt sobbed and Annev knew with preternatural certainty that further torture would not drag the words from the man's throat – not with his mind so close to breaking – and that was an injury Annev's magic could not mend; he saw it in the man's aura, a spiderwebbing crack that threatened to shatter the Dionach's spirit, and he immediately took the knife from Honeycutt's forehead.

'You don't need to say it,' Annev whispered, almost tender. 'I've already guessed the answer. You can just nod – a single nod if I am right.' He laid the crimson rag across the man's scalp, allowing it to absorb the Breathbreaker's blood even as it healed his flesh. The man on the table shuddered with relief.

Annev dreaded the words he was about to say, yet somehow

sensed his guess was correct. 'Dortafola thinks I am the heir of Keos. That is why he doesn't want me harmed. He believes I will ... become Keos. Yes?'

Honeycutt gritted his teeth, and he nodded.

Annev felt as if a great burden had been lifted. Saying those words had pained him, as he'd known it would, but keeping his suspicions bottled inside had been more painful. The self-doubt, the fear and anxiety. They had been eating at him these past months – since leaving Dolyn's forge in Banok, in fact – but he had chosen to ignore those fears, allowing them to gnaw at the back of his mind, feeding on his insecurities.

But now he'd spoken them aloud and Dionach Honeycutt had confirmed it: something about Annev made Dortafola think he was capable of becoming Keos Reborn.

It made sense, too, in some dark and twisted fashion. The prophecy named him as the Vessel, and the Younger Gods hoped to control him – to *possess* him – so they might assume the role of Keos Reborn.

'Dortafola's interest in me: is it solely because of the Hand of Keos?'

'I don't know,' Honeycutt said, without guile. 'I ...' He paused. 'It is you. Something about you specifically. The Hand of Keos is important, but it is not his primary interest.'

A chill ran through Annev as he considered the implications of that statement: Dortafola did not want to find Annev because of the Hand of Keos, nor did Neruacanta hunt him because of it ...

Odar's beard! They think I am the next Keos. Dortafola wants to help me and Neruacanta wants to kill me ... because they both think I'm Keos Reborn.

Chapter Eighty

Annev spun from the table and vomited. As his stomach pitched and writhed, he had flashes of memory: every moment he'd felt the darkness inside him. When he'd shown the potential for violence. During Ancient Dorstal's artifact identification test, when he had thought the Rod of Healing was a dark rod. When he'd nearly thrown Lemwich over the ledge of the Academy's rooftop. When he had pinned Fyn and tortured him with the stumble-stick. Most damning of all: unleashing the destructive power of the Hand of Keos. He'd been terrified by it ... yet part of him had also revelled in it.

Burn them all, he thought, remembering the words that had fuelled his anger. *Break them. Kill them. Burn them.*

Burn them all.

Annev wiped the vomit from his mouth and reassessed his actions over the last few days. Had he tortured Honeycutt out of necessity or had he been fuelled by a darker motive?

I am not *Keos,* he told himself. *It doesn't matter what the prophecies say or what Dortafola and Neruacanta believe. I am Annev de Breth, descendant of Breathanas. I am destined to kill Keos,* not *become him.*

He stood and then, as if to prove his own goodness, he returned to the water pail and scooped another ladle of water for the dehydrated Breathbreaker. Honeycutt drank with enthusiasm and Annev was careful to spoon the water in such a way that he spilled less of the precious liquid.

'If Saltair is a Siänar, why did he try to kill me?' Annev asked once the ladle had been emptied.

'Saltair is more of a mercenary than a true believer, but he's still loyal to Dortafola. Perhaps he received conflicting orders.'

'From who?'

'One of King Cheng's consuls. Phoeba Ondina Anabo. She serves as consul between King Cheng and King Lenka in Luqura. I sometimes use her to contact the lizardman.'

Annev nodded, filing the name away for a future interrogation. 'So you think Consul Anabo gave Saltair other orders.'

'Possibly.'

'Why?'

'Because she works closely with the House of Rocas, who are patrons of the Shadow God. Also, Neruacanta has been making inroads with the King of Innistiul. If he persuaded Cheng to act on his behalf, Cheng could have countermanded my instructions.'

'Couldn't Neruacanta speak directly to Saltair?'

'Not without upsetting the equilibrium between him and Dortafola. Rules of etiquette must be followed. The God-king has the Legions of Keos and the First Vampyr has his Siänar. If one tried to influence the other ...' Honeycutt shivered. 'It can't happen. Though Neruacanta would almost certainly try to manipulate things through the use of a third party.'

'Sounds like I need to speak to Anabo, then.'

'Yes,' Honeycutt said, his eyes seeming to light with fervour. 'You should talk to her. She can answer the questions I cannot.'

'I believe I will.'

Honeycutt licked his lips. 'You'll let me go then?'

'That depends,' Annev said, though he very much doubted that possibility. 'What was your plan before I captured you?'

'I've told you: to save you from Holyoak. Once I discovered he had you trapped in his mind palace, I had to kill him and flee the Enclave.'

'No, I meant what was your plan after leaving the Enclave?'

Honeycutt hesitated, and his aura suddenly shifted from compliant to deceitful.

'Don't try to lie,' Annev said, lifting his knife.

'No, of course not.' The pale green aura shifted back to a dull blue. 'There was a situation in Banok,' he said, speaking slowly. 'I had hoped to use it to lure you and your companions away from Quiri.'

'Lure us? You mean the message from Banok ... about the siege and the Sons of Damnation?'

'Yes. I had arranged for your friends to learn of it just before I fled the Enclave. The plan was for one of the Siänar to intercept you between Quiri and Banok.'

'Intercept me,' Annev said, his temper slowly rising. 'And my friends? What would have happened to Therin and Titus?'

'I ... don't know. No other instruction was given.'

Annev nodded, understanding. 'You would have let them die.'

'No!' Honeycutt protested, though his aura and his heartbeat showed he was lying. 'They are resourceful boys. I'm sure they could have escaped.'

Annev tried to keep his anger in check, and Honeycutt misread the silence as hesitation, as doubt. 'Will you let me go now? Please? I swear I will not come for you again.'

No, you will send your servants instead, Annev thought, his mood darkening. *You will not come for me personally, but you also won't stop trying to capture me. Not until you've bound me and delivered me to your master.*

Dortafola and his Siänar. Neruacanta and his legions. The Younger Gods and their servants. They were all hunting him, and they would continue to hunt him so long as he ran. Annev could only escape by fighting back. He could only stop the hunt if he became the hunter.

I'll need to find Anabo, Annev thought, making his way back to the dragonscale cloak. *She's the next in line – her and Saltair – and then I'll have to find the vampyr and kill him, too. That's the only way I can stop him from sending more Siänar after me. Or maybe I need to use him to counter Neruacanta ...?* Annev didn't know. It was all too much of a mess – too many players in the game and too many threads to untangle – but if Annev *cut* some of those threads, perhaps he could see his way through it; if he removed some of the players, perhaps he could win the game.

Annev draped the bloody cloak over the Dionach's shivering

body, its natural magic reflecting Honeycutt's body heat back to himself.

'Thank you,' the priest said, interpreting Annev's actions as a sign of good intent. 'I promise I will not bother you again. Thank you.'

Annev ignored the man's words, reflecting instead on how much death had come from Honeycutt's actions, both directly and indirectly. All the Dionachs Tobar assassinated in their beds and on the roads because he had allowed it. Half the people of Chaenbalu and perhaps Sodar himself had died because of Honeycutt and Holyoak.

No, Annev could not let Jayar go. He would not repeat the mistakes of leaving the Academy's surviving masters and ancients alive. The people of Banok were now paying the price for Annev's mercy.

He did save my life back in Quiri, though. And he kept Holyoak from killing me. That deserves something, doesn't it? Some small chance of mercy?

'You're going to leave now,' Annev said, slicing the ropes that bound Honeycutt to the table. 'You're going to leave ... and I will never see you again.'

'Of course,' Honeycutt promised. 'Never again, I swear.'

'You will tell Dortafola to stop sending his assassins after me, and then you will submit yourself to the judgement of the Enclave.'

'Submit ... myself.'

'Yes,' Annev said, sawing through the last rope. 'Do you promise to do that?'

'I ... yes. Yes, of course. I promise.'

He was lying, of course – Annev didn't need the Inquisitor ring to see that. The man simply saw his chance to escape and was taking it.

Honeycutt pulled the sticky cloak over his shoulders then pulled it tight around his naked body. Annev stepped back to the pail of water and the bucket of blood, his face a mask as the man slithered off the table like the serpent he was. Honeycutt peered into the gloom, his eyes searching for Annev in the candlelit dimness. He stepped towards the door and licked his lips.

'May I ... have another drink of water?'

'Of course,' Annev said, mimicking the man's tone. 'Help yourself.'

Honeycutt took a cautious step towards the pail of water. Then another. He stopped within an arm's reach of Annev then bent to pick up the ladle.

Annev saw the Breathbreaker's intent before he even moved to strike. Despite warning Honeycutt about his precognitive powers and his preternatural ability to sense guile, the man had decided to tempt fate and attack Annev when he seemed weak, merciful.

But Annev was not merciful. Before Honeycutt could draw his glyph, Annev snapped out with his knife and sliced the man's elbow at the artery.

'Shit!' the priest squeaked, his opposite hand trying to stem the flow of blood.

Annev stepped in close and slapped the Rod of Artificing against the man's bicep, the cool metal absorbing the man's blood.

Honeycutt's eyes popped open as he tried to resist. 'What are you doing!' he shouted, his voice hoarse. 'What is that?'

Annev held the man tight, unanswering, as the artifact slowly absorbed the priest's lifeblood. Honeycutt tried to resist, but he flopped impotently in Annev's arms. Annev could feel the cursed prosthetic grow warm with the rage he fought to keep in check.

No, Annev thought, *I won't burn him. I am* not *Keos. His death would be meaningless, but this ... this has purpose.* He released Honeycutt and the man staggered back, his face drawn as he clutched his bleeding arm and pulled the cloak tight around his naked body.

'What the hell are you doing?' he demanded. 'I've done noth-ing—'

'I told you: I know when you're lying,' Annev said, holding the rod aloft as it drank in the blood slicking its surface.

Honeycutt stumbled. 'You ... what? You think you'll use it to track me?' The priest twisted the scales of Annev's cloak, its red surface still slick with the blood Annev had painted on it. 'You can try. But I have ways of hiding my blood trail. You forget that I've worked with Inquisitors! Whatever artifact you use, I *know* how this magic works.'

Annev let the man draw closer to the door. The wand had absorbed all the blood now, and its tip had begun to glow a pale red, like a dull ember.

Honeycutt suddenly seemed to realise what Annev held in his glowing hand.

'That's a Minor Rod of Artificing. You ... want to use my blood to make an artifact?' He gave a weak smile which became an insane laugh. 'Well, good luck with that. You might be able to track me with that magic ring' – he gestured to the red-brown band on Annev's right hand – 'but that rod will never share its powers with you. You'd have to be Terran – an *Artificer*.' He shook his head, more emphatic, and growing more confident as his fingers brushed the door handle. More than a score of steps lay between him and Annev now, and he no doubt felt himself safe. 'You'll have less luck with that than you do with glyph-speaking.' He was starting to gloat. 'It doesn't matter what clever idea you've got – whatever artificery you're thinking of – it won't work.' He sneered at him. 'Dortafola will have you. One way or another, you are his.'

'I didn't use your blood to find you, Jayar – or Valdemar or whoever you are – I used your *magic,* and you can't run from that.'

The priest frowned, then he gritted his teeth and began to cast the spell that would void the air in Annev's lungs. Annev waited until Honeycutt had spent his *quaire,* activating the glyph – and then he snuffed it out with a twitch of the Rod of Artificing. Honeycutt collapsed like a marionette with its strings cut, his final reserve of magic spent.

Annev closed the distance between them while the man caught his breath. The Dionach's face was ghostly white, dry and ashy, and his lips were cracked and bleeding.

'Kill me,' he croaked. 'End it.'

Annev gave it ten heartbeats, then spoke with the same soothing voice he had used to torture the man. 'In my classes at the Academy,' he began, speaking slowly, 'I was taught that even the humblest rod could kill a person ... if misused.'

Honeycutt was still breathing heavily. 'I ... don't understand.'

'I didn't either,' Annev admitted, his brow furrowed. 'Not until

Holyoak trapped me in my room. Not until I was threatened with death – when I *needed* to know. I used the wand to untangle the magic in the painting – to unravel the *quaire* you had invested in it. It was difficult. It's probably impossible without the Hand of Keos magnifying its magic, but I've got better since then. I've been practising – learning the craft, as it were. It's fascinating.'

Honeycutt's eyes slid down to stare at the red glowing rod held in Annev's golden hand. 'Artificing is one of the most difficult magics,' he coughed, blood flecking his lips. 'I should know. I was bonded with an Artificer ... when I made the ageless covenant. Even so, I can barely—'

'I'm not sure I know how to artifice,' Annev said, staring at the rod. 'I've been experimenting, but I've yet to use someone's blood to make something new or extraordinary – much less to craft something permanent. My one success was an accident. In fact, the only thing I've learned – the only thing I've become really good at – is unmaking things.'

Honeycutt's eyes filled with terror. 'You can't—'

'I *can*. It's not that difficult once you've dispelled the *quaire* and found the blood-talent strain ... and these past few days, I've learned that *t'rasang* is infinitely easier to work with.' He looked down at Honeycutt, his eyes cold. 'People are a lot like artifacts, when you get right down to it. Lots of threads connecting the soul, the mind and the body. Dolyn tried to explain it to me once, but I didn't understand then – I couldn't *see* it.'

'Dolyn? Who is—'

'I see it now, though,' Annev continued, ignoring the half-naked Dionach. He studied the threads that bound the man's mind, body and spirit together – the great tapestry that made Honeycutt who he was. Then, using the wand to guide him, Annev began to pull on those threads.

And Honeycutt began to scream.

As he had done during the days and nights of torture, Annev ignored him – or, more specifically, he ignored the part of him that viewed the Dionach as anything more than a tangled piece of string. He had already learned everything the man knew, and the traitorous Breathbreaker had admitted he would continue to threaten Annev and his friends if he were allowed to live.

It was all very unfortunate, but it still had to be done.

Annev kept reminding himself that as he pulled the threads of *t'rasang* from the man's body. He reminded himself of it when the blood began to pour from Honeycutt's eyes, when the flesh and muscle dripped from his bones and began to spatter the stones and dragonscale cloak with their soupy gore. He reminded himself when the gurgling screams had stopped and the warehouse no longer echoed with them.

And now, he thought, *the great experiment begins.*

Annev took a breath and shifted the Rod of Artifcing to his left hand. With his focus heightened by the magic rings and the untapped power of the mythic prosthetic, Annev channelled his will and continued pulling on the threads of *t'rasang*, coolly observing what happened as he did.

Blood came first. Then flesh and muscle. Bones were last, though they melted just as easily, clattering to the ground before pooling into a steaming soup of gristle and marrow. Annev sought out every string and thread, examining them as he pulled, tugged and twisted. As he did, he felt a stirring of knowledge unlock inside him. In just five minutes, he learned more about *t'rasang* and human anatomy than he had in all his time with Sodar. Even so, the new-found knowledge gave rise to a thousand questions he had been too ignorant to ask before. What were these white threads connecting the soul and spirit to the body? Was that *lumen* travelling along them? What did that mean? When Annev severed them, did Honeycutt feel their loss? Did he feel anything now? Did he even exist?

The metaphysical questions would take a lifetime to unravel, but the physics of a man's body were far simpler – like a puzzle. The way the muscles and tendons connected, contracting and expanding, pulling this way and that. It was a work of art, like witnessing a master painter deconstruct his magnum opus. Such genius. Such *beauty*.

Distracted, Annev turned his attention to the blood-soaked cloak now lying in a heap on the floor. Honeycutt had never thought to ask why Annev had given it to him, nor had the priest been awake when Annev had first experimented on it with gathered blood.

He had made mistakes at first – even now Annev could see the discolored scales where he had first failed to penetrate the garment's natural magic enchantments – but he'd eventually broken through with the Rod of Artificing. Once prepared, the thin scales seemed to soak up Honeycutt's blood like a sponge – until they didn't. Annev hadn't understood – not at first – but comprehension slowly dawned, enhanced by the intuitive promptings of the codavora ring.

Annev used those same promptings now as he gathered the remainder of Honeycutt's essence into the cloak. The bone marrow seemed quickest to join, eager to unite with the foreign fabric and give it new life. Honeycutt's blood filled in the rest, though it persisted in sliding off the discoloured grey scales, a reminder to Annev of his failures.

Annev doubled down. He swept aside the *quaire* and *lumen* then dug deep until he found the faint, pink strands of magic – the familiar, undeniable threads of blood-talent.

Using his wand like a weaver's bobbin, Annev guided the threads into the interlocking scales of the magic cloak, deftly merging them with the innate magical protection afforded by the firedrake's scales. The garment had proven to be a perfect item for experimentation, for while it possessed several natural enchantments, it was not itself a forged artifact, leaving Annev a clean slate for his experimental artificing attempts.

As the final thread of blood-talent settled into the tiny scales, Annev felt as if something clicked into place. It had felt the same when attaching his old prosthetic to his body, as though something were suddenly locking together, fusing into a single piece. He felt it now and knew with perfect certainty that the ritual was complete: he had used Honeycutt's blood-talent – his very essence – to forge an artifact.

Annev carefully lifted the cloak from the ground, red flakes of dried blood flitting away as the garment shifted in his hand. He whipped it in the air, shaking the carmine motes of dust to the wind. A red cloud billowed up from the cloak and a flash of white showed beneath the surface. Annev shook it again, more violently, and the red dragonscales were suddenly gone, replaced by a bone-white pattern that was stark amidst the grey discoloured scales. There were more of the latter now – no doubt a sign of Annev's imperfect artificing skills – and they outnumbered the white scales by nearly three to one.

No, Annev thought, the artifact was not perfect ... but he *had* made one. His suspicions about the rod and its use had been correct, and he had made a genuine Terran artifact.

Annev's fist tightened around the garment. *A Terran artifact*, he thought. *This is not Darite magic ... this is* Terran *magic. Does that mean I'm Terran? Was Sodar lying to me about my parents? If my father was a Darite and my mother an Ilumite, how can I use Terran magic?*

It made no sense, but there it was all the same. He had made an artifact and that meant ... he was an Artificer.

Annev's breath caught in his throat and the tears came unbidden to his eyes. He had convinced himself he had no magic – Sodar had taught him for so long and he had failed so often, he had thought it impossible. Even during his final days in Chaenbalu, Annev had thought his ability to use artifacts was somehow cheating, that he was merely using a tool someone else had forged: he was not a mage, not an artisan or a Dionach or a wizard; he was just a boy using someone else's magic.

In the Enclave of the Dionachs Tobar, he'd been forced to watch his friends succeed where he had failed. As they conjured the magic that had always eluded him, he'd felt angry, frustrated, and envious. Alone, like an outcast instead of a brother. He did not fit in. He was not one of them.

And now this – Annev was an *Artificer*. He had a place for himself and a name for his talent. Sodar had been right – Annev *did* possess the talent for magic – but it had not been the magic they had expected.

Annev should have known. He should have guessed that his ability to use artifacts so efficiently – so *powerfully* – was a sign of something ... but he had neither known nor understood. He had no Terran instructors, no Master Artificers to teach him the secrets of the art. He might never have discovered that power without Holyoak's attack in his bedchamber. Faced with death, with no hope of escape or salvation, he had been forced to save himself by dismantling the ward woven into the painting. He had become good at that – the unmaking of things – but that in itself had never seemed like true magic.

But now Annev held the tangible evidence of his calling. He was an Artificer, a mage just like Urran, the fabled artisan who had forged Sodar's sack of holding. He was an Artificer, and he had used Honeycutt's blood-talent to forge something for himself: to weave in the Breathbreaker ability that had protected Annev from his fall from the Enclave's window. He could have done more than that, but it had been difficult to weave more than one intention into the fabric of the dragonscale garment, and he had not wanted to conjure vapours of mist, to carry a shroud of silence wherever he walked or to void the air in someone else's lungs; he had only thought of that feeling, moments before smashing into the earth, and he had imagined the gust of wind that had seemingly repelled him from an otherwise fatal fall. He had recalled how Therin had used his powers to cause the water droplet to float in the air, and he concentrated on that.

With an uneasy sense of anticipation, Annev pulled the grey-white cloak over his shoulders, its brilliant red sheen bleached entirely away. He pulled the hood over his head and fastened the clasp around his neck ... and then he tentatively reached out with his magic.

The red flakes of dust billowed up from ground near Annev's feet and he felt himself suddenly lifted from the earth. One foot. Three feet. Five. He held himself there, floating in the air with the cloak whipping about him, and he recognised the pattern of the white-grey scales: the fringes of the cloak were now bleached bone-white and a mantle of snowy scales marked the breast and back of the garment in what looked like a 'V'.

It looks like a magpie, he thought, a shiver running down his spine. *I'm no longer the phoenix ... I'm the magpie.* Annev felt a chill and he shuddered as he hovered back down towards the floor.

The artifact had worked – the *magic* had worked – and Annev had been the one to forge it.

Annev's boots settled onto the wet stones where Honeycutt had once stood, but instead of a pool of red sludge or a smear of dried-black blood, there was only a puddle of greyish-yellow water. The man himself was gone. Annev had pulled every thread of *t'rasang* from the priest's body, stitching its essence into the cloak he now wore. He had twisted and tucked, rending and pulling until the *quaire* in the man's blood separated into air and water. Annev shifted his gaze and saw a faint glow of *lumen* hanging like a cloud around his knees, hovering above the watery remains of Honeycutt's former body, then it too dispersed. Annev wondered, had he watched the man's soul retreat into the afterlife ... or was it merely a trick of the candlelight?

Annev waited for his stomach to lurch at the thought – for some physical sign of regret or remorse at what he had done – but his gut surprised him by holding its peace. His heart likewise thumped softly in his chest, seemingly unburdened by his actions.

What have I done? Annev thought, trying to summon the guilt he did not feel. *I killed a man ... and I feel nothing.* Perhaps it was because Honeycutt had been willing to sacrifice his friends – to kill Sodar and Therin and Titus and anyone else who stood between him and his goals? Perhaps it was because Honeycutt would not have stopped hunting him, that there was literally no other way to stop him? Perhaps it was because Annev had *wanted* to kill him – because it was just, and because he deserved it.

Annev looked down at his golden fist and the Rod of Artificing still clutched tightly in his palm. On the back of his hand, just above the image of the smoking anvil and hammer, he read the words Keos had etched there: AUT INVENIAM VIAM AUT FACIUM.

Either find a way or make one.

Annev tucked the rod back into his cloak then opened his hand so he could read the second inscription on his palm: MEMENTO SEMPER. NUMQUAM OBLIVISCI.

Always remember. Never forget.

Annev would not forget – not about Sodar, or his friends at

the Academy, or anyone else Dortafola and Neruacanta had hurt while trying to reach him. He would remember Honeycutt and Oyru, both gone now. He would remember Saltair and Consul Anabo – and, thanks to Honeycutt's information, he knew exactly where to find them. He would remember the Younger Gods and their puppets – both those he had vanquished, like Janak Harth and Kelga the wood-witch, and those he would soon face, like the House of Rocas. He would even return to Banok and turn out the Sons of Damnation. He would remember them *all*, allies and enemies, because he was going to hunt anyone who planned to hurt him and his friends. He was going to find them and neutralise them … and kill them … but only so he might keep his friends and himself safe.

He looked down at the faint grey smear on the floor, still waiting for his conscience to chime in and correct his course, but he felt only the conviction that he was right. These people would not stop hunting him until he began hunting them.

I'm not a bad person, he told himself. *I'm just doing what needs to be done.*

And Annev knew what needed to happen next: he had to find Dortafola and stop him from sending more of his Siänar. Before that, he would likely have to find and kill the lizardman, Saltair, and convince Consul Anabo to stop meddling in Terran politics. But not before he learned which of the Younger Gods or Neruacanta's agents had influenced them. That would give him a whole new chain of people to find, interrogate … and possibly kill …

And if they must die, he thought, *their deaths should serve a purpose. If I must kill in order to save lives, I should use those deaths as an opportunity to learn more about artificing. Choosing not to do so would be a waste, one which forfeits both knowledge and power … and I'll need more of both to confront Dortafola and Neruacanta.* Annev thought all of this and knew his instincts were correct, yet some distant part of him quaked at the implications of his logic. Was it his conscience? Or was it the fear of being alone … of no longer having someone to tell him when he had strayed? No more Elders or Ancients to blame. No priests or Dionachs to tell him he'd crossed a line.

Am I becoming the thing I hate? he wondered, watching as the grey pool of matter trickled towards a drain in the corner of the warehouse. *Am I killing monsters . . . or am I becoming one?*

Annev waited for his conscience to respond, but there was only silence.

Chapter Eighty-One

It took Consul Phoeba Ondina Anabo almost a full day to travel from King Cheng's court in central Innistiul to the island's south- ern shores, and from there to the northern beaches of Odarnea. After navigating the channel's choppy waters, she was usually too sick to travel beyond the coastal town of Neahmar and so had to endure a room at the only inn that seemed not to be lice-ridden. After two more days in a carriage navigating the provinces, she was then obliged to spend a night in Quiri, before booking a river voyage south to Luqura. If King Cheng felt generous – which was not often – or if a diplomatic mission required haste, she would then secure the services of a hedge witch or water wizard to guarantee smooth currents and favourable winds for the final leg of her journey. Such self-taught sorcerers lacked the formal training of the Dionachs, but a competent one could still help her shave a day or more from the typical four-day voyage. Having a genuine Breathbreaker or Shieldbearer was even better, for if the boat were swift and the captain departed early, she could reach Luqura's northern gate before nightfall on the second day – and travelling home with the current was even faster.

Such extravagances were hard to arrange, though, and expen- sive besides. Especially since King Cheng was as miserly as he was shrewd – and Magistrate Bliven seemed to take especial delight in underfunding her travels.

'An entire rotten week,' she spat, her seasickness already tickling at her as she contemplated boarding another vessel on the morrow. 'Two days eating dust in that bloody carriage. I'll barely have time to bathe and sleep ... and now Bliven is suggesting I skip the night in Quiri altogether? That'll be the day. If he advances the issue any more with King Cheng, I'll have Elar cut out the man's tongue and put it in a jar next to his balls.'

'Magistrate Bliven,' Jaffa asked, trotting behind with the two heavy bags. 'He keeps his balls in a jar?'

Anabo stood on the street in front of their destination, her face screwed up in distaste. 'Damned if I know, Jaffa. What do they usually do with a eunuch's balls?'

The Ilumite manservant set the bags down in front of the sprawling two-storey inn. 'I was never told. I believe mine were fed to the pigs, though I can't confirm that. I'm certain they were not kept in jars.'

Anabo groaned. 'It was a figure of speech, Jaff – a joke. You have those in Ilumea, don't you?'

Jaffa was half listening. 'What would be the point of saving them, anyway? They would spoil unless you pickled them, and that would be a waste of good vinegar.'

'Jaffa,' Anabo said, rubbing her temples, 'must you always take things so literally? It's infuriating.'

'I'm certain it is, madame.'

Anabo tucked a strand of black hair behind her ear and sighed. 'Just take care of the rotting rooms, will you? And have Alan send up hot water for the tub. I'm *caked* in dust.'

'Dusted.'

'Mm?'

'You have been *dusted* with dust. Caked implies a thick layer, or perhaps mud, and since you're not—'

'Just pay for the rooms and bring up the damn hot water, Jaffa – then I don't want to see you again till morning.'

'As you wish, Consul Anabo.'

'You're bleeding right, it is.' She flung open the door then and flew past the innkeeper's desk, ignoring Alan's courteous nod and enquiry about the nature of the roads to the north. Jaffa stepped between them, his tall, heavily muscled body blocking the inn-keep behind his long, walnut-stained desk. The eunuch offered some apologies on behalf of his mistress and then Phoeba was out of earshot, already focused on the glory of the forthcoming bathwater. The mainland was too cold for her liking, and people were too formal besides. But then, that was her job, wasn't it? To put up with the cooler weather and the colder pleasantries, so King Cheng didn't have to leave the comforts of his palace and his concubines.

Anabo gritted her teeth and breezed up the stairs to the second floor. Perhaps that was what she needed: a nice compliant concubine. It had been ages since her last one ran away, and she'd been so busy haggling with Bliven over travel and lodging that she'd forgotten to requisition another. She'd have to make that a priority when she returned. Perhaps Guildmaster Whalen would donate one to her in the interim.

She kept a stately room further down the corridor on retainer at the Stag and Oak. *And Keos take that damn treasurer if he thinks I'll give this up. He's not the one who has to spend a week on dusty roads and shit-filled rivers. He's not the one who has to check for lice every time he stops in Neahmar or who has to put up with . . .*

Anabo flung open the door and the sight within took her breath away: clean linens, a freshly made bed, scented candles, soap and a steaming tub of hot water.

'Alan, you bastard,' she breathed, inhaling the scent of jasmine and juniper. 'Thank the gods. Thank stoic Odar and radiant Lumea and their bloody brother Keos.' She moaned with delight, already anticipating the warmth. 'Jaffa!' she called down. 'You can cancel the hot water! Alan did something right for once. I'll see you in the morning!' She slammed the door before her manservant could reply and began stripping off her travel cloak and skirts. She was half naked before she realised the window was open and a gentle breeze was billowing the curtains. She huffed, strode over to the window and closed the shutters with a satisfying click. She could still feel the breeze through the green-painted wooden slats, though, and it sent goose pimples up her flesh. She shivered, more in anticipation of the bath than out of any chill – then she stripped off the rest of her clothes and slipped into the tub with a moan.

'Yes,' she hissed, leaning back and closing her eyes. 'Thank the ever-loving gods.'

'You don't really strike me as the pious type.'

Anabo shot up from the water, her left arm slapped across her breasts out of an instinct that thirty years in Innistiul had never quite driven from her. 'Who the dreck are you?' she shouted, her head spinning to find the speaker. 'What are you doing in here? Get the hell out!'

The young man stepped from the shadows behind the curtains and pulled back the grey-white hood of his cloak. Had she really not seen him before? Had she not noticed him while she stood so close to the window? The goose pimples returned again, now magnified tenfold.

'I'm here on behalf of Dionach Honeycutt.'

Anabo frowned and she slowly eased back into the steamy water. 'Are you now? That's interesting. Jayar never told me you'd be coming.'

'No?'

Anabo looked at the stranger with fresh eyes. He was handsome enough – medium build, light brown hair, wide shoulders and a youthful face. Yes, she was tempted to ask the Guildmaster for someone like this. Something about his eyes ... dark blue and piercing. She broke her gaze, though she felt he should be the one looking away.

'You're a Breathbreaker then?'

The candles in the room flickered and the young man rose to hover in mid-air.

Anabo sniffed. 'You're just showing off. Still, I could use a Breathbreaker tomorrow ... and the day after. I'm taking a river barge south to Luqura and I'd kill for a favourable wind. Think you could arrange that?'

'No.'

'Why? Got somewhere better to be?' She raised her brow archly then leaned back until her chest peeked above the waters. 'I could make it worth your while, and I promise Jayar won't mind if you're gone for a few days.'

'My understanding ... is that your promises aren't worth very much.'

'I'm a diplomat. I make a lot of promises and I'm prone to

break a few now and then. I assure you, I can't keep track of them all. Why are you here?'

'Honeycutt asked you to pass a message to the mercenary Saltair – one about a boy named Annev de Breth.'

'The lizardman?' Anabo snorted. 'That's hardly an offence. If the Empire were a brothel, he'd be the bordello's favourite whore, at least here in the north—' The water in the tub suddenly felt ice-cold as she remembered the contents of Honeycutt's message. The boy's name and the memories it brought with it. *Keos*, she swore, *if this one can read minds as well as—*

'I can.'

Anabo slapped the water, realising she'd already given herself up. 'Dammit! You should really have to announce when you're mindwalking. It's not fair to the rest of us liars.' She squinted at the grey-garbed stranger who still floated in the air, his cloak rippling softly about him.

'What's your interest in Annev de Breth?'

The consul snorted. 'Nothing – at least not for myself. Saltair was in charge of it.'

'And what orders did you give him?'

'The ones Honeycutt paid me to pass along.'

'No, you rescinded those and gave him a new set of orders. What were they?'

Damn. 'If you know I rescinded them, you'll know what the new orders were – or you could just read my mind.'

'You're blocking me – or trying to.'

'And am I succeeding?'

The stranger shrugged. 'You're right. I already know your replacement orders. I just wanted you to confirm them.'

Anabo narrowed her eyes. 'No,' she said, calling the young man's bluff. 'You only *think* you know. That's why you want me to confirm it.' She smiled. 'I may not read minds, but I can read people, and you ... you don't even work for Honeycutt, do you?'

He averted his gaze – she had guessed correctly then – and now that she considered it, he seemed more a boy than a man. Eighteen or nineteen? Surely no more than twenty. His features were strange, too. Ilumite? Darite? Hard to say. There may even be some Terran blood mixed in there. And was his left hand larger than the right? Difficult to tell with the single black glove he wore. Probably a padded gauntlet.

'Who are you really?' she asked. 'You're a Breathbreaker, but not one of Jayar's, and a Mindwalker ... so you're a dualist. Very interesting.' Her eyes suddenly grew flat. 'Now cut the shit. Holyoak sent you to check up on me, so I guess he wants to know why the boy is still alive. Well, you can tell him I've been in Innistiul and none of the keokum's messages have reached me. So Saltair's either neck-deep in one of his schemes or he's dead. Elar has been keeping me updated, and I'll check on it myself when I get to Luqura.' She paused. 'Which you could speed along if you decided to come with me.'

The young man pretended to hesitate, but Anabo already knew which way the coin would fall. She had a talent for reading people, men especially. Her mother had whispered it came from an Ilumite ancestor. This one had decided. He would come. She just needed to give him the right reasons.

'My previous offer still stands,' she said, arching her back enticingly and thinking lusty thoughts to prevent this Mindbreaker ... this Breathwalker ... from learning she had no way to pay him except information, favours and—

'Blood.'

Anabo sat up in the water. 'Excuse me?'

'Ten vials of blood. One from you. One from your manservant ... and eight more of my choosing.'

The consul blinked. 'Blood?' she repeated. 'Just blood. Nothing else?' She shrugged suggestively. The boy was young, true, but she'd had younger ... and it was a long way to Luqura, even with magical assistance. She'd made her own decision, that she didn't want to wait for a concubine from Guildmaster Whalen – not when she had the genuine article right in front of her.

'Ten vials of blood,' he repeated, 'and ... some information.'

Phoeba Ondina Anabo sighed. Information was her most prized asset outside of coin, and it always seemed to cost her more than she bargained. Sex was so much cheaper when people deigned to accept it in payment. Maybe she was losing her touch. Maybe she was just getting older – though forty hardly seemed old to her. She licked her lips. So bedding this one would be a challenge. She had time, and he'd have to take breaks to regain whatever essence he tapped to use his arcane magic. She smiled seductively. 'So you'll come with me then? We can talk to Saltair, and you can report back to Holyoak yourself?'

'Yes,' he said. 'I'll come.'

'And you'll help speed our voyage with your wind magic. As much as you can? As much as you … are able?'

Again that hesitation. 'If you get me the blood I request, yes.'

Anabo frowned. What in the name of Keos did he want with blood? She supposed it was cheaper than sex – if not nearly as much fun. 'I'll get you the blood. One small vial from me. One from Jaffa.' She shook her head, knowing it would be difficult to explain to her manservant. Fortunately, she didn't have to explain. She could simply command. 'I can't promise you the eight other vials without knowing whose you want.'

'I understand. I still want your word you'll do everything you can to get them.'

Anabo gave the young man her most captivating smile. 'Of course, of course.' He knew how little her word was worth, of course. They were just playing games now, and these were games she knew how to play. 'What should I call you?'

'Magpie.'

'Ah,' Anabo purred. 'I *thought* that pattern looked familiar.' She nodded at Magpie's cloak and he slowly floated back to the ground. She smiled again, more wickedly this time. That skill would be *very* useful on the voyage. She wondered what other skills he had … 'Do you have anywhere to be, Master Magpie? I could use some help scrubbing my—'

'I'll see you tomorrow morning. Riverside wharf. The Crested Cormorant. Bring the vials of blood.'

'Mm. I'll see what I can arrange.' She began soaping herself and could feel his eyes on her again. That was good. That was what she wanted. 'Did *you* arrange all this?' she asked, her sudsy fingers gesturing at the candles, the linens, and the hot water. 'Alan is not usually so thoughtful. Were you hoping to catch me off my guard? Vulnerable?'

Magpie didn't answer. Anabo slowly stood then and, with a sultry smile, she turned to face the young man. It was then she saw the shutters stood open and Holyoak's messenger had already gone. Anabo might have been disappointed by that, but instead she only felt the thrill of a challenge. This would be far more fun than another concubine – they never lasted long once things got interesting anyway. And if things went well, who knew? Perhaps she'd even keep her promise about the blood.

'Strange bird,' she muttered, easing herself back into the water. 'Not like any of the ones Holyoak sent before.' She wondered what that meant. Surely nothing good, since he was asking about Saltair. That meant this one – this Magpie – was special. More dangerous, no doubt, and it made her second-guess her promise to give him her blood.

Something about him gave her pause, as if his eyes could pierce into her soul and see the secrets buried there. She supposed that wasn't her imagination either, not with a Breathwalker … or Mindbreaker. Damn, but she hated dualists, especially the ones who could read minds. It made her work so much harder.

But then, the challenge was part of the fun. She detested long boat rides and bumpy carriages, but the choppy waters and dusty roads were only half the bother. It was the boredom that made her want to claw out her eyes or cut out her manservant's dry tongue. Give her an interesting companion, though – someone with a little charisma, a little mystery – and just about any voyage became tolerable, even enjoyable.

She guessed that the next three days would be full of surprises.

Part Six

To Kryss Jakasen and the Keepers of the Flame,

I pray that my letter finds you well – whether in Banok or Luqura or wherever your travels take you. Likewise, I thank you for your kind request to join you and your companions in Banok later this season.

I must decline. Noble though your quest may be, local troubles in the Brotherhood require my full attention at this time. If I am able to reconcile the current issues in Quiri quickly, I may still send another member of my Order to join your Council, but I would strongly urge against meeting in Banok. Recent reports suggest the township is besieged by a coordinated assault from local bandits.

I have news regarding one of your companions, though it is not the pleasant kind. The soothsayer Jian Nikloss died shortly after joining my company. May it be some consolation to know his death was a valiant one, his life given in the defence of others.

In regards to Annev, you are correct in guessing the young man was recently in my Enclave, but I am sorry to say he has since departed. I gave him your letter, so perhaps he will decide of his own accord to aid you in your quest. If he does, I advise caution in his presence and recommend you be respectful of his personal traumas (as I'm certain you would be). To do otherwise might have disastrous consequences for both you and your companions.

May the light of Lumea and the winds of Odar protect you,

Arch-Dionach Reeve
High Order of the Dionachs Tobar

Chapter Eighty-Two

Alcoran approached the embers of the fading fire with all the trepidation of a dog begging for scraps. The summer night wasn't all that cold, but he coveted much of what the small caravan shared: companionship, warmth, a sense of peace. There had been very little peace during the campaign in Borderlund – not among its commanders or the squabbling nobility, and certainly not along the front lines adjacent to the Kuar River and the Terran armies in Daogort. It had been madness. Greed and bloodlust and chaos. He'd lost most of his troops and his left eye on his first run at the Black Wall, and the company had never recovered. All the glory he'd envisioned, all the clever strategies he'd planned – it had all gone down the garderobe. Barely a handful of his men had held their ground, and all of them had been slaughtered. Alcoran had only escaped because he'd been smart enough to place his command at the back, and he'd been one of the first to flee when the rock golem began hurling boulders at the scattered company. He still wasn't sure where the arrow had come from – probably one of his own gutless men – and having been shot, he'd reacted in fear and stabbed the first person he'd stumbled into. As it turned out, that had been the company's medic – a herbalist they'd conscripted just outside of Lochland – and he'd had no one to tend to the damaged organ after that.

There'd been no peace since then. Not from the injury, which was currently weeping pus beneath the bandage, and not from the other officers in Borderlund's conscript army. It had been a farce from the beginning, and now Alcoran just wanted a little peace from this sleepy caravan.

Peace, and all of their possessions.

'Evening, folks,' Alcoran drawled in an approximation of the local accent. 'Sorry to disturb. Might I trouble you to share the warmth of your fire?' He swept into a bow with a dramatic flourish, his broad-rimmed hat tilted to cover his missing eye.

'It's late, friend,' said an elderly man sitting on a stump close to the campfire. 'We don't know you. Might be better if you pushed on.'

Alcoran straightened, having expected that. 'I won't share your company, then. But spare me some news from out west? I've just come from the east. The war with Daogort has spread all across Borderlund. The Terrans are making forays into any villages near the Kuar, and our valiant soldiers are hoping for aid from Greater Luqura or Lochland. Do you have news? Or have other affairs kept the Empire's soldiers away from their sister kingdom?'

The old man exchanged a look with the woman tending a pot of food banked in the coals – bacon and root stew by the smell of it. Alcoran fought the urge to lick his lips.

'You're from Borderlund then? Your accent ... sounded like you were from the capital.'

Damn, Alcoran thought. He was getting sloppy. Being hungry would do that to a man, not to mention being in constant pain. 'Yes. Born in Banok but my business keeps me in Borderlund – at least it used to. Tell me. How fares the King's Road?'

The old man whispered something to the woman and slowly stood. She ran off to one of the four tents set up just beyond the fire and soon two men and an older lad had joined them.

'Do you know anyone in Banok?' the old man whispered, his quivering lips seeming to chew his words. 'Any family there? Loved ones?'

Cursed Keos.

What did this old man expect? Was Alcoran going to have to make up a family there before he could sit at a fire? Alcoran fought the urge to scowl and instead forced a disarming smile. He was used to getting his own way, and it pained him to be unable

763

to order folks around. That had been the beauty of the army. Before he could think up a clever response, though, the old man continued.

'If you do,' he said, looking apologetic, 'then you should know they're in a bad way right now. So bad Borderlund probably won't see any soldiers coming to their aid – not till word gets to the capital and other parts of the Empire.'

Alcoran hadn't expected this answer. 'In a bad way? How so?'

The older man indicated a broad-chested fellow who was of a height with Alcoran. He stood in his nightshirt and britches, he carried no weapons, and he had a haunted look about him. The man next to him was stockier, had hair so dark it seemed black, and an angry scar crossed his cheek and chin. The taller man patted the scarred one on his shoulder and nodded in greeting to Alcoran, unembarrassed by his state of undress.

'I'm John Stout and this is my brother, Jacob. We just came from Banok. Barely escaped with the shirts on our backs.'

'Escaped?' Alcoran tilted his head, still trying to make sense of the tale they were telling him. 'Surely the Terrans haven't come this far into the Empire?'

John shook his head. 'I don't think so ... but maybe? We were overrun by the Sons of Damnation – and they didn't sound like foreigners. They knew the city, knew our ways and our speech, but they were dressed funny, and they said they'd come to liberate the village from evil. We didn't know what to make of them, wrote them off as zealots from Quiri ... but then they seized the Harth family's keep and started making demands of the governor. Acted like they were running the village. Governor sent the town guard ... and they didn't come back. They formed a militia, and they didn't return either. Some folks went for help and ... well, we didn't see them again, neither. When others finally did come, it was more strangers and monsters – and they were there to help the Sons of Damnation. The whole place has gone to hell and the remaining townsfolk are being held hostage – forced to serve the man who leads the Sons.'

'Strangers and monsters,' Alcoran repeated, forgetting for a moment why he had come to the small encampment. 'And ...

Sons of Damnation?' He scratched his short red beard, hunger receding to the back of his mind. 'And you don't know who they are?'

The shorter man, Jacob, shook his head. 'We weren't keen on finding out. We decided to send for help – to sneak out of the village and find someone who might help take back the city – but no one cares. Everyone's concerned about their own problems, like the war in the east or the famine in the south. We heard no aid would be coming from the capital, so we're taking our case to the king of Paldron.'

Alcoran laughed – he couldn't help it. The irony was too amusing. 'King Alpenrose wouldn't sell you his own piss, much less spare you a company of soldiers.'

'But ... the people are desperate. The soldiers are gone. The only folk left are shopkeeps and farmers. Merchants and artisans. They aren't warriors! And the people controlling the city ... they've got magic. The Sons said they hate it, but they use it to keep people in line. Even the mercenaries they've hired – half of them use shadow magic and the others ... they're rotting demons. Their flesh is more metal and stone than skin and bone!'

'You have my sympathy – truly, you do – but no aid will be coming. Borderlund has its fists full on the Black Wall. Our numbers are thin. Conscripts are fleeing, abandoning the war and seeking safety elsewhere. If they aren't helped soon, the Terrans will cross the Kuar and start sacking Paldron itself.' Alcoran huffed. 'If these men – these Sons of Damnation – aren't harming you, you should count yourselves lucky. And if they aren't friends of the Terrans, maybe they'll protect you from the war that's about to come.'

The old man's face paled. 'If that is the case, then we are truly in dark times.'

You don't know the half of it, Alcoran thought, feeling a tiny pang of guilt for what his band of soldiers was about to do to these folks. Times were tough all around, though, and only the fittest were going to survive. He tipped his hat low over his bandaged eye and made sure to stay out of the firelight. His men should be in position now ... yet something stayed his hand.

'Lord Stout,' Alcoran said, addressing the elder of the two young men. 'You said these Sons of Damnation aren't letting folk in or out. How did you escape?'

'We can't take much credit for it,' the taller man said. 'These warlocks – the shadow men helping the Sons of Damnation – they wear grey and purple clothing and masks, and they spy on us townsfolk for the Sons of Damnation ... but there's a resistance forming. They've got a leader, too – one who uses magic – and she helped us waylay two of these warlocks and take their clothes.'

Alcoran frowned. '*She?* There's a witch leading your militia?'

'Not just one' – Jacob interrupted – 'there are *three*! One who speaks to the plants, one who doesn't speak at all, and one who charms the warlocks with her witching song.'

John elbowed his younger brother, shushing him. 'They aren't witches. They're just ... well, they're helping us. And we're fighting back, with or without King Lenka and King Alpenrose.'

Alcoran nodded, his tongue drawing across the bottom of his front teeth. 'These mercenaries. Any notion why they're helping these Sons of Damnation?'

John and Jacob exchanged a look that suggested they knew exactly what Alcoran was asking, but they didn't seem eager to share that information. Perhaps they weren't as stupid as Alcoran hoped.

'Only rumours,' John said, speaking for them both. 'We heard about some kind of gold – liquid gold, I guess. I don't know why that'd be so special, but word of it got out soon after the Sons came to Banok, and the mercenaries started appearing pretty quickly.'

'Huh. Liquid gold.' Alcoran shrugged. 'Seems like it'd be more valuable as simple coin. Easier to transport, too. Still ... gold is gold. When folk offer it, others will take it.' He hesitated. 'Anyone else taking this gold? Any of your townsfolk helping these Sons?'

'You mean has anyone turned traitor?' Jacob spat then ran his finger along the side of his savaged cheek. 'Vilhelm Stenger decided he'd take some of that gold – he signed on to help the Sons keep order in the town – but we made an example of him. Forrest Bower and Josie Ladle, too. Banok folks don't take kindly to traitors.'

Alcoran was satisfied. 'Sounds like you folk have your affairs in order then. And this old gaffer here ... no relation to you?'

The young men shook their heads as the old man spoke. 'I can speak for myself. Me and Mirella found the boys just before nightfall. They were tired and needed help, so we took them in. We'll take them as far as Trizgard.'

'I just came from there,' Alcoran said, grunting. 'It hasn't been touched by the war yet, that's why I was surprised by trouble in Banok.'

'Eh, that's some good news at least. We're from Luqura and don't usually trade beyond Banok – too many bandits on the King's Road.' He sniffed. 'But there's no trade in Banok these days, so we've got to chance Trizgard.'

Alcoran clucked his tongue. 'Bandits, eh? Yes ... that really is a sad tale.' Alcoran took off his black felt hat and waved its wide brim in front of his face.

'Hm?' The old man squinted at him in the pale glow of the fire as John and Jacob stared aghast at the blood-soaked bandage wrapped around half of Alcoran's face. 'Here now, what's—'

An arrow blossomed from the gaffer's chest and he fell backward into the coals of the fire. A heartbeat later, five more arrows sprang from Jacob's chest and John's neck and groin. Mirella opened her mouth to scream as the two young men fell – but Alcoran was faster. He dashed forward with his long knife in one hand, the other slipping over her mouth. She bit down hard on his palm, but he ignored the pain and slashed hard at her jugular, cutting her windpipe and spilling her lifeblood down her dress.

Alcoran waited, panting in the near-darkness, but no one else stirred from their tents. Slowly, the other soldiers began trickling in from the edge of the treeline and the ditch by the roadside. Fifteen soldiers in all. Not the best from his old company, but the toughest, the meanest and the ones smart enough to stay alive. He nodded to all of them, his missing eye pulsing with savage agony beneath the filthy bandage. He hoped to the gods the infection didn't spread ...

'Should be half a dozen more in those tents,' he whispered. 'You know what to do.' The others slunk away, their short bows disappearing to be replaced by shortswords and daggers. Alcoran tore a strip of cloth from the dead woman's dress, used it to clean his knife, then ambled over to the simmering pot of stew. Using the same piece of bloody cloth, he eased the lid off the pot and sniffed at the boiling bacon, parsnips and potatoes.

While Alcoran searched for a spoon or a ladle, shouts went up along the cluster of tents behind him. Men, women, and at least one child. Alcoran tsked at that. The King's Road was no place for children after dark. There were bandits about, after all.

'There it is,' Alcoran exclaimed, snatching the charred ladle from the shadows next to the campfire. He smacked it against his leg, shaking off the ash, then scooped up the stew. He raised it to his mouth, blowing to cool it, and savoured the smell of the thick cottage bacon. It'd been so long since he'd had pork that wasn't rancid, or salted, and he imagined the texture of it, the root vegetables mixing with the flavour. He tested it with his tongue, then blew on the ladleful again. Just a little cooler. If he ate quickly, there'd be less to share with his men. He hoped it would take them a while to loot the tents, wagon and corpses.

'Banok's under siege or something, lads. They've got mercenary work if you're up for it, though.' He turned an ear towards his men as he blew on the stew and slurped noisily at its thick gravy. Damn it was good. Too hot by half, but burning his tongue was a small price to pay for the delicious broth.

'Or we can stay on the road,' Alcoran continued, his body huddled over the pot, the steaming ladle raised to his lips. 'Lots of folk will be coming this way now Banok is off-limits to traders. Easy pickings.'

Alcoran stopped. Why had it gone so quiet? He peered over his shoulder and spied the rent and tattered oilcloth, the tents shredded and dismantled. None of his men were in sight, though: only the dead, their voices as silent as the grave.

So where were his men? Alcoran squinted into the darkness. The bodies ... there were too many bodies. Almost a score of them.

On instinct, Alcoran spun around and splashed the hot stew into his silent attacker's face. The young man hissed, his short sword swinging wide. The stranger didn't blink, though – in fact, he didn't close his eyes at all; instead, the steaming liquid glistened on the hard leather skin of his scarred cheekbones, evaporating under the heat of the man's fiery, unblinking eyes.

'Gods,' Alcoran breathed.

The shortsword swung again and Alcoran raised his long knife to parry. Instead of blocking the sword, though, the silvery blade seemed to pass right through it, striking Alcoran on the shoulder and severing his arm at the clavicle.

'Keos,' Alcoran swore, his left hand dropping the wooden ladle and clutching at the pulsing artery beneath his armpit. He'd seen wounds like this on the battle front – killing wounds.

The young man's blade bit into his neck, its edge as cold as winter's ice. Alcoran tried to raise his hand to staunch the flow of blood but neither of his limbs responded. Instead, the world seemed to spin around him, as though he were tumbling through the air. His head crashed into the coals of the dying campfire and he watched, confused, upside down, dying, as his headless body toppled to the ground in front of him.

Chapter Eighty-Three

'They've gone to Banok,' Kenton said, appearing like a wraith in the gloom of the Brakewood. 'Worse, they've put my original plan into action, though I can't fathom why. None of them were keen on pursuing it to begin with. Without a leader, that lot would bicker indefinitely.'

Kiara looked as if none of that was news to her. 'The masters and ancients of Chaenbalu were never very good at improvising. They're just bandits. All they know is theft and living off the labour of others.'

'This is different,' Kenton said, hanging his Cloak of Secrets from the branch of a nearby spruce. 'They're still calling themselves the Sons of Damnation – as if they want people to know who they are and what they're doing – and they've taken the whole town hostage.'

'Hmm.' Kiara looked up from the shadepool she'd been studying. 'That *is* different. But five men are keeping the town hostage? How?' Kenton frowned in response and Kiara's eyes narrowed. 'Whose help have they secured to do it?'

'They've hired mercenaries. Strange ones with shadow magic, like that assassin who visited Chaenbalu with his demons.'

Kiara huffed. 'There is a small faction of Dorchnok's warriors in Luqura. They're servants of one of the noble houses. I can't see why they'd help the Sons of Damnation seize control of a township, though. There's no profit in it.'

'It gets worse,' Kenton said. 'I think they have *ferrumen* helping them.'

'*Ferrumen?*' Kiara jumped up from her stump and strode over to Kenton. 'You're certain?'

'Reasonably certain. They could be golems … but I think not. Their descriptions are too similar to the monsters that attacked Chaenbalu.'

'But these are *ferrumen*. Not *feurog*?'

Kenton nodded. 'It seems that, like the shadow-warriors, the *ferrumen* have been persuaded to help the Sons of Damnation take control of Banok.'

'Could they be fugitives from the failed attack on Chaenbalu?'

'No,' Kenton said, his gaze turning to take in the dead village at the heart of the Brake. 'They were all killed – all those who joined the attack on the village, anyway. These other *ferrumen* must be a separate force from the one that attacked.'

'But they will still be servants of Cruithear,' Kiara mused. She slowly turned and stared into the trees behind him, her attention unfocused, thinking before she turned her grey eyes on Kenton. 'You have guessed what this means.'

'Mercenaries don't work for free, and I can only think of one thing that would persuade the *ferrumen* to help the Sons. The men on the road even said the soldiers are being paid in *liquid gold*.'

'*Aqlumera*,' Kiara said, frowning. 'Yes, and I'm sure that would convince the shadow assassins to help, too. Ather and the rest must have stolen it before the *ferrumen* attacked, which also explains why we've been unable to locate them. Blood of Tacharan! We spent all that effort protecting the Vault from Cruithear's minions and then your entourage just went ahead and handed it to them.'

'Not *my* entourage – not any more, anyway. If Ather went into the Vault to steal *aqlumera*, then I would bet Tosan is leading them now. And he liked the idea of possessing Banok.'

'I don't follow your logic.'

'Tosan's spirit was still guarding the *aqlumera* pool,' Kenton said, replacing the black wrapping that covered his glowing eyes. 'He would have attacked anyone who approached the pool without protection, and I doubt any of them could have fought him off.'

'A sensible explanation, though I wish there were another one.

If Tosan has begun selling the liquid in exchange for mercenary services, it will make it that much harder to reclaim the substance.'

'Reclaim it?' Kenton tilted his head in confusion, then he realised the implication in Kiara's words. 'You want me to go and steal it back. Before it's distributed to the mercenaries.'

'Easier than trying to steal it back from the Cult of Cruithear or these shadowmen.' Kiara nodded. 'It's one target. One task. One mission. Go to Banok and retrieve the *aqlumera* from the Sons of Damnation.'

'And what if Tosan is controlling them?'

'So what if he is? The *aqlumera* is all that matters. Annev will be drawn to it and Myjun will be drawn to him. When he gets his hands on it, Annev will use the *aqlumera* to forge a new artifact – a powerful one, almost as strong as the diamagi.'

'The what?'

'The Hammer of Keos, the Flute of Lumea, and the Staff of Odar. The three most powerful artifacts in existence. Many times more powerful than the Hand of Keos – and you've seen the destruction that wrought on the Academy.'

'So Annev will have the Hand of Keos ... and this new artifact. Which will make him magnitudes stronger.'

'Yes, but *you* have grown stronger, too. Both in your magic and your inventory of artifacts.' The witmistress smiled. 'Besides, you do not need to concern yourself with Annev. He is my affair and no longer your enemy – but if he dies, so does Myjun.'

'How is she? Have you seen her recently?'

Kiara tilted her hand as if sensing the wind or weighing the balance of fate on her palm. 'The shadepools here do not offer the same clarity as the fountain of *aqlumera*. I can sometimes see her ... but not well. Not often.'

'Does she persist in her desire to enter the World of Dreams?' Kiara nodded and Kenton cursed. 'If she does enter, will your magic still work? Will I still be able to track her progress?'

'Probably not. If I could access the Vault, perhaps. But with this?' She gestured at the smoky black surface pooling about her ankles. '*Aqlumera* pierces all veils and touches all realms, but the shadepools are tied directly to the Realm of Shadows. It only borders the Dream World, so the shadepools might provide a few glimpses, but they would be indistinct and infrequent.'

'But her armour . . . the ironwood skin. You said it was imbued with shadow magic. Would that not make it easier to observe her through the shadepools?'

'It is and it does – but that is the only reason we have not lost sight of her entirely. She is more than a continent away, and in another realm. You are lucky I am able to glimpse her at all. Once Oyru takes her to the World of Dreams, I expect we will be entirely blind to her.'

Kenton clenched his fist, brooding. What if he lost her? What if she didn't come back? The thought sickened him, not so much because of his love for the girl-turned-assassin, but because she was his single remaining purpose in life. The thought of losing that frightened him more than he dared acknowledge, and so he persisted in this obsession. If he could save her, perhaps all his suffering would be for something.

'So how can we view them?' he asked, his eyes flaring, betraying his emotions.

'Short of dreamwalking?' Kiara shrugged. 'I suspect your Cloak of Secrets could take you there, if you trusted its magic to transport yourself to other realms – but I cannot accompany you. My affairs tie me to this world – and without a guide, such risks seem unwise.' She hesitated. 'Do you carry anything that would allow us to look into another's dreams?'

Kenton consulted his memory ring for any such artifacts. He shook his head. 'I have no such thing. If there was one in the Vault, I did not encounter it.'

'Mm. Then we must content ourselves with the glimpses we steal from the shadepools.'

'You mentioned dreamwalking,' Kenton pressed, pacing around the black pool of placid shadows. 'Can you teach me?'

'It is not a skill I cared to learn. A few Seers and Shadowcasters have been known to dreamwalk, but it is mainly practised by Kroseran Voidweavers and the Darite mind-mages: the Stormcallers and the Mindwalkers. Beyond those three castes, it is a dangerous skill to hone, whose rewards rarely outweigh the risks.'

'Then I will assume Myjun is in danger,' Kenton snapped, though he fought to remain calm. 'If they have travelled to the World of Dreams, Oyru's magic will be less potent there ... and he'll be less capable of protecting her.'

Kiara snorted. 'Don't worry about Myjun. She is more than capable of protecting herself – at least until she attempts to kill Annev, and that is why you will be here to stop her.'

'But she *will* be in danger,' Kenton pressed. 'More so than in the Shadowrealm.'

Kiara sighed. 'Yes, but she will survive. She may not be the same woman when she returns, but she will survive. Put yourself at ease. She will still return here to confront Annev.'

'But only if the *aqlumera* is here.'

'Yes.'

Kenton grunted. 'I only have your word on that – your word and this prophecy. And what is that exactly?'

Kiara seemed to have been waiting for Kenton to ask that question. 'Before a year has passed, Annev will be enlisted to build an artifact – a sword – but forging it will require a certain quantity of *aqlumera*. If he finds it *anywhere* except Chaenbalu, he will not return to the village ... and neither will Myjun. However, if he can find no other *aqlumera*, he *will* return to the Vault of Damnation. He will forge the sword, and Myjun will come there to kill him. You must be there to stop her, or her life will be forfeit.'

'And if the sword is forged elsewhere?' he asked, staring into the rippling shadepool. 'What will happen then?'

'Then she will be taken the Gods only know where ... beyond your reach, I suspect.'

Kenton stared into darkness, hoping his supernatural vision might pierce the mists of shadow without the witmistress's aid – but they refused to yield to him.

'She kills Annev, doesn't she? In your prophecy? If she finds him, they both die.'

Kiara hummed beside him. 'Your eyes are beginning to see more than this world, Cursed One. Soon you will be able to prophesy, too.'

Kenton shook his head. 'I've enough curses. I do not care to

774

burden myself with more.' He paused. 'But that is something you could teach me, isn't it? You could show me how to see more than this world. Perhaps even peer into the Shadowrealm.'

'I suspect I could teach you more than that, even. Peering into shadows is only the beginning. With the proper training and the aid of your altered sight, I expect you could see the patterns of Fate himself.'

'Himself?'

'The plots of Tacharan. The God of Death. The God of Doom. He works the loom of fate to weave the pattern of our lives.'

Kenton snorted. 'You don't really believe that, do you?'

'I do.'

Kenton and the iron-haired woman were of a height, and he fancied he could almost peer into the woman's soul. Finally he made up his mind. 'I will learn your magics then, witch. Teach me what you can ... but I will not worship your God. I will not chant his prayers or sacrifice lives to him.'

'Nor does he ask for them – not yet. We can begin your training when you return from Banok.'

'And you are certain Myjun will not return before then?'

'As certain as I can be, when the future is never clear. By my estimations, it will be a month or more before either Annev or Myjun returns to Chaenbalu. When they do, Annev will be surrounded by his companions, and it is unlikely Oyru will allow Myjun to attack. They will wait until the sword is forged, when Annev's friends abandon him and his allies desert him and he is weakest. That is when you must intervene. That is how you will save Myjun's life.'

'I swore I would kill Annev.' Kenton had a look of disgust on his face. 'Instead I must save his life – worse, save him from Myjun, whom I would deny nothing.'

'If you wish to save her life ... yes.'

'I see. And how exactly does she die? How does Annev's death lead to hers?'

Kiara hesitated. 'I don't know. Down that path, I see death – a touch of necromancy maybe, but if so, it is a form I am unfamiliar with. Perhaps Myjun sacrifices her own life to kill Annev? Perhaps

Oyru kills her afterwards. Perhaps it is something I cannot foresee or foretell – but do not try to circumvent Fate in this matter, Lord of Damnation. It will bring you ruin. Chade Thornbriar would tell you the same ... if anyone could find him.'

'Then I believe I've got some priceless liquid to recover in Banok.' He moved to leave but Kiara laid a hand on his shoulder.

'Beware of the mercenaries, but be especially careful of Elder Tosan. If the man is truly there, do not underestimate him. I thought his hatred of magic was so great that I never considered he might have experimented with it himself – but I should have seen that he would. Whatever his plans are, they will be extensive. The sorrows of Banok's townsfolk attest to that.'

'And what do I care for them?' Kenton said, shrugging her hand away. 'I've already saved those people from Janak Harth and his Rod of Compulsion – he would have ensnared the entire population if Fyn, Annev and I hadn't stopped him. Besides, if Tosan is plaguing the town he'll be too busy to anticipate my arrival ... but as you say not to underestimate him, I will assume the opposite is true. Tosan is expecting me. Even so, I will reclaim the *aqlumera* and I will return here with speed. If Tosan interferes, I will kill him.'

'And leave the people of Banok alone to face the mercenaries and your Sons of Damnation?'

'They can burn in the forge of Keos for all I care.'

Kiara smiled. 'You say you will make no sacrifices to Tacharan, but already you pledge to do his work.'

Her words made Kenton glare at the old witmistress. But Kiara was contemplating the shadepools and had already dismissed him from her thoughts. He stared at her for a long while, his vision penetrating her bones, but still the woman did not turn to face him. He shook his head in consternation and started to plan his approach to Banok.

It's just like when Fyn, Annev and I left for Janak's palace, he mused. It felt like a lifetime ago, but it had only been a few months: he remembered the paths they had trod, the banter they had shared, the hatred for Annev that he'd kept to himself. He remembered, too, how conflicted he had felt about killing Master Duvarek

– the one person who had shown him an ounce of kindness at the Academy. Tosan had ordered him to kill the Master of Shadows, though Annev had tried to find a way around it. Remembering that, Kenton felt his anger towards Annev cool a little further and his hatred of the former headmaster rise to a new peak: Tosan had given the order to teach Kenton and his mentor a lesson, to prove no one was above the will of the Academy – and now the Academy was gone and it had all been for nothing anyway.

If you really are in Banok, Elder Tosan, then you'd best hide. I'm taking back the aqlumera *you stole and I'm taking your head in vengeance. I'm going to send you back to damnation where you belong.*

Chapter Eighty-Four

The grey ring of Dorchnok's Eye was just peeking above the horizon when Oyru called a halt. Myjun crested the short hill only a few steps behind him and saw they were several miles northeast of the Alltaran mountains, almost where they had first encountered the witherkin. As Oyru stopped, Myjun eased herself to the ground, both physically and mentally fatigued from their ceaseless pace throughout the umbral night.

'I shall sink quickly into sleep,' she murmured, both longing for the rest that true sleep might bring and fearing what might come of it.

'And I will speedily join you,' Oyru said, kneeling formally beside her. He opened his mouth to say more, but hesitated.

'Speak your mind,' Myjun said. 'What vexes you?'

'I have not slept in a decade,' the assassin explained, eyes fixed on the sloping patch of earth ahead of them. 'I do not know ...' His words faded and he stared into the void.

'Are you meditating?' Myjun asked finally. 'That is not what we discussed these many miles we have walked, or what we agreed upon.'

'Not meditating,' Oyru said, almost sheepish. 'Thinking – though perhaps that is little different to meditation.' He shook his head as if waking from a dream. 'I don't know what we will encounter in the World of Dreams. I don't know how to kill the witherkin. And I certainly don't know what I will do if confronted with Oraqui's spectre.'

'And that frightens you.' Oyru met her gaze, a hard glint in his single eye. Myjun nodded. 'You have forced me to face the unknown countless times. You have dashed me on the rocks of uncertainty. I have been broken and rebuilt. Surely you are no stranger to the unknown.'

The assassin shrugged. 'Perhaps not.'

'Did you know whether we would survive the eidolons when I jumped into that first crevice?'

'No.'

'But you came after me anyway – you *saved* me.'

Oyru touched the crushed socket of his missing eye. 'Growing stronger means testing our limits. It means sacrificing our weaker parts in exchange for something greater.'

'And if we break beyond repair, does that mean we have found our ultimate limit? Does that make us for ever less than we once were?'

Oyru was silent, his hand sliding from his cheekbone and then resting at his side.

'I don't know,' he said at last, his gaze distant. 'Perhaps.'

'You don't believe that.'

His gaze suddenly returned to her, meeting the green eyes beneath her mask. 'Why do you say that?'

'Because you have broken me so many times. Because I have learned that every failure is a gift that grants a new beginning. While success teaches you nothing except that you have not yet discovered your limits.'

'And what have your failures taught you?'

'That I have no limits, so long as I make a new beginning.'

A slow smile crept across the assassin's face, its warmth faint and unfamiliar.

'Let us sleep then, and discover what new beginnings await us.'

No more words were exchanged between the master and his former apprentice. Instead, they lay down beside one another, with the familiarity of an old couple. Their eyes closed, and as the exhaustion of the unending days and nights seeped into them, they allowed the somnumbra to saturate them, penetrating so deeply that their physical bodies slipped into another world of darker shadows and deeper dreams.

Myjun awoke so sharply it set her heart racing. Instinctively, she raised her hands to her face to touch her golden prison of a mask, but when her fingertips touched her face she found it as soft and malleable as real flesh.

'It's gone,' she whispered, afraid to open her eyes. 'How is it gone?'

'Because this is a dream,' Oyru said, standing somewhere off to her left, 'and because it is not actually gone.'

Myjun opened her eyes to see the assassin holding a gilded mirror in front of her face. Myjun flinched, afraid to look, until her curiosity got the better of her. She gazed at the polished reflection in the mirror and gasped.

'It's me,' she breathed, her fingers returning to her face. 'It's me, but ...'

'It's not exactly you, is it?'

Myjun's eyes traced the bounce of her wavy auburn hair, clean and combed. She stared at her cool green eyes, shining like emeralds, her flawless skin, its surface gleaming like pure gold yet soft as true flesh.

'What devilry is this?'

'Our dreams are what we make of them,' Oyru said, slowly lowering the mirror. 'We are an image of ourselves, but we cannot wholly control that image.' As the gilded mirror lowered, she saw that the Shadow Reborn's face had also changed: instead of a black mask covering a pale face, the black wrapping had been pulled down to his neck and his cheeks held the fresh tint of life; blood pumped beneath the shade's once bloodless flesh, and his missing eye had repaired itself.

Myjun stared at him, momentarily breathless. Was this how Oyru had looked as a man instead of a half-man? Or was this only his perception of himself – a dream among dreams?

'Nothing you see here is real,' he said, as if answering her question. 'This is a projection of our thoughts, imposed on a reality that only exists here.' He gestured at the void around them. 'Here ... and in the minds of those who touch this realm when they sleep.'

'What about us? Aren't we here physically?'

Oyru slowly nodded. 'We are. If you returned to the Shadowrealm right now, you would not find us slumbering on the ground. We are truly present here. We have physically transported ourselves to a new plane of existence, tabibito.'

'So where are the nightmares and the dreamscapes? There's nothing here.'

'Such things must be summoned. Cognitive energy must be spent to lure them here and they must be shaped by the dreamer. We have summoned no one and invested no such energy, so the world remains empty. More barren than even the Shadowrealm.'

'But surely people in the physical world are dreaming now? Someone, somewhere is sleeping right now. Why do we not see their dreams?'

'Because the Cognitive Realm is a vast ocean where the concept of space differs from the physical world and the Shadowrealm.' Oyru gestured at the endless darkness. 'A dreamwalker can travel this plane with ease because they are not moored by a physical body. They project their mind across the dreamscape and travel wherever their thoughts take them. A Voidweaver could do the same, though they might bring their body with them – but space and time bend themselves to suit the will and the needs of such creatures. For us ... well, we are anchored to the point where we fell asleep. For the landscape to change, we must create that change ourselves, or have it imposed upon us by another being. That is not likely to happen without a strong mental or spiritual connection. So we wait.'

'Wait for the witherkin?'

'For him ... or our own nightmares.'

Myjun squinted at the starless sky and then again at the featureless ground, unable to tell where one ended and the other began. She reached out, searching for anything that would give her a sense of depth, but she found only open air.

'I feel dizzy,' she said, sitting down. 'I feel like I'm falling, but there is ground beneath my feet. I feel like I should be able to see where the earth and the sky meet ... this is madness.'

'Yes. I suspect it is. In fact ...' Oyru reached out and touched what appeared to be a solid black wall. Then he pressed his body against it ... and began crawling up it. When he was satisfied, he rose to his feet and stood perpendicular to the plane Myjun stood upon.

'How in the Nine Hells did you do that?'

Oyru smiled. 'I cannot bend space and time like the Voidweavers, but a little of their blood runs through my veins. This is the only trick I can do with their magic – and the only place I can do it.'

'Can I learn?'

He shook his head. 'Perhaps if the darkness were made of light, but here ... this is a place of entropy. A facet of the Shadowrealm. I think not even a dreamwalker could do this.'

The assassin pressed his fingers against the blackness and began to climb again, and then walked along another wall. From where Myjun stood, it looked as if he was walking on the ceiling.

'Rot and hell!' she swore. 'Stop that!'

Oyru raised a foot, placed it on something solid, then lifted himself up as though he were climbing a stair – except this stair led down towards Myjun instead of up towards the sky. He took another step and then another. His last and final step placed him on equal footing with Myjun ... except she stood right side up and he walked beneath her. She stepped away and Oyru followed, his feet treading the same ground as her, but on an inverted plane. When she finally stopped moving, Oyru walked until his feet rested beneath hers. He looked down – or up – and so did she.

'What happens if I try to take your hand?' Myjun asked, afraid to try. 'Will I detach from the ground I'm standing on ... or will we be unable to penetrate the plane we're anchored to?'

'Try it and find out.'

Myjun leaned further forward and tentatively reached out a hand. Oyru did the same but with more confidence. When their fingers met where the ground should have been, there was no barrier between them and their hands locked together.

'This is madness,' Myjun whispered, her mind still reeling. 'How is this possible?'

'It's all part of the landscape, Myjun. It's all a dream. It's what we make of it.' He nodded at her with his chin. 'Want to try lifting your feet off the floor?'

'You mean, do I want to try and swing from your hand?'

'Sure.'

Myjun inhaled deeply, still battling a sense of vertigo. 'Why not.' She lifted her left foot from the floor but still felt gravity anchoring her to her plane. When she jumped, though, she tumbled into Oyru's arms as gravity reorientated itself and she landed on his plane.

'Well,' he said, his tone dry, 'that was educational.'

'And what exactly did we learn?'

'I have no idea.'

A grey shadow began to coalesce in the air beside them. Myjun saw it a half instant before Oyru did and leapt from his arms, her soulblades popping into existence.

'The witherkin! He's here!'

Oyru's twin flyssas materialised in his hands. 'Our weapons may still be ineffective against it,' he warned, pacing away from Myjun and drawing the creature's attention. As if to test his theory, Oyru swept outward with both his swords and cleaved Yohan's ghost in two. The spectre's eyes burned white with anger and his mouth opened in a voiceless scream.

'Dammit,' he swore, dodging as the witherkin lunged for him. 'Your turn,' he shouted, rolling safely away from the ghoul's attack.

With the witherkin's back to her, Myjun lunged and drove her soulfire blades into the creature. It howled, a shriek more visceral than any scream she'd heard in the Physical Realm, and its eyes burned with bright yellow heat. Its outline turned to glowing ash and then the spectre's ephemeral form blew away like vapour in the wind.

Myjun stared at the spot where the witherkin had stood. 'Is that it? Is it ... gone?'

'It would appear so,' Oyru said, rising to his feet. 'Well done, tabibito.'

Myjun stared at her knives, her brow furrowed. 'That seemed too easy. When I struck it ... I didn't feel any resistance. It was as if there was nothing there at all.'

'And how did it feel the first time you attacked it? Was it any different when we stood together in the Shadowrealm and you tried to kill it?'

'No,' Myjun admitted, though the ease of her kill still bothered her. 'It just felt so ... unsatisfying.'

'Do not forget that this one lost his soul to the eidola. Only his cognitive mind remained, so destroying him could not feed your soulfire blades as it does in the physical world.'

Myjun slowly nodded. 'Yes, that must be it.' She sighed. 'It was so unfulfilling, though. After all that time avoiding it in the Shadowrealm, we come here and—' She snapped her fingers. 'Gone. Just like that.'

'You do not give yourself enough credit, Myjun. My flyssas did not harm the creature. If you had not been here to kill the witherkin, I would have had no recourse against him. It is luck that has saved us this day – luck, and your mastery of your powers.'

'Perhaps.' She turned her eyes on the shapeless darkness surrounding them and squinted at the bright sun beginning to rise up out of the void. 'Oyru,' she said, her stomach twisting into a knot. 'Did you summon that?'

Oyru shook his head, his eyes squinting to block the sudden rays of sunshine. 'That is not my doing, tabibito.'

'This isn't more Voidweaver magic?'

'No – and this is not a dream I have summoned.'

'Then what ... what is it?' They both stared at the light, growing brighter and hotter as it shot like a star across the starless void.

'Did you imagine this sunrise?' Oyru asked, now covering his face from the furnace of the burning orb above their heads. 'Did you *summon* it?'

'No!' Myjun screamed, now turning her back on the sun and searching for a place to hide. But there was none. The void was as empty as it had always been.

'This way!' Oyru shouted and a deep cave formed in front of him. He pulled her inside and together they huddled in the shadows beneath the fire that scoured the world beyond.

'I don't understand,' Myjun said, sweating. 'If neither of us summoned it—'

'Then it must be another person's dream,' Oyru finished, though he seemed uncertain. 'If a dreamwalker slept nearby – not physically perhaps, but if their mind had focused on one of us – then the fire would follow us here.' He shied from the light illuminating the front of the cave, his face turned towards the deeper darkness of their shallow hole. 'The dreamwalker must have thought of us – of me or you – while dreaming of fire and flame. That would bring everything together here. Us and the ball of fire.'

'You don't seem very certain!' Myjun snapped. Oyru hunched deeper into the shadows of the cave, away from the heat. 'What is happening!' She was desperate. 'How do we stop it?'

'We could try to wait it out,' Oyru said, his voice calm though his clothing had begun to smoulder, 'but I fear the fire may cook us alive before its heat diminishes.'

Myjun huddled with him at the back of the shallow cave. 'Can we run?'

'There is nowhere to run to.'

'So what does that leave?'

'Same as always,' Oyru said, his eyes locking on hers. 'We arm ourselves ... and we fight.'

Before Myjun could answer, the assassin pursed his lips and opaque shadows bled out of his pupils, the conjuror's eyes went as dark as liquid night ... and then the blackness continued to flow from his sockets, across his face and dripping down his body. As the blackness shifted to cover his entire body, Oyru's thin plates of shadow armour blossomed into thick scales of nether plate and void shards. He was a black knight – a warrior of shadows and darkness. Still squinting in the glare of the sun outside their cave, the Shadow Reborn stepped into the light and allowed the fire to wash over him, consuming him.

Myjun screamed. It was happening *again* – and once again, she was too slow to stop it; Annev had incinerated her father with the power of his golden hand, and now she watched again as this sun tore through the half-man's nether plate. Oyru turned towards her at the last instant, his shadow armour melted away – and then the shadow mage disappeared in a cloud of ash and smoke.

'No! Noooo!'

Beyond the cave, the intense light continued to beat down.

Heat flowed inside the cave mouth, as if from some infernal forge.

Myjun stopped screaming. Not because her anguish had ended, but because it hurt too much to breathe the fiery air inside her cave.

Is this how it was for Annev? she thought, curling up in the farthest recesses of the subterranean den. *He huddled behind that shield wall and watched his mentor burn alive ... and he did the same to my father.*

She relived the memory she had fought so hard to forget: Annev raising his golden arm, catching the flames in the palm of his hand, her father fighting the will of a crippled boy possessed by the power of Keos himself then withering beneath the flames reflected back at him, his flesh melting, her own skin searing as she dived for cover.

Above her head, the walls of the cave began to crack, letting in more light and heat.

Light, she thought. *I can manipulate the light.* That *is what Oyru has been unable to teach me. I can bend it. Shape it. Own it. Perhaps I can even reflect it?*

Still squinting in the brightness that surrounded her, Myjun found her centre and began to hum. It was instinctive. Natural. She found her emotions and, rather than trying to tame them or wield them, she flowed with them, allowing her voice to capture her feelings. Her anger was there, as it always was, but this time it was not a barrier to her other emotions. She finally mourned her father, feeling the grief that had so often been tinged with her own self-hatred and disgust. This time, however, the feeling was pure. A simple keening for the father she had known, and the void left by his loss. She felt her heady, youthful love for Annev – and her confusion on discovering he was crippled. There was loss there, too. The loss of what might have been. Of trust. Of his friendship. She had felt the same way when Kenton had been scarred ... but this was worse. It was a secret Annev had kept from her, not some punishment inflicted by the gods.

And then he'd killed her father. She saw it more clearly now – his rage at Sodar's death, his sense of her betrayal – and she saw his subsequent rage reflected in her own emotions. When she had been fighting and killing the monsters in the Vosgar, she had been fighting him. When she had been slaughtering innocents in Hentingsfort, she had been murdering him. When she had killed the eidolons on the shadow planes, she had been battling him.

And in battling him – in fighting the *symbol* of her hatred – Myjun realised she had been fighting herself.

Myjun opened her eyes and stared fully into the light that was crushing her sanctuary, crumbling its walls around her. She felt the waves of heat licking at her chitin-covered flesh – and clarity struck. Her humming rose into a wordless tune, and then the melody streamed from her golden lips, its tune bittersweet and strong. She wrapped herself in its music, wrapped the world in its song, and she felt the terrible light of the demon sun move with it, reflecting around her, bending with her word and her will. She wove a tapestry of emotion and light, *lumen* and lightfire – and then she stood and walked into the light.

Ani. The word echoed in her mind, both a name and a calling. *Ainnevog.* She wove it into her song, her pitch and timbre matching the emotions she couldn't express any other way.

Annev.

The sun winked out like a candle in the dark and Myjun stood alone in the darkness, her skin glowing like molten fire.

Chapter Eighty-Five

Annev.

The word echoed in Annev's mind, rousing him from sleep. He'd been dreaming again, the same nightmare he had been fighting since Sodar had died. He saw the molten fire of Tosan's hellfire wand, saw the destruction of the Academy. He watched in horror as he turned his flames on Myjun. She had stood in terror, watching the destruction approach her. He had sealed his mind to the voices that threatened to overtake him – and then she had fallen into the crevasse, screaming his name.

Annev.

He blinked and saw where he was. Creaking wood and lapping water. A dark hull and the fetid smell of an unwashed mattress and dried blood.

Honeycutt's blood, Annev thought, remembering how callously he had used it to paint his dragonscale cloak – and a good thing he had, too, for its magic had proven invaluable. Less than an hour after boarding the *Crested Cormorant* he had been tasked with climbing the ship's rigging and hastening the massive ship's journey upriver towards Luqura. Using Honeycutt's Breathbreaker powers via his cloak, Annev had harnessed the wind and directed it into the great river barge's sails, adding to the labours of the oarsmen. As he worked, he had worried that the magic might tire or that his reserves of *quaire* might be depleted, but the garment seemed unaffected by the constraints of Darite magic; like all artifacts, its magical reserves seemed to be without limit. But Anabo could not know that, so whenever the woman questioned his stamina – usually through some sexual innuendo – Annev would acquiesce and retire to drink water, rest and regain his strength.

Annev rose from his pallet and stood, fumbling in the dark before remembering to magnify the power of his Inquisitor ring. Once the artifact's magic shifted his vision into gradations of red, he soon identified the dark burgundy outlines of the barge's stained wood, the thatch of maroon and scarlet marking the straw pallet where he had slept and the residual heat that still lingered amidst the soft hay. A copper chamber pot gleamed just beyond his feet, perfectly positioned to trip him, and Annev stepped around the receptable with cautious ease. Thinking better of it, he stooped to relieve himself.

Too much bloody water, Annev thought, as he shuddered and shook the excess fluid from his body. *Must have drunk a gallon of the damned stuff.* He rebuttoned his trousers and picked up the dark outline of his steel vambrace, Toothbreaker.

After Anabo had silently questioned the abnormal size of his gloved prosthetic back in Quiri, Annev had taken to hiding his gloved golden hand with Sodar's old battle buckler – a peculiar combination of shield and vambrace with prongs near the fist and elbow that allowed him to fight unarmed, should he need to. The sailors aboard the Cormorant had stared at first, clearly uncomfortable with Annev's decision to carry the weapon, yet after a full day of filling the barge's sails, the crew seemed to have accepted Annev's eccentricities, no longer eyeing his strange shield or the eerie charcoal-and-white magpie cloak.

Enjoying the warmth of his magic garment, Annev slid aside the wooden bar locking his door and stepped into the narrow confines of the ship's bowels. A dim lantern hung at the opposite end of the tight corridor and he felt his way towards it, and the stepladder that led above ship. The stars overhead greeted him, and Annev realised he had slept through first and second watch.

Perhaps using the artifact does drain me somehow, he mused, surprised that he had slept so long. *Or perhaps I've been pushing myself too hard.*

'Good morning, Master Magpie.'

'Is it truly morning if the stars are still out, Jaffa?' Annev stood at the railing, his gaze locked on the heavens above him, searching for answers. Anabo's slave approached from behind.

'For farmers and manservants, it is. We rise before the dawn and complete most of our labours before others have eaten their breakfast.'

Annev nodded. It had been the same for Sodar. 'Are your labours complete, then?'

'Nearly. The consul did not know when you would return to deck, but she bid me give these to you when you did.' Jaffa shifted an ornate leather tube on his back, its cap sealed with the royal crest of Innistiul, then he opened his sand-coloured cloak and took out a shiny black object with a white beak and feathered edges.

'A magpie mask?' Annev asked, surprised. He accepted it. 'When did Consul Anabo have time to procure this?'

'Shortly after your first meeting. She had planned to give it to you last night as a token of her appreciation, but she grew bored waiting for you and retired to her chambers.'

'And did the consul hope I would *wear* it to her chambers?' Annev asked, guessing the woman's intentions.

Jaffa shrugged, though a tiny smile tugged at the corner of his mouth. 'I cannot speak for the consul, milord ... though I suspect you have the right of it.'

Annev knew precisely what the seductive consul had intended by the gift. 'Phoeba has yet to pay me the initial price she promised, yet she hopes to win me over with bedroom gifts?'

Jaffa's smile did not falter.

Annev nodded, turning the eccentric mask over in his hands. The work was exquisite, carved from something that felt like polished wood ... but the magic of his copper ring showed him the truth of the mask's origin. 'This is bone,' he said, holding the magpie mask aloft with his right hand. 'Carved from a skull, possibly human. It was lacquered black and then the ivory beak was affixed to the nose – probably taken from the tusk of some animal.'

'The merchant swore it was crafted from a Bloodlord's head.' Annev turned to see the consul climbing the ladder behind him.

She wore a gossamer-blue nightdress laced with gold, the fabric pulled tight around her curved body. 'The Bloodlord's skull,' she continued, 'and the talons of the harpy that slew him.'

'The hunter and its prey?' Annev offered.

Anabo smiled. 'They grappled and killed each other ... so who can say which is which?'

'Or whether your merchant was telling the truth?' Annev countered, taking care not to stare at the woman's plunging neckline.

'Jacy is the best artisan in Quiri,' Anabo said, her fingers teasing the lace of her frock. 'She's an exquisite craftswoman who procures the most exotic resources for her projects.' She stepped closer, her lacquered fingernails tapping the cheekbones of the mask while her palms softly brushed the back of his right hand. 'I guarantee it's genuine. Do you not like it?' She said this last with a slight pout to her lips.

Annev's eyes tightened and he had to fight not to frown at the woman's obvious advances. He sensed a touch of magic there, too, as he had during their first encounter. She definitely had a strain of magic bound up in her blood, and that made Annev covet it.

'The mask is exquisite – but it is not the payment we agreed on. Ten vials of blood, including one from you and one from your manservant.'

'And eight more of your choosing,' Anabo finished, her eyebrow rising as her lips pursed into a full pout. Even as she spoke, though, her fingers slipped down to her cleavage and removed a glass vial of scarlet liquid. 'I had hoped to give this to you last night ... among other things.'

Annev took the vial, suspicious. 'This is your blood?' he asked, uncorking its contents and inhaling the odour.

The consul nodded slowly. 'As promised.'

Annev touched the tip of his index finger to the top of the vial, upended it and sniffed the crimson liquid clinging to his fingertip. He shook his head. 'Whose blood is this? It's not yours.'

Anabo opened her mouth as if to protest then hesitated. 'Well, as I said, Jacy Ashbury deals in only the most exotic resources. The vial of blood was another gift. With my compliments.'

Annev sniffed again then pressed a drop of blood to his tongue.

Jaffa gasped, his eyes widening. Anabo seemed to as well, though her exclamation transformed into a soft moan of pleasure. Annev gritted his teeth, trying not to roll his eyes. Did the woman's seductions never cease? Or was she truly aroused by his licking a stranger's blood?

For his own part, Annev felt the bile rise in his gut as he realised he was doing exactly what Jian Nikloss had when attempting to read his fate. He fought his private revulsion, though, and forced himself to focus on the magic sitting on his tongue. The copper Inquisitor ring seemed to tingle on his finger, and he felt something akin to mindwalking at the Enclave. The world did not shatter or shake beneath his feet, though, nor did his mind shift to another world; instead, he caught a glimpse of the man whose blood he had just tasted. He saw in a flash what had killed him – a monstrous bird with a woman's face and breasts, razor-sharp fangs, and ivory talons. He watched it strike the Bloodlord as it swooped from the sky, and saw them grapple with each other. He tasted the coppery tang of blood as the talons ripped into his throat. He felt the Bloodlord's magic rise as he seized the creature in his gauntleted hands, snapping the bird's foot and turning its own blood against it.

Then Annev was the harpy who had dived from the sky to attack the man below her. He felt the screams in her throat as she cawed and cackled, felt the fear as her own blood turned against her, like a thousand knives turning on her from within her feathered body. He felt the man's throat crush beneath her talons and the harpy's body explode outward with the force of the Bloodlord's magic.

Annev gasped, breathing hard. He sealed the vial and turned back to the consul. 'I will accept this as one of the eight vials,' he said, slipping the bottle into the breast pocket of his tunic. 'But you still owe me your own blood and that of your servant.' Annev nodded respectfully to Jaffa and the man bowed in return.

'How did you know?' Anabo asked, unabashed and seemingly unashamed of the lie she had told. 'How could you tell?'

Annev raised the magpie mask to his face, his fingers knotting the leather cord behind his head. 'That's my secret,' he said, settling the Bloodlord's skull over his eyes. 'Thank you for the gift.'

Then he bowed, turned, and walked over to climb the ratlines up the ship's mainmast to drive the ship forward again.

When the sun had fully risen above the horizon and the barge was sailing at a good clip down the length of the North Tocra River, Annev released the magic winds and shakily climbed back down to the *Cormorant*'s deck. As expected, Jaffa waited for him, though Anabo was nowhere in sight.

'The consul invites you to take breakfast with her,' Jaffa said, answering Annev's unspoken question.

Annev adjusted his mask. He had originally worn it to draw Anabo's ire – to make a statement that he could not be seduced or bought – but the hours he had spent clinging to the ship's rigging had given him time to wonder at other uses for the curio. If he used his own artificing powers and applied the Terran mage's blood to the mask, would he be able to harness the Bloodlord's powers as he had with the dragonscale cloak and Honeycutt's magic? Annev suspected he could, though he had much less blood to work with.

'I'll join her below deck,' Annev said, and Jaffa led the way down the hatch, beneath the promenade deck, down another level and into the ship's galley where a small table seated Consul Anabo and the ship's captain, Ezias Iosua, a swarthy slave-trader from Innistiul.

'Captain Iosua,' Jaffa said, bowing to the stout Innistiulman. 'Master Magpie is here to break his fast.'

'Please sit,' Iosua said, nodding at the chair to his left, across from the consul. 'We were just discussing your prodigious efforts to move the *Cormorant* upriver. Very impressive. We've more than doubled our typical speed and Consul Anabo was wagering we might reach Luqura before nightfall. I doubted you could keep your present pace up. More likely tomorrow morning?'

Annev accepted the compliment and took his seat beside the captain, noting that Anabo had changed into yet another garment – this time a saffron dress more befitting of her diplomatic station, though the cut was on the line between professional and scandalous. He noted, too, that the captain's attention was more fixed on the consul's chest than on Annev's garish face mask.

'Odar alone knows the limits of my strength, but I hope not to test those today. With proper breaks for rest and refreshment, I expect we'll reach Luqura just after nightfall.'

The captain glanced at Annev. 'Excellent, excellent.' He snapped his fingers and a blonde woman in tan robes brought a steaming bowl of broth to the table and ladled the contents into the wide cups before the captain, the consul, and Annev.

Annev raised an eyebrow, leaned closer to his cup and caught the sweet smell of creamed potatoes and steamed clams. His mouth was beginning to water when he noticed the red slave's brand scarring the Ilumite woman's cheek, and the scent soured for him, remembering the pain when Elar Kranak had pressed his own slave brand into Annev's chest. Without thinking, he traced the raised flesh beneath his tunic. He had healed the injury mere minutes after its formation, but the scar from the slave's brand still remained.

'Fisherman's mulligan,' Captain Iosua said, spooning the thick broth to his lips. 'A delicacy from Quiri that has been perfected in Innistiul. Delicious.'

Annev nodded, drawn back to the present. He pulled off his bone mask and, realising his shield-bracer would be difficult to hold under the table, he tugged it off too. Then, being careful to keep his gloved hand hidden, he began spooning up some of the hot soup. The chowder was good – just a hint of seafood mellowed by the potatoes and cream – and he quickly took another spoonful.

'Master Magpie is speechless, methinks,' Anabo teased, winking across the table.

'Hungry,' Annev said, taking another swallow. 'I've only had cold rations for the last few days. It's good to have something hot running down my throat.' The consul snorted and Annev wondered: had the innuendo been a slip, or were the consul's overt advances finally getting the better of him?

'Nothing like warm soup to fill the belly,' Iosua said, oblivious.

Annev drained the cup in front of him. 'Very good mulligan,' he said, setting his spoon inside the cup. 'Never tasted its like.'

'The soup in Quiri pales in comparison!'

'Ah – yes, I think so.'

The captain slapped the table, satisfied. 'It is one of the wonders of Innistiul! Tell me, Master Magpie. Have you been to the Ivory Isle?'

Annev raised an eyebrow, careful to maintain his guise. 'My tasks with the Brotherhood have taken me to many places ... but never for long. I expect I'm not acquainted with even a fraction of Innistiul's treasures.'

Iosua grunted in agreement. 'Few truly are. We are mostly known for our exports from Ilumea,' he said, gesturing to the scarred slave beside the table. 'Very few travellers take the time to explore our salt mines, our plentiful coasts and endless beaches. A handful come in search of ivory, but they soon discover it is our sands that give Innistiul its title, not the bones of some boar-bear or oliphaunt.' He tsked, then slurped another mouthful of salty chowder.

Anabo cleared her throat. 'Actually, Innistiul was originally the home of both animals, but they were hunted to extinction long ago. Their bones earned the Ivory Isles their name ... even though they are no more. We are left with sand and slaves.'

'And fisherman's mulligan!' Iosua shouted, tossing back the dregs of his cup.

'Hardly a treasure,' Anabo said, taking a polite sip of her chowder, 'but I suppose we have our trade routes. Herbs and exotic animals from Ilumea. Spiced wines and silks from Terra Majora. Red gold and silver from New Terra. Ironwood from Alltara. Grain and horseflesh from Greater Luqura and Southmarch.' She peered at Annev. 'Luqura may be the crossroads of the west, but Innistiul is the shipping capital of the north. We are more cosmopolitan than the other kingdoms in the Empire, and with our ocean access to Ilumea and Terra Majora, we are invaluable allies and essential trading partners.'

Annev nodded as if all of this made sense to him. 'Terra Majora,' he repeated, his feigned nonchalance hiding his actual interest in the conversation. 'What have you seen of that continent?'

'Nothing, I'm afraid. As consul to Luqura, my sphere of influence – and my opportunities for travel – are limited. What I do control, though, I control entirely. I know the ways of Luqura as fluently as my own home, and my power is equal to either King Cheng or King Lenka.'

Annev shrugged her boast away, though he found the consul's comment to be more interesting than her reference to the old Terran continent. 'Surely a diplomat cannot compete with the genuine power of a king or queen? Your title is bestowed by King Cheng, you are only acting in his name.'

Anabo's eyes tightened before she smiled patronizingly at Annev. 'Of course, my power does not exceed that of the king himself – nor does it approach the influence of God-king Neruacanta – but it is often my word that sways the will of kings. '

Annev bowed in acquiescence, sensing this was sensitive territory. 'I mean no offence, Consul Anabo.'

'No offence taken,' Anabo said, still smiling.

Like a viper watching her prey, Annev thought, studying her eyes. *You aren't a seductress – that's a mask you wear to hide the serpent lurking inside. I'll need to be careful with you, Mistress Anabo. Very, very careful.*

Something flickered behind the consul's eyes and she suddenly switched her attention to the ship's captain. 'A second course?'

'Quite right!' Iosua snapped his fingers and Jaffa brought in a long plate – nearly six feet in length. Atop the dish lay a sizzling sturgeon, its flesh smoked and salted.

'That's enormous!' Annev blurted, surprised by the size of the fish, which nose-to-tip nearly equalled him in height. 'Where did you find such a beast?'

'Right here in the Tocra!' Iosua laughed, pounding the surface of the table. 'Didn't know they grew in your own backyard, did you?'

Annev slowly shook his head, and he immediately wondered if the admission might somehow clue the consul in on his false identity. 'I'm afraid I haven't had the pleasure.'

'It seems you have denied yourself so many pleasures,' Anabo said, teasing the tines of her fork between her fingertips. 'You really should experience more that the world has to offer.'

As Annev met her gaze, the sense that he was being hunted by a dangerous predator redoubled. He swallowed. 'I'm afraid my days at the Enclave were not very ... inclusive.'

Anabo's smile broadened. 'That is something we shall have to remedy.'

The captain drew his belt knife and sliced down to decapitate the enormous sturgeon. 'Grab some flesh while it's hot!' the captain commanded.

The consul glanced at Iosua, saw that the man had missed the double meaning entirely, and then winked at Annev, failing to suppress her smile. 'Yes. We mustn't let such tender meat go to waste. Don't you agree, Master Magpie?'

Annev took a long draft from the cup at his side then rose from the table. 'I'm afraid I should get back to my post at the mainsail. The sooner we reach Luqura, the sooner we can all return home.'

Captain Iosua raised his cup in salute to Annev. 'Don't push yourself too hard, Master Magpie. If we reach Luqura before nightfall, I'll owe Mistress Anabo a whole lunari!'

Chapter Eighty-Six

Annev groaned as he climbed down the rigging, his muscles knotted and sore from clinging to the thick rope ladder. He was shivering, too, for though the magic dragonscale cloak trapped his body heat and kept his core warm, he still felt the chill air blowing across the waters, and his hands, face and feet were not immune to the winds.

He had been watching the deck below for half an hour, watching for the predatory consul, and had only descended when he was certain Anabo had gone below deck.

Would it really be so bad if she caught me in her snare? Surely there are worse things than having a beautiful woman massage the kinks out of my muscles? Even as he stomped down onto the main deck, though, he knew that he was fooling himself. Anabo had made her intentions quite clear, and the moment she discovered Annev's golden prosthetic, she would discern his identity. Thinking of this, he briskly rubbed his gloved fingers together, then strapped Toothbreaker on.

Instead of heading down to the galley where either Anabo or Jaffa would spot him, Annev climbed the steps to the promenade deck and stared out over the ship's stern. Without his magical assistance, he could already see the rowers' pace slowing as the barge went from a steady clip upstream to a slow struggle against the current. He rubbed his hands together again and watched the riverbanks, wondering what kind of towns lay between Luqura and Quiri. He wondered, too, whether his friends had gone ahead with their asinine plan to leave the Enclave and try to help the besieged townsfolk in Banok.

'May Odar watch over you, brothers,' he whispered to the wind, 'wherever you are.'

'Do you think he really listens to your prayers?'

Annev froze, not needing to turn to see who was addressing him. 'I don't know,' Annev said truthfully, not moving his gaze from the receding shoreline. 'I've never been that devout ... but my mentor was a true believer. I think many of his views rubbed off on me, but I never swallowed the whole fish, if you catch my meaning.'

'I think I do,' Anabo said, gliding up beside him. She leaned over the rail, her own gaze fixed on the rushing river as it streamed out behind the ship's hull. 'The people of Innistiul have never been especially religious – we leave that to the Enclave and the priesthood in Quiri – but we do have our superstitions and traditions.'

'Such as?' Annev asked, genuinely curious.

Anabo shrugged. 'They say King Cheng's bloodline is uniquely blessed to rule the isle, but few people truly believe it. If they did, there would be fewer assassination attempts and nobles trying to seize control from the royal family.'

Annev grunted, trying to remember where Sraon's lineage fit into the tapestry of Innistiul politics. 'What about you? Where does the Anabo bloodline fit?'

The consul turned her attention from the waves and fixed him with a glare that, for once, was not seductive – it was suspicious. 'You ask as if you don't already know?' She quirked an eyebrow. 'Or perhaps this is your weak attempt at small talk?'

Annev felt himself blush beneath the magpie mask and he fought the urge to lick his lips, for his mouth was not covered by the grisly artifact. 'You're a diplomat,' Annev said, trying to piece together an appropriate response. 'I assume the position is not hereditary.'

'It is not.'

'So what is your lineage?'

Anabo's lips pursed and Annev saw this had been the wrong thing to ask. 'People of no consequence.'

'Of course. My apologies if I was too forward.'

The consul sniffed. 'Too forward would be refreshing, since

you keep rebuffing my advances without directly turning me down. Perhaps it is I who should apologise for being too forward?'

Annev met the woman's gaze and saw she was not being coy or making another attempt at seduction. She seemed genuinely apologetic, which made Annev feel guilty.

'How did you become consul to two of the Empire's most powerful kingdoms?'

Anabo chuckled. 'I'm persuasive, manipulative, seductive, and I get what I want. That's a skill – an especially valuable one for a diplomat – and I capitalised on it. I made myself invaluable to important people and did whatever I needed to, to get ahead – without, before you ask, sleeping with all the men on the isle. Or even half of them. I'm a sensual woman with a healthy sexual appetite, but I'm selective. I don't throw myself at every boy dangled in front of me.'

Annev sputtered, stifling an embarrassed laugh. 'I didn't mean to imply—'

'Yes, you did – and I'm not offended. Many have made the same mistake before, and I'm always quick to correct it. I've had Jaffa cleave a few more insistent men from their cocks, in the past. Word gets around fast, and then you can pursue the few that genuinely interest you.'

'I see.'

'Do you?'

Annev met her gaze and once more saw her seductive danger. 'I'm flattered by your interest, Consul – really, I am – but my presence here is purely professional. Surely you understand that.'

Anabo smiled, her eyes crinkling and hinting at the true age hidden behind her artfully applied make-up. 'I suppose I do – but you still haven't rejected me outright.'

'Isn't that what I just did?'

'You said your interest was professional ... while wearing a mask designed for the bedroom, which I gifted you. And you've requested payment in blood. A very sensual price if I do say so myself.' She tilted her head coquettishly. 'Would you like to draw that sample now ... in my bedroom? Perhaps you'd enjoy that.'

'No. I'll leave that to you, and trust I will have it before we arrive in Luqura. I have business to attend to when we arrive.'

'How very mysterious,' she said, licking her lips. 'Just as well, I suppose, that I have my own errands to run. Politics, you understand.'

Annev wondered if this were a good time to ask the consul her business in Greater Luqura's capital. He held off, suspecting that 'Master Magpie' might already know Anabo's reasons for hastening to Luqura. She had implied as much.

'Where will you go first?' he finally asked, leading with the most innocent question.

'To the palace. Cheng's orders come first – as do those from our mutual friend in New Terra – and I understand Tiana Rocas is keen to speed her coronation. I'd hate to be the reason it was held up.'

Coronation? Annev thought, schooling his reaction. *But that means . . .*

A glimpse into her mind with the codavora ring confirmed his guess: King Lenka was dead – and Tiana Rocas was to be crowned Queen of Greater Luqura. *But how can that be?* Annev wondered, turning his gaze back to the river's winding shores.

'How soon?'

'Things will proceed swiftly. The Guild and the nobility are all in line, and this was prepared well in advance of Lenka's passing. Dante Turano has even prepared some special gladiatorial matches for the coronation.' Annev nodded as if all of this weren't news to him and she eyed him sideways. 'Will you be there? I haven't seen you in the Undercity before. If you haven't experienced its pleasures, I can introduce you to them. I dare say Dante's bazaar of delights rivals even the black markets of Quiri and Innistiul – but don't tell *him* I said that. He's got a big enough ego as it is, and I don't want him to think I actually enjoy his little games.' She smirked as though this were some private joke Annev would understand.

'I wouldn't mind seeing the Undercity . . . but first I need to visit Saltair. We have some unfinished business.'

'The phoenix boy? If anyone has seen him or knows where he's hiding, Tiana Rocas will. She uses Saltair as often as we do.'

Annev was grateful for the information. 'Could Dante be helpful, with his knowledge of the Undercity?'

Anabo grinned. 'I'm sure Dante knows *something*. Between him and Tiana's Watchers they know every dark secret in that city – but if you were fishing for an invitation, you can just ask. I'd be more than happy for the company.' She moistened her lips, leaning forward. 'Then again, maybe I should seek a companion who's more amenable to *my* interests?' She arched an eyebrow and Annev couldn't help but chuckle.

'You really are relentless.'

'You noticed.'

Annev's cheeks turned red at the images dancing through the woman's mind. *She wants to win. She thinks of me as a conquest.* He wondered how long he could play this game before the entire Master Magpie ruse collapsed. *If she catches a glimpse of my hand . . .*

'I'd love to accompany you,' he said, impulsively. 'To Dante's party, and to the palace.'

Anabo narrowed her eyes. 'The palace wasn't part of the invitation . . . but I suppose I can be generous. Tiana will be there, so you could talk to her about Saltair.'

'My thoughts exactly.'

'Mm. Wonderful. It's a date then.'

Annev forced a smile, though he suddenly felt like an animal in a trap. 'I suppose it is.' He instantly regretted making the commitment.

'Tell me,' he continued, purposefully avoiding the consul's gaze, 'what is that tube Jaffa carries on his back?'

The consul's eyes narrowed for a fraction of second. 'Cheng's sovereign writ,' she said smoothly. 'The consul from Paldron will have a similar writ from King Alpenrose. With two writs and a simple majority of Luqura's nobles, Tiana can be crowned Queen of Greater Luqura.'

Annev feared he should have already known that. The consul gave no indication that he had misspoken, though, so he almost let it pass. Only his paranoia prompted him to use the codavora ring's mindwalking powers again ... and instead of a coherent string of words, the golden serpent from the codavora ring allowed him to glimpse the woman's emotions: suspicion, anger and uncertainty.

Bollocks. She suspects something. I shouldn't have asked so many questions. Then again, Annev thought, could he turn those suspicions to his advantage? *Can I read her mind, to tell her something that only Neruacanta's agent would know ... ?*

'Is King Cheng still comfortable with his part in the arrangement?' Annev asked, taking a gamble that there was such an arrangement.

The consul's face was a mask. 'More or less. Why? Is Neruacanta open to renegotiating our terms?'

Annev searched the consul's mind for some indication of the terms she was talking about and this time he got his answer.

'We could use more of that red gold,' Anabo thought. *'Or maybe he's referring to Cheng's proposal to seed the southern territories with Terran slaves ...'*

Like plucking a drunken bird from the air.

'The God-king has been considering King Cheng's proposal about Terran slaves. He thinks it may have merit.'

Anabo's eyes lit up. 'That's good. Obviously we wouldn't move too many at once, but with the war in Borderlund we have a cover story for our sudden surplus of Terran stock.' She paused. 'What's changed, though? The last messenger said Daogort could not spare any soldiers.'

Annev smiled as he repeated the words echoing in the consul's mind: '"The day our soldiers give up their weapons and pretend to be house servants is the day I consecrate myself a eunuch."'

Anabo laughed. 'Yes! That's exactly what Cammack said. So, what changed?'

'Word got around and Neruacanta had the man consecrated on the spot – the God-king doesn't appreciate his servants making such unilateral decisions.'

The consul's eyes widened. 'I suppose that answers my other question then.'

'Which was?'

'Why he sent you. Cammack was working out fine – a little crass at times, but no worse than most of the men I work with. If he's been castrated, though ... Bah. I've seen what the man lost. His wife won't miss it. You, though ...' She tapped Annev's chest. 'I'd like to make some comparisons. Maybe tonight?'

Annev bowed low, his magpie mask hiding the blush from his cheeks. 'I'm flattered Consul Anabo, but I really must preserve my strength if I'm to bring the *Cormorant* into port before nightfall.'

She groaned. 'We don't *have* to arrive before dark, you know. Even if we bribe the guards to let us through the gate, we'll be stuck inside the river lock till morning.' Her fingers traced his shoulders. 'Slow down. Let me massage the kinks out of those muscles.'

Annev wondered if the woman had been reading his thoughts. *Of course not. She's not a Mindwalker ... but can she sense my emotion? I really need to be more careful around her.* A thought occurred to him. *She knows whether I'm interested or not. That's why she keeps pressing me to join her. She knows I'm reluctant ... but curious, and she thinks she can break me.* He chided himself for not understanding earlier. Hells, the consul probably thought he was teasing her – and, if Annev were honest, perhaps he was. He was seventeen years old and curious. He just didn't want to satisfy that curiosity with a woman he barely knew, let alone one who had been asked to kill him.

What am I thinking? There is zero chance of my bedding this woman – not unless I want to show her the Hand of Keos and blast this ship to smithereens. He exhaled slowly and cleared all thoughts and feelings of flattery, interest or lust from his mind. *Stay focused. Find Tiana Rocas and Dante Turano. Get them to talk. Find Elar and Saltair ... and kill them.*

That last thought drove all thought of intimacy or seduction from his mind.

'Forgive me, Consul, but I really must decline. My only interest is in reaching Luqura and meeting with Saltair. Neruacanta's tasks don't leave me much opportunity for pleasure.'

'All the more reason why you should indulge now,' Anabo said, though her heart wasn't in it this time; it was a token resistance.

'Thank you, but no. Good afternoon.' He nodded, then glided across the promenade deck with a subtle flourish of his magpie cloak. Behind him, he could feel the consul's eyes burning into his back.

She's not giving up that easily, Annev realised, consulting the co-davora ring one last time. *She doesn't understand why I keep refusing her and she's going to keep trying to seduce me until I give a concrete reason for rejecting her.*

Annev sighed, then readjusted the vambrace covering his left arm. *Maybe I'll take her advice and sleep a bit longer. If what she says about the river gate is true, we'll be stuck in the lock all night and I'll be out of convenient excuses to fend off her advances. If I manage to sleep half the way there, that's a few less hours I'll have to avoid the consul.*

Chapter Eighty-Seven

Myjun stood alone in the dark, the gleam of her burnished skin the only light in the world. Her mentor was gone, taken by some force she did not understand, and she was trapped in the World of Dreams.

Alone.

The blackness was suffocating. The silence oppressive. Oyru had said this plane held the thoughts and dreams of those in the physical world, but what she had experienced so far felt like a nightmare.

I'm trapped. He tried to fight the light and it killed him ... and now I'm alone.

Or was she? Oyru had disappeared, but did that mean his life had been extinguished? He had said the Spirit World lay just beyond this plane of existence – perhaps it even overlapped the plane on which she now stood?

Yes. Yohan had been killed by the eidolons after being dragged into the Shadowrealm, but *he* had not died – and if the chandler's mind and spirit had survived, surely the Shadow Reborn would not be so easily vanquished. His spirit was here. Some form or essence of the half-man must still be lingering ... searching for a release ... or searching for the spirit of his dead lover.

Oraqui, Myjun thought, remembering her name. *He went to Reocht na Skah to find her, and he would descend to the World of Spirits again to seek her out ... but he would not do so quickly.* Oyru had been afraid of what he might find here; he would be even more afraid to descend further. His instinct had always been to cling to life, to any shred that remained to him, so he had to be here ... somewhere.

But how do I summon him? she wondered. *How do I bring him back?*

A conviction suddenly struck her – not a thought, so much as an intuition. A feeling. A sense that he would find her ... if she could find Oraqui. Without knowing precisely why, she began to hum a voiceless tune that reflected her emotions.

As she sang, the light emanating from Myjun's golden skin began to coalesce around her, its diffuse rays concentrating into a white light that seemed to saturate her flesh and bones. She imagined herself as *he* would see *her*. Beautiful yet dangerous, every bit his equal in magic and might. Proud and imperious. She still wore the golden mask, and her flesh remained the grey-blue of her ironwood armour, but now her hair gleamed like the sun. She remembered how Oyru had burned her – how painful it had been, though she had endured it, and how pleased they had both been when she had completed the ritual of ash and embers. She drew on the memory ... imagining it was not her being burned but Oraqui. Imagined *being* Oraqui: Auramancer and Lightslinger. Consort to Oyru and betrayer of his home and family. Bane of his household, secret mistress of the warrior Gevul. A traitor, who had sold Oyru's life and family for a secret that only she knew.

With her eyes still closed, Myjun could sense another presence accompanying her now – a spirit ... a life-force. She knew who it was without opening her eyes, for their spirits seemed to be communing intuitively with one another; Myjun sensed the woman's disdain, her imperiousness and her vanity. She sensed, too, her curiosity. Why had Myjun summoned her? How was she so close to the World of Spirits yet not dead? The spirit recognised Myjun's mask, too, for when she saw it, her feelings mirrored Myjun's own: dread and hatred paired with the lust for power and the intoxicating magic that fuelled the artifact. Myjun found she coveted Oraqui's unconquerable spirit, her powerful auramancy and her mastery of bending light in ways that Myjun could barely imagine, let alone attempt. In some ways, they were complete opposites – in others, they were mirror images.

Myjun opened her eyes – both her physical eyes and the literal windows to her soul – and she seized the connection between herself and the disembodied spirit. Oraqui hesitated for an instant, but then her will and aura was merged with Myjun's ... and they became one.

The light emanating from Myjun's skin dimmed and the darkness around her began to coalesce into something more solid. Tendrils of smoke wafted up from the ground and began weaving themselves into the form of a man with ashen skin and hair as dark as night.

Oraqui watched, detached as her former lover rose from the land of the dead and greeted her with hollow eyes.

'Oraqui.'

'Oyru,' Myjun replied, though it was not her voice she heard but one deeper and more resonant; the voice of a woman with a secret the world would never know. It held a thousand unspoken conversations and a hundred unsung songs. It held the malice of death and a spite for life. It spoke of a love for the half-man standing beside her, tainted by resentment, pain and hatred.

'I have been searching for you.'

'But I have not sought you,' Myjun said, her voice still not her own. 'We were never destined to meet again, not in this life or the next. But this one has summoned me with her magic ... and I see she has brought you, too.'

'The tabibito,' Oyru said, his eyes shining with tears. 'You ... are her. She is you.'

Oraqui nodded. 'I have possessed her – she shares enough of my blood that it is possible, and she has also invited me to do so. You understand what this means?'

'Yes,' Oyru said, tears trickling down his face. 'It means we are together again. Finally, we can be together ... for ever.'

'No.' The word struck like a hammer against a glass anvil.

'No?' Oyru repeated, not understanding. 'But ... Oraqui ...'

'I have not dispossessed your tabibito,' the woman said, ignoring him. 'And I will not let you sully her.'

'But you are sharing her body?'

'I am.' She raised an eyebrow. 'What is she to you, anyway? A

808

consort? A lover?' The question hissed from Myjun's lips, though the words were not hers and the lips themselves remained hidden behind the gold perfection of her mask.

'She is ... a gift. A new body for your spirit – or a companion in the darkness.'

'You do not love her, then.'

Oyru shook his head. 'Not as I have loved you.'

Oraqui tilted her head and cackled, her eyes cruel beneath the Mask of Gevul's Mistress. 'So you *do* love her, if only a little.'

The Shadow Reborn hesitated. 'She is my tabi no tomo ... my apprentice.'

'Your companion in the dark.'

'No! *You* are my companion in the dark. Only you ... always you.'

She scoffed as if it made no difference. 'You trained this child. Then you brought her here and expected me to inhabit her? To wear her skin? Why? So we can use her body as our mutual plaything? So we can repeat the mistakes of our past?' Oraqui shook her head, her contempt ill-concealed behind the mask. The emotion radiated from her aura and was projected by her posture, by her very presence. 'Why would I consent to that? What makes you think I would ever *want* that?'

The assassin lowered his face. 'I have searched for you, Oraqui. All these years. For a thousand lifetimes, I have thought only of you.'

'And I have tried to forget you.' She sniffed. 'You know the girl – your *companion*? Do you know what she thinks of you?'

The assassin nodded. 'She has nothing but contempt for me.'

Oraqui's eyes sparkled with a mixture of malice and pleasure. 'That is the irony, Oyru. This poor girl ... she is actually beginning to *love* you. You have tainted and tortured her and she loves you for it. She despises you, yes – hates you, most likely – but she accepts your abuse and sees it as some kind of ... justice. Some perverse version of love.' She cackled again, her mocking laugh echoing into the void. 'I don't know which of you is more pathetic.'

Oyru blinked, his love and delight to see her beginning to

809

crack. 'Why do you say these hateful things? Why can you not simply speak the truth?'

'The *truth*? Ha! What would you know of truth? You are so far removed from it, you have lied to her every step of the way to win her aid, to bring her here; you've even lied about your plans for back in the physical world.'

'I did not *ask* her to come here. It was her proposal. I merely assented.'

'Is that how it was?' the woman purred, pacing lithely around the assassin. 'And was it *her* idea to come here ... or was it an idea you *planted*?'

The assassin looked away.

Oraqui laughed, her tone dripping with mockery and condescension. 'Let me see how you did it.'

Myjun felt something brush her psyche – her *soul*. It was so feather-light and precise that she almost didn't notice, but neither could she forget it. In that briefest moment, Myjun saw the woman behind the mask. She saw Oraqui for who she was now, and who she had been. She saw, too, how easily the woman had manipulated the *lumen* and lightfire – the secrets that Myjun couldn't fully grasp, let alone master. She gasped at the sudden glimpse of knowledge – and then the woman was gone.

'Ah,' Oraqui continued. 'There it is. You frightened her with ... a *witherkin*. How delicious! All these years and you have no new tricks. Still conjuring shadows to frighten your lessers. Still hiding in those shadows when around your betters.' She sniffed. 'Pathetic.'

Oyru's face darkened. 'She would not have come otherwise.'

'Of course not! Because she is *smart* – smarter than you, anyway.' She tsked. 'You tricked her, Oyru, just as you tricked me. Just as you've tricked other innocents in our little love affair, bringing them to the Shadowrealm and, when I did not heed your call, to the World of Dreams. This is the first time you've brought a sacrifice to the Crossroads, though. Even then, I would have stayed away ... but *she* called for me. She called and I didn't realise it was on your behalf.' She sighed. 'Enough, Oyru. I made my choice.'

The assassin refused to listen. 'Why did you do it, *anata*? You were one of us ... part of our family. How could you betray us?'

Oraqui scoffed. 'How could I not? Your line carried the blood of the Voidweavers, Oyru. Gevul was right to eradicate you – I just happened to be his means for achieving it.'

'And you failed,' Oyru whispered, his spine straightening. 'Some strain of the old magic still remains. It survives still in Luqura, in the Noble House of Rocas – and Thornbriar himself has not tasted death.'

'Bah!' Oraqui waved him off as if it made no difference. 'It was one reason among many, *koibito*. You had given me all you could – and Gevul had not. My choice was clear.'

'So you had to *enslave* yourself to him? You were so proud ... until you debased yourself by joining that monster – by *serving* him.' He spat. 'Why? The woman I loved would have never sunk so low.'

Oraqui stopped pacing. 'He never told you?' she whispered, the malice almost absent from her voice.

'Who?'

'Dortafola.'

Now Oyru froze. 'What did he do? What did that monster do to you?'

Oraqui shook her head. 'Gevul didn't give me the mask. It was your master, Oyru. It was the vampyr ... Dortafola gave it to me.'

Oyru slumped down, his face as bloodless as the snow. 'He couldn't ... he wouldn't.'

'He did.' Oraqui dragged her fingernails down the length of her metal jaw. 'He bid me wear it. He said either I would conquer it ... or it would conquer me.'

'But ... why? When you donned the mask, I had not even *met* the vampyr. What did he want ... how could he have known?'

'I don't know, *anata*. What's more, I don't care. I put the mask on, I failed to conquer its magic, and then Gevul conquered me.' She shrugged. 'Now you know.' She looked away, and her golden mask began to glow.

'I must return to the World of Spirits, Oyru. I cannot stay here – nor would I if I could.' She laid a hand on the half-man's shoulder and Myjun saw that her blue-black chitin skin now shone with the shimmer of gold.

'Wait,' Oyru said, looking up, his eyes desperate. 'Stay with me. We can rebuild what we have broken.'

'These are the Crossroads, Oyru. Nothing stays here. Nothing is permanent. We are all only transitioning.' As Myjun spoke, her voice became higher, at once sweeter and less exotic. It was her own voice, she realised; Oraqui was fading away. Yet even as her aura faded, the light around Myjun began to grow, first emanating from her golden skin and then shining to fill the darkness around them.

'Goodbye, *koibito*.'

The halo of *lumen* grew until it filled the space between them – and then it burst in a dazzling flash of colour. When the light faded, Myjun felt whole once more: Oraqui was gone, and her body and soul were her own once more.

Chapter Eighty-Eight

Oyru stared at her, his face a picture of pain and sorrow. Then his lip curled and he screamed into the darkness – not with words, but with pure anguish.

Myjun saw the assassin slowly transform as he screamed. She saw his back straighten and his face darken as a black mask stretched up from his neck and wrapped around the bottom half of his face. When he turned to look at her, the assassin's eyes were as cold and empty as the landscape.

'Come,' he intoned, his voice more hollow than it had ever been, his apathy seemingly infinite.

'Where?' Myjun asked, still disorientated after Oraqui's possession.

'If we can find the way, we will return to the World of Dreams.'

'But ...' Myjun looked at the endless void surrounding them. 'Aren't we *in* the World of Dreams?'

'No, this is the Crossroads. It is a place of transition before one passes on to the World of Spirits. Somehow, when you faced the flames, they brought you here to join me and then you summoned ... her.'

Myjun still had more questions than answers. 'The witherkin ... it was not real.'

He shook his head. 'It was just a trick of shadow. More than an illusion, but less than an actual eidolon.'

Myjun turned the events of the past few weeks over in her mind, understanding.

'You lured me here as a sacrifice to her.'

'Yes,' he said, without hesitation. 'I have tried before, but never got so close. The others ... they did not survive the journey through the Shadowrealm, or they failed to summon Oraqui in the Dream World. In the end, we had to return to the surface.'

'And what happened to those others?'

'I killed them. Then I began again.'

Myjun hardly believed how calmly he admitted it. 'You would have done the same to me. You *tried* to do the same to me.'

'But you were different,' Oyru said. 'You always were. I sensed it from the beginning, and you proved it today. You are the only one who descended to the Place Between Worlds. You are the only one who had the power to bring Oraqui to the Crossroads.'

Myjun sniffed. 'Which scarcely matters, since you intended to gift my body to her all along.'

The Shadow Reborn shrugged. 'I assumed you would fail, just like the others. Then I planned to bring you back to the Empire so we could hunt Annev. I never broke my promise.'

Myjun's eyes narrowed. 'Oraqui implied that you had something else in mind ... that this was another lie.'

'She did,' Oyru admitted, 'but you saw what she has become. Hate and envy. Spite and malice. She was not always that way.' He turned away, his eyes distant. 'She is no longer the woman I loved. That woman died at Gevul's hands. Possibly even before that.' He sighed, head shaking. 'When we return to the physical world, I will have a long conversation with my employer.'

'Dortafola? The vampyr?'

Oyru glanced at her out of the corner of his eye. 'The timelines don't match up. He could never have known about Oraqui to give her the mask, not even with Gevul serving as his Siänar in Krosera. It just ... it doesn't make sense.' He turned back to the desolate landscape, brooding.

'How do we return?'

'Mm?'

'To the physical world?' Myjun said. 'You implied that you knew a way back.'

The assassin suddenly grew weary. 'I know how to transition

from the Dream World – not the Place Between – and even then, it's difficult. I did not lie about that.'

'You *did* lie about that. You said you didn't know how to return from the World of Dreams.'

Oyru shrugged again, his behaviour almost sulky. 'It doesn't matter, since we aren't in the World of Dreams. We're at the Crossroads, and it's only a matter of time before we're swept on to the next plane of existence.'

Myjun sucked in a sharp intake of breath. 'You're talking about the World of Spirits.'

'I am.'

'But . . . that means we'll be dead. That's where spirits go. That's where the *dead* go.'

'It is.'

'So . . . how do we escape from there? How do we cheat death?'

'There is no cheating death,' Oyru said, his eyes peering intently into the void. 'Only the gods can travel between the Crossroads and the Spirit World without paying death's toll. Whatever we are – whatever shades or monsters we've become – we're still mortals. We're still subject to the laws of life and death.'

'So that's it, then? We're just dead.'

Oyru shook his head. 'There are a few places where the Crossroads touch the physical world – and one in particular where all the planes connect at once.'

Myjun stared at him, her heart thudding in her chest. 'Reocht na Skah.'

The assassin nodded. 'If I were a Voidweaver, I could take us there now. I could shift us to another plane or even another time . . . but I am just a Shadowcaster – and a half-man, besides. We have shifted too far from the physical world for me to access the greater depth of my magic.' He chewed his lip. 'To ascend, we must dive deeper still. We must go to Takarania, to the Heart of the Void, and hope we can escape its endless eddies.'

'No – no, no, no, *no*. You said time moves differently there – that a thousand lifetimes can pass in the space of a day. You said you were *trapped* there, until Dortafola came to rescue you.'

'It is as you say, yet I know of no other way. If we remain

815

here for too long, we will perish, our souls will be swept into the World of Spirits and we will be done. No more chances to escape. No more quests for revenge. It will all have been for nothing.'

Myjun glared at the assassin, for though the corrupting power of the mask was at its weakest here, her hatred towards him overwhelmed everything she had felt on the surface. Everything during her training, all the frustrations and resentments she had harboured, they all paled in comparison to this hatred.

He was planning to sacrifice me to Oraqui, and if that failed he would have killed me. He was never going to let me hunt Annev. He was always lying to me. Everything he's been telling me has been a lie. And now, she thought, *because of his lies, we are trapped here. Either dead or damned for eternity. Filthy. Bloody. Half-man.*

She had been in awe of him and had been frightened of him. She had feared what he claimed to be and the mystery that surrounded him. He had been the Shadow Reborn – a ghost and a shade, an assassin that was more nightmare than flesh. But now she saw the truth of it: Oyru was still human ... if that. A half-man, who relied on tricks to get what he wanted. He hid in the shadows, afraid of himself and his past. Too afraid to embrace his own death and too weak to accept he could not have the one thing he still desired. He was a liar – just as she had always accused him of being – and for all the magic that he possessed, he was barely a shadow of the monster he claimed to be. The legend. The myth. It was a lie that he told himself and others, hoping as the eidolons did that he might find a new life in the mimicry of it.

And now she saw the truth of it. She was no longer afraid of him. No longer in awe of his powers, or of what he might teach her. She had outgrown him, and she saw the small man that hid behind the terrible mask of the Siänar assassin.

Unfortunately, she still needed him to help her escape.

'We're going to Reocht na Skah,' Myjun said, struggling to keep her rage in check. '*Now.* No more wasting time. No more tricks. You're going to take us there, by the fastest route possible. And we're going to find a way out.'

The assassin nodded, his expression thoughtful. 'There is ... one possibility. One chance of escape that does not involve travelling to Reocht na Skah and imperilling our souls.'

'Well, for Odar's sake, spit it out!'

The half-man frowned. 'The thing is, it's not really up to us. It's up to Dorchnok.'

'Dorch ... the Shadow God?'

'Sionnach Dorchadas – Dorchnok. The Shadow Fox. Clesaiche. The God of Thieves, Travellers and Assassins. Lord of the Forgotten. Reluctant God of the Kroserans. The Younger God of Shadows.'

Myjun snorted. 'You're lying again. More made-up stories. More witherkin.' She shook her head. 'I swear, Oyru, I will kill you if—'

'This is his home,' Oyru said, ignoring her. 'I told you before. The stories about him ferrying lost souls back to the land of the living – they speak of these Crossroads. This is where he roams. If he is likely to hear our prayers anywhere, it is here.'

'But you said you no longer believe in him.'

'I said I no longer worshipped him, not that he doesn't exist.'

'Why would he listen? Why would Dorchnok give a rat's arse about either of us?'

'He doesn't. He is whimsical and enigmatic, and worshipping him doesn't make it any more likely he'll pay attention to you. Probably the opposite, at least in my experience.'

'Sounds like an arsehole.'

'Yes. You're starting to catch on.'

She rolled her eyes. 'So how do we get his attention?'

Oyru blinked. 'I ... am not sure. I would suggest praying but, well, he has never spoken to me, so I do not know that prayer is the best way.'

'Have you tried cursing his name?'

'Many, many times.'

Myjun sniffed, scanning the void of the Crossroads. 'Have you tried just calling for him?' She began to shout into the darkness. 'Dorchnok! Shadow fox. You grey bastard! Come out here and help us.'

Silence.

'I doubt insulting a god is the best way to earn his favour,' Oyru said, his tone dry.

'It's a good way to get his attention, though.' She looked around. 'I don't want to spend an eternity stuck in Reocht na Skah, I don't want to die, and I don't want to spend my last breath screaming into an endless abyss.' She huffed. 'Did those stories ever describe how those travellers found Dorchnok – or how *he* found *them*?'

Oyru considered it. 'Most did not, but then many of those who shared such stories were probably lying.' He paused. 'There is one story, though – more of a legend, really. The Tale of Chiad Thornbriar.'

'Tell me.'

The assassin looked dubious. 'It is a long story and some of its parts are in dispute. Though some other parts are at least a little reliable.' He eased himself to the floor. 'Chiad Thornbriar is one of my ancestors – a distant one, but still a relative. The main branch of his family were Voidweavers, whereas the descendants in my family line were all Shadowcasters.'

'What is a Voidweaver? You have mentioned this term before but not explained it.'

'A shadow mage, one whose powers are more elemental than metaphysical. Legend says those with the talent could bend space and warp time. They were the original travellers – those with the power to traverse the planes of existence – who frequently used that power to meddle in the affairs of others.'

'And where are those Voidweavers now?' Myjun asked. 'Dead?'

Oyru nodded. 'They have been systematically wiped out by the ruling dynasties and others who were afraid of their powers. Gevul the Terrible was the last to combat them, though by his time they had already ceased to exist as true mages. Some few still possessed the talent, but they had no education in how to use it. Gevul's prejudice against my family and our magic was nothing but pure zealotry.'

'Fine,' Myjun said, waving him off. 'Get to the point. Who is this Thornbriar and how did Dorchnok help him escape?'

'Thornbriar was a savant among the Voidweavers. Most of his kind could only master a single strand of a single strain of magic

– teleportation, gravitation, planeswalking, time fluctuation – but Thornbriar had a talent for it all. They say he could even walk the streams of time as if they were corridors in a great palace. To someone like that, all other magics became impotent: whatever you achieved against him, he could simply go back in time and undo. Whatever plans you made to harry him, he could go forward and view those plans and then respond in kind.' He shook his head. 'No man should ever be given such power, yet the gods gave it to Thornbriar.'

'So how did he get trapped here?' Myjun asked, pacing in front of her mentor.

'He was tricked ... by Dorchnok himself, no less.'

Myjun blinked. 'I thought you said Dorchnok helped him *escape*.'

'He did.'

Myjun waited for an explanation but Oyru teased her by remaining silent. Finally, she sighed. 'Why the contradiction?' she asked. 'Why would he trap Thornbriar only to free him?'

'Because,' Oyru said, a flicker of amusement in his eyes, 'Dorchnok is a capricious arsehole who does whatever he pleases. His actions are not bound by reason.'

Myjun frowned. 'No, I don't believe that. Dorchnok isn't a mad god.' She paused. 'That's not one of his titles, is it?'

'No,' Oyru said, scratching his chin. 'Sometimes they call Tacharan the Mad God ... but not Dorchnok. I suppose he has his own internal set of rules – though they are a mystery.'

Myjun grunted. 'All right. So Dorchnok traps Thornbriar at these Crossroads. Then what?'

'Some stories say Thornbriar challenged Dorchnok to a game. That the Voidweaver bested the Younger God and so won his freedom. Or a boon of his choosing. Or the wish of his heart.' Oyru sniffed. 'As I said, it varies between the tellings.'

'But Thornbriar *did* escape?' She looked around. 'I mean, otherwise, he'd still be here.'

'Assuming he actually existed, then yes. Thornbriar escaped.'

'And Dorchnok helped him.'

'So they say.'

'Do any of the stories suggest other ways of escape?'

Oyru seemed to consider this. 'Only two that I know of. In the first, Thornbriar outwits the Younger God and usurps his powers. Dorchnok is trapped at the Crossroads and Thornbriar takes up his mantle, masquerading as the Younger God.'

'And the second story?'

'It is just as far-fetched. In it, Dorchnok is charmed by Thornbriar and offers to let the Voidweaver take a turn at being the God of Mischief. In exchange, Dorchnok promises to wear the man's skin and make him a legend among his people – well, a greater legend than he already was. Thornbriar agrees and Dorchnok runs off with the man's body, leaving Thornbriar to wander the wastes as a dispossessed soul.'

'That doesn't make any sense either. If that's what Dorchnok wanted, he could have just sent Thornbriar to the World of Spirits.'

The Shadow Reborn hesitated, and finally he nodded. 'You may be right. Still, I wouldn't put it past Dorchnok. He's—'

'Capricious. You keep saying that.' Myjun glowered at him. 'As always, none of what you said seems helpful.'

'I didn't think it would be.' He arranged his legs and feet before him, as if to meditate, then closed his eyes.

'So you've given up.'

'I endured a hundred lifetimes in Reocht na Skah – but only because I hoped to find Oraqui. That kept me sane. Kept me alive.' His eyes opened. 'Now I have nothing ... less than nothing, perhaps. Only your hatred and scorn, and the whisper of cold vengeance against Dortafola.' He shrugged, apathetic. 'It doesn't matter. I will not take you to Takarania or the Heart of the Void ... and so we will wait, and let death claim us, and transition to the World of Spirits.'

Myjun looked at him in disgust. 'Stay here and die then. I'm going to fight tooth and nail, teeth and claw, until I escape this place. If that means travelling to Reocht na Skah, I will find a way there. If it means enduring a hundred thousand lifetimes in the Heart of the Void, I will do it. I *will* return to the physical world – and then I'm going to kill Annev de Breth. No more delays. No more tests. No more lies.'

'And no guide?' Oyru asked, glowering. 'No mentor?'

'Every day I have listened to you is a day I've been driven further from my goal. Everything – the training, the travelling, the stories, the lies – it was all so you could kill me ... for a woman who despised and betrayed you.'

'Yes,' he admitted. 'Even were we not here for Oraqui, I would have used you to capture Annev – and I would never have allowed you to kill him. He was always promised to Dortafola.'

'And now that you know Dortafola betrayed you.'

Oyru blinked his single, unmutilated eye. Something shifted in his aura, too, and Myjun saw the assassin was resigned to dying in this place, and that resignation allowed him to speak the truth he had hidden from himself. What's more, he sensed Myjun's intentions, and had no desire to stop her.

'Before seeing Oraqui,' Oyru said, 'I would not have let you kill Annev. I would have fulfilled my oaths to my master and broken my promises to you.'

'And now?' Myjun whispered, stepping behind the assassin, straining not to let her resentment show through her mask. 'Now that you know, would you have forsaken the vampyr and allowed me to kill Annev?'

Oyru slowly exhaled, his gaze staring into the endless void. 'No, nakama. There is no meaning to any of this now. No loyalty. I expect that I would have killed you. I would have taken your life just so I could remember that feeling of loss – so I could relive that pain of losing her ... one last time.' The half-man bowed his head. 'Oraqui's words,' he whispered. 'When she said you cared for me ... that kindness cut me deeper than any hatred you might have harboured.'

'But I do hate you,' Myjun whispered. Then she hummed – not a scream this time, but a sad song of bitterness and longing – and as she did, her soulblades materialised in her hands. 'I cared for you,' she breathed, '*and* I hated you.'

'And now you understand what I felt for Oraqui.' The space of a heartbeat passed and then the Shadow Reborn straightened, his gaze looking forward once more. 'Our battle would have been legendary, *nakama*. I cannot say who would have won.'

Myjun shook her head. 'Another lie, conjuror.'

Oyru lowered his black face wrap – and smiled. 'May Dorchnok guide you on your journey, tabibito.'

Myjun plunged her soulfire daggers through the assassin's neck and back. He gasped – though it almost sounded like a laugh – and then his single unblemished eye winked into fire and ash. The Shadow Reborn slumped forward, and as he fell, his body disintegrated into shadows and smoke. They did not reform, and when the mists had cleared Myjun stood alone at the Crossroads of life and death.

'I will find my own way back,' she promised herself, tasting the soul she had just consumed. 'Whether it takes ten years or ten lifetimes to do it. Even if I have to take on a god to return and take my revenge.' She looked around the void, thinking on all that had occurred, her fate in her own hands for the first time. She shrugged. 'Hey, Dorchnok!'

Silence.

'Dorchnok,' she shouted, imbuing her voice with the resonance of her newly discovered magic. 'Arsehole, trickster god!' She lent more power still to her voice, feeling it resonate throughout this world, seeking connection. 'Do you want to play a game?'

There was a tremendous rumble and Myjun shrieked as the ground suddenly dropped away. She was falling through the endless abyss of the Crossroads, her body no longer tethered to any plane or sense of gravity.

'I'm always up for a game,' a disembodied voice answered.

Myjun tried to shift in the air, spinning her body towards the speaker – and as she tried, she realised she was suspended in the void, neither standing nor falling but . . . floating.

Myjun finally spotted another figure in the darkness, though his own clothes and hair were nearly as dark as the void itself: his locks were tight ringlets that seemed to glisten with oil and his white face was even paler than Oyru's. He had a close-cropped goatee that reminded her of her father's neatly groomed beard, and his eyes sparkled with purple iridescent light.

'But first,' the Younger God said, stepping towards her, 'we must discuss the stakes. And perhaps introductions are in order.'

He extended a gloved hand towards Myjun. 'I'm Clesaiche. You can call me Dorchnok, though – most everybody does these days.'

He smiled and Myjun saw a glint of something otherworldly in the man's eyes. Something dark. Something more dangerous than anything she had seen on her travels with the Kroseran assassin.

If this wasn't a mad god, it was the next closest thing.

Chapter Eighty-Nine

The old farmer pulled his wagon up short just as Banok's silhouette crested the horizon.

'There 'tis, boys. I won't go no farther with all the trouble on these roads, but you can walk the rest of the way. Take care in that city. If half the rumours are true, you'd be better steering clear of that place.'

'Thank you, gaffer,' Titus said, nodding politely to the old man. 'We'll do fine from here. And anyway, we have friends inside those walls who need our help.'

The farmer grunted, swished the corncob pipe in his mouth and spat. 'Well, be off with you, then. If you're not headed to Trizgard or Paldron, this is as far as I can take you.'

'You're sure you won't take payment?' Titus asked for perhaps the fourth time.

The gaffer smiled, his chapped lips peeling back to reveal teeth that were half yellow. 'Now, now. I was already headin' this way. I said that, didn't I? And anyway, you two have kept me good company these past few days. Bandits are less willin' to rob an old man with his two grandsons. Either of us alone, though, would be a temptin' target.' He cackled as if laughing at a private joke then waved Titus off.

'Well, thank you anyway,' Titus said, half bowing as he gathered up his pack and then leapt down from the fat man's cart. Before leaving, he stopped to scratch the ears of the mule that had pulled the two boys, the farmer and his wagon all the way from Southern Odarnea, through Corlin and Ankyr, past Luqura and east towards Banok. It was hard to imagine their journey without the old traveller, who had made a tough road significantly easier. 'We really do owe you for the food, though.'

'Bah.' Again, the farmer waved them off. 'You brought that coney in and washed the pots and pans. Seems a fair trade for the vegetables you ate and the water I boiled – and besides, conversation is the currency I trade in, and you boys had plenty o' that.'

Titus nodded, wondering if they had said too much about their affairs to the old farmer. He had a kind soul and a warm heart, though there was also something unsettling about him that Titus had never quite put his finger on. When they had first approached the gaffer about catching a ride south, Titus had attempted some mindwalking to discern the old man's nature, and he'd not found so much as a menacing thought in his head – which meant he was either very skilled at projecting his mental defences, or he was exactly as he seemed: a kindly old farmer moving west after having sold his farm and most of his worldly possessions.

No, Titus thought, *that's not right. The farmer approached us.* He tried to think back on their first meeting, just minutes after they had swum to shore and begun walking the southern road towards Luqura. *He waved and asked if we needed a ride.* The memory seemed strange, for Titus had started to think they had selected the farmer on guessing he was heading towards Banok, but that wasn't right.

'Good luck with your quest, lads!' The old man waved to them, then slapped his reins and the cart lurched forward. Titus watched him go, distracted as he tried to recall the details of the last few days.

We didn't even ask his name. Or had he given it to them? *Carraig . . . Cragcarac?* He thought hard, trying to remember if they had given their own names, but the details were lost to him. Titus shook his head, confused by the whole trip and elated about having reached their destination.

'Well, he was a nice fellow,' Therin said, slapping Titus on the back. 'He even gave me this.' Therin held up a bracelet made from interlocking pieces of black and white stone. 'Pretty thing, eh?'

Titus stared at the jewellery, at a loss for words. 'What the hell just happened to us?'

'Hmm?' Therin frowned at him, genuinely confused. 'What do you mean? We made it to Banok!' He watched Titus for any sign of enthusiasm. Not getting any, he continued. 'We escaped the Enclave's quarantine and nearly got killed by some pirates. Then we escaped from them and had a quiet journey south with a mild-mannered pedlar.'

'He was a farmer ... wasn't he?'

Therin rubbed his jaw. 'You know, I don't ... huh. I don't remember. Seemed like a pedlar to me. With his wagon full of wares?'

'I thought those were his possessions from Quiri. He sold his farm and was moving south.'

'Or east?'

For a long while, the boys stared at each other.

'Right then,' Therin said, swallowing. 'Let's not dwell on it. The important thing is we're here, and we can make sure Brayan's all right.'

'Assuming he's still alive,' Titus muttered. 'Honestly, the more time passes, the more certain I am he's dead. I've been trying to reach out to him this entire trip and I haven't had any success. It's like he's not there at all – like he's fallen off the edge of the world.'

Therin wrapped the smaller boy in a bear hug ... though the height difference between them wasn't quite so large any more. 'Come on, Titan. Brayan's either there or he's not. If he is, we'll find him and take care of him. If he's not ... well, the people of Banok need our help too. If the Academy's masters are causing this trouble, then it falls to us to put it right.'

Titus was surprised by the other boy's conviction. 'Why did you really want to come to Banok, Therin?'

'Huh?'

'Come on,' he said, punching the boy on the arm. 'You've never been altruistic, you were never close to Brayan, and you don't know anyone in Banok. Why would you agree to leave the Enclave when you were doing so well there?'

Therin studied their dusty travel clothes. 'You're right. That wasn't the main reason I came – not at first. It was to do with Annev.'

'With Annev?'

Therin nodded. 'I was certain he would lead the charge to Banok. He's always been that way, you know? The first one to volunteer for the hard jobs. The first one to sacrifice something if it needed doing.' He scratched the stubble on his upper lip. 'When Annev didn't want to come, I ... I don't know. I sort of panicked. I thought, if *he's* not going to help, then who will?'

'Yeah,' Titus said, finally admitting to himself how disappointed he'd been when Annev had chosen not to come with them. 'I understand that.'

'Do you? Because you're just like Annev, Titus – if anything, you're worse. I mean, that's not a bad thing. You're selfless to a fault. But me?' He shook his head. 'I've never had to be the good one – the selfless one – because you or Annev were always the first to volunteer. I *liked* that. I like knowing things will work out. It's different now, though. Annev is ... well, he's not the same – even *you* aren't the same.'

Titus had been feeling the changes for a while, but he was surprised that Therin had noticed. 'We're not kids any more, Therin. The Academy was our home and it was destroyed. Our mentors turned out to be monsters, and we've had to find our own way since leaving Chaenbalu. Even when we were at the Enclave – even when the Brotherhood promoted me to become a Dionach Tobar ...' He shrugged. 'No one is here to protect us – Annev was right about that – and no one is here to protect these people either. You know what Reeve said when I asked permission to come here? When I said Banok needed our help?'

'I didn't know you asked.'

'He told me it was none of our affair,' Titus said. 'He said the Brotherhood was spread too thin and it was too dangerous outside the Enclave. I told him these people were innocent – that this was our fault – and he told me to go back to my room and study.'

Therin stared at him, eyes wide. 'What did you do?'

'I was angry. I felt he knew I was referring to Brayan, and he still didn't care. Maybe I should have said something – should have pressed the issue – but I didn't ... I went back to my room and tried to contact Brayan by mindwalking, but I failed. I tried to reach Annev, but he pushed me away. So, I just ... floated. I let my mind wander and see where it led me. My thoughts kept drifting back to Banok and – I swear I'm not making this up – I could actually *see* the people in the city. I could hear their thoughts and feelings.'

'Did you see Faith?'

'Huh?' Titus said, awoken from his memories. 'Faith. No, she's ... Therin, she's dead.'

'But we *saw* her, Titus. We saw her ghost. First in the Brakewood and then in Banok.'

'I didn't see Faith, Therin. She died back in Chaenbalu, with all the other witgirls, when the monsters attacked and the Academy collapsed.' He laid a hand on his friend's shoulder. 'Is that the other reason you came to Banok? Do you think Faith is still alive?'

Therin pulled away, his face flushed. 'Forget it,' he said, his tone morose, and he seemed on the verge of tears. 'Just ... let's go. Banok needs us – the *people* of Banok need us. It doesn't matter if Brayan is there, or Faith, or anyone else from Chaenbalu. Those people *need* us, and no one else is coming to help them.'

Titus smiled. 'You're right. We can do this ... right?'

'Yeah. I mean, I think so. Don't you?'

Titus took a deep breath and slowly let it out. 'Honestly, I'm not sure. The masters and ancients ... they've always been superior to us in every way. But we have magic now – *real* magic – and I bet the folks in Banok will help us, too. We don't have to do it alone.'

'You're right,' Therin said, and took a step towards the looming town walls. 'Come on. We need to get the lay of the land before it gets dark.'

Titus hurried to follow him, falling in step. 'I have a plan, you know.'

Therin smiled. 'Well, that's a relief. I was worried I might have to come up with one.' He ruffled Titus's hair and then they broke into a jog without another word.

Chapter Ninety

Kenton had been scouting the Banok rooftops for almost six hours before he felt satisfied with his conclusions. Even so, he had a difficult time admitting what he was seeing: the township of Banok had completely changed, and not for the better.

Near as Kenton could tell, the city had been divided into quarters, with each section being ruled by a different faction. In the southeast, the Cult of Cruithear had taken over the artisans' shops and sent their *ferrumen* to keep order in the streets. In the northwest, shadow mages in purple and grey uniforms patrolled the rooftops and alleys, so thoroughly that Kenton had been spotted twice and had to circle back using his wits, his avatar skills and a bit of magical help.

Janak's palace stood in the northeast quadrant and was guarded by a handful of each of the former groups along with, Kenton thought, most of the Sons of Damnation; but no matter how many trips he made around the city's walls, or how closely he watched the dead merchant's keep, he had only glimpsed two of his former avatar colleagues: Ancient Denithal, whose white robes stood out like a beacon, and Master Edra, who made no effort to hide. *Master Der could be anywhere, though,* Kenton thought. *With his training and all that magic I gave him from the Vault, he could be standing ten feet away and I'd probably not spot him.* Realising the truth of that, Kenton shuffled back into the shadows of the twin chimneys he stood between.

No sign of Murlach, he continued, cataloguing his thoughts, *which means he's probably inside, with Ather.* That made sense. The former

Master of Engineering would be difficult to hide in his hulking exoskeleton, and he had always preferred tinkering with a new project to any form of guard duty or actual avatar work. Ather's absence also seemed to confirm Kenton's suspicion that he had been possessed by Elder Tosan's disembodied spirit.

He's in there, Kenton thought, studying the keep's sandstone walls. *It's the strongest and most defensible section of the city, and it's loaded with all those artifacts Janak never turned over to the Academy – whichever ones weren't burned in his study, anyway.*

Having almost been possessed by Tosan himself, Kenton knew the old headmaster's mind better than anyone: he'd be unable to resist either the treasures of Janak's palace or the power it represented, especially when it was essentially abandoned. *So how can I get in there?* Kenton wondered. He still hadn't seen a pattern for the *ferrumen* and other mercenaries patrolling the keep, though he thought the guard had changed at least once.

'Damnation,' Kenton muttered under his breath. In a few more minutes, the Orvanish mages and Kroseran Shadowcasters would perform another rooftop sweep. He'd have to leave his post then and, most likely, that was when they'd change the guards patrolling the palace itself. *If I try to go in while they sweep the rooftop, I'll see them coming … but I can't look in all directions at once. I won't know exactly when or from which direction the new guards will be coming … which is as good as being blind.* He didn't like that notion, but he was beginning to think such a gamble was his only chance of entering the keep undetected.

Kenton glanced into the final quadrant of the city. It was the poorest section of town, though Banok wasn't especially rich or poor, and it harboured the fewest mercenaries. Kenton had wondered why, when he'd first dropped over Banok's walls, until he'd seen there was some kind of resistance in that area; the townspeople simply didn't allow any of the other factions to stick around for too long. Kenton hadn't paid close enough attention to know who was organising it, but someone in that quadrant of the city was using magic – not to support the takeover of the Lords of Damnation, but to end it. Given what Kenton had observed, the resistance had figured out a way to take out the *ferrumen*, their mineral-laden bodies popping up as effigies on every street corner and plaza. When that happened, the Orvanes sent more of their number into the southwest quadrant to retrieve their fallen comrades. That rescue mission often became a fight ... and the new *ferruman* was strung up with the others, like some kind of macabre festival decoration. He'd seen it play out half a dozen times in as many hours – and always without a single loss to the resistance.

Kenton focused his attention on the poorly lit quadrant. The resistance was somewhere inside those ramshackle homes, and Kenton would bet his Cloak of Secrets that the three witches leading the townsfolk were the reason those *ferrumen* kept disappearing; their magic was the only way simple villagers could even the odds against wizards wielding shadow magic or soldiers made from metal and stone.

Kenton waited until the guards patrolling the uppermost terraces of Janak's keep had circled around to the back, then he popped out of his shadows and scurried down from the rooftops to the streets below. Once on the ground, he made a beeline for the southwestern section of the city, an idea forming in his mind.

'What are they?' Therin asked, peering around the corner of the abandoned tannery. 'Are those the same creatures that attacked Chaenbalu?'

'They look like it,' Titus whispered, also being careful to stay out of sight, 'but they don't act like it. They're not feral, they're on patrol ... and I saw more on Miller Road.'

'How do you know which one is Miller Road?'

'They've got signs.' Titus pointed to the dank piece of wood near the corner of the intersection, the glyphs painted on it. 'This one is Samak Street.'

Therin grunted, obviously impressed. 'I guess that's the kind of inanity you've got to think up when you have more than two streets in your village.'

'Quiri did it, too – and Luqura.'

'Really? I never noticed.' Both boys flinched as, with no warning, one of the shops on the opposite side of the street exploded into a ball of fire.

'Blood and ashes! Did you see that?'

'Hard not to,' Titus whispered. 'That's can't be good. We should get out of here.'

'Agreed,' Therin said, as the soldiers turned back to investigate the blaze. 'The *feurog* are crawling all over this part of town. We should head back to the southwest. It felt quieter there.'

'Right,' Titus said, watching the distant conflagration. 'We should find Dolyn's shop and see if Brayan—'

'Hey! What are you doing out here?'

As one, Titus and Therin turned to see an imposing woman with bronze skin and a long spear standing directly behind them. Firelight flickered across the street and Titus realised her flesh wasn't simply an earthy brown; it was accented with stripes of bronze and scraps of brass metal. She wore a thick cotton tunic, a shirt made of steel rings, and she stood with her legs wide, blocking the road behind them as she levelled her spear.

'You boys have anything to do with that?' She gestured towards the fire with the head of her spear, its movement drawing their attention like the head of a circling viper.

'That wasn't us,' Titus protested, his tongue feeling thick in his throat.

'That so? What's inside those bags?'

'Er ...'

'We were just stretching our legs,' Therin interjected, a foolish smile plastered on his face. 'You know how it is.'

'It's after curfew,' the guard snapped, her attention split between the boys' faces and the travel sacks they carried. 'And why go for a stroll carrying those? Planning to sneak out?'

'Ah ...' Therin was speechless, and that silence seemed enough to convict them.

'Empty your bags,' she ordered.

Therin froze while Titus swallowed his fear and complied with the command, untying the drawstring and emptying his bag's contents onto the street. His canteen tumbled out, along with two apples, his bedroll, some scraps of paper and a change of clothes. When Titus saw the papers hit the ground, he cursed under his breath and drew a questioning gaze from Therin.

The guard took a step closer then poked her spear at the scraps of parchment. 'What are those?'

Titus felt his cheeks burn hot. They were his practice attempts, before forging Arch-Dionach Reeve's signature back at the Enclave; having managed a superior forgery, Titus had kept the wasted paper, thinking it might prove useful. Now, he wished he had burned it.

'It's just, uh ... just notes.'

'Right,' the guard said, unconvinced. 'Step away from the bag – and you, empty yours.' She pointed her spear at Therin and the other boy slowly opened his sack. As he did, the woman began to unroll the damning pieces of parchment.

'Run!' Titus shouted. In the same instant that Therin took off, he leapt forward and grabbed the shaft of the woman's spear. The guard didn't let go, so Titus used his weight and leverage to push the unbalanced woman over. He overcorrected, though, and the guard used their momentum to pull Titus with her, propelling him into the air and throwing him over her head.

Titus crashed to the ground and immediately rolled to his feet. The guard was a heartbeat behind him and he used that advantage to sprint in the opposite direction to Therin.

Gotta make it ... to the wall, he puffed, his thoughts matching the pace of his exertions. *Gotta make it ... to an alley ...*

'Stop!'

Titus did not stop. Instead, he sprinted harder, searching for an escape, for some shred of salvation. So intent was he, in fact, that he didn't notice when the ground split open in front of him and he fell headlong into the pit that hadn't been there a second ago.

Chapter Ninety-One

Kenton edged into the hallway outside Janak Harth's former study, the pungent smell of charcoal and charred flesh still fresh in his mind, though it had been months since that fateful retrieval mission. He fancied he could smell it still, the acrid scent hanging thick in the air. He took a deep breath and tried to ignore the memory of fire and corpses. At the same time, he felt his head swoon and his vision suddenly went black. His hands flew up to his face—

But no. Everything was fine – well, as fine as it could be, with eyes that glowed with golden fire. A cursory glance showed that the magical fires that had consumed Janak's study had somehow been contained to just the top floor, their infernal flames frustrated by strips of brass etched with runes, strategically placed in the stone floor, walls and ceiling. Even so, Kenton could see where the undying flames had eaten at the mortar and sandstone.

When Kenton reached the arch marking the entrance to Janak's study, he expected there to be nothing left of the grey door he, Fyn and Annev had once passed through. Instead, he found the melted hinges and the dross of superheated sandstone – but the ironwood door seemed almost perfectly preserved, barely charred and not marred in any significant way.

'Damn,' he breathed, touching the portal. 'That's … that's not right.' Kenton shook his head, idly wondering if there might be some better use for the wood than discarding it in some dead merchant's hallway. He had to leave the wood there, though he made a mental note of its location and properties, being careful to store the memory in his Ring of Remembrance.

Kenton stepped through the doorway, his emotions flooded with more memories of the night he had betrayed Annev and left him to die in this room. His eyes scanned the floor, searching for the prosthetic that Annev must have left behind. Instead he found the charred armour Master Duvarek had been wearing – the armour he'd been wearing when Kenton drove Mercy through his visor and killed him. He stepped closer to blackened armour, knowing it had once been a beautiful bronze, but he did not stoop to look inside at the remains of the Master of Shadows.

'You deserved better than this, Dove. I'm sorry we had to kill you.' He knelt down beside the blackened armour and placed two fingers on the corpse's chest. 'Go with the gods, Duvarek – and be at peace. I promise, I'll find Tosan and send him to hell alongside you.'

As Kenton stood, his gaze followed the charred manacle and chain still attaching Duvarek's arm to the other manacle, lying discarded on the floor. Kenton picked it up and examined the artifact, knowing it should have contained Annev's original prosthetic arm. He found only ashes.

'I looked for it, too.' The voice came from the doorway, and though it sounded like Master Ather, Kenton knew who really spoke.

'It was the first thing I did after taking the keep,' the voice continued. 'I wanted to prove he was a liar – I knew it already, but I needed to see it for myself.' Soft boots crunched the charred wood and vitrified stone behind Kenton.

'I guessed you would come here, too. I knew you would, actually, except this time you came looking for these.'

Kenton finally turned and what he saw made his heartbeat quicken. Ather stood before him, a leather bandolier draped over his shoulder – and sparkling inside that bandolier, protected by twelve magically enchanted vials, was the stolen *aqlumera*.

'Hello, Elder Tosan.'

The dispossessed headmaster smiled using Ather's lips, the master's pencil-thin moustache replaced with a close-cropped goatee. 'I knew you would guess where I'd gone.' He opened his arms

835

wide, gesturing to their surroundings. 'Do you like what we've done with the place?'

'If the rest of the keep is anything like this room, I'd have to say no. Janak Harth was a pretentious prick, but at least he knew how to decorate.'

Tosan's smile widened. 'Funny boy. I was referring to Banok. When I'm through with the town, I think it will be an upgrade from Chaenbalu. We'll have all Janak's artifacts – those from his basement anyway, since the ones from this room were destroyed or damaged – plus we'll have everything we can bring back from the Vault of Damnation, and almost four times the population to do our bidding. More farmers. More artisans. More avatars.' He stepped further into the room, his lavender gloves tracing sinuous lines in the ash-covered walls.

'You know the best part, though?' Tosan continued, peering sideways at Kenton. 'We no longer need to *hide* our magic – we no longer need to fight what is *natural* to us.' He pointed at Kenton. 'We're the same, you know. Both cursed with the taint of Keos – or blessed with Odar's gift, if you choose to see it that way. We're both smart enough to keep our abilities hidden from those who wouldn't understand, from those who would claim we were keokum who had made a pact with Keos – but we knew the truth. We *knew* it, and we didn't let the Academy's traditions prevent us from becoming better versions of ourselves.'

Kenton snorted. 'If I'd told you I had a talent for magic back in Chaenbalu, you would have stoned me, skewered me and flayed me alive.'

'Yes,' Tosan admitted, taking another step closer. 'And you would have deserved it, too, for being stupid enough to reveal yourself.'

'You're not the Tosan I knew. What's changed?'

'Being dead, Master Kenton. I no longer have reason to be ashamed – and I should never have allowed someone else's ideologies to influence what I knew for myself to be true. The Academy was useful, and its orthodoxy was mostly correct, but I had always known it was flawed. I believed that *I* was that flaw ... at least at first. It took me many years to unlearn that – and it took dying to stomp it out completely. I no longer fear my own magic, and I'm certain there are few that can be trusted to wield it.'

'Like Annev?' Kenton said, turning squarely to face the old headmaster. 'He had magic and you punished him for it. You tried to execute him for it.'

'He destroyed the Academy,' Tosan growled.

'After your accusations, yes, not before. How are we any different from him?'

Tosan's face was stony. 'Annev deserved death. He bore the taint of Keos – a missing *arm* – for which he should have died as an infant. We are *nothing* like him. If he had died, maybe my wife would still be alive.'

Kenton remembered that searing memory from Tosan's attempt to possess his body. In that struggle many of the headmaster's secrets had spilled into Kenton's psyche, replacing some of his own. His identity had nearly been subsumed by the former Eldest of Ancients. 'Did you kill Ather, then ... or is his spirit still floating around in there somewhere?'

'His spirit is gone – thankfully – but a lot of his memories remain. It's peculiar, actually. I find I'm sometimes adopting his mannerisms, which might have been helpful if I had wanted anyone to believe I was a conceited dandy.' He snorted, showing exactly what he thought of that idea.

'You dress like one,' Kenton said, pointing to Tosan's brightly coloured waistcoat and gloves.

'Only because they're useful – only because they're *artifacts*. Thank you for these, by the way. They've proved very useful.' He waggled the fingers of his gloves in Kenton's direction. 'Taking over Banok would have been much harder without these little gems. Not quite as effective as that Rod of Compulsion you failed to steal for us, but not without their uses.'

'Is that how you got those mercenaries to help you?' Kenton asked, taking another step closer, his magic eyes shifting between the bandolier of *aqlumera* and Tosan's grinning face.

Tosan nodded. 'Just a light touch and they become very susceptible to my suggestions. Those I meet in person, that is. The rest are here for something more ... tangible – but you guessed that already, didn't you?' Kenton watched as Tosan lifted a gloved finger and tapped one of the vials slung across his chest. 'These are very valuable, you know. I'd known that back at the Academy, when material wealth had no appeal to me. I had wanted to cheat death itself!' He gestured to his stolen face. 'And now that I've done that, I'm finding that wealth and riches have their uses.'

'You and I both know your spell backfired. You weren't trying to preserve your soul in that fountain of *aqlumera*. You were trying to possess someone else's body – just like Bron Gloir – and you failed. You would have been trapped in there for ever if Ather, or myself, or someone else hadn't gone down to the Vault and accidentally freed you.'

Tosan frowned. 'A minor error in my calculations. Bron Gloir had talents I do not possess – and I *was* successful. I cheated death itself, Master Kenton. The final barrier. The last obstacle. I am *immortal*.'

'Until someone else kills Ather's body, anyway. Then what? You're going to fly back to that *aqlumera* puddle? Jump into the nearest person's body, just like Bron Gloir does in the stories? Or will you just go to hell, where you should have been this whole time?'

Tosan's mouth twisted into a sneer, though he forced it into a perverse kind of smile. 'You really shouldn't antagonise me, you know, especially since I came here offering an olive branch.'

'Why in Odar's name would I want an olive branch?'

'It's a *metaphor*, you idiot. The stories ...' Tosan waved a hand, dismissing him. 'Never mind. You were never very well read. My point is I came here offering peace – a chance to join me and your little Sons of Damnation. I'm offering you a *place* here, Kenton. A chance to be truly great. Just imagine it: not locked away inside some dusty Vault cataloguing artifacts, but at my side. The first to be raised to a new Order of Ancients.'

'Denithal is already an ancient.'

'Bah! Forget him. He's been demoted. You, though ... we could do great things here. With your talent for finding and identifying artifacts, the Order would be unstoppable.' He stepped closer – almost close enough to touch now – and stared intently at Kenton.

'The Order of Ancients is dead, Elder Tosan. It died the instant you took over – when you killed Elders Winsor and Grimm.'

Tosan was distracted by the accusation, and Kenton lunged for the bandolier around his neck. But just as his fingers were about to close around the leather strap, Kenton felt his hand bounce away, his fingertips sliding just above the vials of *aqlumera* and the mustard-yellow waistcoat beneath them. He tried to attack or cripple Tosan – his legs, his head – but again Kenton encountered a shield protecting the former headmaster.

Tosan stepped back, his attention back in the moment. 'Ah. Did you not notice this other artifact?' He touched the yellow vest. 'Just another foppish garment to the untrained eye, but one that protects me in ways that other artifacts cannot.'

'A shield protecting your body ... and protecting you from theft. But how?' Kenton couldn't understand. 'I would have noticed it ... would have sensed it.'

'No, you wouldn't.' Tosan opened his waistcoat to reveal a piece of black fabric woven into the vest. When Kenton looked at it, he felt his eyes unfocus, his magic vision unable to penetrate the plain-looking fabric.

'What devilry is this?'

'I think it's called illusory cloth. It's designed to hide artifacts from detection – and I suspect it's how that cursed priest hid Annev's prosthetic from me for all those years.' He smiled, then rebuttoned his waistcoat. 'The garment forms a barrier of air – one that protects my entire body – and the lining repels all forms of scrying and magical detection. I can hide anything I want inside a pocket and your damnable eyes won't see a thing.' So saying, he slipped a gloved hand inside his breast pocket and withdrew a thin wooden wand. As soon as the artifact cleared the waistcoat, Kenton saw it for what it was ... but his supernatural ability to identify the artifact seemed muddled somehow. He could hear the echo of blood–magic in the wand, but its intent was obscured. *Die ... rot ... sleep.* Was this how a normal person felt when they identified an artifact? Even before the *aqlumera* had changed his vision, Kenton had been skilled at identification, but that ability seemed muted now.

Kenton retreated, his mind working furiously on his next course of action. Tosan had come prepared, it seemed; in one blow, he had neutralised Kenton's greatest advantage while apparently making himself immune to any damage or theft.

Dammit.

Kenton turned to flee, but ran headlong into a dark shadow that had been creeping up behind him.

'Hello, Master Kenton. Long time no see, eh?'

It was Der, of course, the Academy's former Master of Stealth, only Kenton hadn't noticed his shadowy, shapeshifting presence. How was that possible? His eyes should have alerted him to any magic artifacts in the room.

'You're wondering how we knew you'd come here – how we neutralised your magic vision and kept you from seeing Der, Edra, and Denithal.'

Kenton spun and saw the other Sons of Damnation emerge from the shadows in the room, from the ashes covering the walls and the soot staining the stone floor.

What in the five hells is happening?

'You must be feeling a little disorientated just now? You can thank Ancient Denithal for that.' Tosan watched him through Ather's eyes. 'Surely you noticed that odour amidst the smoke and ash? That pungent aroma of cooked meat?'

Kenton frowned then realised he *had* noticed it – when his vision had first gone black. Had he been poisoned?

Dammit.

Tosan's smile morphed into a grin. 'There it is. You're starting to understand now. It's a concoction I had Denithal make specifically for you. A gas that mimics the properties of the illusory cloth. You inhaled quite a bit of it in the corridor.' He sighed contentedly. 'It doesn't really do anything else – it won't harm you or kill you – it just inhibits magical scrying.'

'Are you reading my thoughts?' Kenton whispered, backing into a corner as his vision continued to blur. Keos, was he going *blind*?

'Yes,' Tosan said. 'Janak kept a really very useful treasure hoard; he kept back far more than we guessed. Murlach's down there right now getting it all sorted.'

Gotta stall him, Kenton thought, *at least until my vision returns.* Tosan laughed aloud and Kenton swore, realising the former headmaster had just heard his own thoughts. That would take some getting used to – and he didn't have that kind of time.

'So this ...' he tried, 'it was all just a trap. That's why you left Duvarek's body here. You wanted to lure me here.'

'I really did want you to join us, Kenton. Those eyes of yours are so incredibly valuable, I don't think you realise what a gift you've been given – that's why I didn't want Denithal's poison to be permanent. It'll wear off eventually.' He shrugged. 'But I may as well take them from you since it's clear you'll never join us. You still blame me for Duvarek's death.' He stepped forward and nudged the magic suit of armour containing the dead man's corpse. 'It wasn't me, you know. It was all you. I sent you here, but you held the sword. You used its magic. The only person you have to blame is yourself.' Tosan raised the Death Wand and pointed it in his direction. 'I can rid you of that guilt, you know? One touch of this and you won't have to live with it any more.'

Kenton's head swivelled between Tosan and the approaching masters. He was trapped. With all the artifacts he'd stolen from the Academy's Vault, he was still trapped. The masters' artifacts would neutralise his advantages, and his magic eyesight was all but gone. He could see a faint blur of light and shadows now ... but that was growing darker by the second. In a few more seconds he would be completely blind. He had nowhere to go. No escape.

No – there was still one escape route, if he dared try.

Tosan's brow furrowed in consternation just as Kenton knew with certainty what he had to do.

'Stop him!'

Tosan stepped forward with his Death Wand in the same instant Kenton wrapped himself in his Cloak of Secrets.

I'm sorry, Myjun, Kenton thought, wondering if he could still save the girl's life and prevent Kiara's prophecy from unfolding; he hadn't reclaimed the *aqlumera*, so there was no guarantee he would see her again. If she found Annev while he was lost in the void, she would probably die ... and it would be his fault.

Tosan hesitated, his Death Wand beginning to hum in his fist. 'Wait!' he shouted. 'My daughter is *alive*?'

In spite of his situation, his near-blindness and being so close to death, Kenton smiled; it seemed both his departure and his final thoughts would frustrate Tosan – and that was some consolation, even if the cloak killed him. Tosan seemed to sense Kenton's thoughts, and a rage stormed across his stolen face. 'Seize him!'

The Sons of Damnation surged forward once more, Der and Edra attempting to rip his cloak from his body.

Still clutching the garment, and with Myjun's unknown fate at the forefront of his mind, Kenton grasped his own wand and prayed it would be enough to keep him from being trapped in the void by the cloak – then he fell into its blackness, the physical world disappearing with a soft pop and a flash of ethereal grey light.

Chapter Ninety-Two

Therin licked the rune stone hanging around his neck and activated the glyph that would lift him off the ground. Nearly weightless and gliding on a pad of voided air, he sped along the streets of Banok, heading southwest and away from the woman who had surprised them.

Titus. Gods be good, he'd forgotten about Titus!

Therin wheeled about, caroming off the wall of a two-storey house as he curved around in the direction his best friend had headed.

If anything happens to him, I'll never forgive myself. 'Hold on, Titan,' Therin whispered to the night air. 'I'm coming. Just hold on.'

Therin whipped around a second street corner and found himself staring straight at the blaze that had drawn the attention of every patrol in the neighbourhood. Therin stopped cold in his tracks, realising that several of the assembled soldiers had metal or stone bodies ... just like those back in Chaenbalu. He pushed back his fear, then searched for the street where he had abandoned his friend.

There, he thought. *That's the corner.* He edged beneath the shadowy eaves of an overhanging rooftop and edged closer, hoping for a glimpse of Titus.

Something reached out from the darkness and wrapped itself around his neck, legs and arms. Therin tried to scream, but an enormous flower bud slapped into his face and began blossoming inside his mouth. He coughed, first trying to expel the malevolent plant, then trying to chew through its thick stem.

'Pull him inside.'

The voice was soft – a woman's, if he didn't miss his guess – and suddenly Therin was dragged through the door of an abandoned building. More vines wrapped around his wrists and ankles, and Therin gave up on breathing through his mouth and concentrated on sucking air through his nostrils.

'Set him against the wall there.'

Therin flew into a wall as the unseen plants that had swarmed him grew to lift his feet from the earth and bind him to the wall, their thick vines hanging him in the darkness of the empty chamber.

'Luathas. Give us light.'

Luathas. Why did that name sound so familiar? Therin tried to remember but could only recall a vague memory of a small woman playing a flute and ... a juggler? Yes, that was it. He'd juggled twelve knives at once. An Ilumite merrymaker called ... Red-beard? Red-toe?

'*Refum!*' Therin screamed from behind his gag. 'Refum, Refum!' The blossom retreated, no longer pressing against his tongue, and Therin gulped a chestful of air.

'What's he saying?' the feminine voice asked again.

That voice, Therin thought. *Why does that voice sound so familiar?*

Light suddenly bloomed inside the small chamber, accompanied by the faint music of a tin whistle. Therin blinked and saw he was suspended within a net of vines stretching up from the dirt floor and wrapping around the exposed wooden beams over his head. He looked around for the source of the music, and immediately spotted the Ilumite flautist, Luathas.

'Red-thumb!' Therin shouted, before the blossom was shoved back into his mouth.

An exotic-looking woman dressed in leaves, flowers and intricate vines glanced between Therin and the merrymaker. 'Luathas, do you know this boy?'

The mute Ilumite woman tilted her head, still not taking her lips from the tin whistle she was playing. Then she nodded.

The plant woman sniffed. 'Friend or foe?'

The music took on a pleasant melody, its tone light and airy.

'Friend then – and a silly one, if I judge your tone right.'

Luathas inclined her head and continued to play. As Therin watched, he noticed that the light from the room seemed to come not from any normal light source, but from the woman herself. Moreover, its flickering patterns seemed to bend and shift according to the tune and rhythm of her music.

'Therin?'

That voice again. Therin twisted in place, his limbs fighting his living bindings, and he glimpsed the young woman who had addressed him – not a ghost, but a real, live human being.

It was Faith.

Titus lay in the darkness, his mind fuzzy as he tried to recall where he was and how he had got here.

That metal woman, he thought. *That soldier ... she opened that pit and it swallowed me whole. But how?* Magic was the obvious answer, of course, but that did nothing to explain where he was now or who had taken him hostage.

I must be underground. Somewhere with no light at all. It's cold ... but not too damp. What does that mean? He chewed his lip, trying to figure out how he was going to get out of here – wherever here was. *I hope Therin got away,* he thought. *If he's still out there, he'll bring help.* He swallowed. Therin would bring help. He *had* to bring help. He wouldn't just abandon him ... would he?

Something shifted in the darkness and Titus pulled his legs close to his body. 'Hello?' he coughed, his voice feeling dry and scratchy. 'Who – who's there?'

'I am,' croaked a disused voice, withered but masculine. 'I am here – and now, so are you.'

'Who are you?'

'A prisoner, like yourself. Left here to die, like yourself. Left here to be born again.'

Titus shifted against the cold stones until his back was pressed tight against the wall. Whoever this stranger was, he didn't sound right at all. 'My name is Titus,' he began, his voice sounding smaller and more scared than he would have liked. 'I'm ... I'm looking for someone. Have you met a man named Brayan?'

845

'I have met many people in my lifetimes. I suppose it likely that one of them was named Brayan. Or Bram. Or Brenn. Probably all of them.'

'Right,' Titus whispered, realising he was imprisoned with a madman. 'Well, thanks anyway.'

'You're going to die.'

'What?' Titus stumbled against the wall and tripped on something soft just to his right. He steadied himself, reaching out a hand, and felt the cold, clammy sensation of dead flesh.

'Keos!' Titus swore, jumping back from where the corpse lay. 'What is that? Is that a *body*? Is there a dead person in here with us?'

'Aye, that used to be me. I'm sorry about that. I don't have much control over which bodies I take, or what happens once I leave them.' The stranger sighed, a wealth of emotion revealed in the single sound.

'What do you mean "that used to be you"?'

Another world-weary sigh. 'You wouldn't believe me if I told you. Trust me. I'm going to die ... and then, so will you. I don't have any control over it and I'm sorry it's going to happen – but there it is. It happened to him when I died last time and it will happen to you next.'

'Who was he?'

'Mm? Oh, no one important. They wouldn't send anyone *important* down here – not if they want to keep me chained.'

'You're ... wearing chains?'

Somewhere in the darkness, the mad prisoner chuckled. 'No, boy. Just a figure of speech. No key will free me. No hammer can break me. I am a prisoner in every body I inhabit, and I always will be.'

Silence.

'Do ... do you think ...'

'Do I think what?'

Titus was becoming more and more certain. 'You think you're Bron Gloir ... don't you?' Again, the silence – a silence so long and so eerie, Titus knew he'd guessed right.

846

'What do you know of me, boy?' the man asked after what seemed like an eternity. 'And who are you to ask?'

'My name's Titus – just Titus, sir.'

Sir? Why had he called him *sir*? Did Titus actually believe he was a knight – the last of the legendary Halcyon Knights – or did it seem wise to be respectful towards a madman? He swallowed hard and knew with perfect certainty it was the latter.

'Titus,' the madman repeated. 'I shall try to honour your name when I possess your body, but please forgive me when I expel your soul. It is beyond my control and I would gladly give my own life to save yours – but fate, it seems, will never give me that satisfaction.'

Bloody burning bones, Titus thought, keeping an equal distance between himself, the madman and the half-frozen corpse. *I am going to die down here.*

Chapter Ninety-Three

Despite it being only mid-afternoon, Annev slept long and hard after retiring to his berth. He was awakened briefly by the sound of moving furniture, but did not even bother to open his eyes.

'Take it off.'

The words seemed to float to him in a dream, and Annev instantly imagined it was the consul, who had cornered him and forced him to disrobe.

'No,' he protested, but only gently. 'It's important that I ...'

That he what? Suddenly, Annev couldn't recall exactly *what* was so important. The gentle splash of water echoed nearby, and Annev shifted uncomfortably in his sleep. Something shifted beneath him – or was it beside him? – and he heard a gasp.

'It's *him*. The golden hand. The *Vessel*.'

Annev's eyes immediately shot open. Instead of the familiar darkness of his narrow quarters, he was met with the eerie glow of yellow light shining to his left.

The Hand of Keos. Someone had removed his protective glove.

In the faint glow of the prosthetic's infernal light, Annev saw who had broken into his room: Captain Iosua, Consul Anabo, Jaffa, and three of the river barge's more muscular oarsmen.

Rot and hell.

Despite the restricted confines of the tiny berth, Annev sprang to his feet and snatched up the nearest weapon he could find – Toothbreaker, lying just beyond the edge of his pallet. With a feral roar, he slammed the sharpened tines of the vambrace's forearm into the gut of the first man who tried to seize him. The oarsman crumpled in a heap, entangled with those behind him, and Annev spun to face Captain Iosua's heavy cudgel. The club rocked against his skull and sent Annev tripping back to the floor. Someone else grabbed his arms and legs, and Annev had a flashback to a similar struggle with Fyn and the other bullies back at Chaenbalu's Academy.

'Use these,' Anabo said, and something metallic clinked beside his head. Handcuffs? Manacles? Before he could divine which, a thick iron band clamped down around his right wrist and then another pair locked tight around his ankles.

'It's too big!' Iosua shouted, struggling with Annev's left hand. 'The binding won't close!'

Annev struggled and earned a club to his skull a second time. He smelled blood, and stars and darkness swam before his eyes.

'Careful! If you kill him, I'll kill you.'

'He gutted one of my men!' Iosua whined. 'Besides, I thought you wanted him dead.'

Anabo grunted from somewhere off to Annev's right. 'True, but ... there are some questions I want answered first.'

Annev laughed. He didn't mean to – the situation certainly didn't warrant any humour – but the irony that he was about to be abducted, tortured and killed, just as he'd murdered Dionach Honeycutt, wasn't lost on him.

He opened his eyes and saw the consul's manservant had already dragged the injured oarsman out of the room. Captain Iosua wrestled with Annev's left hand – not the wisest decision, though Annev wasn't struggling at the moment. Meanwhile, Anabo stood above him, her chest heaving with a sadistic thrill.

'You didn't order Jaffa to castrate those men,' Annev guessed, guided by the codavora ring. 'You did it yourself.'

The consul smiled, though there was nothing charitable in it – the mask of the seductress had finally fallen away. 'I did, and I'll do the same to you before Captain Iosua and his men feed your guts to the sturgeons.' She licked her lips, held up the bone magpie mask and tossed it to the floor. 'Pretending to be one of Neruacanta's messengers, hmm? Very bold – incredibly so. Stupid, too.'

'What ... gave me away?' Annev panted, dizzy from the repeated blows to his head.

'You should have known what Jaffa carried inside that messenger tube. Cammack approved the writ and brought it to King Cheng himself. Anyone replacing Cammack would have known that ... so it was clear you weren't actually his replacement. That, and you kept your left hand hidden. I *knew* there was something strange about it.'

Annev's chin lolled to his chest and one of the oarsmen slapped him across the face. A spark of anger kindled in his chest, and he suddenly felt fires brewing inside his soul.

Damn them.

'Cut off his shirt.'

The second oarsman complied, drawing a knife from his belt and slicing Annev's tunic from navel to neck. The steel nicked Annev's ribs and he winced at the tiny flash of pain.

This isn't going to end well, Annev thought, *not for any of us.*

'He's got Elar's mark!' the captain jeered. 'It's him for sure. He said he burned the bastard with his brand.'

Anabo nodded. 'The hand was confirmation enough, but the brand seals it.' She eyed Annev like a serpent about to swallow its prey. A slim dagger suddenly appeared in her hand and Annev struggled to stay alert.

'You were, uh ... going to question me?'

The consul hesitated. 'No. No, I think I've changed my mind. Elar and Saltair have already fouled things up, and it seems Holyoak did, too. Pity. He was so easy to manipulate, and it takes a long time to corrupt someone as thoroughly as I did that man.' Anabo leaned forward, pressed the knife to Annev's throat, kissed him full on the lips, and then bit him. When she drew back she was grinning, her lips stained with his blood.

'Goodbye, Master Magpie. I'll treasure our foreplay, even if we didn't get to—'

Light flashed – bright and brilliant – and the air boomed and crackled with the release of energy. At the same instant, heat and fire blossomed from Annev's palm, consuming the room and everything in it.

Annev swooned, still disorientated. To his left, he felt the ashy pulp of Captain Iosua's body, his ruined arms still feebly clutching the cursed Hand of Keos. Annev shook the man off, his head still reeling, and felt another pulse of dizziness overtake him.

What have I done?

'Phoeba,' he muttered, struggling to rise to his shackled feet. Was the consul still alive? Could he salvage *anything* from this?

Something wet and cold rushed against Annev's feet and he had his answer: he'd blown a hole through the side of the ship. He blinked, realised the bright light in his palm had not been extinguished, and fought to rein in the cursed artifact. The light sputtered, no longer blinding, and he glimpsed his surroundings.

Hell and damnation! Annev swore, suddenly seeing the charred flesh of the oarsmen and the remains of the former consul: the top half of the woman's face had been immolated by the power of the golden gauntlet ... yet the blood from Annev's lips seemed to have preserved the woman's sensual mouth.

Bile rose in Annev's throat and he fought the urge to retch. Instead of vomiting though, he felt another surge of fire blast forth from the Hand of Keos, tearing through the ship's hull and doing further damage to the structure of the vessel. The river barge rocked beneath his feet and Annev heard the rapid patter of a dozen feet converging on his location.

I have to get out of here, he thought. *I have to get these rotting manacles off and swim for the bleeding shore!* More water flowed around Annev's ankles and he fought the instinct to panic. Another flare from the Hand of Keos pulsed outward and a hole the size of his head flooded more water into the lower decks of the ship. Instead of fleeing to the upper levels, though, Annev made himself focus. *I need to melt the bindings or else I won't be able to swim for shore.* Using the golden prosthetic, he grasped the shackle binding his left foot and sent heat into the metal band wrapping his ankle.

'Ouch! Blood and ashes,' Annev swore, releasing the iron band that had seared his ankle, but not melted away as he'd hoped. Cool river water splashed around his foot, immediately cooling the hot metal, and he gritted his teeth in both pain and relief.

The chains, he thought. *I can melt the links.* Once more he leaned over, this time grasping the metal links between his shackles. With a moment's focus, he sent the power of the cursed artifact into the chain and he felt the handful of iron links fall away in his hands, the red-hot metal crumbling into molten iron and glowing dust, which were swiftly cooled by the water surging around his legs. Annev groaned with relief, now able to walk about the flooded cabin. His left hand took the dangling manacle still chained to his right wrist and melted those links, too. He still wore the bands on his right hand and ankles, but they no longer bound him or prevented movement. He was free.

Before Annev could celebrate, more water surged into the room, sloshing up to his knees. The planks beneath his feet began to shift and he felt the bow and stern start to crack and separate. The force of the ship breaking apart shot huge splinters of wood across the cabin and Annev scrambled to grab his sodden supplies, in particular the magpie cloak, his bloody vambrace and his flamberge, Retribution. He strapped these on in the time it took the river water to flood the room up to his chest, and he had to climb the walls and exit through the broken ceiling to reach the main deck of the sinking barge. As he did so, he spotted the lacquered bone mask fashioned from the Bloodlord's skull and snatched it from the churning waters.

I'm not sure I can swim to safety, he thought, floundering with the extra weight of his cloak, his weapons, and the iron manacles clamped around his right wrist and ankles. *But perhaps ... perhaps I don't need to swim.*

Grasping the hem of his cloak, Annev summoned the Breathbreaker magic he had used to propel the *Cormorant* upriver and used its power to fling his body across the sinking ship, through the air and over onto the eastern shoreline of the Tocra river. He landed heavily on the muddy embankment and immediately dropped Toothbreaker and his flamberge to the earth, gasping for breath, barely able to believe he had escaped either the conflagration or the ruined ship.

Looking back from the shore, Annev saw that the *Cormorant*'s crew hadn't been half so lucky. The slaves chained to the oars had gone down with the barge, unable to free themselves from their benches. The sailors had fared a little better, though only a few of them were paddling towards either shore. One man struggled to reach the west bank, but quickly succumbed to the river's current and his own injuries, sinking beneath the North Tocra's churning waters. Two more – a man and a woman – struggled to reach the eastern shore where Annev stood. They got farther than the first man, clinging to flotsam from the *Cormorant*'s sunken wreckage, but it was clear the woman had been badly burned and the man had suffered a head injury.

Should I help them ... or kill them? It was a dark, pragmatic thought, whispered by the same inner voice that suggested he betray Titus and Therin in the final Test of Judgement. Back then Annev had decided he could find another path, another way to make things right. But that decision had backfired and he had nearly lost everything. What would happen now, if he allowed those sailors to reach the shore? If they made their way to Luqura and shared the news of the *Cormorant*'s wreck, he'd lose any advantage of surprise and his enemies in the capital would begin searching for him.

But if no news reached the city? If the deaths of Honeycutt, Holyoak and Anabo remained secret a little while longer? Surely that would be to his advantage while he searched for Saltair and the other Siänar? And if Tiana Rocas and Dante Turano were part of the plots against Annev, keeping his identity secret would be yet another advantage.

Annev looked down at the Hand of Keos, which was now glowing faintly with its characteristic light, all signs of its unholy fire quenched by the waters of the Tocra. Annev looked out at the injured sailors who were now a hundred paces from the shore. He felt his conscience warring with his sense of practicality and he silenced them both, listening only to the slow beat of his heart.

The male sailor succumbed to his injuries, slipping from the broken mast he clung to and dropping beneath the surface of the river. Annev breathed a tiny sigh of relief, one decision having been made for him – but the female sailor was dogged in her attempts to reach the shore.

She's going to make it, he realised, his heart rising into his throat.

Without thinking, Annev stooped down to the muddy embankment and placed his left hand in the cool waters of the Tocra. He focused his emotions into the artifact, and he summoned a portion of the heat and flame that had destroyed the *Crested Cormorant*.

The water around Annev's hand began to boil, and as it did he quested out with his hand. He watched as a column of liquid fire erupted from his fist and churned through the water, a jet of steam trailing in its wake. The pillar of boiling water slammed into the sailor at the same instant she let go of her makeshift raft, and both she and the flotsam sank beneath the river waves.

Annev pulled his hand from the water and watched as the waters cooled. The woman did not resurface.

He felt the chill of apathy settle over him, something he had become all too familiar with while torturing Honeycutt in the derelict warehouse. Distantly, he understood why his actions and her death had been necessary – and therefore justifiable – yet he felt another part of him reject the reality of what he had just done.

They were Anabo's allies, Annev reminded himself, *and that means they share the guilt of her crimes. She was going to kill me, and every sailor on that ship would have helped her do it. It was necessary.*

Necessary.

Chapter Ninety-Four

Annev stood from the water's edge and collected his vambrace and long sword. After securing both, he slid the magpie mask into place and then called upon the magic of his cloak. After all of his practice directing wind into the *Cormorant*'s mainsail, he felt more confident in his ability to control the powers of the magpie cloak, and he used it now to skim the surface of the water and search for any more survivors. He saw a handful of floating bodies, but none moved or demonstrated any signs of life.

On his second sweep, Annev spotted Anabo's manservant Jaffa amidst the wreckage and he swooped in to take a closer look. The eunuch had somehow salvaged the barge's only rowboat, but his arms and chest were badly blistered and a splinter of wood pierced his abdomen. From the glimpse he got, though, Annev could not immediately discern whether the manservant was still breathing. He flew closer still, finally touching down inside the boat, and spied the treasures the eunuch had rescued: a purse overflowing with red-gold Terran coins and the leather messenger tube, still sealed with King Cheng's royal sigil.

Keeping one eye on Jaffa, Annev scooped up the fallen coins and retied the bulging purse, tucking it into the depths of his cloak. He reached for the messenger tube last of all, but when his hands brushed against the oiled leather casing, the manservant's eyes flew open and he slapped a bloody hand against the bottom of the rowboat.

'Phoeba,' Jaffa gasped, clutching his wounded stomach. 'Did she survive?'

Annev kept his right hand on the leather tube. 'I'm sorry, Jaffa. This wasn't part of the plan.'

The eunuch groaned with a mixture of physical pain and spiritual anguish. 'She was the only thing that mattered to me in this world ... and *you* took her from me.'

Annev's fist clenched in a burst of defensive rage. 'I never intended for this to happen,' he repeated, picking up the messenger tube and slinging it over his back. 'These people – your mistress and the people she serves – *they* have been trying to kill *me*. They destroyed my home ... killed everyone in my village. *They* started this.'

'And so,' the eunuch said, slumped in the boat, 'you have finished it.'

'Not by half,' Annev said. 'This—' He gestured at the wreckage strewn round them, at the sunken barge and the charred bodies bobbing in the water. 'This was self-defence, not revenge. I would not have killed these people if it hadn't been necessary.'

'Was it necessary to kill that sailor?' Jaffa pressed on, seeing Annev's flash of guilt, more certain of himself. 'Yes, I saw what you did, Master Magpie. You're no different from those who hunt you. You'll preserve your own life at the cost of others and justify whatever actions make that possible.' He spat, and there was blood in it.

'You know nothing—'

'And you are a thief, besides,' Jaffa continued, his breathing becoming more laboured. 'You steal from me ... from my lady ... from our king.' He gestured weakly at the purse tied to Annev's belt and the messenger tube slung across his back. Then he smiled. 'Do not tell me it is right or necessary or just. I have heard these platitudes before, these weak justifications.' He snorted derisively. 'You are a villain, Master Magpie, though you refuse to acknowledge it. I have worked with enough of them to know when I see one. You intend to kill me – so do it. End this charade and finish what you started.'

Annev stared at the dying manservant before turning to survey the carnage that surrounded them both. The eunuch's words echoed Elder Tosan and Myjun's accusations when they had called him a ring-snake and a Son of Keos. It repeated Kenton and Fyn's accusations that he was selfish, manipulative or hypocritical. Even Titus and Therin, ostensibly his only friends in the world, had parted saying the same. Jaffa's words felt worse, though, for here and now they carried the sting of truth.

I am not a monster, Annev told himself, though he did not voice his protest aloud. Instead, he knelt beside the manservant and began examining his wound.

'What are you doing?'

'Trying to save your life, you ball-less bastard. Now stop fighting me and let me see your injury.'

Jaffa slowly lowered his bloody hands from his abdomen. 'You killed my mistress, the barge captain and everyone aboard our ship. You robbed me when you thought I was dead and now you want to *heal* me?' He shook his head in protest. 'That is not how virtue works, Magpie.' The eunuch drew his long belt knife from his sheath. Annev tensed, expecting an attack, but instead Jaffa tossed the knife to him.

'Stop pretending to be noble and put an end to this.'

Annev hesitated, then he took the weapon. His eyes met Jaffa's and the man glared at him, prepared to meet his death. Annev sighed, rose to his feet and dropped the dagger into the water. The eunuch swore in a language Annev did not recognise.

'Why? Why not just kill me? Must I throw myself into the water? Am I so far beneath you that I cannot receive a clean death?'

'What language was that?' Annev demanded, his hands unwinding the bloody scarf around his neck. 'I would have recognised Old Darite and that didn't sound like Terran. Was it Ilumite?'

'Ildari,' the eunuch snapped, scowling. 'It is the language of slaves in Innistiul.'

'You are Ilumite then – or part Ilumite.'

'Yes.'

Annev was unsurprised, then he leaned forward and yanked the splinter of wood from beneath Jaffa's ribs. The eunuch screamed and a stream of blood spurted from the wound. Jaffa slapped his hands to his side, cursing, but Annev forced his hands away and pressed the tattered remnants of the Shirt of Regeneration against the injury. The wound immediately began to close and within moments it had stopped. Jaffa gasped, his eyes blinking with renewed clarity.

'You ... healed me.' He shook his head, confused. 'Why would you do this?'

'Do you still wish to go to Luqura or will you return home?' Annev asked, ignoring the question.

Jaffa blinked. 'My home was with the consul, as her property. Without her I have no home.'

'So what will you do?' Annev repeated. 'Are you required to report her death? Do you wish to remain a slave? Or would you free yourself and return to Ilumea?'

Jaffa scoffed. 'You are naive, Magpie. I was born in Innistiul – not Ilumea – and I was raised in the royal palace. If I return there and report Consul Anabo's death, I will be killed for not having protected her – or not having died with her. So you see, you have not saved my life. You have only delayed my death.'

'Only if you choose to go back. Wouldn't you rather be free? The Luqurans might—'

'I would rather you had not killed my mistress.'

'Well, I did!' Annev shouted. 'She's *gone*. She tried to kill me and I melted half her face off and I'm not sorry for doing it.'

And he wasn't – that was perhaps the most surprising thing about it: Annev had felt guilty for destroying the *Cormorant* and had been conflicted about killing the sailor ... but he felt no remorse for the consul's death. Instead, he felt a tiny sense of closure, an impression that he was gradually making things better, even if his methods seemed terrible.

'I must go to Luqura,' Jaffa said, his tone resigned. 'And I must go with King Cheng's sovereign writ.' He gestured to the messenger tube on Annev's back. 'Without that, it will not matter what defence I give. I will be killed.'

Annev withdrew the bandage from the man's stomach, his thoughts racing as he tucked the bloody rag into his bottomless sack for later experimentation. 'I cannot give it to you,' Annev said, his mind descending into a dark place of cold logic and cruel necessity. 'And I cannot let you go to Luqura ... though it seems you refuse to go anywhere else.'

'Just so.'

Annev stared into Jaffa's eyes. 'Your actions threaten my life and my mission – you realise that. If I let you go, your Guild will send more of their assassins after me.'

'Yes.'

'I cannot allow that.'

'And I cannot deviate from my course,' Jaffa said, unflinching.

Annev's lip curled, for though he did not hate the man, he despised what he represented. It reminded him of Tosan and his unrelenting war against any who were deemed unwhole or impure – a blind obedience to a flawed ideology. Worse, Jaffa believed his actions and his motives were just – that *he* was the one in the right and that Annev was evil for opposing him.

'So be it,' Annev said, and slammed his golden fist into the boat's hull. Splinters of wood exploded around them and the eunuch dived into the waters, attempting to swim for shore.

Annev rose into the air using the magic of his cloak and hovered above the waters, his path angling to meet the manservant before he reached the Tocra's shore. As Jaffa's pace began to flag, Annev slowed with him, gently gliding along behind him as he matched the river current. The man visibly tired, and Annev moved forward to hover just above Jaffa's head, letting the windstream from his cloak pound into the eunuch's head and shoulders. A vortex of water churned around the manservant, holding him in place and drowning him in waves of water. Annev held his position, only glancing down once to confirm he was still above his target. The second time he looked down, Jaffa had disappeared beneath the surface. Annev waited for another minute. Then two.

Something cold settled into his gut. It did not taste like guilt, but it weighed him down all the same: he had killed a man in cold blood – a man whose only crime had been loyalty to a dead mistress, and being trapped by his fate.

It had to be done, he told himself, the coldness spreading to his chest and gut. *He left me no choice. I had to do it.*

Annev surveyed the wreckage of the *Crested Cormorant* once

more, pushing himself as high as the cloak would take him – almost seven feet above the river. From that vantage and using the supernatural vision of his Inquisitor ring, Annev could just make out the sunken barge resting at the bottom of the Tocra. The bodies had cooled in the river's waters – all except Jaffa's, which was bobbing face-down in the current. There would be no witnesses sharing news of the consul's fate with anyone in Luqura. The wreck was far enough from the capital that no homes or villages dotted the shores of the wide river. No one had seen anything. For once, fate seemed to be aiding Annev, no matter how dark his actions might be.

Annev dropped down to hover just above the river and the spray from the water and wind began to mist his boots. He angled himself until the bulk of his magic was propelling him forward, sending him upstream towards Luqura. Freed of having to propel the massive river barge, Annev flew across the water at a break-neck pace. Drops of water beaded around his magpie mask and flew along the lacquered feathers carved into the bone artifact.

Not an artifact, Annev reminded himself, *not yet. Not until I fuse it with the Terran mage's blood.*

Then again, Annev thought, perhaps that wouldn't be necessary. The mask had been carved from the Bloodlord's skull. A trace of the man's blood-talent might still reside in the core of the mask. Perhaps that would be enough to manipulate the magic threads and form something more ... permanent.

But he could worry about that later. For now, he had to reach Luqura before dawn – a task he felt confident he could achieve at his current pace. He'd gain admittance as Master Magpie, an enigmatic lord from ... somewhere. Innistiul? That would explain the writ he carried on his back. Or perhaps he should continue pretending to be an agent of the God-king Neruacanta. Annev wasn't sure, but he had no intention of entering the city as himself. In fact, his best option might be to levitate over the city wall and enter Luqura unannounced.

Once inside I can seek out Tiana and Dante, and find out where Saltair is hiding. And if they can tell me anything about who hunts me, I'll pursue those leads, too, until none of my enemies remain behind me.

Then I can go on to Banok and clean up the mess I left there. Hells, I could go to Daogort and roust out the God-king himself, and finally put an end to this madness.

And it was madness – Annev had no illusions about that; even his own plans for retribution had a taste of insanity about them – but Annev no longer feared the people he was facing or the lengths to which he might need to go to stop them.

If I must be a monster, he thought, *then I will be the kind that hunts the others. I will be the villain that destroys all other villains.*

The cold knot resting in his stomach seemed to untwist then, and he felt at peace with the decisions he had made over the past week.

He was not a hero, nor would he try to be one.

He was not a virtuous saviour, or even the prophesied descendant of Breathanas.

He was just ... himself. Annev de Breth. Ring-snake. Magpie. Phoenix. He was the Master of Sorrows: a saviour and a destroyer. And he was not afraid of the fate that awaited him. Whether in darkness or light, life or death, he would follow his heart and never waver from what needed to be done.

And right now, Annev needed to go to the capital and hunt out some monsters.

Epilogue

Kiara knelt beside the altar she had built in the heart of the Brakewood, her strong fingers clutching the ceremonial knife she carried for exactly this occasion.

Lying on the grey stone in front of her was one of Cruithear's fallen children – an abomination, a twisted one.

A *feurog*.

This creature had been a man once, and the magic that strengthened him had also crippled and deformed him: scabs of stone grew like scales across his chest and abdomen; soft veins of steel threaded his muscles like glimmering bands of silver sinew. In time, those would harden and petrify the poor creature, paralysing him until Death himself claimed him. Such a waste. Such a shame. Fortunately, Kiara was here to give that death a purpose; it would no longer be meaningless, and it was coming much, much sooner.

The abomination's eyelids began to flutter. Before it could regain control of the rest of its muscles, Kiara sliced her blade deep into the monster's abdomen. The *feurog* tried to scream, but only managed a strangled whimper. Kiara paid it no heed, her attention focused on its intestines, liver and spleen. She poked, prodded and twisted, her fingers entwining with the bloody entrails as her Yomad magic seeped into the dying monster's bowels. Some of the organs had a metallic sheen to them, though they still yielded to the edge of her magically honed knife. Finally, Kiara felt the blood-magic reach out to her, as light and cool and potent as the touch of a wraith as it travelled up her arms, through her heart and up to the sclera of her eyes. If she looked into a mirror just then, she knew her pupils would appear cloudy white – a temporary side effect of her Seer magic. Kiara felt her skin tighten, too, her flesh losing some of its elasticity and her face becoming ever more skeletal. This was another unfortunate side effect and one that would be regrettably permanent. Such were the costs of peering into Fate's flowing rivers, particularly without a pool of *aqlumera* to aid in her scrying.

As soon as her eyes were fully saturated, Kiara drew out a damp rag. Until a few minutes ago, the cloth had been stained with Kenton's dried blood – which she had been circumspect about obtaining. Kiara placed the bloody scrap in her mouth and sucked until she tasted the familiar tang of rust and iron.

Images flashed across her field of vision. Imagined scents filled her nose, replacing the coppery smell of Kenton's dried blood and the foul odour of whatever the *feurog* had recently digested. She caught fragments of thoughts – words and sentences, rhymes and riddles. Despite her years of experience interpreting the whispers of Fate, Kiara grappled with the prophecy, wrestling with its meaning, attempting to bind it to her will and her memory.

Kenton, she thought, then asked her question aloud: 'Has the boy reclaimed the *aqlumera*?' The answer came almost immediately.

The Cursed Leader has failed to reclaim what was lost.

Kiara bowed in gratitude to Tacharan. The Younger God of Fate had answered her swiftly – and with uncharacteristic clarity – and though she did not like the answer she received, she knew better than to express her ire. She considered enquiring after the boy's fate, but it would be a difficult subject to navigate. Much better to keep her questions specific.

'Where is Kenton now?'

He has lost himself in turn and finds himself where all things go that are lost.

Damn. That was as vague an answer as she'd ever received – or perhaps it was very specific. It was hard to tell, with Fate. Kiara slipped another loop of intestines between her fingers and sifted through the blood-magic, searching for clarity.

'When will he return?'

Yes.

Blood and ashes. The augury was already degrading. Kiara had feared as much, and while she had three more unconscious *feurog* lying on separate stone tables, she had a limited quantity of Kenton's blood and a similarly limited quantity of Annev's. She had tasted a good deal of it since the boy's imprisonment, but it wouldn't last for ever. Sooner rather than later, she'd be unable to divine anything related to the Vessel ... and she would be as blind to his presence as she had been for these past seventeen years.

Kiara moved to the second table, her bloody knife already separating flesh and muscle in her attempt to divine Annev's future. When Kiara placed this second rag in her mouth, she knew this would be the last augury she would divine regarding Annev's fate; she'd taken the bloody rag from Brayan and Titus after they had tended to the boy's wounds and placed him in the Academy's dungeons, and the blood-magic was nearly spent. She sucked and chewed, mixing the blood with water and saliva, trying to awaken a sense of the boy's fate in her mind. Finally, something kindled, and she latched onto the magic, using the dying *feurog* in front of her as a focal point.

The witmistress opened her mouth, prepared to ask her questions – then hesitated. There might only be enough magic for one question. Best to make it a good one.

'What must I do to help Annev forge the Sword of Seeking?'

Kiara's past auguries had told her the boy would forge the sword using the *aqlumera* from Chaenbalu's Vault, and that her aid would be critical if she were to gain his trust – but some of that *aqlumera* had been stolen, and the matter of Annev's involvement was now in doubt. If Kiara was to help him, she would need to know where to find him. And if she was to help him forge the artifact and earn his trust, she would need to offer invaluable aid.

Open the Vault of Damnation, Fate whispered. *Inside its flooded chamber, you will find the help you seek. Bring it to Banok and the Vessel will construct the diamagus.*

Another imperfect answer. Of the thousands of artifacts inside the Vault, Kiara could barely guess what might aid Annev and bind his will to her own. But the instruction to open the Vault was clear enough. Perhaps knowing the answers would be inside would prove enough. More concerning was the omission of Annev's location and Kiara's involvement in his prophesied creation.

If I go to Banok, will Annev be there? There is no mention of where the sword will be forged. Must I lead him back to the fountain of aqlumera *– assuming he does not come here on his own?*

But Kiara could work with this information. She understood, better than any, how to manipulate Fate's web. If she could open the Vault, Kiara could take a portion of the *aqlumera* for herself and take *it* to Banok. If she encountered the Vessel, she could offer him the *aqlumera* as an act of goodwill along with the pledge of her allegiance. Perhaps that was even what the prophecy intended.

Perhaps . . . but probably not. Fate rarely made any task easy for her.

Kiara looked down the line at the two remaining *feurog*. It had been difficult to find any after their attack on Chaenbalu, but Kiara knew their burrows and the creatures were slowly returning to their network of tunnels beneath the Brakewood. Even so, it had taken two days to find these four sacrifices, and she would need to use these last two carefully so that she did not delay her trip to Banok hunting for more.

But what to ask? She needed to know which items to take from the Vault, and she needed a way to open it – with the connecting tunnels all flooded, it would be dangerous to attempt any sort of digging.

The nechraict, Kiara thought with a sigh. The cost for using her necromancy would be high – she had been very careful not to dabble in its usage while at the Academy – but she couldn't waste time hunting for more *feurog* to aid her. Resurrecting their dead bodies would be much easier, despite the cost.

It must be done.

She moved to the third *feurog* – a female whose stone tumours had transformed her body into a misshapen lump of hardened flesh and crystallised bone. Her eyes were open, and she watched Kiara with undisguised horror.

'Shhh,' she whispered. 'I've severed your spinal cord to keep you from moving. It'll be over soon.'

Once she had the woman's bowels wrapped between her fingers, Kiara studied them with her next question held firmly in her mind.

'What must I take from the Vault of Damnation and bring to Banok ... ?' She considered being more specific – mentioning her intent to help Annev forge the Sword of Seeking – but that often backfired. When you were dealing with Fate, you had to walk the line between being too vague and getting an answer you couldn't use, or being too specific and getting no answer at all.

The air that hissed between the *feurog*'s paralysed lips matched the cadence of Tacharan's eventual answer: *Take the lamp marked by Odar ... the smith marked by Keos ... and the essence of life and death*.

It was never an easy answer ... but it was good enough.

Kiara looked down at the fourth *feurog*, intending to ask when she needed to go to Banok, only to realise the creature had bled to death while she'd been studying the first three auguries.

Well, she consoled herself, *at least I have four fresh bodies to help with the digging.*

Kiara ignored the water pulsing from the mouth of the excavated tunnel and instead examined her skeletal hands: before that summer they'd held the beauty and strength of life, but her use of magic over these past few months had drained away that vitality; Kiara looked thin, almost sickly, and her hands were an ashen grey tone in place of their usual healthy pink. It was the cost of her magic, which she'd managed to stave off for many, many years.

The cost of using her necromancy had been much worse: white bones now showed beneath the translucent skin covering her thin fingers, and her eyes had sunken into her skull. She was a far cry from the striking Grey Lady, as her witgirls and witwomen had once called her. Her magic was twisting her, revealing her to be like the necromancers and lich lords of Takarania and Terra Majora.

But she had chosen to pay the price.

Once the water had drained away, Kiara stepped around the enslaved corpses that had dug her path into the Vault of Damnation.

They had been the first bodies to spew out of the tunnel mouth, with the first violent blast of draining water, and a stream of bloated corpses had soon followed – a grisly reminder of how Kenton had won his campaign against the *ferrumen* and their mage-priests.

Using the light of a single torch, Kiara navigated the sodden warren until she found the secret entrance Kenton had used to enter the otherwise impenetrable Vault of Damnation.

'Hello, High Priestess Ciarán.'

'*You!*' Kiara hissed in shock, recognising the voice that greeted her from within the Vault of Damnation. 'How are you *alive*? After all these weeks ... how have you survived?'

Dolyn Smith climbed down from the bier she'd been sitting on and gestured at the pewter and limestone jars sitting at the foot of the *aqlumera* fountain. 'The metal one makes barley cakes – palatable, but dry – and the stone one generates water.' She gestured behind her. 'There's a black one back there I've been using to relieve myself. Not sure where it goes, but it keeps the stink out of the chamber.' The priestess stretched and walked over to Kiara. 'Do I have you to thank for trapping me in here?'

'Our Master of Curses. He said the leader of the *ferrumen* was dead – that he had eliminated everyone who had attacked the village – but hiding inside the Vault would have hidden you from his magic.'

'So you didn't know it was me? You didn't guess ... or use your magic?'

'I guessed Cruithear might send his high priestess – and that if he had, you were certainly dead. I don't bother to divine the answer to every question, Dolyn. You know the costs of our magic as well as anyone.'

Dolyn shrugged, her hands rising to show Kiara the scars burned there – the marks from where Annev had burned her with the Hand of Keos. 'I am well acquainted with the cost of our magics, Ciarán.'

Kiara stared at the red scars burned into the woman's open palms. 'You touched it, then ... the Hand of Keos.'

'I did. The Vessel came to me and asked if I could assist him in removing the Hand. I tried, and failed. This was my punishment.' She lowered her hands. 'I would have killed him right there and harvested it from his corpse ... but Cruithear's spirit stayed me.'

Kiara chuckled. 'You mean you were afraid he might destroy you, and Banok too.'

Dolyn nodded. 'It did not seem wise to attack him directly. I tried to assassinate him instead, but using a crossbow proved difficult with my injuries ... and he had companions with him. Other servants of the gods.'

Kiara had foreseen this. The priests of the Younger and Elder Gods would be drawn to the Vessel of Keos. 'Of course you failed. The prophecies state he must forge the Sword of Seeking – he must *end* the Silence of the Gods.'

'Him or his hand, Ciarán? We do not believe as you do – and I answer to *Cruithear*, not Tacharan. I will not be conned into helping your master achieve his goals.'

'And how are Cruithear's plans working out for you?' Kiara snapped, her patience at an end. 'First you siphon the tainted *aqlumera* from beneath our village and try to make your perverse *ferrumen* – and then you abandoned your failures.'

'They were imperfect – and they knew the risks.'

'You turned Janak Harth against us and attempted to start a war between Banok and Chaenbalu,' Kiara continued, her anger rising, 'and for what? For this?' She gestured at the glowing pool of liquid magic. 'You know it is forbidden to forge with it.'

'And yet you claim the Vessel will use the *aqlumera* to forge the Sword of Seeking!' Dolyn scoffed. 'Hypocrite.'

'The Vessel bears the Hand. He is the only one who can safely risk its dangers. You've seen what the *aqlumera* can do. You've seen how it can corrupt and kill.'

'And I have seen how it can heal – I've seen it can transform mundane soldiers into living golems! I will not be denied its power, nor will Cruithear.'

'Bah!' Kiara waved a hand, dismissing the iron-headed fool. 'You're as stubborn as your Ironborn.' She frowned, her attention momentarily drawn back to the corpse on the bier at the centre of the room. 'Is that Brayan?'

'He ... was my guide,' Dolyn admitted.

'You tricked him into bringing you here.'

'I had no *choice*,' Dolyn protested, sounding anguished. 'When the Vessel left Banok, he left the quartermaster to help me. Brayan ... was kind. He helped me with my work.'

'Brayan was always tender-hearted,' Kiara agreed, 'and you took advantage of that.'

Dolyn looked towards the bier. 'I ... did. I tried to convince him that only magic could heal my hands – Chaenbalu's magic – but he refused to bring me here. "Only if it was a matter of life and death," he said ... so I poisoned him, and convinced him the cure lay in Chaenbalu's Vault. I think he even believed me – and so he became our guide, and we passed through Chaenbalu's circle of protection. I expected to find the village abandoned. I had hoped ... I had *thought* ...' She shuddered. 'What did you *do*, Kiara? What demons did you send to attack us?'

'Just our Master of Curses – him and his brainwashed lapdog – but that was enough. Kenton decimated you and your precious *ferrumen*.' She sniffed, not hiding her disdain. 'You should have stayed in Banok, Dolyn. With a little patience, you would have met with Annev when we came to forge the Sword of Seeking. We would have brought you to this very room.' She gestured at the shelves of artifacts and the churning pool of liquid magic. 'You acted in haste – and Brayan paid for it with his life.'

Dolyn's head bowed in sorrow, but then she sneered. '*You* dare to lecture *me* about the cost of lives? You, who sacrificed your entire village to protect your dark secrets? Do not judge the blood I have spilled or spent. Your hands are no cleaner than mine.'

'On that, we can agree,' Kiara said, her demeanour still cool. She frowned. 'Why did you stay? Why not burrow your way out with your magic?'

Dolyn gestured at the concave walls and domed ceiling. 'Magic protects this place. I can't shape the stone here.'

'But the trapdoor? Surely you could have swum out through one of the flooded tunnels?'

'I tried. I swam in search of an escape, but every exit was sealed.' She lifted her dirty tunic to show her skin, scaled with white marble and flakes of greenish-white platinum. 'I lacked the strength to shape the stone walls. I can't even slow the transmutation without proper food to replace the minerals my body has lost,' she explained. 'I need meat and milk, and other things that I can't get locked underground in a flooded chamber.'

'Of course – and you shall have them.'

'You're ... letting me go?'

'I need your help,' Kiara snapped, 'to forge the Sword of Seeking – and so does Annev. He will be in Banok soon, and we will need to be ready to greet him.'

Dolyn's brow furrowed, suspicious. 'Why would I do that? I tried to kill him!'

'But he doesn't know that,' Kiara said, completing the other woman's thoughts. 'And before you try to barter with me, you should know you cannot have the Hand of Keos, nor will I allow you to capture the Vessel. I have already promised him to Tacharan, and if you obstruct me in this, we will become enemies.'

'Then there is nothing you can offer me.'

'Oh no?' Kiara gestured at the fountain and its rainbow-hued contents. 'As much *aqlumera* as you can carry, in exchange for helping Annev forge the diamagus when it is time.'

The high priestess of the Orvanes grunted, considering. 'That ... is a tempting offer.'

'Stop being coy. You know the value of what I offer.'

'And what's to stop me from killing you and escaping through the tunnel you just opened?'

'Fate,' Kiara crooned, her voice sure.

The smith frowned at Kiara's cryptic answer, but eventually she nodded. 'Cruithear curse me, but ... very well.'

'Good,' Kiara said. 'There are some enchanted jars on that shelf. Take as many as you can. They'll be needed to forge the sword.' She moved between the shelves, guided by a preternatural sense of intuition. Halfway down the third shelf, she squatted down and found a worn leather satchel containing the other item she sought – a brass lamp engraved with a thousand runes in Old Darite.

'What's that?' Dolyn asked, drawing close to peer over the witmistress's shoulder.

'A lamp,' Kiara said, dropping it into her apron pocket.

'Anything significant about it?'

'The Dionachs Tobar think it houses the Oracle of Odar.'

'They *think* it does? What does it actually hold?'

Kiara smiled, her eyes sparkling with the secrets that only a High Priestess of Tacharan could know. 'My sweet Dolyn, you wouldn't believe me if I told you – and *this* is a secret I'll take to my grave.'

THE END

Appendix

The Luquatran Magic System

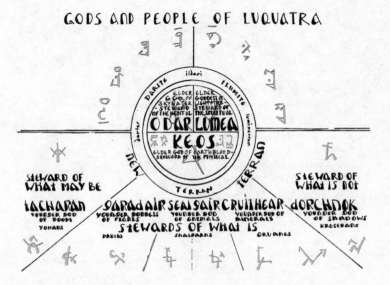

GODS AND PEOPLE OF LUQUATRA

Prime Magic

AURAMANCER
telempath

can project emotions onto others and change or augment them; aura projection

STORMCALLER
thought projection

can telepathically speak by "pushing" thoughts into others' minds; blunt force psychic attacks

SOULRIDER
empath

can sense and adopt others' emotional auras; can drain life forces; aura absorption

ARTIFICER
makes artifacts

can create magic artifacts by infusing matter with another artisan's blood-talent

MINDWALKER
mind reading

can telepathically hear by "pulling" thoughts from others' minds & can steal memories and siphon willpower

INQUISITOR
detects lies; healer; tracker

can detect lies by pulse; self-healing; supernatural tracking by tasting or smelling blood; blood divination

EARTHSHAPER
shapes earth

can reform any mineral or vegetable they touch & can move and transform transform nearby earth

BREATHBREAKER
"voided-air" bubbles; fog

can change water to vapor & form bubbles of "voided" air; can create sound bubbles & gusts of wind

BLOODLORD
hemokinesis

can compress blood into a telepathic weapon & can puppeteer someone who is bleeding

LIGHTSLINGER
fire balls, lightning; illusions

can throw light globes, lightning, and fireballs & can bend light to create mirror illusions

SHIELDBEARER
"air" blades, shields; ice

can change water to ice & form and manipulate shards of "condensed" skywater

BLADESINGER
fire blades; invisibility

can create "aura" constructs & can turn invisible by bending light around body

= pushing/expanding

= pulling/condensing

= Odar
Elder God of Skywater
Steward of the Mental
Darite

= Lumea
Elder Goddess of Lightfire
Steward of the Spiritual
Ilumite

= Keos
Elder God of Earthblood
Steward of the Physical
Terran

= metaphysical

= elemental

New Terran Magic

descendants of Keos, a subset of Trasang and Earthblood

STONESMITH
shapes stone & metal

can shape and move stone and metal by touching it; some can move nearby earth without any physical contact

IRONBORN
changes self into stone & metal

can transform one's self into stone or metal; some can transform others into stone or metal

SKINCHANGER
animal shapeshifter

can adopt the physical characteristics of other animals & can shapeshift into a single "spirit" animal

FORGEMASTER
both Stonesmith & Ironborn

SOWER
controls plants

can shape and move nearby plants & can accelerate or suspend plant growth

BEASTMASTER
animal empath

can spiritually communicate with other animals, hear their thoughts, and see through their senses

SPEAKER
senses through plants

can feel nearby plant life forces and sense through them & can harvest memories of plants

SHAMAN
both Skinchanger & Beastmaster

TREEHEART
both Sower & Speaker

YOUNGER GOD OF MINERALS
CRUITHEAR

YOUNGER GOD OF ANIMALS
SEALGAIR

YOUNGER GODDESS OF PLANTS
GARADAIR

YOUNGER GOD OF SHADOWS
DORCHADR

YOUNGER GOD OF DEATH
TACHARAN

VOIDWEAVER
manipulates space-time

can increase matter density and gravitational attraction between objects; can create portals & manipulate time

NECROMANCER
necromancy

can reanimate dead organic matter, commune with the dead, and sense dying and death; unnaturally long-lived

SHADOWCASTER
shadow mage

can decrease matter density and gravitational attraction between objects; can phase into the shadow realm, slowing time & can create shadow constructs

SEER
divination

can predict the future with relatively high accuracy; limited scrying and precognition, unnaturally long-lived

DARK LORD
both Voidweaver & Shadowcaster

MARROW-LICH
both Necromancer & Seer

= outward elemental

= inward metaphysical

= Stewards of What Is

= Steward of What May Be

= Steward of What Is Not

Acknowledgements

Please allow me to heap an unseemly amount of praise on my UK editor, Gillian Redfearn, whose keen eye, sage advice and uncanny wisdom helped me shape this rough story into something special. When I worried that *Master Artificer* was getting too long for the publisher, she was the person who assured me the story was good and that I should stay the course. It takes an immense amount of trust to do that – both for an editor and her publisher – and I feel uniquely blessed to be allowed that trust and privilege. To that end, I'd also like to give a special thanks to the people at Gollancz, Blackstone, and all my other foreign publishers who have believed in me, my writing, and this series.

The second person I'd like thank is my wonderful wife Collette, whose sacrifices have enabled me to be an author and to sneak away from my kids long enough to write my dratted books. I have said before that Co doesn't much like anything to do with SFF – but she does believe in my writing; she knows it makes me happy, and it makes a lot of other people happy to read it. Thanks for the cheerleading, Coco.

Which leads me back to those amazing kids – I love you guys. Hopefully when you are older, you'll be able to read these books and appreciate why your dad locked himself in his office all those times. And to Tord – who is old enough to read these books now – please know that I love and support you, and I treasure our time exploring other people's fantasy stories together.

I'd also like to thank three of the people in the background whose unrecognized contributions make my storytelling all the more epic. If you are reading the ebook, hardback, or paperback for Master Artificer, you should know that most of the hand-written maps, symbols, and ephemera in this book were illustrated by my good friend Jared Sprague – and we spent a lot of hours discussing and refining those illustrations so they could accurately represent the world I imaged. Special attention should also be given to Jen Elliott – who, at the time of this acknowledgement, is the lead artist for the Forgotten Realms TTRPG; Jen illustrated the phenomenal graphic in the appendix that explains the rules and categories for the Prime and New Terran magic systems in The Silent Gods. If you haven't seen it, please allow your eyes to feast on her talents (and go check out her other artwork).

The third person I'd like to thank is Peter Kenny, my absolutely amazing audiobook narrator. If you are listening to his narration, you may lack the ability to see the maps and appendix graphics I previously mentioned, but in exchange you get to hear Peter's incredible vocal talents as he brings my characters, my world, and my story to life. In addition to his legendary narrative skills, Peter is also one of the kindest people I've met in the publishing industry (or anywhere else for that matter), and I'm delighted to call him my friend.

Lastly, I'd like to thank my agent Danny Baror. If it weren't for Danny, no one would have heard these stories – either domestic-ally or internationally – and his belief in my talents as a storyteller is invaluable. Cheers and thanks to all.

Credits

Justin Call and Gollancz would like to thank everyone at Orion who worked on the publication of *Master Artificer* in the UK.

Editorial
Gillian Redfearn
Brendan Durkin

Copy editor
Abigail Nathan

Proofreader
Gabriella Nemeth

Audio
Paul Stark
Amber Bates

Contracts
Anne Goddard
Paul Bulos
Jake Alderson

Design
Lucie Stericker
Joanna Ridley
Nick May

Editorial Management
Charlie Panayiotou
Jane Hughes
Alice Davis

Finance
Jennifer Muchan
Jasdip Nandra
Afeera Ahmed
Elizabeth Beaumont
Sue Baker

Marketing
Lucy Cameron

Production
Paul Hussey

Publicity
Will O'Mullane

Sales
Jen Wilson
Esther Waters
Victoria Laws
Rachael Hum
Ellie Kyrke-Smith
Frances Doyle
Georgina Cutler

Operations
Jo Jacobs
Sharon Willis
Lisa Pryde
Lucy Brem